Her Write
HIS NAME

THOEMMES

THE STORY OF ELIZABETH
and
OLD KENSINGTON

Anne Isabella Thackeray

With a new Introduction by
Esther Schwartz-McKinzie

THOEMMES PRESS

© Thoemmes Press 1995

Published in 1995 by
Thoemmes Press
11 Great George Street
Bristol BS1 5RR
England

ISBN 1 85506 388 3

This is a reprint of the 1876 and 1873 Editions
© Introduction by Esther Schwartz-McKinzie 1995

Publisher's Note

These reprints are taken from original copies of each book.
In many cases the condition of those originals is not perfect,
the paper, often handmade, having suffered over time and
the copy from such things as inconsistent printing pressures
resulting in faint text, show-through from one side of a leaf
to the other, the filling in of some characters, and the break
up of type. The publisher has gone to great lengths to ensure
the quality of these reprints but points out that certain
characteristics of the original copies will, of necessity, be
apparent in reprints thereof.

INTRODUCTION

For scholars of the nineteenth century, the decades
following 1860 tend to have a special appeal. In many
ways, these were progressive years: reforms in
education, working conditions and laws governing
marriage, voting and property were changing the social
texture of England, and the rise of an affordable and
prolific press (after the paper duty was abolished in
1861) meant that a highly literate populace could, to a
hitherto unparalleled degree, become involved in the
questions and debates of the day. Prominent among
these debates was the changing role of women, many of
whom were expressing their desires in print, using both
the journalistic essay and the novel as a way of making
their claims and of investigating what these changes
meant to them. This is not to say that all women
writers were feminists (many, in fact, wrote only to
oppose the newly formed suffrage movement), but that
in writing for publication they were challenging the
traditional family and gender roles that were thought to
hold English society together. Such challenges did not
go unrewarded. Scholars recovering the work of late
nineteenth-century women writers often cite negative
contemporary reviews as an index of an author's
radicalism. Even writers whom we do not, by today's
standards, recognize as 'feminists' provoked tremendous hostility, and the language used to denounce them is
often revealing: they were 'unfeminine women', or

worse, 'hysterical man haters' who should not be invited into decent homes. But what of the writers who were embraced by the nineteenth-century critics, and even held up as models for female authorship? How did they negotiate the hostile terrain of the public press to achieve both popularity and respectability? More importantly, what was or is the value of their work and what can we, over a century later, get out of reading it?

Anne Isabella Thackeray, later Lady Anne Thackeray Ritchie, was probably the best-known 'good girl' to achieve literary stature after 1860. As the daughter of William Makepeace Thackeray, she commanded a certain amount of respect from the literary world, and it would be fair to say that his name contributed to, was even – after she published her biographical intro-ductions to his collected works in 1899, commemo-rating his hundredth birthday – considered the most important subject of *her write*. Indeed Ritchie's relationships with and intimate knowledge of the male writers who were her father's contemporaries, especially Browning, Tennyson and Ruskin, would become the basis of the memoirs which assured her prolonged popularity and (as Thackeray died before he could provide an inheritance for his daughters) financial independence. It has been easy, in this light, for critics to dismiss her as the privileged daughter of a literary 'great' whose connections are more interesting than her career, or even as a woman who articulated the status quo by defining herself in relation to great men. However, such analysis denies the success that Ritchie achieved in her own *right* as a novelist, social commen-tator and biographer of women as well as of men. Despite the very real merits of novels like *Story of Elizabeth* (1863) and *Old Kensington* (1873) –

explicitly concerned with female subjects and subjectivity – Hester Thackeray Fuller's desire (articulated in 1951) that critics explore her mother's innovative 'approach to fiction',[1] has gone almost completely unfulfilled. Commentary on Ritchie tends to emphasize her famous father, and Carol Hanbery MacKay's efforts to call attention to her literary style – particularly with the 1988 republication of the *Centenary Biographical Introductions* – have received little notice, perhaps because the text itself asks readers to think more about Thackeray than about its writer.[2] Reviving interest in Thackeray near the end of her own career, Ritchie, in effect, subordinated her own writerly identity to stand (more than ever) in the shadow of his celebrated personality. Ironically, the last major work of her fifty-year oeuvre has ensured her limited reputation as a dutiful daughter who, in Swinburne's words, produced 'the most perfect memorial ever raised to the fame and to the character of any great writer on record'.[3]

Born in London in 1837, Ritchie was named after her paternal grandmother, Anne Carmichael-Smyth, and her mother, Isabella Shawe Thackeray. Both women would have profound impact on Ritchie, though they would be absent during much of her growing up. Winifred Gerin, in her moving and well-researched biography *Anne Thackeray Ritchie*, has detailed the events that shaped Ritchie's unique

[1]   Hester Thackeray Fuller and Violet Hammersley, *Thackeray's Daughter, Some Recollections of Anne Thackeray Ritchie* (Dublin: Euphorion Books, 1951), p. 101.

[2]   Carol Hanbery MacKay, Peter Shillingsburg and Julia Maxey, *The Two Thackerays, Anne Thackeray Ritchie's Centenary Biographical Introductions to the Works of William Makepeace Thackeray* (New York: AMS Press, 1988).

[3]   Algernon Charles Swinburne, 'Charles Dickens', *Quarterly Review*, vol. 196 (1902), p. 39.

perspective, and particularly the formulations of womanhood and femininity that would later find expression in her work.[4] Early tragedies – including the death of her infant sister and the attempted suicide of her mother (who was permanently institutionalized following post-partum depression in 1840) – left the family broken and (with Isabella's medical expenses) broke. Still struggling to establish himself as a writer, Thackeray left 'Anny' and her younger sister Harriet, known as 'Minny', in his mother's care in Paris. Though they had to face hardships, France was a rich resource for a child's imagination, and Thackeray – whose philosophy of education was based on stimulating that faculty – encouraged his eldest to take in its atmosphere. Paris would, in fact, be the setting of Ritchie's first novel, *The Story of Elizabeth*, inspired in part by her teenage rebellion against her Calvinist grandparents. While Ritchie's childhood was, as Gerin puts it, 'shockingly' lacking in conventional schooling, her liberal access to literature usually forbidden to girls (most notably novels by Dickens and Brontë) fortified her religious scepticism and independence of mind. By the time she, at fifteen, became her father's 'secretary amanuensis', she had already decided on a literary career and her participation in Thackeray's creative process stimulated confidence in her own imaginative power.

Precocious and warm-spirited, Ritchie – by her father's account – assumed primary caretaking and nurturing responsibilities when the family reunited in London in 1846. Isabella's illness left her the eldest female in the Thackeray home, and she immediately

---

[4] Winifred Gerin, *Anne Thackeray Ritchie, A Biography* (Oxford: Oxford University Press, 1981).

became surrogate 'wife' and mother to her father and adoring sister. This experience set the tone for Ritchie's later life, as she would fill these roles for numerous people, including her own mother (whom she supported until her death in 1894), her governess' orphaned children, her niece (after Minny died in childbirth in 1875), Leslie Stephen (Minny's bereft husband), and Virginia Woolf, who was the child of Stephen's second marriage. During a century characterized by women's rebellions against their traditional gender roles, Ritchie – well before she became a wife and mother in fact, in 1877 – embraced them to perhaps even an unusual degree. While she never overtly identified herself with the feminist movement, she did, as breadwinner and literary celebrity, extend herself beyond the traditional domain of women. Implicitly rather than explicitly supporting the efforts of women who (as the narrator of *Old Kensington* comments) 'cry out in print' because their 'vitality cannot be repressed',[5] she preferred to focus on the hardships of women whose values and experiences were similar to her own. Both *The Story of Elizabeth* and *Old Kensington* feature heroines who, like Ritchie, become caretakers, endure losses and, through their experiences, learn to take control of their situations. In her treatment of human subjects, fictional or real, Ritchie projected the sense that women's sympathetic powers were valuable and necessary, a cause for celebration. Though not directly engaged in the debates about what women should be or do, her prose gave these ideas renewed genuineness, and thereby subtly reappropriated an ideal which had been typically used to

---

[5] *Old Kensington. A Novel*, p. 73.

oppress women in order to say something about their value and importance. By Ritchie's death in 1919, her novels were already long out of print, though her *Centennial Introductions* remained, as now, a 'must read' for Thackeray scholars. Hester Fuller briefly revived the interest of women readers when she published her mother's letters in 1924, making them feel, as Muriel Kent later recalled, 'that they had gained a friend with a tender heart and discerning spirit'.[6] This impression is consistent with the interests and the thematic concerns that characterize Ritchie's work, particularly her fascination with women's lives, desires, ambitions and hardships. Women writers and artists were often the subjects of her pen: Mrs Barbauld, Mrs Opie, Felicia Felix, Maria Edgeworth, Elizabeth Gaskell, Elizabeth Barrett Browning, Fanny Kemble and Margaret Oliphant are only a few of the 'Modern Sibyls' (the phrase that would title her 1883 essay collection), to whom she paid tribute. Her interest in women artists who (like Ritchie now) were facing obscurity sometimes baffled critics who would have preferred to know more about Thackeray's 'circle'. Surprised that anyone should care about Mrs Barbauld and Mrs Opie, the Saturday Review in 1883 asserted that they were 'both dead and buried, nor can anything revive an interest in their works'.[7] In fact, revival does not appear to have been what Ritchie (keenly aware of reigning literary standards) was aiming for. Her discussions tend to be 'personal rather than literary',[8] and express her desire

---

[6] Muriel Kent, 'Anne Thackeray Ritchie', *The Cornhill Magazine*, vol. 155 (1937), p. 706.

[7] 'A Book of Sibyls', *Saturday Review*, vol. 56 (1883), p. 545.

[8] *ibid.*

to show that women were acting in and contributing to the world, and that their personal as well as their professional struggles held meaning. Loosely focused on why and how these women wrote – as a means of self-expression, to support families, often answering at once to numerous and conflicting demands on their time and energy – these biographical essays implicitly suggest a need, on the part of a writer so intimately associated with a literary father, to recover her literary mothers. Perhaps more importantly, they provided women readers with a mirror through which to recognize something of their own 'life' and experiences in a market-place that was relatively new to them and, at times, unwelcoming.

Ritchie's treatment by Victorian biographers suggests something not only about what it means for women artists to be in the shadows of great men, but also about why she was so sought after as a memorialist. Whether or not she knew her subjects, her objective (often achieved by intensive research) was to convey something of the personalities that informed their lives. Reviewers praised her ability to create 'living records' of 'our friends and England's', so unlike the usual 'trifling' accounts that tended towards gossip and lacked 'gentleness'.[9] A number of the memorials published after her death in 1919 provide a real contrast to her own style, subjecting her to the carelessness against which she had shielded so many writers from her own and the previous generation. Remembering her as an 'airier, more feminine' (and therefore as a watered-down) version of her father, *The Cornhill*, comparing her to Henry Charles Beeching, concludes in praise of

---

[9] 'The Old Saloon', *Blackwood's Magazine*, vol. 152 (1892), p. 852.

Beeching who 'most admirably upheld'[10] Thackeray's tradition. Similarly, the *Dictionary of National Biography*, listing her under her husband's name, commented that 'it is in social life rather than in literature that her position was unique'.[11] Even more generous reviewers, like Howard Sturgis, extolled Richmond Ritchie as 'perhaps rather more than [his wife's] intellectual equal', and hinted that he may have 'helped her with her own work'.[12] In reality, Ritchie's most prolific and successful period occurred before her marriage to Richmond, whose proposal she accepted late in life, long after she had been recognized as a woman of letters. What's more, their marriage appears not to have conformed to traditional patterns, as Ritchie was her husband's acknowledged mentor, senior to him by sixteen years. While critics had always looked for 'traces' of her father, most (including George Eliot) credited Ritchie during her lifetime with an interesting and pleasing style – a combination of precision and 'diffuseness', of realism and impressionism – that was uniquely her own.

Ritchie's entrance into the literary scene was not much different than that of any other aspiring writer of the day. Her early essays and first novel, *The Story of Elizabeth*, were published anonymously, 'without any trumpets',[13] and there is no question that their positive reception was won independently of her father. Though

---

[10] 'In Memoriam, Anne Thackeray Ritchie and Henry Charles Beeching', *The Cornhill Magazine*, vol. 47 (1919), p. 447.

[11] Lord Blake and C. S. Nicholls, *Dictionary of National Biography* (Oxford: Oxford University Press, 1990), p. 463.

[12] Howard Sturgis, 'Anne Isabella Thackeray (Lady Ritchie)', *The Cornhill Magazine*, vol. 47 (1919), p. 455.

[13] 'The Old Saloon', *Blackwood's Magazine*, vol. 152 (1892), p. 852.

she would later turn exclusively to essay writing, fiction was Ritchie's first passion; she produced 'several novels and a play' in her early teens, causing her alarmed parent to insist that she put off 'scribbling' and read *'other* people's books'[14] instead. *The Story of Elizabeth,* which ran serially in the *Cornhill* ten years later, suggests that Ritchie had done more than this. By late adolescence (when most of the novel was written), she had absorbed – even formulated a response to – the debates about questions of literary form and function, and about female authorship. In addition, she had taken possession of the themes and subject matter that would be more fully explored in *Village on the Cliff* four years later, and given their most mature expression in *Old Kensington* in 1873. The first and third novels, reprinted here, are most interesting for their still-familiar visions of girlhood, and for their rendering of how young, fairly sheltered women learn to 'read' the world and become self-aware actors in it. Far from presenting an idyllic picture of the experience of women in Victorian society, Ritchie exposes her heroines to a number of disillusionments, mostly pertaining to the unethical and pecuniary operations of the marriage market. Her sense that women are 'ripened' rather than defeated by their trials becomes particularly important in *Old Kensington,* where a number of reversals – more succinctly emphasized than in *Story of Elizabeth* – take place. These reversals have to do with moving her heroines from powerlessness to subtle positions of power, most markedly in their dealings with men. More unusual is

---

[14] Hester Thackeray Ritchie, *Thackeray and His Daughter, The Letters and Journals of Anne Thackeray Ritchie, with Many Letters of William Makepeace Thackeray* (New York: Harper & Brothers, 1924), p. 124.

Ritchie's portrayal of women's relationships to each other, as in both novels she recuperates old maids and maiden aunts (typically villainized in Victorian social fiction) as the nurturers and advisors of her maturing heroines. While neither novel emphasizes the changing status of women in Victorian England in the way that New Women novels would by the 1890s – though 'Dolly' of *Old Kensington* does have her own latch key – they do represent a uniquely female response to the concerns about literary production that accompanied these changes. The role of literature – its relationship to national identity and the character of society – was a major topic of the period, and nearly everyone had something to say about who should be reading and writing what. The alarm sounded by William Wordsworth in 1849 had, with the rise of the 'Sensation School of Art', become a roaring siren by 1860. Modern taste, to the poet's thinking, had been blunted by the conditions of modern life: war, urban crowding, industrialization with its consequent 'uniformity of occupation', had combined to produce, in the average citizen, a 'craving for extraordinary incident', 'a degrading thirst for outrageous stimulation'. In supplying this thirst, artists and writers – particularly the authors of 'frantic novels' – were failing in their responsibility to society, feeding the vicious trend and ignoring the higher purposes of art to uplift mankind.[15] Implicit here is the assumption that people are influenced by what they read, and this assumption would remain vital to the ideas of authorship and literary

[15] William Wordsworth, 'Preface to the Second Edition of *Lyrical Ballads*', in Hazard Adams (editor), *Critical Theory Since Plato* (Fort Worth: Harcourt, Brace Janovich College Publishers, 1992), p. 439.

merit over the following decades. While sensationalism was not exclusively a female phenomenon (Wilkie Collins is perhaps most immediately associated with the term), women's writing and reading were, given the Victorian's ideas about gender, of special concern; and women were doing more of both than ever before. In a series of *Blackwood's* reviews published in the early 1860s, Margaret Oliphant called attention to this fact: 'nowadays', she wrote, 'stains of ink linger on the prettiest of fingers', but far from exciting celebrity, women's fiction was disparaged as 'a branch of female industry not more important than Berlin wool'. Yet Oliphant pointed to what she saw as a telling paradox: 'though we laugh at it, sneer at it, patronize it, we continue to read, or somebody does', and soaring subscriptions to *Mudie's* underlined her claim.[16]

Why were women so involved in the production and reading of what Oliphant called 'sensational monsters'? Sally Mitchell has discussed this phenomenon in terms of what the situations, characters and emotions that dominated women's literature of the 1860s indicate about 'the way women felt about the society in which they lived'. Typically lacking in satire or in 'overt social comment',[17] these tear-stained fictions nonetheless express a great deal about the frustrations and fantasies of their women writers and readers. Mitchell's sense of how authors like Mrs Henry Woods and Rhoda Broughton projected 'emotional analyses'[18] of the culture that evoked those frustrations helps to explain their tremendous popularity – and the corresponding

[16] Margaret Oliphant, 'Novels', *Blackwood's Magazine*, vol. 94 (1863), p. 168.

[17] Sally Mitchell, 'Sentiment and Suffering: Women's Recreational Reading in the 1860s', *Victorian Studies*, vol. 21 (1977), p. 31.

[18] *ibid.*, p. 34.

censure with which they met. If women sympathized with persecuted heroines of sentimental, sensationalistic literature, then this was – in the eyes of the critics – a dangerous sort of sympathy. Building on Mitchell's reading, Kate Flint has analysed the 'prescriptive attitude' towards women's fiction that developed (at least in part) as a response to literary sensationalism. Wordsworth's warning against the state of 'savage torpor' threatening the modern mind applied, or so it seems, especially to women. This had to do both with 'the circumstances of women's lives' and with the 'physiological and psychological ways in which [they] were held to differ from men'.[19] Driven by instinct and intuition rather than by intellect and reason, women's virtue – their ability to empathize, identify with and even to 'live in' others – was also their greatest weakness, and women already impatient of 'old restraints' were in particular danger when picking up a volume of *East Lynne*. In short, they were capable of failing to distinguish fiction from reality, of neglecting husband and home in favour of novel-reading; or worse, of attempting, Madame Bovary-like, to act out fantastic plots of romance and seduction. Sensation novels therefore promoted a cruel misuse of women's God-given sympathetic capacities, and their writers were guilty not only of degrading literature, but of degrading home, family and society.

It is no surprise that, with women's fiction under this kind of attack, serious women writers of the mid-century responded by attempting to establish their own definitions and standards for what was genuinely good

---

[19] Kate Flint, 'The Woman Reader and the Opiate of Fiction: 1855–1870', in Jeremy Hawthorn (editor), *The Nineteenth Century British Novel* (Stratford-Upon-Avon: Edward Arnold, 1986), p. 50.

women's writing, and this did not necessarily mean either turning wholly to or wholly away from male literary standards. Committed as much as their male contemporaries to the notion that literature should have 'worthy purpose',[20] they were particularly concerned with the role that their work played in their readers' lives. To be sure, Oliphant lamented the 'confused moral world'[21] of women's novels, and blamed the serialization of fiction on the writers' need to produce 'strong effects' that clouded the reader's judgement.[22] But if literature could be a force for 'moral obliquity', so could it be a source of health and inspiration. The assumption that novels could actually help real women to cope by providing realistic role models was implicit in the thinking of writers like Oliphant, Dinah Craik and (as we will see) Ritchie. Rather than rejecting the notion that women, by nature, identified with fictional heroines, they embraced it as a cause for celebration *when* writers rose to the occasion. Craik's 1861 review of *Mill on the Floss* suggests the centrality of this idea in the analysis by women of women's literature. Remarking on the obvious 'perfection', power and breadth of the novel, Craik nonetheless expresses a feeling of betrayal: Maggie Tulliver dies in the end because, as Eliot created her, she simply could not live in the world. What then 'is to become of the hundreds of clever girls' like Maggie who read the novel? And how is it that Eliot, in the same text, can call on older

---

[20] William Wordsworth, 'Preface to the Second Edition of *Lyrical Ballads*', in Hazard Adams (editor), *Critical Theory Since Plato* (Fort Worth: Harcourt, Brace Janovich College Publishers, 1992), p. 438.

[21] Margaret Oliphant, 'Novels', *Blackwood's Magazine*, vol. 94 (1863), p. 169.

[22] Margaret Oliphant, 'Sensation Novels', *Blackwood's Magazine*, vol. 91 (1862), p. 568.

women to be the 'refuge and rescue of early stumblers' when, in portraying death as the only 'escape from all pain', she fails the task?[23]

While Eliot and Craik here represent diverse approaches to fiction writing, they shared similar concerns over the quality of women's literature in general, and these concerns had specifically to do with their ideas about realism. For Craik, Eliot's realism was wonderful in its skill, yet too much 'vividness' was distressing in such powerless heroines, since they lacked an ability to deal with their circumstances or simply to *live*. Her criticism of young writers who – like Prometheus playing with fire – 'little dream' of their awesome responsibility, strikes (to say the least) a weighty moral tone.[24] Equally serious and intimidating were Eliot's famous complaints against 'silly women novelists' five years earlier. Embarrassed by what she saw as their carelessness, Eliot disparaged women for falling short of the authoritative standards for literary realism into which she put her 'strongest effort'.[25] For her, 'a sense of the responsibility involved in publication, and an appreciation of the sacredness of the writer's art' were no less than 'moral qualities'.[26] Defending the cause of female education and authorship, Eliot blamed the mass of women writers whose works – in failing to express these qualities – cast doubt on the intellect and moral soundness of their gender. Her own commitment to realism, her ideal of

---

[23] Dinah Craik, 'To Novelists – And a Novelist', *Macmillan's Magazine*, vol. 3 (1861), p. 445.

[24] *ibid.*, p. 442.

[25] George Eliot, from chapter 17 of *Adam Bede* in Dorothy Van Ghent, *The English Novel* (New York: Harper & Row, 1953), p. 209.

[26] George Eliot, 'Silly Novels By Lady Novelists', *Westminster Review*, vols. 65–6 (1856), p. 254.

giving 'a faithful account of men and things as they have mirrored themselves on my mind', carried with it a Wordsworthian sensibility. Like occupants of 'the witness box, narrating...experience on oath',[27] Eliot believed that writers should truly (in so far as it is possible) reflect the human condition and that in doing so, they could elevate humanity. Furthermore, women's novels had, Eliot hinted, a significant role to play as, at their best, they achieved 'a precious specialty, lying quite apart from masculine aptitudes and experience'.[28]

These then were the issues and imperatives faced by Ritchie – a young woman with serious literary ambitions – when she began her publishing career in 1860. What is most interesting about *The Story of Elizabeth* (which the *Cornhill* ran alongside Eliot's *Romola* in 1862) is not so much any unusual turn of plot or radicalness of style, but Ritchie's already mature engagement in the concerns that occupied critics like Eliot and Craik. Centred – as *Old Kensington* would be ten years later – on the complications of girlhood, growing up and the marriage market, the novel spoke to the experiences of average women, and Ritchie's insistence on the 'commonness' of her heroines projected (if subtly) a philosophy not dissimilar to Eliot's. More fully articulated in Ritchie's essay *Heroines and Their Grandmothers* (1865), this philosophy was no mere echo of a famous father (though his influences are certainly present), but a response to the criticism being levelled at women writers and readers who, as Ritchie explained, had developed a preference for 'analysis of emotion instead

---

[27] George Eliot, from chapter 17 of *Adam Bede* in Dorothy Van Ghent, *The English Novel* (New York: Harper & Row, 1953), p. 209.

[28] Eliot, 'Silly Novels By Lady Novelists', *Westminster Review*, vols. 65–6 (1856), p. 254.

of analysis of character, the history of feeling instead of the history of events'.[29] Women's writing had, she realized, undergone a transformation by which the Victorians were both fascinated and appalled, and there were reasons for the change: these had to do with women's lives, and with their need to find their own otherwise 'silent struggles' given voice in literature. Like Craik, Ritchie believed that heroines had a real purpose, but by 1860, modern heroines – with their extravagant suffering and sensational fates – had fallen into disrepute. The recovery of heroines from 'sensation sentiment'[30] was a problem that Ritchie (whose own 'Elizabeth' she admitted, could be a bit 'tempestuous'), felt called upon to deal with.

Where critics like Eliot expressed anger and impatience with women who indulged in sensation conventions, Ritchie viewed her contemporaries in a more generous light. Instead of condemning the 'sensation feeling' that seemed to be 'required by modern taste',[31] she asked 'for what reason are such stories written?' The answers, for Ritchie, lay in fiction's ability to engage women's sympathies, to express sorrows so intense that they seem 'for a minute as if they [are] one's own', and through this empathetic experience, 'to cheer one in dull hours, to soothe, to interest, and to distract from weary thoughts from which it is at times a blessing to escape'.[32] More than escape however, Ritchie saw novels as a source of nourishment and strength, especially when readers

---

[29] Anne Isabella Thackeray (Ritchie), 'Heroines and Their Grandmothers', *The Cornhill Magazine*, vol. 11 (1865), p. 632.

[30] *ibid.*, p. 631.

[31] *ibid.*, p. 630.

[32] *ibid.*, p. 637.

recognized their own experiences and longings reflected in the pages of an absorbing book. The increase in the production of novels was neither a source of despair or mystery to her, but a natural result of 'the necessity for expression' on the part of writers and readers for whom fiction provided 'a bond of common pain and pleasure, of common fear and hope, and love and weakness'. In Ritchie's view, women writers were not to be rebuked for writing novels that are 'like tears...the vent and relief of many a chafing spirit',[33] but gently directed to reconsider what the negative influence of too many tears might be. Modern heroines represented a liberation from the emotional reserve of literary forbears like Jane Bennett, but such liberation carried with it another risk. 'Our danger is now, not of expressing and feeling too little, but of expressing more than we feel.'[34] In Ritchie's analysis, the damage occurred on two levels: while overly morbid and introspective heroines suggested a too tragic, even 'strained and affected' view of life to their readers, 'sensation feeling' also represented a departure from literary integrity when such heroines lacked realism; or in other words, when they expressed themselves *so much* that expression 'depreciated in value'.[35]

Ritchie's own fiction is best described as the product of these insights into the value of women's writing and its problems. Asserting that there is 'no comparison between the interest excited by facts...with the interest

---

[33] Anne Isabella Thackeray (Ritchie), 'Heroines and Their Grandmothers', *The Cornhill Magazine*, vol. 11 (1865), p. 639.

[34] Anne Isabella Thackeray, Lady Ritchie, *A Book of Modern Sibyls: Mrs Barbauld, Miss Edgeworth, Mrs Opie, Miss Austen* (New York: Harper & Brothers, 1883). From 'Miss Austen', originally published in *The Cornhill Magazine* in 1871.

[35] Anne Isabella Thackeray (Ritchie), 'Heroines and Their Grandmothers', *The Cornhill Magazine*, vol. 11 (1865), pp. 631, 640.

of feeling and emotion',[36] she stressed her kinship with
her contemporaries while also seeking to bridge the gap
between their work and the more 'reserved' realism of
Jane Austen. In this, she was responding to what she
perceived as the needs of her readers, as well as to the
critical concerns about the form and 'influences' of literature. While the circumstances of sensation heroines –
abused women, deprived heiresses, outcasts – tended to
be as inflated as their emotions, Ritchie self-consciously
formulated her characters as universal types; they are
typically, as in *Old Kensington*, healthy and 'for the
most part, foolish young folks just beginning their
lives'.[37] They are neither poverty stricken nor well-to-
do, neither particularly blessed in nor thwarted by their
families. Elizabeth Gilmour and Dorothea Vanborough
are beautiful without being glamorous, intelligent but
young women with a lot to learn. What and how they
learn is the gist of these novels, and Elizabeth and Dolly
differ from sensation types in that while they too suffer
hardships and betrayals, they finally – as real women
need to do – make sense of their worlds. The reviews of
Elizabeth and *Old Kensington* suggest something about
what a welcome relief such untrendy heroines were.
Ritchie's novels were received as timely protests 'against
the falsehood in art which is so prevalent among novel
writers of the present period... the falsity of extremes'.[38]
In plainer terms, her heroines are neither hysterics nor
'Cinderellas'; made to experience 'those trials that come

[36] Anne Isabella Thackeray (Ritchie), 'Heroines and Their Grandmothers',
The Cornhill Magazine, vol. 11 (1865), p. 632.

[37] *Old Kensington. A Novel*, p. 83.

[38] 'Miss Thackeray's "Old Kensington"', *Edinburgh Review*, vol. 138
(1873), p. 166.

to everybody in real life',[39] they achieved a high degree
of realism by contemporary standards.

To the twentieth-century reader this emphasis in the
critique of Ritchie may seem surprising. Particularly in
Old Kensington, one is more likely to be struck by her
ability to project a sense of atmosphere and mood than
by her adherence to traditional conventions for realism.
Ritchie's digressions (on the quality of sunlight, the feel
of a ruined garden) convey something about her
heroine's way of perceiving the world, and this method
of rendering experience would gain legitimacy in the
following decades, especially with Henry James' formulations of impressionism. Referring directly to Ritchie's
model and to her advice to the (then) novice – 'Try to
be one of those people on whom nothing is lost!'[40] –
James's 'The Art of Fiction' (1884) would argue that
'impressions *are* experience', and impressionism a more
real way of describing it. The reviews of Ritchie suggest
that her style influenced readers to identify with and
believe in her heroines, and James's references to the
'woman of genius' who advised him in his youth tend to
confirm Hester Fuller's claim that her mother's
influence was far-reaching, and that her work 'opened
wide a door through which a whole host' of writers
would come.[41] Focused on the inner lives of these
heroines, Ritchie's novels highlight issues that still move
women – a sense of duty to family and love relationships, a longing for sympathy, the emphasis on female

---

[39] 'Miss Thackeray's "Old Kensington"', p. 182.

[40] James E. Miller, *Theory of Fiction: Henry James* (Lincoln: University of
Nebraska Press, 1972), p. 35.

[41] Hester Thackeray Fuller and Violet Hammersley, *Thackeray's Daughter,
Some Recollections of Anne Thackeray Ritchie* (Dublin: Euphorion
Books, 1951), p. 101.

beauty over intellect and education, the pressures to be 'good', self-sacrificing, *married*. For Ritchie's contemporary readers, her ability to create heroines whose experiences of these matters were believable, wrought plainly and without exaggeration, had considerable power. Oliphant was the first to call attention to this quality in *The Story of Elizabeth*. Free from 'ideal mists', the merit of the book, she claimed, lay in a 'certain wonderful realism' and in a 'force of line and colour' so vivid that women readers will have difficulty putting it down: 'It will call back ghosts of recollections to the hearts of women who were once girls, and know what it means; and it bears every mark of deep veracity as a study of true life.'[42] The reviewers of *Old Kensington* would echo this feeling, stressing Ritchie's 'deep psychological insight' in 'the delineation of her own sex'.[43] In that they were 'common' women with *common sense*, Ritchie's heroines projected an idea of what women were that women could appreciate: they allowed female reviewers – in saying *these* portraits 'may be true'[44] – to stake a claim in opposition to the rhetoric (bolstered by women's sensation fiction), that associated women with irrationality.

What Ritchie was most well-known for – other than, of course, her famous paternity – was her ability to inspire empathetic feeling in her readers. This may account for her focus on biography writing after *Old Kensington*, even though the novel was particularly successful and went through five editions. Commentary on Ritchie suggests that – despite her turn away from

[42] Margaret Oliphant, 'Novels', *Blackwood's Magazine*, vol. 94 (1863), p. 176.

[43] 'Miss Thackeray's "Old Kensington"', p. 183.

[44] Margaret Oliphant, 'Novels', *Blackwood's Magazine*, vol. 94 (1863), p. 171.

novels – the emotional involvement she was capable of inspiring was considered equally valuable when achieved through fictive characters. Fitzwilliam Stephen described the experience of reading Ritchie's books, in 1867, as having a 'moral effect': 'each…is, from first to last, the expression of the feeling of intense sympathy with everyone whom the authoress regards as beautiful or good or wise.'[45] In the same vein, Howard Sturgis borrowed Ritchie's own analysis of 'great' writers (from her paper on Ruskin) to describe her forte, an aptitude for 'reaching hearers at once, giving straight from [herself] and not in reflections from other minds'. Eulogizing Ritchie in 1919, Sturgis regretted that few readers were still familiar with her novels, but speculated that Ritchie's 'great gift of genuine sympathy' – a 'sap-stirring' and 'life-giving' quality – might still lead to their establishment as classics.[46] In short, Ritchie fulfilled an ideal of authorship held dear by her contemporaries. The 'great value' of books, wrote an earlier admirer in 1873, is 'to rouse a sluggish nature into the activity of feeling, and if a novelist were called upon for his *raison d'etre* he could scarcely find a better one than this'.[47] Where sensation writers relied upon hideous secrets and revelations to stimulate empathy and interest, Ritchie effectively relied upon a simpler vision of the world as she knew it, and her characters were recognizably (as Oliphant noted) 'within the range of [their author's] observation and

---

[45] Fitzwilliam Stephen, 'The Village on the Cliff', *Fraser's Magazine*, vol. 76 (1867), p. 499.

[46] Howard Sturgis, 'Anne Isabella Thackeray (Lady Ritchie)', *The Cornhill Magazine*, vol. 47 (1919), p. 452.

[47] 'Miss Thackeray's "Old Kensington"', p. 184.

experience'.[48] This explains why even the harshest critics of women's writing, among them George Eliot, made 'an exception' of 'Miss Thackeray's stories', which Eliot reported to *Blackwood's* in 1870, 'I cannot resist when they come near me'.[49]

In reviewing these commentaries, we can begin to understand better Ritchie's accomplishment: emotional intensity, the inspiration of sympathy and identification with fictional characters – these were, to the sensation-weary Victorians, the mine fields of women's literature. Yet, Ritchie trespassed the danger grounds without causing any undue explosions. Evoking these types of responses without the 'violence' of sensation conventions, she reclaimed the 'virtue' of women's sympathetic powers, at the same time that she reminded her contemporaries of the Wordsworthian ideal so prominent in the thinking of artists like Eliot: 'one of the best services in which...a writer can be engaged', the poet had advised the nation, was to 'enlarge' the ability of the mind to be 'excited' without the 'gross' and degrading influences of shock effect.[50] Meeting this criterion, Ritchie quietly affirmed the notion that art was capable of refining and educating taste away from sensationalism. As a female writer who answered to her culture's paranoias about literary production, she became not only a model of authorship but of Womanhood; in short, a literary 'good girl' whose respectability went unchallenged despite what modern readers, after recon-

[48] Margaret Oliphant, 'Novels', *Blackwood's Magazine*, vol. 94 (1863), p. 171.

[49] Winifred Gerin, *Anne Thackeray Ritchie, A Biography* (Oxford: Oxford University Press, 1981), p. 163.

[50] William Wordsworth, 'Preface to the Second Edition of *Lyrical Ballads*', in Hazard Adams (editor), *Critical Theory Since Plato* (Fort Worth: Harcourt, Brace Janovich College Publishers, 1992), p. 439.

sidering *The Story of Elizabeth* and *Old Kensington*, are likely to recognize as pointed critiques of the Victorians' thinking about gender. As in Ritchie's biographies and memorials of women writers, her fiction expresses an implicit sense of women's importance to each other in and outside of family circles, as consolers, role models and protectors. While both novels adhere to traditional marriage plot formulas, on a deeper level they express a fantasy of surrogate motherhood whereby older women become the mechanisms for moving the stories forward to just conclusions. In this, they are more gratifying versions of the fantasy by which Craik measured Eliot: that of the older woman who provides 'refuge' and safe-harbour to young 'stumblers'. Though Elly and Dolly are forced to deal with 'bad' mothers – a convention commonly used in female-authored Victorian fiction – both heroines are taken in by older women, and the bonds between them displace 'romance' as the emotional centre of the narratives. The prevalence of 'bad' mothers in Victorian literature has been interpreted as an indication of heightened tension between generations of women whose opportunities and values were changing with the times. *Elizabeth* and *Old Kensington* illustrate this tension at the same time that they place terrific value on the ability of mature women to guide their less experienced friends. While both heroines are required to surpass the attitudes of mothers who understand and evaluate themselves (and their daughters) only in terms of their relationships with men, the maiden aunts and widows to whom they turn are content to live independently, without husbands. Significantly, their examples make marriage a matter of choice, not fate – an issue with which Ritchie (who refused a number of proposals, including Richmond's, until her fortieth year) was familiar. More than this, Ritchie movingly figures these female bonds as crucial to her heroine's emotional and spiritual development. Both Elizabeth and Dolly long for connection with various mother figures who shape their dreams, and who help them to rethink their identities in ways that negotiate the novels' traditional marriage conclusions.

Plots in which women desire each other's sympathy more than they do men are perhaps as subversive as anything else in Victorian literature. Ritchie was no feminist (at least not in any usual sense), but what she claimed to know about human nature has feminist overtones. While her heroines never discuss their feelings about other women (or, as in the style of Jane Austen, about very much at all), their actions reveal a good deal about what Ritchie thought women needed and wanted. Surely Elly needs to be married, to escape a tedious home life and to 'grow up'; her 'half-glad, half-reluctant' choice of John Dampier is closely aligned with these (albeit unconscious) motivations. While the young women of sensation fiction fantasized about mysterious potential husbands, Elly's marriage fantasy takes on an unusual twist. In fact, Elly's attraction to John from the start has more to do with his aunt than with him, and 'Miss Dampier, knitting in the sunshine'[51] usurps his place in her dreams of future happiness. Later when Elly is sick, she sees her friend (not her 'lover') in 'dim dreams' that seem almost to call the rescuing older woman to her bedside. Having 'lost' John, she gains a new mother who – and this is most interesting – literally rewrites Elly's story from within the novel.

---

[51] *The Story of Elizabeth*, p. 29.

The Dampier family (after Elly learns that John is engaged to an heiress) perceive her in conventional terms: she is 'artful', a 'mad girl' whose illness is designed to trap John. However, through the novel's old maids, Ritchie turns the sensation conventions for female hysteria on their heads. Playfully foiling the melodrama of Elly's 'fever' (the result of sleeping in wet clothes as much as of John's rejection), Ritchie gives Elly's sharp-sighted servant, Francoise (who has also been her particular friend) the last word: young women are more resilient than they are given credit for, and the relatives who are prepared for Elly's death act absurdly. In terms of plot, Elly's fever is important because it gives Miss Dampier the opportunity to step in, to assert her love for Elly and to determine, 'against all opposition', that 'she shall be made happy' (in part, an expression of loyalty to her own deceased mother whom Elly resembles).[52] Adopting Elly as her 'heroine', she edits the Dampiers' version of events to tell a contrasting story 'in her quiet, pleasant, old-fashioned way...of all that had been happening'. Doing so, she allows Elly to be seen fully, as a young woman whose character is refined by her disappointments; more than this, the refuge provided by Miss Dampier allows Elly to envision another (unmarried) life for herself, and to offer John to 'the other woman' (Elly's former schoolmate) whose subsequent rejection of him utterly deflates his domineering presumptions and 'superior' status.

By the time she created Dorothea Vanborough, Ritchie's concern with the role that female bonds play in women's lives had noticeably deepened. The opening pages of *Old Kensington* amplify this theme, as well as

[52] *Story of Elizabeth* , pp. 126–7.

the critique of the marriage market already developed in *Story of Elizabeth*. Beginning again with her heroine's early childhood, Ritchie focuses on Dolly's fascination with the stories told by her aunt, Lady Sarah – a widow whose history, Ritchie ironically remarks, has been 'concisely detailed' in the church registry recording father's and husband's names. Lady Sarah's stories however, bring to life the female ancestors she shares with her niece, even a centuries-old 'golden-brown grandmother' whose features and name Dolly has inherited, and whose portrait will (much later) become her aunt's legacy to her. The plot of *Old Kensington* turns on Dolly's loyalty to this old aunt-mother, which (in ways she cannot predict) ultimately saves her from unhappiness. In short, Dolly's fiancé is a composite of misogynist attitudes, and when she 'disobeys' him in order to nurse Lady Sarah on her deathbed she initiates the chain of events that free her from him. Forced to rebel against the future husband whose refrain '*you belong to me*', seemed less troubling at first, Dolly re-evaluates the 'general rule' he espouses: 'a woman's work is to follow her husband…to give up her old ties and associations.'[53] Yet other women, including Dolly's future in-laws, nurture her and support her rejection of this 'rule'. One such woman – the organizer of a military hospital – steps in to 'rescue' Dolly at the height of her crisis, and to offer a more authentic view of human relationships that confirms Dolly's 'disobedience' to masculine authority: her way of loving has a terrific resonance when she tells Dolly 'we seem to belong to each other'.[54]

---

[53] *Old Kensington. A Novel*, pp. 334–5.

[54] *ibid.*, p. 428.

As in the *Story of Elizabeth*, Ritchie, formulating this far more complex and sophisticated plot, enacts a reversal of power whereby her heroine – largely due to the influence of these older women – becomes the agent of her own fate. For women, becoming active agents means discarding (at least in part) the ideals of love and marriage with which Victorian girls were indoctrinated. In her first 'romance', Dolly accepts an entirely passive role, concluding that 'indeed if he loves me, I must love him'.[55] She takes control of her life (and her self-image) when she subverts this idea of female loyalty and uses it to free herself. Professing her 'unworthiness' and lack of proper femininity, Dolly averts victim status by confessing to the fiancé who has been unfaithful *in fact* that she has been unfaithful in spirit. Having relinquished her male 'protector' to another woman, she is able to pursue a more genuine relationship – with a man who has looked to her as an advisor and teacher – obviously based on the model provided by her surrogate mothers. In *Old Kensington*, Dolly is rewarded with happiness not because she has been a 'true woman', but because she has learned to negotiate the ideals of womanhood that threatened to oppress her. Where *Story of Elizabeth* (the ending of which was rewritten to please Thackeray) was not originally intended to follow the traditional marriage resolution formula, Ritchie uses marriage in this later novel to suggest that emotional and intellectual freedom need not be radical concepts for women. Given that most women still did want to marry in 1873, Dolly is a realistic model for women's development; she is in fact 'no uncommon type', a sort of everywoman whose

---

[55] *Old Kensington. A Novel*, p. 224.

name is, Ritchie concludes, 'one that I gave her…but her real names are many, and are those of the friends whom we love'.[56]

Esther Schwartz-McKinzie
Philadelphia, 1995

[56] *Old Kensington. A Novel*, p. 529.

BIBLIOGRAPHY

Flint, Kate. 'The Woman Reader and the Opiate of Fiction: 1855–1870', in Jeremy Hawthorn (editor), *The Nineteenth Century British Novel*, Stratford-Upon-Avon: Edward Arnold, 1986.

Fuller, Hester Thackeray and Violet Hammersley. *Thackeray's Daughter, Some Recollections of Anne Thackeray Ritchie*, Dublin: Euphorion Books, 1951.

Gerin, Winifred. *Anne Thackeray Ritchie, A Biography*, Oxford: Oxford University Press, 1981.

Kent, Muriel. 'Anne Thackeray Ritchie', *The Cornhill Magazine*, vol. 155 (1937) pp. 766–73.

MacKay, Carol Hanbery, Peter Shillingsburg and Julia Maxey. *The Two Thackerays, Anne Thackeray Ritchie's Centenary Biographical Introductions to the Works of William Makepeace Thackeray*, New York: AMS Press, 1988.

Miller, James E. *Theory of Fiction: Henry James*, Lincoln: University of Nebraska Press, 1972.

Mitchell, Sally. 'Sentiment and Suffering: Women's Recreational Reading in the 1860s', *Victorian Studies*, vol. 155 (1977) pp. 29–45.

Ritchie, Hester Thackeray. *Thackeray and His Daughter, The Letters and Journals of Anne Thackeray Ritchie, with Many Letters of William Makepeace Thackeray*, New York: Harper & Brothers, 1924.

Van Ghent, Dorothy. *The English Novel*, New York: Harper & Row, 1953.

Wordsworth, William. 'Preface to the Second Edition of *Lyrical Ballads*', in Hazard Adams (editor), *Critical Theory Since Plato*, Fort Worth: Harcourt, Brace Janovich College Publishers, 1992.

CONTEMPORARY ESSAYS, REVIEWS, MEMORIALS:

Blake, Lord and C. S. Nicholls. *Dictionary of National Biography*, Oxford: Oxford University Press, 1990.

Craik, Dinah. 'To Novelists – And a Novelist', *Macmillan's Magazine*, vol. 3 (1861) pp. 441–8.

Eliot, George. 'Silly Novels By Lady Novelists', *Westminster Review*, vols. 65–6 (1856) pp. 243–54.

Oliphant, Margaret. 'Sensation Novels', *Blackwood's Magazine*, vol. 91 (1862) pp. 564–84.

Oliphant, Margaret. 'Novels', *Blackwood's Magazine*, vol. 94 (1863) pp. 168–83.

Sturgis, Howard. 'Anne Isabella Thackeray (Lady Ritchie)', *The Cornhill Magazine*, vol. 47 (1919) pp. 447–65.

Stephen, Fitzwilliam. 'The Village on the Cliff', *Fraser's Magazine*, vol. 76 (1867) pp. 491–503.

Swinburne, Algernon Charles. 'Charles Dickens', *Quarterly Review*, vol. 196 (1902) p. 39.

Thackeray, Anne Isabella, Lady Ritchie. 'Heroines and Their Grandmothers', *The Cornhill Magazine*, vol. 11 (1865) pp. 630–40.

Thackeray, Anne Isabella, Lady Ritchie. *A Book of Modern Sibyls: Mrs Barbauld, Miss Edgeworth, Mrs Opie, Miss Austen.* New York: Harper & Brothers, 1883.

Thackeray, Anne Isabella, Lady Ritchie. *Story of Elizabeth.* London: Smith, Elder, and Co., 1876.

Thackeray, Anne Isabella, Lady Ritchie. *Old Kensington. A Novel.* London: Smith, Elder, and Co., 1873.

'Miss Thackeray's "Old Kensington"', *Edinburgh Review*, vol. 138 (1873) pp. 166–86.

'A Book of Sibyls', *Saturday Review*, vol. 56 (1883) pp. 544–6.

'The Old Saloon', *Blackwood's Magazine*, vol. 152 (1892) pp. 852–8.

'In Memoriam, Anne Thackeray Ritchie and Henry Charles Beeching', *The Cornhill Magazine*, vol. 47 (1919) pp. 444–8.

THE
STORY OF ELIZABETH,

BY

MISS THACKERAY

LONDON

SMITH, ELDER, & CO., 15 WATERLOO PLACE

1876

JULIA MARGARET CAMERON

THE

STORY OF ELIZABETH.

CHAPTER I.

If singing breath, or echoing chord,
To every hidden pang were given,
What endless melodies were poured
As sad as earth, as sweet as heaven!

THIS is the story of a foolish woman, who, through her
own folly, learnt wisdom at last; whose troubles—they
were not very great, they might have made the happiness
of some less eager spirit—were more than she knew how
to bear. The lesson of life was a hard lesson to her.
She would not learn, she revolted against the wholesome
doctrine. And while she was crying out that she would
not learn, and turning away and railing and complaining
against her fate; days, hours, fate, went on their course.
And they passed unmoved; and it was she who gave way,
she who was altered, she who was touched and torn by
her own complaints and regrets.

B

Elizabeth had great soft eyes and pretty yellow hair, and a sweet flitting smile, which came out like sunlight over her face, and lit up yours and mine, and any other it might chance to fall upon. She used to smile at herself in the glass, as many a girl has done before her ; she used to dance about the room, and think, ' Come life, come life, mine is going to be a happy one. Here I am awaiting, and I was made handsome to be admired, and to be loved, and to be hated by a few, and worshipped by a few, and envied by all. I am handsomer than Lætitia a thousand times. I am glad I have no money as she has, and that I shall be loved for myself, for my *beaux yeux.* One person turns pale when they look at him. Tra la la, tra la la!' and she danced along the room singing. There was no carpet, only a smooth polished floor. Three tall windows looked out into a busy Paris street paved with stones, over which carriages, and cabs, and hand-trucks were jolting. There was a clock, and artificial flowers in china vases on the chimney, a red velvet sofa, a sort of *étagère* with ornaments, and a great double-door wide open, through which you could see a dining-room, also bare, polished, with a round table and an oilcloth cover, and a white china stove, and some wax-work fruit on the sideboard, and a maid in a white cap at work in the window.

Presently there came a ring at the bell. Elizabeth stopped short in her dance, and the maid rose, put down her work, and went to open the door; and then a voice, which made Elizabeth smile and look handsomer than ever, asked if Mrs. and Miss Gilmour were at home?

Elizabeth stood listening, with her fair head a little bent, while the maid said, '*No, sare*,' and then Miss Gilmour flushed up quite angrily in the inner room. and would have run out. She hesitated only for a minute, · and then it was too late; the door was shut, and Clementine sat down again to her work.

'Clementine, how dare you say I was not· at home?' cried Elizabeth, suddenly standing before her.

'Madame desired me to let no one in in her absence,' said Clementine, primly. 'I only obeyed my orders. There is the gentleman's card.'

'Sir John Dampier' was on the card, and then, in pencil, 'I hope you will be at home in Chester Street next week. Can I be your *avant-courier* in any way? I cross to-night.'

Elizabeth. smiled again, shrugged her shoulders, and said to herself, 'Next week; I can afford to wait better than he can, perhaps. Poor man! After all, *il y en a bien d'autres*;' and she went to the window, and, by leaning out, she just caught a glimpse of the Madeleine and of Sir John Dampier walking away; and then presently she saw her mother on the opposite side of the street, passing the stall of the old apple-woman, turning in under the archway of the house.

Elizabeth's mother was like her daughter, only she had black eyes and black hair, and where her daughter was wayward and yielding, the elder woman was wayward and determined. They did not care much for one another, these two. They had not lived together all their lives, or learnt to love one another, as a matter of course; they were too much alike, too much of an age : Elizabeth was eighteen, and her mother thirty-six. If Elizabeth looked twenty, the mother looked thirty, and she was as vain, as foolish, as fond of admiration as her daughter. Mrs. Gilmour did not own it to herself, but she had been used to it all her life—to be first, to be made much of; and here was a little girl who had sprung up somehow, and learnt of herself to be charming—more charming than she had ever been in her best days; and now that they had slid away, those best days, the elder woman had a dull, unconscious discontent in her heart. People whom she had known, and who had admired her but a year or two ago, seemed to neglect her now and to pass her by, in order to pay a certain homage to her daughter's youth and brilliance : John Dampier, among others, whom she had known as a boy, when she was a young woman. Good mothers, tender-hearted women, brighten again and grow young over their children's happiness and success. Caroline Gilmour suddenly became old, somehow, when she first witnessed her daughter's triumphs, and she felt that the wrinkles were growing under her wistful eyes, and

that the colour was fading from her cheeks, and she
gasped a little sigh and thought, ' Ah! how I suffer!
What is it? what can have come to me?' As time
passed on, the widow's brows grew darker, her lips set
ominously. One day she suddenly declared that she was
weary of London and London ways, and that she should
go abroad; and Elizabeth, who liked everything that was
change, that was more life and more experience—she had
not taken into account that there was any other than
the experience of pleasure in store for her—Elizabeth
clapped her hands and cried, ' Yes, yes, mamma; I am
quite tired of London and all this excitement. Let us go
to Paris for the winter, and lead a quiet life.'

'Paris is just the place to go to for quiet,' said Mrs.
Gilmour, who was smoothing her shining locks in the
glass, and looking intently into her own dark gloomful
eyes.

'The Dampiers are going to Paris,' Elizabeth went
on; 'Lady Dampier and Sir John, and old Miss Dampier
and Lætitia. He was saying how he wished you would
go. We could have such fun! *Do* go, dear, pretty mamma!'

As Elizabeth spoke, Mrs. Gilmour's dark eyes brightened, and suddenly her hard face melted; and, still looking at herself in the glass, she said, ' We will go if you
wish it, Elly. I thought you had had enough of balls.'

But the end of the Paris winter came, and even then
Elly had not had enough : not enough admiration, not

enough happiness, not enough new dresses, not enough of
herself, not enough time to suffice her eager, longing
desires, not enough delights to fill up the swift flying
days. I cannot tell you—she could not have told you
herself—what she wanted, what perfection of happiness,
what wonderful thing. She danced, she wore beautiful
dresses, she flirted, she chattered nonsense and sentiment,
she listened to music ; her pretty little head was in a
whirl. John Dampier followed her from place to place ;
and so, indeed, did one or two others. Though she was
in love with them all, I believe she would have married
this Dampier if he had asked her, but he never did. He
saw that she did not really care for him ; opportunity did
not befriend him. His mother was against it ; and then,
her mother was there, looking at him with her dark reproachful eyes—those eyes which had once fascinated and
then repelled him, and that he mistrusted so and almost
hated now. And this is the secret of my story ; but for
this it would never have been written. He hated, and she
did not hate, poor woman ! It would have been better, a
thousand times, for herself and for her daughter, had she
done so. Ah me ! what cruel perversion was it, that the
best of all good gifts should have turned to trouble, to
jealousy and wicked rancour ; that this sacred power of
faithful devotion, by which she might have saved herself
and ennobled a mean and earthly spirit, should have turned
to a curse instead of a blessing !

There was a placid, pretty niece of Lady Dampier,
called Lætitia, who had been long destined for Sir John.
Lætitia and Elizabeth had been at school together for
a good many dreary years, and were very old friends.
Elizabeth all her life used to triumph over her friend,
and to bewilder her with her careless, gleeful ways, and
yet win her over to her own side, for she was irresistible,
and she knew it. Perhaps it was because she knew it so
well that she was so confident and so charming. Lætitia,
although she was sincerely fond of her cousin, used to
wonder that her aunt could be against such a wife for her
son.

'She is a sort of princess,' the girl used to say; 'and
John *ought* to have a beautiful wife for the credit of the
family.'

'Your fifty thousand pounds would go a great deal
further to promote the credit of the family my dear,' said
old Miss Dampier, who was a fat, plain-spoken, kindly old
lady. 'I like the girl, though my sister-in-law does not;
and I hope that some day she will find a very good husband.
I confess that I had rather it were not John.'

And so one day John was informed by his mother, who
was getting alarmed, that she was going home, and that
she could not think of crossing without him. And
Dampier, who was careful, as men are mostly, and wanted
to think about his decision, and who was anxious to do the

very best for himself in every respect—as is the way with
just, and good, and respectable gentlemen—was not at all
loth to obey her summons.

Here was Lætitia, who was very fond of him—there
was no doubt of that—with a house in the country and
money at her bankers'; there was a wayward, charming,
beautiful girl, who didn't care for him very much, who
had little or no money, but whom he certainly cared for.
He talked it all over dispassionately with his aunt—so
dispassionately that the old woman got angry.

'You are a model young man, John. It quite affects
me, and makes me forget my years to see the admirable
way in which you young people conduct yourselves. You
have got such well-regulated hearts, it's quite a marvel.
You are quite right; Tishy has got 50,000l., which will
all go into your pocket, and respectable connections, who
will come to your wedding, and Elly Gilmour has not a
penny except what her mother will leave her—a mother
with a bad temper, and who is sure to marry again; and
though the girl is the prettiest young creature I ever set
eyes on, and though you care for her as you never cared
for any other woman before, men don't marry wives for
such absurd reasons as that. You are quite right to have
nothing to do with her; and I respect you for your noble
self-denial.' And the old lady began to knit away at a
great long red comforter she had always on hand for her
other nephew the clergyman.

'But, my dear aunt Jean, what is it you want me to do?' cried John.

'Drop one, knit two together,' said the old lady, cliquetting her needles.

She really wanted John to marry his cousin, but she was a spinster still and sentimental; and she could not help being sorry for pretty Elizabeth; and now she was afraid that she had said too much, for her nephew frowned, put his hands in his pockets, and walked out of the room.

He walked downstairs, and out of the door into the Rue Royale, the street where they were lodging ; then he strolled across the Place de la Concorde, and in at the gates of the Tuileries, where the soldiers were pacing, and so along the broad path, to where he heard a sound of music, and saw a glitter of people. Tum te tum, bom, bom, bom, went the military music ; twittering busy little birds were chirping up in the branches ; buds were bursting ; colours glimmering ; tinted sunshine flooding the garden, and the music, and the people ; old gentlemen were reading newspapers on the benches ; children were playing at hide-and-seek behind the statues ; nurses gossiping, and nodding their white caps, and dandling their white babies ; and there on chairs, listening to the music, the mammas were sitting in grand bonnets and parasols, working, and gossiping too, and ladies and gentlemen went walking up and down before them. All the windows of the Tuileries were ablaze with the sun ; the terraces were beginning to gleam with crocuses and spring flowers.

As John Dampier was walking along, scarcely noting all this, he heard his name softly called, and turning round he saw two ladies sitting under a budding horse-chestnut tree. One of them he thought looked like a fresh spring flower herself smiling pleasantly, all dressed in crisp light grey, with a white bonnet, and a quantity of bright yellow crocus hair. She held out a little grey hand and said,

' Won't you come and talk to us ? Mamma and I are tired of listening to music. We want to hear somebody talk.'

And then mamma, who was Mrs Gilmour, held out a straw-coloured hand, and said, ' Do you think sensible people have nothing better to do than to listen to your chatter, Elly ? Here is your particular friend, M. de Vaux, coming to us. You can talk to him.'

Elizabeth looked up quickly at her mother, then glanced at Dampier, then greeted M. de Vaux as pleasantly almost as she had greeted him.

' I am afraid I cannot stay now,' said Sir John to Elizabeth. I have several things to do. Do you know that we are going away immediately ? '

Mrs. Gilmour's black eyes seemed to flash into his face as he spoke. He felt them, though he was looking at Elizabeth, and he could not help turning away with an impatient movement of dislike.

'Going away! Oh, how sorry I am!' said Elly.
'But, mamma, I forgot—you said we were going home,
too, in a few days; so I don't mind so much. You will
come and say good-by, won't you?' Elizabeth went on,
while M. de Vaux, who had been waiting to be spoken to,
turned away rather provoked, and made some remark to
Mrs. Gilmour. And then Elizabeth seeing her opportunity, and looking up frank, fair, and smiling, said
quickly, 'To-morrow at _three_, mind—and give my love to
Lætitia,' she went on, much more deliberately, ' and my
best love to Miss Dampier! and oh, dear! why does one
ever have to say good-by to one's friends? Are you sure
you are all really going?'

' Alas!' said Dampier, looking down at the kind young
face with strange emotion and tenderness, and holding
out his hand. He had not meant it as good-by yet, but
so Elly and her mother understood it.

' Good-by, Sir John ; we shall meet again in London,'
said Mrs. Gilmour.

' Good-by,' said Elly, wistfully raising her sweet eyes.

As he walked away, he carried with him a bright
picture of the woman he loved, looking at him kindly,
happy, surrounded with sunshine and budding green
leaves, smiling and holding out her hand ; and so he saw
her in his dreams sometimes ; and so she would appear to
him now and then in the course of his life ; so he sometimes sees her now, in spring-time, generally when the

trees are coming out, and some little chirp of a sparrow or some little glistening green bud conjures up all these old bygone days again.

Mrs. Gilmour did not sleep very sound all that night. While Elizabeth lay dreaming in her dark room, her mother, with wild-falling black hair, and wrapped in a long red dressing-gown, was wandering restlessly up and down, or flinging herself on the bed or the sofa, and trying at her bedside desperately to sleep, or falling on her knees with clasped outstretched hands. Was she asking for her own happiness at the expense of poor Elly's? I don't like to think so—it seems so cruel, so wicked, so unnatural. But remember, here was a passionate selfish woman, who for long years had had one dream, one idea; who knew that she loved this man twenty times—twenty years—more than did Elizabeth, who was but a child when this mad fancy began.

'She does not care for him a bit,' the poor wretch said to herself over and over again. 'He likes her, and he would marry her, if—if I chose to give him the chance. She will be as happy with anybody else. I could not bear this—it would kill me. I never suffered such horrible torture in all my life. He hates me. It is hopeless; and I—I do not know whether I hate him or I love him most. How dare she tell him to come to-morrow, when she knew I would be out. She shall not see him. We will neither of us see him again; never—oh! never. But I shall suffer, and she will forget. Oh! if I could forget!' And then she would fall down on her knees again; and because she prayed, she blinded herself to her own wrong-doings, and thought that heaven was on her side.

And so the night went on. John Dampier was haunted with strange dreams, and saw Caroline Gilmour more than once coming and going in a red gown and talking to him, though he could not understand what she was saying; sometimes she was in his house at Guildford; sometimes in Paris; sometimes sitting with Elly up in a chestnut-tree, and chattering like a monkey; sometimes gliding down interminable rooms and opening door after door. He disliked her worse than ever when he woke in the morning. Is this strange? It would have seemed to me stranger had it not been so. We are not blocks of wax and putty with glass eyes, like the people at Madame Tussaud's; we have souls, and we feel and we guess at more than we see round about us, and we influence one another for good or for evil from the moment we come into the world. Let us be humbly thankful if the day comes for us to leave it before we have done any great harm to those who live their lives alongside with ours. And so the next morning Caroline asked her daughter if she would come with her to M. le Pasteur Tourneur's at two. 'I am sure you would be the better for listening to a good man's exhortation,' said Mrs. Gilmour.

'I don't want to go, mamma. I hate exhortations,'
said Elizabeth, pettishly; 'and you know how ill it made
me last Tuesday. How can you like it—such dreary,
sleepy talk? It gave me the most dreadful headache.'

'Poor child,' said Mrs. Gilmour, 'perhaps the day may
come when you will find out that a headache is not the
most terrible calamity. But you understand that if you
do not choose to come with me, you must stay at home.
I will not have you going about by yourself, or with any
chance friends—it is not respectable.'

Elly shrugged her shoulders, but resigned herself with
wonderful good grace. Mrs. Gilmour prepared herself
for her expedition : she put on a black silk gown, a plain
bonnet, a black cloak. I cannot exactly tell you what
change came over her. It was not the lady of the Tuileries
the day before; it was not the woman in the red dressing-
gown. It was a respectable, quiet personage enough, who
went off primly with her prayer-book in her hand, and
who desired Clementine on no account to let anybody in
until her return.

'Miss Elizabeth is so little to be trusted,' so she explained quite unnecessarily to the maid, 'that I cannot
allow her to receive visits when I am from home.'

And Clementine, who was a stiff, ill-humoured woman,
pinched her lips and said, 'Bien, madame.'

And so when Elizabeth's best chance for happiness
came to the door, Clementine closed it again with great

alacrity, and shut out the good fortune, and sent it away.
I am sure that if Dampier had come in that day and
seen Elly once more, he could not have helped speaking
to her and making her and making himself happy in
so doing. I am sure that Elly, with all her vanities and
faults, would have made him a good wife, and brightened
his dismal old house; but I am not sure that happiness
is the best portion after all, and that there is not something better to be found in life than mere worldly prosperity.

Dampier walked away, almost relieved, and yet disappointed too. 'Well, they will be back in town in ten
days,' he thought, 'and we will see then. But why the
deuce did the girl tell me three o'clock, and then not be
at home to see me?' And as ill-luck would have it, at
this moment, up came Mrs. Gilmour. 'I have just been
to see you, to say good-by,' said Dampier. 'I was very
sorry to miss you and your daughter.'

'I have been attending a meeting at the house of my
friend the Pasteur Tourneur,' said Mrs. Gilmour; 'but
Elizabeth was at home—would not she see you?' She
blushed up very red as she spoke, and so did John
Dampier; her face glowed with shame, and his with vexation.

'No; she would not see me,' cried he. 'Good-by,
Mrs. Gilmour.'

'Good-by,' she said, and looked up with her black eyes;

but he was staring vacantly beyond her, busy with his own reflections, and then she felt it was good-by for ever.

He turned down a wide street, and she crossed mechanically and came along the other side of the road, as I have said; past the stall of the old apple-woman; advancing demurely, turning in under the archway of the house.

She had no time for remorse. ' He does not care for me,' was all she could think; ' he scorns me——he has behaved as no gentleman would behave.' (Poor John!—in justice to him I must say that this was quite an assumption on her part.) And at the same time John Dampier, at the other end of the street, was walking away in a huff, and saying to himself that ' Elly is a little heartless flirt; she cares for no one but herself. I will have no more to do with her. Lætitia would not have served me so.'

Elly met her mother at the door. ' Mamma, how *could* you be so horrid and disagreeable?—*why* did you tell Clementine to let no one in?' She shook back her curly locks, and stamped her little foot, as she spoke, in her childish anger.

' You should not give people appointments when I am out of the way,' said Mrs. Gilmour, primly. ' Why did you not come with me? Dear M. Tourneur's exposition was quite beautiful.'

' I hate Monsieur Tourneur!' cried Elizabeth; ' and I should not do such things if you were kind, mamma, and liked me to amuse myself and to be happy; but you sit there, prim and frowning, and thinking everything wrong that is harmless; and you spoil all my pleasure; and it is a shame—and a shame—and you will make me hate you too;' and she ran into her own room, banged the door, and locked it.

I suppose it was by way of compensation to Elly that Mrs. Gilmour sat down and wrote a little note, asking Monsieur de Vaux to tea that evening to meet M. le Pasteur Tourneur and his son.

Elizabeth sat sulking in her room all the afternoon, the door shut; the hum of a busy city came in at her open window; then the glass panes blazed with light, and she remembered how the windows of the Tuileries had shone at that time the day before, and she thought how kind and how handsome Dampier looked, as he came walking along, and how he was worth ten Messieurs de Vaux and twenty foolish boys like Anthony Tourneur. The dusky shadows came creeping round the room, dimming a pretty picture.

It was a commonplace little *tableau de genre* enough— that of a girl sitting at a window, with clasped hands, dreaming dreams more or less silly, with the light falling on her hair, and on the folds of her dress, and on the blazing petals of the flowers on the balcony outside, and then overhead a quivering green summer sky. But it is a little picture that nature is never tired of reproducing; and,

C

besides nature, every year, in the Royal Academy, I see half-a-dozen such representations.

In a quiet unconscious sort of way, Elly made up her mind, this summer afternoon—made up her mind, knowing not that perhaps it was too late, that the future she was accepting, half glad, half reluctant, was, maybe, already hers no more, to take or to leave. Only a little stream, apparently easy to cross, lay, as yet, between her and the figure she seemed to see advancing towards her. She did not know that every day this little stream would widen and widen, until in time it would be a great ocean lying between them. Ah! take care, my poor Elizabeth, that you don't tumble into the waters, and go sinking down, down, down, while the waves close over your curly yellow locks.

' Will you come to dinner, mademoiselle? ' said Clementine, rapping at the door with the finger of fate which had shut out Sir John Dampier only a few hours ago.

' Go away ! ' cries Elizabeth.

' Elizabeth ! dinner is ready,' says her mother, from outside, with unusual gentleness.

' I don't want any dinner,' says Elly ; and then feels very sorry and very hungry the minute she has spoken. The door was locked, but she had forgotten the window, and Mrs. Gilmour, in a minute, came along the balcony, with her silk dress rustling against the iron bars.

' You silly girl ! come and eat,' said her mother, still

strangely kind and forbearing. 'The Vicomte de Vaux is
coming to tea, and Monsieur Tourneur and Anthony; you
must come and have your dinner, and then let Clementine
dress you; you will catch cold if you sit here any longer;'
and she took the girl's hand gently and led her away.

For the first time in her life, Elizabeth almost felt as
if she really loved her mother; and, touched by her kindness, and with a sudden impulse, and melting, and blushing,
and all ashamed of herself, she said, almost before she knew
what she had spoken, 'Mamma, I am very silly, and I've
behaved very badly, but I did so want to see him again.'

Mrs. Gilmour just dropped the girl's hand. 'Nonsense,
Elizabeth; your head is full of silly school-girl notions. 1
wish I had had you brought up at home instead of at Mrs.
Straightboard's.'

'I wish you had, mamma,' said Elly, speaking coldly
and quietly; 'Lætitia and I were both very miserable
there.' And then she sat down at the round table to
break bread with her mother, hurt, wounded, and angry.
Her face looked hard and stern, like Mrs. Gilmour's; her
bread choked her; she drank a glass of water, and it
tasted bitter, somehow. Was Caroline more happy? did
she eat with better appetite? She ate more, she looked
much as usual, she talked a good deal. Clementine was
secretly thinking what a good-for-nothing, ill-tempered
girl mademoiselle was; what a good woman, what a good
mother was madame. Clementine revenged some of

c 2

madame's wrongs upon Elizabeth, by pulling her hair
after dinner, as she was plaiting and pinning it up.   Elly
lost her temper, and violently pushed Clementine away,.
and gave her warning to leave.

Clementine, furious, and knowing that some of the
company had already arrived, rushed into the drawing--
room with her wrongs. 'Mademoiselle m'a poussée,.
madame; mademoiselle m'a dit des injures; mademoiselle
m'a congédiée——' But in the middle of her harangue,
the door flew open, and Elizabeth, looking like an empress,.
bright cheeks flushed, eyes sparkling, hair crisply curling,.
and all dressed in shining pink silk, stood before them.

CHAPTER II.

But for his funeral train which the bridegroom sees in the distance,
Would he so joyfully, think you, fall in with the marriage procession?
But for that final discharge, would he dare to enlist in that service?
But for that certain release, ever sign to that perilous contract?

I DON'T think they had ever seen anybody like her before, those two MM. Tourneurs, who had just arrived; they both rose, a little man and a tall one, father and son; and besides these gentlemen, there was an old lady in a poke bonnet sitting there too, who opened her shrewd eyes and held out her hand. Clementine was crushed, eclipsed, forgotten. Elizabeth advanced, tall, slim, stately, with wide-spread petticoats; but she began to blush very much when she saw Miss Dampier. For a few minutes there was a little confusion of greeting, and voices, and chairs moved about, and then—

'I came to say good-by to you,' said the old lady, 'in case we should not meet again. I am going to Scotland in a month or two—perhaps I may be gone by the time you get back to town.'

'Oh, no, no! I hope not,' said Elizabeth. She was very much excited, the tears almost came into her eyes.

' We shall most likely follow you in a week or ten days,' said Mrs. Gilmour, with a sort of laugh; 'there is no necessity for any sentimental leave-taking.'

' Does that woman mean what she says?' thought the old lady, looking at her; and then turning to Elizabeth again she continued: 'There is no knowing what may happen to any one of us, my dear. There is no harm in saying good-by, is there? Have you any message for Lætitia or Catherine?'

'Give Lætitia my very best love,' said Elly, grateful for the old lady's kindness; 'and—and I was very, very sorry that I could not see Sir John when he came to-day so good-naturedly.'

'He must come and see you in London,' said Miss Dampier, very kindly still. (She was thinking, 'She does care for him, poor child.')

'Oh, yes! in London,' repeated Mrs. Gilmour; so that Elly looked quite pleased, and Miss Dampier again said to herself, 'She is decidedly not coming to London. What can she mean? Can there be anything with that Frenchman, De Vaux? Impossible!' And then she got up, and said aloud, 'Well good-by. I have all my old gowns to pack up, and my knitting, Elly. Write to me, child, sometimes!'

'Oh, yes, yes!' cried Elizabeth, flinging her arms round the old lady's neck, kissing her, and whispering, 'Good-by, dear, dear Miss Dampier.'

At the door of the apartment, Clementine was waiting, hoping for a possible five-franc piece. 'Bon soir, madame,' said she.

'Oh, indeed,' said Miss Dampier, staring at her, and she passed out with a sort of sniff, and then she walked home quietly through the dark back-streets, only, as she went along, she said to herself every now and then, she hardly knew why, 'Poor Elly—poor child!'

Meanwhile, M. Tourneur was taking Elizabeth gently to task. Elizabeth was pouting her red lips and sulking, and looking at him defiantly from under her drooped eyelids; and all the time Anthony Tourneur sat admiring her, with his eyes wide open, and his great mouth open too. He was a big young man, with immense hands and feet, without any manners to speak of, and with thick hair growing violently upon end. There was a certain distinction about his father which he had not inherited. Young Frenchmen of this class are often singularly rough and unpolished in their early youth; they tone down with time however, as they see more of men and of women. Anthony had never known much of either till now; for his young companions at the Protestant college were rough cubs like himself; and as for women, his mother was dead (she had been an Englishwoman, and died when he was ten years old), and old Françoise, the *cuisinière*, at home, was almost the only woman he knew. His father was more used to the world and its ways: he fancied he scorned them all, and yet the pomps and vanities and the pride of life had a horrible attraction for this quiet pasteur. He was humble and ambitious: he was tender-hearted, and hard-headed, and narrow-minded. Though stern to himself, he was weak to others, and yet feebly resolute when he met with opposition. He was not a great man; his qualities neutralized one another, but he had a great reputation. The Oratoire was crowded on the days when he was expected to preach, his classes were thronged, his pamphlets went through three or four editions. Popularity delighted him. His manner had a great charm, his voice was sweet, his words well chosen; his head was a fine melancholy head, his dark eyes flashed when he was excited. Women especially admired and respected Stephen Tourneur.

Mrs. Gilmour was like another person when she was in his presence. Look at her to-night, with her smooth black hair, and her grey silk gown, and her white hands busied pouring out his tea. See how she is appealing to him, deferentially listening to his talk. I cannot write his talk down here. Certain allusions can have no place in a little story like this one, and yet they were allusions so frequently in his thoughts and in his mouth that it was almost unconsciously that he used them. He and his brethren like him have learned to look at this life from a loftier point of view than Elly Gilmour and worldlings like her, who feel that to-day they are in the world and

of it, not of their own will, indeed—though they are glad
that they are here—but waiting a further dispensation.
Tourneur, and those like him, look at this life only in
comparison with the next, as though they had already
passed beyond, and had but little concern with the things
of to-day. They speak chiefly of sacred subjects; they
have put aside our common talk, and thought, and career.
They have put them away, and yet they are men and
women after all. And Stephen Tourneur, among the rest,
was a soft-hearted man. To-night, as indeed often before,
he was full of sympathy for the poor mother who had so
often spoken of her grief and care for her daughter, of her
loneliness. He understood her need ; her want of an
adviser, of a friend whom she could reverence and defer to.
How meekly she listened to his words, with what kindling
interest she heard him speak of what was in his heart
always, with what gentleness she attended to his wants.
How womanly she was, how much more pleasant than any
of the English, Scotch, Irish old maids who were in the
habit of coming to consult him in their various needs and
troubles. He had never known her so tender, so gentle,
as to-night. Even Elly, sulking, and beating the tattoo
with her satin shoes, thought that her mother's manner was
very strange. How could any one of the people sitting
round that little tea-table guess at the passion of hopelessness, of rage, of despair, of envy, that was gnawing at the
elder woman's heart? at the mad, desperate determination

she was making? And yet every now and then she said
odd, imploring things—she seemed to be crying wildly for
sympathy—she spoke of other people's troubles with a
startling earnestness.

De Vaux, who arrived about nine o'clock, and asked
for a *soupçon de thé*, and put in six lumps of sugar, and
'so managed to swallow the mixture, went away at ten,
without one idea of the tragedy with which he had been
spending his evening—a tragical farce, a comedy—I know
not what to call it.

Elly was full of her own fancies; Monsieur Tourneur
was making up his mind; Anthony's whole head was rustling with pink silk, or dizzy with those downcast, bright, bewildering blue eyes of Elly's, and he sat stupidly counting
the little bows on her skirt, or watching the glitter of the
rings on her finger, and wishing that she would not look
so cross when he spoke to her. She had brightened up
considerably while De Vaux was there; but now, in truth,
her mind was travelling away, and she was picturing to
herself the Dampiers at their tea-table—Tishy, pale and
listless, over her feeble cups; Lady Dampier, with her fair
hair and her hook nose, lying on the sofa; and John in
the arm-chair by the fire, cutting dry jokes at his aunt.
Elly's spirits had travelled away like a ghost, and it was
only her body that was left sitting in the little gaudy
drawing-room; and, though she did not know it, there
was another ghost flitting alongside with hers. Strangely

enough, the people of whom she was thinking were assembled together very much as she imagined them to be. Did they guess at the two pale phantoms that were hovering about them'? Somehow or other, Miss Dampier, over her knitting, was still muttering, 'Poor child!' to the click of her needles; and John Dampier was haunted by the woman in red, and by a certain look in Elly's eyes, which he had seen yesterday when he found her under the tree.

Meanwhile, at the other side of Paris, the other little company was assembled round the fire; and Mrs. Gilmour, with her two hands folded tightly together, was looking at M. Tourneur with her great soft eyes, and saying, ' The woman was never yet born who could stand alone, who did not look for some earthly counsellor and friend to point out the road to better things—to help her along the narrow thorny way. Wounded, and bruised, and weary, it is hard, hard for us to follow our lonely path.' She spoke with a pathetic passion, so that Elizabeth could not think what had come to her. Mrs. Gilmour was generally quite capable of standing, and going, and coming, without any assistance whatever. In her father's time, Elly could remember that there was not the slightest need for his interference in any of their arrangements. But the mother was evidently in earnest to-night, and the daughter quite bewildered. Later in the evening, after Monsieur de Vaux was gone, Mrs. Gilmour got up from her chair and flung open the window of the balcony. All the stars of heaven shone splendidly over the city. A great, silent, wonderful night had gathered round about them unawares; a great calm had come after the noise and business of the careful day. Caroline Gilmour stepped out with a gasping sigh, and stood looking upwards; they could see her grey figure dimly against the darkness. Monsieur Tourneur remained sitting by the fire, with his eyes cast down and his hands folded. Presently he too rose and walked slowly across the room, and stepped out upon the balcony; and Elizabeth and Anthony remained behind, staring vacantly at one another. Elizabeth was yawning and wondering when they would go.

'You are sleepy, miss,' said young Tourneur, in his French-English.

Elly yawned in a very unmistakable language, and showed all her even white teeth :—'I always get sleepy when I have been cross, Mr. Anthony. I have been cross ever since three o'clock to-day, and now it is long past ten, and time for us all to go to bed : don't you think so ?'

'I am waiting for my father,' said the young man. 'He watches late at night, but we are all sent off at ten.'

' "We!"—you and old Françoise ?'

'I and the young Christians who live in our house, and study with my father and read under his direction. There are five, all from the south, who are, like me, preparing to be ministers of the gospel.'

Another great wide yawn from Elly.

'Do you think your father will stop much longer—if so, I shall go to bed. Oh, dear me!' and with a sigh she let her head fall back upon the soft cushioned chair, and then, somehow, her eyes shut very softly, and her hands fell loosely, and a little quiet dream came, something of a garden and peace, and green trees, and Miss Dampier knitting in the sunshine. Click, click, click, she heard the needles, but it was only the clock ticking on the mantel-piece. Anthony was almost afraid to breathe, for fear he should wake her. It seemed to him very strange to be sitting by this smouldering fire, with the stars burning outside, while through the open window the voices of the two people talking on the balcony came to him in a low murmuring sound. And there opposite him Elly, asleep, breathing so softly and looking so wonderfully pretty in her slumbers. Do you not know the peculiar peaceful feeling which comes to anyone sitting alone by a sleeping person? I cannot tell which of the two was for a few minutes the most tranquil and happy.

Elly was still dreaming her quiet, peaceful dreams, still sitting with Miss Dampier in her garden, under a chestnut-tree, with Dampier coming towards them, when suddenly some voice whispered 'Elizabeth' in her ear, and she awoke with a start of chill surprise. It was not Anthony who had called her, it was only fancy; but as she woke he said,—

' Ah ! I was just going to wake you.'

What had come to him. He seemed to have awakened
too—to have come to himself suddenly. One word which
had reached him—he had very big sharp ears—one word
distinctly uttered amid the confused murmur on the balcony, brought another word of old Françoise's to his mind.
And then in a minute—he could not tell how it was—it
was all clear to him. Already he was beginning to learn
the ways of the world. Elly saw him blush up, saw his
eyes light with intelligence, and his ears grow very red ;
and then he sat up straight in his chair, and looked at her
in a quick, uncertain sort of way.

' You would not allow it,' said he, suddenly, staring at
her fixedly with his great flashing eyes. ' I never thought
of such a thing till this minute. Who ever would ? '

' Thought of what ? What are you talking about ? '
said Elly, startled.

' Ah ! that is it.' And then he turned his head impatiently : ' How stupid you must have been. What can
have put such a thing into his head and hers. Ah, it is so
strange I don't know what to think or to say ; ' and he sank
back in his chair. But, somehow or other, the idea which
had occurred to him was not nearly so disagreeable as he
would have expected it to be. The notion of some other
companionship besides that of the five young men from the
south, instead of shocking him, filled him with a vague,
delightful excitement. ' Ah ! then she would come and

live with us in that pink dress,' he thought. And meanwhile Elizabeth turned very pale, and she too began dimly to see what he was thinking of, only she could not be quite sure. 'Is it that I am to marry him?' she thought; 'they cannot be plotting that.'

'What is it, M. Anthony?' said she, very fierce. 'Is it——they do not think that I would ever—ever dream or think of marrying you?' She was quite pale now, and *her* eyes were glowing.

Anthony shook his head again. 'I know that,' said he ; 'it is not you or me.'

'What do you dare to imply?' she cried, more and more fiercely. 'You can't mean—you would never endure, never suffer that—that——' The words failed on her lips.

'I should like to have you for a sister, Miss Elizabeth,' said he, looking down ; 'it is so *triste* at home.'

Elly half started from her chair, put up her white hands, scarce knowing what she did, and then suddenly cried out, 'Mother! mother!' in a loud, shrill, thrilling voice, which brought Mrs. Gilmour back into the room. And Monsieur Tourneur came too. Not one of them spoke for a minute. Elizabeth's horror-stricken face frightened the pasteur, who felt as if he was in a dream, who had let himself drift along with the feeling of the moment, who did not know even now if he had done right or wrong, if he had been carried away by mere earthly

impulse and regard for his own happiness, or if he had been
led and directed to a worthy helpmeet, to a Christian
companion, to one who had the means and the power to
help him in his labours. Ah, surely, surely he had done
well, he thought, for himself, and for those who depended
on him. It was not without a certain dignity at last, and
nobleness of manner, that he took Mrs. Gilmour's hand,
and said—

'You called your mother just now, Elizabeth; here
she is. Dear woman, she has consented to be my best
earthly friend and companion, to share my hard labours;
to share a life poor and arduous, and full of care, and
despised perhaps by the world; but rich in eternal hope,
blessed by prayer, and consecrated by a Christian's faith.'
He was a little man, but he seemed to grow tall as he
spoke. His eyes kindled, his face lightened with enthusiasm. Elizabeth could not help seeing this, even while
she stood shivering with indignation and sick at heart.
As for Anthony he got up, and came to his father and
took both his hands, and then suddenly flung his arms
round his neck. Elizabeth found words at last:

'You can suffer this?' she said to Anthony. 'You
have no feelings, then, of decency, of fitness of memory
for the dead. You, mamma, can degrade yourself by a
second marriage? Oh! for shame, for shame!' and she
burst into passionate tears, and flung herself down on a
chair. Monsieur Tourneur was not used to be thwarted,

to be reproved; he got very pale, he pushed Anthony gently aside, and went up to her. 'Elizabeth,' said he, 'is this the conduct of a devoted daughter; are these the words of good will and of peace, with which your mother should be greeted by her children? I had hoped that you would look upon me as a friend. If you could see my heart, you would know how ready I am; how gladly I would love you as my own child,' and he held out his hand. Elly Gilmour dashed it away.

'Go,' she said; 'you have made me wretched; *I* hate your life and your ways, and your sermons, and we shall all be miserable, every one of us; I know well enough it is for her money you marry her. Oh, go away out of my sight.' Tourneur had felt doubts. Elizabeth's taunts and opposition reassured him and strengthened him in his purpose. This is only human nature, as well as pasteur nature in particular. If everything had gone smoothly, very likely he would have found out a snare of the devil in it, and broken it off, not caring what grief and suffering he caused to himself in so doing. Now that the girl's words brought a flush into his pale face and made him to wince with pain, he felt justified, nay, impelled to go on—to be firm. And now he stood up like a gentleman, and spoke:

'And if I want your mother's money, is it hers, is it mine, was it given to me or to her to spend for our own use? Was it not lent, will not an account be demanded hereafter? Unhappy child! where have you found already such sordid thoughts, such unworthy suspicions? Where is your Christian charity?'

'I never made any pretence of having any,' cried Elizabeth, stamping her foot and tossing her fair mane. 'You talk and talk about it and about the will of heaven, and suit yourselves, and break my heart, and look up quite scandalized, and forgive me for my wickedness. But I had rather be as wicked as I am than as good as you.'

'Allons, taisez-vous, Mademoiselle Elizabeth!' said Anthony, who had taken his part; 'or my father will not marry your mother, and then *you* will be in the wrong, and have made everybody unhappy. It is very, very sad and melancholy in our house; be kind and come and make us happy. If I am not angry, why should you mind? but see here, I will not give my consent unless you do, and I know my father will do nothing against my wishes and yours.'

Poor Elizabeth looked up, and then she saw that her mother was crying too; Caroline had had a hard day's work. No wonder she was fairly harassed and worn out. Elizabeth herself began to be as bewildered, as puzzled, as the rest. She put her hand wearily to her head. She did not feel angry any more, but very tired and sad. 'How can I say I think it right when I think it wrong? It is not me you want to marry, M. Tourneur; mamma is old enough to decide. What need you care for what a silly

girl like me says and thinks? Good-night, mamma; I
am tired and must go to bed. Good-night, Monsieur
Tourneur. Good-night, M. Anthony. Oh, dear!' sighed
Elizabeth, as she went out of the room with her head hanging, and with pale cheeks and dim eyes. You could hardly
have believed it was the triumphant young beauty of an
hour ago. But it had always been so with this impetuous,
sensitive Elizabeth; she suffered as she enjoyed, more
keenly than anybody else I ever knew; she put her whole
heart into her life without any reserve, and then, when
failure and disappointment came, she had no more heart
left to endure with.

I am sure it was with a humble spirit that Tourneur
that night, before he left, implored a benediction on
himself and on those who were about to belong to him.
He went away at eleven o'clock with Anthony, walking
home through the dark, long streets to his house, which
was near one of the gates of the city. And Caroline sat
till the candles went out, till the fire had smouldered
away, till the chill night breezes swept round the room,
and then went stupefied to bed, saying to herself, 'Now
he will learn that others do not despise me, and I—I will
lead a good life.'

CHAPTER III.

Le temps emporte sur son aile
Et le printemps et l'hirondelle,
Et la vie et les jours perdus ;
Tout s'en va comme la fumée,
L'espérance et la renommée,
Et moi qui vous ai tant aimée,
Et toi qui ne t'en souviens plus !

A LOW, one-storied house standing opposite a hospital,. built on a hilly street, with a great white *porte-cochère* closed and barred, and then a garden wall ; nine or ten windows only a foot from the ground, all blinded and shuttered in a row ; a brass plate on the door,. with *Stephen Tourneur* engraved thereon, and grass and chickweed growing between the stones and against the white walls of the house. Passing under the archway, you come into a grass-grown courtyard ; through an iron grating you see a little desolate garden with wall-flowers and stocks, and tall yellow weeds all flowering together, and fruit-trees running wild against the wall. On one side there are some empty stables, with chickens pecketting in the sun. The house is built in two long low wings ; it has a dreary moated-grange sort of look ; and see, standing at one of the upper windows, is not that

Elizabeth looking out? An old woman in a blue gown and a white coif is pumping water at the pump, some miserable canaries are piping shrilly out of green cages, the old woman clacks away with her sabots echoing over the stones, the canaries cease their piping, and then nobody else comes. There are two or three tall poplar-trees growing along the wall, which shiver plaintively; a few clouds drift by, and a very distant faint sound of military music comes borne on the wind.

'Ah, how dull it is to be here! Ah, how I hate it, how I hate them all!' Elizabeth is saying to herself; 'There is some music, all the Champs Elysées are crowded with people, the soldiers are marching along with glistening bayonets and flags flying. Not one of them thinks that in a dismal house not very far away there is anybody so unhappy as I am. This day year—it breaks my heart to think of it—I was nineteen; to-day I am twenty, and I feel a hundred. Oh, what a sin and shame it is to condemn me to this hateful life. Oh, what wicked people these good people are. Oh, how dull, oh, how stupid, oh, how prosy, oh, how I wish I was dead, and they were dead, and it was all over!'

How many weary yawns, I wonder, had poor Elizabeth yawned since that first night when M. Tourneur came to tea? With what distaste she set herself to live her new life I cannot attempt to tell you. It bored her, and wearied and displeased her, and she made no secret of

her displeasure, you may be certain. But what annoyed
her most of all, what seemed to her so inconceivable that
she could never understand or credit it, was the extraordinary change which had come over her mother. Mme.
Tourneur was like Mrs. Gilmour in many things, but so
different in others that Elly could hardly believe her to
be the same woman. The secret of it all was a love of
power and admiration, purchased no matter at what sacrifice, which had always been the hidden motive of Caroline's
life. Now she found that by dressing in black, by looking stiff, by attending endless charitable meetings,
prayer-meetings, religious meetings, by influencing M.
Tourneur, who was himself a man in authority, she could
eat of the food her soul longed for. 'There was a man
once who did not care for me, he despised me,' she used
to think sometimes; 'he liked that silly child of mine
better; he shall hear of me one day.'

Lady Dampier was a very strong partisan of the
French Protestant Church. Mme. Tourneur used to hope
that she would come to Paris again and carry home with
her the fame of her virtues, and her influence, and her
conversion; and in the meanwhile the weary round of
poor Elly's daily existence went on. To-day, for two
lonesome hours, she stood leaning at that window with the
refrain of the distant music echoing in her ears long after
it had died away. It was like the remembrance of the
past pleasures of her short life. Such a longing for sym-

pathy, for congenial spirits, for the pleasures she loved so dearly, came over her, that the great hot tears welled into her eyes, and thé bitterest tears are those which do not fall. The gate bell rang at last, and Clementine walked across the yard to unbolt, to unbar, and to let in Monsieur Tourneur, with books under his arm, and a big stick. Then the bell rang again, and Madame Tourneur followed, dressed in prim scant clothes, accompanied by another person even primmer and scantier than herself; this was a widowed step-sister of M. Tourneur's who, unluckily, had no home of her own, so the good man received her and her children into his. Lastly, Elizabeth, from her window, saw Anthony arrive with four of the young Protestants, all swinging their legs and arms. (The fifth was detained at home with a bad swelled face.) All the others were now coming back to dinner, after attending a class at the Pasteur Boulot's. They clattered past the door of Elly's room—a bare little chamber, with one white curtain she had nailed up herself, and a straight bed and a chair. A clock struck five. A melancholy bell presently sounded through the house, and a strong smell of cabbage came in at the open window. Elly looked in the glass; her rough hair was all standing on end curling, her hands were streaked with chalk and brick from the window, her washed-out blue cotton gown was creased and tumbled. What did it matter? she shook her head, as she had a way of doing, and went downstairs as she was. On the way she met two untidy-looking little girls, and then clatter, clatter, along the uncarpeted passage, came the great big nailed boots of the pupils; and then at the dining-room door there was Clementine in a yellow gown—much smarter and trimmer than Elizabeth's blue cotton—carrying a great long loaf of sour bread.

Madame Tourneur was already at her post, standing at the head of the table, ladleing out the cabbage soup with the pieces of bread floating in every plate. M. Tourneur was eating his dinner quickly; he had to examine a class for confirmation at six, and there was a prayer-meeting at seven. The other prim lady sat opposite to him with her portion before her. There was a small table-cloth, streaked with blue, and not over clean; hunches of bread by every plate, and iron knives and forks. Each person said grace to himself as he came and took his place. Only Elizabeth flung herself down in a chair, looked at the soup, made a face, and sent it away untasted.

'Elizabeth, ma fille, vous ne mangez pas,' said M. Tourneur, kindly.

'I can't swallow it!' said Elizabeth.

'When there are so many poor people starving in the streets, you do not, I suppose, expect us to sympathise with such pampered fancies?' said the prim lady.

Although the sisters-in-law were apparently very good

friends, there was a sort of race of virtue always being run between them, and just now Elly's shortcomings were a thorn in her mother's side, so skilfully were they wielded by Mrs. Jacob. Lou-Lou and Tou-Tou, otherwise Louise and Thérèse, *her* daughters, were such good, stupid, obedient, uninteresting little girls, that there was really not a word to say against them in retort; and all that Elly's mother could do, was to be even more severe, more uncompromising than Madame Jacob herself. And now she said,—

' Nonsense, Elizabeth; you must really eat your dinner. Clementine, bring back Miss Elizabeth's plate.'

M. Tourneur looked up—he thought the soup very good himself, but he could not bear to see anybody distressed. ' Go and fetch the bouillie quickly, Clementine. Why should Elizabeth take what she does not like? Rose,' said he to his sister, ' do you remember how our poor mother used to make us breakfast off—*porridge* I think she called it—and what a bad taste it had, and how we used to cry?'

' We never ungratefully objected to good soup,' said Rose. 'I make a point of never giving in to Lou-Lou and Tou-Tou when they have their fancies. I care more for the welfare of their souls than for pampering their bodies.'

' And I only care for my body,' Elly cried. ' Mamma, I like porridge, will you have some for me?'

'Ah! hush! hush! Elizabeth. You do not think what you say, my poor child,' said Tourneur. 'What is mere eating and drinking, what is food, what is raiment, but dust and rottenness? You only care for your body!—for that mass of corruption. Ah, do not say such things, even in jest. Remember, that for every idle word——'

'And is there to be no account for spiteful words?' interrupted Elizabeth, looking at Mrs. Jacob.

Monsieur Tourneur put down the glass of wine he was raising to his lips, and with sad, reproachful glances, looked at the unruly step-daughter. Madame Jacob, shaking with indignation, cast her eyes up and opened her mouth, and Elizabeth began to pout her red lips. One minute and the storm would have burst, when Anthony upset a jug of water at his elbow, and the stream trickled down and down the table-cloth. These troubled waters restored peace for the moment. Poor Tourneur was able to finish his meal, in a puddle truly, but also in silence. Mrs. Jacob, who had received a large portion of the water in her lap, retired to change her dress, the young Christians sniggered over their plates, and Anthony went on eating his dinner.

I don't offer any excuse for Elizabeth. She was worried, and vexed, and tried beyond her powers of endurance, and she grew more wayward, more provoking every day. It is very easy to be good-natured, good-tempered, thankful and happy, when you are in the country you love,

among your own people, living your own life. But if you
are suddenly transplanted, made to live someone else's
life, expected to see with another man's eyes, to forget
your own identity almost, all that happens is, that you do
not do as you were expected. Sometimes it is a sheer
impossibility. What is that rare proverb about the shoe?
Cinderella slipped it on in an instant; but you know her
poor sisters cut off their toes and heels, and could not
screw their feet in, though they tried ever so. Well, they
did their best; but Elly did not try at all, and that is
why she was to blame. She was a spoiled child, both by
good and ill fortune. Sometimes, when she sat sulking,
her mother used to look wondering at her with her black
eyes, without saying a word. Did it ever occur to her
that this was *her* work, that Elizabeth might have been
happy now, honoured, prosperous, well loved, but for a
little lie which had been told—but for a little barrier
which had been thrown, one summer's day, between her
and John Dampier? Caroline had long ceased to feel
remorse—she used to say to herself that it would be much
better for Elizabeth to marry Anthony, she would make
anybody else miserable with her wayward temper. Anthony was so obtuse, that Elizabeth's fancies would not try
him in the least. Mrs. Gilmour chose to term obtuseness
a certain chivalrous devotion which the young man felt
for her daughter. She thought him dull and slow, and
so he was; but at the same time there were gleams of

shrewdness which came quite unexpectedly, you knew not whence; there was a certain reticence and good sense of which people had no idea. Anthony knew much more about her and about his father than they knew about him. Every day he was learning to read the world. Elly had taught him a great deal, and he in return was her friend always.

Elly went out into the courtyard after dinner, and Anthony followed her—one little cousin had hold of each of his hands. If the little girls had not been little French Protestant girls, Elizabeth would have been very fond of them, for she loved children; but when they ran up to her, she motioned them away impatiently, and Anthony told them to go and run round the garden. Elizabeth was sitting on a tub which had been overturned, and resting her pretty dishevelled head wearily against the wall. Anthony looked at her for a minute.

'Why do you never wear nice dresses now,' said he at last, 'but this ugly old one always?'

'Is it not all vanity and corruption?' said Elizabeth, with a sneer; 'how can you ask such a question? Everything that is pretty is vanity. Your aunt and my mother only like ugly things. They would like to put out my eyes because they don't squint; to cut off my hair because it is pretty.'

'Your hair! It is not at all pretty like that,' said Anthony; 'it is all rough, like mine.'

Elizabeth laughed and blushed very sweetly. 'What is the use, who cares?'

'There are a good many people coming to-night,' said Anthony. 'It is our turn to receive the prayer-meeting. Why should you not smooth your curls and change your dress?'

'And do you remember what happened once, when I did dress, and make myself look nice?' said Elizabeth, flashing up, and then beginning to laugh.

Anthony looked grave and puzzled; for Elizabeth had caused quite a scandal in the community on that occasion. No wonder the old ladies in their old dowdy bonnets, the young ones in their ill-made woollen dresses, the preacher preaching against the vanities of the world, had all been shocked and outraged, when after the sermon had begun, the door opened, and Elizabeth appeared in the celebrated pink silk dress, with flowers in her hair, white lace falling from her shoulders, a bouquet, a gold fan, and glittering bracelets. Mme. Jacob's head nearly shook off with horror. The word was with the Pasteur Boulot, who did not conceal his opinion, and whose strictures introduced into the sermon were enough to make a less hardened sinner quake in her shoes. Many of the great leaders of the Protestant world in Paris had been present on that occasion. Some would not speak to her, some did speak very plainly. Elizabeth took it all as a sort of triumph, bent her head, smiled, fanned herself, and when ordered out of the room at last by her mother, left it with a splendid curtsey to the Rev. M. Boulot, and thanked him for his beautiful and improving discourse. And then, when she was upstairs in her own room again, where she had been decking herself for the last hour—the tallow candle was still spluttering on the table—her clothes all lying about the room—she locked the door, tore off her ornaments, her shining dress, and flung herself down on the floor, crying and sobbing as if her heart would break. ' Oh, I want to go ! I want to go ! Oh, take me away !' she prayed and sobbed. ' Oh, what harm is there in a pink gown more than a black one ! Oh, why does not John Dampier come and fetch me ? Oh, what dolts, what idiots, those people are ! What a heart-broken girl I am ! Poor Elly, poor Elly, poor, poor girl !' said she, pitying herself, and stroking her tear-stained cheeks. And so she went on, until she had nearly worn herself out, poor child. She really was almost heart-broken. This uncongenial atmosphere seemed to freeze and chill her best impulses. I cannot help being sorry for her, and sympathising with her against that rigid community down below, and yet, after all, there was scarcely one of the people whom she so scorned who was not a better Christian than poor Elizabeth, more self-denying, more scrupulous, more patient in effort, more diligent,—not one of them that did not lead a more useful life than hers. It was in vain that her mother had offered her classes in the schools, humble neighbours to visit, sick people to tend.

'Leave me alone,' the girl would say. 'You know how I
hate all that cant!' Mme. Tourneur herself spent her
whole days doing good, patronising the poor, lecturing
the wicked, dosing the sick, superintending countless charitable communities. Her name was on all the committees,
her decisions were deferred to, her wishes consulted. She
did not once regret the step she had taken; she was a
clever, ambitious, active-minded woman; she found herself busy, virtuous, and respected; what more could she
desire? Her daughter's unhappiness did not give her any
very great concern. 'It would go off in time,' she said.
But days went by, and Elly was only more hopeless, more
heart-broken; black lines came under the blue eyes; from
being a stout hearty girl, she grew thin and languid.
Seeing her day by day, they none of them noticed that
she was looking ill, except Anthony, who often imagined
a change would do her good; only how was this to be
managed? He could only think of one way. He was
thinking of it, as he followed her out into the courtyard
to-day. The sun was low in the west, the long shadows of
the trees flickered across the stones. Say what he would,
the blue gown, the wall, the yellow hair, made up a pretty
little piece of colouring. With all her faults, Anthony
loved Elly better than any other human being, and would
have given his life to make her happy.

'I cannot bear to see you so unhappy,' said he, in
French, speaking very simply, in his usual voice. 'Eliza-

beth, why don't you do as your mother has done, and marry a French pasteur, who has loved you ever since the day he first saw you? You should do as you liked, and leave this house, where you are so miserable, and get away from aunt Rose, who is so ill-natured. I would not propose such a scheme if I saw a chance for something better; but anything would be an improvement on the life you are leading here. It is wicked and profitless, and you are killing yourself and wasting your best days. You are not taking up your cross with joy and with courage, dear Elizabeth. Perhaps by starting afresh——' His voice failed him, but his eyes spoke and finished the sentence.

This was Anthony's scheme. Elly opened her round eyes, and looked at him all amazed and wondering. A year ago it would have been very different, and so she thought as she scanned him. A year ago she would have scorned the poor fellow, laughed at him, tossed her head, and turned away. But was this the Elly of a year ago? This unhappy, broken-spirited girl, with dimmed beauty, dulled spirits, in all her ways so softened, saddened, silenced. It was almost another person than the Elizabeth Gilmour of former times, who spoke, and said, still looking at him steadfastly, 'Thank you, Anthony; I will think about it, and tell you to-morrow what—what I think.'

Anthony blushed, and faltered a few unintelligible words, and turned away abruptly, as he saw Madame

Jacob coming towards them. As for Elly, she stood quite still, and perfectly cool, and rather bewildered, only somewhat surprised at herself. ' Can this be me?' she was thinking. ' Can that kind fellow be the boy I used to laugh at so often? Shall I take him at his word? Why not—— ? '

But Madame Jacob's long nose came and put an end to her wonderings. This lady did not at all approve of gossiping; she stepped up with an enquiring sniff, turned round to look after Anthony, and then said, rather viciously, '' Our Christian brothers and sisters will assemble shortly for their pious Wednesday meetings. It is not by exchanging idle words with my nephew that you will best prepare your mind for the exercises of this evening. Retire into your own room, and see if it is possible to compose yourself to a fitter frame of mind. Tou-Tou, Lou-Lou, my children, what are you about?'

' I am gathering pretty flowers, mamma,' shouted Lou-Lou.

' I am picking up stones for my little basket,' said Tou-Tou, coming to the railing.

' I will allow four minutes,' said their mother, looking at her watch. 'Then you will come to me, both of you, in my room, and apply yourselves to something more profitable than filling your little baskets. Elizabeth, do you mean to obey me?'

Very much to Madame Jacob's surprise, Elizabeth

E

walked quietly before her into the house without saying
one word. The truth was, she was preoccupied with other
things, and forgot to be rebellious. She was not even rebellious in her heart when she was upstairs sitting by the
bedside, and puzzling her brains over Anthony's scheme.
It seemed a relief certainly to turn from the horrible
monotony of her daily life, and to think of his kindness.
He was very rough, very uncouth, very young; but he was
shrewd, and kind, and faithful, more tolerant than his
father,—perhaps because he felt less keenly;—not sensitive, like him, but more patient, dull over things which
are learnt by books, but quick at learning other not less
useful things which belong to the experience of daily life.
When Elly came down into the réfectoire where they were
all assembled, her mother was surprised to see that she had
dressed herself, not in the objectionable pink silk, but in
a soft grey stuff gown, all her yellow hair was smooth and
shining, and a little locket hung round her neck tied with
a blue ribbon. The little bit of colour seemed reflected
somehow in her eyes. They looked blue to-night, as they
used to look once when she was happy. Madame Tourneur
was quite delighted, and came up and kissed her, and said,
' Elly, this is how I like to see you.'

Madame Jacob tossed her head, and gave a rough pull
at the ends of the ribbon. ' *This* was quite unnecessary,'
said she.

' Ah !' cried Elly, ' you have hurt me.'

' Is not that the locket Miss Dampier gave you ? ' said Madame Tourneur. ' You had best put such things away in your drawer another time. But it is time for you to take your place.'

CHAPTER IV.

Unhappier are they to whom a higher instinct has been given, who struggle to be persons, not machines; to whom the universe is not a warehouse, or at best a fancy bazaar, but a mystic temple and hall of doom.

A NUMBER of straw chairs were ranged along the room, with a row of seats behind, for the pasteurs who were to address the meeting.

The people began to arrive very punctually: One or two grand-looking French ladies in cashmeres, a good many limp ones, a stray man or two, two English clergymen in white neckcloths, and five or six Englishwomen in old bonnets. A little whispering and chattering went on among the young French girls, who arrived guarded by their mothers. The way in which French mothers look after their daughters, tie their bonnet-strings, pin their collars, carry their books and shawls, &c., and sit beside them, and always answer for them if they are spoken to, is very curious. Now and then, however, they relax a little, and allow a little whispering with young companions. There was a low murmur and a slight bustle as four pasteurs of unequal heights walked in and placed themselves in the reserved seats. M. Stephen Tourneur followed and took his place. With what kind steadfast glances he greeted his audience! Even Elizabeth could not resist the charm of his manner, and she admired and respected him, much as she disliked the exercise of the evening.

His face lit up with Christian fervour, his eyes shone and gleamed with kindness, his voice, when he began to speak, thrilled with earnestness and sincerity. There was at times a wonderful power about the frail little man, the power which is won in many a desperate secret struggle, the power which comes from a whole life of deep feeling and honest endeavour. No wonder that Stephen Tourneur, who had so often wrestled with the angel and overcome his own passionate spirit, should have influence over others less strong, less impetuous than his own. Elly could not but admire him and love him, many of his followers worshipped him with the most affecting devotion; Anthony, his son, loved him too, and would have died for him in a quiet way, but he did not blindly believe in his father.

But listen! What a host of eloquent words, of tender thoughts come alive from his lips to-night. What reverent faith, what charity, what fervour! The people's eyes were fixed upon his kind, eloquent face, and their hearts all beat in sympathy with his own.

One or two of the Englishwomen began to cry. One French lady was swaying herself backwards and forwards

in rapt attention; the two clergymen sat wondering in
their white neckcloths.   What would they give to preach
such sermons?   And the voice went on uttering, entreating, encouraging, rising and sinking, ringing with passionate cadence.   It ceased at last, and the only sounds in the
room were a few sighs, and the suppressed sobs of one or
two women.   Elizabeth sighed among others, and sat very
still with her hands clasped in her lap.   For the first time
in her life she was wondering whether she had not perhaps
been in the wrong hitherto, and Tourneur, and Madame
Jacob, and all the rest in the right—and whether happiness was not the last thing to search for, and those things
of which he had spoken, the first and best and only neces-
sities.   Alas! what strange chance was it that at that
moment she raised her head and looked up with her great
blue eyes, and saw a strange familiar face under one of the
dowdy English bonnets—a face, thin, pinched, with a
hooked nose, and sandy hair—that sent a little thrill to
her heart, and made her cry out to herself eagerly, as a
rush of old memories and hopes came over her, that happiness was sent into the world for a gracious purpose, and
that love meant goodness and happiness too sometimes.
And, yes—no—yes—that was Lady Dampier! and was
John in Paris, perhaps? and Miss Dampier? and were
the dear, dear old days come back? . . .

After a few minutes the congregation began to sing a
hymn, the English ladies joining in audibly with their

queer accents. The melody swayed on, horribly out of tune and out of time, in a wild sort of minor key. Tou-Tou and Lou-Lou sang, one on each side of their mother, exceedingly loud and shrill, and one of the clergymen attempted a second, after which the discordance reached its climax. Elly had laughed on one or two occasions, and indeed I do not wonder. To-day she scarcely heard the sound of the voices. Her heart was beating with hope, delight, wonder; her head was in a whirl, her whole frame trembling with excitement, that increased every instant. Would M. Boulot's sermon never come to an end? Monsieur Bontemps' exposition, Monsieur de Marveille's reports, go on for ever and ever?

But at last it was over : a little rustling, a little pause, and all the voices beginning to murmur, and the chairs scraping; people rising, a little group forming round each favourite pasteur, hands outstretched, thanks uttered, people coming and going. With one bound Elly found herself standing by Lady Dampier, holding both her hands, almost crying with delight. The apathetic English lady was quite puzzled by the girl's exaggerated expressions. She cared very little for Elly Gilmour herself : she liked her very well, but she could not understand her extraordinary warmth of greeting. However, she was carried away by her feelings to the extent of saying, 'You must come and see us to-morrow. We are only passing through Paris on our way to Schlangenbad for Lætitia ; she has been

sadly out of health and spirits lately, poor dear. We are
at the Hôtel du Louvre. You must come and lunch with
us. Ah! here is your mother. How d'ye do, dear Madam
Tourneur? What a privilege it has been! What a treat
Mossu Tourneur has given us to-night. I have been quite
delighted, I assure you,' said her ladyship, bent on being
gracious.

Mme. Tourneur made the most courteous of salutations.
' I am glad you came, since it was so,' said she.

'I want you to let Elly come and see me,' continued
Lady Dampier; 'she must come to lunch; I should be so
glad if you would accompany her. I would offer to take her
to the play, but I suppose you do not approve of such
things any more.'

' My life is so taken up with other more serious duties,'
said Mme. Tourneur, with a faint superior smile, 'that I
have little time for mere worldly amusements. I cannot
say that I desire them for my daughter.'

' Oh, of course,' said Lady Dampier. 'I myself——but
it is only *en passant*, as we are all going on to Schlangenbad in two days. It is really quite delightful to find
you settled here so nicely. What a privilege it must be
to be so constantly in Mossu Tourneur's society!'

Madame Tourneur gave a bland assenting smile, and
turned to speak to several people who were standing near.
'Monsieur de Marveille, are you going? Thanks, I will
be at the committee on Thursday without fail. Monsieur

Boulot, you must remain a few minutes; I want to consult you about that case in which la Comtesse de Glaris
takes so deep an interest. Lady Macduff has also written
to me to ask my husband's interest for her. Ah, Lady
Sophia! how glad I am you have returned; is Lady Ma-
tilda better?'

'Well, I'll wish you good-by, Madame Tourneur,' said
Lady Dampier, rather impressed, and not much caring to
stand by quite unnoticed while all these greetings were
going on. 'You will let Elly come to morrow?'

'Certainly,' said Mme. Tourneur. 'You will understand how it is that I do not call. My days are much
occupied. I have little time for mere visits of pleasure
and ceremony. Monsieur Bontemps, one word——'

'Elly, which is the way out?' said Lady Dampier,
abruptly, less and less pleased, but more and more impressed.

'I will show you,' said Elly, who had been standing
by all this time, and she led the way bare-headed into the
court, over which the stars where shining tranquilly.
The trees looked dark and rustled mysteriously along the
wall, but all heaven was alight. Elly looked up for an
instant, and then turned to her companion and asked her,
with a voice that faltered a little, if they were all together
in Paris?

'No; Miss Dampier is in Scotland still,' said my lady.
It was not Miss Dampier's name of which Elizabeth

Gilmour was longing to hear, she did not dare ask any more ; but it seemed as if a great weight had suddenly fallen upon her heart, as she thought that perhaps, after all, he was not come; she should not hear of him ; see him, who knows, perhaps never again ?

Elly tried to unbar the great front door to let out her friend ; but she could not do it, and called to old Françoise, who was passing across to the kitchen, to come and help her. And suddenly the bolt, which had stuck in some manner, gave way, the gate opened wide, and as it opened Elly saw that there was somebody standing just outside under the lamp-post. The foolish child did not guess who it was, but said 'Good-night,' with a sigh, and held out her soft hand to Lady Dampier. And then, all of a sudden, the great load went away, and in its place came a sort of undreamt-of peace, happiness, and gratitude. All the stars seemed suddenly to blaze more brightly ; all the summer's night to shine more wonderfully; all trouble, all anxiousness, to melt away ; and John Dampier turned round and said,—

'Is that you, Elizabeth ? '

'And you ? ' cried Elly, springing forward, with both her hands outstretched. 'Ah ! I did not think who was outside the door.'

'How did you come here, John ? ' said my lady, very much flustered.

'I came to fetch you,' said her son. 'I wanted a walk,

and Letty told me where you were gone.' Lady Dampier
did not pay much attention to his explanations; she was
watching Elly with a dissatisfied face; and glancing round
too, the young man saw that Elly was standing quite still
under the archway, with her hands folded, and with a look
of dazzled delight in her blue eyes that there was no mistaking.

'You don't forget your old friends, Elly?' said he.

'I! never, never,' cried Elizabeth.

'And I, too, do not forget,' said he, very kindly, and
held out his hand once more, and took hers, and did not
let it go. 'I will come and see you, and bring Lætitia,'
he added, as his mother looked up rather severely. 'Good-
night, dear Elly? I am glad you are unchanged.'

People, however slow they may be naturally, are
generally quick in discovering admiration, or affection, or
respectful devotion to themselves. Lady Dampier only
suspected, her son was quite sure of poor Elly's feelings,
as he said good-night under the archway. Indeed he knew
a great deal more about them than did Elizabeth herself.
All she knew was that the great load was gone; and she
danced across the stones of the yard, clapping her hands
in her old happy way. The windows of the salle were
lighted up. She could see the people within coming and
going, but she did not notice Anthony, who was standing
in one of them. He, for his part, was watching the little
dim figure dancing and flitting about in the starlight.

Had he, then, anything to do with her happiness? Was he indeed so blessed? His heart was overflowing with humble gratitude, with kindness, with wonder. He was happy at the moment, and was right to be grateful. She was happy, too—as thoroughly happy now, and carried away by her pleasure, as she had been crushed and broken by her troubles. 'Ah! to think that the day has come at last, after watching all this long, long, cruel time! I always knew it would come. Everybody gets what they wish for sooner or later. I don't think anybody was ever so miserable as I have been all this year, but at last—at last——' No one saw the bright, happy look that came into her face, for she was standing in the dark outside the door of the house. She wanted to dream, she did not want to talk to anybody; she wanted to tell herself over and over again how happy she was; how she had seen him again; how he had looked; how kindly he had spoken to her. Ah! yes, he had cared for her all the time; and now he had come to fetch her away. She did not think much of poor Anthony; if she did, it was to say to herself that somehow it would all come right, and everybody would be as well contented as she was. The door of the house opened while she still stood looking up at the stars. This time it was not John Dampier, but the Pasteur Tourneur, who came from behind it. He put out his hand and took hold of hers.

'You there, Elizabeth! Come in, my child; you will

be cold.' And he drew her into the hall, where the Pasteurs Boulot and De Marveille were pulling on their cloaks and hats, and bidding everybody good-night.

The whole night Elizabeth lay starting and waking —so happy that she could not bear to go to sleep, to cease to exist for one instant. Often it had been the other way, and she had been thankful to lay her weary head on her pillow, and close her aching eyes, and forget her troubles. But all this night she lay wondering what the coming day was to bring forth. She had better have gone to sleep. The coming day brought forth nothing at all, except, indeed, a little note from Lætitia, written on a half-sheet of paper, which was put into her hand about eleven o'clock, just as she was sitting down to the *déjeûner à la fourchette.*

> 'Hôtel du Rhin, Place Vendôme,
> 'Wednesday Evening.

'My dear Elizabeth,— I am so disappointed to think that I shall not perhaps see you after all. Some friends of ours have just arrived, who are going on to Schlangen-bad to-morrow, and aunt Catherine thinks it will be better to set off a little sooner than we had intended, so as to travel with them. I wish you might be able to come and breakfast with us about nine to-morrow ; but I am afraid this is asking almost too much, though I should greatly enjoy seeing you again. Good-by. If we do not meet now, I trust that on our return in a couple of months we may be more fortunate, and see much of each other.   We start at ten, and shall reach Strasbourg about eight.

‘ Ever, dear Elizabeth,

‘ Affectionately yours,

‘ LÆTITIA MALCOLM.’

‘ What has happened ? ’ said Madame Tourneur, quite frightened, for she saw the girl’s face change and her eyes suddenly filling with tears.

‘ Nothing has happened,’ said Elizabeth.   ‘ I was only disappointed to think I should not see them again.’   And she put out her hand and gave her mother the note.

‘ But why care so much for people who do not care for you ? ’ said her mother.   ‘ Lady Dampier is one of the coldest women I ever knew ; and as for Lætitia, if she loved you in the least, would she write you such a note as this ? ’

‘ Mamma ! it is a very kind note,’ said Elizabeth.   ‘ I know she loves me.’

‘ Do you think she cried over it, as you did ? ’ said her mother.   ‘ “ So disappointed ”—“ more fortunate on our return through Paris ” ? ’

‘ Do not let us judge our neighbours so hastily, my wife,’ said M. Tourneur.   ‘ Let Elizabeth love her friend. What can she do better ? ’

Caroline looked up with an odd expression, shrugged her shoulders, and did not answer.

Until breakfast was over, Elly kept up pretty well; but when M. Tourneur rose and went away into his writing-room, when Anthony and the young men filed off by an opposite door, and Mme. Tourneur disappeared to look to her household duties—then, when the room was quiet again, and only Madame Jacob remained sewing in a window, and Lou-Lou and Tou-Tou whispering over their lessons, suddenly the canary burst out into a shrill piping jubilant song, and the sunshine poured in, and Elly's heart began to sink. And then suddenly the horrible reality seemed realised to her. . . .

They were gone—those who had come, as she thought, to rescue her. Could it be true—could it be really true? She had stood lonely on the arid shore waving her signals of distress, and they who should have seen them, never heeded, but went sailing away to happier lands, disappearing in the horizon, and leaving her to her fate. That fate which—it was more than she could bear. It seemed more terrible than ever to her to-day. . . . Ah! silly girl, was her life as hard as the lives of thousands struggling along with her in the world, tossed and broken against the rocks, while she, at least, was safely landed on the beach? She had no heart to think of others. She sat sickening with disappointment, and once more her eyes filled up with stinging tears.

'Lou-Lou, Tou-Tou, come up to your lessons,' said Mrs. Jacob. 'I do not wish you to see such a wicked

example of discontent.' The little girls went off on tip-
toe ; and when these people were gone, Elizabeth was left
quite alone.

' I daresay I am very wicked,' she was saying to herself.
' I was made wicked. But this is more than I can bear—
to live all day with the people I hate, and then when I do
love with my whole heart, to be treated with such cruel
indifference—such coldness. He *ought* to know, he must
know that he has broken my heart. Why does he look
so kindly, and then forget so heartlessly? . . .'

She hid her face in her hands, and bent her head over
the wooden table. She did not care who knew her to be
unhappy—what pain her unhappiness might give. The
person who was likely to be most wounded by her poig-
nant grief came into the room at the end of half-an-hour,
and found her sitting still in the same attitude, with her
head hanging, and her tears dribbling on the deal table.
This was enough answer for poor Anthony.

' Elizabeth,' he faltered, ' I see you cannot make up
your mind.'

' Ah ! no, no, Anthony, not yet,' said Elizabeth ; ' but
you are the only person in the world who cares for me ; and
indeed, indeed, I am grateful.'

And then the poor little head sank down again overwhelmed with its load of grief.

' Tell me, Elizabeth, is there anything in the world I
can do to make you more happy ? ' said Anthony. ' My

prayers, my best wishes are yours. Is there nothing else?'

'Only not to notice me,' said Elly; 'only to leave me alone.'

And so Anthony, seeing that he could do nothing, went away very sad at heart. He had been so happy and confident the night before, and now he began to fear that what he longed for was never to be his. Poor boy, he buried his trouble in his own heart, and did not say one word of it to father, or mother, or young companions.

Five or six weeks went by, and Elly heard no more of the Dampiers.. Every day she looked more ill, more haggard ; her temper did not mend, her spirits did not improve. In June the five young men went home to their families. M. and Madame Tourneur went down to Fontainebleau for a week. Anthony set off for the South of France to visit an uncle. He was to be ordained in the autumn, and was anxious to pay this visit before his time should be quite taken up by his duties. Clementine asked for a holiday, and went off to her friends at Passy ; and Elly remained at home. It was her own fault : Monsieur Tourneur had begged her to come with them ; her mother had scolded and remonstrated, all in vain. The wayward girl declared that she wanted no change, no company, that she was best where she was. Only for a week? she would stay, and there was an end of it. I think the secret was, that she could not bear to quit Paris, and waited and waited, hoping against hope.

'I am afraid you will quarrel with Madame Jacob,' said her mother, as she was setting off.

'I shall not speak to her,' said Elly; and for two days she was as good as her word. But on the third day, this salutary silence was broken. Madame Jacob, coming in with her bonnet on, informed Elizabeth that she was going out for the afternoon.

'I confess it is not without great apprehensions, lest you should get into mischief,' says the lady.

'And pray,' says Elly, 'am I more likely to get into mischief than you are? _I_ am going out.'

'You will do nothing of the sort,' says Madame Jacob.

'I will do exactly as I choose,' says Elizabeth.

In a few minutes, a battle royal was raging; Tou-Tou and Lou-Lou look on, all eyes and ears; old Françoise comes up from the kitchen, and puts her head in at the door.

Madame Jacob was desiring her, on no account, to let Elizabeth out that afternoon, when Lou-Lou said, 'There, that was the street-door shutting;' and Tou-Tou said, 'She is gone.' And so it was.

The wilful Elizabeth had brushed past old Françoise, rushed up to her own room, pulled out a shawl, tied on her bonnet, defiantly, run down stairs and across the yard, and, in a minute, was walking rapidly away without once looking behind her. Down the hill, past the hospital—they were carrying a wounded man in at the door as she passed, and she just caught a glimpse of his pale face, and turned shrinking away. Then she got into the Faubourg St. Honoré, with its shops and its cab-stands, and busy people coming and going; and then she turned up the Rue d'Angoulême. In the Champs Elysées the afternoon sun was streaming ; there was a crowd, and, as it happened, soldiers were marching along to the sound of martial music. She saw an empty bench, and sat down for a minute to regain breath and equanimity. The music put her in mind of the day when she had listened at her window—of the day when her heart was so heavy and then so light—of the day when Anthony had told her his scheme, when John Dampier had waited at the door : the day, the only one —she was not likely to forget it—when she had been so happy, just for a little. And now—— ? The bitter remembrance came rushing over her ; and she jumped up, and walked faster and faster, trying to escape from it.

She got into the Tuileries, and on into the Rue de Rivoli, but she thought that people looked at her strangely, and she turned homewards at last. It was lonely, wandering about this busy city by herself. As she passed by the columns of St. Philip's Church, somebody came out, and the curtain swung back, and Elly, looking up, saw a dim quiet interior, full of silent rays of light falling from the yellow windows and chequering the marble. She stopped,

and went in with a sudden impulse. One old woman was
kneeling on the threshold, and Elly felt as if she, too,
wanted to fall upon her knees. What tranquil gloom, and
silence, and repose! Her own church was only open at
certain hours. Did it always happen that precisely at
eleven o'clock on Sunday mornings she was in the exact
frame of mind in which she most longed for spiritual com-
munion and consolation? To be tightly wedged in between
two other devotees, plied with *chaufferettes* by the pew-
opener, forced to follow the extempore supplications of the
preacher—did all this suffice to her wants? Here was
silence, coolness, a faint, half-forgotten smell of incense,
there were long, empty rows of chairs, one or two people
kneeling at the little altars, five or six little pious candles
burning in compliment to the various saints and deities to
whom they were dedicated. The rays of the little candles
glimmered in the darkness, and the foot-falls fell quietly
along the aisle. I, for my part, do not blame this poor
foolish heart, if it offered up a humble supplication here
in the shrine of the stranger. Poor Elly was not very
eloquent; she only prayed to be made a good girl and to
be happy. But, after all, eloquence and long words do
not mean any more.

She walked home, looking up at the sunset lines which
were streaking the sky freshly and delicately; she thought
she saw Madame Jacob's red nose up in a little pink cloud,
and began to speculate how she would be received. And

she had nearly reached her own door, and was toiling wearily up the last hilly piece of road, when she heard some quick steps behind ; somebody passed, turned round, said, ' Why, Elly ! I was going to see you.'

In an instant, Elly's blue eyes were all alight, and her ready hand outstretched to John Dampier—for it was he.

CHAPTER V.

In looking backward, they may find that several things which were not
the charm have more reality to this groping memory than the charm itself
which embalmed them.

HE had time to think, as he greeted her, how worn she
looked, how shabbily she was dressed. And yet what a
charming, talking, brightening face it was. When Elly
smiled, her bonnet and dress became quite new and
becoming, somehow. In two minutes he thought her
handsomer than ever. They walked on, side by side, up·
the hilly street. She, trying to hide her agitation,.
asked him about Lætitia, about his mother, and dear Miss:
Dampier.

'I think she does care for me still,' said Elly; 'but
you have all left off.'

'My dear child,' said he, 'how can you think anything so foolish.'

'I have nothing else to do,' said Elly, plaintively; 'all!
day long I think about those happy times which are gone.
I thought you had forgotten me when you did not come.'

Dampier laughed a little uneasily. 'I have had to
take them to their watering-place,' said he; 'I could not.

help it. But tell me about yourself. Are you not comfortable ? ' he asked.

' I am rather unhappy,' said Elizabeth. ' I am not good, like they are, and oh ! I get so tired ; ' and then she went on and told him what miserable days she spent, and how she hated them, and she longed for a little pleasure, and ease, and happiness.

He was very much touched, and very, very sorry. ' You don't look well,' he said. ' You should have some amusement—some change. I would take you anywhere you liked. Why not come now, for a drive ? See, here is a little open carriage passing. Surely, with an old friend like me, there can be no harm.' And he signed to the driver to stop.

Elizabeth was quite frightened at the idea, and said, ' Oh, no, no ! indeed.' Whereas Dampier only said, ' Oh, yes ! indeed, you must. Why, I knew you when you were a baby—and your father and your grandmother—and I am a respectable middle-aged man, and it will do you good, and it will soon be a great deal too dark for any of your pasteurs to recognise you and report. We have been out riding together before now—why not come for a little drive in the Bois ? Why not ? '

So said Elly to herself, doubtfully ; and she got in, still hesitating, and in a minute they were rolling away swiftly out at the gates of Paris, out towards the sunset— so it seemed to Elizabeth—and she forgot all her fears.

The heavens glowed overhead; her heart beat with intensest enjoyment. Presently, the twilight came falling with a green glow, with stars, with evening perfumes, with lights twinkling from the carriages reflected on the lakes as they rolled past.

And so at last she was happy, sometimes silent from delight, sometimes talking in her simple, foolish way, and telling him all about herself, her regrets, her troubles—about Anthony. She could not help it—indeed, she could not. Dampier, for his part, cried out at the notion of her marrying Anthony, made fun of him, laughed at him, pitied him. The poor fellow, now that she compared him to John Dampier, did indeed seem dull and strangely uncouth, and commonplace.

'Marry that cub,' said Sir John; 'you mustn't do it, my dear. You would be like the princess in the fairy tale, who went off with the bear. It's downright wicked to think of such a thing. Elizabeth, *promise* me you won't. Does he ever climb up and down a pole? is he fond of buns? is he tame? If your father were alive, would he suffer such a thing? Promise me, Elly, that you will never become Mrs. Bruin.'

'Yes; I promise,' said Elly, with a sigh. 'But he is so kind. Nobody is as——' And then she stopped, and thought, 'Yes; here was some one who was a great deal kinder.' Talking to Dampier was so easy, so pleasant, that she scarcely recognised her own words and sentences:

it was like music in tune after music out of tune : it was
like running on smooth rails after rolling along a stony
road : it was like breathing fresh air after a heated stifling
atmosphere. Somehow, he met her half-way ; she need
not explain, recapitulate, stumble for words, as she was
forced to do with those practical, impracticable people at
home. He understood what she wanted to say before she
had half finished her sentence; he laughed at her fine
little jokes ; he encouraged, he cheered, he delighted her.
If she had cared for him before, it was now a mad adoration which she felt for this man. He suited her ; she felt
now that he was part of her life—the better, nobler, wiser
part ; and if he was the other half of her life, surely, somehow, she must be as necessary to him as he was to her.
Why had he come to see her else ? Why had he cared for
her, and brought her here ? Why was his voice so gentle,
his manner so kind and sympathetic ? He had cared for
her once, she knew he had ; and he cared for her still, she
knew he did. If the whole world were to deceive her and
fail her, she would still trust him. And her instinct was
not wrong : he was sincerely and heartily her friend. The
carriage put them down a few doors from M. Tourneur's
house, and then Elly went boldly up to the door and rang
at the bell.

'I shall come at four o'clock to-morrow, and take you
for a drive,' said John ; 'you look like another woman
already.'

' It is no use asking Madame Jacob,' said Elly ; ' she
would lock me up into my room.   I will come somehow.
How shall I thank you ? '

' By looking well and happy again.   I shall be so glad
to have cured you.'

' And it is so pleasant to meet with such a kind doctor,'
said Elly, looking up and smiling.

' Good-by, Elly,' repeated Sir John, quite affected by
her gentle looks.

Old Françoise opened the door.   Elly turned a little
pale.

' Ah, ha ! vous voilà,' says the old woman ; ' méchante
fille, you are going to get a pretty scolding.   Where have
you been ? '

' Ah, Françoise ! ' said Elly, ' I have been so happy.   I
met Sir John Dampier : he is an old, old friend.   He took
me for a drive in the Bois.   Is Madame Jacob very, very
angry ? '

' Well, you are in luck,' says the old woman, who
could never resist Elizabeth's pretty pleading ways; ' she
came home an hour ago and fetched the children, and
went out to dine in town, and I told her you were in your
room.'

' Ah, you dear kind old woman ! ' said Elly, flinging
her arms round her neck, and giving her a kiss.

' There, there ! ' said the unblushing Françoise; ' I
will put your couvert in the salle.'

'Ah! I am very glad. I am so hungry, Françoise,' said Elly, pulling off her bonnet, and shaking her loose hair as she followed the old woman across the courtyard.

So Elizabeth sat down to dine off dry bread and cold mutton. But though she said she was hungry, she was too happy to eat much. The tallow candle flickered on the table. She thought of the candles in St. Philip's Church; then she went over every word, every minute which she had spent since she was kneeling there. Old Françoise came in with a little cake she had made her, and found Elizabeth sitting, smiling, with her elbows on the table. 'Allons, allons!' thought the old cook. 'Here, eat, mamzelle,' said she; 'faut plus sortir sans permission— hein?'

'Thank you, Françoise. How nice! how kind of you!' said Elizabeth, in her bad French—she never would learn to talk properly; and then she ate her cake by the light of the candle, and this little dim tallow wick seemed to cast light and brilliance over the whole world, over her whole life, which seemed to her as if it would go on for ever and ever. Now and then a torturing doubt, a misgiving, came over her, but these she put quickly aside.

Madame Jacob was pouring out the coffee when Elly came down to breakfast next morning, conscious and ashamed, and almost disposed to confess. 'I am surprised,' said Madame Jacob, 'that you have the impudence to sit down at table with me;' and she said it in such an acid tone that all Elly's sweetness, and ashamedness, and penitence turned to bitterness.

'I find it very disagreeable,' says Elly; ' but I try and resign myself.'

'I shall write to my brother about you,' continued Madame Jacob.

'Indeed!' says Elizabeth. 'Here is a letter which he has written to me. What fun if it should be about you!' It was like Tourneur's handwriting, but it did not come from him. Elly opened it carelessly enough, but Tou-Tou and Lou-Lou exchanged looks of intelligence. Their mother had examined the little missive, and made her comments upon it:—

> 'Avignon, Rue de la Clochette,
> 'Chez le Pasteur Ch. Tourneur.

'My dear Elly,—I think of you so much and so constantly that I cannot help wishing to make you think of me, if only for one minute, while you read these few words. I have been telling my uncle about you; it is he who asks me why I do not write. But there are some things which are not to be spoken or to be written—it is only by one's life that one can try to tell them; and you, alas! do not care to hear the story of my life. I wonder will the day ever come when you will listen to it?

'I have been most kindly received by all my old friends down in these parts. Yesterday I attended the service in

the Temple, and heard a most soul-stirring and eloquent
oration from the mouth of M. le Pasteur David. I receive cheering accounts on every side. A new temple has
been opened at Beziers, thanks to the munificence of one
of our *coréligionnaires*. The temple was solemnly opened
on the Monday of the Pentecost. The discourse of dedication was pronounced by M. le Pasteur Borrel, of Nismes.
Seven pasteurs *en robe* attended the ceremony. They tell
me that the interdiction which had weighed for some
years upon the temple at Fouqueure (Charente) has been
taken off, and that the faithful were able to reopen their
temple on the first Sunday in June. Need I say what
vivid actions of grace were uttered on this happy occasion?
A Protestant school has also been established at Montau-
ban, which seems to be well attended. I am now going
to visit two of my uncle's *confrères*, MM. Bertoul and
Joseph Aubré. Of M. Bertoul I have heard much good.

'Why do I tell you all this? Do you care for what I
care? Could you ever bring yourself to lead the life which
I propose to lead? Time only will show, dear Elizabeth.
It will also show to you the faithfulness and depth of my
affection.

'A. T.'

Elly put the letter down with a sigh, and went on
drinking her coffee and eating her bread. Madame Jacob
hemmed and tried to ask her a question or two on the

subject, but Elly would not answer. Elly sometimes wondered at Anthony's fancy for her, knowing how little suited she was to the way of life she was leading; she was surprised that his rigid notions should allow him to entertain such an idea for an instant. But the truth was that Anthony was head over ears in love with her, and thought her perfection at the bottom of his heart.

Poor Anthony! This is what he got in return for his letter :—

'My dear Anthony,—It cannot be—never—never. But I do care for you, and I mean to always. For you are my brother in a sort of way.

'I am your affectionate, grateful

'ELLY.

'P.S.—Your father and my mother are away at Fontainebleau. Madame Jacob is here, and more disagreeable than anything you can imagine.'

And so it was settled; and Elly never once asked herself if she had been foolish or wise; but, after thinking compassionately about Anthony for a minute or two, she began to think about Dampier, and said to herself that she had followed his advice, and he must know best; and Dampier himself, comfortably breakfasting in the coffee-room of the hotel, was thinking of her, and, as he thought, put away all unpleasant doubts or suggestions. 'Poor

little thing! dear little thing!' he was saying to himself.
' I will not leave her to the tender mercies of those fana-
tics. She will die—I see it in her eyes—if she stays there.
My mother or aunt Jean must come to her help ; we must
not desert her. Poor, poor, little Elly, with her wistful
face ! Why did not she make me marry her a year ago?
I was very near it.'

He was faithful next day to his appointment, and Elly
arrived breathless. ' Madame Jacob had locked her up
in her room,' she said, only she got out of window and
clambered down by the vine, and here she was. ' But it
is the last time,' she added. ' Ah ! let us make haste ; is
not that Françoise ? ' He helped her in, and in a minute
they were driving away along the Faubourg. Elly let
down the veil. John saw that her hand was trembling,
and asked if she was afraid ?

' I am afraid, because I know I am doing wrong,' said
Elly ; ' only I think I should have died for want of fresh
air in that hateful prison, if I had not come.'

' You used to like your little apartment near the
Madeleine better,' said Dampier ; ' that was not a prison.'

' I grow sick with regret when I think of those days,'
Elly said. ' Do you know that day you spoke to us in the
Tuileries was the last happy day in my life, except——'

' Except ? ' said Dampier.

' Except yesterday,' said Elly. ' It is so delightful to
do something wrong again.'

'Why should you think that this is doing wrong?'
said Dampier. 'You know me, and can trust me—can't
you, Elly?'

'Have I shown much mistrust?' said Elly, laughing;
and then she added more seriously, 'I have been writing
to Anthony this morning—I have done as you told me.
So you see whether I trust you or not.'

'You have refused him?' said Dampier.

'Yes; are you satisfied?' said Elly, looking with her
bright blue-eyed glance.

'He was unworthy of you,' cried Dampier, secretly
rather dismayed to find his advice so quickly acted upon.
What had he done? would not that marriage, after all,
have been the very best thing for Elly perhaps? He
was glad and sorry, but I think he would rather have been
more sorry and less glad, and have heard that Elly had
found a solution to all her troubles. He thought it necessary to be sentimental; it was the least he could do,
after what she had done for him.

'Why wouldn't you let me in when I came to see you
one day long ago, just before I left Paris?' he asked
suddenly. 'Do you know what I wanted to say to you?'

Elly blushed up under her veil. 'Mamma had desired
Clementine to let no one in. Did you not know I would
have seen you if I could?'

'I knew nothing of the sort,' said Dampier, rather
sadly. 'I wish—I wish—I had known it.' He forgot

that, after all, that was not the real reason of his going away without speaking. He chose to imagine that this was the reason—that he would have married Elly but for this. He forgot his own careful scruples and hesitations; his doubts and indecision; and now to-day he forgot everything, except that he was very sorry for Elly, and glad to give her a little pleasure. He did not trouble himself as to what people would say of her—of a girl who was going about with a man who was neither her brother nor her husband. Nobody would know her. The only people to fear were the people at home, who should never hear anything about it. He would give her and give himself a little happiness, if he could; and he said to himself that he was doing a good action in so doing; he would write to his aunt about her, he would be her friend and her doctor, and if he could bring a little colour in those wasted cheeks and happiness into those sad eyes, it would be wicked and cruel not to do so.

And so, like a quack doctor, as he was, he administered his drug, which soothed and dulled her pain for the moment, only to incre e and hasten the progress of the cruel malady which was estroying her. They drove along past the Madeleine, along the broad glittering Boulevards, with their crowds, their wares, people thronging the pavements, horses and carriages travelling alongside with them; the world, the flesh, and the devil jostling and pressing past.

'There is a theatre,' cried Elly, as they came to a sudden stop. 'I wonder, shall I ever go again? What fun it used to be.'

'Will you come to-night?' asked Dampier, smiling, 'I will take care of you.'

Elly, who had found her good spirits again, laughed and clasped her hands. 'How I should like it. Oh! how I wish it was possible, but it would be quite, quite impossible.'

'Have you come to think such vanities wrong?' said Dampier.

'Not wrong. Where is the harm? Only unattainable. Imagine Madame Jacob; think of the dragons, who would tear me to pieces if they found me out—of Anthony—of my step-father.'

'You need not show them the play-bill,' said Dampier, laughing. 'You will be quite sure of not meeting any of the pasteurs there. Could you not open one of those barred windows and jump out? I would come with a ladder of ropes, if you will let me.'

'I should not want a ladder of ropes,' said Elly; 'the windows are quite close to the ground. What fun it would be! but it is quite, quite impossible, of course.'

Dampier said no more. He told the driver to turn back, and to stop at the Louvre; and he made her get out, and took her upstairs into the great golden hall with the tall windows, through which you can see the Seine as it rushes under the bridges, and the light as it falls on the ancient stately quays and houses, on the cathedral, on the towers of Paris. It was like enchantment to Elly; all about the atmosphere was golden, was bewitched. She was eagerly drinking her cup of happiness to the dregs, she was in a sort of glamour. She hardly could believe that this was herself.

They went and sat down on the great round sofa in the first room, opposite the ' Marriage of Cana,' with ' St. Michael killing the Dragon' on one side, and the green pale wicked woman staring at them from behind : the pale woman with the unfathomable face. Elly kept turning round every now and then, fascinated by her cold eyes. Dampier was a connoisseur, and fond of pictures, and he told Elizabeth all about those which he liked best ; told her about the painters—about their histories. She was very ignorant, and scarcely knew the commonest stories. How she listened ; how she treasured up his words, how she remembered, in after days, every tone as he spoke, every look in his kind eyes! He talked when he should have been silent, looked kind when he should have turned his eyes away. What cruel kindness ! what fatal friendship ! He imagined she liked him; he knew it, indeed: but he fancied that she liked him and loved him in the same quiet way in which he loved her—hopelessly, regretfully, resignedly. As he walked by her side along these wonderful galleries, now and then it occurred to him that, perhaps, after all, it was scarcely wise ; but he put the thought quickly away, as I have said already, and blinded himself, and said, surely it was right. They were standing before a kneeling abbess in white flannel, painted by good old Philip of Champagne, and laughing at her droll looks and her long nose, when Sir John, happening to turn round, saw his old acquaintance De Vaux coming directly towards them with his eye-glasses stuck over his nose, and his nose in the air. He came up quite close, stared at the abbess, and walked on without apparently seeing or recognising them. Elly had not turned her head, but Dampier drew a long breath when he was gone. Elly wondered to see him looking so grave when she turned round with a smile and made some little joke. 'I think we ought to go, Elly,' said he. 'Come; this place will soon be shut.'

They drove home through the busy street, once more, through the golden sunset. They stopped at the corner by the hospital, and Elly said 'Good-by,' and jumped out. As Elly was reluctantly turning to go away, Dampier felt that he *must* see her once more ; that he *couldn't* part from her now. 'Elly,' he said, 'I shall be here at six o'clock on Friday. This is Tuesday, isn't it? and we must go to the play just once together. Won't you come? Do, please, come.'

'Shall I come? I will think about it all to-morrow,' said Elly, 'and make up my mind.' And then Dampier watched the slim little figure disappear under the doorway.

Fortune was befriending Elly to-day. Old Françoise had left the great door open, and now she slipped in and ran up to her own room, where she found the key in the lock. She came down quite demurely to dinner when Lou-Lou came to summon her to the frugal repast.

All dinner-time she thought about her scheme, and hesitated, and determined, and hesitated, and wished wistfully, and then suddenly said to herself that she would be happy her own way, come what might. 'We will eat, drink, and be merry,' said Elly to herself, with a little wry face at the cabbage, 'for to-morrow we die.'

And so the silly girl almost enjoyed the notion of running wild in this reckless way. Her whole life, which had been so dull and wearisome before, glittered with strange happiness and bewildering hope. She moved about the house like a person in a dream. She was very silent, but that of late had been her habit. Madame Jacob looked surprised sometimes at her gentleness, but thought it was all right, and did not trouble herself about much else besides Tou-Tou's and Lou-Lou's hymns and lessons. She had no suspicion. She thought that Elizabeth's first escapade had been a mere girlish freak; of the second she knew nothing; of the third not one dim imagination entered her head. She noticed that Elly did not eat, but she looked well and came dancing into the room, and she (Mme. Jacob) supposed it was all right. Was it all right ? The whole summer nights Elly used to lie awake with wide-open eyes, or spring from her bed, and stand for long hours leaning from her window, staring at the stars and telling them all her story. The life she was leading was one of morbid excitement and feverish dreams.

CHAPTER VI.

What are we sent on earth for? Say to toil,
Nor seek to leave the tending of the vines,
For all the heat of day till it declines,
And death's mild curfew shall from work assoil.

MADAME JACOB had a friend at Asnières, an old maiden lady, Tou-Tou's godmother, who was well to do in the world, with her 200*l.* a year, it was said, and who lived in a little Chinese pagoda by the railway. Now and then this old lady used to write and invite Tou-Tou and Lou-Lou and their mother to come and see her, and you may be sure her invitations were never disregarded.

Mme. Jacob did look at Elizabeth rather doubtfully when she found on Wednesday morning the usual ill-spelt, ill-written little letter. But, after all, Tou-Tou's prospects were not to be endangered for the sake of looking after a young woman like Elizabeth, were she ten times more wayward and ill-behaved, and so the little girls were desired to make up their paquets. It was a great event in Mme. Jacob's eyes; the house echoed with her directions, Françoise went out to request assistance, and came back with a friend, who helped her down with the box. The little girls stood at the door to stop the omnibus, which was to take them to the station. They were off at last. The house door closed upon them with a satisfactory bang, and Elly breathed freely and ran through the deserted rooms clapping and waving her hands, and dancing her steps, and feeling at last that she was free. And so the morning hours went by. Old Françoise was not sorry either to see everybody go. She was sitting in the kitchen in the afternoon peeling onions and potatoes, when Elly came wandering in in her restless way, with her blue eyes shining and her curly hair pushed back. What a tranquil little kitchen it was, with a glimpse of the courtyard outside, and the cocks and the hens, and the poplar-trees waving in the sunshine, and the old woman sitting in her white cap busy at her homely work. Elly did not think how tranquil it was, but said to herself as she looked at Françoise, how old she was, and what a strange fate hers, that she should be there quietly peeling onions at the end of her life. What a horrible fate, thought Elizabeth, to be sitting by one's grave, as it were, paring vegetables and cooking broth to the last day of one's existence. Poor Françoise! And then she said out loud, ' Françoise, tell me, are cooks like ladies ; do they get to hate their lives sometimes ? Are you not tired to death of cooking *pot-au-feu* ? '

' I am thankful to have *pot-au-feu* to cook,' said Françoise. ' Mademoiselle, I should like to see you *éplu-*

cher vegetables sometimes, as I do, instead of running about all day. It would be much better for you.'

'Ecoutez, Françoise,' said Elly, imploringly; 'when I am old like you, I will sit still by the fire; now that I am young I want to run about. I am the only young person in this house. They are all old here, and like dead people, for they only think of heaven.'

'That is because they are on the road,' said Françoise. 'Ah! they are good folks—they are.'

'I see no merit in being good,' Elizabeth said, crossly, sitting down on the table and dabbling her fingers in a bowl of water, which stood there; 'they are good because they like it. It amuses them, it is their way of thinking — they like to be better than their neighbours.'

'*Fi donc*, Elizabeth!' said Françoise. 'You do not amuse them; but they are good to you. Is it Anthony's way of thinking when he bears with all your caprices? When my master comes home quite worn out and exhausted, and trudges off again without so much as waiting for his soup, if he hears he is wanted by some poor person or other, does he go because it pleases him, or because he is serving the Lord in this world, as he hopes to serve Him in the next?'

Elly was a little ashamed, and said, looking down, 'Have you always lived here with him, Françoise?'

'Not I,' said Françoise; 'ten years, that is all. But that is long enough to tell a good man from a bad one.

Good people live for others, and don't care about themselves. I hope when I have known you ten years, that
you too will be a good woman, mademoiselle.'

'Like Madame Jacob?' said Elly.

Françoise shrugged her shoulders rather doubtfully,
and Elly sat quite still watching her. Was it not strange
to be sitting there in this quiet everyday kitchen, with a
great unknown world throbbing in her heart. 'How little
Françoise guesses,' thought Elly; 'Françoise, who is only
thinking of her marmite and her potatoes.' Elly did not
know it, but Françoise had a very shrewd suspicion of what
was going on in the poor little passionate heart. 'The
girl is not suited here,' thought the old woman. 'If she
has found someone, so much the better; Clementine has
told me something about it. If madame were to drive
him off again, that would be a pity. But I saw them
quite plainly that day I went to Martin, the chemist's,
driving away in that little carriole, and I saw him that
night when he was waiting for his mother.'

So old Françoise peels potatoes, and Elly sits wondering and saying over to herself, 'Good people live for
others.' Who had she ever lived for but for herself? Ah!
there was one person whom she would live and die for now.
Ah! at last she would be good. 'And about the play?'
thought Elly; 'shall I go—shall I send him word that I
will not? There is no harm in a play; why should I not
please him and accept his kindness? it is not the first

time that we have been there together. I know that plays
are not wrong, whatever these stupid people say. Ah!
surely if happiness is sent to me, it would be wicked to
turn away, instead of being always—always grateful all
my life.' And so, though she told herself that it could
not be wrong to go, she forgot to tell herself that it was
wrong to go with him; her scruples died away one by one;
once or twice she thought of being brave and staying away,
and sending a message by old Françoise, but she only
thought of it.

All day long, on Friday, she wandered about the empty
house, coming and going, like a girl bewitched. She went
into the garden; she picked flowers and pulled them to
pieces, trying to spell out her fate; she tried to make a
wreath of vine-leaves, but got tired, and flung it away.
Old Françoise, from her kitchen window, watched her
standing at the grating and pulling at the vine; but the
old woman's spectacles were somewhat dim, and she did
not see Elly's two bright feverish eyes and her burning
cheeks from the kitchen window. As the evening drew
near, Elly's cheeks became pale, and her courage nearly
failed her, but she had been three days at home. Monsieur and Madame Tourneur were expected the next
morning; she had not seen Dampier for a long, long time
—so it seemed to her. Yes, she would go; she did not
care. Wrong? Right? It was neither wrong nor right,
—it was simply impossible to keep away. She could not

think of one reason in the world why she should stop.
She felt a thousand in her heart urging, ordering, com-
pelling her to go. She went up to her own room after
dinner, and began to dress, to plait, and to smoothe her
pretty curly hair. She put on a white dress, a black lace
shawl, and then she found that she had no gloves. Some
of her ancient belongings she kept in a drawer, but they
were not replaced as they wore out. And Elly possessed
diamond rings and bracelets in abundance; but neither
gloves, nor money to buy them. What did it matter?
She did not think about it twice; she put on her shabby
bonnet and ran downstairs. She was just going out, when
she remembered that Françoise would wonder what had
become of her, and so she went to the kitchen-door, opened
it a little way, and said, 'Good-night, Françoise! don't
disturb me to-night, I want to get up early to-morrow.'

Françoise, who had invited a friend to spend the evening, said, 'Bon soir, mamzelle!' rather crossly,—she did
not like her kitchen invaded at all times and hours,—and
then Elly was free to go.

She did not get out by the window, there was no need
for that, but she unfastened it, and unbarred the shutter
on the inside, so that, though everything looked much as
usual on the outside, she had only to push, and it would
fly open.

As she got to the door, her heart began to beat, and
she stopped for an instant to think. Inside, here, where

she was standing, was dulness, weariness, security, death; outside, wonderful happiness, dangerous happiness, and life —-so it seemed to her. Inside were cocks and hens, and ser- mons, weary exhortations, old Françoise peeling her onions. Outside, John Dampier waiting, the life she was created for, fresh air, congenial spirits, light and brightness,—and heaven there as well as here, thought Elly, clasping her hands ; heaven spreading across the housetops as well as over this narrow courtyard. ' What shall I do ? Oh ! shall I be forgiven ? Oh ! it will be forgiven me, surely, surely ! ' the girl sighed, and, with trembling hands, she undid the latch, and went out into the dusky street.

The little carriole, as Françoise called it, was waiting, a short way down, at the corner of the hospital; and Dampier came to meet her, looking very tall and straight through the twilight. She wondered at his grave, anxious face; but, in truth, he too was exceedingly nervous, though he would not let her know it : he was beginning to be afraid for her, and had resolved that he would not take her out again ; it might, after all, be unpleasant for them both ; he had seen De Vaux, and found out, to his annoyance, that he had recognised them in the Louvre the day before, and had passed them by on purpose. There was no knowing what trouble he might not get poor Elly into. And, besides, his aunt Jean was on her way to Paris. She had been keeping house for Will Dampier, she wrote, and she was coming. Will was on his way to Switzerland, and she should cross with him.

That very day John had received a letter from her, in answer to the one he had written about Elly. He had written it three days ago; but he was not the same man he had been three days ago. He was puzzled, and restless, and thoroughly wretched, that was the truth, and he was not used to be unhappy, and he did not like it. Elly's face haunted him day and night; he thought of her continually; he tried, in vain, to forget her, to put her out of his mind. Well, on the whole he was glad that his aunt was coming, and very glad that his mother and Lætitia were still away, and unconscious of what he was thinking about.

'So you did not lose courage?' he said, as they were driving off. 'How did you escape Madame Jacob?'

'I have been all alone,' said Elly, 'these two days. How I found courage to come I cannot tell you. I don't quite believe that it is I myself who am here. It seems impossible. I don't feel like myself. I have not for some days past. All I know is, that I am certain those horrible long days have come to an end.' John Dampier was frightened—he hardly knew why—when he heard her say this.

'I hope so, most sincerely,' said he. 'But, after all, Elly, we men and women are rarely contented; and there are plenty of days, more or less tiresome, in store for me and for you, I hope. We must pluck up our courage and go through with them. You are such a sensitive, weak-minded little girl that you will go on breaking your heart a dozen times a day to the end of your life.'

Dampier looked very grave as he spoke, though it was too dark for her to see him. He was angry and provoked with himself, and an insane impulse came over him to knock his head violently against the sides of the cab. Insane, do I say? It would have been the very best thing he could have done. But they drove on all the same: Elly in rapture. She was not a bit afraid now. Her spirits were so high and so daring that they would carry her through anything; and when she was with Dampier she was content to be happy, and not to trouble herself with vague apprehensions. And she was happy now: her eyes danced with delight, her heart beat with expectation, she seemed to have become a child again, she was not like a woman any more.

' Have you not a veil?' said Dampier, as they stopped before the theatre. There was a great light, a crowd of people passing and repassing; other carriages driving up.

' No,' said Elly. ' What does it matter? Who will know me?'

' Well, make haste. Here, take my arm,' said Sir John, hurriedly; and he hastily sprang down and helped her out.

' Look at the new moon,' said Elly, looking up smiling.

'Never mind the new moon. Come, Elly,' said Dampier. And so they passed on into the theatre.

Dampier was dreading recognition. He had a feeling that they would be sure to come against someone. Elly feared no one. When the play began she sat entranced, thrilling with interest, carried away. *Faust* was the piece which they were representing; and as each scene was played before her, as one change after another came over the piece, she was lost more and more in wonder. If she looked up for an instant it was to see John Dampier's familiar face opposite; and then outside the box, with its little curtain, great glittering theatre-lights, crystals reflecting the glitter, gilding, and silken drapery; everywhere hundreds of people, silent, and breathless too, with interest, with excitement. The music plays, the scene shifts and changes, melting into fresh combinations. Here is *Faust*. Listen to him as he laments his wasted life. Of what use is wisdom? What does he care for knowledge? A lonely man without one heart to love, one creature to cherish him. Has he not wilfully wasted the best years of his life? he cries, in a passion of rage and indignation —wasted them in the pursuit of arid science, of fruitless learning? Will these tend him in his old age, soothe his last hours, be to him wife, and children, and household, and holy home ties? Will these stand by his bedside, and close his weary, aching eyes, and follow him to his grave in the churchyard?

Faust's sad complaint went straight to the heart of his hearers. The church bell was ringing up the street. Fathers, mothers, and children were wending their way obedient to its call. And the poor desolate old man burst into passionate and hopeless lamentation.

It was all so real to Elly that she almost began to cry herself. She was so carried away by the play, by this history of Faust and of Margaret, that it was in vain Dampier begged her to be careful, to sit back in the shade of the curtain, and not to lean forward too eagerly. She would draw back for a minute or two, and then by degrees advance her pretty, breathless head, turning to him every now and then. It was like a dream to her. Like a face in a dream, too, did she presently recognise the face of De Vaux, her former admirer, opposite, in one of the boxes. But Margaret was coming into the chapel with her companions, and Elly was too much interested to think of what he would think of her. Just at that moment it was Margaret who seemed to her to be the important person in the world.

De Vaux was of a different opinion ; he looked towards them once or twice, and at the end of the second act, Dampier saw him get up and leave his seat. Sir John was provoked and annoyed beyond measure. He did not want him, De Vaux, least of all people in the world. Every moment he felt as he had never felt before—how wrong it was to have brought Elly, whom he was so fond

H

of, into such a situation. For a moment he was undecided, and then he rose, biting his lips, and opened the door of the box, hoping to intercept him; but there was his Mephistopheles, as ill luck would have it, standing at the door ready to come in.

'I thought I could not be mistaken,' De Vaux began, with a smirk, bowing, and looking significantly from one to the other. 'Did you see me in the gallery of the Louvre the other day?'

Elly blushed up very red, and Dampier muttered an oath as he caught sight of the other man's face. He was smiling very disagreeably. John glanced a second time, hesitated, and then said, suddenly and abruptly, 'No, you are not mistaken. This is Miss Gilmour, my *fiancée*, M. de Vaux. I dare say you are surprised that I should have brought her to the play. It is the custom in our country.' He did not dare look at Elly as he spoke. Had he known what else to say he would have said it.

De Vaux was quite satisfied, and instantly assumed a serious and important manner. The English miss was to him the most extraordinary being in creation, and he would believe anything you liked to tell him of her. He was prepared to sit down in the vacant chair by Elizabeth, and make himself agreeable to her.

The English miss was scarcely aware of his existence. Faust, Margaret, had been the whole world to her a minute ago. Where was she now? . . . where were they? . . .

Was she the actress? and were they the spectators looking on? . . . Was that the Truth which he had spoken? Did he mean it? Was there such wonderful, wonderful happiness in store for a poor little wretch like herself? Ah! could it be—could it be true? Her whole soul shone in her trembling eyes, as she looked up for one instant, and upturned her flashing, speaking, beaming face. Dampier was very pale, and was looking vacantly at the stage. Margaret was weeping, for her troubles had begun. Mephistopheles was laughing, and De Vaux chatting on in an agreeable manner, with his hat between his knees. After some time, he discovered that they were not paying attention to one single word he was saying; upon which he rose in an *empressé* manner, wished them good-by politely, and went away, very well pleased with his own good breeding. And then, when he was gone, when the door was shut, when they were alone together, there was a silence, and Elly leant her head against the side of the box; she was trembling so that she could not sit up. And Dampier, looking white and grey in the face somehow, said, in an odd, harsh voice,—

'Elly, you must not mind what I was obliged to say just now. You see, my dear child, that it doesn't do. I ought never to have brought you, and I could think of no better way to get out of my scrape than to tell him that lie.'

'It was—it was a lie?' repeated Elly, slowly raising herself upright.

'What could I do?' Sir John continued, very nervously and exceedingly agitated. 'Elly, my dear little girl, I could not let him think you were out upon an unauthorised escapade. We all know how it is, but he does not. You must, you do forgive me—only say you do.'

'And it is not true?' said Elly, once more, in a bewildered, piteous way.

'I—I belong to Lætitia. It was settled before we came abroad,' faltered Dampier; and he just looked at her once, and then he turned away. And the light was gone out of her face; all the sparkle, the glitter, the amazement of happiness. Just as this shining theatre, now full of life, of light, of excitement, would be in a few hours black, ghastly, and void. John Dampier did not dare to look at her again—he hesitated, he was picking and choosing the words which should be least cruel, least insulting; and while he was still choking and fumbling, he heard a noise outside, a whispering, as the door flew open. Elly looked up and gave a little low plaintive cry, and two darkling, frowning men in black coats came into the box.

They were the Pasteurs Boulot and Tourneur.

Who cares to witness, who cares to read, who cares to describe scenes such as these? Reproach, condemnation, righteous wrath, and indignation, and then one crushed, bewildered, almost desperate little heart.

She was hurried out into the night air. She had time to say good-bye, not one other word. He had not stretched out a hand to save her. The play was going on, all the people were sitting in their places, one or two looked up as she passed by the open doors. Then they came out into the street; the stars were all gone, the night was black with clouds, and a heavy rain was pouring down upon the earth. The drops fell wet upon her bare, uncovered head. 'Go under shelter,' said the Pasteur Boulot; but she paid no heed, and in a minute a cab came up, the two men clasped each other's hands in the peculiar silent way to which they were used. Boulot walked away. And Elly found herself alone, inside the damp vehicle, driving over the stones. Her stepfather had got upon the box; he was in a fury of indignation, so that he could not trust himself to be with her.

His indignation was not what she most feared. Another torturing doubt filled her whole heart. Her agony of hopelessness was almost unendurable: she was chilled through and through, but she did not heed it—and faint, and sick, and wearied, but too unhappy to care. Unhappy is hardly the word—bewilderment, a sort of crushed dull misery, would better describe her state. She felt little remorse : she had done wrong, but not very wrong, she thought. She sat motionless in the corner of the jolting cab, with the rain beating in at the open window, as they travelled through the black night and the splashing streets.

By what unlucky chance had M. Boulot been returning home along the Boulevards about half-past seven, at the very moment when Elly, jumping from the carriage, stopped to look up at the little new moon? He, poor man, could hardly believe his eyes. He did not believe them, and went home wondering, and puzzling, and asking himself if that audacious girl could be so utterly lost as to set her foot in that horrible den of iniquity. Ah! it was impossible; it was some one strangely like her. She could not be so lost—so perverted. But the chances were still against Elly; for when he reached the modest little apartment where he lived, his maid-servant told him that M. Tourneur had been there some time, and was waiting to see him. And there in the study, reading by the light of the green lamp, sat Tourneur, with his low-crowned hat lying on the table. He had come up on some business connected with an appointment he wanted to obtain for Anthony. His wife was to follow him next day, he said, and then he and Boulot fell to talking over their affairs and Anthony's prospects and chances.

'Poor Anthony, he has been sorely tried and proved of late,' said his father. 'Elizabeth will never make him happy.'

'Never—never—never!' cried Boulot. 'Elizabeth!—

she!—the last person in the world a pastor ought to think
of as a wife!'

'If she were more like her mother,' sighed Tourneur.

'Ah! that would be different,' said Boulot; 'but the
girl causes me deep anxiety, my friend. Hers is, I fear
an unconverted spirit. Her heart is of this world; she
requires much earnest teaching. Did you take her to
Fontainebleau with you?'

'She would not come,' said Tourneur; 'she is at home
with my sister, Madame Jacob; or rather by herself, for
my sister went away a day or two ago.'

'Tourneur, you do not do wisely to leave that girl
alone; she is not to be trusted,' said the other, suddenly
remembering all his former doubts. And so, when
Tourneur asked what he meant, he told him what he had
seen. The mere suspicion was a blow for our simple-
minded pasteur. He loved Elly; with all her waywardness,
there was a look in her eyes which nobody could resist.
In his heart of hearts he liked her better for a daughter-
in-law than any one of the decorous young women who were
in the habit of coming to be catechized by him. But to
think that she had deceived him, to think that she had
forgotten herself so far, forgotten his teaching, his wishes,
his firm convictions, sinned so outrageously! Ah, it was
too much; it was impossible, it was unpardonable. He
fired up, and in an agitated voice said that it could not be;
that he knew her to be incapable of such horrible conduct,

and then seizing his hat, he rushed downstairs and called
a carriage which happened to be passing by.

'Where are you going?' asked Boulot, who had
followed him, somewhat alarmed.

'I am going home, to see that she is there. Safe in
her room, and sheltered under her parents' roof, I humbly
pray. Far away from the snares, and dangers, and tempta-
tions of the world.'

Alas! poor Elly was not at home, peacefully resting
or reading by the lamp light. Françoise, to be sure, told
them she was in bed, and Tourneur went hopefully to her
door and knocked—

'Elly,' he cried, 'mon enfant! êtes-vous là, ma fille?
Répondez, Elizabeth!' and he shook the door in his agitation.

Old Françoise was standing by, holding the candle;
Boulot was leaning against the wall. But there came no
answer. The silence struck chill. Tourneur's face was
very pale, his lips were drawn, and his eyes gleamed as he
raised his head. He went away for a minute and came
back with a little tool; it did not take long to force back
the lock—the door flew open, and there was the empty
room all in disorder! In silence truly, but emptiness is
not peace always, silence is not tranquillity; a horrible
dread and terror came over poor Tourneur; Françoise's
hand, holding the light, began to tremble guiltily. Boulot
was dreadfully shocked—

'My poor friend ! my poor friend ! ' he began.

Tourneur put his hand to his head—

' How has this come to pass—am I to blame ? ' said he.
' Oh ! unhappy girl, what has she done ?—how has she brought this disgrace upon us ? ' and he fell on his knees by the bedside, and buried his head in the clothes—kneeling there praying for Elly where she had so often knelt and poured out all her sad heart. . . .

Elly, at that minute—sitting in the little box, wondering, delighted, thrilling with interest, with pleasure— did not guess what a strange scene was taking place in her own room at home ; she did not once think of what trouble, what grief, she was causing to others, and to herself, poor child, most of all. Only a few minutes more—all the music would cease abruptly for her ; all the lights go out ; all the sweetness turn to gall and to bitterness. Nearer and nearer comes the sad hour, the cruel awakening ; dream on still for a few happy minutes, poor Elly !—nearer and nearer come these two angry silent men, in their black, sombre clothes—nearer and nearer the cruel spoken word which will chill, crush, and destroy. Elizabeth's dreams lasted a little longer, and then she awoke at last.

CHAPTER VII.

Not a flower, not a flower sweet,
  On my black coffin let there be strown ;
Not a friend, not a friend greet
  My poor corpse where my bones shall be thrown.
A thousand, thousand sighs to save,
  Lay me, oh ! where
Sad true lover never find my grave,
  To weep there.

It was on the evening of the Monday after that Miss Dampier arrived in Paris, with her bonnet-box, her knitting, her carpet-bag. She drove to Meurice's, and hired a room, and then she asked the servants there who knew him whether Sir John Dampier was still staying in the house. They said he had left the place some time before, but that he had called twice that day to ask if she had arrived. And then Miss Dampier, who always liked to make herself comfortable and at home, went up to her room, had the window opened, light brought, and ordered some tea. She was sitting at the table in her cap, in her comfortable black gown, with her knitting, her writing-desk, her books, all set out about the room. She was pouring out tea for herself, and looking as much at home as if she had lived there for months, when the door opened, and her nephew walked in. She was delighted to see him.

'My dear Jack, how good of you to come,' said the old lady, looking up at him, and holding out her hand. 'But you don't look well. You have been sitting up late and racketing. Will you have some tea to refresh you? I will treat you to anything you like.'

'Ah! don't make jokes,' said Dampier. 'I am very unhappy. Look here, I have got into the most horrible scrape; and not myself only.' And the room shook, and the tea-table rattled, as he went pacing up and down the room with heavy footsteps. 'I want to behave like a gentleman, and I wake up one morning and find myself a scoundrel. Do you see?'

'Tell me about it, my dear,' said Miss Dampier, quietly.

And then poor John burst out and told all his story, confounding himself, and stamping, flinging himself about into one chair after another. 'I meant no harm,' he said. 'I wanted to give her a little pleasure, and this is the end. I think I have broken her heart, and those *pasteurs* have murdered her by this time. They won't let me see her; Tourneur almost ordered me out of the house. Aunt Jean, do say something; do have an opinion.'

'I wish your cousin was here,' said Miss Dampier; 'he is the parson of the family, and bound to give us all good advice; let me write to him, Jack. I have a certain reliance on Will's good sense.'

'I won't have Will interfering with my affairs,' cried the other, testily. 'And you—you will not help me, I see?'

'I will go and see Elizabeth,' said Miss Dampier, 'to-night, if you like. I am very, very sorry for her, and for you too, John. What more can I say? Come again in an hour, and I will tell you what I think.'

So Miss Dampier was as good as her word, and set off on her pilgrimage, and drove along the lighted streets, and then past the cab-stand and the hospital to the house with the shuttered windows. Her own heart was very sad as she got out of the carriage and rang at the bell. But looking up by chance, she just saw a gleam of light which came from one of the upper windows and played upon the wall. She took this as a good omen, and said to herself that all would be well. Do you believe in omens? The light came from a room where Elly was lying asleep, and dreaming gently,—calm, satisfied, happy for once, heedless of the troubles, and turmoils, and anxieties of the waking people all round about her. She looked very pale, her hands were loosely clasped, the light was in the window, flickering; and meanwhile, beneath the window, in the street, Miss Dampier stood waiting under the stars. She did not know that Elly saw her in her dim dreams, and somehow fancied that she was near.

The door opened at last. How black the courtyard looked behind it! ' What do you want ?' said Clementine, in a hiss. ' Who is it ?'

' I want to know how Miss Gilmour is,' said Miss Dampier, quite humbly, ' and to see Monsieur or Madame Tourneur.'

' Vous êtes Madame Dampierre,' said Clementine. ' Madame est occupée. Elle ne reçoit pas.'

' When will she be disengaged?' said the old lady.

' *Ma foi !*' said Clementine, shrugging her shoulders, ' that I cannot tell you. She has desired me to say that she does not wish to see anybody.' And the door was shut with a bang. Elly woke up, startled from her sleep ; and old Françoise, happening to come into the room, carried the candle away.

Miss Dampier went home very sad and alarmed, she scarcely knew why. She wrote a tender little letter to Elly next day. It was :—

' Dear Child,—You must let me come and see you. We are very unhappy, John and I, to think that his imprudence has caused you such trouble. He does not know how to beg you to forgive him—you and M. Tourneur and your mother. He should have known better ; he has been unpardonably thoughtless, but he is nearly broken-hearted about it. He has been engaged to Lætitia for three or four months, and you know how long she has loved him.

Dearest Elly, you must let me come and see you, and perhaps one day you may be trusted to the care of an old woman, and you will come home with me for a time, and brighten my lonely little house. Your affectionate old friend, 'JEAN DAMPIER.'

But to this there came no answer. Miss Dampier went again and could not get in. She wrote to Madame Tourneur, who sent back the letter unopened. John Dampier walked about pale and haggard, and remorseful.

One evening he and his aunt were dining in the public room of the hotel, and talking over this affair, when the waiter came and told them that a gentleman wanted to speak to Miss Dampier, and the old lady got up and went out of the room. She came back in an instant, looking very agitated. 'John!' she said—'oh, John!' and then began to cry. She could not speak for a minute, while he, quite frightened for his part, hastily went to the door. A tall young man was standing there, wrapped in a loose coat, who looked into his face and said—

'Are you Sir John Dampier? My sister Elizabeth would like to see you again. I have come for you.'

'Your sister Elizabeth!' said Dampier, looking surprised.

The other man's face changed as he spoke again. 'I am Anthony Tourneur; I have come to fetch you, because it is her wish, and she is dying, we fear.'

The two men stood looking at one another for one horrible moment, then Dampier slowly turned his face round to the wall. In that one instant, all that cruel weight which had almost crushed poor Elly to death came and fell upon his broad shoulders, better able, in truth, to bear it, than she had ever been.

He looked up at last. 'Have I done this?' said he to Tourneur, in a sort of hoarse whisper. 'I meant for the best.'

'I don't know what you have done,' said the other, very sadly. 'Life and death are not in your hands or mine. Let us pray that our mistakes may be forgiven us. Are you ready now?'

Elly's visions had come to an end. The hour seemed to be very near when she should awake from the dream of life. Dim figures of her mother, her step-father, of old Françoise, came and stood by her bed-side. But how far-off they appeared; how distant their voices sounded. Old Françoise came into her room the morning after Elly had been brought home, with some message from Tourneur, desiring her to come downstairs and speak to him : he had been lying awake all night, thinking what he should say to her, praying for her, imploring grace, so that he should be allowed to touch the rebellious spirit, to point out all its errors, to bring it to the light. And, meanwhile, Elly, the rebellious spirit, sat by her bedside in a sort of bewildered misery. She scarcely told herself

why she was so unhappy. She wondered a little that
there was agony so great to be endured; she had never
conceived its existence before. Was he gone for ever—
was it Lætitia whom he cared for? 'You know that I
belong to Lætitia,' he had said. How could it be? all
heaven and earth would cry out against it. Lætitia's—
Lætitia, who cared so little, whô was so pale, and so cold,
and so indifferent? How could he speak such cruel
words? Oh, shame, shame! that she should be so made
to suffer. ' A poor little thing like me,' said Elly, ' lonely
and friendless, and heart-broken.' The pang was so sharp
that it seemed to her like physical pain, and she moaned,
and winced, and shivered under it—was it she herself or
another person that was here in the darkness? She was
cold too, and yet burning with thirst; she groped her way
to the jug, and poured out a little water, and drank with
eager gulps. Then she began to take off her damp
clothes; but it tired her, and she forgot to go on; she
dropped her cloak upon the floor, and flung herself upon
the bed, with a passionate outcry. Her mouth was dry
and parched, her throat was burning, her hands were
burning too. In the darkness she seemed to see his face
and Lætitia's glaring at her, and she turned sick and
giddy at the sight; presently, not theirs only, but a hundred others—Tourneur's, Boulot's, Faust's, and Mephistopheles'—crowding upon her and glaring furiously. She
fell into a short, uneasy sleep once, and woke up with a

moan as the hospital clock struck three. The moon was
shining into her room, ineffably grey, chill, and silent,
and as she woke, a horror, a terror, came over her—her
heart scarcely beat; she seemed to be sinking and dying
away. She thought with a thrill that her last hour was
come; the terror seemed to bear down upon her, nearer
and closer and irresistible—and then she must have fallen
back senseless upon her bed. And so when Françoise
came with a message in the morning, which was intended
to frighten the rebellious spirit into submission, she found
it gone, safe, far away from reproach, from angry chiding
and the poor little body lying lifeless, burnt with fierce
fever, and racked with dull pain. All that day Elly was
scarcely sensible, lying in a sort of stupor. Françoise,
with tender hands, undressed her and laid her within the
sheets; Tourneur came and stood by the poor child's bedside. He had brought a doctor, who was bending over
her.

'It is a sort of nervous fever,' said the doctor, 'and I
fear that there is some inward inflammation as well; she
is very ill. This must have been impending for some
time past.'

Tourneur stood, with clasped hands and a heavy heart,
watching the changes as they passed over the poor little
face. Who was to blame in this? He had not spoken
one word to her the night before. Was it grief? was it
repentance? Ah me! Elly was dumb now, and could not

I

answer. All his wrath was turned against Dampier; for
Elly he only felt the tenderest concern. But he was too
unhappy just now to think of his anger. He went for
Madame Tourneur, who came back and set to work to
nurse her daughter; but she was frightened and agitated,
and seemed scarcely to know what she was about. On the
morning of the second day, contrary to the doctor's expec-
tations, Elly recovered her consciousness; on the third
day she was better. And when Tourneur came into the
room, she said to him, with one of her old pretty, sad
smiles, 'You are very angry with me, are you not? You
think I ought not to have gone to the play with John
Dampier?'

'Ah, my child,' said Tourneur, with a long-drawn,
shivering sigh, 'I am too anxious to be angry.'

'Did he promise to marry you, Elly?' said Madame
Tourneur, who was sitting by her bedside. She was looking so eagerly for an answer that she did not see her husband's look of reproach.

'How could he?' said Elly, simply. 'He is going to
marry Lætitia.'

'Tell me, my child,' said Tourneur, gently taking her
hand, 'how often did you go with him?'

'Three times,' Elly answered, faintly. 'Once to the
Bois, and once to the Louvre, and then that last time;'
and she gasped for breath. Tourneur did not answer, but
bent down gently, and kissed her forehead.

It was on that very day that Dampier called. Elly seemed somehow to know that he was in the house. She got excited, and began to wander, and to call him by his name. Tourneur heard her, and turned pale, and set his teeth as he went down to speak to Sir John. In the evening the girl was better, and Anthony arrived from the south. And I think it was on the fifth day that Elly told Anthony that she wanted to see Dampier once again.

' You can guess how it has been,' she said, ' and I love him still, but not as I did. Anthony, is it not strange? Perhaps one is selfish when one is dying. But I want to see him—just once again. Everything is so changed. I cannot understand why I have been so unhappy all this time. Anthony, I have wasted all my life; I have made nobody happy—not even you.'

' You have made me love you, and that has been my happiness,' said Anthony. ' I have been very unhappy too ; but I thank heaven for having known you, Elly.'

Elly thought that she had but a little time left. What was there in the solemn nearness of death that had changed her so greatly? She had no terror : she was ready to lie down and go to sleep like a tired child in its mother's arms. Worldly! we call some folks worldly, and truly they have lived for to-day and cared for to-day ; but for them, as for us, the great to-morrow comes, and then they cease to be worldly—is it not so? Who shall say

that such and such a life is wasted, is purposeless ? that
such and such minds are narrow, are mean, are earthly ?
The day comes, dawning freshly and stilly, like any other
day in all the year, when the secret of their life is ended,
and the great sanctification of Death is theirs.

Boulot came to see Tourneur, over whom he had great
influence, and insisted upon being shown to Elizabeth's
bedside. She put out her hand and said, 'How-d'ye-do,
Monsieur Boulot ?' very sweetly, but when he had talked
to her for some little time, she stopped him and said,—
'You cannot know how near these things seem, and how
much more great, and awful, and real they are, when you
are lying here like me, than when you are standing by
another person's sick bed. Nobody can speak of them to
me as they themselves speak to me.' She said it so
simply, with so little intention of offence, that Boulot
stopped in the midst of his little sermon, and said farewell
quite kindly and gently. And then, not long after he was
gone, Anthony came back with the Dampiers.

They walked up the wooden stairs with hearts that
ached sorely enough. Miss Dampier was calm and composed again ; she had stood by many a death-bed—she was
expecting to go herself before very long—but John was
quite unnerved. Little Elly, whom he had pitied, and
looked down upon, and patronised, was she to be to him
from this minute a terror, a life-long regret and remorse ?
—he could hardly summon courage to walk into the room

when the door was opened and Anthony silently motioned him to pass through it.

And yet there was nothing very dreadful. A pale, sweet face lying on the little white bed; the gentle eyes, whose look he knew so well, turned expectantly towards him; a cup with some flowers; a little water in a glass by the bedside; an open window; the sun setting behind the poplar-trees.

Old Françoise was sitting in the window, sewing; the birds were twittering outside. John Dampier thought it strange that death should come in this familiar guise—tranquilly, with the sunset, the rustling leaves of the trees, the scent of the geraniums in the court below, the cackle of the hens, the stitching of a needle—he almost envied Elly, lying resting at the end of her journey: Elly, no longer the silly little girl he had laughed at, chided, and played with—she was wise now, in his eyes.

She could not talk much, but what she said was in her own voice and in her old manner,—' You kind people, to come and see me,' she said, and beckoned to them to approach nearer.

Miss Dampier gave her nephew a warning touch; she saw how agitated he was, and was afraid that he would disturb Elizabeth. But what would he not have done for her? He controlled himself, and spoke quietly, in a low voice—

' I am very grateful to you, dear Elly, for sending for

me. I was longing to hear about you. I want to ask you
to forgive me for the ill I have done you. I want to tell
you just once that I meant no harm, only it was such a
pleasure to myself that I persuaded myself it was right.
I know you will forgive me. All my life I will bless you.'
And his head fell as he spoke.

'What have I to forgive?' faltered Elly. 'It seems
so long ago!—Faust and Margaret, and those pleasant
drives. Am I to forgive you because I loved you? That
was a sort of madness; but it is gone. I love you still,
dear John, but differently. I am not mad now, but in
my senses. If I get well, how changed it will be—if I
die——'

If she died? Dampier, hating himself all the while,
thought, with a chill pang, that here would be a horrible
solution to all his perplexities. Perhaps Elly guessed
something of what was passing in his mind, for she gave
him her hand once more, and faltered,—

'My love to Lætitia,' and, as she spoke, she raised
her eyes, with the old familiar look in them.

It was more than he could bear; he stooped and
kissed her frail, burning fingers, and then, with scorched,
quivering lips, turned aside and went softly out of the
room. Anthony and Madame Tourneur were standing
outside, and as Dampier passed she looked at him piteously,
and her lips trembled too, but she did not speak. It
seemed to him somehow—only he was thinking of other

things—as if Elly's good and bad angels were waiting there. He himself passed on with a hanging head; what could he say to justify himself?—his sorrow was too real to be measured out into words, his penitence greater almost than the offence had been. Even Tourneur, whom he met in the courtyard, almost forgave him as he glanced at the stricken face that was passing out of his house into the street.

After he was gone, Elly began to wander. Françoise, who had never taken such a bad view of Elly's condition as the others, and who strongly disapproved of all this leave-taking, told Miss Dampier that if they wanted to kill her outright, they need only let in all Paris to stare at her, as they had been doing for the last two days; and Miss Dampier, meekly taking the hint, rose in her turn to go. But Elly, from her bed, knew that she was about to leave her, and cried out piteously, and stretched out her hands, and clutched at her gown.

'Faut rester,' whispered Françoise.

'I mean to stay,' said Miss Dampier, after a moment's deliberation, sitting down at the bedside and untying her bonnet.

Under her bonnet she wore a little prim cap, with loops of grey ribbon; out of her pocket she pulled her knitting and a pair of mittens. She folded up her mantlet and put it away; she signed to Françoise to leave her in charge. When Tourneur came in he found her installed, and as much at home as if she were there by rights. Elly wished it, she told him, and she would stay were ten pasteurs opposed to it.

Tourneur reluctantly consented at last, much against his will. It seemed to him that her mother ought to be Elly's best nurse, but Madame Tourneur eagerly implored him to let Miss Dampier remain; she seemed strangely scared and helpless, and changed and odd. 'Oh, if you will only make her well!' said she to the old Scotch-woman.

'How can I make her well?' Miss Dampier answered. 'I will try and keep her quiet, that is the chief thing; and if M. Tourneur will let me, I should like to send for my old friend, Dr. Bertin.'

And her persistency overcame Tourneur's bewildered objections; her quiet good sense and determination carried the day. Doctor Bertin came, and the first doctor went off in a huff, and Elly lay tossing on her bed. What a weary rack it was to her, that little white bed! There she lay, scorched and burning—consumed by a fierce fire. There she lay through the long days and the nights, as they followed one by one, waiting to know the end. Not one of them dared think what that end might be. Doctor Bertin himself could not tell how this queer illness might turn; such fevers were sometimes caused by mental dis-quietude, he said. Of infection there was no fear; he came day after day, and stood pitifully by the bedside.

He had seen her once before in her brilliance and health ; he had never cared for her as he did now that she was lying prostrate and helpless in their hands.

Madame Jacob had carried off her children at the first alarm of fever ; the house was kept darkened and cool and quiet ; and patient Miss Dampier sat waiting in the big chair for good or for ill fortune. Sometimes of an evening she would creep downstairs and meet her nephew in the street outside and bring him news.

And besides John, there was poor Anthony wandering about the house, wretched, anxious, and yet resigned. Often, as a boy, he had feared death ; the stern tenets to which he belonged made him subject to its terrors, but now it seemed to him so simple a thing to die, that he wondered at his own past fears. Elly thought it a simple thing to die, but of this fever she was weary—of this cruel pain and thirst and misery ; she would moan a little, utter a few complaining words, and wander off into delirium again. She had been worse than usual one evening, the fever higher. It was a bad account that Miss Dampier had to give to the doctor when he came, to the anxious people waiting for news. All night long Elly's kind nurse sat patiently in the big arm-chair, knitting, as was her way, or sometimes letting the needles fall into her lap, and sitting still with clasped hands and a wistful heart. The clocks of the city struck the dark hours as they passed—where these Elly's last upon earth ? Jean Dampier sadly wondered. The stars set behind the poplar-trees, a night breeze came shivering now and then through the open window. The night did not appear so very long; it seemed hastening by, dark and silent, relentless to the wearied nurse; for presently, before she knew it almost, it seemed as if the dawn had begun; and somehow, as she was watching still, she fell asleep for a little. While she slept the shadows began to tremble and fade, and fly hither and thither in the death-like silence of the early morning, and when she awoke it was with a start and a chill terror, coming, she knew not whence. She saw that the room was grey, and black no longer. Her heart began to beat, and with a terrified glance she looked round at the bed where Elly was lying.

She looked once, and then again, and then suddenly her trembling hands were clasped in humblest thanksgiving, and the grey head bent lower and lower.

There was nothing to fear any more. Elly was sleeping quietly on her pillow, the fiery spots had faded out of her cheeks, her skin looked fresh and moist, the fever had left her. Death had not yet laid his cold hand on the poor little prey, he had not come while the nurse was sleeping—he had not called her as yet. I speak in this way from long habit and foolishness. For in truth, had he come, would it have been so sad, would it have been so hard a fate—would it have been death with his skeleton's head, and his theatrical grave-clothes, and his scythe, and his hour-glass? Would it have been this, or simply the great law of Nature working peacefully in its course — only the seed falling into the ground, only the decree of that same merciful Power which sent us into the world?—us men and women, who are glad to exist, and grateful for our own creation, into a world where we love to tarry for a while?

Jean Dampier, sitting there in the dawning, thought something of all this, and yet how could she help acknowledging the mercy which spared her and hers the pang of having fatally injured this poor little Elly, whom she had learnt to love with all her tender old heart? It seemed a deliverance, a blessing a hundred times beyond their deserts.

She had been prepared for the worst, and yet she had shrunk with terror from the chastisement. Now, in this first moment of relief—now that, after all, Elly was, perhaps, given back to them, to youth, to life—she felt as if she could have borne the blow better than she had ever dared to hope. The sun rose, the birds chirped freshly among the branches, the chill morning spread over the city. Sleepers began to stir, and to awake to their daily cares, to their busy life. Elizabeth's life, too, began anew from this hour.

Someone said to me just now that we can best make others happy by the mere fact of our own existence; as she got well day by day, Elly found that it was so. How had she deserved so much of those about her? she often wondered to herself. A hindrance, a trouble, a vexation to them, was all she had ever been; and yet as one by one they came to greet her, she felt that they were glad. Anthony's eyes were full of tears; Tourneur closed his for an instant, as he uttered a silent thanksgiving—she herself did not know how to thank them all.

And here, perhaps, my story ought to end, but in truth it is not finished, though I should cease to write it down, and it goes on and on as the years go by.

CHAPTER VIII.

Move eastward, happy earth, and leave
   Yon orange sunset, waning slow
From fringes of the faded eve.
   O happy planet, eastward go,
   Till over thy dark shoulder glow
Thy silver sister-world, and rise
   To glass herself in dewy eyes,
     That watch me from the glen below.

AND so she had left all behind, Elizabeth thought. Paris,
the old house, mother, stepfather, and pasteur, the courtyard, the familiar wearisome life, the dull days breaking
one by one, John Dampier, her hopeless hopes, and her
foolish fancies—she had left them all on the other side
of the sea for a time, and come away with kind Miss
Dampier.

Here, in England, whither her good friend had brought
her to get well, the air is damp with sea breezes; the
atmosphere is not keen and exciting as it is abroad; the
sky is more often grey than blue; it rarely dazzles and
bewilders you with its brilliance; there is humidity and
vegetation, a certain placidity and denseness, and moisture
of which some people complain. To Elizabeth—nervous,

eager, excitable—this quiet green country, these autumn mists, were new life. Day by day she gained strength, and flesh, and tone, and health, and good spirits.

But it was only by slow degrees that this good change was effected ; weaknesses, faintnesses, relapses,—who does not know the wearisome course of a long convalescence ?

To-night, though she is by way of being a strong woman again, she feels as if she was a very very old one, somehow, as she sits at the window of a great hotel looking out at the sunset. It seems to her as if it was never to rise again. There it goes sinking, glorying over the sea, blazing yellow in the west. The place grows dark ; in the next room through the open door her white bed gleams chilly ; she shudders as she looks at it, and thinks of the death-bed from which she has scarce risen. There are hours, especially when people are still weak and exhausted by sickness, when life seems unbearable, when death appears terrible, and when the spirit is so weary that it seems as if no sleep could be deep enough to give it rest. 'When I am dead,' thought Elizabeth ; 'ah me ! my body will be at rest, but I myself, shall I have forgotten—do I want to forget . . . ?'

Meanwhile Miss Dampier, wrapped in her grey cloak, is taking a brisk solitary little walk upon the wooden pier which Elly sees reflected black against the sea. Aunt Jean is serenely happy about her charge ; delighted to have carried her off against all opposition ; determined that somehow or other she shall never go back; that she shall be made happy one day.

It is late in the autumn. Tourists are flocking home; a little procession of battered ladies and gentlemen carrying all sorts of bundles, and bags, and parcels, disembarks every day; and then another procession of ladies and gentlemen goes to see them land. Any moment you may chance to encounter some wan sea-sick friend staggering along with the rest of the sufferers, who are more or less other people's friends. The waves wash up and down, painted yellow by the sunset. There is no wind, but it has been blowing hard for a day or two, and the sea is not yet calm. How pleasant it is, Miss Dampier thinks; chill, fresh, wholesome. This good air is the very thing for Elly. Along the cliffs the old lady can see the people walking against the sky like little specks. There are plenty of fishing-boats out and about. There is the west still blazing yellow, and then a long grey bank of clouds; and with a hiss and a shrill clamour here comes the tossing dark-shadowed steamer across the black and golden water. All the passengers are crowding on deck and feebly gathering their belongings together; here the *Frederick William* comes close alongside, and as everybody else rushes along the pier to inspect the new comers, good old Jean trots off, too, to see what is what. In a few minutes the passengers appear, slowly rising through a trap like the ghost in the *Corsican Brothers.*

First, a lilac gentleman, then a mouldy green gentleman (evidently a foreigner), then an orange lady.

Then a ghostly blue gentleman, then a deadly white lady, then a pale lemon-coloured gentleman, with a red nose.

Then a stout lady, black in the face, then a faltering lady's-maid, with a band-box.

Then a gentleman with an umbrella.

Jean Dampier is in luck to-night, as, indeed, she deserves to be: a more kindly, tender-hearted, unselfish old woman does not exist—if that is a reason for being lucky—however, she has been my good friend for many a long year, and it is not to-day that I am going to begin to pay her compliments.

I was saying she is in luck, and she finds a nephew among the passengers—it is the gentleman with the umbrella; and there they are, greeting one another in the most affectionate manner.

The Nephew.—'Let me get my portmanteau, and then I will come and talk to you as much as you like.'

The Aunt.—'Never mind your portmanteau, the porter will look after it. Where have you been, Will? Where do you come from? I am at the "Flag Hotel," close by.'

The Nephew.—'So I hear.'

The Aunt.—'Who told you that?'

The Nephew.—'A sour-faced woman at Paris. I asked for you at Meurice's, and they sent me to this Madame

Tourneur. She told me all about you. What business is it of yours to go about nursing mad girls ? '

Aunt Jean.—' Elly is not mad. You have heard me talk of her a hundred times. I do believe I saved her life, Will ; it was my business, if anybody's, to care for her. Her heart was nearly broken.'

The Nephew.—' John nearly broke her heart, did he ? I don't believe a word of it' (*smiling very sweetly*). ' You are always running away with one idea after another, you silly old woman. Young ladies' hearts are made of india-rubber, and Lady Dampier says this one is an artful— designing—horrible—abominable——'

Aunt Jean (*sadly*).—' Elly nearly died, that is all. You are like all men, Will——'

The Nephew (*interrupting*).—' Don't ! Consider, I'm just out of the hands of the steward. Let me have something to eat before we enter into any sentimental discussion. Here (*to a porter*), bring my portmanteau to the hotel.— Nonsense (*to a flyman*), what should I do with your carriage ? '

Will Dampier was a member of the Alpine Club, and went year by year to scramble his holiday away up and down mountain sides. He was a clergyman, comfortably installed in a family living. He was something like his cousin in appearance, but, to my mind, better looking, browner, broader, with bright blue eyes and a charming smile. He looked like a gentleman. He wore a clerical

K

waistcoat. He had been very much complimented upon his good sense; and he liked giving advice, and took pains about it, as he was anxious not to lose his reputation. Now and then, however, he did foolish things, but he did them sensibly, which is a very different thing from doing sensible things foolishly. It seems to me that is just the difference between men and women.

Will was Miss Dampier's ideal of what a nephew should be. They walked back to the hotel together, chattering away very comfortably. He went into the coffee-room and ordered his dinner, and then he came back to his aunt, who was walking on the lawn outside. Meanwhile the sun went on setting; the windows lighted up one by one. It was that comfortable hour when people sit down in little friendly groups and break bread, and take their ease, the business of the day being over. Will Dampier and his aunt took one or two turns along the gravel path facing the sea; he had twenty minutes to wait, and he thought they might be well employed in giving good counsel.

'It seems to me a very wild scheme of yours, carrying off this unruly young woman,' he began; 'she will have to go home sooner or later. What good will you have done?'

'I don't know, I'm sure,' says Miss Dampier, meekly; 'a holiday is good for us at all times. Haven't you enjoyed yours, Will?'

'I should rather think I had. You never saw any-thing so pretty as Berne the other morning as I was coming away. I came home by the Rhine, you know. I saw aunt Dampier and Tishy for an hour or two.'

'And did you see John at Paris?'

'No; he was down at V——, staying with the M——s. And now tell me about the young lady with the heart. Is she upstairs tearing her hair? Aunt Dampier was furious.'

'So she had heard of it?' said Miss Dampier, thought-fully. And then she added rather sharply, 'You can tell her that the young lady is quite getting over her fancy. In fact, John doesn't deserve that she should remember him. Now, listen, Will, I am going to tell you a story.' And then, in her quiet, pleasant, old-fashioned way, she told him her version of all that had been happening.

Will listened and laughed, and said, 'You will think me a brute, but I agree with aunt Dampier. Your young woman has behaved as badly as possible; she has made a dead set at poor John, who is so vain that any woman can get him into her clutches.'

'What do you mean?' cries the aunt, quite angry.

'If she had really cared for him, would she have for-gotten all about him already? I warn you, aunt Jenny; I don't approve of your heroine.'

'I must go and look after my heroine,' says Miss Dam-pier, dryly. 'I dare say your dinner is ready.'

But Will Dampier, whose curiosity at all events was excited, followed his aunt upstairs and along the passage, and went in after her as she opened a door; went into a dim chill room, with two wide-set windows, through which the last yellow streaks of the sunset were fading, and the fresh evening blast blew in with a gust as they entered. It was dark, and nothing could be seen distinctly, only something white seemed crouching in a chair, and as the door opened they heard a low sobbing sigh, which seemed to come out of the gloom; and then it was all very silent.

'Elly, my dear child,' said Miss Dampier, 'what is the matter?'

There was no answer.

'Why don't you speak?' said the kind old lady, groping about, and running up against chairs and tables.

'Because I can't speak without crying,' gasps Elly, beginning to cry. 'And it's so ungrateful——'

'You are tired, dear,' says aunt Jean, 'and cold'—taking her hand; and then turning round and seeing that her nephew had come in with her, she said, 'Ring the bell, Will, and go to your dinner. If you will tell them downstairs to send up some tea directly I shall be obliged to you.' William Dampier did as he was bid, and walked away considerably mollified towards poor Elly. 'One is so apt to find fault with people,' he was thinking. 'And there she was crying upstairs all the time, poor wretch.'

He could never bear to see a woman cry. ˙ His parish-
ioners—the women, I mean—had found this out, and used
to shed a great many tears when he came to see them.
He had found them out—he knew that they had found
him out, and yet as sure as the apron-corner went up, the
half-crown came out of the pocket.

9.30.—*Reading Room, Flag Hotel, Boatstown.*—Mr.
William Dampier writing at a side-table to a married
sister in India. Three old gentlemen come creaking in;
select limp newspapers, and take their places. A young
man who is going to town by the 10.30 train lies down on
the sofa and falls asleep, and snores gently. A soothing
silence. Mr. Dampier's blunt pen travels along the thin
paper. . . . ' What a dear old woman aunt Jenny is.
How well she tells a story. Lady Dampier was telling
me the same story the other day. I was very much bored,
I thought each one person more selfish and disagreeable
than the other. Now aunt Jenny takes up the tale. The
personages all brighten under her friendly old spectacles,
and become good, gentle-hearted, romantic, and heroic all
at once—as she is herself. I was a good deal struck by
her report of poor John's sentimental imbroglio. I drank
tea with the imbroglio this evening, and I can't help
rather liking her. She has a sweet pretty face, and her
voice, when she talks, pipes and thrills like a musical
snuff-box. Aunt Jenny wants her for a niece, that is
certain, and says that a man ought to marry the wife he

likes best. You are sure to agree to that; I wonder
what Miles says? But she's torn with sympathy, poor
old dear, and first cries over one girl, and then over
the other. She says John came to her one day at Paris
in a great state of mind, declared he was quite determined
to finish with all his uncertainty, and that he had made
up his mind to break with Lætitia, and to marry Elizabeth,
if she was still in her old way of thinking. Aunt Jean
got frightened, refused to interfere, carried off the young
lady, and has not spoken to her on the subject. John,
who is really behaving very foolishly, is still at Paris,
and has not followed them, as I know my aunt hoped he
would have done. I can't help being very sorry for him.
Lady Dampier has heard of his goings on. A Frenchman
told some people, who told some people, who—you know
how things get about. Some day when I don't wish it,
you will hear all about me, and write me a thundering
letter all the way from Lucknow. There is no doubt
about the matter. It would be a thousand pities if John
were to break off with Lætitia, to speak nothing of the
cruelty and the insult to the poor child.

'And so Rosey and Posey are coming home. I am
right sorry for their poor papa and mamma. I hope you
have sometimes talked to my nieces about their respectable
uncle Will. They are sure to be looked after and happy
with aunt Jenny, but how you will be breaking your hearts
after them! A priest ought perhaps to talk to you of one

consolation very certain and efficacious. But I have always found my dear Prue a better Christian than myself, and I have no need to preach to her.'

Will Dampier wrote a close straight little handwriting; only one side of his paper was full, but he did not care to write any more that night: he put up his letter in his case, and walked out into the garden.

It was a great starlight night. The sea gloomed vast and black on the horizon. A few other people were walking in the garden, and they talked in hushed yet distinct voices. Many of the windows were open and alight. Will looked up at the window of the room where he had been to see his aunt. That was alight and open, too, and some one was sitting with clasped hands, looking at the sky. Dampier lit a cigar, and he, too, walked along gazing at the stars, and thinking of Prue's kind face as he went along. Other constellations clustered above her head, he thought; between them lay miles of land and sea, great countries, oceans rushing, plains arid and unknown; vast jungles, deserted cities, crumbling in a broiling sun; it gave him a little vertigo to try and realise what hundreds of miles of distance stretched between their two beating hearts. Distance so great, and yet so little; for he could love his sister, and think of her, and see her, and talk to her, as if she was in the next room. What was that distance which could be measured by miles, compared to the immeasurable gulf that separates each one of us from the nearest and dearest whose hands we may hold in our own ?

Will walked on, his mind full of dim thoughts, such as come to most people on starlight nights; when constellations are blazing, and the living soul gazes with awe-stricken wonder at the great living universe, in the midst of which it waits, and trembles, and adores. 'The world all about has faded away,' he thought, 'and lies dark and dim, and indistinct. People are lying like dead people stretched out, unconscious on their beds, heedless, unknowing. Here and there in the houses, a few dead people are lying like the sleepers. Are they as unconscious as the living?' He goes to the end of the garden, and stands looking upward, until he cannot think longer of things so far above him. It seems to him that his brain is like the string of an instrument, which will break under the passionate vibration of harmonies so far beyond his powers to render. He goes back into the house. Everything suddenly grows strangely real and familiar, and yet it seemed, but a moment ago, as if to-day and its cares had passed away for ever.

CHAPTER IX.

To humbler functions, awful Power,
 I call Thee: I myself commend
Unto thy guidance from this hour.
 Oh, let my weakness have an end.
Give unto me, made lowly wise,
The spirit of self-sacrifice—
The confidence of reason give,
And in the light of truth *thy bondman* let me live.
Ode to Duty.

ELLY had a little Indian box that her father had once given to her. It served her for a work-box and a treasure casket. She kept her scissors in it and her ruby ring; some lavender, a gold thimble, and her father's picture. And then in a lower tray were some cottons and tapes, one or two letters, a pencil, and a broken silver chain. She had a childish habit of playing with it still, sometimes, and setting it to rights. It was lying on the breakfast-table next morning when Will Dampier came in to see his aunt. Miss Dampier, who liked order, begged Elly to take it off, and Dampier politely, to save her the trouble, set it down somewhere else, and then came to the table and asked for some tea. The fishes had had no luck that morning, he told them; he had been out in a boat since seven o'clock, and brought back a basketful. The sea air made them hungry, no doubt, for they came by dozens —little feeble whiting—and nibbled at the bait. 'I wish you would come,' he said to his aunt; 'the boat bobs up and down in the sunshine, and the breeze is delightfully fresh, and the people come down on the beach and stare at you through telescopes.' As he talked to his aunt he glanced at Elly, who was pouring out his tea; he said to himself that she was certainly an uncommonly pretty girl; and then he began to speculate about an odd soft look in her eyes. 'When I see people with that expression,' he wrote to his sister, 'I always ask myself what it means? I have seen it in the glass, sometimes, when I have been shaving. Miss Gilmour was not looking at me, but at the muffins and tea-cups. She was nicely dressed in blue calico; she was smiling; her hair trim and shiny. I could hardly believe it was my wailing banshee of the previous night.' (What follows is to the purpose, so I may as well transcribe a little more of Will's letter.) 'When she had poured out my tea, she took up her hat and said she should go down to the station, and get *The Times* for my aunt. I should have offered my services, but aunt Jean made me a sign to stay. What for, do you think? To show me a letter she had received in the morning from that absurd John, who cannot make up his mind. "I do not," he says, "want you to talk poor Elly into a *grande passion*. But if her feelings are unchanged,

I will marry her to-morrow, if she chooses; and I daresay Tishy will not break her heart. Perhaps you will think me a fool for my pains; but I shall not be alone in the world. What was poor little Elly herself when she cried for the moon?" This is all rodomontade; John is not acting fairly by Lætitia, to whom he is bound by every possible promise.

'My aunt said just now that it would be hard for Tishy if he married her, liking Elizabeth best: and there is truth in that. But he mustn't like her best; Miss Gilmour will get over her fancy for him, and he must get over his for her. If he had only behaved like a man and married her right off two years ago, and never hankered after the flesh-pots of Egypt, or if he had only left her alone to settle down with her French pasteur——

' "If—if," cried my aunt, impatiently, when I said as much—(you know her way)—"he has done wrong and been sorry for it, Will, which of us can do more? I doubt whether you would have behaved a bit better in his place." '

This portion of Mr. Will's letter was written at his aunt's writing-book immediately after their little talk. Elly came in rosy from her walk, and Will went on diligently, looking up every now and then with the sense of *bien-être* which a bachelor experiences when he suddenly finds himself domesticated and at home with kind women.

Miss Dampier was sitting in the window. She had got *The Times* in her hand, and was trying to read. Every now and then she looked up at her nephew, with his curly head bent over his writing, at Elly leaning lazily back in her chair, sewing idly at a little shred of work. Her hair was clipped, the colour had faded out of her cheeks, her eyes gleamed. Pretty as she was, still she was changed—how changed from the Elizabeth of eighteen months ago whom Miss Dampier could remember! The old lady went on with her paper, trying to read. She turned to the French correspondent, and saw something about the Chamber, the Emperor, about Italy; about M. X——, the rich banker, having resolved to terminate his existence, when fortunately his servant enters the room at the precise moment when he was preparing to precipitate himself . . . 'The servant to precipitate . . . the window . . . the . . . poor Tishy! At my age I did think I should have done with sentimental troubles. Heigho! heigho!' sighs Miss Dampier.

Elly wanted some thread, and rose with a soft rustle, and got her box and came back to her easy chair. Out of the window they could see all the pleasant idle business of the little seaport going on, the people strolling in the garden, or sitting in all sorts of queer corners, the boats, the mariners (I do believe they are hired to stand about in blue shirts, and shake their battered old noses as they prose for hours together). The waiter came and took away the breakfast, William went on with his letter, and Miss Dampier, with John's little note in her pocket, was, as I

say, reading the most extraordinary things in *The Times*
all about her own private concerns. Nobody spoke for
some ten minutes, when suddenly came a little gasp, a
little sigh from Elly's low chair, and the girl said, ' Aunt
Jean! look here,' almost crying, and held out something
in her thin hand.

' What is it, my dear?' said Miss Dampier, looking up
hastily, and pulling off her spectacles: they were dim
somehow and wanted wiping.

' Poor dear, dearest Tishy,' cried Elly, in her odd
impetuous way. ' Why does he not go to her? Aunt
Jean, look here, I found it in my box—only look here;'
and she put a little note into Miss Dampier's hand.

Will looked up curiously from his writing. Elly had
forgotten all about him. Miss Dampier took the letter,
and when she had read what was written, and then turned
over the page, she took off her glasses again with a click,
and said, ' What nonsense!'

And so it was nonsense, and yet the nonsense touched
Elizabeth, and brought tears into her eyes. They came
faster and faster, and then suddenly remembering that she
was not alone, and ashamed that Dampier should see her
cry again, she jumped up with a shining, blushing, tear-
dimmed tender face, and ran away out of the room. Aunt
Jean looked at Will doubtfully, then hesitated, and gave
him the little shabby letter that had brought these bright

tears into the girl's eyes.   Dear old soul! she made a sort
of confessor of her nephew.

·   The confessor saw a few foolish words which Lætitia
must have written days ago, never thinking that her poor
little words were to be scanned by stranger eyes—written
perhaps unconsciously on a stray sheet of paper.   There
was 'John. Dear John! Dear, dearest! I am so hap. . .
John and Lætitia.   John, my jo.   Goose and gander.'
And then, by some odd chance, she must have folded the
blotted sheet together and forgotten what she had written,
and sent it off to Elly Gilmour, with a little careless note
about Schlangenbad, and 'more fortunate next time,' on
the other side.

'Poor little Letty!' thought Dampier, and he doubled
the paper up, and put it back into the lavender box as the
door opened, and Miss Gilmour came back into the room.
She had dried her eyes, she had fastened on her grey shawl.
She picked up her hat, which was lying on the floor, and
began pulling on two very formidable looking gauntlets
over her slim white hands.   'I am going for a little walk,'
she said to Miss Dampier.   'Will you'—hesitating and
blushing—'direct that little note of Lætitia's to Sir
John? I am going along the cliff towards the pretty
little bay.'

Will was quite melted and touched.   Was this the
scheming young woman, against whom he had been

warned? the woman who had entangled his cousin with her wiles?

'Aunt Jenny,' he says, with a sudden glance, 'are you going to tell her why John Dampier does not go to Lætitia?'

'Why does he not go?' Elly repeats, losing her colour a little.

'He says that if you would like him to stay, he thinks he ought not to go,' says Jean Dampier, hesitating, and tearing corners off *The Times* newspaper.

Will Dampier turned his broad back and looked out of window. There was a moment's silence. They could hear the tinkling of bells, the whistling of the sea, the voices of the men calling to each other in the port: the sunshine streamed in: Elly was standing in it, and seemed gilt with a golden background. She ought to have held a palm in her hand, poor little martyr!

It seemed a long time, it was only a minute, and then she spoke; a sweet honest blush came deepening into Elizabeth's pale cheeks: 'I don't want to marry him because I care for him,' she said, in a thrilling pathetic voice. 'Why should Lætitia, who is so fond of him, suffer because I behaved so badly?' The tears once more came welling up into her eyes. 'I shall think I ought to have died instead of getting well,' she said. 'Aunt Jean, send him the little note; make him go, dear aunt Jean.'

Miss Dampier gave Elly a kiss; she did not know

what to say; she could not influence her one way or another.

She wrote to John that morning, taking good care to look at the back of her paper first.

'Flag Hotel, Boatstown, Nov. 15th.

'My dear Jack,—I had great doubts about communicating your letter to Elizabeth. It seemed to me that the path you had determined upon was one full of thorns and difficulties, for her, for you, and for my niece Lætitia. But although Elly is of far too affectionate a nature ever to give up caring for any of her friends, let me assure you that her feelings are now only those of friendly regard and deep interest in your welfare. When I mentioned to her the contents of your letter (I think it best to speak plainly), she said, with her eyes full of tears, that she did not want to marry you—that she felt you were bound to return to Lætitia. She had been much affected by discovering the enclosed little note from your cousin. I must say that the part which concerns you interested me much, more so than her letter to her old friend. But she was evidently pre-occupied at the time, and Elly, far from feeling neglected, actually began to cry, she was so touched by this somewhat singular discovery. Girl's tears are easily dried. If it lies in my power she shall yet be made happy.

'There is nothing now, as you see, that need prevent your fulfilling your engagements. You are all very good

children, on the whole, and I trust that your troubles are
but fleeting clouds that will soon pass away. That you
and Lætitia may enjoy all prosperity is the sincere hope
and desire of your

'Affectionate old aunt,

'J. M. DAMPIER.'

Miss Dampier, having determined that she had written
a perfectly impartial letter, put it up in an envelope, rang
the bell, and desired a waiter to post it.

Number twenty-three's bell rang at the same moment;
so did number fifteen; immediately after a quantity of
people poured in by the eleven o'clock train; the waiter
flung the letter down on his pantry table, and rushed off
to attend to half-a-dozen things at once, of which posting
the note was not one.

About three o'clock that afternoon Miss Dampier in
her close bonnet was standing in the passage talking to a
tall young man with a black waistcoat and wide-awake.

'What are you going to do?' he said. 'Couldn't we
go for a drive somewhere?'

'I have ordered a carriage at three,' said Miss Dampier, smiling. 'We are going up on the hills. You
might come, too, if you liked it.' And when the carriage
drove up to the door there he was, waiting to hand her in.

He had always, until he saw her, imagined Elly a
little flirting person, quite different from the tall young

L

lady in the broad hat, with the long cloak falling from
her shoulders, who was prepared to accompany them. She
had gone away a little, and his aunt sent him to fetch her.
She was standing against the railing, looking out at the
sea with her sad eyes. There was the lawn, there was the
sea, there was Elly. A pretty young lady always makes a
pretty picture; but out of doors in the sunshine she looks
a prettier young lady than anywhere else, thought Mr.
Will, as Elizabeth walked across the grass. He was not
alone in his opinion; more than one person looked up as
she passed. He began to think that far from doing a
foolish thing his aunt had shown her usual good sense in
taking such good care of this sad, charming, beautiful
young woman. It was no use trying to think ill of her.
With such a face as hers, she has a right to fall in love
with anybody she pleases, he thought; and so, as they
were walking towards the carriage, Will Dampier, thinking
that this was a good opportunity for a little confidential
communication, said, somewhat in his professional manner,
'You seem out of spirits, Miss Gilmour. I hope that you
do not regret your decision of this morning.'

'Yes, I do regret it,' said poor Elly; and two great
tears came dribbling down her cheeks. 'Do you think
that when a girl gives up what she likes best in the world
she is not sorry? I am horribly sorry.'

Will was very much puzzled how to answer this unexpected confidence. He said, looking rather foolish,

'One is so apt to ask unnecessary questions. But, take my word for it, you have done quite right, and some day you will be more glad than you are now.'

I must confess that my heroine here got exceedingly cross.

'Ah, that is what people say who do not know of what they are talking. What business of yours is my poor unlucky bruised and broken fancy?' she said. 'Ah! why were you ever told? What am I? What is it to you?'

All the way she sat silent and dull, staring out at the landscape as they went along; suffering, in truth, poor child, more than either of her companions could tell; saying goodbye to the dearest hope of her youth, tearing herself away from the familiar and the well-loved dreams. Dreams, do I say? They had been the Realities to her, poor child! for many a day. And the realities had seemed to be the dreams.

They drove along a straight road, and came at last to some delighful fresh downs, with the sea sparkling in the distance, and a sort of autumnal glow on the hills all about. The breeze came in fresh gusts, the carriage jogged on, still up hill, and Will Dampier walked alongside, well pleased with the entertainment, and making endless jokes at his aunt. She rather liked being laughed at; but Elly never looked up once, or heeded what they said. They were going towards a brown church, that was standing on the top of a hill. It must have been built by the Danes

a thousand years ago. There it stood, looking out at the
sea, brown, grim, solitary, with its graveyard on the hill-
side. Trees were clustering down in a valley below; but
here, up above, it was all bleak, bare, and solitary, only
tinted and painted by the brown and purple sunshine.

They stopped the carriage a little way off, and got out
and passed through a gate, and walked up the hill-top.
Elly went first, Will followed, and Miss Dampier came
slowly after. As Elly reached the top of the hill she
turned round, and stood against the landscape, like a
picture with a background, and looked back and said—

'Do you hear?'

The organ inside the church was playing a chaunt,
and presently some voices began chaunting to the playing
of the organ. Elly went across the graveyard, and leant
against the porch, listening. Five minutes went by: her
anger was melting away. It was exquisitely clear, peaceful, and tranquil here, up on this hill where the dead people
were lying among the grass and daisies. All the bitterness
went away out of her heart, somehow, in the golden glow.
She said to herself that she felt now, suddenly, for the
first time, as if she could bury her fancy and leave it behind her in this quiet place. As the chaunt went on, her
whole heart uttered in harmony with it, though her lips
were silent. She did not say to herself, what a small thing
it was that had troubled her: what vast combinations were
here to make her happy; hills, vales, light, with its won-

drous refractions, harmony, colour; the great ocean, the great world, rolling on amid the greater worlds beyond!

But she felt it somehow. The voices ceased, and all was very silent.

'O give thanks,' the Psalm began again; and Elly felt that she could indeed give thanks for mercies that were more than she had ever deserved. When she was at home with her mother she thought—just now the thought of returning there scarce gave her a pang—she should remember to-day all the good hopes, good prayers, and aspirations which had come to her in this peaceful graveyard up among the hills. She had been selfish, discontented, and ungrateful all her life, angry and chafed but an hour ago, and here was peace, hers for the moment; here was tranquil happiness. The mad, rash delight she had felt when she had been with John Dampier was nothing compared to this great natural peace and calm. A sort of veil seemed lifted from her eyes, and she felt, for the first time, that she could be happy though what she had wished for most was never to be hers—that there was other happiness than that which she had once fancied part of life itself. Did she ever regret the decision she had made? Did she ever see occasion to think differently from this? If, in after times, she may have felt a little sad, a little lonely now and then—if she may have thought with a moment's regret, of those days that were now already past and over for ever—still she knew she had done rightly when she determined to bury the past with all kindness, with reverend hands. Somehow, in some strange and mysterious manner, the bitterness of her silly troubles had left her—left her a better girl than she had been ever before. She was more good, more happy, more old, more wise, now, and, in truth, there was kindness in store for her, there were suns yet to shine, friendly words to be spoken, troubles yet to be endured, other than those sentimental griefs which had racked her youth so fiercely.

While they were all on the hill-top the steamer came into the port earlier than on the day when Will Dampier arrived. One of the passengers walked up to the hotel and desired a waiter to show him to Miss Dampier's room. It was empty, of course; chairs pushed about, windows open, work and books on the table. The paper was lying on the floor—the passenger noticed that a corner had been torn off; a little box was open on the table, a ruby ring glittering in the tray. 'How careless!' he thought; and then went and flung himself into a great arm-chair.

So! she had been here a minute ago. There was a glove lying on a chair; there were writing materials on a side-table, a blotting-book open, pens with the ink scarcely dry; and in this room, in this place, he was going to decide his fate—rightly or wrongly he could not tell. 'Lætitia is a cold-blooded little creature,' he kept saying to himself; 'this girl, with all her faults, with all her impulses, has a heart to break or to mend. My mother will learn too late that I cannot submit to such dictation. By Jove, what a letter it is!' He pulled it out of his pocket, read it once more, and crumpled it up and threw it into the fireplace. It was certainly not a very wise composition— long, vicious, wiry tails and flourishes. 'John, words cannot,' &c. &c. 'What Lady Tomsey,' &c. &c. 'How horror-struck Major Potterton,' &c. &c.; and finally concluded with a command that he should instantly return to Schlangenbad; or, failing this, an announcement that she should immediately join him, *wherever* he might be!

So Sir John, in a rage, packed up and came off to Boatstown—his mother can follow him or not, as she chooses; and here he is walking up and down the room, while Elly, driving over the hills, is saying farewell, farewell, goodbye to her old love for ever.

Could he have really cared for anybody? By some strange contradiction, now that the die is cast, now that, after all these long doubts and mistrusts, he has made up his mind, somehow new doubts arise. He wonders whether he and Elly will be happy together? He pictures stormy scenes; he intuitively shrinks from the idea of her unconventionalities, her eagerness, her enthusiasm. He is a man who likes a quiet life, who would appreciate a sober, happy home — a gentle, equable companion, to greet him quietly, to care for his tastes and his ways, to sympathise, to befriend him. Whereas now it is he who will have to

study his companion all the rest of his life; if he thwart
her she will fall ill of sorrow, if he satisfy her she will ask
more and more; if he neglect her—being busy, or weary,
or what not—she will die of grief; if he want sympathy
and common sense, she will only adore him.   Poor Elly!
it is hard upon her that he should make such a bugbear
of her poor little love.   His courage is oozing out at his
finger-ends.   He is in a rage with her, and with himself,
and with his mother, and with his aunt.   He and everybody else are in a league to behave as badly as possible.
He will try and do his duty, he thinks, for all that, for my
hero is an honest-hearted man, though a weak one.   It is
not Lady Dampier's letter that shall influence him one
way or another; if Elly is breaking her heart to have him,
and if Letty doesn't care one way or the other, as is likely
enough, well then he will marry Elizabeth, he cries with
a stout desperation, and he dashes up and down the room
in a fury.

And just at this minute the waiter comes in, and says
Miss Dampier has gone out for a drive, and will not be
back for some time.   Mr. Dampier is staying in the house,
but he has gone out with her, and who shall he say?
And Sir John, looking up, gives his name and says he will
wait.

Upon which the waiter suddenly remembers the letter
he left in his pantry, and, feeling rather guilty, proposes
to fetch it.   And by this time Elly, and Will, and Miss

Dampier have got into the carriage again and are driving homewards.

There was a certain humility about Elly, with all her ill-humours and varieties, which seemed to sweeten her whole nature. Will Dampier, who was rather angry with her for her peevishness, could not help forgiving her, when, as he helped her out of the carriage in the courtyard, she said,—

'I don't quite know how to say it—but I was very rude just now. I was very unhappy, and I hope you will forgive me;' and she looked up. The light from the hills was still in her face.

'It was I who was rude,' says Will, goodnaturedly holding out his hand; and of course he forgave her.

The band was playing, the garden was full of people; but aunt Jenny was cold, and glad to get home. The ladies went upstairs: Will remained down below, strolling up and down in the garden with the rest of the people; but at five o'clock the indefatigable bell began to ring once more; the afternoon boat was getting up its steam, and making its preparations to cross over to the other side.

Will met a friend of his, who was going over in it, and he walked down with him to see him off. He went on board with him, shook hands, and turned to come away. At that minute some one happened to look round, and Will, to his immense surprise, recognised his cousin. That was John; those were his whiskers; there was no doubt about it.

He sprang forward and called him by name. 'John,' he said, 'you here?'

'Well!' said John, smiling a little, 'why not me, as well as you? are you coming across?'

'Are you going across?' said Will, doubtfully.

'Yes,' the other answered; 'I came over on business; don't say anything of my having been here. Pray remember this. I have a particular reason.'

'I shall say nothing,' said Will. 'I am glad you are going, John,' he added, stupidly. 'I think I know your reason—a very nice, pretty reason too.'

'So those women have been telling you all about my private affairs?' said Sir John, speaking quick, and looking very black.

'Your mother told me first,' Will said. 'I saw her the other day. For all sakes, I am glad you are giving up all thoughts of Elly Gilmour.'

'Are you?' said John, dryly. They waited for a minute in awkward silence, but as they were shaking hands and saying 'Goodbye,' suddenly John melted and said, 'Look here, Will, I should like to see her once more. Could you manage this for me? I don't want her to know, you know; but could you bring her to the end of the pier? I am going back to Letty, as you see, so I don't think she need object.'

Will nodded, and went up the ladder and turned towards the house without a word, walking quickly and hurrying along. The band in the garden burst out into a pretty melancholy dance tune. The sun went down peg by peg into the sea; the steamer still whistled and puffed as it got up its steam.

Elly was sitting alone. She had lighted a candle, and was writing home. Her hat was lying on a chair beside her. The music had set her dreaming; her thoughts were far away, in the dismal old home again, with Françoise, and Anthony, and the rest of them. She was beginning to live the new life she had been picturing to herself; trying to imagine herself good and contented in the hateful old home; it seemed almost endurable just at this minute, when suddenly the door burst open, and Will Dampier came in with his hat on.

'I want you to come out a little way with me,' he said. 'I want you to come and see the boat off. There's no time to lose.'

'Thank you,' said Elly, 'but I'm busy.'

'It won't take you five minutes,' he said.

She laughed. 'I am lazy, and rather tired.'

Will could not give up. He persisted : he knew he had a knack of persuading his old women at home; he tried it on Miss Gilmour.

'I see you have not forgiven me,' he said ; 'you won't trust yourself with me.'

'Yes, indeed,' said Elly; 'I am only lazy.'

The time was going. He looked at his watch; there were but five minutes—but five minutes for John to take leave of his love of many a year; but five minutes and it would be too late. He grew impatient.

'Pray, come,' he said. 'I shall look upon it as a sign that you have forgiven me. Will you do me this favour? —will you come? I assure you I shall not be ungrateful.'

Elly thought it odd, and still hesitated; but it seemed unkind to refuse. She got up, fetched her hat and cloak, and in a minute he was hurrying her along across the lawn, along the side of the dock, out to the pier's end.

They were only just in time. 'You are very mysterious,' said Elly. 'Why do you care so much to see the boat go out? How chilly it is! Are you not glad to be here on this side of the water? Ah! how soon it will be time for me to go back!'

Will did not answer, he was so busy watching the people moving about on board. Puff! puff! Cannot you imagine the great boat passing close at their feet, going out in the night into the open sea; the streaks of light in the west; Elly, with flushed, rosy-red cheeks, like the sunset, standing under the lighthouse, and talking in her gentle voice, and looking out, saying it would be fine to-morrow?

Can't you fancy poor Sir John leaning against a pile

of baggage, smoking a cigar, and looking up wistfully? As he slid past he actually caught the tone of her voice. Like a drowning man who can see in one instant years of his past life flashing before him, Sir John saw Elly—a woman with lines of care in her face,—there, standing in the light of the lamp, with the red streams of sunset beyond, and the night closing in all round about; and then he saw her as he had seen her once—a happy, unconscious girl, brightening, smiling at his coming; and as the picture travelled on, a sad girl, meeting him in the street by chance—a desperate, almost broken-hearted woman, looking up greyly into his face in the theatre. Puff! puff!—it was all over, she was still smiling before his eyes. One last glimpse of the two, and they had disappeared. He slipped away right out of her existence, and she did not even guess that he had been near. She stood unwitting for an instant, watching the boat as it tossed out to sea, and then said, ' Now we will go home.' A sudden gloom and depression seemed to have come over her. She walked along quite silently, and did not seem to heed the presence of her companion.

CHAPTER X.

> . . . Poor forsaken Flos!
> Not all her brightness, sportfulness, and bloom,
> Her sweetness and her wildness, and her wit,
> Could save her from desertion. No ; their loves
> Were off the poise. Love competent
> Makes better bargains than love affluent.

BEFORE he went to bed that night Dampier wrote the end of his letter to Prue.   He described, rather amusingly, the snubbing which Elly had given him, the dry way in which Sir John had received his advances, the glances of disfavour with which aunt Jean listened to his advice. ' So this is all the gratitude one gets for interfering in the most sensible manner.   If you are as ungrateful, Prue, for this immense long letter, I shall, indeed, have laboured in vain.   It is one o'clock.   Bong! there it went from the tower.   Good-night, dear ; your beloved brother is going to bed.   Love to Miles.   Kiss the children all round for their and your affectionate W. D.'

Will Dampier was not in the least like his letter.   I know two or three men who are manly enough, who write gentle, gossiping letters like women.   He was a big, commonplace young man, straight-minded and tender-hearted, with immense energy, and great good spirits. He believed in himself; indeed, he tried so heartily and conscientiously to do what was right, that he could not help knowing more or less that he was a good fellow. And then he had a happy knack of seeing one side of a question, and having once determined that so and so was the thing to be done, he could do so and so without one doubt or compunction. He belonged to the school of athletic Christianity. I heard someone once say that there are some of that sect who would almost make out cock-fighting to be a religious ceremony. William Dampier did not go so far as this; but he heartily believed that nothing was wrong that was done with a Christian and manly spirit. He rode across country, he smoked pipes, he went out shooting, he played billiards and cricket, he rowed up and down the river in his boat, and he was charming with all the grumbling old men and women in his parish, he preached capital sermons —short, brisk, well-considered. He enjoyed life and all its good things with a grateful temper, and made most people happy about him.

One day, Elly began to think what a different creed Will Dampier's was from her stepfather's, only she did not put her thoughts into words. It was not her way.

Tourneur, with a great heart, set on the greatest truth, feeling the constant presence of those mightier dispensations, cared but little for the affairs of to-day: they seemed to him subordinate, immaterial; they lost all importance

from comparison to that awful reality that this man had
so vividly realised to himself.   To Dampier, it was through
the simple language of his daily life that he could best
express what good was in him.   He saw wisdom and
mercy, he saw order and progression, he saw infinite
variety and wonder in all natural things, in all life, at
all places and hours.   By looking at this world, he could
best understand and adore the next.

And yet Tourneur's was the loftier spirit : to him
had come a certain knowledge and understanding, of which
Dampier had scarce a conception.   Dampier, who felt less
keenly, could well be more liberal, more forbearing.   One
of these two told Elly that we were put into the world to
live in it, and to be thankful for our creation ; to do our
duty, and to labour until the night should come when no
man can work.   The other safe, sadly, you are born only
to overcome the flesh, to crush it under foot, to turn away
from all that you like most, innocent or not.   What do I
care ?   Are you an immortal spirit, or are you a clod of
earth ?   Will you suffer this all-wondrous, all-precious
gift should be clogged, and stifled, and choked, and destroyed, maybe, by despicable daily concerns ?   Tourneur
himself set an example of what he preached by his devoted,
humble, holy, self-denying-life.   And yet Elly turned
with a sense of infinite relief to the other creed : she could
understand it, sympathise with it, try to do good, though
to be good was beyond her frail powers.   Already she was

learning to be thankful, to be cheerful, to be unselfish, to be keenly penitent for her many shortcomings.

As the time drew near when an answer to her note might be expected, Miss Dampier grew anxious and fidgety, dropped her stitches, looked out for the post, and wondered why no letter came. Elly was only a little silent, a little thoughtful. She used to go out by herself and take long walks. One day Will, returning from one of his peregrinations, came upon her sitting on the edge of a cliff staring at the distant coast of France. It lay blue, pale, like a dream-country, and glimmered in the horizon. Who would believe that there was reality, busy life in all earnest going on beyond those calm, heavenly-looking hills ! Another time his aunt sent him out to look for her, and he found her at the end of the pier, leaning against the chain, and still gazing towards France.

In his rough, friendly manner he said, ' I wish you would look another way sometimes, Miss Gilmour, up or down, or in the glass even. You make me feel very guilty, for to tell the truth I—I advised John——'

' I thought so,' Elly cried, interrupting. ' And you were quite right. I advised him too,' she said, with a smile. ' Don't you think he has taken your advice ? '

Will looked down uncomfortably. ' I think so,' he said, in a low tone.

And, meanwhile, Miss Dampier was sitting in the window and the sunshine, knitting castles in the air.

M

'Suppose he does not take this as an answer? Suppose Lætitia has found somebody else, suppose the door opens and he comes in, and the sun shines into the room, and then he seizes Elly's hand, and says, "Though you give me up, I will not give up the hope of calling you mine," and Elly glances up bright, blushing, happy. . . Suppose Lady Dampier is furious, and dear Tishy makes peace? I should like to see Elizabeth mistress of the dear old house. I think my mother was like her. I don't approve of cousins' marriages . . . How charming she would look coming along the old oak gallery!' Look at the old maid in the window building castles in the air through her spectacles. But it is a ridiculous sight; she is only a fat, foolish old woman. All her fancies are but follies flying away with caps and jingling bells—they vanish through the window as the door opens and the young people come in.

'Here is a letter for you the porter gave me in the hall,' said Will, as carelessly as he could; Jean saw Elly's eyes busy glancing at the writing.

'My dear Aunt Jean,—Many thanks for your note, and the enclosure. My mother and Lætitia are with me, and we shall all go back to Friar's Bush on Thursday. Elly's decision is the wisest under the circumstances, and we had better abide by it. Give her my love. Lætitia knows nothing, as my mother has had the grace to be silent.

'Yours affectionately, J. C. D.

'P.S.—You will be good to her, won't you?'

Miss Dampier read the note imperturbably, but while she read there seemed to run through her a cold thrill of disappointment, which was so unendurable that after a minute she got up and left the room.

When she came back, Elly said with a sigh, ' Where is he ? '

' At Paris,' said Miss Dampier. ' They have saved him all trouble and come to him. He sends you his love, Elly, which is very handsome of him, considering how much it is worth.'

' It has been worth a great deal to me,' said Elly, in her sweet voice. ' It is all over ; but I am grateful still and always shall be. I was very rash; he was very kind. Let me be grateful, dear aunt Jean, to those who are good to me.' And she kissed the old woman's shrivelled hand.

Miss Gilmour cheered up wonderfully from that time. I am sure that if she had been angry with him, if she had thought herself hardly used, if she had had more of what people call self-respect, less of that sweet humility of nature, it would not have been so.

As the short, happy, delightful six weeks which she was to spend with Miss Dampier came to an end, she began to use all her philosophy and good resolves to reconcile herself to going home. Will Dampier was gone. He had only been able to stay a week. They missed him. But still they managed to be very comfortable together

Tea-talk, long walks, long hours on the sands, novels and story-books, idleness and contentment—why couldn't it go on for ever? Elly said. Aunt Jean laughed and said they might as well be a couple of jelly-fish at once. And so the time went by, but one day just before she went away, Mr. Will appeared again unexpectedly.

Elly was sitting in the sun on the beach, throwing idle stones into the sea. She had put down her novel on the shingle beside her. It was 'Deerbrook,' I think—an old favourite of Jean Dampier's. Everybody knows what twelve o'clock is like on a fine day at the sea-side. It means little children, nurses in clean cotton gowns, groups of young ladies scattered here and there; it means a great cheerfulness and tranquillity, a delightful glitter, and life, and light: happy folks plashing in the water, bathing-dresses drying in the sun, all sorts of aches, pains, troubles, vanishing like mist in its friendly beams. Elly was thinking: 'Yes, how pleasant and nice it is, and how good, how dear aunt Jean is! Only six months, and she says I am to come to her in her cottage again.' (Splash a stone goes into the water.) 'Only six months! I will try and spend them better than I ever spent six months before. Eugh! If it was not for Mme. Jacob . . . . I really do love my stepfather, and could live happily enough with him.' (Splash.) Suddenly an idea came to Elly—the Pasteur Boulot was the idea. 'Why should not he marry Mme. Jacob? He admires her immensely. Ah! what fun that would be!' (Splash, splash—a couple of stones.) And then, tramp, tramp, on the shingle behind her, and a cheery man's voice says, ' Here you are!'

Elly stares up in some surprise, and looks pleased, and attempts to get up, but Will Dampier—he was the man—sits down beside her, opens his umbrella, and looks very odd. ' I only came down for the day,' he said, after a little preliminary talk. ' I have been with aunt Jean; she tells me you are going home to-morrow.'

' Yes,' says Elly, with a sigh; ' but I am to come back again and see her in a little time.'

' I am glad of that,' says the clergyman. ' What sort of place do you live in at Paris?'

' It is rather a dull place,' says Elly. ' I'm very fond of my stepfather; besides him, there is Anthony, and five young pupils, there is an old French cook, and a cross maid, and my mother, and a horri—— a sister of Monsieur Tourneur's, and Tou-Tou and Lou-Lou, and me.'

' Why, that is quite a little colony,' said Dampier. ' And what will you do there when you get back?'

' I must see,' said the girl, smiling. ' Till now I have done nothing at all; but that is stupid work. I shall teach Tou-Tou and Lou-Lou a little, and mind the house if my mother will let me, and learn to cook from Françoise. I have a notion that it may be useful some day or other.'

' Do, by all means,' said Will; ' it is a capital idea. But as years go on, what do you mean to do? Tou-Tou and Lou-Lou will grow up, and you will have mastered the art of French cookery——'

' How can you ask such things?' Elly said, looking out at the sea. ' I cannot tell, or make schemes for the future.'

' Pray forgive me,' said Will, ' for asking such a question, but have you any idea of marrying M. Anthony eventually ? '

' He is a dear old fellow,' said Elly, flushing up. ' I am not going to answer any such questions. I am not half good enough for him—that is my answer.'

' But suppose—— ? '

' Pray don't suppose. I am not going to marry anybody, or to think much about such things ever again. Do you imagine that I am not the wiser for all my experience ? '

' Are you wise now ? ' said Will, still in his odd manner.

' Look at that pretty little fishing-smack,' Elly interrupted.

' Show it,' he went on, never heeding, ' by curing yourself of your fancy for my cousin John ; by curing yourself, and becoming some day a really useful personage and member of society.'

Elly stared at him, as well she might.

'Come back to England some day,' he continued, still looking away, 'to your home, to your best vocation in life, to be happy, and useful, and well-loved,' he said, with a sweet inflexion in his voice; 'that is no very hard fate.'

'What are you talking about?' said Elly. 'How can I cure myself? How can I ever forget what is past? I am not going to be discontented, or to be particularly happy at home. I am going *to try*—to try and do my best.'

'Well, then, do your best to get cured of this hopeless nonsense,' said Mr. William Dampier, 'and turn your thoughts to real good sense, to the real business of life, and to making yourself and others happy, instead of wasting and maudling away the next few best years of your life, regretting and hankering after what is past and unattainable. For some strong minds, who can defy the world, and stand alone without the need of sympathy and sustainment, it is a fine thing to be faithful to a chimera,' he said, with a pathetic ring in his voice. 'But I assure you infidelity is better still sometimes, more human, more natural, particularly for a confiding and uncertain person like yourself.' Was he thinking of to-day as he spoke? Was he only thinking of Elly, and preaching only to her?

'You mean I had better marry him?' said Elly, while her eyes filled up with tears, and she knocked one stone against another. 'And yet aunt Jean says, "No!"—that I need not think of it. It seems to me as if I—I had rather jump into the sea at once,' said the girl, dashing the stones away, ' though I love him dearly, dear old fellow ! '

' I did not exactly mean M. Anthony,' said Will, looking round for the first time and smiling at her tears and his own talk.

Elizabeth was puzzled still. For, in truth, her sad experience had taught her to put but little faith in kindness and implications of kindness—to attach little meaning to the good-nature and admiration a beautiful young woman was certain to meet with on every side. It had not occurred to her that Will, who had done so little, seen her so few times, could be in love with her ; when John, for whom she would have died, who said and looked so much, had only been playing with her, and pitying her as if she had been a child; and she said, still with tears, but not caring much—

' I shall never give a different answer. I believe you are right, but I have not the courage to try. I think I could try and be good if I stay as I am ; but to be bound and chained to Anthony all the rest of my life—once I thought it possible ; but now—— You who advise it do not know what it is.'

' But I never advised it,' Will said ; ' you won't understand me. Dear Elizabeth, why won't you see that it is of myself that I am speaking ? '

Elly felt for a moment as if the sea had rushed up suddenly, and caught her away on its billows, and then the next moment she found that she was only sitting crying in the sun, on the sands.

' Look here : every day I live, I get worse and worse,' she sobbed. ' I flirt with one person after another—I don't deserve that you should ever speak to me again—I can't try and talk about myself—I do like you, and—and yet I know that the only person I care for really is the one who does not care for me ; and if I married you to-morrow, and I saw John coming along the street, I should rush away to meet him. I don't want to marry him, and I don't know what I want. But, indeed, I have tried to be good. You are stronger than me, don't be hard upon me.'

' My dear little girl,' said Will, loyally and kindly, ' don't be unhappy; you have not flirted with me. I couldn't be hard upon you if I tried: you are a faithful little soul. Shall I tell you about myself ? Once, not so very long ago, I liked Tishy almost as well as you like John. There, now, you see that you have done no great harm, and only helped to cheer me up again, and I am sure that you and I will be just as good friends as ever. As for John,' he added, in quite a different tone, ' the sooner you forget all about him the better.'

Will took her hand which was lying limp on the shingle, said ' Goodbye,' took up his umbrella, and walked away.

And so, by some strange arrangement, Elly put away

from her a second time the love of a good and honourable man, and turned back impotently to the memory—it was no more—of a dead and buried passion. Was this madness or wisdom? Was this the decree of fate or of folly?

She sat all in a maze, staring at the sea and the wavelets, and in half an hour rushed into the sitting-room, flung her arms round Miss Dampier's neck, and told her all that happened.

CHAPTER XI.

Of all the gifts of Heaven to us below, that felicity is the sum and the chief. I tremble as I hold it, lest I should lose it, and be left alone in the blank world without it. Again, I feel humiliated to think that I possess it: as hastening home to a warm fireside, and a plentiful table, I feel ashamed sometimes before the poor outcast beggar shivering in the street.

ELLY expected, she did not know why, that there would be some great difference when she got back to the old house at Paris. Her heart sank as Clementine, looking just as usual, opened the great door, and stepped forward to help with the box. She went into the courtyard. Those cocks and hens were pecketting between the stones, the poplar-trees shivering, Françoise in her blue gown came out of the kitchen : it was like one of the dreams which used to haunt her pillow. This sameness and monotony was terrible. Already in one minute it seemed to her that she had never been away. Her mother and father were out. Mme. Jacob came downstairs with the children to greet her and see her. Ah ! they had got new frocks, and were grown—that was some relief. Tou-Tou and Lou-Lou were not more delighted with their little check black-and-white alpacas than Elly was.

Anthony was away—she was glad. After the first shock the girl took heart and courage, and set herself to practise the good resolutions she had made when she was away. It was not so hard as she had fancied to be a little less ill-tempered and discontented, because you see she had really behaved so very badly before. But it was not so easy to lead the cheerful devoted life she had pictured to herself. Her mother was very kind, very indifferent, very unhappy, Elizabeth feared. She was ill too, and out of health, but she bore great suffering with wonderful patience and constancy. Tourneur looked haggard and worn. Had he begun to discover that he could not understand his wife, that he had not married the woman he fancied he knew so well, but some quite different person? Ill-temper, discontent, he could have endured and dealt with; but a terrible mistrust and doubt had come into his heart, he did not know how or when, and had nearly broken it.

A gloom seemed hanging over this sad house; a sort of hopeless dreariness. Do you remember how cheerful and contented Caroline had been at first? By degrees she began to get a little tired now and then—a little weary. All these things grew just a little insipid and distasteful. Do you know that torture to which some poor slaves have been subjected? I believe it is only a drop of water falling at regular intervals upon their heads. At first they scarcely heed it, and talk and laugh; then they become silent; and still the drop falls and drips. And then they moan and beg for mercy, and still it falls; and then scream out with horror, and cry out for death, for this is more than they can bear—but still it goes on falling. I have read this somewhere, and it seems to me that this applies to Caroline Tourneur, and to the terrible life which had begun for her.

Her health failed, and she daily lost strength and interest in the things by which she was surrounded; then they became wearisome. Her tired frame was not equal to the constant exertions she had imposed upon herself; from being wearisome, they grew hateful to her; and, one by one, she gave them up. Then the terrible sameness of a life in which her heart was no longer set, seemed to crush her down day by day : a life never lived from high and honourable motives, but for mean and despicable ends; a life lofty and noble to those who, with great hearts and good courage, knew how to look beyond it, and not to care for the things of the world, but dull and terrible beyond expression to a woman whose whole soul was set amidst the thorns and thistles ; and who had only rushed by chance into this narrow path blindfold with passion and despair.

Now she has torn the bandage off her eyes; now she is struggling to get out of it, and beating against the thorns, and wearily trying to trace back her steps. Elly used to cry out in her childish way. Caroline, who is a woman, is silent, and utters not one word of complaint; only her cheeks fall away and her eyes glare out of great black rings.

Elly came home blooming and well, and was shocked and frightened at first to see the change which had come over her mother. She did not ask the reason of it, but, as we all do sometimes, accepted without much speculation the course of events. Things come about so simply and naturally that people are often in the midst of strangest histories without having once thought so, or wondered that it should be. Very soon all the gloomy house, though she did not know it, seemed brightened and cheered by her coming home. Even Mme. Jacob relented a little when she heard Tou-Tou and Lou-Lou's shouts of laughter one day coming through the open window. The three girls were at work in the garden. I do not know that they were doing much good except to themselves. It was a keen, clear, brilliant winter morning, and the sun out of doors put out the smouldering fires within.

The little girls were laughing and working with all their hearts. Elly was laughing too, and tearing up dried old plants, and heaping broken flower-pots together. Almost happy, almost contented, almost good. . . . And there is many a worse state of mind than this. She was sighing as she laughed, for she was thinking of herself, pacing round and round the neglected garden once not so long ago ; then she thought of the church on the hill-top, then of Will Dampier, and then of John, and then she came upon a long wriggling worm, and she jumped away and forgot to be sentimental. Besides working in the garden, she set to teaching the children in her mother's school. What this girl turned her hand to, she always did well and thoroughly. She even went to visit some of the sick people, and though she never took kindly to these exercises, the children liked to say their lessons to her, and the sick people were glad when she came in. She was very popular with them all; perhaps the reason was, that she did not do these things from a sense of duty, and did not look upon the poor and the sick, as so many of us do, as a selfish means of self-advancement; she went to them because it was more convenient for her to go than for anybody else—she only thought of their needs, grumbled at the trouble she was taking, and it never occurred to her that this unconsciousness was as good as a good conscience.

My dear little Elizabeth! I am glad that at last she is behaving pretty well. Tourneur strokes her head sometimes, and holds out his kind hand to her when she comes into his room. His eyes follow her fondly as if he were her father. One day she told him about William Dampier. He sighed as he heard the story. It was all ordained for the best, he said to himself. But he would have been glad to know her happy, and he patted her cheek and went into his study.

Miss Dampier's letters were Elly's best treasures: how eagerly she took them from Clementine's hands, how she tore them open and read them once, twice, thrice! No novels interest people so much as their own—a story in which you have ever so little a part to enact thrills, and excites, and amuses to the very last. You don't skip the reflections; the descriptions do not weary. I can fancy Elly sitting in a heap on the floor, and spelling out Miss Dampier's; Tou-Tou and Lou-Lou looking on with respectful wonder.

But suddenly the letters seemed to her to change. They became short and reserved; they were not interesting any more. Looked for so anxiously, they only brought disappointment when they came, and no word of the people about whom she longed to hear, no mention of their doings. Even Lady Dampier's name would have been welcome. But there was nothing. It was in vain she read and re-read so eagerly, longing and thirsting for news.

Things were best as they were, she told herself a hundred times; and so, though poor Elly sighed and wearied, and though her heart sank, she did not speak to anyone of her trouble: it was a wholesome one, she told herself, one that must be surmounted and overcome by patience. Sometimes her work seemed almost greater than her strength, and then she would go upstairs and cry a little bit and pity herself, and sop up all her tears, and then run round and round the garden once or twice, and come back, with bright eyes and glowing cheeks, to chatter with Françoise, to look after her mother and Stephen Tourneur, to scold the pupils and make jokes at them, to romp with the little girls.

One day she found her letter waiting on the hall-table, and tore it open with a trembling hope. . . . Aunt Jean described the weather, the pigsty, made valuable remarks on the news contained in the daily papers, signed herself, ever her affectionate old friend. And that was all. Was not that enough? Elly asked herself, with such a sigh. She was reading it over in the doorway of the salle-à-manger, bonneted and cloaked, with all the remains of the mid-day meal congealing and disordered on the table.

'Es-tu prête, Elizabeth?' said Tou-Tou, coming in with a little basket—there were no stones in it this time. 'Tiens, voilà ce que ma tante envoie à cette pauvre Madame Jonnes.'

Madame Jonnes was only Mrs. Jones, only an old woman dying in a melancholy room hard-by—in a melancholy room in a deserted street, where there were few houses, but long walls, where the mould was feeding, and yellow placards were pasted and defaced and flapping in shreds, and where Elly, picking her little steps over the stone, saw blades of grass growing between them. There was a *chantier*—a great wood-yard—on one side; now and then a dark doorway leading into a black and filthy court, out of which a gutter would come with evil smells, flowing murkily into the street; in the distance, two figures passing; a child in a nightcap, thumping a doll

N

upon a kerbstone ; a dog snuffing at a heap ; at the end
of the street the placarded backs of tall houses built upon
a rising ground ; a man in a blouse wheeling a truck, and
singing out dismally ; and meanwhile, good old Mrs.
Jones was dying close at hand, under this black and crumbling doorway, in a room opening with cracked glass-doors
upon the yard.

She was lying alone upon her bed ; the nurse they
had sent to her was gossiping with the porter in his lodge.
Kindly and dimly her eyes opened and smiled somehow at
the girl, out of the faded bed, out of a mystery of pain,
of grief, and solitude.

It was a mystery indeed, which Elizabeth, standing
beside it, could not understand, though she herself had
lain so lately and so resignedly upon a couch of sickness.
Age, abandonment, seventy years of life—how many of grief
and trouble ? As she looked at the dying, indifferent face,
she saw that they were almost ended. And in the midst
of her pity and shrinking compassion Elly thought to herself that she would change all with the sick woman, at
that minute, to have endured, to have surmounted so
much.

She sat with her till the dim twilight came through
the dirty and patched panes of the windows. Even as she
waited there her thoughts went wandering, and she was
trying to picture to herself faces and scenes that she could
not see. She knew that the shadows were creeping round

about those whom she loved, as quietly as they were rising here in this sordid room. It was their evening as it was hers; and then she said to herself that they who made up so large a part of her life must, perforce, think of her sometimes : she was part of their lives, even though they should utterly neglect and forget and abandon her ; even though they should never meet again from this day ; though she should never hear their names so much as mentioned ; though their paths should separate for ever. For a time they had travelled the same road——ah ! she was thankful even for so much ; and she unconsciously pressed the wasted hand she was holding : and then her heart thrilled with tender, unselfish gladness as the feeble fingers tried to clasp hers, and the faltering whisper tried to bless.

She came home sad and tired from her sick woman's bedside, thinking of the last kind gleam of the eyes as she left the room. She went straight upstairs and took off her shabby dress, and found another, and poured out water and bathed her face. Her heart was beating, her hands trembling. She was remembering and regretting ; she was despairing and longing, and yet resigned, as she had learnt to be of late. She leant against the wall for a minute before she went down ; she was dressed in the blue dress, with her favourite little locket hanging round her neck. She put her hand tiredly to her head ; and so she stood, as she used to stand when she was a child, in a sort of dream, and almost out of the world.

And as she was waiting a knock came at the door. It was Clementine who knocked, and who said, in the sing-song way in which Frenchwomen speak—' Mademoiselle, voilà pour vous.'

It was too dark to see anything, except that it was another familiar-looking letter. Elly made up her mind not to be disappointed any more, and went downstairs leisurely to the study, where she knew she should find Tourneur's lamp alight. And she crossed the hall and turned the handle of the door, and opened it and went in.

The lamp, with its green shade on the table, lit up one part of the room, but in the duskiness, standing by the stove and talking eagerly, were two people whom she could not distinguish very plainly. One of them was Tourneur, who looked round and came to meet her, and took her hand; and the other . . . .

Suddenly her heart began to beat so that her breath was taken away. What was this? Who was this——? What chance had she come upon? Such mad hopes as hers, were they ever fulfilled? Was this moment, so sudden, so unlooked for, the one for which she had despaired and longed; for which she had waited and lived through an eternity of grief? Was it John Dampier into whose hand Tourneur put hers? Was she still asleep and dreaming one of those delighting but terrible dreams, from which, ah me! she must awake? In this dream she heard the pasteur saying, ' Il a bien des choses à vous dire, Elizabeth,' and then he seemed to go away and to leave them.

In this dream, bewildered and trembling, with a desperate effort, she pulled her hand away, and said, 'What does it mean? Where is Tishy? Why do you come, John? Why don't you leave me in peace?'

And then it was a dream no longer, but a truth and a reality, when John began to speak in his familiar way, and she heard his voice, and saw him before her, and— yes, it was he ; and he said, ' Tishy and I have had a quarrel, Elly. We are nothing to one another any more, and so I have come to you—to—to—tell you that I have behaved like a fool all this time.' And he turned very red as he spoke, and then he was silent, and then he took both her hands and spoke again: ' Tell me, dear,' he said, looking up into her sweet eyes,—' Elly, tell me, would you—won't you—be content with a fool for a husband?' And Elizabeth Gilmour only answered, ' Oh, John, John!' and burst into a great flood of happy tears : tears which fell raining peace and calm after this long drought and misery ; tears which seemed to speak to him, and made him sad, and yet happier than he had ever dreamt of or imagined ; tears which quieted her, soothed her, and healed all her troubles.

Before John went away that night, Elly read Miss Dampier's letter, which explained his explanations. The old lady wrote in a state of incoherent excitement.—It

was some speech of Will's which had brought the whole
thing about.

' What did he say ? ' Elly asked, looking up from the
letter, with her shining eyes.

Sir John said, ' He asked me if I did not remember
that church on the hill, at Boatstown ? We were all out
in the garden, by the old statue of the nymph. Tishy
suddenly stopped, and turned upon me, and cried out,
when was I last at Boatstown ? And then I was obliged
to confess, and we had a disagreeable scene enough, and
she appealed to William—gave me my congé, and I was
not sorry, Elly.'

' But had you never told her about——? '

' It was from sheer honesty that I was silent,' said Sir
John ; ' a man who sincerely wishes to keep his word
doesn't say, " Madam, I like someone else, but I will
marry you if you insist upon it ; " only the worst of it is,
that we were both uncomfortable, and I now find she suspected me the whole time.   She sent me a note in the
evening.   Look here : '—

The note said—

' I have been thinking about what I said just now in the
garden.   I am more than ever decided that it is best we
two should part.   But I do not choose to say goodbye to
you in an angry spirit, and so this is to tell you that I
forgive you all the injustice of your conduct to me.

Everybody seems to have been in a league to deceive me, and I have not found out one true friend among you all. How could you for one moment imagine that I should wish to marry a man who preferred another woman? You may have been influenced and worked upon; but for all that I should never be able to place confidence in you again, and I feel it is best and happiest for us both that all should be at an end between us.

'You will not wonder that, though I try to forgive you, I cannot help feeling indignant at the way in which I have been used. I could never understand exactly what was going on in your mind. You were silent, you equivocated; and not you only, everybody seems to have been thinking of themselves, and never once for me. Even William, who professes to care for me still, only spoke by chance, and revealed the whole history. When he talked to you about Boatstown, some former suspicions of mine were confirmed, and by the most fortunate chance two people have been saved from a whole lifetime of regret.

'I will not trust myself to think of the way in which I should have been bartered had I only discovered the truth when it was too late. If I speak plainly, it is in justice to myself, and from no unkindness to you; for though I bid you farewell, I can still sincerely sign myself,

'Yours affectionately,

'LÆTITIA.'

Elly read the letter, and gave it back to him, and sighed, then smiled, then sighed again, and then went on with Miss Dampier's epistle.

For some time past Jean Dampier wrote she had noticed a growing suspicion and estrangement between the engaged couple. John was brusque and morose at times, Tishy cross and defiant. He used to come over on his brown mare, and stop at the cottage gate, and ask about Elly, and then interrupt her before she could answer and change the talk. He used to give her messages to send, and then retract them. He was always philosophising and discoursing about first affections. Lætitia, too, used to come and ask about Elly.

Miss Dampier hoped that John himself would put an end to this false situation. She did not know how to write about either of them to Elly. Her perplexities had seemed unending.

'But I also never heard that you came to Boatstown,' Elly said.

'And yet I saw you there,' said John, 'standing at the end of the pier.' And then he went on to tell her a great deal more, and to confess all that he had thought while he was waiting for her.

Elly passed her hand across her eyes with the old familiar action.

'And you came to Boatstown, and you went away

·when you read Tishy's writing, and you had the heart to be angry with me?' she said.

'I was worried, and out of temper,' said John. 'I felt I was doing wrong when I ran away from Tishy. I blamed you because I was in a rage with myself. I can't bear to think of it. But I was punished, Elly. Were you ever jealous?' She laughed and nodded her head 'I daresay not,' he went on; 'when I sailed away and saw you standing so confidentially with Will Dampier, I won't try and tell you what I suffered. I could bear to give you up—but to see you another man's wife——Elly, I know you never were jealous, or you would understand what I felt at that moment.'

When their *tête-à-tête* was over they went into the next room. All the family congratulated them, Madame Tourneur among the rest; she was ill and tired that evening, and lying on the yellow Utrecht velvet sofa. But it was awkward for them and uncomfortable, and John went home early to his inn. As Elly went up to bed that night Françoise brought her one other piece of news—Madame Jonnes was dead. They had sent to acquaint the police. But Elly was so happy, that, though she tried, she could not be less happy because of this. All the night she lay awake, giving thanks and praise, and saying over to herself, a hundred times, 'At last—at last!'

At last! after all this long rigmarole. At last! after all these despairing adjectives and adverbs; at last! after all these thousands of hours of grief and despair. Did not that one minute almost repay her for them all? She went on telling herself, as I have said, that this was a dream—from which she need never awake. And I, who am writing her story, wonder if it is so—wonder if even to such dreams as these there may not be a waking one day, when all the visions that surround us shall vanish and disappear for ever into eternal silence and oblivion. Dear faces—voices whose tones speak to us even more familiarly than the tender words which they utter! It would, in truth, seem almost too hard to bear, if we did not guess—if we were not told—how the love which makes such things so dear to us endures in the eternity out of which they have passed.

Happiness like Elly's is so vague and so great that it is impossible to try to describe it. To a nature like hers, full of tenderness, faithful and eager, it came like a sea, ebbing and flowing with waves, and with the sun shining and sparkling on the water, and lighting the fathoms below. I do not mean to say that my poor little heroine was such a tremendous creature that she could compass the depths and wide extent of a sea in her heart. Love is not a thing which belongs to any one of us individually; it is everywhere, here and all round about, and sometimes people's hearts are opened, and they guess at it, and realise that it is theirs.

Dampier came early next morning, looking kind and

happy and bright, to fetch her for a walk; Elly was all blue ribbons and blue eyes; her feet seemed dancing against her will, she could hardly walk quietly along. Old Françoise looked after them as they walked off towards the Bois de Boulogne; Tou-Tou and Lou-Lou peeped from their bedroom window. The sun was shining, the sky had mounted Elly's favourite colours.

CHAPTER XII.

O blessed rest, O royal night!
  Wherefore seemeth the time so long
Till I see yon stars in their fullest light,
  And list to their loudest song?

WHEN I first saw Lady Dampier she had only been married a day or two. I had been staying at Guildford, and I drove over one day to see my old friend Jean Dampier. I came across the hills and by Coombe Bottom and along the lanes, and through the little village street, and when I reached the cottage I saw Elly, of whom I had heard so much, standing at the gate. She was a very beautiful young woman, tall and straight, with the most charming blue eyes, a sweet frank voice, and a taking manner, and an expression on her face that I cannot describe. She had a blue ribbon in her hair, which was curling in a crop. She held her hat full of flowers ; behind her the lattices of the cottage were gleaming in the sun; the creepers were climbing and flowering about the porch.

All about rose a spring incense of light, of colour, of perfume. The country folks were at work in the fields and on the hills. The light shone beyond the church spire, beyond the cottages and glowing trees. Inside the cottage, through the lattice, I could see aunt Jean nodding over her knitting.

She threw down her needles to welcome me. Of course I was going to stay to tea—and I said that was my intention in coming. As the sun set, the clouds began to gather, coming quickly we knew not whence ; but we were safe and dry, sitting by the lattice and gossiping, and meanwhile Miss Dampier went on with her work.

Elly had been spending the day with her, she told me. Sir John was to come for her, and presently he arrived, dripping wet, through the April shower which was now pouring over the fields.

The door of the porch opens into the little dining-room, where the tea was laid : a wood fire was crackling in the tall cottage chimney. Elizabeth was smiling by the hearth, toasting cakes with one hand and holding a book in the other, when the young man walked in.

He came into the room where we were sitting and shook hands with us both, and then he laughed and said he must go and dry himself by the fire, and he went back.

So Jean Dampier and I sat mumbling confidences in the inner room, and John and Elly were chattering to one another by the burning wood logs.

The door was open which led, with a step, into the dining-room, where the wood fire was burning. Darkness was setting in. The rain was over, the clouds swiftly breaking and coursing away, and such a bright, mild-eyed little star peeped in through the lattice at us two old maids in the window. It was a shame to hear, but how could we help it? Out of the fire-lit room the voices came to us, and when we ceased chattering for an instant, we heard them so plainly—

'I saw Will to-day,' said a voice. 'He was talking about Lætitia. I think there will be some news of them before long. Should you be glad?'

'Ah! so glad. I don't.want to be the only happy woman in the world.'

'My dearest Elly!' said the kind voice. 'And you will never regret——And are you happy?'

'Can you ask?' said Elly. 'Come into the porch, and I will tell you.' And then there was a gust of fresh rain-scented air, and a soft rustle, and the closing click of a door. And then we saw them pass the window, and Jean clasped my hand very tightly, and flung her arms round my neck, and gave me a delighted kiss.

'You dear, silly woman,' said I, 'how glad I am they are so happy together.'

'I hope she won't catch cold,' said Jean, looking at the damp walks. 'Could not you take out a shawl?'

'Let her catch cold!' said I; 'and in the meantime give me some tea, if you please. Remember, I have got to drive home in the dark.'

So we went into the next room. Jean rang for the candles. The old silver candlesticks were brought in by Kitty on a tray.

'Don't shut the curtains,' said Miss Dampier; 'and come here, Mary, and sit by the fire.'

While Elizabeth and John Dampier were wandering up and down in the dark damp garden, Jenny and I were comfortably installed by the fire drinking hot, sweet tea, and eating toasted cakes, and preserves, and cream. I say *we,* but that is out of modesty, for she had no appetite, whereas I was very hungry.

'Heigho!' said Jean, looking at the fire. 'It's a good thing to be young, Mary. Tell me honestly: what would you give——'

'To be walking in the garden with young Dampier,' said I (and I burst out laughing), 'without a cloak, or an umbrella, or india-rubbers? My dear Jenny, where are your five wits?'

'Where indeed?' said Jean, with another sigh. 'Yet I can remember when you used to cry instead of laughing over such things, Mary.'

Her sadness had made me sad. Whilst the young folks were whispering outside, it seemed as if we two old women were sitting by the fire and croaking the elegy of all youth, and love, and happiness. 'The night is coming for you and me, Jenny,' I said. 'Dear me, how quickly.'

'The night is at hand,' echoed she softly, and she passed

her fingers across - her eyes, and then sighed, and got up slowly and went to the door which opened into the porch. And then I heard her call me. ' Come here ! ' she said, ' Mary ! ' And then I, too, rose stiffly from my chair, and went to her. The clouds had cleared away. From the little porch, where the sweetbriar was climbing, we could see all the myriad worlds of heaven, alight and blazing, and circling in their infinite tracks. An awful, silent harmony, power and peace, and light and life eternal—a shining benediction seemed to be there hanging above our heads. ' This is the night,' she whispered, and took my hand in hers.

And so this is the end of the story of Elizabeth Gilmour, whose troubles, as I have said, were not very great; who is a better woman, I fancy, than if her life had been the happy life she prophesied to herself. Deeper tones and understandings must have come to her out of the profoundness of her griefs, such as they were. For when other troubles came, as they come to all as years go by, she had learnt to endure and to care for others, and to be valiant and to be brave. And I do not like her the less because I have spoken the truth about her, and written of her as the woman she is.

I went to Paris a little time ago. I saw the old grass-grown court; I saw Françoise and Anthony, and Tou-Tou and Lou-Lou, who had grown up two pretty and modest and smiling young girls. The old lady at Asnières had done what was expected, and died and left her fortune to Tou-Tou, her god-daughter. (The little Chinese pagoda is still to let.) Poor Madame Jacob did not, however, enjoy this good luck, for she died suddenly one day, some months before it came to them. But you may be sure that the little girls had still a father in Tourneur, and Caroline too was very kind to them in her uncertain way. She loved them because they were so unlike herself—so gentle, and dull, and guileless. Anthony asked me a great many questions about Elizabeth and her home, and told me that he meant to marry Lou-Lou eventually. He is thin and pale, with a fine head like his father, and a quiet manner. He works very hard, he earns very little—he is one of the best men I ever knew in my life. As I talked to him, I could not but compare him to Will Dampier and to John, who are also good men. But then they are prosperous and well-to-do, with well-stored granaries, with vineyards and fig-trees, with children growing up round them. I was wondering if Elizabeth, who chose her husband because she loved him, and for no better reason, might not have been as wise if she could have appreciated the gifts better than happiness, than well-stored granaries, than vineyards, than fig-trees, which Anthony held in his hand to offer? Who shall say? Self-denial and holy living are better than ease and prosperity? But for that reason some people wilfully turn away from the mercies of Heaven, and call the angels devils, and its gracious bounties temptation.

Anthony has answered this question to himself as we all must do. His father looks old and worn. I fear there is trouble still under his roof—trouble, whatever it may be, which is borne with Christian and courageous resignation by the master of the house: he seems, somehow, in these later years to have risen beyond it. A noble reliance and peace are his; holy thoughts keep him company. The affection between him and his son is very touching.

Madame Tourneur looks haggard and weary; and one day, when I happened to tell her I was going away, she gasped out suddenly—'Ah! what would I not give——' and then was silent and turned aside. But she remains with her husband, which is more than I should have given her credit for.

And so when the appointed hour came, I drove off, and all the personages of my story came out to bid me farewell. I looked back for the last time at the courtyard with the hens pecketting round about the kitchen door; at the garden with the weeds and flowers tangling together in the sun; at the shadows falling across the stones of the yard. I could fancy Elizabeth a prisoner within those walls, beating like a bird against the bars of the cage, and revolting and struggling to be free.

The old house is done away with and exists no longer. It was pulled down by order of the Government, and a grand new boulevard runs right across the place where it stood.

OLD KENSINGTON

BY

MISS THACKERAY

'Nice place, isn't it?' said Ponto; 'quiet and unpretending'

SECOND EDITION

LONDON

SMITH, ELDER, & CO., 15 WATERLOO PLACE

1873

OLD KENSINGTON

MISS THACKERAY

By the Pollards.

T'is life whereof our nerves are scant,
Oh ! life, not death, for which we pant,
More life and fuller that I want.

ALFRED TENNYSON.

A DEDICATION

TO SOME NEW FRIENDS.

—•◇•—

SOMETIMES new friends meet one along the mid-way of life, and come forward with sweet unknown faces and with looks that seem strangely familiar to greet us.

To some of these new friends I must dedicate my story. It was begun ten years ago, and is older than my god-daughter Margie herself, who is the oldest among them. She is playing with her sister and her little cousins in the sunny Eton nurseries. Harry has a crown on. Annie is a queen who flies on errands. Ada and Lilly are Court ladies.

My neighbour Dolly and the little Dorotheas, however, have a first right to a presentation copy. It is true that the little ones cannot read, but they need not regret it; for Margie will take them on her knee and show them the pictures, and Georgie and Stella and Molly shall stand round too, and dark-eyed little Margaret can tell them her own sweet little stories, while Francis chimes in from the floor. Eleanor cannot talk, but she can sing; and so can our Laura at home, and her song is her own; a sweet home song; the song

of all children to those who love them.   It tells of the past, and
one day brings it back without a pang; it tells of a future, not
remorselessly strange and chill and unknown, but bound to us by a
thousand hopes and loving thoughts—a kingdom-come for us all,
not of strangers, but of little children.   And meanwhile Laura
measures the present with her soft little fingers as she beats time
upon her mother's hand to her own vague music.

8, SOUTHWELL GARDENS: *March* 20, 1873.

CONTENTS.

LIST OF ILLUSTRATIONS.

OLD KENSINGTON.

CHAPTER I.

BRICKS AND IVY.

From the ivy where it dapples
A grey ruin, stone by stone,
Do you look for grapes and apples,
Or for sad green leaves alone?
—E. B. Browning.

A QUARTER of a century ago the shabby tide of progress had
not spread to the quiet old suburb where Lady Sarah
Francis's house was standing, with its many windows dazzling
as the sun travelled across the old-fashioned housetops
to set into a distant sea of tenements and echoing life.
The roar did not reach the old house. The children could
listen to the cawing of the rooks, to the echo of the hours,
as they struck on from one day to another, vibrating from
the old square tower of the church. At night the strokes
seemed to ring more slowly than in the day. Little Dolly
Vanborough, Lady Sarah's niece, thought each special hour
had its voice. The church clock is silent now, but the
rooks caw on undisturbed from one spring to another in the
Old Kensington suburb. There are tranquil corners still, and
sunny silent nooks, and ivy wreaths growing in the western

B

sun; and jessamines and vine-trees, planted by a former
generation, spreading along the old garden-walls. But
every year the shabby stream of progress rises and engulfs
one relic or another, carrying off many and many a landmark
and memory. Last year only, the old church was standing,
in its iron cage, at the junction of the thoroughfares. It
was the Church of England itself to Dolly and George Vanborough in those early church-going days of theirs. There
was the old painting of the lion and the unicorn hanging
from the gallery; the light streaming through the brown
saints over the communion-table. In after-life the children
may have seen other saints more glorious in crimson and in
purple, nobler piles and arches, but none of them have ever
seemed so near to heaven as the old Queen Anne building;
and the wooden pew with its high stools, through which
elbows of straw were protruding, where they used to kneel
on either side of their aunt, watching with awe-stricken faces
the tears as they came falling from the widow's sad eyes.

Lady Sarah could scarcely have told you the meaning of
those tears as they fell—old love and life partings, sorrows
and past mercies, all came returning to her with the familiar
words of the prayers. The tears fell bright and awe-stricken
as she thought of the present—of distances immeasurable—
of life and its inconceivable mystery; and then her heart
would warm with hope perhaps of what might be to come,
of the overwhelming possibilities—how many of them to her
lay in the warm clasp of the child's hand that came pushing
into hers!—For her, as for the children, heaven's state was
in the old wooden pew. Then the sing-song of the hymn
would flood the old church with its homely cadence.

Prepare your glad voices;
Let Hisreal rejoice,

sang the little charity children ; poor little Israelites, with blue stockings, and funny woollen knobs to their fustian caps, rejoicing, though their pastures were not green as yet, nor was their land overflowing with milk and honey. However, they sang praises for others, as all people do at times, thanks be to the merciful dispensation that allows us to weep, to work, to be comforted, and to rejoice with one another's hearts, consciously or unconsciously, as long as life exists.

Every lane, and corner, and archway had a childish story for Dolly and her brother—for Dolly most especially, because girls cling more to the inanimate aspects of life than boys do. For Dolly the hawthorn bleeds as it is laid low and is transformed year after year into iron railings and areas, for particulars of which you are requested to apply to the railway company, and to Mr. Taylor, the house-agent. In those days the lanes spread to Fulham, white with blossom in spring, or golden with the yellow London sunsets that blazed beyond the cabbage-fields. In those days there were gardens, and trees, and great walls along the high-road that came from London, passing through the old white turnpike. There were high brown walls along Kensington Gardens, reaching to the Palace Gate ; elms spread their shade, and birds chirrupped, and children played behind them.

Dolly Vanborough and her brother had had many a game there, and knew every corner and haunt of this sylvan world of children and ducks and nursemaids. They had knocked their noses against the old sun-dial many and many a time. Sometimes now, as she comes walking along the straight avenues, Dolly thinks she can hear the echo of their own childish voices whooping and calling to one another as they used to do. How often they had played with their big cousin, Robert

Henley, and the little Morgans, round about the stately
orange-house, and made believe to be statues in the
niches!

'I am Apollo,' cries George Vanborough, throwing himself into an attitude.

'Apollo!' cries Robert, exploding with schoolboy wit:
'an Apollo-guy, you mean.'

Dolly does not understand why the Morgan boys laugh
and George blushes up furiously. When they are tired of
jumping about in the sun, the statues straggle homewards,
accompanied by Dolly's French governess, who has been
reading a novel on a bench close by. They pass along the
front of the old palace that stands blinking its sleepy windows across elmy vistas, or into tranquil courts where sentries
go pacing. Robert has his grandmother living in the
Palace, and he strides off across the court to her apartments.
The children think she is a witch, and always on the watch
for them, though they do not tell Robert so. The Morgans
turn up Old Street, and George and Dolly escort them
so far on their way home. It is a shabby street, with
shops at one end and old-fashioned houses, stone-stepped,
bow-windowed at the other. Dear Old Street! where an
echo still lingers of the quaint and stately music of the past,
of which the voice comes to us like a song of Mozart, sounding above the dreamy flutterings of a Wagner of the present!
Little Zoe Morgan would linger to peep at the parrot that
lived next door in the area, with the little page-boy, who
always winked at them as they went by; little Cassie would
glance wistfully at a certain shop-front where various medals
and crosses were exposed for sale. There were even in those
days convents and Catholics established at Kensington, and
this little repository had been opened for their use.

When they have seen the little Morgans safe into their old brown house—very often it is John Morgan who comes to the door to admit them—(John is the eldest son, the curate, the tutor, the mainstay of the straggling establishment)—Dolly and her brother trudge home through the Square, followed by Mademoiselle, still lost in her novel. The lilacs are flowering behind the rusty rails, the children know every flagstone and window; they turn up a passage of narrow doorways and wide-eaved roofs, and so get out into the high-road again. They look up with friendly recognition at the little boy and girl in their quaint Dutch garb standing on their pedestals above the crowd as it passes the Vestry-hall; then they turn down a sunshiny spring lane, where ivy is growing, and bricks are twinkling in the western sunshine; and they ring at a gateway where an iron bell is swung. The house is called Church House, and all its windows look upon gardens, along which the sunshine comes flowing. The light used to fill Dolly's slanting wooden school-room at the top of the house. When the bells were ringing, and the sun-flood came in and made shadows on the wall, it used to seem to her like a chapel full of music.

George wanted to make an altar one day, and to light Lady Sarah's toilet candles, and to burn the sandal-wood matches; but Dolly, who was a little Puritan, blew the matches out and carried the candles back to their places.

' I shall go over to the Morgans,' said George, ' since you are so disagreeable.'

Whether Dolly was agreeable or not, this was what George was pretty sure to do.

CHAPTER II.

DUTCH TILES.

O priceless art ! O princely state,
E'en while by sense of change opprest,
Within to antedate
Heaven's age of fearless rest.

—J. H. Newman.

There are many disconnected pictures in Dorothea Vanborough's gallery, drifting and following each other like the images of a dissolving-view. There are voices and faces changing, people whom she hardly knows to be the same appearing and disappearing. Looking back now-a-days through a score or two of years, Dorothea can see many lights crossing and reflecting one another, many strange places and persons in juxtaposition. She can hear, as we all can, a great clamour of words and of laughter, cries of pain and of sorrow and anger, through all of which sound the sacred voices that will utter to her through life—and beyond life she humbly prays.

Dorothea's pictures are but mist and fancy work, not made of paint and canvas as is that one which hangs over the fire-place in the wainscot dining-room at Church House in Kensington, where my heroine passed so much of her life. It is supposed by some to be a Van der Helst. It represents a golden brown grandmother, with a coiffe and a ruffle and a

grand chain round her neck, and a ring on her forefinger,
and a double-winged house in the background. This
placid-faced Dutchwoman, existing two centuries ago, has
some looks still living in the face of the Dorothea Vanborough of these days. Her descendants have changed their
name and their dress, cast away their ruffles, forgotten the
story of their early origin; but there is still a something that
tells of it: in Dolly's slow quaint grace and crumpled bronze
hair, in her brother George's black brows, in their aunt Lady
Sarah Francis's round brown eyes and big ears, to say nothing
of her store of blue Dutch china. Tall blue pots, with dragon
handles, are ranged in rows upon the chimney-board under
the picture. On either side of the flame below are blue
tiles, that Lady Sarah's husband brought over from the
Hague the year before he died. Abraham, Jonah, Noah,
Balaam tumbling off his blue ass; the whole sacred history is
there, lighted up by the flaring flame of the logs.

When first George and Dolly came to live in the old
house, then it was the pictures came to life. The ass began
to call out Balaam! Balaam! The animals to walk two by
two (all blue) into the ark. Jonah's whale swallowed and
disgorged him night after night, as George and Dolly sat at
their aunt's knee listening to her stories in the dusk of the
'children's hour;' and the vivid life that childhood strikes
even into inanimate things, awakened the widow's dull
heart and the silent house in the old by-lane in Kensington.

The lady over the fire-place had married in King Charles's
reign; she was Dorothea Vanborough and the first Countess
of Churchtown. Other countesses followed in due course, of
whom one or two were engraved in the passage overhead;
the last was a miniature in Lady Sarah's own room, her
mother and my heroine's grandmother; a beautiful and

wilful person, who had grievously offended by taking a
second husband soon after her lord's demise in 1806.
This second husband was himself a member of the Vanborough family, a certain Colonel Stanham Vanborough,
a descendant of the lady over the chimney-piece. He was
afterwards killed in the Peninsula. Lady Sarah bitterly
resented her mother's marriage, and once said she would
never forgive it. It was herself that she never forgave for
her own unforgiveness. She was a generous-hearted woman,
fantastic, impressionable, reserved. When her mother died
soon after Colonel Vanborough, it was to her own home that
Lady Sarah brought her little step-brother, now left friendless, and justly ignored by the peerage, where the elder
sister's own life was concisely detailed as ' dau. John Vanborough, last Earl of Churchtown, b. 1790, m. 1807, to
Darby Francis, Esq., of Church House, Kensington.'

Young Stanham Vanborough found but a cold welcome
from Mr. Francis, but much faithful care and affection,
lavished, not without remorse, by the sister who had been so
long estranged. The boy grew up in time, and went out
into the world, and became a soldier as his father had
been. He was a simple, straightforward youth, very fond
of his sister, and loth to leave her, but very glad to be
his own master at last. He married in India, the daughter
of a Yorkshire baronet, a pretty young lady, who had
come out to keep her brother's house. Her name was
Philippa Henley, and her fortune consisted chiefly in golden
hair and two pearly rows of teeth. The marriage was not
so happy as it might have been ; trouble came, children
died, the poor parents, in fear and trembling, sent their one
little boy home to Lady Sarah to save his life. And then,
some three years later, their little daughter Dolly was making

her way, a young traveller by land and by sea coming from
the distant Indian station, where she had been born, to
the shelter of the old house in the old by-lane in Kensington. The children found the door open wide and
the lonely woman on her threshold looking out for them.
Mr. Francis was dead, and it was an empty house by this
time, out of which a whole home had passed away.
Lady Sarah's troubles were over, leaving little behind; the
silence of mid-life had succeeded to the loving turmoils and
jealousies and anxieties of earlier days, only some memories
remained of which the very tears and words seem wanting
now and then, although other people may have thought
that if words failed the widow, the silent deeds were there
that should belong to all past affection.

One of the first things Dolly remembers is a landing-
place one bitter east-winded morning, with the white blast
blowing dry and fierce from the land, and swirling out to
sea through the leafless forest of shipping; the squalid
houses fast closed and double-locked upon their sleeping
inmates: the sudden storms of dust and wind; the distant
clanking of some awakening pail, and the bewildered ayah,
in her rings and bangles, squatting on the ground and
veiling her face in white muslin.

By the side of the ayah stands my heroine, a little puppy-
like girl, staring as Indian children stare, at the strange
dismal shores upon which they are cast; staring at the lady
in the grey cloak, who had come on board with her
papa's face, and caught her in her arms, and who is her
Aunt Sarah; at the big boy of seven in the red mittens,
whose photograph her papa had shown her in the veran-
dah, and who is her brother George; at the luggage as
it comes bumping and stumbling off the big ship; at

the passengers departing. The stout little gentleman, who used to take her to see the chickens, pats Dolly on the head, and says he shall come and see her; the friendly sailor who carried her on shore shakes hands, and then the clouds close in, and the sounds and the faces disappear. . . .

Presently, into Dolly's gallery come pleasanter visions of the old house at Kensington, to which Lady Sarah took her straight away, with its brick wall, and ivy creepers, and many-paned windows, and the stone balls at either side of the door—on one of which a little dark-eyed girl is sitting, expecting them.

'Who is dat?' says little three-year-old Dolly, running up, and pulling the child's pinafore, to make sure that she is *real.*

Children believe in many things, in fairies, and sudden disappearances; they would not think it very strange if they were to see people turn to fountains and dragons in the course of conversation.

'That is a nice little girl like you,' said Lady Sarah, kindly.

'A nice little girl lite me?' said Dolly.

'Go away,' says the little strange girl, hiding her face in her hands.

'Have you come to play wiss me? My name is Dolliciavanble,' continues Dolly, who is not shy, and quite used to the world, having travelled so far.

'Is that your name? What a funny name,' says the little girl, looking up. 'My name is Rhoda, but they call me Dody at our house. I'se four years old.'

Dolly was three years old, but she could not speak quite plain; she took the little girl's hand and stood by the ayah, watching the people passing and repassing, the carriage being unpacked, Lady Sarah directing and giving people money, George stumping about in everybody's way, and then, somehow, everything and everybody seems going up and down stairs, and in confusion; she is very tired and sleepy, and forgets all the rest.

Next day Dolly wakes up crying for her papa. It is not the ship any more. Everything is quite still, and her crib does not rock up and down. ' I sought he would be here,' said poor little Dolly, in a croaking, waking voice, sitting up with crumpled curls and bright warm cheeks. It is not her papa, but Aunt Sarah, who takes her up and kisses her, and tries to comfort her, while the ayah, Nun Comee, who has been lying on the floor, jumps up and dances in her flowing white garment and snaps her black fingers, and George brings three tops to spin all at once. Dolly is interested, and ceases crying and begins to smile and to show all her little white teeth.

Lady Sarah rarely smiled. She used to frown so as not to show what she felt. But Dolly from the first day had seemed to understand her ; she was never afraid of her ; and she used to jump on her knee and make her welcome to the nursery.

' *Is* you very pretty ? ' said little Dolly one day, looking at the grim face with the long nose and pinched lips. ' I think you is a very ugly aunt.' And she smiled up in the ugly aunt's face.

' O Dolly! how naughty ! ' said Rhoda, who happened to be in Dolly's nursery.

Rhoda was a little waif *protégée* of Lady Sarah's. She came from the curate's home close by, and was often sent in to play with Dolly, who would be lonely, her aunt thought, without a companion of her own age ; Rhoda was Mr. Mor-

gan's niece, and a timid little thing; she was very much
afraid at first of Dolly; so she was of the ayah, with her
brown face and earrings and monkey hands; but soon the
ayah went back to India with silver pins in her ears, taking
back many messages to the poor child-bereft parents, with a
pair of Dolly's shoes, as a remembrance, and a couple of
dolls for herself as a token of good-will from her young
mistress. They were for her brothers, Nun Comee said, but
it was supposed that she intended to worship them on her
return to her native land.

The ayah being gone, little Rhoda soon ceased to be
afraid of Dolly, the kind, merry, helpful little playmate, who
remained behind, frisking along the passages and up and
down the landing-places of Church House. She was much
nicer, Rhoda thought, than her own real cousins the
Morgans in Old Street.

As days go by, Dolly's pictures warm and brighten from
early spring into summer-time. By degrees they reach
above the table and over and beyond the garden roller.
They are chiefly of the old garden, whose brick walls seem
to enclose sunshine and gaudy flowers all the summer
through; of the great Kensington parks, where in due
season chestnuts are to be found shining among the
leaves and dry grasses; of the pond, where the ducks are
flapping and diving; of the house, which was little Rhoda's
home. This was the great bare house in Old Street, with
plenty of noise, dried herbs, content, children without end,
and thick bread-and-butter. There was also cold stalled
ox on Sundays at one.

In those days life was a simple matter to the children;
their days and their legs lengthened together; they loved,
they learned, and they looked for a time that was never to

be—when their father and mother should come home and live with them again, and everybody was to be happy. As yet the children thought they were only expecting happiness.

George went to school at Frant, near Tunbridge Wells, and came home for the holidays. Dolly had a governess too, and she used to do her lessons with little Rhoda in the slanting schoolroom at the top of Church House. The little girls did a great many sums, and learnt some French, and read little Arthur's *History of England* to everybody's satisfaction.

Kind Lady Sarah wrote careful records of the children's progress to her brother, who had sent them to the faithful old sister at home. He heard of the two growing up with good care and much love in the sunshine that streamed upon the old garden; playing together on the terrace that he remembered so well; pulling up the crocuses and the violets that grew in the shade of the white holly-tree. George was a quaint, clever boy, Sarah wrote; Dolly was not so quick, but happy and obedient, and growing up like a little spring flower among the silent old bricks.

Lady Sarah also kept up a desultory correspondence with Philippa, her sister-in-law. Mrs. Vanborough sent many minute directions about the children; Dolly was to dine off cold meat for her complexion's sake, and she wished her to have her hair crimped; and George was to wear kid-gloves and write a better hand; and she hoped they were very good, and that they sometimes saw their cousin Robert, and wrote to their uncle, Sir Thomas Henley, Henley Court, Smokethwaite, Yorkshire: and she and dear papa often and often longed for their darlings. Then came presents—a spangled dress for Lady Sarah, and silver ornaments for Dolly, and an Indian sword for George, with which he nearly cut off Rhoda's head.

CHAPTER III.

And after April when May follows,
And the white-throat builds, and all the swallows,
. . And buttercups the little children's dower.
                                        —R. BROWNING.

IN those days, as I have said, the hawthorn spread across the
fields and market-gardens that lay between Kensington and
the river. Lanes ran to Chelsea, to Fulham, to North
End, where Richardson once lived and wrote in his garden-house. The mist of the great city hid the horizon and
dulled the sound of the advancing multitudes; but close at
hand, all round about the old house, were country corners
untouched—blossoms instead of bricks in spring-time, summer shade in summer. There were strawberry-beds, green,
white, and crimson in turn. The children used to get many
a handful of strawberries from Mr. Penfold, the market-
gardener at the end of the lane, and bunches of radish when
strawberries were scarce. They gathered them for themselves on a bank where paving-stones and coal-holes are
now and a fine growth of respectable modern villas. I
believe that in those days there were sheep grazing in
Kensington Gore. It is certain that Mr. Penfold kept Al-
derneys in the field beyond his orchard; and that they used

to come and drink in a pond near his cottage. He lived with his wife and his daughter, under an old tiled roof, and with a rose-tree growing on the wall. In the window of the cottage a little card was put up, announcing that " Curds-and-whey were to be had within," and the children some-times went there to drink the compound out of Emma Pen-fold's doll's tea-things. The old pond was at the garden-gate: there was a hedge round about it, and alder-trees starting up against the sunset, and the lanes, and orchards beyond. The water reflected the sunset in the sky and the birds flying home to the sound of the evening bells. Sometimes Emma would come out of the cottage, and stand watching the children play. She was a pretty girl, with rosy cheeks and dark soft eyes. It was a quaint old corner, lonely enough in the daytime ; but of evenings, people would be passing—labourers from their work, strollers in the fields, neighbours enjoying the air. The cot-tage must have been as old as Church House itself. It was chiefly remarkable for its beautiful damask rose-trees, of which the red leaves sprinkled the threshold, across which pretty Emma Penfold would step. I think it was for the sake of the rose-tree that people sometimes stopped and asked for curds-and-whey. Emma would dispense the hor-rible mixture, blushing beneath her basket-work plaits.

Sometimes in May mornings the children would gather hawthorn branches out of the lanes, and make what they liked to call garlands for themselves. The white blossoms looked pretty in Rhoda's dark hair ; and Mademoiselle, coming to give them their music-lesson, would find the little girls crowned with May-flower wreaths. It was hard work settling down to lessons on those days. How slowly the clocks ticked when the practice hour began ; how the little

birds would come hopping on the window-ledge, before Dolly
had half finished her sum ; how cruel it was of Mademoiselle
to pull down the blind and frighten the poor little birds
away. Many pictures in Dolly's gallery belong to this bit of
her life. It seems one long day as she looks back to it, for
when the sun set Dolly too used to be put to bed.

As for little Rhoda she would be sent back to Old Street.
When prayers were over, long after Dolly was asleep, she
would creep upstairs alone to the very top of the house, and
put herself to bed and blow out her own candle if Zoe did
not come for it. How bare and chill and lonely it was to be
all by oneself at the top of that busy house ! 'I don't think
they would come, even if I screamed,' Rhoda would think
as she lay staring at the cupboard-door, and wondering if
there was any one behind it.

Once the door burst open and a great cat jumped out, and
Rhoda's shriek brought up one of John Morgan's pupils, who
had been reading in his room.

'Is anything the matter ? ' said the young man at the
door.

'Oh, no, no—o ! Please don't say I screamed ? ' said
little Rhoda, disappearing under the bed-clothes.

'Silly child ! ' (This was Aunt Morgan's voice in the
passage.) 'Thank you, Mr. Raban, I will go to her. A
little girl of ten years old frightened at a cat ! For shame,
Rhoda ! There—go to sleep directly,' and her Aunt Morgan
vigorously tucked her up and gave her a kiss.

The Morgans were a cheerful and noisy household ; little
Rhoda lived there, but she scarcely seemed to belong to it :
she was like a little stray waif born into some strange nest full
of active, early, chirping birds, all bigger and stronger than
herself. The Rev. John Morgan was master of the nest,

which his step-mother kept in excellent order and ruled with
an active rod. There were two pupils, two younger brothers,
two sisters, and Rhoda Parnell, the forlorn little niece they
had adopted. Downstairs the fat parlour-maid and the old
country cook were established, and a succeeding generation
of little charity-boys, who were expected by Mrs. Morgan to
work in the garden, go errands, and learn their catechisms,
while blacking the young gentlemen's boots in a vault-like
chamber set apart for that purpose.

Mrs. Morgan was a thrifty woman, and could not bear to
think of time or space being wasted, much less comestibles.
Her life had been one long course of early rising, moral and
physical rectitude. She allowed John to sit in an arm-chair,
but no one else if she could help it. When poor little Rhoda
was tired, she used to go up to the room she shared with
Zoe, her youngest cousin, and lie down on the floor. If Zoe
told her mother, a message would come immediately for
Rhoda to help with the poor flannel.

This poor flannel was Mrs. Morgan's own kingdom. She
used to preside over passive rolls of grey and blue. She
could cut out any known garment in use in any civilized
community. She knew the right side of the stuff, the right
way to turn the scissors. She could contrive, direct, turn
corners, snip, snap on occasions, talking the whole time ; she
was emphatic always. In her moments of relaxation she
dearly loved a whisper. She wore a front of curls with a
velvet band and Kensington-made gowns and shoes. Cassie
and Zoe, when they grew up to be young ladies, used to
struggle hard for Knightsbridge fashions. The Kensington
style was prim in those days. The ladies wore a dress somewhat peculiar to themselves and cut to one pattern by the
Misses Trix in their corner house. There was a Kensington

world (I am writing of twenty years ago) somewhat apart
from the big uneasy world surging beyond the turnpike—a
world of neighbours bound together by the old winding
streets and narrow corners in a community of vener-
able elm-trees and traditions that are almost levelled
away. Mr. Awl, the bootmaker, in High Street, exhibited
peculiar walking-shoes long after high-heels and kid brode-
kins had come into fashion in the metropolis. The last time
I was in his shop I saw a pair of the old-fashioned, flat,
sandalled shoes, directed to Miss Vieuxtemps, in Palace
Green. Tippets, poke-bonnets, even a sedan-chair, still
existed among us long after they had been discarded by
more active minds. In Dolly's early days, in Kensington
Square itself, high-heels and hoops were not unknown ; but
these belonged to ladies of some pretension, who would come
in state along the narrow street leading from the Square,
advancing in powder, and hoops, and high-heeled shoes—
real hoops, real heels, not modern imitations, but relics
unchanged since the youth of the ghost-like old sisters.
They lived in a tall house, with a mansard roof. As the
children passed they used to look up at the cobweb-windows,
at the narrow doorway with its oaken daïs, and the flagged
court and the worn steps. Lady Sarah told Dolly that Mrs.
Francis had known Talleyrand, when he was living there in
one of the old houses of the Square. At any time it would
be easy to conjure up ghosts of great people with such in-
cantations of crumbling wall and oaken device and panel.
Not Talleyrand only, but a whole past generation, still lives
for us among these quaint old ruins.

The Kensington tradespeople used to be Conservative, as
was natural, with a sentry in the High Street, and such a
ménagerie of lions and unicorns as that which they kept

over their shop-fronts. They always conversed with their customers while they measured a yard of silk or sold a skein of thread across their counters. Dolly would feel flattered when Mr. Baize found her grown. Even Lady Sarah would graciously reply to his respectful inquiries after her health on the rare occasions when she shopped herself. Mrs. Morgan never trusted anybody with her shopping.

'*I* always talk to Baize,' she would say, complacently, coming away after half-an-hour's exchange of ideas with that respectable man. She would repeat his conversation for the benefit of her son and his pupils at tea-time. 'I think tradespeople are often very sensible and well-informed persons,' said Mrs. Morgan, 'when they do not forget themselves, Mr. Raban. Radical as you are, you must allow that Kensington tradespeople are always respectful to the clergy— our position is too well established; they know what is due to us,' said Mrs. Morgan gravely.

'They don't forget what is due to themselves,' said Mr. Raban, with an odd sort of smile.

'That they don't,' said Robert Henley, who was Morgan's other pupil at that time. 'I daresay Master George wishes they would; he owes a terrible long bill at Baize's for ties and kid-gloves.'

Presently came a ring at the bell. 'Here he is,' cries John, starting up hastily. 'No more tea, thank you, mother.'

George Vanborough used also to read with John Morgan during the holidays. The curate's energy was unfailing; he slaved, taught, panted, and struggled for the family he had shouldered. What a good fellow he was! Pack clouds away, no shades or evil things should come near him as he worked; who ever piped to him that he did not leap, or call

to him that he did not shout in answer. With what
emphasis he preached his dull Sunday sermon, with what
excitement he would to his admiring sisters and mother read
out his impossible articles in the *Vestryman's Magazine* or
elsewhere, how liberally he dashed and italicised his sentences, how gallantly he would fly to his pen or his pulpit in
defence of friend or in attack of foe (the former being flesh
and blood, and the latter chiefly spiritual). And then he
was in love with a widow—how he admired her blue and
pink eyes ; he could not think of marrying until the boys
were out in the world and the girls provided for. But with
Joe's wit and Tom's extraordinary powers, and the girls'
remarkable amiability, all this would surely be settled in the
course of a very short time.

The Morgan family was certainly a most united and
affectionate clan. I don't know that they loved each other
more than many people do, but they certainly believed in
each other more fervently. They had a strange and special
fascination for George, who was not too young to appreciate
the curate's unselfishness.

The younger Morgans, who were a hearty, jolly race, used
to laugh at George. Poor boy, he had already begun to
knock his head, young as it was, against stone walls ; his
schoolfellows said he had cracked it with his paradoxes. At
twelve he was a stout fellow for his age, looking older than
he really was. He was slow and clumsy, he had a sallow
complexion, winking blue eyes, a turn-up nose, and heavy
dark eyebrows ; there was something honest and almost
pathetic at times in the glance of these blue eyes, but he
usually kept them down from shyness as well as from vanity,
he didn't dare look in people's faces, he thought he should
see them laughing at him. He was very lazy, as sensitive

people often are; he hated games and active amusements;
he had a soft melancholy voice that was his one endowment,
besides his gift for music; he could work when he chose, but
he was beginning life in despair with it, and he was not
popular among his companions; they called him conceited,
and they were right; but it was a melancholy conceit, if they
had but known it. The truth was, however, that he was too
ugly, too clever, too clumsy to get on with boys of a simpler
and wholesomer mind. Even John Morgan, his friend and
preceptor, used to be puzzled about him and distressed at
times. 'If George Vanborough were only more like his own
brothers, there would be something to be done with him,'
thought honest John as those young gentlemen's bullet-heads
passed the window where the pupil and his preceptor were at
work. If only—there would be a strange monotony in
human nature, I fancy, if all the 'if onlys' could be realised,
and we had the moulding of one another, and pastors and
masters could turn assenting pupils out by the gross like the
little chalk rabbits Italian boys carry about for sale.

Dolly was very well contented with her brother just as he
was. She trusted his affection, respected his cleverness, and
instinctively guessed at his vanities and morbidities. Even
when she was quite a child, Dolly, in her sweet downright
way, seemed to have the gift of healing the wounds of her
poor St. Sebastian, who, when he was a little boy, would
come home day after day smarting and bleeding with the
arrows of his tormentors. These used to be, alternately,
Lady Sarah herself, Cassie Morgan, and Zoe, the two boys
when they were at home for the holidays, and little Rhoda,
whom he declared to be the most malicious of them all.
The person who treated George with most sympathy and
confidence was Mrs. Morgan, that active and garrulous old

lady, to whom anybody was dear who would listen to the praises of her children.

Robert Henley, as I have said, was also studying with John Morgan. He had just left Eton. Lady Sarah asked him to Church House at her sister-in-law's request; but he did not often find time to come and see them. He used to be tramping off to Putney, where he and his friend Frank Raban kept a boat; or they would be locked up together with ink and blots and paper in John Morgan's study. Raban was older than Henley. He was at College, but he had come up for a time to read for his degree.

Old Betty, the cook at John Morgan's, was a Yorkshire woman, and she took a motherly interest in the pupils. She had much to say about young Mr. Raban, whose relations she knew in Yorkshire. Betty used to call Frank Raban 'a noist young man.'

'He's Squoire's hair and grandsun loike,' she told Rhoda and Dolly one day. 'They cannot do n' less nor roast a hox when 'a cooms t' hage.'

After this Rhoda used to stand on tiptoe and respectfully peep through the study window at the heads and the books and the tobacco-smoke within; but there was a big table in the way, and she could never see much more than her own nose reflected in the glass. Once or twice, when George was in the way, as a great favour he would be allowed to accompany the young men in one of their long expeditions in big boots. They would come home late in the evening, tired and hungry and calling out for food. At whatever hour they came old Betty had a meal of cold meat and cake for them, of which George partook with good appetite. At Church House, if George was late for dinner he had to wait for tea and thin bread-and-butter at eight o'clock. Lady

Sarah, who had fought many a battle for George's father, now—from some curious retrospective feeling—seemed to feel it her duty to revive many of her late husband's peculiarities, and one of them was that nothing was to be allowed to interfere with the routine of the house. Routine there was none at the curate's, although there were more hours, perhaps, than in any other house in Old Street. The sun rose and set, the seasons drifted through the back garden in changing tints and lights, each day brought its burden, and the dinner-time was shifted to it.

CHAPTER IV.

AN AFTERNOON AT PENFOLD'S.

Whilst yet the calm hours creep,
   Whilst flowers are gay,
Whilst eyes that change ere night
   Make glad the day,
Whilst yet the calm hours creep,
Dream thou, and from thy sleep
Then wake to weep.

To this day Dolly remembers the light of a certain afternoon in May when all was hot and silent and sleepy in the
school-room at Church House. The boards cracked, the
dust-moats floated ; down below, the garden burnt with that
first summer glow of heat that makes a new world out of
such old, well-worn materials as twigs, clouds, birds, and the
human beings all round us. The little girls had been at
work, and practised, and multiplied, and divided again ;
they had recollected various facts connected with the reign
of Richard the Second. Mademoiselle had suppressed many
a yawn, Dolly was droning over her sum—six and five made
thirteen—over and over again. 'That I should have been,
that thou shouldst have been, that he shouldst have been,'
drawled poor little Rhoda. Then a great fly hums by, as the
door opens, and Lady Sarah appears with a zigzag of sunlight shooting in from the passage—a ray of hope. Lady

Sarah has her bonnet on, and a sort of put-away-your-lessons-children face.

Is there any happiness like that escape on a summer's day from the dull struggle with vacuity, brown paper-covered books, dates, ink-blots, cramps, and crotchets, into the open air of birds, sounds, flowers, liberty everywhere? As the children come out into the garden with Lady Sarah, two butterflies are flitting along the terrace. The Spanish jessamine has flowered in the night, and spreads its branches out fragrant with its golden drops. Lady Sarah gathers a sprig and opens her parasol. She is carrying a book and a shawl, and is actually smiling. The pigeons go whirring up and down from their pigeon-cote high up in the air. Four o'clock comes sounding across the ivy-wall, the notes strike mellow and distinct above the hum of human insects out and about. Half Lady Sarah's district is sunning itself on the door-steps, children are squatting in the middle of the road. The benches are full in Kensington Gardens, so are the steamers on the river. To these people walking in their garden there comes the creaking sound of a large wheel-barrow, and at the turn of the path they discover Mr. Penfold superintending a boy and a load of gravel. Mr. Penfold is a cheerful little man, with gloomy views of human nature. According to Penfold's account there were those (whoever they might be) who was always a plotting against you. They was hup to everything, and there was no saying what they was not at the bottom of. But Penfold could be heven with them, and he kep' hisself to hisself, and named no names. Dolly felt grateful to these unknown beings when she heard Mr. Penfold telling Lady Sarah they had said as how that Miss Dorothea 'ad been makin' hinquiry respectin' of some puppies. He did not know as how she wished it generally know'd, but he might mention as he 'ad two nice pups down at his place, and Miss Dorothea was welcome to take her choice.

It is a dream Dolly can scarcely trust herself to contemplate. Lady Sarah does not say no, but she looks at her watch, telling Dolly to run back to the house, and see if the post is come in, and continues graciously, 'I am much obliged to you, Penfold; I have no doubt Miss Dorothea will be glad to have one of your puppies. What is your daughter doing? Is she at home?'

'Yes, my lady,' says Penfold, mysteriously pointing over his shoulder with his thumb. 'They would have 'ad us send the gurl away, but she is a good gurl, though she takes her own way, and there are those as puts her hup to it.'

'We all like our own way, without anybody's suggestions,' said Lady Sarah, smiling. Then Dolly comes flying from the house, and tumbles over a broom-stick, so that she has to stop to pick up her handful of letters.

'Thank you, my dear: now if you like we will go and see the puppies,' says Aunt Sarah. 'No Indian letter' (in a disappointed voice). 'I wish your mother would ——. Run on, Dolly.'

So Dolly runs on with Rhoda, thinking of puppies, and Lady Sarah follows thinking of her Indian letter, which is lying under the laurel-tree where Dolly dropped it, and where Penfold presently spies it out and picks it up, unconscious of its contents. After examining the seal and some serious thought, he determines to follow the trio. They have been advancing in the shadow of the hedges, through the gaps of which they can see people at work in the sunshiny cabbage-fields. Then they come to Earl's Court, and its quaint old row of houses, with their lattices stuffed with spring-flowers, and so to the pond by the road-side (how cool and deep it looked as they passed by), and then by the wicket-gate they wander into Penfold's orchard, of which some of the trees are still in flower, and where Lady Sarah is soon established on the stump of a tree. Her magazine pages flutter as the warm, sweet winds come blowing from across the fields—the shadows travel on so quietly that you cannot tell when they go or whither. There is no sound but a little calf bleating somewhere. Rhoda is picking daisies in the shade, Dolly is chirping to herself by the hedge that separates the orchard from the Penfolds' garden. There is a ditch along one part of the hedge, with a tangle of grass and dock-leaves and mallows; a bird flies out of the hedge, close by Dolly's nose, and goes thrilling and chirping up into the sky, where the stars are at night; the daisies and butter-cups look so big, the grass is so long and so green; there are two purple flowers with long stalks close at hand, but Dolly does not pick them; her little heart seems to shake like the bird's song, it is all so pretty; the dandelions are like lamps burning. She tries to think she is a bird, and that she lives in the beautiful hedges.

From behind the hawthorn hedge some voices come that Dolly should certainly know. . . .

'You'll believe me another time,' cries some one, with a sort of sniff, and speaking in tones so familiar that Dolly, without an instant's hesitation, sets off running to the wicket-gate, which had been left open, and through which she now sees, as she expects, George with his curly head and his cricketing cap standing in the Penfolds' garden, and with him her cousin Robert, looking very tall as he leans against a paling, and talks to Mrs. Penfold. There is also another person whom Dolly recognises as Mr. Raban, and she thinks

of the 'hox,' as she gazes with respect at the pale young
man with his watch-chain and horseshoe pin. He has a
straw hat and white shoes and a big knobstick in his hand,
and nodding to Robert, he strides off towards the cottage.
Dolly watches him as he walks in under the porch : no doubt
he is going to drink curds and whey, she thinks.

'Why, Dolly! are *you* here?' says Robert, coming
towards her.

'Missy is often here,' says Mrs. Penfold, looking not
over-pleased. 'Is Mrs. Marker with you, my dear?'

Dolly would have answered, but from the farther end of
the garden behind Mrs. Penfold, two horrible apparitions
advance, rusty black, with many red bobs and tassels
dangling, and deliberate steps and horrible crinkly eyes.
Old Betty would call them Bubbly Jocks; Dolly has no
name for them, but shrinks away behind her big cousin.

'Here are Dolly's bogies,' says George, who is giving himself airs on the strength of his companionship and his short
cut. 'Now then, Dolly, they are going to bite like ghosts.'

'Don't,' cried Dolly.

'Are you afraid of turkeys, Dolly! Little girls of
eight years old shouldn't be afraid of anything,' said Rhoda,
busy with her flowers. Alas! Rhoda's philosophy is not
always justified by subsequent experience. It is second-
hand, and quoted from Mrs. Morgan.

'We are going to see the puppies,' says Dolly, recovering
her courage as the turkey-cocks go by. 'Won't you come,
Robert?'

'Puppies!' said Robert. 'Are you fond of puppies,
Dolly? My Aunt Henley says she prefers them to her own
children.'

'So should I,' says Dolly, opening her eyes.

DOLLY VANBOROUGH.

Presently Robert and Dolly come back, with two little fuzzy heads wildly squeaking from Dolly's lap, and old Bunch, the mother of the twins, following, half-agonised, half-radiant. They set the little staggering bundles down upon the ground, and Dolly squats in admiration while Robert goes off upon his business, and Mrs. Penfold hurries back into the house as Mr. Penfold appears crossing the lane.

Mr. Penfold was gone: Dolly was still watching with all-absorbed eyes, when George started up. 'I say, Dolly! look there at Aunt Sarah.'

Aunt Sarah! What had come to her, and how strange she looked walking through the orchard with a curious rapid step, and coming towards the open wicket-gate, through which the children could see her. Her bonnet was falling off her face, her hair was pushed back, she came very quick, straight on, looking neither to the right nor to the left, with her fixed eyes and pale cheeks. Penfold seemed hurrying after her; he followed Lady Sarah into the garden, and then out again into the road. She hardly seemed to know which way she went.

What had happened? Why didn't she answer when Dolly called her? As she passed so swiftly, the children thought that something must have happened; they did not know what. George set off running after her; Dolly waited for a minute.

'Why did she look so funny?' said Rhoda, coming up.

'I don't know,' said Dolly, almost crying.

'She had a black-edged letter in her hand,' said Rhoda, 'that Mr. Penfold brought. When people think they are going to die they write and tell you on black paper.'

Then Mrs. Penfold came running out of the cottage with a shriek, and the children running too, saw the gardener catch Aunt Sarah in his arms, as she staggered and put out her hands. When they came up, she lay back in his arms scarce conscious, and he called to them to bring some water from the pond. No wonder Dolly remembered that day, and Aunt Sarah lying long and straight upon the grass by the road-side. The letter had fallen from her hand, they threw water upon her face; it wetted her muslin dress, and her pale cheeks; a workman crossing from the field, stood and looked on awhile; and so did the little children from the carpenter's shed up the road, gazing with wondering eyes at the pale lady beginning to move again at last and to speak so languidly.

The labourer helped to carry her into the cottage as she revived. George had already run home for Marker. Dolly and Rhoda, who were shut out by Mrs. Penfold, wandered disconsolately about the garden and into the orchard again, where Aunt Sarah's parasol was lying under the tree, and her book thrown face downwards: presently the little girls came straggling back with it to the garden-house once more.

The parlour door was shut close when they reached it, the kitchen door was open. What was that shrill shivering cry? Who could it be? Perhaps it was some animal, thought Dolly.

In the kitchen some unheeded pot was cooking and boiling over; the afternoon sun was all hot upon the road outside, and Bunch and the puppies had lain down to sleep in a little heap on the step of the house.

Long, long after, Dolly remembered that day, everything as it happened: Marker's voice inside the room; young Mr.

Raban passing by the end of the lane talking to Emma Penfold. (Mrs. Penfold had unlocked the back-door, and let them out.) After a time the shrill sobs ceased ; then a clock struck, and the boiling pot in the kitchen fell over with a great crash, and Rhoda ran to see, and at that moment the parlour door opened, and Lady Sarah came out, very pale still and very strange, leaning; just as if she was old, upon Marker and Mr. Penfold. But she started away and seemed to find a sudden strength, and caught Dolly up in her arms. 'My darling, my darling,' she said, 'you have only me now—only me. Heaven help you, my poor, poor children.' And once more she burst into the shrill sighing sobs. It was Aunt Sarah who had been crying all the time for her brother who was dead.

This was the first echo of a mourning outcry that reached the children. They were told that the day was never to come now of which they had spoken so often; their father would never come home—they were orphans. George was to have a tall hat with crape upon it. Marker went into town to buy Dolly stuff for a new black frock. Aunt Sarah did not smile when she spoke to them, and told them that their mamma would soon be home now. Dolly could not understand it all very well. Their father had been but a remembrance ; she did not remember him less because Lady Sarah's eyes were red and the letters were edged with black. Dolly didn't cry the first day, though Rhoda did ; but in the night when she woke up with a little start and a moan from a dream in which she thought it was her papa who was lying by the pond, Aunt Sarah herself came and bent over her crib.

But next morning the daisies did not look less pretty, nor did the puppy cease to jump, nor, if the truth be told, did Dolly herself; nor would kind Stanham Vanborough have wished it. . . .

Robert came into the garden and found the children with a skipping-rope, and was greatly shocked, and told them they should not skip about.

'I was not skipping,' said Rhoda. 'I was turning the rope for Dolly.'

Dolly ran off, blushing. Had she done wrong? She had not thought so. I cannot say what dim unrealised feelings were in her little heart; longings never to be realised, love never to be fulfilled. She went up into her nursery, and hid there in a corner until Rhoda came to find her, and to tell her dinner was ready.

CHAPTER V.

STEEL PENS AND GOOSE QUILLS.

> Virtue, how frail it is,
> Friendship too rare;
> Love, how it sells poor bliss
> For proud despair.

THE letter announcing poor Stanham's death came from a Captain Palmer, a friend of Stan's, whose ship was stationed somewhere in that latitude, and who happened to have been with him at the time. They had been out boar-hunting in the marshes near Calcutta. The poor Major's illness was but a short one, produced by sunstroke, so the Captain wrote. His affairs were in perfect order. He had been handsomely noticed in the Bengal *Hurkaru*. Of his spiritual state Captain Palmer felt less able to speak. Although not a professed Christian, poor Stanham had for some time past attended the services of the Scotch chapel at Dum Dum, where Mr. McFlaggit had been permitted to awaken many sleepers to a deep sense of spiritual unrest. Captain Palmer believed that Major Vanborough had insured his life for 2,000*l.*, and the widow and children would also be entitled to something from the regimental fund. Captain Palmer then went on to say that he had been attending another deathbed, that of a native gentleman, whose wives and

D

orphan children having been left unprovided for, had been happily brought to see the past errors of their faith and had come forward in a body. They were about to be sent to England under the charge of Miss M'Grudder, who had done so much good work among the Zenanas. Captain Palmer wound up by a friendly offer of assistance and a message from Mrs. Vanborough. She did not feel equal to writing, she was utterly prostrate. She sent fondest love, and would write by the next mail.

So this was the children's first taste of the fruit of the tree of life and death growing in that garden of Eden and childhood through which we all come wandering into life, a garden blooming still,—it may be, in the square before the house,—where little Adams and Eves still sport, innocent and uncareful for the future, gathering the fruits as they ripen in the sunshine, hearing voices and seeing their childish visions, naming the animals as a new creation passes before them.

Lady Sarah longed to get away when her first burst of grief was over. The sleepy, drowsy old place seemed to stifle her with its calm content and sunny indifference. But she wanted to hear more of Philippa's plans before she formed any of her own, and meanwhile she could cry unobserved within the old walls where she had loved poor Stan, and seen him grow up from a boy; no wonder, no triumphant paragon ; but a kindly, gentle, simple creature, whom she had loved with all her heart, as Dolly now loved George, and without whom the world seemed a wanting place— though there were many wiser and more brilliant men left in it than poor Stanham Vanborough. Robert, after some incompetent attempts at consolation, was obliged to return to Cambridge.

Poor Mrs. Vanborough's 'plans' were rather vague, and all crossed one another and came on different scraps of papers, contradicting and utterly bewildering, though good Lady Sarah had docketed them and tied them up together for more convenient reference. They were to write to her by every post, Philippa said. Why could they not come to her? She longed for her children. She scarcely knew how to bear her sorrow. She dreaded the journey, the cold, empty, home-coming, the life in England, so different from what she had dreamed. The doctor said it would be madness for her to move as yet. Her brother, Colonel Henley ('Dear Charles! he was goodness itself'), suggested Italy. Would Lady Sarah consent to this, and meet her with the children? Or would she even come as far as Paris? But there were difficulties in everything everywhere—cruel money difficulties, she was told. There was a lawsuit now coming on in the Calcutta Courts with the insurance office in which poor dear Stan had insured his life. Captain Palmer said her presence was necessary. If it was given against her, she was utterly penniless; and, meanwhile, harassed, detained. . . . Perhaps, on her return, she might take boarders or Indian children—would lady Sarah advertise at once. . . . ? What did George advise? When should she see them all again? Her heart yearned in vain—months might elapse. Dependence she could not bear. Even Sarah's kindness was bitter to her, when she thought of the past. All were kind—all was sad. The poor thing seemed utterly distracted.

Lady Sarah had written that Church House was her home, and that she must come at once to her home and her children.

Mrs. Vanborough wrote that this could not be. Alas,

alas! it was only a bright dream, from which she sometimes awoke (so Philippa wrote) to find herself a mourner in a foreign land, watching the slow progress of the law.

'Why didn't she come?' wrote Lady Henley from the Court. 'When will she come?' the children asked. Her room was ready, the bed was made, the fire burning. Dolly used to pick nosegays for her mamma's toilet-table, and stick pins in the cushion in stars. She made little bags of lavender to scent the great cabinet. It was one of those welcomes that are wasted in life, one of those guest-chambers made ready to which the guest does not come. They look just like any other rooms unless you know their history.

Dolly often followed Marker when she went in to see that all was in order. One day the fire blazed comfortably; although the rain was beating against the window, a gleam of sun came from the inner dressing-room, that looked out cross-ways along the garden. 'Do you think she will come soon, Marker?' Dolly asked, peeping about the room.

'I don't think nothing at all, my dear,' said Marker, poking the fire. 'Why don't you go and play with Miss Rhoda? She came with Mrs. Morgan just now.'

'Is Rhoda here?' cries Dolly, starting off instantly.

Rhoda was there; she had come with her aunt, who was talking to Lady Sarah in the drawing-room.

Mrs. Morgan took a very long time to say what she had to say, and had left Rhoda outside in the hall. The little girls listened to Mrs. Morgan's voice as it went on, and on, and on. They sat on the stairs and played at being ladies too, and Rhoda told Dolly a great many secrets that she was not to tell, in a mysterious whisper just like her aunt's. Mr. Raban was gone away, she said, and he had married somebody, and Aunt Morgan said she should never speak to him again, and Mrs. Penfold came crying, and Aunt Morgan scolded and scolded, and Rhoda thought Emma Penfold was gone too, and just then the drawing-room door opened; Mrs. Morgan came out, looking very busy and bustled off with Rhoda. Lady Sarah cut Dolly's questions very short and forbade her going to the cottage again.

It was the very next day that Dolly and Rhoda met old Penfold walking in the lane, as they were coming home with Mademoiselle.

Gumbo ran to meet him, barking, wagging his tail, and creeping along the ground with delight.

Penfold, who had been passing on, stooped to caress the puppy's head with his brown creased hand, and seeing Dolly, he nodded kindly to her as she walked by with Mademoiselle.

'Has Emma come home to the cottage?' asked Rhoda, lingering.

Penfold frowned. His honest red face turned crimson. 'She's not come back, nor will she,' he said. 'She has got a 'usband now, and she is gone a-travellin', and if they hast you, you can tell them as I said so, Miss Rhoda, nor should I say otherwise if they was here to contradic' me.' He spoke in a fierce defiant way. Mademoiselle called shrilly to the children to come on.

Dolly looked after the old gardener as he slowly walked away down the lane: he looked very old and tired, and she wished her aunt had not told her to keep away from the cottage.

Emma's name was never mentioned; Raban's, too, was forgotten; Mrs. Vanborough still delayed from one reason and another.

*   *   *   *   *

From MRS. VANBOROUGH *to the* LADY SARAH FRANCIS, *Church House, Kensington.*

Bugpore, April 1—, 18—.

DEAREST SARAH,—I fear that you will be totally unprepared (not more so, however, than I was myself) for a great and sudden change in my life of sad regrets (sad and regretful it will ever be), notwithstanding the altered circumstances which fate has forced upon me during the last few months that I have spent in sorrowful retirement, with spirits and health shattered and nerves unstrung. During these long lonely months, weighed down by care and harassed by business, which I was utterly incapable of understanding, I know not what would have become of me if (during my brother's absence on regimental duties) it had not been for the unremitting attention and generous devotion of one without whose support I now feel I could not bring myself to face the struggle of a solitary life. For the sake of my poor fatherless children more even than for my own, I have accepted the name and protection of Captain Hawtry Palmer, of the Royal Navy, a sailor, of a family of sailors. Joanna, my brother's wife, was a Palmer, and from her I have often heard of Hawtry at a time when I little thought . . . You, dearest, who know me as I am, will rejoice that I have found rest and strength in another, though happiness I may not claim.

Captain Palmer is a man of iron will and fervent principle. He must make me good, I tell him, unless sadness and resignation can be counted for goodness. Your poor Philippa is but a faulty creature, frail and delicate, and of little power; and yet, with all my faults, I feel that I am necessary to him, and, wreck as I am, there are those who do not utterly forget me. And, as he says with his quaint humour, there is not much to choose between the saints and sinners of the world. A thousand thousand kisses to my precious children. You will bring them to meet me next year, will you not, when Captain Palmer promises that I shall return to my real home—for your home is my home, is it not?

For the present, I remain on a visit to my friend Mrs. M'Grudder, an intimate friend of Captain Palmer, with one only daughter.

The marriage will not, of course, take place for six weeks. Joanna will describe her brother to you. I am anxious to hear all she says about Hawtry and myself and our marriage. Pray announce my great news to my darlings. Let them write to me without reserve.

Ever, dearest Sarah,

Your very devoted

PHILIPPA.

Poor Lady Sarah read the letter one white, cold, east-windy day, when the sun shone, and the dry, parching wind blew the wreaths of dust along the ground. As she read the curious, heartless words, it seemed to her that the east-wind was blowing into the room,—into her heart,—

drying up all faith in life, all tears for the past, all hope for the future. Had she a heart, this cruel woman, poor Stan's wife and Dolly's mother ? Can women live and be loved, and bear children, and go through life without one human feeling, one natural emotion ; take every blessing of God, and every sacred sorrow, and live on, without knowing either the blessing or the sorrow ? Lady Sarah tore the letter up carefully and very quietly, for Dolly was by her side, and would have asked to see it. She was not angry just then, but cold and sad, unspeakably sad. ' Poor woman !' she thought, ' was this all ; this the end of Stan's tender life devotion ; this the end of his pride and tender trust ?' She could see him now, whispering to Philippa, as they sat together on the old bench by the pond, a handsome pair, people said, and well suited. Well suited ! She got up shivering from her chair, and went to the fire, and threw the letter in, shred by shred, while the sun poured in fierce, and put out the flames.

' Are you cold, Aunt Sarah ?' said Dolly, coming to her side. Sarah moved away. She was afraid that even now it was burnt Dolly might read the cruel letter in the fire. ' For my children's sake !' The little red flames seemed to be crackling the words, as they smouldered among the coals, and a shrill, sudden blast against the window seemed hissing out that Captain Palmer was a man of iron will. As they stood side by side, Lady Sarah looked steadily away from little Dolly's eyes, and told her that her mamma was going to marry again.

Poor Dolly turned the colour of the little flames when her aunt told her. She said nothing, not even to Rhoda, nor to Mrs. Morgan, who called immediately upon hearing the rumour. Lady Sarah was not at home, but Mrs. Morgan came in all the same, and closely questioned Dolly upon the subject.

'What is the gentleman's name, my dear?' she asked.

'I don't know,' said Dolly.

'Why, Mr. Palmer, to be sure,' said Rhoda.

In due time the news came of the marriage, and then poor Aunt Sarah had to wipe her eyes, and to give up writing on black-edged paper. The clocks went round and round, and the earth rolled on, and seasons spread their feasts, and the winds swept them away in turn ; summer burnt into autumn in cloud and vapour. The winter came closing in, and the snow fell thick upon the lanes and the gardens, on the Kensington house-tops and laurel-trees, on the old church tower, and the curate's well-worn waterproof cape, as he trudged to and fro. It fell on the old garden walls and slanting roof of Church House, with little Dolly, safe sheltered within, warming herself by the baked Dutch tiles.

CHAPTER VI.

DOWNSTAIRS IN THE DARK.

D'un linceuil de point d'Angleterre
Que l'on recouvre sa beauté . . .
Que des violettes de parme
Au lieu des tristes fleurs des morts,
Où chaque fleur est une larme,
Pleuvent en bouquets sur son corps.
— T. GAUTIER.

THERE are old houses in other places besides Kensington. Perhaps, it is from early associations that Dolly has always had so great a liking for walls furnished with some upholstery of the past, and set up by strong hands that seem to have had their own secrets for making their work last on. Some of these old piles stand like rocks, defying our lives as they have defied the generations before us. We come upon them everywhere, set upon high hills, standing in wide country-places, crowded into the narrow streets of a city. Perhaps it is the golden Tiber that flows past the old doorways, perhaps it is the Danube rushing by, or the grey Thames running to the marshes, or the Seine as it shines between the banks. There is an old house in the Champs Elysées at Paris where most English people have lived in turn, and to which Dolly's fate brought her when she was about twelve years old.

The prompter rings the bell, and the scene shifts to the
Maison Vâlin, and to one night, twenty years ago, when the
two little girls were tucked up in bed. The dim night-
light was put on the round marble table, the curtains were
drawn, but all the same they could hear the noise of the
horses trampling and the sabots clanking in the courtyard
down below. Lady Sarah had sent her little niece to bed,
and she now stood at the door and said, 'Good-night, my
dears.' The second night-cap was only that of a little stray
school-girl come to spend a holiday, from one of those vast
and dreary establishments scattered all about the deserted
suburbs of the great city: of which the lights were blazing
from the uncurtained drawing-room windows, and its great
semicircle of dark hills flashing.

Lady Sarah had come to Paris to meet Dolly's mamma,
who had been married more than a year by this time, and
who was expected home at last. She was coming *alone*,
she wrote. She had at length received Captain Palmer's
permission to visit her children; but not even her wishes
could induce him to quit his beloved frigate. She should,
therefore, leave him cruising along the Coromandel coast,
and start in January, for which month her passage was
taken. She implored Lady Sarah to meet her in Paris,
where some weeks' rest would be absolutely necessary, she
said, to recruit her strength after the fatigue of her journey;
and Lady Sarah, with some misgiving, yielded to Dolly's
wistful entreaties, and wrote to her old friend the Rev. W.
Lovejoy, of the Marmouton Chapel, to take rooms for her for
a few weeks, during which Dolly might improve her French
accent and her style of dancing (Dolly had been pronounced
clumsy by Mrs. Morgan) in the companionship of little
Rhoda, who had been sent some time before to be established

for a year in a boarding-school near Paris, there to put on the armour of accomplishments that she would require some day in the dismal battle of life.

John Morgan had been loth that the little girl should go; he was afraid the child might feel lonely away from them all; but Rhoda said, very sensibly, that, if she was to be a governess, she supposed she had better learn things. So Rhoda was sent off for a year to Madame Laplanche's, towards the end of which time Lady Sarah came to Paris with Dolly and the faithful Marker in attendance.

Dolly did not trouble her head very much about her accent, but she was delighted to be with her friend again, to say nothing of seeing the world and the prospect of meeting her mother. She went twice a week to Rhoda's school to learn to point her bronze toes and play on the well-worn piano; and then every morning came Madame de St. Honoré, an old lady who instructed Mademoiselle Dolli in the grammar and literature of the country to which she belonged. French literature, according to Madame de St. Honoré, was in one snuffy volume which she happened to possess. Dolly asked no questions, and greatly preferred stray scenes out of *Athalie* and odd pages from *Paul and Virginia* to Noel and Chapsal, and l'Abbé Gaultier's *Geography*. The two would sit at the dining-room table with the windows open, and the cupboards full of French china, and with the head of Socrates staring at them from over the stove.

Mr. Lovejoy had selected for his old friend a large and dilapidated set of rooms, the chairs and tables of which had seen better days, and had been in their prime during the classic furniture period of the Great Napoleon.

The tall white marble clock on the chimney-piece had

struck nine, and Lady Sarah was sitting alone in the carpet-less drawing-room on one of the stiff-backed chairs. It was early times for two girls of eleven and twelve to be popped away out of the world; but Lady Sarah was at that time a strict disciplinarian, and seemed to think that one of the grand objects of life was to go to bed and to be up again an hour in advance of everybody else.

'And so there is only dreaming till to-morrow morning,' thought Dolly, with a dreary wide-awake sigh. Dolly and Henriette her maid had two beds side by side. Dolly used to lie wide-awake in hers, watching the dawn as it streamed through the old-flowered chintz curtains, and the shadows and pictures flying from the corners of the room; or, when the night-light burnt dimly, and the darkness lay heaped against the walls, Dolly, still childish for her age, could paint pictures for herself upon it, bright phantasmagorias woven out of her brain, faces and flowers and glittering sights such as those she saw when she was out in the day-time. Dolly thought the room was enchanted, and that fairies came into it as soon as Henriette was asleep and snoring. To-night little Rhoda was sleeping in the bed, and Henriette and Marker were sitting at work in the next room. They had left the door open; and, presently, when they thought the children were asleep, began a low, mysterious conversation in French.

'She died on Tuesday,' said Henriette, 'and is to be buried to-morrow.'

'She could not have been twenty,' said Marker; 'and a sweet pretty lady. I can't think where it is I have seen such another as her.'

'Pauvre dame,' said Henriette. 'He feels her death very much. He is half-distracted, Julie tells me.'

'Serve him right, the brute! I should like to give it him!' cries the other.

'He looks such a handsome smiling gentleman, that Mr. Rab—Rap—Who could have thought it possible?'

'Oh, they're all smiling enough,' said Marker, who knew the world. 'There was a young man in a grocer's shop——' And her voice sank into confidences still more mysterious.

'When they came to measure her for her coffin,' said Henriette, who had a taste for the terrible, 'they found she had grown since her death, poor thing. Julie tells me that she looks more beautiful than you can imagine. He comes and cries out, "Emma! Emma!" as if he could wake her and bring her to life.'

'Wake her and bring her to life to kill her again, the wretch!' said Marker, 'with his neglect and cruelty.'

'He is very young—a mere boy,' said Henriette. 'The concierge says there was no malice in him; and then he gave her such beautiful gowns! There was a moire-antique came home the day she died, with lace trimmings. Julie showed it me: she expects to get all the things. They were going to a ball at the Tuileries. How beautiful she would have looked!'

'Poor child!' said Marker.

'To die without ever putting it on! Dame, I should not like that; but I should like to have a husband who would buy me such pretty things. I would not mind his being out of temper now and then, and leaving me to do as I liked for a month or two at a time. I should have amused myself, instead of crying all day, as she did. Julie tells me she has tried on the black velvet, and it fits her perfectly.'

'Julie ought to be ashamed of herself,' growled Marker, 'with the poor child lying there still.'

' Not in the least,' said Henriette ; ' Julie was very fond
of her when she was alive—now she is dead—that is another
thing. She says she would not stop in the room for worlds.
She thought she saw her move yesterday, and she rushed
away into the kitchen and had an *attaque de nerfs* in consequence.'

' But did she tell nobody—could it have been true ? '

' Françoise told *him*, and they went in immediately, but
it was all silent as before. I am glad I sleep upstairs : I
should not like to be in the room over that one. It is
underneath there where are *les petites*.'

' She would do no one harm, now or when she was alive,
poor thing,' said Marker. ' I should like to flay that man
alive.'

' That would be a pity, Mrs. Marker,' said Henriette : ' a
fine young man like that ! He liked her well enough, allez !
She cried too much : it was her own fault that she was not
happy.'

' I would rather be her than him at this minute,' said
Marker. ' Why he sulked and sneered and complained of
the bills when he was at home, and went away for days
together without telling her where he was going. I know
where he was : he was gambling and spending her money
on other people—I'd pickle him, I would ! ' said Marker ;
' and I don't care a snap for his looks ; and her heart is as
cold as his own now, poor little thing.'

' It's supper-time, isn't it ? ' yawned Henriette.

Then Dolly heard a little rustle as they got up to go to
their supper, and the light in the next room disappeared,
and everything seemed very silent. The night-light splut-
tered a little, the noises in the courtyard were hushed, the
familiar chairs and tables looked queer and unknown in the

darkness. Rhoda was fast asleep and breathing softly ; Dolly was kicking about in her own bed, and thrilling with terror and excitement, and thinking of what she had heard of the poor pretty lady downstairs. She and Rhoda always used to rush to the window to see her drive off in her smart little carriage, wrapped in her furs, but all alone. Poor little lady ! her unkind husband never went with her, and used to leave her for weeks at a time. Her eyes used to shine through the veil that she always wore when they met her on the stairs ; but Aunt Sarah would hurry past her, and never would talk about her. And now she was dead. Dolly looked at Rhoda lying so still on her white pillow. How would Rhoda look when she was dead, thought Dolly.

'Being asleep is being dead. . . . I daresay people would be more afraid of dying if they were not so used to go to sleep. When I am dying—I daresay I shall die about seventeen—I shall send for John Morgan, and George will come from Eton, and Aunt Sarah will be crying, and, perhaps, mamma and Captain Palmer will be there ; and I shall hold all their hands in mine and say, " Now be friends, for my sake." And then I shall urge George to exert himself more, and go to church on week-days ; and then to Aunt Sarah I shall turn with a sad smile, and say, " Adieu ! dear aunt, you never understood me—you fancied me a child when I had the feelings of a woman, and you sneered at me, and sent me to bed at eight o'clock. Do not crush George and Rhoda as you have crushed me : be gentle with them ; " and then I shall cross my hands over my chest and—and what then ? ' And a sort of shock came over the girl as, perhaps for the first time in her life, she realised the awful awakening. 'Suppose they bury me alive ? It is very common, I know—oh ! no, no, no ; that would be too hor-

rible! Suppose that poor young lady is not dead downstairs—suppose she is alive, and they bury her to-morrow,
and she wakes up, and it is all dark, and she chokes and
cries out, and nobody hears. . . . Surely they will take
precautions?—they will make sure. . . . Who will, I
wonder? Not that wicked husband—not that horrid maid.
That wicked man has gone to gamble, I daresay; and Julie
is trying on her dresses, and perhaps her eyes are opening
now and nobody to see—nobody to come. Ah! this is
dreadful. I must go to sleep and forget it.'

Little Rhoda turned and whispered something in her
dreams; Dorothy curled herself up in her nest and shut her
eyes, and did go to sleep for a couple of hours, and then
woke up again with a start, and thought it must be morning.
Had not somebody called her by name? did not somebody
whisper Dolly in her ear? so loud that it woke her out of a
strange dream : a sort of dream in which strange clanging
sounds rung round and round in the air; in which Dolly
herself lay powerless, gasping and desperate on her bed.
Vainly she tried to move, to call, to utter; no one came.

Julie, in white satin, was looking at herself in the glass;
the wicked husband was standing in the door with a horrible
scowl. Rhoda, somehow, was quietly asleep in her bed.
Ah! no, she, too, was dead; she would never wake; she
would not come and save her. And just then Dolly awoke,
and started up in bed with wide open childish eyes. What
a still quiet room—what a dim light from the lamp—who
had spoken? Was it a warning? was it a call? was this
dream sent to her as a token? as the people in the Bible
dreamt dreams and dared not disobey them? Was this
what was going on in the room below? was it for her
to go down and save the poor lady, who might be calling

to her ? Something within her said ' Go, go,' and suddenly
she found herself standing by the bedside, putting on her
white dressing-gown, and then pattering out bare-footed
across the wooden floors, out into the dark dining-room, out
into the ante-room, all dark and black, opening the front
door (the key was merely turned in the lock), walking downstairs with the dim lamps glimmering and the moonlight
pouring in at the blindless window; and standing at the
door of the apartment below. Her only thought was wonder
at finding it so easy. Then she laid her hand softly on the
lock and turned it, and the door opened, and she found
herself in an ante-room like their own, only carpeted and
alight. The room was under her own: she knew her way
well enough. Into the dark dining-room she passed with a
beating heart, and so came to a door beneath which a ray of
light was streaming. And then she stopped. Was this a
dream ? was this really herself? or was she asleep in bed upstairs ? or was she, perhaps, dead in her coffin? A qualm
of terror came over her—should she turn and go ?—her
knees were shaking, her heart was beating so that she could
hardly breathe ; but she would not turn back—that would
be a thousand times too cowardly. Just then she thought
she heard a footstep in the dining-room. With a shuddering
effort she raised her hand, and in an instant she stood in the
threshold of the chamber. What, was this a sacred chapel?
Silence and light, many flowers, tall tapers burning. It
seemed like an awful dream to the bewildered child: the
coffin stood in the middle of the room, she smelt a faint
odour of incense, of roses, of scented tapers, and then her
heart stood still as she heard a sudden gasping sigh, and
against the light an awful shrouded figure slowly rising and
seeming to come towards her. It was more than she could

E

bear: the room span round, once more the loud clanging sounded in her ears, and poor Dolly, with a shuddering scream, fell to the ground.

*   *   *   *   *

A jumble of whispers, of vinegar, of water trickling down her back, and of an officious flapping wet handkerchief; of kind arms enfolding her: of nurse saying, 'Now she is coming to;' of Lady Sarah answering, 'Poor little thing, she must have been walking in her sleep'—a strange new birth, new vitality pouring in at all her limbs, a dull identity coming flashing suddenly into life, and Dolly opened her eyes to find herself in the nurse's arms, with her aunt bending over her, in the warm drawing-room upstairs. Other people seemed standing about—Henriette and a man whom she could scarcely see with her dim weary eyes, and Julie. Dolly hid her face on the nurse's shoulder.

'Oh, nurse, nurse! have you saved me?' was all she could say.

'What were you doing downstairs, you naughty child?' said Lady Sarah, in her brisk tones. 'Marker heard a noise and luckily ran after you.'

'Oh, Aunt Sarah, forgive me!' faltered Dolly. 'I went to save the lady—I thought if she opened her eyes and there was no one there—and Julie trying on the dresses, and the wicked husband—I heard Henriette telling Marker——Oh, save me, save me!' and the poor little thing burst into tears and clung closer and closer.

'You are all safe, dear,' said Marker, 'and the young lady is at rest where nothing will frighten or disturb her. Hush! don't cry.'

'Poor little thing,' said the man, taking her hand; 'the nuns must have frightened her.' And he raised the

child's hand to his lips and kissed it, and then seemed to go
away.

'I'm ashamed of myself, my lady,' said Marker, 'for
having talked as I did with the chance of the children being
awake to hear me. It was downright wicked, and I should
like to bite my tongue out. Go to bed, Henriette. Be off,
Mamzelle July, if you please.'

'We are all going to bed; but Henriette will get Miss
Dolly a cup of chocolate first,' said Lady Sarah.

Dolly was very fond of chocolate; and this little im-
promptu supper by the drawing-room fire did more to quiet
and reassure her than anything else. But she was hardly
herself as yet, and could only cling to Marker's arm and hide
her face away from them all. Her aunt kissed her once more,
saying, 'Well, I won't scold you to-night; indeed, I am not
sure but that you were quite right to go,' and disappeared
into her own room. Then Henriette carried the candle, and
Marker carried great big Dolly and laid her down by Rhoda
in her bed, and the wearied and tired little girl fell asleep
at last, holding Rhoda's hand.

CHAPTER VII.

CLOUD=CAPPED TOWERS AND GORGEOUS PALACES.

Lo ! what wrong was her life to thee, Death ?
—ROSETTI.

WHEN Dolly awoke next morning Rhoda was dressed and
her bed was empty.   The window had been opened, but the
light was carefully shaded by the old brown curtains.   Dolly
lay quite still; she felt strangely tired, and as if she had
been for a very long journey, toiling along a weary road.
And so she had, in truth ; she had travelled along a road
that no one ever retraces, she had learnt a secret that no one
ever forgets.   Henceforth in many places and hours the
vision that haunts each one of us was revealed to her ; that
solemn ghost of Death stood before her with its changing
face, at once sad and tender and pitiless.   Who shall speak
of it ?   With our own looks, with the familiar eyes of others,
it watches us through life, the good angel and comforter of
the stricken and desolate, the strength of the weak, the
pitiless enemy of home and peaceful love and tranquil days.
But perhaps to some of us the hour may come when we fall
into the mighty arms, feeling that within them is the home
and the love and the peace that they have torn from us.

Dolly was still lying quite quiet and waiting for something

ᴠo happen, when the door opened, and her aunt's maid came in carrying a nice little tray with breakfast upon it.   There was a roll, and some French butter in a white scroll-like saucer, and Dolly's favourite cup.

' My lady is gone out, Miss Dolly,' said Marker, ' but she left word you was not to be disturbed.   It is eleven o'clock, and she is going to take you and Miss Rhoda for a treat when she gets back.'

' A treat!' said Dolly, languidly; 'that will be nice. Marker, I have to push my arms to make them go.'

But when Dolly had had her bath and eaten her breakfast, her arms began to go of themselves.   Once, indeed, she turned a little sick and giddy, for, happening to look out of window into the courtyard below, she saw that they were carrying away black cloths and silver-spangled draperies, which somehow brought up the terror of the night before ; but her nurse kissed her, and made her kneel down and say her prayers, and told her in her homely way that she must not be afraid; that life and death were made by the same Hand, and ruled over by the same Love.   ' The poor young lady was buried this morning, my dear,' said Marker, ' before you were awake.   Your aunt went with the poor young man.'

Marker was a short, stout, smiling old woman.   Lady Sarah was tall and thin, and silent, and scant in dress, with a brown face and grey hair ; she came in, in her black gown, from the funeral, with her shaggy kind eyes red with tears.

' You won't forget, my lady, that you promised the young ladies a treat,' said Marker, who was anxious that Dolly should have something fresh to think of.

' I have not forgotten,' said Dolly's aunt, smiling, as she looked at the two children.   ' Rhoda must get a remem-

brance to take back to school, mustn't she, Dolly? I have
ordered a carriage at two.'

There is a royal palace familiar to many of us of which
the courts are shining and busy, and crowded with people.
Flowers are growing among fountains and foliage, and
children are at play; there is a sight of high gabled roofs
overhead enclosing it, so do the long lines of the ancient
arcades. Some music is playing to which the children are
dancing. In this strange little world the children seem to
grow up to music in beautiful ready-made little frocks and
pinafores, the grown-up people seem to live on grapes
and ices and bonbons, and on the enormous pears displayed
in the windows of the cafés. Everything is more or less
gilt and twinkling,—china flowers bloom delicate and scent-
less; it would seem as if the business of life consisted in
wandering here and there, and sipping and resting to the
sound of music in the shade of the orange-trees, and gazing
at the many wonders displayed; at the gimcracks and trinkets and strings of beads, the precious stones, and the silver
and gold, and the fanciful jewels. Are these things all dust
and ashes? Here are others, again, of imitation dross and
dust, shining and dazzling too; and again, imitations of
imitations for the poorest and most credulous, heaped up in
harmless glitter and array. Here are opera-glasses to detect
the deceptions, and the deceptions to deceive the glasses,—
bubbles of pomp, thinnest gilding of vanity and good-humour.

Some twenty years ago Dorothea Vanborough and a great
many ladies and gentlemen her contemporaries were not the
respectable middle-aged people they are now, but very young
folks standing on tip-toe to look at life, which they gazed at
with respectful eyes, believing all things, hoping all things,
and interested in all things beyond words or the power of

words to describe. My heroine was a blooming little girl, with her thick wavy hair plaited into two long tails. She wore a great flapping hat and frilled trousers, according to the barbarous fashion of the time. Little Rhoda was shorter and slighter, with great dark eyes and a wistful pale face; she was all shabbily dressed, and had no frills like Dolly, or flowers in her hat. The two stood gazing at the portrait of a smiling little Prince with a blue ribbon, surmounted by a wreath of flowers, glazed and enclosed in a gilt-locket. I suppose the little girls of the present[1] bear the same sort of allegiance to the Prince Imperial that Dolly felt for the little smiling Count of Paris of those days. For the King his grandfather, for the Dukes and Princes his uncles, hers was a very vague devotion; but when the old yellow royal coaches used to come by rumbling and shaking along the Champs Elysées, Dolly for one, followed by her protesting attendant, would set off running as hard as she could, and stand at the very edge of the pavement in the hopes of seeing her little smiling Prince peep out of the carriage-window. He was also to be seen in effigy on cups, on pin-boxes, and bonbons, and, above all, to be worn by the little girls in the ornamental fashion I have described. He smiled impartially from their various tuckers; and, indeed, many of the youthful possessors of those little gilt lockets are true to this day to their early impressions.

So both Dolly and Rhoda came to tell Lady Sarah that they had made up their minds, what they most admired.

The widow had been sitting upon one of the benches in the garden, feeling not unlike the skeleton at a feast—a scanty figure in the sunshine, with a heart scarcely attuned to the bustle and chatter around her, but she began to tell

[1] Written before recent events in France.

herself that there must be some use even in the pomps and
vanities of life, when she saw how happy the little girls
looked, how the light had come into Dolly's eyes, and then
she gave them each a solid silver piece out of a purse,
which, contrary to the custom of skeletons, she held ready
in her hand.

'Oh, thank you,' says Dolly ; ' now I can get no end of
things. There's George and Robert and —— '

' It is much better to buy *one* nice thing to take care of
than a great many little ones,' said Rhoda, philosophically.
' Dolly, you don't manage well. I don't want to get everything I see. I shall buy that pretty locket. None of the
girls in my class have got one as pretty.'

' Come along quick then,' said Dolly, ' for fear they
should have sold it.'

They left the Palais Royal at last and drove homewards
with their treasures. Dolly never forgot that evening ; the
carriage drove along through the May-lit city, by teeming
streets, by shady avenues, to the sounds of life and pleasure-
making. Carriages were rolling along with them ; long
lines of trees, of people, of pavements led to a great tri-
umphal archway, over which the little pink clouds were
floating, while an intense sweet thrill of spring rung in the
air and in the spirits of the people. Henriette opened the
door to them when they got home.

' The poor gentleman from below,' she said, ' is waiting
for you in the drawing-room. I told him you would not be
long.'

The gentleman was waiting in the drawing-room as Lady
Sarah came in with the two little girls shyly following. She
would have sent them away, but a sort of shyness habitual

to her made her shrink from a scene or an explanation. It may have been some feeling of the same sort which had induced the widower to go away to the farthest window of the room, where he stood leaning out with his back turned for an instant after they had come in.

Coming in out of the dazzle of the streets, the old yellow drawing-room looked dark and dingy ; the lights reflected from the great amphitheatre without struck on the panelled doors and fusty hangings. All these furnished houses have a family likeness : chairs with Napoleon backs and brass-bound legs, tables that cry *vive l'empire* as plain as tables can utter, old-fashioned secretaries standing demure with their backs against the wall, keeping their counsel and their secrets (if there *are* such things as secrets). The laurel-crowned clocks tick beneath their wreaths and memorials of bygone victories, the looking-glasses placidly relate the faces, the passing figures, the varying lights and changes as they pass before them. To-night a dusky golden light was streaming into the room from behind the hills, that were heaving, so Dolly thought, and dimming the solemn glow of the sky : she saw it all in an instant ; and then, with a throb she recognised this wicked husband coming from the window where he had been standing with his back to them. She had never seen him before so close, and yet she seemed to know his face. He looked very cruel, thought Dolly; he had a pale face and white set lips, and a sort of dull black gleam flashed from his eyes. He spoke in a harsh voice. He was very young—a mere boy, with thick fair hair brushed back from his haggard young face. He might have been, perhaps, about two or three and twenty.

' I waited for you, Lady Sarah. I came to say good-by,' he said, ' I am going back to London to-night. I

shall never forget your ——' His voice broke. 'How good
you have been to me,' he said hoarsely, as he took the two
thin hands in his and wrung them again and again.

The widow's sad face softened as she told him 'to have
trust, to be brave.'

'You don't know what you say,' he said in a common-
place way. 'God bless you.' He was going, but seeing the
two, Dolly and Rhoda, standing by the door looking at him
with wondering faces, he stopped short. 'I forgot,' he said,
still in his hard matter-of-fact voice, 'I brought a cross of
Emma's; I thought she would wish it. It won't bring ill-
luck,' he said, with a ghastly sort of laugh. 'She bore
crosses enough in her life, poor soul, but this one, at least,
had no nails in it. May I give it to your little girl?' he said,
'unless she is afraid to take anything from me.'

Lady Sarah did not say no, and the pale young man
looked vaguely from one to the other of the two little girls
as they stood there, and then he took one step towards Dolly,
who was the biggest, and who was standing, straight and tall
for her age, in her light-coloured dress, with her straw hat
hanging on her arm. I don't know how to write this of my
poor little heroine. If he had seemed more unhappy, if he
had not looked so strangely and spoken so oddly, she might
have understood him better; but as it was, she thought he
was saying terrible things, laughing and jeering and heartless: so judged Dolly in an innocent severity. Is it so?
Are not the children of this world wiser in their generation
than the children of light? Are there not depths of sin and
repentance undreamt of by the pure in spirit? One seems
to grasp at a meaning which eludes one as one strains
at it, wondering what is the sermon to be preached upon
this text. . . . It was one that little Dolly, still playing in

her childish and peaceful valley, could not understand. She might forgive as time went on; she had not lived long enough yet either to forgive or to forget; never once had it occurred to her that any thought of hers, either of blame or forgiveness, could signify to any other human being, or that any word or sign of hers could have a meaning to any one except herself.

Dolly was true to herself, and in those days she used to think that all her life long she would be always true, and always say all she felt. As life grows long, and people, living on together through time and sorrow and experience, realise more and more the complexities of their own hearts, and sympathise more and more with the failings and sorrows of others, they are apt to ask themselves with dismay if it is a reality of life to be less and less uncompromising as complexities increase, less true to themselves as they are more true to others, and if the very angels of God are wrestling and at war in their hearts. All through her life Dolly found, with a bitter experience, that these two angels of charity and of truth are often very far apart until the miracle of love comes to unite them. She was strong and true; in after days she prayed for charity; with charity came sorrow, and doubt, and perplexity. Charity is long-suffering and kind, and thinks no evil; but then comes truth crying out, 'Is not wrong wrong; is not falsehood a lie?' Perhaps it is because truth is not for this life that the two are at variance, until the day shall come when the light shall come, and with the light peace and knowledge and love, and then charity itself will be no longer needed.

And so Dolly, who in those days had scarcely realised even human charity in her innocent young heart, looked up and saw the wicked man who had been so cruel to his wife

coming towards her with a gift in his hand; and as she saw
him coming, black against the light of the sunset, she
shrank away behind Rhoda, who stood looking up with her
dark wistful eyes. The young man saw Dolly shrink from
him, and he stopped short; but at the same instant he met
the tranquil glance of a trustful upturned face, and, with a
sigh, he put the cross (shimmering with a sudden flash of
light) into little Rhoda's soft clasping hand.

'You are not afraid, like your sister? Will you keep it
for Emma's sake?' he said again, in a softer voice.

There was a moment's silence. Lady Sarah, never, at
the best of times, a ready woman, tried to say something,
but the words died away. Dolly looked up, and her eyes
met the flash of the young man's two wild burning eyes.
They seemed to her to speak. 'I saw you shrink away,'
they seemed to say. 'You are right; don't come near me
—don't come near me.' But this was only unspoken
language.

'Good-by,' he said suddenly to Lady Sarah. 'I am glad
to have seen you once more,' and then he went quickly out
of the room without looking back, leaving them all standing
scared and saddened by this melancholy little scene.

The lights were burning deeper behind the hills; the
reflections were darker. Had there been a sudden storm?
No; the sun had set quietly behind Montmartre, where the
poor girl was lying there upon the heights above the city.
Was it Dolly who was trembling, or was it the room that
seemed vibrating to the echo of some disastrous chords that
were still ringing in her ears.

Dolly went to the window and leant out over the wooden
bar, looking down into the rustling glooming lilac garden
below. How sad the scent of the lilac-trees in flower

seemed as it came flooding up! She was still angry, but she was sorry too, and two great tears fell upon the wooden bar against which she was leaning. She always remembered that evening when she smelt lilac in flower.

Rhoda was very much pleased with her cross.

' I shall hang it on a black ribbon,' said the child, ' and always think of the poor gentleman when I wear it ; and I shall tell the girls in class all about him and how he gave it to me.'

' How you took it from him, you mean,' said Lady Sarah, shortly.

' No, indeed, Lady Sarah ; he gave it to me,' cried Rhoda, clutching her treasure quite tight.

CHAPTER VIII.

IMMORTELLES.

O lieb so lang du lieben kannst,
O lieb so lang du lieben magst,
Die Stunde kommt, die Stunde kommt,
Wo du am Graben stehst und klagst.

FRANK RABAN, having left the three standing silent and
sorry in the calm sunset room, ran down to his own apartment on the floor beneath. He was to go back to England
that night: he felt he could not stay in that place any
longer ; the memories seemed to choke him, and to rise up
and madden him. As he came now down the echoing stairs
he heard the voices of his servants : the front door was wide
open. The concierge was standing in the passage in his
shirt-sleeves ; M. Adolphe was discoursing ; a milliner
was waiting with her bill. ' Not two years married,' he
heard them saying ; ' as for him, he will console himself.'
Their loud voices suddenly hushed as he appeared. Adolphe
flung the door open still wider for his master ; but the
master could not face them all, with their curious eyes fixed
upon him, and he turned and fled down-stairs. Only two
years since he. had carried her away from her home in the
quiet suburban cottage—poor Emma, who wanted to be
married, and who had never loved him ! Where was she

now ? Married only two years ! What years ! And now
his remorse seemed almost greater than he could bear. He
crossed the crowded road, heedless of the warning cries of
the drivers, pushing his way across the stream ; then he got
into a deserted country close upon the bustle of the main
thoroughfare (they call it Beaujon), where great walls run
by lonely avenues, and great gates stand closed and barred.
Would they burst open ? Would *she* come out with a pale
avenging face and strike him ? She, poor child ! Whom
did she ever strike in word or thought ? Once he got a
little ease : he thought he had been a very long way, and he
had wandered at last into an ancient lane by a convent wall,
beyond the modern dismal Beaujon, in the friendly older
quarter. Lime-trees were planted in this tranquil place.
There was a dim rain-washed painting upon the wall, a faint
vista of fountains and gardens, the lilac-trees were blooming
behind it, and the vesper song of the nuns reached his ears.
He stood still for an instant, but the song ceased.

The old avenue led back to the great round Place in
front of the Arc ; for, in those days, neither the ride nor the
great new roads were made which now lead thronging to the
Bois. And the tide came streaming to the end of the long
avenue of the Champs Elysées and no farther, and turned
and ebbed away again from the gates of the Douane.
Beyond them, the place was silent. The young man hurried
on, not caring where he went. If I had loved her, if I had
loved her—was the burthen of his remorse. It was almost
heavier than he could bear. There were some children
swinging on the chains that separate the great arch from
the road ; the last rays of the sun were lighting the stones
and the gritty platform ; twilight was closing in. I think
if it had not been for the children, he would have thrown

himself down upon the ground. They screamed shrilly at their play, and the echo from under the great vault gave back their voices. A few listless people were standing about; a countryman spelling out by the dying lights the pompous lists of victories that had been carved into the stone—Jena, Marengo, Austerlitz. Chiller and more death-like came the twilight creeping on : the great carved figures blew their trumpets, waved their stony laurels, of which the shadows changed so many times a day. He staggered to a bench; he said to himself, 'I should like this Arc to fall down upon my head and crush me. I am a devil, I am not a man. I killed her with neglect, with reproach, and suspicion ! But for me she would have been alive now, smiling as when I first saw her. I will go away and never be heard of any more. Go away—how can I go from this curse ? could Cain escape ? ' Then he began to see what was all round about him again, see it distorted by his mad remorse. All the great figures seemed writhing their arms and legs; the long lists of battle seemed like funeral processions moving round and round him, fighting and thundering and running into one another. The Arc itself was a great tomb where these legions lay buried. Was it not about to fall with a stupendous crash ; and would the dead people come rising round about at the blast of the trumpets of stone. Here was an Emperor who had wanted to conquer the whole world, and who had all but attained his object. Here was he, a man who had not striven for victory, but yielded to temptation ; a man who had deserted his post, betrayed his trust, cursed a life that he should have cherished. Though his heart were broken on a wheel and his body racked with pain, that would not mend the past, sanctify it, and renew it again.

A sort of cold sweat lay upon his forehead; some children were playing, and had come up to the stone bench where he was sitting, and were making little heaps of dust upon it. One of them looked into his face and saw him clench his hand, and the little thing got frightened and burst out crying. The other, who was older, took the little one by the hand and led it away.

Of what good was it thinking over the past? It was over. Emma was dead, lying up on the heights towards which Dolly had been looking from her window. He had been to blame; but not to blame as he imagined in his mad remorse and despair. He had been careless and impatient, and hard upon her, as he was now hard upon himself. He had married her from a sense of honour, when his boyish fancy was past. His duty was too hard for him, and he had failed, and now he was free.

It was that very evening—Dolly remembered it afterwards—a letter came from her mother, written on thin lilac paper, in a large and twisted handwriting, sealed and stamped with many Indian stamps. Dolly's mother's letters always took a long time to read; they were written up and down and on different scraps of paper. Sometimes she sent whole bouquets of faded flowers in them to the children, sometimes patterns for dresses to be returned. Henriette brought the evening's mail in with the lamp and the tea-tray, and put the whole concern down with a clatter of cups and saucers on the table before Lady Sarah. There was also a thick blue lawyer-looking letter with a seal. The little girls peeped up shyly as Lady Sarah laid down her correspondence unopened beside her. She was a nervous woman, and afraid of unread letters; but after a little she opened the lilac epistle, and then began to flush, and turned eagerly to the second.

'Who is that from?' Dolly asked at last. 'Is it from Captain Palmer?'

'Her aunt laid one thin brown hand upon the letter, and went on pouring out the tea without speaking. Rhoda looked for a moment, and then stooped over her work once more. Long years afterwards the quiet atmosphere of that lamp-lit room used to come round about Dolly again. The log fire flamed, the clock ticked on. How still it was! the leaves of her book scraped as she turned them, and Rhoda stuck her silken stitches. The roll of the carriages was so far away that it sounded like a distant sea. They were still sitting silent, and Dolly was wondering whether she might speak of the letter again and of its contents, when there came an odd muffled sound of voices and exclamations from the room underneath.

'Listen!' said Rhoda.

'What can it be?' said Dolly, shutting up her book and starting up from her chair as Henriette appeared at the door, with her white cap-strings flying, breathless.

'They were all disputing downstairs,' she said. 'Persons had arrived that evening. It was terrible to hear them.'

Lady Sarah impatiently sent Henriette about her business, and the sounds died away, and the little girls were sent off to bed. In the morning, her aunt's eyes were so red that Dolly felt sure she must have been crying. Henriette told them that the gentleman was gone. 'Milady had been sent for before he left: she had lent him some money,' said Henriette, 'and paid the milliner's bill;' but the strange people who had come had been packing up and carrying off everything, to Julie's disgust.

Events and emotions come very rarely alone, they fly in troops, like the birds. It was that very day that Lady Sarah told Dolly that she had had some bad news—she had lost a great deal of money. An Indian bank had failed in which they all had a share.

'Your mamma writes in great trouble,' said Lady Sarah, reading out from a lilac scrap. ' " Tell my precious Dolly that this odious bank will interfere once more with my heart's longing to see her. Captain Palmer insists upon a cruel delay. I am not strong enough to travel round the Cape as he proposes. You, dear Sarah, might be able to endure such fatigue; but I, alas! have not the power. Once more my return is delayed." '

'Oh, Aunt Sarah, will she ever come?' said Dolly, struggling not to cry. . . . Dolly only cheered up when she remembered that they were ruined. She had forgotten it, in her disappointment, about her mother. 'Are we really ruined?' she said, more hopefully. 'We should not have spent that money yesterday. Shall we have to leave Church House? Poor mamma! Poor Aunt Sarah!'

'Poor Marker is most to be pitied,' said Lady Sarah, 'for we shall have to be very careful, and keep fewer maids, and wear out all our old dresses; but we need not leave Church House, Dolly?'

'Then it is nothing after all,' said Dolly, again disappointed. 'I thought we should have had to go away and keep a shop, and that I should have worked for you. I should like to be your support in your old age, and mamma's too.'

Then Lady Sarah suddenly caught Dolly in her arms, and

held her tight for a moment—quite tight to her heart, that was beating tumultuously.

The next time Rhoda came out of her school for a day's holiday, Lady Sarah took the little girls to a flower-shop hard by. In the window shone a lovely rainbow of sun-rays and flowers; inside the shop were glass globes and china pots, great white sprays of lilacs, lilies, violets, ferns, and hyacinths, and golden bells, stuck into emerald-blue vases, all nodding their fragrant heads. Lady Sarah bought a great bunch of violets, and two yellow garlands made of dried immortelles.

' Do you know where we are going ? ' she asked.

Dolly didn't answer; she was sniffing, with her face buried in a green pot of mignonette.

' May I carry the garlands ? ' said Rhoda, raising her great round eyes. ' I know we are going to the poor lady's grave.'

Then they got into the carriage, and it rolled off towards the heights.

They went out beyond the barriers of the town by dusty roads, with acacia-trees; they struggled up a steep hill, and stopped at last at the gate of the cemetery. All round about it there were stalls, with more wreaths and chaplets to sell, and little sacred images for the mourners to buy for the adornment of the graves. Children were at play, and birds singing, and the sunlight streamed bright. Dolly cried out in admiration of the winding walks, shaded with early green, the flowers blooming, the tombs and the garlands, and the epitaphs, with their notes of exclamation. She began reading them out, and calling out so loudly, that her aunt had to tell her to be quiet. Then Dolly was silent for a little, but she could not help it. The sun shone, the flowers

were so bright; sunshine, spring-time, sweet flowers, all
made her tipsy with delight; the thought of the kind,
pretty lady, who had never passed her without a smile,
did not make her sad just then, but happy. She ran
away for a little while, and went to help some children,
who were picking daisies and tying them by a string.

When she came back, a little sobered down, she found
that her aunt had scattered the violets over a new-made
grave, and little Rhoda had hung the yellow wreath on the
cross at its head.

Dolly was silent, then, for a minute, and stood, looking
from her aunt, as she stood straight and grey before her, to
little Rhoda, whose eyes were full of tears. What was there
written on the cross?—

TO EMMA,
THE WIFE OF FRANCIS RABAN,
AND ONLY DAUGHTER OF DAVID PENFOLD, OF EARLSCOURT,
IN THE PARISH OF KENSINGTON.
DIED MARCH 20, 18—. AGED 22.

'Aunt Sarah,' Dolly cried, suddenly, seizing her aunt's
gown, 'tell me, was that young Mr. Raban from John Morgan's house and Emma from the cottage? When he looked
at me once I thought I knew him, only I didn't know who
he could be.'

'Yes, my dear,' said Lady Sarah; 'I did not suppose
that you would remember them.'

'I remembered,' said Rhoda, nodding her head; 'but I
thought you did not wish me to say so.'

'Why not?' asked Lady Sarah. 'You are always
imagining things, Rhoda. I had forgotten all about them
myself; I had other things on my mind at the time they
married,' and she sighed and looked away.

'It was when Dolly's papa——' Rhoda began.

'Mr. Raban reminded me of Kensington before he left,' said Lady Sarah, hastily, in her short voice. 'I was able to help him, foolish young man. It is all very sad, and he is very unhappy and very much to blame.'

This was their only visit to poor Emma Raban's grave. A few days after, Lady Sarah, in her turn, left Paris, and took Dolly and little Rhoda, whose schooling was over, home to England. Rhoda was rather sorry to be dropped at home at the well-known door in Old Street, where she lived with her Aunt Morgan. Yes, it would open in a minute, and all her old life would begin again. Tom and Joe and Cassie were behind it, with their loud voices. Dolly envied her; it seemed to her to be a noisy elysium of welcoming exclamations into which Rhoda disappeared.

CHAPTER IX.

THE BOW-WINDOWED HOUSE.

You'll love me yet, and I can tarry
  Your love's protracted growing ;
You reared that bunch of flowers you carry,
  From seeds of April's sowing.

RHODA, as she sat at her work, used to peep out of the bow-windows at the people passing up and down the street—a pretty girlish head, with thick black plaits pinned away, and a white frill round the slender throat. Sometimes, when Mrs. Morgan was out, Rhoda would untwist and unpin, and shake down a cloud upon her shoulders ; then her eyes would gleam with a wild wilful light, as she looked at herself in the little glass in the workbox, but she would run away if she heard any one coming, and hastily plait up her coils. The plain-speaking and rough-dealing of a household not attuned to the refinements of more sensitive natures had frightened instead of strengthening hers. She had learnt to be afraid and reserved. She was timid and determined, but things had gone wrong with her, and she was neither brave nor frightened in the right way. She had learnt to think for herself, to hold her own secretly against the universal encroachments of a lively race. She was obliging, and ready to sacrifice her own for others, but when she gave up, she

was conscious of the sacrifice. She could forgive her brother
unto seven times. She was like the disciple, whose sympathy
did not reach unto seventy times seven.

Rhoda was not strong, like Cassie and Zoe. She was
often tired, as she sat there in the window-corner. She could
not always touch the huge smoking heaps that came to table.
When all the knives and forks and voices clattered together,
they seemed to go through her head. The bells and laughter
made her start. She would nervously listen for the boys'
feet clattering down the stairs. At Church House there was
a fresh silence. You could hear the birds chirruping in the
garden all the time Lady Sarah was reading aloud. There
were low comfortable seats covered with faded old chintz and
tapestry. There were Court ladies hanging on the walls.
One wore a pearl necklace; she had dark bright eyes, and
Rhoda used to look at her, and think her like herself, and
wonder. There were books to read and times to read them
at Church House, and there was Dolly always thinking how
to give Rhoda pleasure. If she exacted a certain fealty and
obedience from the little maiden, her rule was different from
Aunt Morgan's. Dolly had no sheets to sew, no dusty cupboards to put straight, no horrible boys' shirts to front or
socks to darn and darn and darn, while their owners were
disporting themselves out of doors, and making fresh work
for the poor little Danaides at home.

To Dolly, Old Street seemed a delightful place. She
never could understand why Rhoda was so unhappy there.
It seemed to Dolly only too delightful, for George was for
ever going there when he was at home. The stillness of
Church House, its tranquil order and cheerful depression,
used to weary the boy; perhaps it was natural enough.
Unless, as Rhoda was, they are constitutionally delicate,

boys and girls don't want to bask all day long like jelly-fish
in a sunny calm ; they want to tire themselves, to try their
lungs; noise and disorder are to them like light and air,
wholesome tonics with which they brace themselves for the
coming struggles of life. Later in life there are sometimes
quite old girls and boys whose vitality cannot be repressed.
They go up mountains and drive steam-engines. They cry
out in print, since it would no longer be seemly for them to
shriek at the pitch of their voices, or to set off running
violently, or to leap high in the air.

'The Morgans' certainly meant plenty of noise and
cheerful clatter, the short tramp of schoolboy feet, huge
smoking dishes liberally dispensed. John Morgan would
rush in pale, breathless, and over-worked ; in a limp white
neckcloth as befitted his calling, he would utter a breathless
blessing on the food, and begin hastily to dispense the
smoking heap before him.

' Take care, John, dear,' cries Mrs. Morgan.

' What ? where ? ' says John. ' Why, George ! come to
lunch ? Just in time.'

It was in John Morgan's study that George established
himself after luncheon. The two windows stood open as far
as the old-fashioned sashes would go. The vine was straggling across the panes, wide-spreading its bronzed and
shining leaves. The sunlight dazzled through the green,
making a pleasant flicker on the walls of the shabby room,
with its worn carpet and old-fashioned cane chairs and deal
book-cases.

A door opened into an inner room, through which George,
by leaning forward from his arm-chair behind the door, can
see Mrs. Morgan's cap-ribbons all on end against the cross-
light in the sitting-room windows. Cassie is kneeling on

the floor, surrounded by piles of garments ; while her brother, standing in the middle of the room, is rapidly checking off a list of various ailments and misfortunes that are to be balanced in the scales of fate by proportionate rolls of flannel and calico.   Good little Cassie Morgan feels never a moment's doubt as she piles her heaps—so much sorrow, so many petticoats; so much hopeless improvidence, so many pounds of tea and a coal-ticket.   In cases of confirmed wickedness, she adds an illuminated text sometimes, and a hymn-book.   Do they ever come up, these hymn-books and bread-tickets cast upon the waters ?   Is it so much waste of time and seed ?   After all, people can but work in their own way, and feel kindly towards their fellow-creatures.   One seed is wasted, another grows up ; as the buried flora of a country starts into life when the fields are ploughed in after years.

' Go on, Cassie,' says Mrs. Morgan : ' Bonker—Wickens —Costello.'

. ' Costello is again in trouble,' says John.   ' It is too bad of him, with that poor wife of his and all those children.   I have to go round to the Court about him now.   Tell George I shall be back in ten minutes.'

' I have kept some clothes for them,' said Cassie.   ' They are such nice little children,' and she looks up flushed and all over ravellings at the relenting curate, who puts Mrs. Costello down in his relief-book.

All over John Morgan's study, chairs and tables, such books are lying, with pamphlets, blue books, black books, rolls and registers, in confusion, and smelling of tobacco.

In this age of good reports and evil reports people seem like the two boys in Dickens's story, who felt when they had docketed their bills that they were as good as paid.   So we

classify our wrongs and tie up our miseries with red tape;
we pity people by decimals, and put our statistics away with
satisfied consciences. John Morgan wrote articles from a
cold and lofty point of view, but he left his reports about all
over the room, and would rush off to the help of any human
being, deserving or undeserving. He had a theory that
heaven had created individuals as well as classes; and at
this very moment, with another bang of the door, he was on
his way to the police-court, to say a good word for the
intemperate Costello, who was ruefully awaiting his trial in
the dark cell below.

George, although comfortably established in the Morgan
study, was also tired of waiting, and found the house
unusually dull. For some time past he had been listening
to a measured creaking noise in the garden; then came a
peal of bells from the steeple; and he went to the window
and looked out. The garden was full of weeds and flowers,
with daisies on the lawn, and dandelions and milkwort
among the beds. It was not trimly kept, like the garden
at home; but George, who was the chief gardener, thought
it a far pleasanter place, with its breath of fresh breeze, and
its bit of blue over-roof. For flowers, there were blush-
roses, nailed against the wall, that Rhoda used to wear in
her dark hair sometimes, when there were no earwigs in
them; and blue flags, growing in the beds among spiked
leaves, and London pride, and Cape jessamine, very sweet
upon the air, and also ivy, creeping in a tangle of leaves
and tendrils. The garden had been planted by the different
inhabitants of the old brown house—each left a token.
There was a medlar-tree, with one rotten medlar upon a
branch, beneath which John Morgan would sit and smoke
his pipe in the sun, while his pupils construed Greek upon

the little lawn. Only Carlo was there now, stretching
himself comfortably in the dry grass (Carlo was one of
Bunch's puppies, grown up to be of a gigantic size and an
unknown species). Tom Morgan's tortoise was also basking
upon the wall. The creaking noise went on after the
chimes had ceased, and George jumped out of window on to
the water-butt to see what was the matter. He had forgotten the swing. It hung from a branch of the medlar-
tree to the trellis, and a slim figure, in a limp cotton dress,
stood clinging to the rope—a girl with a black cloud of
hair falling about her shoulders. George stared in amazement. Rhoda had stuck some vine-leaves in her hair, and
had made a long wreath, that was hanging from the swing,
and that floated as she floated. She was looking up with
great wistful eyes, and for a minute she did not see him.
As the swing rose and fell, her childish wild head went up
above the wall and the branches against the blue, and down
' upon a background of pure gold,' where the Virginian
creeper had turned in the sun. George thought it was a
sort of tune she was swinging, with all those colours round
about her in the sultry summer day. As he leaped down, a
feeling came over him as if it had all happened before, as if he
had seen it and heard the creaking of the ropes in a dream.
Rhoda blushed and slackened her flight. He seemed still to
remember it all while the swing stopped by degrees ; and
a voice within the house began calling, ' Rhoda ! Rhoda ! '

' Oh ! I must go,' said Rhoda, sighing. ' I am wasting
my time. Please don't tell Aunt Morgan I was swinging.'

' Tell her ! ' said George. ' What a silly child you are.
Why shouldn't you swing ? '

' Oh ! she would be angry,' said Rhoda, looking down.
I *am* very silly. I can't bear being scolded.'

' Can't you ? ' says George, with his hands in his pockets.
' I'm used to it, and don't mind a bit.'

' I shouldn't mind it if . . . if I was you, and any one
cared for me,' said Rhoda, with tearful eyes. She spoke in
a low depressed voice.

' Nonsense,' said George ; ' everybody cares for everybody.
Dolly loves you, so—so do we all.'

' Do you ? ' said Rhoda, looking at him in a strange
wistful way, and brightening suddenly, and putting back all
her cloudy hair with her hands. Then she blushed up, and
ran into the house.

When George told Dolly about it, Dolly was very sympathising, except that she said Rhoda ought to have answered
when her aunt called her. ' She is too much afraid of being
scolded,' said Dolly.

' Poor little thing ! ' said George. ' Listen to this,' and
he sat down to the piano. He made a little tune he
called ' The Swing,' with a minor accompaniment recurring
again and again, and a pretty modulation.

' It is exactly like a swing,' said Dolly. ' George, you
must have a cathedral some day, and make them sing all
the services through.'

' I shall not be a clergyman,' said George, gravely. ' It
is all very well for Morgan, who is desperately in love. He
has often told me that it would be his ruin if he were
separated from Mrs. Carbury.'

George, during his stay in Old Street (he had boarded
there for some weeks during Lady Sarah's absence), had
been installed general confidante and sympathiser, and was
most deeply interested in the young couple's prospects. •

' I believe Aunt Sarah has got a living when old Mr.
Livermore dies,' he went on, shutting up the piano and

coming to the table where Dolly was drawing. 'We must get her to present it to John Morgan.'

'But she always says it is for you, George, now that the money is lost,' said Dolly. 'I am afraid it will not be any use asking her. George, how much is prudent ? '

'How much is how much ? ' says George, looking with his odd blue eyes.

'I meant prudent to marry on ? ' says Dolly.

'Oh, I don't know,' says George, indifferently. 'I shall marry on anything I may happen to have.'

'What are you children talking about ? ' said Lady Sarah, looking up from her corner by the farthest chimney-piece. She liked one particular place by the fire, from which she could look down the room at the two heads that were bending together over the round table, and out into the garden, where a west wind was blowing, and tossing clouds and ivy sprays.

'We are talking about prudence in marriage,' says George.

'How can you be so silly ! ' says Lady Sarah, sharply. At which George starts up offended and marches through the window into the garden.

'What is it ? ' said the widow. 'Yes, Dolly, go to him,' she said, in answer to Dolly's pleading eyes. 'Foolish boy ! '

The girl was already gone. Her aunt watched the white figure, flying with wind-blown locks and floating skirts along the ivy wall. Dolly caught her brother up by the speckled holly-tree, and the two went on together, proceeding in step to a triumphant music of sparrows overhead, a wavering of ivy along their path ; soft winds blew everywhere, scattering light leaves ; the summer's light was in the day, and shining from the depth of Dolly's grey eyes. The two went and sat down on the bench by the pond, the old stone-edged pond, that reflected scraps of the blue green overhead ; a couple of gold-fishes alternately darted from side to side. George forgot that he was not understood as he sat there throwing pebbles into the water. Presently the wind brought some sudden voices close at hand, and, looking up, they saw two people advancing from the house, Robert Henley walking by Lady Sarah and carrying her old umbrella.

'Oh, he is always coming,' said George, kicking his heels, and not seeming surprised. 'He is staying with his grandmother at the Palace, but they don't give him enough to eat, and so he drops into the Morgans', and now he comes here.'

'Hush!' said Dolly, looking round.

Robert Henley was a tall, handsome young fellow, about twenty, with a straight nose and a somewhat pompous manner. He was very easy and good-natured when it was not too much trouble ; he would patronise people both younger and older than himself with equally good intentions. George's early admiration for his cousin I fear is now tinged with a certain jealousy of which Robert is utterly unconscious ; he takes the admiration for granted. He comes up and gives Dolly an affable kiss. 'Well, Dolly, have you learnt to talk French ? I want to hear all about Paris.'

'What shall I tell you ?' says simple Dolly, greatly excited. 'We had such a pretty drawing-room, Robert, with harps on all the doors, and yellow sofas, and such a lovely, lovely view.' And Lady Sarah smiled at Dolly's enthusiasm, and asked Robert if he could stay to dinner.

'I shall be delighted,' says Robert, just like a man of the world. 'My grandmother has turned me out for the day.'

CHAPTER X.

A SNOW GARDEN.

Ringed by a bowery, flowery angel brood,
Lilies and vestments and white faces sweet.

For every shrub, and every blade of grass,
And every pointed thorn seemed wrought in glass ;
In pearls and rubies rich the hawthorns show,
While through the ice the crimson berries glow
The spreading oak, the beech, and towering pine,
Glazed over, in the freezing æther shine ;
The frighted birds the rattling branches shun,
That wave and glitter in the distant sun.
                                    —PHILLIPS.

Is it that evening or another that they were all assembled
in the little bow-windowed drawing-room in Old Street
listening to one of Rhoda's interminable ' pieces ' that she
learnt at her French school ?   And then came a quartette,
but she broke down in the accompaniment, and George
turned her off the music-stool.

The doors were open into John's inner room, from which
came a last western gleam of light through the narrow windows, and beyond the medlar-tree.   It would have been dark
in the front room but for those western windows.   In one of
them sat Lady Sarah leaning back in John's old leathern
chair, sitting and listening with her hands lying loosely
crossed in her lap; as she listened to the youthful din

of music and voices and the strumming piano and the laughter. She had come by Dolly's special request. Her presence was considered an honour by Mrs. Morgan, but an effort at the same time. In her endeavours to entertain her guest, Mrs. Morgan, bolt upright in another corner, had fallen asleep, and was nodding her head in this silent inner room. There was noise and to spare in the front room, people in the street outside stopped to listen to the music.

When George began to play it seemed another music altogether coming out of the old cracked yellow piano; smash, bang, crack, he flew at it, thumping the keys, missing half the notes, sometimes jumbling the accompaniment, but seizing the tune and spirit of the music with a genuine feeling that was irresistible.

'Now all together,' cries George, getting excited.

It was an arrangement of one of Mendelssohn's four-part songs. 'As pants the hart,' sang Rhoda, shrill and sweet, leading the way. 'As pants the hart,' sang George, with a sort of swing. 'As pants the hart,' sang Dolly, carefully and restrainedly. She sang with great precision for a child of her age, quietly, steadily; but even her brother's enthusiasm did not inspire her. George flung his whole impulse into his music, and banged a chord at her in indignation at her tameness. John Morgan piped away with a face of the greatest seriousness, following his pupil's lead; he had much respect for George's musical capabilities. Cassie and Zoe sang one part together, and now and then Robert Henley came out with a deep trumpet-like note, placing it when he saw an opportunity. Dolly laughed the first time, but Rhoda's dark eyes were raised admiringly. So they all stood in the twilight, nodding their heads and clearing their voices, happy and harmlessly absorbed. They might have stood for a choir of angels; any one of the old Italian masters might have painted them as they sang, with the addition of lilies and wings, and gold glories, and the little cherubim who seemed to have flitted quite innocently out of ancient mythologies into the Légende Dorée of our own days; indifferently holding the music for a St. Cecilia, or the looking-glass for the Mother of Love.

Dolly, with her flowing locks, stood like a little rigid Raphael maiden, with eyes steadily fixed upon her scroll. Rhoda blushed, and shrilled and brightened. How well a golden glory would have become her dark cloudy hair.

As the room darkened Cassie set some lights, and they held them to read their music by. George kept them all at work, and gave no respite except to Rhoda, whose feelings he feared he had hurt. 'Please come and turn over my music, Rhoda,' he said. 'Dolly's not half quick enough.'

He had found some music in an old box at home the day before, some old-fashioned glees, with a faded and flourishing dedication to the Right Honourable the Countess of Churchtown, and then in faint ink, S. C. 1799.

It was easy music, and they all got on well enough, picking out the notes. Lady Sarah could remember her mother playing that same old ballad of ' Ye gentlemen of England' when she was herself quite a little girl. One old tune after another came, and mingled with Mrs. Morgan's sleeping, Lady Sarah's waking dreams of the past that was her own, and of the future that was to be for others; as the tunes struck upon her ear, they seemed to her like the new lives all about her repeating the old notes with fresh voices and feelings. George was in high good humour, behaving very well until Robert displeased him by taking somebody else's part ; the boy stopped short, and there might have been some discussion, but Mrs. Morgan's fat maid came in with the tray of gingerbread nuts, and the madeira and orange wine, that the hospitable old lady delighted to dispense, and set it down with a jingle in the back-room where the elder ladies were sitting.

This gingerbread tray was the grand closing scene of the entertainment, and Robert affably handed the wine-glasses, and John Morgan, seizing the gingerbread nuts, began scattering them all about the room as he forced them upon his unwilling guests. He had his sermon to finish for the next day, and he did not urge them to remain. There was a little chattering in the hall : Dolly was tied up and kissed and tucked up in her shawl ; Lady Sarah donned a capoche (as I think she called it) ; they stepped out into the little star-lit street, of which the go-to-bed lights were already burning in the upper windows. Higher still was Orion and his mighty company, looking down upon the humble illumination of the zigzag roofs. The door of the bow-windowed house opened to let out the voices. ' Good-night,' cried everybody, and then the door closed and all was silent again, except for the footsteps travelling down the street.

Fifteen or twenty years ago, as I have said, Dolly Vanborough and the other ladies and gentlemen her contemporaries were not the respectable middle-aged people they are now, but for the most part foolish young folks just beginning their lives, looking out upon the world with respectful eyes, arrogant,—perhaps dogmatic, uncertain,— but with a larger belief, perhaps a more heroic desire, than exists among them now. To-day, for a good many of them, expediency seems a great discovery, and the stone that is to turn everything to gold. Take things as you find them, do so and so, not because you feel inclined, or because it is right and generous, but because the neighbours are looking on, it is expected of you; and then, with our old friend the donkey-man, we stagger off, carrying the ass upon our shoulders. I suppose it is a law of nature that the horizon should lower as we climb down the hill of life, only some people look upwards always, ' And stumble among the briers and tumble into the well.' This is true enough, as regards my heroine, who was often in trouble, often disappointed, ashamed, angry, but who will persist in her star-gazing to the end of her journey.

When Dolly was nearly fifteen, her brother George was eighteen, and had just gone to college, starting in high spirits, and with visions of all the letters of the alphabet before him, and many other honourable distinctions. Dolly, dazzled, helped to pack his portmanteau.

' Oh, I wish I was going too!' Dolly said; ' girls never do anything, or go anywhere.'

' Mamma wants you to go to India,' said George.

' But the Admiral won't have me,' says Dolly; ' he wrote to Aunt Sarah about it, and said they were coming home. Are you going to take all these pipes and French novels?'

' I can never study without a pipe,' said George; ' and I must keep up my French.'

Dolly and Lady Sarah were disappointed when George, notwithstanding these appliances for study, returned without any special distinctions. The first Christmas that he came back, he brought Robert Henley with him. The old grandmother in the Palace was dead, and the young man had no longer a lodging in Kensington. The two arrived after dinner, and found Lady Sarah established by the fire in the oak parlour. They had come up driving through a fierce Christmas wind from the station, and were glad of Dolly's welcome and comfortable cups of tea.

When Dolly awoke next morning up in her little room, the whole country was white with snow. The iron wind was gone, the rigid breath of winter had sobbed itself away, the soft new-fallen snow lay heaped on the fields and the hedges, on the fir-trees and laurels. Dolly ran to the window. George and Robert were out in the garden already. Overhead was a blue, high heaven; the white snow-country she could see through her window was sparkling and dazzling white. Sharp against the heavens stood the delicate branches of the trees, prismatic lights were radiating from the sloping lawns, a light veil of fallen drift wreathed the distant coppices; and Dolly, running downstairs soon after, found the dining-room empty, except for the teapot, and she carried her breakfast to the window. She had scarcely finished when George and Robert both came tapping at the pane.

'Come out,' cried George.

'Let her finish her breakfast,' said Robert.

'I've done,' cried Dolly, gaily jumping up and running to fetch her hat and her coat, and to tie up her long skirts. Dolly possessed a warm fur cloak, which had been Lady Sarah's once, in the days of her prosperity, and which became the girl so well that her aunt liked her to wear it. Henley, standing by a frozen cabbage in the kitchen-garden, watched her approvingly as she came along the snowy path. All her brown furs were glistening comfortably; the scarlet feather in her hat had caught the light and reflected it on her hair.

Dolly's hair was very much the colour of seal-skin, two-coloured, the hollows of its rippling locks seemed dark while the crests shone like gold. There was something autumnal in her colours. Dolly's was a brilliant russet autumn, with grey skies and red berries and warm lights. She had tied a scarlet kerchief round her neck, but the snow did not melt for all her bright colours. How pretty it was! leaves lying crisped and glittering upon the white foaming heaps, tiny tracks here and there crossing the pathways, and then the bird-steps, like chainlets lightly laid upon the smooth, white field. Where the sun had melted the snow in some sheltered corner, some red-breasts were hopping and bobbing; the snow-sheets glittered, lying heavy on the laurel-leaves on the low fruit walls.

Robert watched her coming, with her honest smiling face. She stopped at the end of the walk to clear away a corner of the bed, where a little colony of snowdrops were crushed by a tiny avalanche that had fallen upon their meek heads. It was the work of an instant, but in that instant Dolly's future fate was decided.

For, as my heroine comes advancing unconscious through this snow and diamond morning, Henley thinks that is the realization of a dream he has sometimes dreamt, and that the mistress of his future home stands there before him, bright and bonnie, handsome and outspoken. Dorothy rules him with the ascendency of a youthful, indifferent heart, strong in its own reliance and hope; and yet this maiden is not the person that she thinks herself, nor is she the person that Henley thinks her. She is strong, but with an artificial strength not all her own; strong in the love of those round about her, strong in youth and in ignorance of evil.

They walked together down the garden walks and out into the lanes, and home again across the stile. 'Dolly,'

IN THAT INSTANT DOLLY'S FUTURE FATE WAS DECIDED.

said Robert, as they were going in, 'I shall not forget our morning's expedition together—will you, too, promise me —— ?' He stopped short. 'What are those?' he said, sentimentally; 'snowdrops?' and he stooped to pick one or two. Dolly also turned away. 'Here is something that will remind you ——' Robert began.

'And you,' cries Dolly, flinging a great snow heap suddenly into his face and running away. It was very babyish and vulgar, but Robert looked so solemn that she could not resist the impulse. He walked back to the house greatly offended.

CHAPTER XI.

RABAN MEETS THE SHABBY ANGEL.

Christ hath sent us down the angels,
And the whole earth and the skies
Are illumed by altar-candles,
Lit for blessed mysteries.
And a Priest's hand through creation
Waveth calm and consecration. . . .

—E. B. B.

SOMETIMES winter days come in autumn, just as hours of old age and middle age seem to start out of their places in the due rotation of life and to meet us on the way.   One October evening in the following year a damp fog was spreading over London, the lights from the windows streamed faintly upon the thick veils of vapour.   Many noisy shadows were out and about, for it was Saturday night, and the winding Kensington thoroughfare was almost blocked by the trucks and the passers-by.   It was only six o'clock, but the last gleam of light had died away behind the western chimney-tops ; and with the darkness and notwithstanding the fog, a cheerful saturnalia had begun.   A loitering, a clamouring through the clouds of mist, witches with and without broom-sticks, little imps darting through the crowd, flaring trucks drawn up along the road, housewives bargaining their Sunday dinners.   It seemed a confusion of darkness, candles, paper-shades, oranges, and what not. Now and then some quiet West End carriage would roll by, with lamps burning, through the mist, and horses trampling steadily. Here and there, a bending head might be seen in some lighted window —it was before the time of Saturday half-holidays—the forge was blazing and hard at work, clink clank fell the iron strokes, and flames flashed from the furnace.

Beyond the church, and the arch, and the forge, the shop-lights cease, the fog seems to thicken, and a sudden silence to fall upon everything; while the great veils spread along the road, hiding away how many faces, hearths, and homelike rays. There are sometimes whole years in one's life that seem so buried beneath some gloomy shadow ; people come and go, lights are burning, and voices sound, but the darkness hangs over everything, and the sun never seems to rise. A dull-looking broad-shouldered young man with a beard had come elbowing his way through the crowd, looking about him as he came along. After a moment's hesitation he turned up a side lane, looming away out of the region of lamps. It was so black and silent that he thought at first he must have been mistaken. He had been carefully directed, but there seemed no possibility of a house. He could just make out two long walls ; a cat ran hissing along the top of one of them, a wet foggy wind flickered in his face, and a twig broke from some branch overhead. Frank Raban, for it was he, wondered if the people he was in search of could be roosting on the trees or hiding behind the walls this damp evening.

He was turning back in despair when suddenly a door opened, with a flash of light, through the brickwork, and a lantern was held out.

'Good-night,' said a loud, cheerful voice ; 'why, your

street lamp is out; take my arm, Zoe. Go in, Dorothea, you
will catch cold.' And two figures, issuing from the wall like
apparitions in the *Arabian Nights*, passed by hurrying
along—a big, comfortable great-coat and a small dark thing
tripping beside it. Meanwhile, the person who had let them
out peeped for an instant into the blackness, holding the
lantern high up so as to throw its light upon the lane.
There came a sudden revelation of the crannies of an old
brick wall; of creeping, green ivy, rustling in the light
which seemed to flow from leaf to leaf; and of a young
face smiling upon the dim vapours. It was all like the slide
of a magic-lantern passing on the darkness. Raban almost
hesitated to come forward, but the door was closing on the
shining phantasmagoria.

'Does Lady Sarah Francis live here?' he said, coming
up.

The girl started—looked at him. She, in turn, saw a
red beard and a pale face appearing unexpectedly, and with
a not unnatural impulse she half closed the door. 'Yes,'
she said, retreating a step or two towards the house, which
Raban could now see standing ghost-like within the outer
wall. It was dimly lighted, here and there, from the deep
windows; it seemed covered with tangled creepers; over
the open hall door an old-fashioned stone canopy still hung,
dripping with fog and overgrown with ivy.

The girl, with her lantern, stood waiting on the steps.
A blooming maiden, in a dark green dress, cut in some
quaint old-fashioned way, and slashed with black. Her
dress was made of coarse homely stuff, but a gold chain
hung round her neck; it twinkled in the lantern light. Her
reddish-brown hair was pinned up in pretty twists, and some
berries glistend among its coils.

'If you want to *see* Lady Sarah,' she said, a little impatiently, 'come in, and shut the garden door.'

He did as he was bid. She ran up the steps into the house, and stood waiting in the old hall, scanning him still by her lamplight. She had put the lantern on a corner of the carved chimney-sill, from whence its glimmers fell upon oaken panels and black-and-white flags of marble, upon a dark oak staircase winding up into the house.

'Will you go in there?' said the girl, in a low voice, pointing to an open door.

Then she quickly and noiselessly barred and fixed the heavy bolts; her hands slid along the old iron hasps and hooks. Raban stood watching her at work; he found himself comparing her to an ivy plant, she seemed to bloom so freshly in the damp- and darkness, as she went moving hither and thither in her odd green gown. The next minute she was springing up the staircase. She stopped, however, on the landing, and leaned over the banisters to point again, with a stiff quick gesture, to the open door.

Raban at last remembered that he had not given his name. 'Will you kindly say that———'

But the green dress was gone, and Raban could only walk into the dark room, and make his way through unknown passes to a smouldering fire dying on the hearth. On his way he tumbled over a growl, a squeak. Then a chair went down, and a cat gave a yell, and sprang into the hall. It was an odd sort of place, and not like anything that Raban had expected. The usual proprieties of life have this advantage, that people know what is coming, and pull at a wire with a butler or a parlour-maid at the other end of it, who also know their parts and in their turn correspond with an invisible lady upstairs, at the right-hand corner of the drawing room fire-place. She is prepared to come forward with a nice bow, and to point to the chair opposite, which is usually on castors, so that you can pull it forward, and as you sit down you say, ' I daresay you may remember,' or ' I have been meaning to,' or, &c.

But the whole machinery seemed wanting here, and Frank Raban remained in the dark, looking through the unshuttered black windows, or at the smouldering ashes at his feet. At first he speculated on the ivy-maiden, and then as the minutes went by and no one came, his mind travelled back through darkness all the way to the last time he had met Lady Sarah Francis, and the old sickening feeling came over him at the thought of the past. In these last few years he had felt that he must either fight for life or sink for ever. It was through no merit of his own that he had not been utterly wrecked ; that he was here to-night, come to repay the debt he owed ; that, more fortunate than many, he had struggled to shore. Kind hands had been held out to help him to drag safe out of the depths. Lady Sarah's was the first ; then came the younger, firmer grasp of some of his companions, whom he had left but a year or two ago in the old haunts, before his unlucky start in life. It was habit that had taken him back to these old haunts at a time when, by a fortunate chance, work could be found for him to do. His old friends did not fail him ; they asked no questions ; they did not try to probe his wounds ; they helped him to the best of their ability, and stood by him as men stand by each other, particularly young men. No one was surprised when Mr. Raban was elected to one of the tutorships at All Saints'

He had taken a good degree, he had been popular in his time, though now he could not be called a popular man. Some wondered that it should be worth his while to settle down upon so small an inducement. Henley, of St. Thomas's, had refused it when it was pressed upon him. Perhaps Raban had private means. He had lived like a rich man, it was said, after he left college. Poor Frank! Those two fatal years had eaten up the many lean kine that were to follow. All he had asked for now was work, and a hope of saving up enough to repay those who had trusted him in his dismay. His grandfather had refused to see him after his marriage. Frank was too proud a man to make advances, but not too proud to work. He gratefully took the first chance that came in his way. The morning he was elected he went to thank one or two of his supporters. He just shook hands, and said 'Thank you;' but they did not want any fine speeches, nor was Frank inclined to make them.

Three years are very long to some people, while they are short to others. Mrs. Palmer had spent them away from her children not unpleasantly, except for one or two passing differences with the Captain, who had now, it was said, taken to offering up public prayers for Philippa's conversion. Lady Sarah had grown old in three years. She had had illness and money troubles, and was a poor woman comparatively speaking. Her hair had turned white, her face had shrunk, while Dolly had bloomed into brightness, and Frank Raban had grown into middle age, as far as hope and feeling went. There he sat in the warm twilight, thinking of the past—ah, how sadly! He was strong enough for to-day, and not without trust in the future; but he was still almost hopeless when he thought of the past. He had not forgiven himself. His was not a forgiving nature, and as long as he lived, those two fatal years of his life would make part of his sorrowful experience. Once Sarah Francis had tried to tell him—(but many things cannot be understood except by those who have first learnt the language)—that for some people the only possible repentance is to do better. Mere repentance, that dwelling upon past misery and evil doing, which people call remorse, is, as often as not, madness and meaningless despair.

Sometimes Frank wondered now at the irritation which had led him to rebel so furiously at his fate. Poor, gentle fate! he could scarcely understand his impatience with it now. Perhaps, if Emma had lived——

We often, in our blindness, take a bit of our life, and look at it apart as an ended history. We take a phase incomplete, only begun, perhaps, for the finished and irrevocable whole. Irrevocable it may be, in one sense, but who shall say that the past is completed because it is past, any more than that we ourselves are completed because we must die? Frank had not come to look at his own personal misdoings philosophically (as what honest man or woman would), or with anything but shrinking pain, as yet; he could bear no allusion to those sad days.

'You know Paris well, I believe Mr. Raban,' said some young lady. 'How long is it since——'

He looked so odd and angry that she stopped quite frightened. Dark fierce lines used to come under his heavy eyes at the smallest attempt to revive what was still so recent and vivid. If it was rude he could not help it.

He never spoke of himself. Strangers used to think Raban odd and abrupt when he sometimes left them in the middle of a sentence, or started away and did not answer. His old friends thought him changed, but after a great crisis we are used to see people harder. And this one talks, and you think he has told you all ; and that one is silent, and he thinks he has told you nothing. And feelings come and go, the very power to understand them comes and goes, gifts and emotions pass, our inmost feelings change as we go on wandering through the narrow worlds that lie along the commonest commonplaces and ways of life. Into what worlds had poor Frank been wandering as he stood watching the red lights dull into white ashes by the blue tiles of the hearth !

Presently a lantern and two dark heads passed the window.

' Where is he ? ' said a voice in the hall. ' Dolly, did you say Mr. Raban was here ? What ! all in the dark ? '

The voice had reached the door by this time, and some one came and stood there for an instant. How well he remembered the kindly croaking tones ! When he heard them again, it seemed to him as if they had only finished speaking a minute before.

Some one came and stood for an instant at the doorway. No blooming young girl with a bright face and golden head, but a grey-haired woman, stooping a little as she walked. She came forward slowly, set her light upon the table, and then looked at him with a pair of kind shaggy eyes, and put out her long hand as of old.

Raban felt his heart warm towards the shabby face, the thick kindly brows. Once that woman's face had seemed to him like an angel's in his sorest need. Who says angels must be all young and splendid ; will there not be some comforting ones, shabby and tender, whose radiance does not dazzle nor bewilder ; whose faces are worn, perhaps, while their stars shine with a gentle tremulous light, more soothing to our aching, earth-bound hearts than the glorious radiance of brighter spirits? Raban turned very red when he saw his old friend. 'How could you know I was here? You have not forgotten me?' he said; not in his usual reluctant way, but speaking out with a gentle tone in his voice. 'I should have come before, but I——' Here he began to stammer and to feel in his pocket. 'Here it is,' and he pulled out a packet. 'If it hadn't been for you I should never have had the heart to set to work again. I don't know what I should have done,' he repeated, 'but for you.' And then he looked at her for an instant, and then, with a sudden impulse, Raban stopped—as he did so she saw his eyes were glistening—he stooped and kissed her cheek.

'Why, my dear?' said Lady Sarah, blushing up. She had not had many kisses in her life. Some people would as soon have thought of kissing the poker and tongs.

Frank blushed up too and looked a little foolish; but he quickly sobered down again. 'You will find it all right,' said Raban, folding her long thin hand over the little parcel, 'and good-night, and thank you.'

Still Lady Sarah hesitated. She could not bear to take it. She felt as though he had paid her twice over; that she ought to give it back to him, and say, 'Here, keep it. I don't want your money, only your kiss and your friendship. I was glad to help you.' She looked up in his pale face in a strange wistful way, scanning it with her grey eyes. They almost seemed to speak, and to say, 'You don't know how I want it, or I would not take it from you.'

'How changed you are!' she said at last, speaking very slowly. 'I am afraid you have been working too hard to pay me. I oughtn't to——' He was almost annoyed by this wistful persistency. Why did she stand hesitating? Why did she not take it, and put it in her pocket, and have done with it? Now again she was looking at the money with a pathetic look. And meanwhile Raban was wondering, Could it be that this woman cared for money—this woman, who had forced her help upon him so generously? He hated himself for the thought. This was the penalty, he told himself, for his own past life. This fatal suspicion and mistrust of others: even his benefactress was not to be spared.

'I must be going,' he said, starting away in his old stiff manner. 'You will let me come again, won't you?'

'Come again! Of course you will come again,' Lady Sarah said, laying her thin fingers on his arm. 'I shall not let you go now until you have seen my Dolly.' And so saying, she led him back into the hall. 'Go in, you will find her there. I will come back,' said Lady Sarah, abruptly, with her hand on the door-handle. She looked quite old and feeble as she leant against the oak. Then again she seemed to remember herself. 'You—you will not say anything of this,' she added, with a sudden imploring look ; and she opened her thin fingers, still clutching the packet of bank-notes and gold, and closed them again.

Then he saw her take the lantern from the chimney and hurriedly toil up the stairs, and he felt somehow that she was going to hide it away.

What would he have thought if he could have seen her safe in her own room, with the sovereigns spread out upon the bed and the bank-notes, while the poor soul stood eagerly counting over her store. Yes, she loved money, but there were things she loved still more. Sarah Francis, alone in the world, might have been a miser if she had not loved Dolly so dearly—Dolly, who was Stan's daughter. There

H

was always just this difference between Lady Sarah and open-handed people. With them money means little—a moment's weakness, a passing interest. With Lady Sarah to give was doubt, not pleasure ; it meant disorder in her balanced schemes ; it meant truest self-denial: to give was to bestow on others what she meant for Dolly's future ease and happiness ; and yet she gave.

CHAPTER XII.

DOROTHEA BY FIRELIGHT.

The waunut logs shot sparkles out
Towards the pootiest, bless her,
An' leetle fires danced all about
The chiny on the dresser ;
The very room, coz she was in,
Looked warm from floor to ceilin'.
—LOWELL.

LADY SARAH had left Raban to go into the drawing-room
alone. It was all very strange, he thought, and more and
more like a crazy dream. He found himself in a long room
of the colour of firelight, with faded hangings, sweeping
mysteriously from the narrow windows, with some old chan-
deliers swinging from the shadows. It seemed to him,
though he could not clearly see them, that there were ghosts
sitting on the chairs, denizens of the kingdom of mystery,
and that there was a vague flit and consternation in the
darkness at the farther end of the room, when through the
opening door the gleam of the lantern, which by this time
was travelling upstairs, sped on with a long slanting flash.
For a moment he thought the place was empty ; the atmosphere was very warm and still ; the firelight blazed comfortably ; a coal started from the grate, then came a breath, a
long, low, sleepy breath from a far-away corner. Was this

a ghost ?   And then, as his eyes got accustomed, he saw that
the girl who had let him in sat crouching by the fire.   Her
face was turned away ; the light fell upon her throat and the
harmonious lines of her figure.   Raban, looking at her,
thought of one of Lionardo's figures in the Louvre.   But
this was finer than a Lionardo.   What is it in some attitudes
that is so still, and yet that thrills with a coming movement
of life and action ?   It is life, not inanimately resting, but
suspended from motion as we see it in the old Greek art.
That flying change from the now to the future is a wonder
sometimes written in stone; it belongs to the greatest
creations of genius as well as to the living statues and pictures among which we live.

So Dolly, unconscious, was a work of art, as she warmed
her hands at the fire : her long draperies were heaped round
about her, her hair caught the light and burnt like gold.
If Miss Vanborough had been a conscious work of art she
might have remained in her pretty attitude, but being a
girl of sixteen, simple and somewhat brusque in manners,
utterly ignoring the opinions of others, she started up and
came to meet Raban, advancing quick through the dimness
and the familiar labyrinth of chairs.

' Hush—sh ! ' she said, pointing to a white heap in a
further corner, ' Rhoda is asleep; she has been ill, and we
have brought her here to nurse.'   Then she went back in
the same quick silence, brought a light from the table, and
beckoning to him to follow her, led the way to the very
darkest and shadiest end of the long drawing-room, where
the ghosts had been flitting before them.   There was a tall
oak chair, in which she established herself.   There was an
old cabinet and a sofa, and a faded Italian shield of looking-
glass, reflecting waves of brown and reddish light.   Again

Dolly motioned. Raban was to sit down there on the sofa opposite.

Since he had come into the house he had done little but obey the orders he had received. He was amused and not a little mystified by this young heroine's silent imperious manners. He did not admire them, and yet he could not help watching her, half in wonder, half in admiration of her beauty. She, as I have said, did not think of speculating upon the impression she had created : she had other business on hand.

' I knew you at once,' said Dolly, with the hardihood of sixteen, ' when I saw you at the gate.' As she spoke in her girlish voice, somehow the mystery seemed dispelled, and Raban began to realise that this was only a drawing-room and a young lady after all.

' Ever since your letter came last year,' she continued, unabashed, ' I have hoped that you would come, and—and you have paid her the money she lent you, have you not ? ' said the girl, looking into his face doubtfully, and yet confidingly too.

Raban answered by an immense stare. He was a man almost foolishly fastidious and reserved. He was completely taken aback and shocked by her want of discretion—so he chose to consider it. Dolly, unused to the ways of the world, had not yet appreciated those refinements of delicacy with which people envelop the simplest facts of life.

As for Raban, he was at all times uncomfortably silent respecting himself. ' Dolly ' conveyed no meaning whatever to his mind, although he might have guessed who she was. Even if Lady Sarah had not asked it of him, he would not have answered her. Whatever they may say, reserved people pique themselves upon some mental superiority in the reservations they make. Miss Vanborough misinterpreted the meaning of the young man's confused looks and silence.

He had not paid the money! she was sorry. Oh, how
welcome it would have been for Aunt Sarah's sake and for
George's sake! Poor George! how should she ever ask for
money for him now? Her face fell; she tried to speak of
other things to hide her disappointment. Now she wished
she had not asked the question—it must be so uncomfortable for Mr. Raban she thought. She tried to talk on;
one little sentence came jerking out after another, and Raban
answered more or less stiffly. 'Was he not at Cambridge?
Did he know her brother there—George Vanborough?'

Raban looked surprised, and said, 'Yes, he knew a
Mr. Vanborough slightly. He had known him at his tutor's
years before.' Here a vision of a stumpy young man
flourishing a tankard rose before him. Could he be this
beautiful girl's brother?

'Did he know her cousin, Robert Henley?' continued
Dolly, eagerly.

Raban (who had long avoided Henley's companionship)
answered even more stiffly that he did not see much of him.
So the two talked on; but they had got into a wrong key,
as people do at times, and they mutually jarred upon each
other. Even their silence was inharmonious. Occasionally
came a long, low, peaceful breath: it seemed floating on
the warm shadows.

Everything was perfectly commonplace, and yet to
Raban there seemed an element of strangeness and incongruity in the ways of the old house. There was something
weird in the whole thing—the defiant girl, the sleeping
woman, Lady Sarah, with her strange hesitations and
emotions, and the darkness.—How differently events strike
people from different points of view. Here was a common-
place half-hour, while old Sam prepared the seven-o'clock

tea with Marker's help—while Rhoda slept a peaceful little
sleep: to Raban it seemed a strange and puzzling experience,
quite out of the common run of half-hours.

Did he dislike poor Dolly? That off-hand manner was
not Frank Raban's ideal of womanliness. Lady Sarah, with
her chilled silence and restrained emotions, was nearer to it
by far, old and ugly though she was. And yet he could not
forget Dolly's presence for a single instant. He found himself watching, and admiring, and speculating about her
almost against his will. She, too, was aware of this silent
scrutiny, and resented it. Dolly was more brusque and
fierce and uncomfortable that evening than she had ever
been in all her life before. Dorothea Vanborough was one
of those people who reflect the atmosphere somehow, whose
lights come and go, and whose brilliance comes and goes.
Dull fogs would fall upon her sometimes, at others sunlight,
moonlight, or faint reflected rays would beam upon her
world. It was a wide one, and open to all the winds of
heaven.

So Frank Raban discovered when it was too late. He
admired her when he should have loved her. He judged
her in secret when he should have trusted or blamed her
openly. A day came when he felt he had forfeited all right
even to help her or to protect her, and that, while he was
still repenting for the past, he had fallen (as people sometimes do who walk backwards) into fresh pitfalls.

' My cousin Robert has asked me and Rhoda to spend a
day at Cambridge in the spring,' said Dolly, reluctantly
struggling on at conversation.

Frank Raban was wondering if Lady Sarah was never
coming back.

There was a sigh, a movement from the distant corner.

' Did you call me ? ' said a faint, shrill voice, plaintive and tremulous, and a figure rose from the nest of soft shawls and came slowly forward, dispersing the many wraps that lay coiling on the floor.

' Have I been asleep ? I thought Mr. Henley was here ? ' said the voice, confusedly.

Dolly turned towards her. ' No, he is not here, Rhoda. Sit down, don't stand ; here is Mr. Raban come to see us.'

And then in the dim light of the fire and distant candle, Raban saw two dark eyes looking out of a pale face that he seemed to remember.

' Mr. Raban ! ' said the voice.

' Have you forgotten ? ' said Dolly, hastily, going up to the distant sofa. ' Mr. Raban, from Paris ----' she began ; then seeing he had followed her, she stopped ; she turned very red. She did not want to pain him. And Raban, at the same moment, recognised the two girls he had seen once before, and remembered where it was that he had known the deep grey eyes, with their look of cold repulsion and dislike.

' Are you Mr. Raban ? ' repeated Rhoda, looking intently into his face. ' I should have known you if it had not been so dark.' And she instinctively put up her hand and clasped something hanging round her neck.

The young man was moved.

' I ought indeed to remember you,' he said, with some emotion.

And as he spoke, he saw a diamond flash in the firelight. This, then, was the child who had wandered down that terrible night, to whom he had given his poor wife's diamond cross.

Rhoda saw with some alarm that his eyes were fixed upon the cross.

' I sometimes think I ought to send this back to you,' she faltered on, blushing faintly, and still holding it tight-clasped in her hand.

' Keep it,' said Raban, gravely; 'no one has more right to it than you.' Then they were all silent.

Dolly wondered why Rhoda had a right to the cross, but she did not ask.

Raban turned still more hard and more sad as the old memories assailed him suddenly from every side. Here was the past living over again. Though he might have softened to Lady Sarah, he now hardened to himself; and, as it often happens, the self-inflicted pain he felt seemed reflected in his manner towards the girls.

' I know you both now,' he said, gravely, standing up. ' Good-night; will you say good-by to your aunt for me ? '

He did not offer to shake hands; it was Dolly who put out hers. He was very stiff, and yet there was a humble look in his pale face and dark eyes that Dolly could not forget. She seemed to remember it after he was gone.

Lady Sarah came in only a minute after Frank had left. She looked disappointed.

' I have just met him in the hall,' she said.

' Is he gone ? ' said Dolly. ' Aunt Sarah, he is still very unhappy.'

A few minutes afterwards Rhoda said what a pity that Mr. Raban was gone, when she saw how smartly the tea-table was set out, how the silver candlesticks were lighted, and some of the good old wine that George liked sparkling in the decanter. Dolly felt as if Mr. Raban was more dis-agreeable than ever for giving so much trouble for nothing. Rhoda was very much interested in Lady Sarah's visitor, and asked Dolly many more questions when they were alone

upstairs. She had been ill, and was staying at Church
House to get well in quiet and away from the schoolboys.

'Of course one can't ever like him,' Dolly said, 'but one
is very sorry for him. Good-night, Rhoda.'

'No, I don't like her,' said Raban to himself; and he
thought of Dolly all the way home. Her face haunted him.
He dined at his club, and drove to the shabby station in
Bishopsgate. He seemed to see her still as he waited for
his train, stamping by the station fire, and by degrees that
bitter vision of the past vanished away and the present
remained. Dolly's face seemed to float along before him all
the way back as the second-class carriage shook and jolted
through the night, out beyond London fog into a region of
starlit plains and distant glimmering lights. Vision and
visionary travelled on together, until at last the train
slackened its thunder and stopped. A few late Cambridge
lights shone in the distance. It was past midnight. When
Raban, walking through the familiar byways, reached his
college-gates, he found them closed and barred; one gas-
lamp flared—a garish light of to-day shining on the ancient
carved stones and gabions of the past. A sleepy porter let
him in, and as he walked across the dark court he looked up
and saw here and there a light burning in a window, and
then some far-away college-clock clanged the half-hour, then
another, and another, and then their own clock overhead, loud
and stunning. He reached his own staircase at last and opened
the oak door. Before going in, Raban looked up through
the staircase-window at George Vanborough's rooms, which
happened to be opposite his own. They were brilliantly
illuminated, and the rays streamed out and lighted up many
a deep lintel and sleeping-window.

CHAPTER XIII.

LITTLE BROTHER AND LITTLE SISTER.

Go ; when the instinct is stilled, and when the deed is accomplished,
What thou hast done, and shalt do, shall be declared to thee then ;
Go with the sun and the stars, and yet evermore in thy spirit
Say to thyself: ' It is good, yet is there better than it ;
This that I see is not all, and this that I do is but little,
Nevertheless it is good, though there is better than it.'
—A. CLOUGH.

As the actors pass across the stage of life and play their
parts in its great drama, it is not difficult at the outset to
docket them for the most part 'a lawyer,' 'a speculator,' 'an
amiable person,' 'an intelligent, prosy man,' 'a parson,' &c.;
but after watching the piece a little (on this all-the-world
stage it is not the play that ends, but the actors and specu-
lators that come and go), we begin to see, that although
some of the performers may be suited to their parts, there
are others whose characters are not so well cast to the
piece—Robert Henley, for instance, who is not quite in his
element as a very young man. But every one is in earnest
in a certain fashion upon this life-stage, and that is why
we find the actors presently beginning to play their own
characters, instead of those which they are supposed to
represent—to the great confusion, very often, of the drama
itself. We have all read of a locksmith who had to act the

part of a king; of a nephew who tried to wear his uncle's
cocked hat; of a king who proclaimed himself a god; and
of the confusion that ensued; and it is the same in private
as in public life, where people are set to work experiments
in love, money, sermon, hay, or law-making, with more or
less aptitude for the exercise—what a strange jumble it is!
Here is the lawyer making love to his client, instead of
writing her will; the lover playing on the piano while his
mistress is expecting him; the farmer, while his crops are
spoiling, pondering on the theory of original sin. Among
women, too, we find wives, mothers, daughters, and even
professed aunts and nieces, all with their parts reversed by
the unkind freaks of fate. Some get on pretty well, some
break down utterly. The higher natures, acting from a
wider conception of life, will do their best to do justice to
the character, uncongenial though it may be, which happens
to be assigned to them. Perhaps they may flag now and
then, specially towards the middle of the performance; but
by degrees they come to hear the music of 'duty done.'
And duty is music, though it may be a hard sort of fugue,
and difficult to practise—one too hard, alas, for our poor
George as yet to master. Henley, to be sure, accomplished
his ambitions; but then it was only a one-fingered scale
that he attempted.

Dolly's was easy music in those early days of her life: at
home or in Old Street the girl herself and her surroundings
were in a perfect harmony. Dolly's life was a melody
played to an accompaniment of loving tones and tender
words among the tranquil traditions of the old house and
the old ivy-grown suburb in which it stood. Rhoda used to
wonder why people cared so much for Dolly, who was so
happy, who never sacrificed herself, but did as she liked,

and won all hearts to her, even Robert Henley's, thought
Rhoda, with a sigh. As for Dolly, she never thought about
her happiness, though Rhoda did. The girl's life sped on
peacefully among the people who loved her. She knew she
meant so well that it had not yet occurred to her that she
might make mistakes in life and fail, and be sorry some day
like other folks. Rhoda, comparing her own little back-
garret life in the noisy Morgan household with her friend's,
used to think that everybody and everything united to spoil
her. Dolly was undoubtedly Dorothea Regina—ruler of the
household—a benevolent tyrant. The province of the teapot was hers—the fortress of the store-room. She had her
latch-key. Old Marker and George were the only people
who ever ventured to oppose her. When they did so, Dolly
gave in instantly with a smile and a sweet grace that was
specially her own. She was a somewhat impetuous and self-
diffident person in reality, though as yet she did not know
what she was. In looks she could see a tall and stately
maiden, with a sweet, round, sleepy face, reflected in the
glass, and she took herself for granted at the loving valua-
tion of those about her, as people, both old and young, are
apt to do.

Dolly was one of those persons who travel on eagerly
by starts, and then sit down to rest.   Notwithstanding
her impetuous, youthful manner, she was full of humility
and diffidence, and often from very shyness and sincerity
she would seem rude and indignant when she was half-
frightened at her own vehemence ; then came passionate
self-reproach, how passionate none can tell but those who,
like Dolly Vanborough, seem to have many selves and many
impulses, all warring with one another. There are two
great classes of women—those who minister, and those who

are taken care of by others; and the born care-takers and
workers are apt to chafe in early life, before people will
recognise their right to do. Something is wrong, tempers
go wrong, hearts beat passionately, boil over, ache for
nothing at all; they want to comfort people, to live, to
love, to come and go, to feel they are at work. It may
be wholesome discipline for such natures to live for years
in a kingdom of education of shadows and rules. They
may practise their self-denial on the keys of the piano, they
may translate their hearts' interest into German exercises
and back into English again; but that is poor work, and
so far the upper classes pay a cruel penalty unknown to
girls of a humbler birth. And so time goes on. For some
a natural explanation comes to all their nameless difficulties. Others find one sooner or later, or the bright edge
of impatient youth wears off. Raban once called Dolly a
beautiful sour apple. Beautiful apples want time and
sunshine to ripen and become sweet. If Dolly blamed
others, she did not spare herself; but she was much beloved,
and, as I have said, she meant so well that she could
not help trusting in herself.

Something of Dolly's life was written in her face, in
her clear, happy eyes, in her dark and troubled brow.
Even as a girl, people used to say that she had always
different faces, and so she had for the multitude; but for
those who loved her it was always the same true, trusting
look, more or less worn as time went on, but still the
same. She had a peculiar, sudden, sweet smile, that went
to the very heart of the lonely old aunt, who saw it often.
Dolly never had the training of repression, and perhaps
that is why, when it fell upon her in later life, the lesson
seemed so hard. She was not brilliant. She could not

say things like George. She was not witty. Though she loved to be busy, and to accomplish, Dolly could not do things like Rhoda—clearly, quickly, completely. But how many stupid people there are who have a touch of genius about them. It would be hard to say in what it consists. They may be dull, slow, cross at times, ill-informed, but you feel there is something that outweighs dulness, crossness, want of information.

Dorothy Vanborough had a little genius in her, though she was apt to look stupid and sulky and indifferent when she did not feel at her ease. Sometimes when reproved for this, she would stand gaping with her grey eyes, and looking so oddly like her Aunt Sarah that Mrs. Palmer, when she came home, would lose all patience with her. There was no knowing exactly what she was, her mother used to say. One day straight as an arrow—bright, determined; another day, grey and stiff, and almost ugly and high-shouldered. ' If Dolly had been more taking,' said Mrs. Palmer, judging by the light of her own two marriages, ' she might have allowed herself these quirks and fancies; but as it was, it was a pity.' Her mother declared that she did it on purpose.

Did she do it on purpose? In early life she didn't care a bit what people thought of her. In this she was a little unwomanly, perhaps, but unwomanly in the best and noblest sense. When with time those mysterious other selves came upon her that we meet as we travel along the road, bewildering her and pointing with all their different experiences, she ceased to judge either herself or others as severely; she loved faith and truth, and hated meanness and dissimulation as much as ever. Only, being a woman too honest to deceive herself, she found she could no longer apply the precepts that she had used once to her satisfaction. To hate the devil and all his works is one thing, but to say who is the devil and which are his works is another.

As for George Vanborough, his temper was alternately uproarious and melancholy: there was some incongruity in his nature that chafed and irritated him. He had abilities, but strange and cross-grained ones, of no use in an examination for instance. He could invent theories, but somehow he never got at the facts; he was rapid in conclusion, too rapid for poor Dolly, who was expected to follow him wherever he went, and who was sometimes hard put to it, for, unlike George, her convictions were slower than her sympathies.

A great many people seem to miss their vocations because their bodies do not happen to fit their souls. This is one of the advantages of middle age: people have got used to their bodies and to their faults; they know how to use them, to spare them, and they do not expect too much. George was at war with himself, poor fellow: by turns ascetic and self-indulgent, morbid, and over-confident. It is difficult to docket such a character, made up of all sorts of little bits collected from one and another ancestor; of materials warring against each other, as we have read in Mr. Darwin.

George's rooms at Cambridge were very small, and looked out across the green quadrangle at All Saints'. Among other instincts, he had inherited that of weaving his nest with photographs and old china, and lining it comfortably from Church House. There were papers and music-books, tankards (most of them with inscriptions), and a divining crystal. The old windows were deep and ivy-grown: at night they would often be cheerfully lighted up. 'Far too often,' say George's counsellors.

'I should like to entertain well enough,' says Henley, with a wave of the hand, 'but I can't afford it prudently. Bills have a knack of running up, particularly when they are not paid,' the young man remarks, with great originality, 'and then one can't always meet them.'

George only answers by a scowl from his little ferret eyes. 'You can pay your own bills twice over if you like,' he grunts out impatiently ; 'mine don't concern you.'

Robert said no more ; he had done his part, and he felt he could now face Dolly and poor Lady Sarah of the bleeding purse with a clear conscience ; but he could not help remembering with some satisfaction two neatly tied-up bundles of bills lying with a cheque-book in his despatch-box at home. He was just going when there came a knock at the door, and a pale man with a red beard walked in and shook hands with George, then somewhat hesitatingly with his companion, and finally sat down in George's three-sided chair.

Need I say that this was Raban, who had come to recommend a tutor to George? Was it to George or to Dorothea that Raban was so anxious to recommend a tutor?

George shrugged his shoulders, and did not seem in the least grateful.

Henley delayed a moment. 'I am glad you agree with me,' he said. 'I also have been speaking to my cousin on the subject.'

Raban bowed in the shy way peculiar to him. You never could tell if he was only shy or repelled by your advances.

'You and I have found the advantage of a good coach all our lives,' the other continued, with a subdued air of modest

I

triumph. It seemed to say, ' You will be glad to know that
I am one of the most rising men of the University;' and at
the same time Robert looked down apologetically at poor
scowling George, who was anything but rising, poor fellow,
and well up to his knees in the slough of despond. Nor was
it destined that Robert Henley was to be the man to pull
him out. Although he had walked over from St. Thomas's
to do so, he walked back again without having effected his
purpose.

' I did not know, till your sister told me, that Mr. Henley
was your cousin,' said Raban, as Robert left the room.

' Didn't you ? ' said George. ' I suppose you did not see
any likeness in me to that grenadier with the cameo nose ? '
and turning his back abruptly upon Raban, he began
strumming Yankee-doodle on the piano, standing as he
played, and putting in a quantity of pretty modulations. It
was only to show off; but Raban might have been tempted
to follow Henley downstairs if he had not caught sight of a
photograph of a girl with circling eyes in some strange old-
fashioned dress, with a lantern in her hand. It was the work
of a well-known amateur, who has the gift of seizing expression as it flies, and giving you a breathing friend, instead of
the image of an image. But it was in vain the young
professor stayed on, in vain that he came time after time
trying to make friends with young Vanborough and to urge
him to work. He once went so far as to write a warning
letter to Lady Sarah. It did no good, and only made Dolly
angry. At Christmas, George wrote that he had not passed,
and would be home on the 23rd. He did not add that he
had been obliged to sign some bills before he could get
away.

George came home ; with or without his laurels, he was

sure of an ovation.   Dolly, by her extra loving welcome,
only showed her disappointment at his want of success.

The fatted calf was killed, and the bottle of good wine was
opened.   ' Old Sam insisted on it,' said Lady Sarah, who had
got into a way of taking shelter behind old Sam when she
found herself relenting.   It was impossible not to relent
when Dolly, hearing the cab-wheels, came with a scream of
delight flying down the staircase from George's room, where
she had been busy making ready.   A great gust of cold wind
burst into the hall with the open door, by which George was
standing, with his bag, a little fussy and a little shy ; but
Dolly's glad cry of welcome and loving arms were there to
reassure him.

' Shut the door,' said Dolly, ' the wind will blow us away.
Have you paid your cab?'   As she spoke the horse was
turning round upon its haunches, and the cab was driving
off, and a pale face looked out for an instant.

' It's no matter,' said George, pushing to the door. ' Raban
brought me.   He is going on to dine somewhere near.'

' Horrid man!' said Dolly.   ' Come, George, and see
Aunt Sarah.   She is in the drawing-room.'

Lady Sarah looked at George very gravely over her knitting, and her needles began to tremble a little.

' What do you wish me to say, George?   That you failed
because you couldn't or because you wouldn't try?'

' Some one must fail,' said George.

' It is not fair upon me,' said Lady Sarah, ' that you
should be the one.   No, Dolly, I am not at all unkind.'

I have said very little of the changes and economies
that had been made at Church House, they affected Lady
Sarah and Dolly so little; but when George came home, even
in disgrace, a certain difference was made in the still ways

of the house.   Old Sam's niece, Eliza Twells, stayed all day,
and was transformed into a smiling abigail, not a little
pleased with her promotion.   One of Lady Sarah's old grey
gowns was bestowed upon her.   A cap and ribbons were concocted by Dolly; the ribbons were for ever fluttering in and
out of the sitting-room, and up and down the passages.
There was a sound of voices now, a show of life. Dolly could
not talk to herself all through the long months when George
was away; but when she had him safe in his little room
again the duet was unceasing.

Eliza Twells down below in the pan-decorated kitchen, in
all the excitement of her new dignities, kept the ball going.
You could hear old Sam's chuckles all the way upstairs, and
the maiden's loud, croaking, cheerful voice.

'It's like a saw-mill,' said George, 'but what is that?'

'That is Eliza laughing,' said Dorothea, laughing herself;
'and there is dear old Marker scolding.   Oh! George, how
nice it is to have you home again; and then, as most happy
vibrations bring a sadder after-tone, Dolly sighed and
stopped short.

'Disgrace *is* hard to bear,' said George moodily.

'Disgrace!   What do you mean?' wondered Dolly, who
had been thinking of something quite apart from those unlucky examinations—something that was not much, and yet
she would have found it hard to put her thought into words.
For how much there is that is not in words, that never happens quite, that is never realised altogether; and yet it is as
much part of our life as anything else.

CHAPTER XIV.

RAG DOLLS.

And slight Sir Robert, with his watery smile
And educated whisker.

THESE were days not to be forgotten by Dolly or by her
aunt. Don't we all know how life runs in certain grooves,
following phases of one sort or another? how dreams of
coming trouble haunt us vaguely all through a night? or,
again, is it hope that dawns silently from afar to lighten our
hearts and to make sweet visions for us before we awake to
the heat of the day?

It was all tranquil progress from day to day. Raban
came to see them once or twice while George was away. It
seemed all peace and silence during those years in the old
house, where the two women lived so quietly each their own
life, thinking their own thoughts. Rumours came now and
then of Mrs. Palmer's return; but this had been put off so
often, from one reason or another, that Dolly had almost
ceased to dwell upon it. She had settled down to her daily
occupations. John Morgan had set her to work in one of
his districts. She used to teach in the Sunday-school, help
her aunt in a hundred ways. This eventful spring she went
into Yorkshire with Marker and a couple of new gowns, on a

visit to her uncle, Sir Thomas Henley, at Smokethwaite. She enjoyed herself extremely, and liked her uncle and the girls very much. Her aunt was not very kind; 'at least, not so kind as I'm used to,' said Dolly afterwards. They had gone for long walks across the moors; they had ridden for twenty miles one day. She had seen her mother's picture, and slept in the room that used to be hers when she was a girl, and her cousin Norah had taken her about; but her Aunt Henley was certainly very cross and always saying uncomfortable things, and she was very glad to be home again, and didn't want to go away for years and years. Robert Henley had been there for a couple of days, and had come up to town with her. Jonah Henley was a very kind, stupid boy, not at all like Robert. He was very friendly to Dolly, and used to confide in her. He had made his mother very angry by insisting upon going into the Guards.

'She asked my advice,' said Dolly. 'She wanted to know if I didn't think it a foolish, idle sort of life.'

'And what did you say?' said Lady Sarah.

'I said that it might be so for some people who were clever and thoughtful, but that he seemed to have no interests at all, and never opened a book.'

'My dear child,' cried Lady Sarah, 'no wonder Lady Henley was annoyed!'

'Oh, dear me! I am so very sorry,' cries Dolly, penitently, as she walked along. They were going along one of the narrow alleys leading to the Square.

Day after day Lady Sarah used to leave home and trudge off with her basket and her well-known shabby cloak —it was warm and green like the heart that beat under it —from house to house, in and out, round and about the nar-

On the Step of a Rag Shop

row little Kensington streets. The parents, who had tried to
impose upon her at first, soon found that she had little sympathy for pathetic attitudes, and that her quick tongue paid
them back in their own coin.   They bore no malice.   Poor
people only really respect those who know them as they are,
and whose sympathy is personal and not ideal.   Lady Sarah's
was genuine sympathy ; she knew her flock by name, and
she spared no trouble to help those who were trying to help
themselves.   The children would come up shyly when they
saw the straight, scant figure coming along, and look into
her face.   Sometimes the basket would open and red apples
would come out—shining red apples in the dirty little back
streets and by-lanes behind Kensington Square.   Once
Robert Henley, walking to Church House, across some back
way, came upon his aunt sitting on an old chair on the step
of a rag-shop with a little circle of children round her, and
Dolly standing beside her, straight and upright.   Over her
head swung the legless form of a rag doll, twirling in
the wind.   On one side of the door was some rhymed
doggerel about ' Come, cookey, come,' and bring ' your
bones,' plastered up against the wall.   Lady Sarah, on the
step, seemed dispensing bounties from her bag to half-a-
dozen little clamorous, half-fledged creatures.

'My dear Lady Sarah, what does this mean ? ' said
Robert, trying to laugh, but looking very uncomfortable.

'I was so tired, Robert, I could not get home without
resting,' said Lady Sarah, 'and Mr. Wilkins kindly brought
me out a chair.   These are some of my Sunday-school
children, and Dolly and I were giving them a treat.'

'But really this is scarcely the place to —— If any one
were to pass—if—— Run away, run away, run away,' said
Mr. Henley affably to the children, who were all closing

in a ragged phalanx and gazing admiringly at his trousers.
'I'll get you a cab directly,' said the young man, looking up
and down. 'I came this short cut, but I had no idea ——'

'There are no cabs anywhere down here,' said Dolly,
laughing. 'This is Aunt Sarah's district; that is her soup-
kitchen.' And Dolly pointed up a dismal street with some
flapping washing-lines on one side. It looked all empty and
deserted, except that two women were standing in the doorways of their queer old huddled-up houses. A little further
off came a branch street, a blank wall, and some old Queen
Anne railings and doorways leading into Kensington Square.

'Good-by, little Betty,' said Lady Sarah, getting up
from her old straw chair, and smiling.

She was amused by the young man's unaffected dismay.
Philanthropy was quite in Henley's line, but that was,
Robert thought, a very different thing from familiarity.

'Now then, Betty, where's your curtsey?' says Dolly;
'and Mick, sir!'

Mick grinned, and pulled at one of his horrible little
wisps of hair. The children seemed fascinated by the 'gentleman.' They were used to the ladies, and, in fact, accustomed to be very rude to Dolly, although she was so severe.

'If you will give me an arm, Robert,' said Lady Sarah,
'and if you are not ashamed to be seen with me ——'

'My dear Lady Sarah!' said Robert, hastily, offering his
arm.

'Now, children, be off,' says Dolly.

'Please, sir, won't you give us 'napeny?' said Mick,
hopping along with his little deft, bare feet.

'Go away,—for shame, Mick!' cried Dolly again, while
Henley impatiently threw some coppers into the road, after
which all the children set off scrambling in an instant.

' Oh, Robert, you shouldn't have done that,' cried Dolly, rushing back to superintend the fair division of kicks and halfpence.

Robert waited for her for a moment, and looked at her as she stood in her long grey cloak, with a little struggling heap at her feet of legs and rags and squeaks and contortions. The old Queen Anne railings of the corner house, and the dim street winding into rags, made a background to this picture of modern times: an old slatternly woman in a night-cap came to her help from one of the neighbouring doorways, and seizing one of the children out of the heap, gave it a cuff and dragged it away. Dolly had lifted Mick off the back of a smaller child—the crisis was over.

' Here she comes,' said Lady Sarah, in no way discomposed.

Robert was extremely discomposed. He hated to see Dolly among such sights and surroundings. He tried to speak calmly as they walked on, but his voice sounded a little cracked.

' Surely,' he said, ' this is too much for you at times. Do you go very often ? '

' Nearly every day, Robert,' said Dorothea. ' You see what order I have got the children into.'

She was laughing again, and Henley, as usual, was serious.

' Of course I cannot judge,' said he, ' not knowing what state they were in originally.' Then he added, gravely turning to Lady Sarah, ' Don't you somehow think that Dolly is very young to be mixed up with a— rag-shops and wickedness ? '

' Dolly is young,' said her aunt, not over pleased ; ' but she is very prudent, and I am not afraid of her pawning her clothes and taking to drink.'

'My dear aunt, you don't suppose I ever thought of such a possibility,' Robert exclaimed. 'Only ladies do not always consider things from our point of view, and I feel in a certain degree responsible and bound to you as your nearest male protector (take care—here is a step). I should not like other people, who might not know Dolly as we do, to imagine that she was accustomed already to ——'

'My dear Robert,' said Lady Sarah, 'Dolly has got an aunt and a brother to take care of her; do you suppose that we would let her do anything that we thought might hurt her in other people's opinion? Dolly, here is Robert horrified at the examples to which you are exposed. He feels he ought to interfere.'

'You won't understand me,' said Robert, keeping his temper very good-naturedly. 'Of course I can't help taking an interest in my relations.'

'Thank you, Robert,' said Dolly, smiling and blushing.

Their eyes met for an instant, and Robert looked better pleased. It was a bright delightful spring morning. All the windows were shining in the old square, there was a holiday thrill in the air, a sound of life, dogs barking, people stirring and coming out of their hiding-places, animals and birds exulting.

Dolly used to get almost tipsy upon sunshine. The weather is as much part of some people's lives as the minor events which happen to them. She walked along by the other two, diverging a little as they travelled along, the elder woman's bent figure beating time with quick fluttering footsteps to the young man's even stride. Dolly liked Robert to be nice to her aunt, and was not a little pleased when he approved of herself. She was a little afraid of him. She felt that beneath that calm manner there were many secrets that she had not yet fathomed. She knew how good he was, how he never got into debt. Ah me! how she wished George would take pattern by him. Dolly and Rhoda had sometimes talked Robert over. They gave him credit for great experience, a deep knowledge of the world (he dined out continually when he was in town), and they also gave him full credit for his handsome, thoughtful face, his tall commanding figure. You cannot but respect a man of six foot high.

So they reached the doorway at last. The ivy was all glistening in the sunshine, and as they rang the bell they heard the sound of Gumbo's bark in the garden, and then came some music, some brilliant pianoforte-playing, which sounded clear and ringing as it overflowed the garden-wall and streamed out into the lane.

'Listen! Who can that be playing?' cries Dolly, brightening up still brighter, and listening with her face against the ivy.

'George,' says Robert. 'Has George come up again?'

'It's the overture to the *Freischütz*,' says Dolly, conclusively; 'it *is* George.'

And when old Sam shuffled up at last to open the door, he announced, grinning, that 'Mr. Garge had come, and was playing the peanner in the drawing-room.'

At the same moment, through the iron gate, they saw a figure advancing to meet them from the garden, with Gumbo caracolling in advance.

'Why there is Rhoda in the garden,' cries Dolly. 'Robert, you go to her. I must go to George.'

CHAPTER XV.

GEORGE'S TUNES.

> . . Sing our fine songs that tell in artful phrase
> The secrets of our lives, and plead and pray
> For alms of memory with the after time.
> —O. W. H.

THERE is George sitting at the old piano in the drawing-room. The window is wide open. The Venetian glass is dazzling over his head, of which the cauliflower shadow is thrown upon the wall. By daylight, the old damask paper looks all stained and discoloured, and the draperies hang fainting and turning grey and brown and to all sorts of strange autumnal hues in this bright spring sunshine.

The keys answer to George's vigorous fingers, while the shadow bobs in time from side to side. A pretty little pair of slim gloves and a prayer-book are lying on a chair by the piano; they are certainly not George's, nor Eliza Twells', who is ostensibly dusting the room, but who has stopped short to listen to the music. It has wandered from the *Freischütz* overture to *Kennst Du das Land?* which, for the moment, George imagines to be his own composition. How easily the chords fall into their places! how the melody flows loud and clear from his fingers! (It's not only on the piano that people play tunes which they imagine to be their own.)

As for Eliza, she had never heard anything so beautiful in all her life.

'Can it play hymn toones, sir?' says she, in a hoarse voice.

Hymn tunes! George goes off into the Hundredth Psalm. The old piano shakes its cranky sides, the pedals groan and creak, the music echoes all round ; then another shadow comes floating along the faded wall, two fair arms are round his neck, the music stops for an instant, and Eliza begins to rub up the leg of a table.

'How glad I am you have come; but *why* have you come, George—oughtn't you to be reading?'

'Oh,' says George, airily, 'I have only come for the day. Look here : have you ever heard this Russian tune? I've been playing it to Miss Parnell ; I met her coming from church.'

'Miss Parnell? Do you mean Rhoda?' said Dolly, as she sits down in the big chair and takes up the gloves and the prayer-book, which opens wide, and a little bit of fresh-gathered ivy falls out. It is Rhoda's prayer-book, as Dolly knows. She puts back the ivy, while George goes on playing.

'How pretty!' says she, looking at him with her two admiring eyes, and raising her thick brows.

George, much pleased with the compliment, goes on strumming louder than ever.

'Robert is here,' says Dolly, still listening. 'He is in the garden with Rhoda.'

'Oh, is he?' says George, not over-pleased.

It was at this moment that Lady Sarah came to the garden-window, still in her district equipments. Eliza Twells, much confused by her mistress's appearance, begins to dust wildly.

'How d'ye do, George?' said his aunt, coming up to him. 'We didn't expect you so soon again.'

George offered his cheek to be kissed, and played a few chords with his left hand.

'I hadn't meant to come,' he said; 'but I was up at the station this morning, seeing a friend off, and as the train was starting I got in. I've got a return-ticket.'

'Of course you have,' said Lady Sarah, 'but where will you get a return-ticket for the time you are wasting? It is no use attempting to speak to you. Some day you will be sorry;' and then she turned away, and walked off in her gleaming goloshes, and went out at the window again. She did not join Robert and Rhoda, who were pacing round and round the garden walk, but wandered off her own way alone.

'There!' says George, looking up at Dolly for sympathy.

Dolly doesn't answer, but turns very pale, and her heart begins to beat.

'It is one persecution,' cries George, speaking for himself, since Dolly won't speak for him. 'She seems to think she has a right to insult me—that she has bought it with her hateful money.'

He began to crash out some defiant chords upon the piano.

'Don't, dear,' said Dolly, putting her hand on his. 'You don't know,' she said, hesitating, 'how bitterly disappointed Aunt Sarah has been when—when you have not passed. She is so clever herself. She is so proud of you. She hopes so much.'

'Nonsense,' said George, hunching up sulkily. 'Dolly, you are for ever humbugging. You love me, and perhaps others appreciate me a little; but not Aunt Sarah. She don't care that' (a crash) 'for me. She thinks that I can bear insult like Robert, or all the rest of them who are after her money-bags.'

He was working himself up more and more, as people do who are not sure they are right. He spoke so angrily that Dolly was frightened.

'Oh, George,' she said, 'how can you say such things; you mustn't, do you hear? not to me—not to yourself. Of course Robert scorns anything mean, as much as you do. Her savings! they all went in that horrid bank. She does not know where to go for money sometimes, and we ought to spare her, and never to forget what we do owe her. She denies herself every day for us. She will scarcely see a doctor when she is ill, or take a carriage when she is tired.'

Dolly's heart was beating very quick; she was determined that, come what might, George should hear the truth from her.

'If you are going to lecture me, too, I shall go,' said George; and he got up and walked away to the open window, and stood grimly looking out. He did not believe Dolly; he could not afford to believe her. He was in trouble; he wanted money himself. He had meant to confide in Dolly; that was one of the reasons why he had come up to town. He should say nothing to her now. She did not deserve his confidence; she did not understand him, and always sided with her aunt. 'Look here, I had better give the whole thing up at once,' he said, sulkily; 'I don't care to be the object of so many sacrifices.' As he stood there glowering, he was unconsciously watching the two figures crossing the garden and going towards the pond; one of them, the lady, turned, and seeing him at the window, waved a distant hand in greeting. George's face cleared. He would join Rhoda; it was no use staying here.

As he was leaving the room poor Dolly looked up from the arm-chair in which she had been sitting despondently: she had tears in her heart though her eyes were dry: she wanted to make friends. 'You know, George,' she said, ' I *must* say what I think true to you. Aunt Sarah grudges nothing —— '

' She makes the very most,' says George, stopping short, ' of what she does, and so do you; ' and he looked away from Dolly's entreating face.

Again poor Dolly's indignation masters her prudence. ' How can you be so mean and ungrateful ? ' she says.

' Ungrateful ! ' cries George, in a passion ; ' you get all you like out of Aunt Sarah ; to me she doles out hard words and a miserable pittance, and you expect me to be grateful. I can see what Robert and Frank Raban think as well as if they said it.'

Dolly sprang past him and rushed out of the room in tears.

' Dolly ! Dolly ! forgive me, do forgive me ! I'm a brute,' says George, running after her,—he had really talked on without knowing what he said—' please stop ! '

' Dolly ! ' cries Lady Sarah from the breakfast-room.

Dolly went flying along the oak hall and up the old staircase and across the ivy window. She could not speak. She ran up to her room, and slammed the door, and burst out sobbing. She did not heed the voices calling then, but in after days, long, long after, she used to hear them at times, and how plainly they sounded, when all was silent— ' Dolly, Dolly ! ' they called. People say that voices travel on through space,—they travel on through life, and across time,—is it not so ? Years have passed since they may have been uttered, but do we not hear them again and again, and answer back longing into the past ?

Meanwhile poor Dolly banged the door in indignation. She was glad George was sorry, but how dared he suspect her? How dared Mr. Raban—Mr. Raban, who did not pay his debts—What did she care?—What did they know? *They* did not understand how she loved her brother in her own way, her very own; loving him and taking care for him and fighting his battles. . . .

'Oh, George, how cruel you are,' sobbed poor Dolly, sitting on her window-sill. The warm sun was pouring through the open casement, spreading the shadow of the panes and the framework upon the carpetless floor; in a corner of the window a little pot of mignonette stood ready to start to life; a bird came with the shadow of its little breast upon the bars, and chirruped a cheerful chirp. Dolly looked up, breathed in the sun and the bird-chirp, how could she help it? Then her wooden clock struck, it distracted her somehow, and her indignation abated; the girl got up, bathed her red eyes, and went to the glass to straighten her crisp locks and limp tucker. 'Who is knocking?—come in,' said Dolly. She did not look round, she was too busy struggling with her laces: presently she saw a face reflected in the glass beside her own, a pale brown face with black hair and slow, dark eyes, and close little red lips.

'Why, Rhoda, have you come for me?' said Dolly, looking round, sighing and soothed.

At the same time a voice from the garden below cried out, 'Dolly, come down. Have you forgiven me?'

'Yes, George,' said Dolly, looking out from her window.

'Here, let me help you,' cried Rhoda. 'Dolly, Mr. Robert and your brother sent me to find you.'

CHAPTER XVI.

A WALKING PARTY.

Not wholly in the busy world,
Nor quite beyond it,
Blooms the garden that I love;
News from the teeming city comes to it,
In sound of funeral or marriage bells.

THE young people were starting for another walk that afternoon. Rhoda and Dolly were holding up their parasols and
their white dresses out of the dust. They were half-way
down the sunshiny lane when they met Frank Raban (of
whom they had been speaking) coming to call at Church
House.

'You had much better come along with us, Frank,' said
George, who was always delighted to welcome his friends,
however soon he might quarrel with them afterwards.

'I have an appointment at five o'clock,' said Raban,
hesitating, and with a glance at Miss Vanborough, who was
standing a little apart, and watching the people passing up
and down the road.

'Five o'clock!' said George; 'five o'clock is ever so far
away—on board a steamer, somewhere in the Indian Ocean;
the passengers are looking over the ship's side at the por-
poises. Where is your appointment?'

'Do you know a place called Nightingale Lane?' said Frank.

'I know Nightingale Lane; it is as good a place as any other. Come, we will show you the way;' and, putting his arm through Frank's, George dragged him along.

'I wish George had not asked him,' said Robert, in a low voice. 'There were several things I wanted to consult you about, Dolly! but I must get a quiet half-hour. Not now, at some better opportunity.'

'Why, Robert!' said Dolly; 'what can you have to say that will take half-an-hour!' She was, however, much flattered that Robert should wish to consult her, and she walked along brightly.

It was a lovely spring afternoon: people were all out in the open air; the little Quaker children who lived in the house at the corner of the terrace were looking out of window with their prim little bonnets, and Dolly, who knew them, nodded gaily as she passed. She was quite happy again. Robert had looked at her so kindly. She was in charity with the whole world. She had scarcely had a word of explanation with George, but she had made it up with him in her heart. When he asked her for a second help of cold pie at luncheon, she took it as a sign of forgiveness. They went on now by the brown houses of Phillimore Terrace, until they reached a place where the bricks turn into green leaves, and branches arch overhead, and two long avenues lead from the ancient high road of the Trinobants all the way to the palatine heights of Campden Hill.

When they were in the avenue, the young people went and stood under the shade of a tree. George was leaning against the iron rail that separates the public walk from the park beyond. They were standing with their feet on the turf in

K 2

a cris-cross of shadow, of twigs, and green blades sprouting between. Beyond the rail the lawns and fields sloped to where the old arcades and the many roofs and turrets of Holland House rose, with their weather-cocks veering upon the sky. Great trees were spreading their shadows upon the grass. Some cows were trailing across the meadow, and from beyond the high walls came the echo of the streets without—a surging sound of voices and wheels, a rising tide of life, of countless feet beating upon the stones. Here, behind the walls, all was sweet and peaceful afternoon, and high overhead hung a pale daylight moon.

' Are not you glad to have seen this pretty view of the old house, Mr. Raban ? ' said Dolly to Frank, who happened to be standing next to her. ' Don't you like old houses ? ' she added, graciously, in her new-found amenity.

' I don't know,' said Frank. ' They are too much like coffins and full of dead men's bones. Modern lath and plaster has the great advantage of being easily swept away with its own generation. These poor old places seem to me all out of place among omnibuses and railway whistles.'

' The associations of Holland House must be very interesting,' said Robert.

' I hate associations,' said Frank, looking hard at Dolly. ' To-day is just as good as yesterday.'

Dolly looked surprised, then blushed up.

It is strange enough, after one revelation of a man or woman, to meet with another of the same person at some different time. The same person and not the same. The same voice and face, looking and saying such other things, to which we ourselves respond how differently. Here were Raban and Dolly, who had first met by a grave, now coming together in another world and state, with people laughing

and talking; with motion, with festivity. Walking side by
side through the early summer streets, where all seemed life,
not death; hope and progress, not sorrow and retrospect—
for Dolly's heart was full of the wonder of life and of the
dazzling present. After that first meeting, she had begun to
look upon the Raban of to-day as a new person altogether, a
person who interested her, though she did not like him.
Even Dorothea in her softest moods seemed scarcely to thaw
poor Frank. When he met her, his old, sad, desperate self
used to rise like a phantom between them—no wonder he
was cold, and silent, and abrupt. He could talk to others—
to Rhoda, who wore his poor wife's shining cross, and had
stood by her coffin, as he thought, and who now met him
with looks of sympathy, and who seemed to have forgotten
the past. To Miss Vanborough he rarely spoke; he barely
answered her if she spoke to him; and yet I don't think
there was a word or look of Dolly's that Raban ever forgot.
All her poor little faults he remembered afterwards; her impatient ways, and imperious gestures, her hasty impulse and
her innocent severity. What strange debtor and creditor
account was this between them?

There are some people we only seem to love all the more
because they belong to past sorrow. Perhaps it is that they
are of the guild of those who are initiated into the sad secrets
of life. Others bring back the pain without its consolation;
and so Dolly, who was connected with the tragedy of poor
Frank Raban's life, frightened him. When, as now, he
thought he had seen a remembering look in her eyes, the
whole unforgettable past would come before him with cruel
vividness. She seemed to him like one of the avenging angels
with the flaming swords, ready to strike. Little he knew
her! The poor angel might lift the heavy sword, but it

would be with a trembling hand. She might remember, but
it was as a child remembers—with awe, but without judgment. The little girl he had known had pinned up her locks
in great brown loops ; her short skirts now fell in voluminous
folds ; she was a whole head taller, and nearly seventeen : but
if the truth were told, I do not think that any other particular change had come to her, so peaceful had been her
experience. Frank was far more changed. He had fought a
hard fight with himself since that terrible day he had sat under
the arch in the twilight. He had conquered Peace in some
degree, and now already he felt it was no longer peace that
he wanted, but more trouble. Already, in his heart, he
rebelled at the semi-claustration of the tranquil refuge he
had found, where the ivy buttresses and scrolled iron gateways seemed to shut out wider horizons. But hitherto
work was what he wanted, not liberty. He had made debts
and difficulties for himself during that wild, foolish time
at Paris! These very debts and difficulties were his best
friends now, and kept him steady to his task. He accepted
the yoke, thankful for an honest means of livelihood. He
took the first chance that offered, and he put a shoulder to
the old pulley at which he had tugged as a boy with a dream
of something beyond, and at which he laboured as a man
with some sense of duty done. He went on in a dogged,
hopeless way from day to day. He is a man of little faith,
and yet of tender heart.

Some one says that the world is a mirror that reflects
the faces that we bring to the surface. Frank's scepticisms
met him at every turn. He even judged his own ideal ; and as
he could not but think of Dolly every hour of the day, he
doubted her unceasingly. There seemed scarcely a respon-
sive chord left to him with which to vibrate to the song of

those about him. Until he believed in himself again, he could not heartily believe in others.

Others, meanwhile, were happily not silent because of his reserve, and were chattering and laughing gaily. Rhoda was sitting on the shady corner of a bench, George was swinging his legs on the railing. Dolly did not sit down. She was not tired; she was in high spirits. By degrees, she seemed to absorb all her companion's life and brightness. So Raban thought as he glanced from Rhoda's pale face to Miss Vanborough's beaming countenance. Dolly's brown hair was waving in a pretty drift, her violet ribbons seemed to make her grey eyes look violet. She had a long neck, a long chin; her white ample skirt almost hid Rhoda as she sat in her corner. The girl shifted gently from her seat, and slid away when Dolly—Dolly sobering down—began to tell some of Lady Sarah's stories of Holland House and its inmates.

'There was beautiful Lady Diana Rich,' said Dorothea, pointing with her gloved hand.

'Don't say Diana,' cries George; 'say Diāna.'

'She was walking in the Park,' continues his sister, unheeding the interruption, 'when she met a lady coming from behind a tree dressed, as she was herself, in a habit. Then she recognised herself,' Dolly said, slowly, opening her grey eyes; 'and she went home, and she died within a——'

Dolly, hearing a rustle, looked over her shoulder, and her sentence broke down. A white figure was coming from behind the great stem of the elm-tree, near which they were standing. In a moment, Dolly recovered herself, and began to laugh.

'Rhoda!' she said. 'I did not know you had moved. I thought you were my fetch.'

'No; I'm myself, and I don't like ghost stories,' said Rhoda, in her shrill voice. 'They frighten me so, though I don't believe a word of them. Do you, Mr. Raban?'

'Not believe!' cries George, putting himself in between Frank and Rhoda. 'Don't you believe in the White Lady of Holland House? She flits through the rooms once a year all in white satin, on the day of her husband's execution. They cut off his head in a silver nightcap, and she can't rest in her grave when she thinks of it.'

'Poor ghost!' said Dolly. 'I'm so sorry for ghosts. I sometimes think I know some live ones,' the girl added, looking at Frank unconsciously, and with more softness than he had believed her capable of.

'The first Lord Holland was a Rich,' said Henley, tapping with his cane upon the iron bars. 'He must have been the father of Lady Diana. He married a Cope. The Copes built the house you know. I believe Aubrey de Vere was the original possessor of the property. It then passed to the monks of Abingdon.'

'What a fund of information!' said George, laughing. 'Raban is immensely impressed.'

Raban could not help smiling; but Dolly interposed. She saw that her cousin was only half pleased by the levity with which his remarks were received. 'What had Lord Holland done?' she asked.

'He betrayed everybody,' said Robert; 'first one side, then another. He earned his fate—he was utterly unreliable and inconsistent.'

'How can an honest man be anything else?' cried George, with his usual snort, rushing to battle. 'No honest men are consistent. Take Sir Robert Peel, take Oliver Cromwell. Lord Holland joined the Commonwealth, and then gave his head to save the King's. It was gloriously inconsistent.'

'For my part,' Robert answered, with some asperity, 'I must confess that I greatly dislike such impulsive characters. They are utterly unscrupulous. . . .'

'Some consciences might have been more scrupulously consistent than Lord Holland's, and kept their heads upon their shoulders,' said Raban, drily.

Dolly wondered what he meant, and whether he was serious. He spoke so shortly that she did not always understand him.

'I am sure I shall often change my mind,' she said, to her cousin.

'You are a woman, you know,' answered Henley, mollified by her sweet looks.

'And women need not trouble themselves about their motives?' said Frank, speaking in his most sententious way, and ignoring Henley altogether.

'Their motives don't concern anybody but themselves,' cried Dolly, rather offended by Frank's manner. He seemed to look upon her as some naughty child, to be constantly reproved and put down. He was not half so kind to her as he was to Rhoda, whom he was now helping on with a shawl. Why did he dislike her? Dolly wondered. She couldn't understand anybody disliking her. Perhaps it says well for human nature, on the whole, that people are so surprised to find themselves odious to others.

Just then some church-bell began to ring for evening service. Five o'clock had come to Kensington, and George proposed that they should walk on with Raban to the house in Nightingale Lane.

'This way, Rhoda,' he said; 'are you tired? Take my arm.'

Rhoda, however, preferred tripping by Dolly's side.

A painter lived in the house to which Raban was going. It stood, as he said, in Nightingale Lane, within garden-walls. It looked like a farm-house, with its many tiles and chimneys, standing in the sweet old garden fringed with rose-bushes. There were poplar-trees and snowball-trees, and may-flowers in their season, and lilies-of-the-valley growing in the shade. The lawn was dappled with many shadows of sweet things. From the thatched porch you could hear the rural clucking of poultry and the lowing of cattle, and see the sloping roof of a farm-house beyond the elms. Henley did not want to come in ; but Dolly and Rhoda had cried out that it was a dear old garden, and had come up to the very door, smiling and wilfully advancing as they looked about them.

The old house—we all know our way thither—has stood for many a year, and seen many a change, and sheltered many an honoured head. One can fancy Addison wandering in the lanes round about, and listening to the nightingale ' with a much better voice than Mrs. Tofts, and something of Italian manners in her diversions ; ' or Newton, an old man with faded blue eyes, passing by on his way from Pitt House, hard by. Gentle Mrs. Opie used to stay here, and ugly Wilkes to come striding up the lane in the days of Fox and Pitt and fiery periwigs. Into one of the old raftered rooms poor Lord Camelford was carried to die, when he fell in his fatal duel with Mr. Best in the meadows hard by. Perhaps Sir Joshua may have sometimes walked across from Holland House, five minutes off, where he was, a hundred years ago, painting two beautiful young ladies. Only yesterday I saw them ; one leant from a window in the wall, the other stood without, holding a dove in her extended

UNDER THE RUSTIC PORCH.

hand ; a boy was by her side. Those ladies have left the
window long since ; but others, not less beautiful, still come
up Nightingale Lane, to visit the Sir Joshua of our own time
in his studios built against the hospitable house. My
heroine comes perforce, and looks at the old gables and elm-
trees, and stands under the rustic porch. Robert was
seriously distressed.

'Do come away,' said he ; 'suppose some one were to
see us.'

Rhoda, with a little laugh, ran down one of the garden-
walks, and George went after her. Dolly stood leaning up
against the doorway. She paid no attention to Robert's
remonstrance, and was listening, with upraised eyes, to the
bird up in the tree. Frank's hand was on the bell, when, as
Robert predicted, the door suddenly opened wide. A servant,
carrying papers and parcels, came out, followed by a lady in
a flowing silk dress, with a lace hood upon her head, and by
a stately-looking gentleman, in a long grey coat ; erect, and
with silver hair and a noble and benevolent head.

'Why is not the carriage come up?' said the lady to
the servant, who set off immediately running with his parcels
in his arms; then seeing Dolly, who was standing blushing
and confused by the open door, she said kindly, 'Have you
come to see the studios?'

'No,' said Dolly, turning pinker still: 'it was only the
garden, it looked so pretty; we came to the door with
Mr. Raban.'

'I had an appointment with Mr. Royal,' said Raban, also
shyly, 'and my friends kindly showed me the way.'

'Why don't you take your friends up to see the
pictures?' said the gentleman. 'Go up all of you now that
you are here.'

'My servant shall show you the way,' said the lady, with
a smile, and as the servant came back, followed by a carriage,
she gave him a few parting directions. Then the Councillor
and the lady drove off to the India Office as hard as the
horses could go.

It was a white-letter day with Dolly. She followed the
servant up an oak passage, and by a long wall, where flying
figures were painted. The servant opened a side door into a
room with a great window, and my heroine found herself in
better company than she had ever been in all her life before.
Two visitors were already in the studio. One was a lady
with a pale and gentle face—Dolly remembered it long
afterwards when they met again—but just then she only
thought of the pictures that were crowding upon the walls
sumptuous and silent—the men and women of our day who
seem already to belong to the future, as one looks at the
solemn eyes watching from the canvas. Sweet women's faces
lighted with some spiritual grace, poets, soldiers, rulers, and
windbags, side by side, each telling their story in a well-
known name. There were children too, smiling, and
sketches, half done, growing from the canvas, and here and
there a dream made into a vision, of Justice or of Oblivion.
Of Silence, and lo! Titans from their everlasting hills lie
watching the mists of life; or infinite Peace, behold, an
Angel of Death is waiting against a solemn disc. Dolly
felt as though she had come with Christian to some mystical
house along the way. For some minutes past she had been
gazing at the solemn Angel—she was absorbed, she could
not take her eyes away. She did not know that the painter
had come in, and was standing near her.

'Do you know what that is?' said he, coming up to her.

'Yes,' answered Dolly in a low voice; 'I have only once

seen death. I think this must be it; only it is not terrible, as I thought.'

'I did not mean to make it terrible,' the painter said, struck by her passing likeness to the face at which she was gazing so steadfastly.

Raban also noticed the gentle and powerful look, and in that moment he understood her better than he had ever done before; he felt as if a sudden ray of faith and love had fallen into his dark heart.

Before they left Mr. Royal introduced Dolly to the two ladies who were in the studio. He had painted the head of one of them upon a little wooden panel that leant upon an easel by which the two ladies were standing.

One of them spoke : 'How her children will prize your gift, Mr. Royal ; it is not the likeness only. . . .' 'Life is short; one cannot do all things,' said the painter, quietly. 'I have tried not so much to imitate what I see as to paint people and things as I feel them, and as others appear to me to feel them.'

Dolly thought how many people he must have taught to feel, to see with their eyes, and to understand.

All the way home she was talking of the pictures.

'I saw a great many likenesses which were really admirable,' said Robert. 'I have met several of the people out at dinner.'

Rhoda could not say a single word about the pictures.

'Why, what were you about?' said Dolly, after she had mentioned two or three one after another. 'You don't seem to have looked at anything.'

'You didn't come into the back room, Dolly. I had an excellent cup of tea there,' said George ; 'that kind lady had it sent up for us.'

CHAPTER XVII.

' INNER LIFE.'

The idea of a man's interviewing himself is rather odd to be sure. But then that is what we are all of us doing every day. I talk half the time to find out my own thoughts, as a schoolboy turns his pockets inside out to see what is in them.—O. W. HOLMES.

THE next time Raban came to town, he called again at Church House. Then he began to go to John Morgan's, whom he had known and neglected for years. He was specially kind to Rhoda and gentle in his manner when he spoke to her. Cassie, who had experience, used to joke her about her admirer. Not unfrequently Dolly would be in Old Street during that summer, and the deeply-interested recipient of the girls' confidences.

' Cassie, do you really mean that he has fallen in love with Rhoda ? ' said Dolly. ' Indeed he is not half good enough for her.' But all the same, the thought of his admiration for her friend somewhat softened Dolly's feelings towards Raban.

Rhoda herself was mysterious. One day she gave up wearing her diamond cross, and appeared instead with a pretty pearl locket. She would not say where she had got it. Zoe said it was like Cassie's. ' Had John given it to her ? ' Rhoda shook her head.

Dolly did not like it, and took Rhoda seriously to task.
'Rhoda, how silly to make a mystery about nothing!'
Rhoda laughed.

Except for occasional troubles about George, things
were going well at Church House that autumn. Raban sent
a warning letter once, which made Dolly very angry. The
Admiral talked of coming home in the following spring.
Dolly's heart beat at the thought of her mother's return.
But meanwhile she was very happy. Robert used to come
not unfrequently. Rhoda liked coming when he was there;
they would all go out when dinner was over, and sit upon
the terrace and watch the sun setting calmly behind the
medlar-tree and the old beech walk. Kensington has special
tranquil hours of its own, happy jumbles of old bricks and
sunset. The pigeons would come from next door with a
whirr, and with round breasts shining in the light; the ivy-
leaves stood out green and crisp; the birds went flying overhead and circling in their evening dance. Three together,
then two, then a lonely one in pursuit.

Dolly stood watching them one evening, in the autumn
of that year, while her aunt and Henley were talking. John
Morgan, who had come to fetch Rhoda home, was discoursing, too, in cheerful tones, about the voice of nature
I think it was. 'You do not make enough allowance
for the voice of nature,' the curate was saying. 'You cannot
blame a man because he is natural, because his impulse cries
out against rules and restrictions.' As he spoke a bell in the
ivy wall began to jangle from outside, and Dolly and Rhoda
both looked up curiously, wondering who it could be.

'Rules are absolutely necessary restrictions,' said Henley,
stirring his coffee; 'we are lost if we trust to our impulses.
What are our bodies but concrete rules?'

'I wonder if it could be George?' interrupted Dolly.

'Oh, no,' said Rhoda, quickly, 'because ——' Then she stopped short.

'Because what, Rhoda?' said Lady Sarah, looking at her curiously. The girl blushed up, and seemed embarrassed, and began pulling the ribbon and the cross round her neck. It had come out again the last few days.

'Have you heard anything of George?' Lady Sarah went on.

'How should I?' said Rhoda, looking up; then she turned a little pale, then she blushed again. 'Dolly, look,' she said, 'who is it?'

It was Mr. Raban, the giver of the diamond cross, who came walking up along the side-path, following old Sam. There was a little scrunching of chair-legs to welcome him. John Morgan shook him by the hand. Lady Sarah looked pleased.

'This was kind of you,' she said.

Raban looked shy. 'I am afraid you won't think so,' he said. 'I wanted a few minutes' conversation with you.'

Rhoda opened her wide brown eyes. Henley, who had said a stiff 'How-dy-do?' and wished to go on with the conversation, now addressed himself to Dolly.

'I always doubt the fact when people say that impulse is the voice of one's inner life. I consider that principle should be its real interpretation.'

Nobody exactly understood what he meant, nor did he himself, if the truth were to be told; but the sentence had occurred to him.

'An inner life,' said Dolly, presently, looking at the birds. 'I wonder what it means? I don't think I have got one.'

'No, Dolly,' said Lady Sarah, kindly, 'it is very often only another name for remorse. Not yet, my dear—that has not reached you yet.'

'An inner life,' repeated Rhoda, standing by. 'Doesn't it mean all those things you don't talk about—religion and principles?' she said, faltering a little, with a shy glance at Frank Raban. Henley had just finished his coffee, and heard her approvingly. He was going again to enforce the remark, when Dolly, as usual, interrupted him.

'But there is *nothing* one doesn't talk about,' said the Dolly of those days, standing on the garden-step, with all her pretty loops of brown hair against the sun.

'I wish you would preach a sermon, Mr. Morgan, and tell people to take care of their outer lives,' said Lady Sarah, over her coffee-pot, 'and keep *them* in order while they have them, and leave their souls to take care of themselves. We have all read of the figs and the thistles. Let us cultivate figs; that is the best thing we can do.'

'Dear Aunt Sarah,' said Dolly prettily, and looking up suddenly, and blushing, 'here we all are sitting under your fig-tree.'

Dolly having given vent to her feelings suddenly blushed up. All their eyes seemed to be fixed upon her. What business had Mr. Raban to look at her so gravely?

'I wonder if the cocks and hens are gone to roost,' said my heroine, confused; and, jumping down from the step, she left the coffee-drinkers to finish their coffee.

Lady Sarah had no great taste for art or for *bric-à-brac*. Mr. Francis had been a collector, and from him she had inherited her blue china, but she did not care at all for it. She had one fancy, however,—a poultry fancy,—which harmlessly distracted many of her spare hours. With a cheerful cluck, a pluming, a spreading out of glistening feathers, a strutting

and champing, Lady Sarah's cocks and hens used to awake
betimes in the early morning. The cocks would chaunt
matutinal hymns to the annoyance of the neighbourhood,
while the hens clucked a cheerful accompaniment to the
strains. The silver trumpets themselves would not have
sounded pleasanter to Lady Sarah's ears than this crowing
noise of her favourites. She had a little temple erected for
this choir. It was a sort of pantheon, where all parts of the
world were represented, divided off by various latitudinal
wires. There were crêve-cœurs from the Pyrenees, with
their crimson crests and robes of black satin; there were
magi from Persia, puffy, wind-blown, silent, and somewhat
melancholy: there were Polish warriors, gallant and splendid,
with an air of misfortune so courageously surmounted that
fortune itself would have looked small beside it. Then came
the Dorkings, feathery and speckly, with ample wings outstretched, clucking common-place English to one another.

To-night, however, the clarions were silent, the warriors
were sleepy, the cocks and hens were settling themselves
comfortably in quaint fluffy heaps upon their roosts, with
their portable feather-beds shaken out, and their bills snugly
tucked into the down.

Dolly was standing admiring their strength of mind, in
retiring by broad daylight from the nice cheerful world, into
the dismal darkened bed-chamber they occupied. As Dolly
stood outside in the sunset, peeping into the dark roosting-
place, she heard voices coming along the path, and Lady
Sarah speaking in a very agitated voice.

'Cruel boy,' she said, 'what have I done, what have I left
undone that he should treat me so ill?'

They were close to Dolly, who started away from the hen-
house, and ran up to meet her aunt with a sudden movement.

'What is it? Why is he—— *Who* is cruel?' said Dolly, and she turned a quick, reproachful look upon Raban. What had he been saying?

'I meant to spare you, my dear,' said Lady Sarah, trembling very much, and putting her hand upon Dolly's shoulder. 'I have no good news for you; but sooner or later you must know it. Your brother has been behaving as badly as possible. He has put his name to some bills. Mr. Raban heard of it by chance. Wretched boy! he might be arrested. It is hard upon me, and cruel of George.'

They were standing near the hen-house still, and a hen woke up from her dreams with a sleepy cluck. Lady Sarah was speaking passionately and vehemently, as she did when she was excited; Raban was standing a little apart in the shadow.

Dolly listened with a hanging head. She could say nothing. It all seemed to choke her; she let her Aunt Sarah walk on— she stood quite still, thinking it over. Then came a gleam of hope. She felt as if Frank Raban must be answerable somehow for George's misdemeanours. Was it all true, she began to wonder. Mr. Raban, dismal man that he was, delighted in warnings and croakings. Then Dolly raised her head, and found that the dismal man had come back, and was standing beside her. He looked so humble and sorry that she felt he must be to blame.

'What have you been telling Aunt Sarah?' said Dolly, quite fiercely. 'Why have you made her so angry with my brother?'

'I am afraid it is your brother himself who has made her angry,' said Raban. 'I needn't tell you that I am very sorry,' he added, looking very pale; 'I would do anything I could to help him. I came back to talk to you about it now.'

'I don't want to hear any more,' cried Dolly, with great emotion. 'Why do you come at all? What can I say to you, to ask you to spare my poor George? It only vexes *her*. You don't understand him—how should you?' Then melting, 'If you knew all his tenderness and cleverness?'— she looked up wistfully; for once she did not seem stern, but entreating; her eyes were full of tears as she gazed into his face. There was something of the expression that he had seen in the studio.

'It is because I do your brother full justice,' said Raban, gravely, looking at her fixedly, 'that I have cared to interfere.'

Dolly's eyes dilated, her mouth quivered. Why did she look at him like that? He could not bear it. With a sudden impulse—one of those which come to slow natures, one such as that which had wrecked his life before—he said in a low voice, 'Do you know that I would do anything in the world for you and yours?'

'No, I don't know it,' said Dolly. 'I know that you seem to disapprove of everything I say, and that you think the worst of my poor George; that you don't care for him a bit.'

'The worst!' Raban said. 'Ah! Miss Vanborough, do you think it so impossible to love those people of whose conduct you think the worst?'

She was beginning to speak. He would not let her go on. 'Won't you give me a right to interfere?' he said; and he took a step forward, and stood close up to her, with a pale, determined face. 'There are some past things which can never be forgotten, but a whole life may atone for them. Don't you think so?' and he put out his hand. Dolly did not in the least understand him, or what was in his mind.

'Nobody ever did any good by preaching and interfering,' cried the angry sister, ignoring the outstretched hand. 'How can *you*, of all people —— ?' She stopped short; she felt that it was ungenerous to call up the past: but in George's behalf she could be mean, spiteful, unjust, if need be, to deliver him from this persecution,—so Dolly chose to call it.

She was almost startled by the deep cold tone of Frank's voice, as he answered, 'It is because I know what I am speaking of, Miss Vanborough, that I have an excuse for interfering before it is too late. You, at all events, who remember my past troubles, need not have reminded me of them.'

Heartless, cruel girl, she had not understood him. It was as well that she could not read his heart or guess how cruelly she had wounded him. He would keep his secret henceforth. Who was he to love a beautiful, peerless woman, in her pride and the triumph of her unsullied youth. He looked once more at the sweet, angry face. No, she had not understood him; so much he could see in her clear eyes. A minute ago they had been full of tears. The tears were all dry now; the angel was gone!

So an event had occurred to Dolly of which she knew nothing. She was utterly unconscious as she came sadly back to the house in the twilight. The pigeons were gone to roost. Lady Sarah was sitting alone in the darkling room.

'What a strange man Mr. Raban is, and how oddly and unkindly he talks,' said Dolly, going to the chimney and striking a light.

'What did he say?' said Lady Sarah.

'I don't quite remember,' said Dolly; 'it was all so incoherent and angry. He said he would do anything for us, and that he could never forgive George.'

CHAPTER XVIII.

AN AUTUMN MORNING.

Fain would I but I dare not ; I dare and yet I may not ;
I may although I care not, for pleasure when I play not.
You laugh because you like not ; I jest whenas I joy not ;
You pierce although you strike not ; I strike and yet annoy not.

—THE SHEPHERD'S DESCRIPTION OF LOVE.

THE Palace clock takes up the echo of the Old Church steeple, the sun-dial is pointing with its hooked nose to the Roman figures on its copper face—eleven o'clock says the Palace clock. People go crossing and re-crossing the distant vistas of Kensington Gardens ; the children are fluttering and scampering all over the brown turf, with its autumnal crop of sandwich-papers and orange-peel ; governesses and their pupils are walking briskly up and down the flower-walk that skirts Hyde Park. There is a tempting glitter of horsemanship in the distance, and the little girls glance wistfully towards it, but the governesses for the most part keep their young charges to the iron railings and the varied selection of little wooden boards, with Latin names, that are sprouting all along the tangled flower-beds ; the gravel paths are shaken over with fallen leaves, old, brown, purple—so they lie twinkling as the sun shines upon them.

One or two people are drinking at the little well among the trees where the children are at play.

'Hoy! hugh! houp!' cries little Betty, jumping high into the air, and setting off, followed by a crew of small fluttering rags. What a crisp noise the dead leaves make as the children wade and splash and tumble through the heaps that the gardeners have swept together. The old place echoes with their jolly little voices. The children come, like the leaves themselves, and disport year after year in the sunshine, and the ducks in the round pond feed upon the crumbs which succeeding generations bring from their tables. There are some of us who still know the ducks of twenty years apart. Where is the gallant grey (goose) that once used to chase unhappy children flying agonized before him? Where is the little duck with the bright sparkling yellow eyes and the orange beak? Quick-witted, eager, unabashed, it used to carry off the spoils of the great grey goose itself, too busy careering upon the green and driving all before it, to notice the disappearance of its crusts, although the foolish floundering white ducks, placidly impatient in the pond, would lift up their canary noses and quack notes of warning. One would still be glad to know where human nature finishes and where ducks begin.

Overhead the sky lies in faint blue vaults crossed by misty autumnal streamers; the rooks sweep cawing and circling among the tree-tops; a bell is going quick and tinkling: it comes from the little chapel of the Palace hard by. The old royal bricks and windows look red and purple in the autumn sunlight, against gold and blue vapours, and with canopies of azure and grey.

All the people are coming and going their different ways this October morning. A slim girl, in black silk, is hurrying

along from the wide door leading from the Palace Green.
She stops for an instant to look at the shadow on the old
sun-dial, and then hurries on again; and as she goes the
brazen hour comes striking and sounding from across the
house-roofs of the old suburb. A little boy, playing under
a tree, throws a chestnut at the girl as she hurries by. It
falls to the ground, slipping along the folds of her black silk
dress. At the same moment two young men, who have met
by chance, are parting at the end of one of the long avenues.
The girl, seeing them, stops short and turns back deliberately
and walks as far as the old sun-dial before she retraces her
steps.

How oddly all our comings and goings, and purposes and
cross-purposes combine, fulfil, frustrate each other. It is
like a wonderful symphony, of which every note is a human
life. The chapel bell had just finished ringing, as Rhoda
(for it is Rhoda) turned in through the narrow door leading
to the garden, and John Morgan, with Dolly beside him,
came quickly across the worn green space in front of the
barracks.

' I'm glad I caught you up,' panted good old John, tumbling and flying after Dolly. ' So this is your birthday, and
you are coming to church! I promised to take the duty for
Mr. Thompson this morning. I have had two funerals on,
and I couldn't get home before. We shall just do it. I'm
afraid I'm going too quick for you?'

' Not at all,' said Dolly. I always go quick. I was
running after Rhoda. She started to go, and then Aunt
Sarah sent me after her. Do you know,' Dolly said, ' George,
too, has become so very—I don't know what to call it —— ?
He asked me to go to church more often that day he came
up.'

'Well,' said John, looking at her kindly, and yet a little troubled, 'for myself, I find there's nothing like it; but then I'm paid for it, you know : it is in my day's work. I hope George is keeping to his?'

'Oh, I hope so,' said Dolly, looking a little wistful.

'H'm,' says John, doubtfully; 'here we are. Go round to the left, where you see those people.' And he darts away and leaves her.

· The clock began striking eleven slowly from the archway of the old Palace; some dozen people are assembled together in the little Palace chapel, and begin repeating the responses in measured tones. It is a quiet little place. The world rolls beyond it on its many chariot-wheels to busier haunts, along the great high-roads. As for the flesh and the devil, can they be those who are assembled here? They assemble to the sound of the bell, advancing feebly, for the most part skirting the sunny wall, past the sentry at his post, and along the outer courtyard of the Palace, where the windows are green and red with geranium-pots, where there is a tranquil glimmer of autumnal sunshine and a crowing of cocks. Then the little congregation turns in at a side-door of the Palace, and so through a vestibule, comes into the chapel, of which the bell has been tinkling for some week-day service: it stops short, and the service begins quite suddenly as a door opens in the wall, and a preacher, in a white surplice, comes out and begins in a deep voice almost before the last vibration of the bell has died away. As for the congregation, there is not much to note. There are some bent white heads, there is some placid middle-age, a little youth to brighten to the sunshine. The great square window admits a silenced light; there are high old-fashioned pews on either side of the place, and opposite the communion-

table, high up over the heads of the congregation, a great
square-curtained pew, with the royal arms and a curtained
gallery.   It was like Dugald Dalgetty's hiding-place, one
member of the congregation thought.   She used to wonder
if he was not concealed behind the heavy curtains.   This
reader of the *Legend of Montrose* is standing alone in a big
pew, with one elbow on the cushioned ledge, and her head
resting on her hand.   She has a soft brown scroll of hair,
with a gleam of sunlight in it.   She has soft oval cheeks
that flush up easily, grey eyes, and black knotted eyebrows,
and a curious soft mouth, close fixed now, but it trembles at
a word or a breath.   She had come to meet her friend.   But
Rhoda, who is not very far off, goes flitting down the broad
walk leading to the great summer-house.   It used to stand
there until a year or two ago, when the present generation
carried it bodily away—a melancholy, stately, grandiose old
pile, filling one with no little respect for the people who
raised so stately a mausoleum to rest in for a moment.
There was some one who had been resting there many moments on this particular morning : a sturdy young man,
leaning back against the wall and smoking a cigar.   He
jumped up eagerly when he saw the girl at last, and, flinging
his cigar away, came forward to meet her as she hurried
from under the shade of the trees in which she had been
keeping.

   'At last, you unpunctual girl, he cried, meeting her
and pulling her hand through his arm.   ' Do you know how
many cigars I have smoked while you have been keeping me
waiting ? '

   She did not answer, but looked up at him with a long
slow look.

   'Dear George, I couldn't get away before ; and when I

came just now there was some one talking to you. Your
aunt came, and Dolly, and they stayed, oh, such a time. I
was so cross, and I kept thinking of my poor George waiting
for me here.'

She could see George smiling and mollified as she spoke,
and went on more gaily.

'At last, I slipped away ; but I am afraid Dolly must
have thought it so strange.'

'Dolly !' said George Vanborough, impatiently (for, of
course, it was George, who had come up to town again with
another return-ticket); 'she had better take care and not
keep you from me again. Come and sit down,' said he.
'I have a thousand things to say to you. . . . '

'Oh, George! it must only be for a moment,' said Rhoda,
hesitating ; 'if anybody were to——'

'Nonsense !' cried George, already agitated by the
meeting, and exasperated by his long waiting ; 'you are
always thinking of what people will say ; you have no
feeling for a poor wretch who has been counting the minutes
till he could see you again—who is going to the devil
without you. Rhoda ! I cannot stand this much longer—
this waiting and starving on the crumbs that you vouch-
safe to scatter from your table. What the deuce does it
matter if they *don't* approve ? Why won't you marry me
this minute, and have done with it ? There goes a parson with an umbrella. Shall I run after him and get
him to splice us off-hand?'

Rhoda looked seriously alarmed. 'George, don't talk
like this,' she said, putting her slim hand on his. 'You
would never speak to me again if I consented to anything
so dishonourable ; Lady Sarah would never give you her
living ; she would never forg——'

'My aunt be hanged!' cried George, more and more
excited. 'If she were ever so angry she could not divide
us if we were married. I am not at all sure that I shall-
take her living. I only want to earn enough bread and
butter for you, Rhoda. *Now*, I believe she might starve you
into surrender. Rhoda, take me or leave me, but don't let
us go on like this. A woman's idea of honour, I confess,
passes my comprehension,' said he, somewhat bitterly.

'Can't you understand my not wanting to deceive them
all?' Rhoda said.

'Deceive them all?' said George. 'What are we doing
now? I don't like it. I don't understand it. I am ashamed
to look Dolly in the face when she talks to me about you.
Rhoda, be a reasonable, good, kind little Rhoda.' And the
young fellow wrung the little hand he held in his, and
thumped the two hands both down together upon the seat.

He hurt her, but the girl did not wince. She again
raised her dark eyes and looked fixedly into his face. When
she looked like that she knew very well that George, for one
—poor tamed monster that he was—could never defy her.

'Dearest George, you know that if I could, I would marry
you this moment,' she said. 'But how can I ruin your
whole future :—you, who are so sensitive and ill able to bear
things? How could we tell Lady Sarah just now, when—
when you have been so incautious and unfortunate——?'

'When I owe three hundred pounds!' cried George, at
the pitch of his voice : 'and I must get it from my aunt one
way or another—that is the plain English, Rhoda. Don't
be afraid; nothing you say will hurt my feelings. If only,'
he added, in a sweet changing voice—'if only you love me
a little, and will help a poor prodigal out of the mire——
But no : you virtuous people pass on with your high-minded

scruples, and leave us to our deserts,' he cried, with a sudden change of manner; and he started up and began walking up and down hastily in front of the summer-house.

The girl watched him for an instant—a hasty, stumpy figure going up and down, and up and down again.

' George! George!' faltered Rhoda, frightened—and her tears brimmed over unaffectedly—' haven't you any trust in my love? won't you believe me when I tell you, I—I—— you *know* I would give my life for you if I could!'

George Vanborough's own blue eyes were twinkling. ' Forgive me, darling,' he said, utterly melting in one instant, and speaking in that sweet voice peculiar to him. It seemed to come from his very heart. He sank down by her again. ' You are an angel—there, Rhoda—a thousand thousand miles away from me, though we are sitting side by side; but when you are unhappy, then I am punished for all my transgressions,' said George, in his gentle voice. ' Now I will tell you what we will do : we will tell Dolly all about it, and she will help us.'

' Oh! not Dolly,' said Rhoda, imploring; ' George! everybody loves her, and she doesn't know what it means to be unhappy and anxious. Let us wait a little longer, George : we are happy now together, are we not? You must pass your examination, and take your degree, and it will be easier to tell them then. Come.'

' Come where?' said George.

' There are so many people here,' said Rhoda, ' you mustn't write to me again to meet you. You had much better come and see me at the house.'

' I will come and see you there, too,' said George. ' I met Raban just now. He will be telling them I am in town; he says my aunt wants to see me on business. Confound him!'

'Was that Mr. Raban?' said Rhoda, opening her eyes.
'Oh! I hope he will not tell them.' She led him across the
grass, into a quiet place, deep among the trees, where they
were safe enough; for where so many come and go, two
figures, sitting on a felled trunk, on the slope of a leafy
hollow, are scarcely noticed. The chestnuts fell now and
then plash into the leaves and grasses, the breezes stirred
the crisp leaves, the brown sunset of autumn glow tinted
and swept to gold the changing world : there were still birds
and blue overhead, a sea of gold all round them. George
was happy. He forgot his debts, his dreams, the deaths and
doubts and failures of life—everything except two dark eyes,
a soft harmony of voice and look beside him.

'You are like Mendelssohn's *Songs without Words*,
Rhoda,' said George.

Rhoda didn't answer.

' George, what o'clock is it ? ' she said.

CHAPTER XIX.

KENSINGTON PALACE CHAPEL.

An' I hallus comed to's choorch afoar moy Sally wur deäd,
An' eerd un a bummin' awaäy loike a buzzard clock ower my yeäd,
An' I niver knaw'd whot a meän'd, but I thowt a ad summut to saäy,
An' I thowt a said what a owt to 'a said an' I comed awaäy.

MEANWHILE Dolly, who has been looking for Rhoda in vain, stands alone in the pew, listening to the opening exhortation, and, at the same time, wondering alongside of it, as she used to do when she and Rhoda were little girls at Paris long ago. Her thoughts run somewhat in this fashion :— 'Inner life,' thinks Dolly. 'What is inner life? George says he knows. John Morgan makes it all into the day's work and being tired. Aunt Sarah says it is repentance. Robert won't even listen to me when I speak of it. Have I got it? What am I?' Dolly wonders if she is sailing straight off to heaven at that moment in the big cushioned pew, or if the ground will open and swallow it up one day, like the tents of Korah and Abiram. This is what she is at that instant—so she thinks at least : Some whitewashed walls, a light through a big window; John Morgan's voice echoing in an odd melancholy way, and her own two hands lying on the cushion before her. Nothing more : she can go no farther at that minute towards 'the eternal fact upon which man may front the destinies and the immensities.'

So Dolly, at the outset of life, at the beginning of the longest five years of her life, stands in the strangers' great pew in Kensington Palace Chapel—a young Pharisee, perhaps, but an honest one, speculating upon the future, making broad her phylacteries; and with these, strange flashes of self-realisation that came to puzzle her all her life long—standing opposite the great prayer-books, with all the faded golden stamps of lions and unicorns. It was to please her brother George that Dolly had come to church this Saint's Day. What wouldn't she have done to please him? Through all his curious excursions of feeling he expected her always to follow, and Dolly tried to follow as she was expected.

'For our creation, preservation, and all the blessings of life,' the reader ran on. Dolly was ready enough to be grateful for all these mercies, only she thought that out of doors, in the gardens, she would have felt as grateful as she did now; and she again wondered why it was better to tender thanks in a mahogany box with red stuffings, out of a book, instead of out of her heart, in the open air. 'Can this be because I have no inner life?' thought Dolly, with her vacant eyes fixed on the clergyman. A bird's shadow flitted across the sun-gleam on the floor. Dolly looked up and saw the branch of the tree through the great window, and the blue depths shining, dazzling, and dominant. Then the girl pushed her hand across her eyes, and tried to forget other thoughts as she stood reading out of the big brown prayer-book. Dolly's gloves had fallen over the side of the pew, and were lying in the oak-matted passage-place, at the feet of a little country cookmaid from one of the kitchens

of the Palace, who alternately stared down at the grey
gloves and up at the young lady. The little cook, whose
mistress was away, had wandered in to the sound of the bell,
and sat there with her rosy cheeks like some russet apple
that had fallen by chance into a faded reliquary belonging
to a sumptuous shrine. Was it because it was Saturday,
Dolly wondered, that she could not bring her heart to the
altar?—that the little chapel did not seem to her much
more than an allegory? Are royal chapels only echoes and
allegories? Do people go there to pray real prayers, to
long passionately, with beating hearts? Have dried-up tears
ever fallen upon the big pages of the old books with their
curling *t*'s and florid *s*'s? Books in whose pages King George
the Third still rules over a shadowy realm, Queen Charlotte
heads the Royal Family!

Dolly had started away from her vague excursions when
the Epistle ended. 'Of the tribe of Zabulon twelve
thousand, of the tribe of Joseph twelve thousand, of the
tribe of Benjamin twelve thousand.' . . . It seemed to
Dolly but a part of the state and the ceremony that
oppressed her. As the armies passed before her, she seemed
to hear the chaunt of the multitude, to follow the endless
processions of the elect filing past with the seals on their
triumphant brows, the white robes and palms in their extended hands!

But listen, what is this? John Morgan thundered out
the long lists of the tribes; but his voice softened as he
came to the well-loved gospel of the day:—'Blessed are the
poor, for theirs is the kingdom: blessed are they that mourn,
for they shall be comforted; blessed are the merciful, the
pure, the peacemakers. . . .'

'Are these the real tribes upon earth for whom the

M

blessing is kept? Am I of the tribe of the merciful, of the peacemakers?' Dolly asked herself again. 'How can I make peace?—there is no one angry,' thought the girl; 'and I'm sure no one has ever done me any harm to be forgiven, except—except Mr. Raban, when he spoke to Aunt Sarah so cruelly about George. Ought I to forgive that?' thought the sister, and yet she wished she had not spoken so unkindly. . . .

When the end came there was a rustle. The old ladies got up off their knees, the curtains stirred in the big Dugald Dalgetty pew: Dolly was to meet John Morgan in the outer room, but the old clerk gave her a message to say that Mr. Morgan had gone to the chaplain's, and would meet her in the clock court of the Palace.

'There was a gentleman asking for him just a minute by,' said the old clerk.

So Dolly, instead of filing off with the rest of the congregation, went sweeping along the dark vaulted passages with the sunlight at either end—a grey maiden floating in the shade.

Dolly's dress was demure enough: for though she liked bright colours, by some odd scruples she denied herself the tints she liked. If she sometimes wore a rose or a blue ribbon, it was Lady Sarah who bought them, and who had learnt of late to like roses and blue ribbons by proxy. Otherwise, she let Dolly come, go, dress as she liked best; and so the girl bought herself cheap grey gowns and economical brown petticoats: luckily she could not paint her pretty cheeks brown, nor her bright hair grey. Sometimes Rhoda had proposed that they should dress in black with frill caps and crosses, but this Aunt Sarah peremptorily refused to permit. Lady Sarah was a clever woman, with a horror of attitudinising, and some want of artistic feeling. The poor people whom she visited, Rhoda herself, soon discovered the futility of any of the little performances they sometimes attempted for Lady Sarah's benefit.

Dolly stepped out from the dark passage into the Palace courtyard, with its dim rows of windows, its sentinel, its brasses shining, the old doorways standing at prim intervals with knobs and iron bells, which may be pulled to-day, but which seem to echo a hundred years ago, as they ring across the Dutch court. The little cookmaid was peeping out of her kitchen-door, and gave a kind little smile. Some one else was waiting, pacing up and down that quiet place, where footsteps can be heard echoing in the stillness. But as Dolly advanced, she discovered that it was not John Morgan, as she imagined. The gentleman, who had reached the end of his walk, now turned, came towards her, looking absently to the right and the left. It was the very last person in the whole world she had expected or wished to see. It was Frank Raban, with his pale face, who stopped short when he saw her. They had not met since that day when he had talked so strangely.

If Dolly looked as if she was a little sorry to see Mr. Raban, Mr. Raban also looked as if he had rather not have met Dolly. He gave a glance round, but there was no way by which he could avoid her, unless he was prepared, like harlequin in the pantomime, to take a summersault and disappear through one of the many windows. There was no help for it. They both came forward.

'How do you do, Miss Vanborough?' said Raban, gravely, holding out his hand, and thinking of the last time they had met.

'How do you do?' said Dolly, coldly, just giving him

her fingers. Then melting a little, as people do who have
been over-stiff—'Have you seen George lately? how is he?'
said Dolly, more forgivingly.

Raban looked surprised. 'He is quite well . . . Don't
you—has he not——' he interrupted himself, and then he
went on, looking a little confused: 'I am only in town for
an hour or two. I have been calling at John Morgan's, and
they sent me here to find him. Shall I find Lady Sarah at
home this afternoon?'

Dolly flushed up. In a moment all her coldness was gone.
Something in his manner made her suspect that all was not
well. 'It is something more about George?' she said, frightened, and she fixed her two circling eyes upon the man. Why
was he for ever coming—evil messenger of ill tidings? She
guessed it, she felt it, she seemed to have some second sight
as regards Raban. She almost hated him. A minute ago
she had thought she could forgive him.

Dolly's cheeks flushed in vain, her eyes flashed harmless
lightning.

'Yes, it is about your brother,' said the young man, looking away. 'I have at last been able to make that arrangement to help him, as Lady Sarah wished. It has taken me
some time and some trouble;' and without another word he
turned and walked away towards the passage.

I think this was the first time Dolly had ever been snubbed
in all her life, except by George, and that did not count.

A furtive, quick, yet hesitating footstep flutters after
Frank. 'Mr. Raban,' says Miss Vanborough.

He stopped.

'I did not mean to pain you,' blushing up (she was very
indignant still, and half-inclined to cry. But she was in the
wrong, and bent upon apology). 'I beg your pardon,' she

said, in a lofty, condoning, half-ashamed, half-indignant sort
of way; and she held out her hand.

Frank Raban did not refuse the outstretched hand; he
took it in his, and held it tight for an instant, with a grip
of which he was scarcely aware, and then he dropped it.
' You don't know,' he said, with some emotion,—' I hope you
will never know, what it is to have done another great wrong.
I cannot forget what you said to me that last evening we met ;
but you must learn more charity, and believe that even those
who have failed once may mean to do right another time.'

How little she guessed that, as he spoke, he was thinking
what a madness had been his; wondering what infatuation
had made him, even for one instant, dream they could ever
be anything to one another.

As the two made it up, after a fashion, a bell tinkled
through the court, a door opened, and John Morgan came
running down some worn steps, twirling his umbrella like a
mill.

' Here I am, Dolly. Why, Raban !' he shouts, ' where
do you come from ? Dr. Thompson is better—he kept me
discussing the church-rates. I couldn't get away. You see,
where the proportion of Dissenters —— Will you have an
arm ? '

' No, thank you,' said Dolly.

' ——where the proportion is one-fiftieth of the popula-
tion ——'

The curate, always enthusiastic, seized Raban's arm, and
plunged with him into the very depths of Dr. Thompson's
argument. Dolly lingered behind for a minute, and came
after them, along the passage again and out by a different
way into an old avenue which leads from the Palace stables,
and by a garden enclosed in high brick walls. It used to be

Lady Henley's garden, and Dolly sometimes walked there. Now she only skirted the wall. The sun was casting long shadows, the mists were gone, a sort of sweet balmy ripeness was in the air, as they came out upon the green. The windows of the old guard-house were twinkling; some soldiers were lounging on the grass. Some members of the congregation were opening the wicket-gates of one of the old houses that stood round about in those days, modest dependencies of the Palace, quaint-roofed, with slanting bricks and tiles, and narrow panes, from whence autumnal avenues could be descried.

There is a side-door leading from Palace Green to Kensington Gardens. Within the door stands an old stone summer-house, which is generally brimming over with little children, who for many years past have sat swinging their legs upon the seat.

As Dolly passed the gate she heard a shout, and out of the summer-house darted a little ragged procession, with tatters flying—Mikey and his sister, who had spied their victim, and now pursued her with triumphant cries.

'Tsus!—hi, Mikey!—Miss Vamper!' (so they called her).

'Give us a 'napeny,' says Mikey. 'Father's got no work, mother was buried on Toosdy! We's so 'ungry.'

'Why, Betty,' said Dolly, stopping short, and greatly shocked, 'is this true?'

'Ess,' says little Betty, grinning, and running back through the wicket.

'What did you have for dinner yesterday?' says Dolly, incredulous, and pursuing Betty towards the summer-house.

'Please, Miss, mother give us some bread-and-drippin',' says Mikey, with a caper. 'I mean father did. We's so . . .'

'You mean that you have been telling me a wicked story,' interrupted Dolly. 'I am *very* angry, Mikey. I *never* forgive deception. I shall give you no apples— nothing. I . . . .' She stopped short; her voice suddenly faltered. She stood quite still watching two people, who came advancing down the avenue that led to the little door, arm-in-arm, and so absorbed in each other, that for a minute they did not see that she was standing in the way. It was a chance. If it had not happened then, it would have happened at some other time and place.

Rhoda had waited until the service was over, and in so doing she had come upon the last person whom she wished to see just then. There stood Dolly by the summer-house, with a pale face, confronting her, with the little ragged crew about her knees. Mikey, looking up, thought that for once 'Miss Vamper' was in the tantrums.

Rhoda started back instinctively, meeting two blank wondering eyes, and would have pulled George away, but it was too late.

'Nonsense,' said George; and he came forward, and then they all were quite silent for a minute, George a little in advance, Rhoda lingering still.

'What does this mean?' said Dolly, coldly, speaking at last.

'What does it mean!' George burst out. 'Don't you see us? don't you guess? It is good news, isn't it?—Dolly, she loves me. Have you not guessed it all along—ever since—months ago?'

He was half-distracted, half-excited, half-laughing. His eyes were dim with moisture. Any one might see him. What did he care for the ragged children, the people passing by—those silent crowds that flit through our lives! He came up to Dolly.

' You will be tender to her, won't you, and help her, for my sake, and you will be our friend, Dolly? We had not meant to tell you yet; but you wish us joy, won't you, dear?'

'Tender to her? Help her? What help could she want?' thought Dolly, looking at Rhoda, who stood silent still, but who made a little dumb movement of entreaty. ' Was it George who was asking her to befriend him? Was it George, who had mistrusted her all this long time, and kept her in ignorance . . .?'

' Why don't you answer? Why do you look like that? Do you wonder that I or that anybody else should love her?' he went on eagerly.

'What do you want me to do?' Dolly asked. ' I cannot understand it.'

Her voice sounded hard and constrained: she was hurt and bewildered.

George was bitterly disappointed. Her coldness shocked him. Could it be possible that Rhoda was right and Dolly hard and unfeeling?

Poor Dolly! A bitter wave of feeling seemed suddenly to rise from her heart and choke her as she stood there. So! there was an understanding between them? Did he come to see Rhoda in secret, while she was counting the days till they should meet? Was it only by chance that she was to learn their engagement? They had been stopping up the way; as they moved a little aside to let the people pass, Rhoda timidly laid one hand on Dolly's arm,—' Won't you forgive me? won't you keep our secret?' she said.

' Why should there be any secret?' cried Dolly, haughtily. ' How could I keep one from Aunt Sarah? I am not used to such manœuvrings.'

Rhoda began to cry. George, exasperated by Dolly's manner, burst out with 'Tell her, then! Tell them all—tell them everything! Tell them of my debts! Part us!' he said. 'You will make your profit by it, no doubt, and Rhoda, poor child, will be sacrificed.' He felt he was wrong, but this made him only the more bitter. He turned away from Dolly, and pulled Rhoda's hand through his arm.

'I will take care of you, darling,' he said.

'George! George!' from poor Dolly, sick and chilled.

'Dolly!' cried another voice from without the gate. It was John Morgan's. He had missed her, and was retracing his steps to find her.

Poor weak-minded Dolly! now brought to the trial and found wanting: how could she withstand those she loved? All her life long it was so with her. As George turned away from her, her heart went after him.

'Oh, George! don't look at me so. My profit! You have made it impossible for me to speak,' she faltered, as she moved away to meet the curate and Frank Raban.

'What is the matter? are you ill?' said John Morgan, meeting Dorothea in the doorway. 'Why did you wait behind?'

'Mikey detained me. I am quite well, thank you,' said Dolly, slowly, with a changed face.

Raban gave her a curious look. He had seen some one disappear into the summer-house, and he thought he recognised the stumpy figure.

John Morgan noticed nothing; he walked on, talking of the serious aspect things were taking in the East—of Doctor Thompson's gout—of the church-rates. Frank Raban looked at Dolly once or twice, and slackened his steps to hers. They left her at the corner of her lane.

CHAPTER XX.

RHODA TO DOLLY.

Make denials,
Increase your services : so seem as if
You were inspired to do those duties which
You tender to her. . . .
— CYMBELINE.

DOLLY heard the luncheon-bell ringing as she walked slowly homewards. It seemed to her as if she had been hearing a story which had been told her before, with words that she remembered now, though she had listened once without attaching any meaning to them. Now she seemed to awake and understand it all—a hundred little things, unnoticed at the time, crowded back into her mind and seemed to lead up to this moment. Dolly suddenly remembered Rhoda's odd knowledge of George's doings, her blushes, his constant comings of late: she remembered everything, even to the gloves lying by the piano. The girl was bitterly hurt, wounded, impatient. Love had never entered into her calculations, except as a joke or a far-away impossibility. It was no such very terrible secret after all that a young man and a young woman should have taken a fancy to each other ; but Dolly, whose faults were the faults of inexperience and youthful dominion and confidence, blamed passionately as she would have sympathised. Then in a breath she blamed herself.

How often it happens that people meaning well, as Dolly did, undoubtedly slide into some wrong groove from the over-balance of some one or other quality. Dolly cared too much and not too little, and that was what made her so harsh to George, and then, as if to atone for her harshness, too yielding to his wish—to Rhoda's wish working by so powerful a lever.

Lady Sarah came home late for luncheon, and went up to her room soon after. Dolly gave Frank Raban's message. She herself stopped at home all day expecting George, but no George came, not even Rhoda, whom she both longed and hated to see again. Every one seemed changed to Dolly; she felt as if she was wandering lost in the familiar rooms, as if George and her aunt and Rhoda were all different people since the morning.

'Why are you looking at me, child?' said Lady Sarah, suddenly. Dolly had been wistfully scanning the familiar lines of the well-known face; there was now a secret between them, thought the girl.

Mr. Raban came in the afternoon, as he had announced, and Dolly, going into the oak room, found him there, standing in the shadow, with a bundle of papers under his arm, and looking more like a lawyer's clerk than a friend who had been working hard in their service.

Dolly was leaving the room again, when her aunt called her back for a minute.

'Did George tell you anything of his difficulties the last time he was in town?' Lady Sarah asked from her chimney-corner. 'When was it you saw him, Dolly?' She was nervously tying some papers together that slipped out of her hands and fell upon the floor.

Poor Dolly turned away. There was a minute's silence.

. Dolly flushed crimson. 'I—I don't—I can't tell you,' she said, confusedly.

She saw Frank Raban's look of surprise as she turned. What did she care what he thought of her? What was it to him if she chose to tell a lie and he guessed it? Oh, George! cruel boy! what had he asked?

Frank Raban wondered at Dolly's silence. Since she wished to keep a secret, he did not choose to interfere ; but he blamed her for that, as for most other things; and yet the more he blamed her the more her face haunted him. Those girl's eyes, with their great lights and clouds ; that sweet face, that looked so stern and yet so tender too. When he was away from her he loved her; when he was with her he accused her.

It was a long, endless day. Miss Moineaux was welcome at tea-time, with her flannel bindings and fluttering gossip. It seemed like a little bit of commonplace, familiar every-day coming in. Dolly went to the door with her when she left them, and saw black trees swaying, winds chasing across the dreary sky, light clouds sailing by. The winds rose that night, beating about the house. A chimney-pot fell crashing to the ground ; elm-branches broke off from the trees and were scattered along the parks. Dolly, in her little room, lay listening to the sobs and moans without, to the fierce hands beating and struggling with her window. She fell into a sleep, in which it seemed to her that she was railing and raving at George again : she awoke with a start to find that it was the wind. She dreamt the history of the day over and over. She dreamt of Raban, and somehow he always looked at her reproachfully. She awoke very early in the morning, long before it was time to get up, with penitent, loving words on her lips. Had she been harsh to George? Jealous—was she jealous? Dolly scorned to be jealous, she told herself. It was her hatred of wrong, her sense of justice, that had made her heart so bitter. Poor Dolly had yet to discover how far she fell short of her own ideal. My poor little heroine was as yet on the eve of her long and lonely expedition in life. There might be arid places waiting for her, dreary passes, but there were also cool waters and green pastures along the road. Nor had she yet journeyed from their shade, and from the sound of her companions' voices and the shelter of their protection.

This was Rhoda's explanation. She was standing before Dolly, looking prettier than ever. She held a flower in her hand, which she had offered her friend, who silently rejected it. Rhoda had looked for Dolly in vain in the house. She found her at last, disconsolately throwing crumbs to the fishes in the pond. Dolly stood sulky and miserable, scarcely looking up when Rhoda spoke. They were safe in the garden out of reach of the quiet old guardians of the house. Rhoda began at once.

'He urged it,' said Rhoda, fixing her great dark eyes steadily upon Dolly, 'indeed he did. I said no at first; I would not even let him be bound. One day I was weak and consented to be engaged. I sinned against my own conscience; I am chastised.'

'Sinned?' said Dolly, impatiently; 'chastised? Rhoda, Rhoda, you use long words that mean nothing. Oh! why did you not tell Aunt Sarah from the beginning? She loves George so dearly—so dearly that she would have done anything, consented to everything, and this wretchedness would have been spared. How shall I tell her? How shall

I ever tell her? I can't keep such a secret. Already I
have had to tell a lie.'

'I could not bear to be the means of injuring him,'
Rhoda said, flushing up. 'I daresay you won't understand
me or believe me, but it is true. Indeed, indeed, it is true,
Dolly. Lady Sarah would never forgive him now if he were
to marry me. She does not like me. Dolly, you know it.
I have been culpably foolish; but I will not damage his
future.'

'Of course it is foolish to be engaged,' said Dolly; 'but
there are worse things, Rhoda, a thousand times.'

'Yes,' said Rhoda. 'Dolly, you don't know half. He
has been gambling—dear, foolish boy—borrowing money
from the Jews. Uncle John heard of it through a pupil of
his. He wrote to Mr. Raban. Oh, Dolly, I love him so
dearly, that it breaks my heart. How can I trust him?
How can I? Oh, how difficult it is to be good, and to
know what one should do.'

Rhoda flung herself down upon the wooden bench as she
spoke, leaning her head against the low brick wall, with its
ivy sprays. Dolly stood beside her, erect, indignant, half
softened by the girl's passion, and half hardened when she
thought of the deception that she had kept up. Beyond
the low ivy wall was the lane of which I have spoken, where
some people were strolling; overhead the sky was burning
deep, the afternoon shadows came trembling and shimmering into the pond. Lady Sarah had had a screen of creepers
put up to shelter her favourite seat from the winds; the
great leaves were still hanging to the trellis, gold and
brown.

'If I thought only of myself should I not have told
everybody?' said Rhoda, excitedly, and she clasped her

hands; 'but I feel there is a higher duty to him. I will be his good angel and urge him to work. I will leave him if I stand in his way, and keep to him if it is for good. Do you think I want to be a cause of trouble between him and Lady Sarah? She might disinherit him. It is you she cares for, and not poor George; I heard Mr. Raban say so only yesterday,' cried Rhoda, in a sudden burst of tears. ' He told me so.'

Dolly waited for a moment, and then slowly turned away, leaving Rhoda still sobbing against the bricks. She couldn't forgive her at that instant; her heart was bitter against her. What had she done to deserve such taunts? Why had Rhoda come making dissension and unhappiness between them? It was hard, oh, it was hard. There came a jangling burst of music from the church bells, as if to add to her bewilderment.

' Dear Rhoda,' said Dolly, coming back, and melting suddenly, ' do listen to me. Tell them all. I cannot see one reason against it.'

' Except that we are no longer engaged,' said Rhoda, gravely. ' I have set him free, Dolly; that is what I wanted to tell you. I wrote to him, and set him free; for anything underhand is as painful to me as to you. It was only to please George I consented. Hush! They are calling me.'

Engaged or not, poor Dorothea felt that all pleasure in her friend's company was gone; there was a tacit jar between them — a little rift. Dolly for the first time watched Rhoda with critical eyes, as she walked away down the path that led to the house, fresh and trim in her pretty dress, and her black silk mantlet, and with her flower in her hand. Dolly did not follow her. She thought over every

single little bit of her life after Rhoda had left her, as she
sat there alone, curled up on the wooden seat, with her limp
violet dress in crumpled folds, and her brown hair falling
loose, with pretty little twirls and wavings. Her grey eyes
were somewhat sad and dim from the day's emotion. No,
she must not tell her aunt what had happened until she had
George's leave. She would see him soon; she would beg
his pardon; she would *make* him tell Aunt Sarah. She had
been too hasty. She had spoken harshly, only it was difficult not to be harsh to Rhoda, who was so cold—who seemed
as if she would not understand. All she said sounded so
good, and yet, somehow, it did not come right. Then she
began to wonder if it could be that Rhoda loved George
more than Dolly imagined. Some new glimmer had come
to the girl of late—not of what love was, but of what it
might be. Only Dolly was fresh and prim and shy, as girls
are, and she put the thought far away from her. Love!
Love was up in the stars, she thought hastily. All the
same she could not bring herself to feel cordially to Rhoda.
There was something miserably uncomfortable in the new
relations between them; and Dolly showed it in her manner
plainly enough.

Lady Sarah told Dolly that afternoon that she had
written to George to come up at the end of the week. 'He
has had no pity on us, Dolly,' she said. 'I have some money
that a friend paid back, and with that and the price of a
field at Bartlemere, I shall be able to pay for his pastimes
during the last year.

'Aunt Sarah,' said Dolly suddenly illuminated, 'can't you
take some of my money; do, please, dearest Aunt Sarah.'

'What would be the use of that?' said Lady Sarah. 'I
want the interest for your expenses, Dolly.' She spoke quite

sharply, as if in pain, and she put her hand to her side and went away. If Lady Sarah had not been ill herself and preoccupied, she might have felt that something also ailed Dolly, that the girl was constrained at times, and unlike herself. Dolly only wondered that her aunt did not guess what was passing before her, so patent did it seem, now that she had the key.

One day Marker persuaded her mistress to go to a doctor. Lady Sarah came back with one of those impossible prescriptions that people give. Avoid all anxiety; do not trouble yourself about anything; live generously; distract yourself when you can do so without fatigue.

Lady Sarah came home to find a Cambridge letter on the table, containing some old bills of George's, which a tradesman had sent on to her; a fresh call from the unlucky bank in which Mr. Francis had invested so much of her money: an appeal from Mikey's fever-stricken cellar, and a foreign scented letter, that troubled her more than all the rest together :—

Trincomalee, September 25, 18—.

DEAREST SARAH,—I have many and many a time begun to write to you of all, only to destroy bitter records of those sorrows which I must continue to bear *alone*. Soon we shall be leaving this ill-fated shore, where I have passed so many miserable years gazing with longing eyes at the broad expanse lying so calm and indifferent before me.

Before long Admiral Palmer sails for England. He gives up his command with great reluctance, and returns *vià* the Cape; but I, in my weak state of health, dare risk no longer delay. Friends—kind, good friends, Mrs. and Miss M'Grudder—have offered to accompany me overland, sharing all expenses, and visiting Venice and Titian's—the great master's glorious works—*en route*, to say nothing of Raphael, and Angelo the divine. We shall rest a week at Paris. I feel that after so long a journey utter prostration will succeed to the excitement which carries me through where I see others, more robust than myself, failing on every side. And then I am in rags—a study for Murillo himself! I cannot come among you all until my wardrobe is replenished. How I look forward to the time when I shall welcome my Dorothea—ours, I may say—for you have been all but a mother to her. On my return I trust to find some corner to make my nest; and for that purpose I should wish to spend a week or two in London, so as to be within easy reach of all. Sarah,

N

my first husband's sister, will you help me ; for the love of 'auld lang syne,' will you spare a little corner in your dear old house?   Expensive hotels I cannot afford.   My dear friends here rgree that Admiral Palmer's ungraciously-given allowances are beggarly and unworthy of his high position.   How differently dear Stan would have wished him to act!   Silver and gold have I none— barely sufficient for my own dress.   Those insurances were most unfairly given against the widow and the orphan.   Tell my darlings this; tell them, too, that all that I have is theirs.   When I think that for the last six years, ever.since my second marriage, a tyrant will has prevented me from folding them to my heart, indignation nearly overcomes the prudence so foreign to my nature.   Once more, fond love to you, to my boy, and to *ma fille ;* and trusting before long to be once more at home,

Ever your very affectionate
PHILIPPA.

P.S.—Since writing the above few lines, I find that my husband wishes to compass my death.   He again proposes my returning with him by the Cape. Sarah, will you spare me the corner of a garret beneath your roof?

The letter was scented with some faint delicious perfume. ' Here, take it away,' says Lady Sarah. ' Faugh ! Of course she knows very well that she can have the best bedroom, and the dressing-room for her maid ; and you, my poor Dolly, will have a little amusement and some one better fitted to——'

' Don't,' cries Dolly, jumping forward with a kiss.

CHAPTER XXI.

CINDERS.

'Mid the wreck of IS and WAS,
Things incomplete and purposes betrayed
Make sadder transits o'er thought's optic glass
Than noblest objects utterly decayed !

DOLLY went to afternoon church the day George was expected. When she came home she heard that her brother was up-stairs, and she hurried along the passage with a quick-beating heart, and knocked at his door. It was dark in the passage, and Dolly stood listening—a frightened, grey-eyed, pent-up indignation, in a black dress, with her bonnet in her hand. There was a dense cloud of smoke and tobacco in the room when Dolly turned the lock at last, and she could only cough and blink her eyes. As the fumes cleared away, she saw that George was sitting by the low wooden fireplace. He had been burning papers. How eagerly the flames leaped and travelled on, in bright blue and golden tongues, while the papers fell away black and crackling and changing to cinder. Dolly looked very pale and unlike herself. George turned with a bright haggard sort of smile.

' Is that you, Dolly ? ' he said. ' Come in ; the illumina-tion is over. You don't mind the smell of tobacco. I have been burning a box of cigars that Robert gave me. He knows no more about cigars than you do.'

' Oh, George,' cried Dolly. ' Is this all you have to say, after making us so unhappy—— ? '

'What do you want me to say?' said George, shrugging his shoulders.

'I want you to say that you have told her everything, and that there are no more concealments,' Dolly cried, getting angry. 'When Aunt Sarah asked me about you last I felt as if it was written in my face that I was lying.'

He was going to answer roughly, but he looked up at Dolly's pale agitated face, and was sorry for her. He spoke both kindly and crossly.

'Don't make such a talk, Dolly, and a fuss. We have had it out—John Morgan—council of state—she has been— she has been—'—his voice faltered a little bit—' a great deal kinder than I deserve or had any reason to expect, judging by *you*, Dolly. It's not *your* business to scold, you know.'

'And she knows all,' said Dolly, eagerly and brightening.

'She knows all about my debts,' said George, expressively. 'She is going to let me try once more for the next scholarship. She shan't be disappointed this time. However, the past is past, and can't be helped. I've been burning a whole drawer full of it . . .' And he struck his foot into the smouldering heap.

People think that what is destroyed is over, forgetting that what has been is never over, and that it is in vain you burn and scatter the cinders of many a past hope and failure, and of a debt to pay, a promise broken. Debts, promises, failures are there still. There were the poems George had tried to write, the account-books he had not filled up, the lists of books he had not read, a dozen mementoes of good intentions broken.

'And did you not tell Aunt Sarah about Rhoda?' repeated Dolly, disappointed. 'Oh, George, what does Rhoda mean when she says you are no longer engaged? What does it all mean?'

'It means, it means,' said George, impatiently, 'that I am an idiot, but I am not a sneak; and if a woman trusts me, I can keep her counsel, so long as you don't betray me, Dolly. Only there are some things one can't do, not even for the woman one loves.' Then he looked up suddenly, and seeing Dolly's pained face, he went on: 'Dolly, I think you would cut off your head if I were to ask you for it: Rhoda won't snip off one little lock of hair. Poor dear, she is frightened at every shadow. She has given me back this,' he said, opening his hand, which he had kept closed before, and showing Dolly a little pearl locket lying in his palm. Then he went on in a low voice, looking into the fire, 'I love her enough, God knows, and I would tell the whole world, if she would let me. But she says no—always no; and I can trust her, Dolly, for she is nearer heaven than I am. It is her will to be silent,' he said, gently; 'angels vanish if we would look into their faces too closely. She would like me to have a tranquil spirit, such as her own; she thinks me a thousand times better than I am,' said George, 'and if I did as she wishes, I could be happy enough, but not contented.' Dolly wondered of what he was thinking, as he went on pacing up and down the room. 'I cannot tell lies to myself, not even for her sake. I cannot take this living as she wishes. If I may not believe in God my own way, I should blaspheme and deny Him, while I confessed Him in some one else's words. You asked me one day if I had an inner life, Dolly,' George said, coming back to the oak chimney-piece again. 'Inner life is only one's self and the responsibility of this one life to the Truth. Sometimes I think that before I loved Rhoda I was not all myself, and though the truth was the same it did not concern me in the same degree, and I meant to do this or that as it might be most advisable. Now, through loving her, Dolly, I seem to have come to something beyond us both, and what is advisable don't seem to matter any more. Can you understand this?'

'Yes, George,' said Dolly, looking at him earnestly—his sallow face had flushed up, his closed eyes had opened out. Dolly suddenly flung her arms round his neck and kissed him. She felt proud of her brother as she listened to him. She had come to blame, she remained to bless him. Ah, if every one knew him as well as she did. She was happier than she had been for many a day, and ready to believe that George could not be wrong. She could not even say no that evening after dinner, when George proposed that they should go over to the Morgans'.

'Go, my dears,' said Lady Sarah; and Dolly got up with a sort of sigh to get her bonnet. Just as they were starting, her cousin Robert walked in unexpectedly, and proposed to accompany them. He had come in with a serious face, prepared to sympathise in their family troubles, and to add a few words in season, if desired, for George's benefit. He found the young man looking most provokingly cheerful and at home, Lady Sarah smiling, and if Dolly was depressed she did not show it, for, in truth, her heart was greatly lightened. The three walked off together.

'We shall not be back to tea,' said Robert, who always liked to settle things beforehand. But on this occasion Mrs. Morgan's hospitable teapot was empty for once. The whole party had gone off to a lecture and dissolving views in the Town Hall. The only person left behind was Tom

Morgan, who was sitting in the study reading a novel, with his heels on the chimney-piece, when they looked in.

'Good-night, Tom,' said Dolly, with more frankness than necessary; 'we won't stay, since there is only you.'

'Good-evening,' said Robert, affably. And they came out into the street again. He went on: 'I am sorry John Morgan was not at home. I want him to fix some time for coming down to Cambridge. You must come with him, Dolly. I think it might amuse you.'

'Oh, thank you,' says Dolly, delighted.

This prospect alone would have been enough to make her walk back enjoyable, even if George had not been by her side; if it had not been so lovely a night; if stars had not burnt sweet and clear overhead; if soft winds had not been stirring. The place looked transformed, gables and corners standing out in sudden lights. They could see the dim shade of the old church, and a clear green planet flashing with lambent streams beyond the square tower. Then they escaped from the crowd and turned down by the quiet lane where Church House was standing gabled against the great Orion. They found the door ajar when they reached the ivy gate; the hall door, too, was wide open, and there seemed to be boxes and some confusion.

'Oh, don't let us go in; come into the garden,' said Dolly, running to the little iron garden-gate inside the outer wall. There was a strange glimmer behind the gate against which the slim white figure was pushing. The garden was dark, and rustling with a trembling in the branches. A great moon had come up, and was hanging over London, serenely silvering the housetops and spires; its light was rippling down the straight walks of which the gravel was glittering.

'Yes, come,' said George, and the three young people flitted along to their usual haunt by the pond.

'What is that?' said Dolly, pointing in the darkness; 'didn't somebody go by?' She was only a girl in her teens, and still afraid of unseen things.

'A rat,' cried George, dashing forward.

'Oh, stop,' from Dolly.

'Don't be a goose,' said Robert; and as he spoke George met them, flourishing an old garden shawl of Lady Sarah's, which had been forgotten upon the bench. He flung it weirdly down upon the gravel walk. '"Dead for a ducat, dead,"' said he. Then he started forward with a strange moonlight gleam upon his face. '"This counsellor is now most still, most secret, and most grave,"' he said, '"who was in life a foolish prating knave."' His voice thrilled, he got more and more excited.

Robert began to laugh: 'What is that you are acting?' he said.

'Acting?' cried George, opening his eyes; '"that skull had a tongue in it and could sing once." "Dost thou think Alexander looked o' this fashion i' the earth ——?"'

'Do be quiet,' said Henley, impatiently. 'Is not some one calling?'

Some one was calling: lights were appearing and disappearing; the drawing-room window was wide open, and their aunt stood on the terrace making signs, and looking out for them.

'Look, there goes a falling star,' said George.

'Ah! who is that under the tree?' cried Dolly again, with a little shriek. 'I knew I had seen some one move;' and as she spoke, a figure emerging from the gloom came nearer and nearer to them, almost running with two extended arms ; a figure in long flowing garments, silver in the moon-light, a woman advancing quicker and quicker.

'Children, children !' said a voice. 'It is I,—George—your mother ! Don't you know me—darlings ? I have come. I was looking for you. Yes, it is I, your mother, children.'

Dolly's heart stood still, and then began to throb, as the lady flung her arms round Robert, who happened to be standing nearest.

'Is this George ? I should have known him anywhere,' she cried.

Was this their mother ? this beautiful, sweet, unseen woman, this pathetic voice ?

Dolly had seized George's hand in her agitation, and was crunching it in hers. Robert had managed to extricate himself from the poor lady's agitated clutch.

'Here is George. I am Robert Henley,' he said. 'But, my dear aunt, why—why did you not write ? I should have met you. I ——'

It was all a strange confusion of moonlight, and bewil-derment, and of tears, presently, for Mrs. Palmer began to cry and then to laugh, and finally went off into hysterics in her son's arms.

CHAPTER XXII.

MRS. PALMER.

Le Baron—' Je vais m'enfermer pour m'abandonner à ma douleur. Dites-lui,
s'il me demande, que je suis enfermé et que je m'abandonne à ma douleur . . '
—A. DE MUSSET.

WHEN they were a little calmed down, when they had left
the moon and the stars outside in the garden, and were all
standing in a group in the drawing-room round the chair in
which Mrs. Palmer had been placed, Dolly saw her mother's
face at last. She vaguely remembered her out of the long
ago, a very young and beautiful face smiling at her : this
face was rounder and fuller than the picture, but more
familiar than her remembrance. Mrs. Palmer was a stout
and graceful woman, with a sort of undulating motion
peculiar to her, and with looks and ways some of which
Dolly recognised, though she had forgotten them before.
There was a strong likeness to Dolly herself, and even a little
bit of George's look when he was pleased, though poor
George's thick complexion and snub nose were far, far re-
moved from any likeness to that fair and delicate countenance. Dolly gazed admiringly at the soft white hand, with
the great Louis-Quinze ring upon the forefinger. Though
Mrs. Palmer had come off a journey in semi-hysterics, she
was beautifully dressed in a black silk dress, all over rippling

waved flounces, that flowed to her feet. She was leaning back in the chair, with half-closed eyes, but with a tender, contented smile.

'I knew you would take me in,' she said to Lady Sarah. 'I felt I was coming home—to my dear sister's home. See,' she said, 'what dear Stan gave me for my wedding-gift. I chose it at Lambert's myself. We spared no expense. I have never taken off his dear ring;' and she put out her soft hand and took hold of Lady Sarah's mitten. 'Oh, Sarah, to think—to think——'

Lady Sarah shrunk back as usual, though she answered not unkindly: 'Not now, Philippa,' she said, hastily. 'Of course this house is your home, and always open to you; at least, when we know you are coming. Why did you not write? There is no bed ready. I have had the maids called up. If Admiral Palmer had let me know——'

'He did not know,' said Mrs. Palmer, getting agitated. 'I will tell you all. Oh, Dolly, my darling, beware how you marry; promise me——'

'He did not know?' interrupted Lady Sarah.

Dolly's mother got more and more excited.

'I had some one to take care of me,' she said. 'My old friend Colonel Witherington was on board, and I told him everything as we were coming along. I telegraphed to you, did I not? But my poor head fails me. Oh, Sarah, exile is a cruel thing; and now, how do I know that I have not come home too soon?' she said, bursting into tears. 'If you knew all——'

'You shall tell us all about it in the morning, when you are rested,' said Lady Sarah, with a glance at Robert.

'Yes, in the morning, yes,' said Mrs. Palmer, looking relieved, and getting up from her chair, and wiping her eyes.

'How good you are to me! Am I to have my old room where I used to stay as a girl? Oh, Sarah, to think of my longings being realised at last, and my darling children—dear Stan's children—there actually before me.' And the poor thing, with a natural emotion, once more caught first one, then the other, to her, and sat holding her son's hand in both hers. When he tried to take it away she burst into fresh tears; and, as a last resource, Marker was summoned.

Poor Mrs. Palmer! her surprise had been something of a failure; George was not expansive, nor used to having his hand held: the boy and girl were shy, stiff, taken aback. Aunt Sarah was kind, but cross and bewildered: Mrs. Palmer herself exhausted after twelve hours' railway journey, and vaguely disappointed.

'It was just like her,' said Lady Sarah, wearily, to Marker, as they were going upstairs some two hours later, after seeing Mrs. Palmer safe into her room, and bolting the doors, and putting out the lights of this eventful evening. 'What can have brought her in this way?'

Marker looked at her mistress with her smiling round face. 'The wonder to me was whatever kept her away so long from those sweet children, to say nothing of you, my lady.'

'She has chosen to make other ties,' said Lady Sarah; 'her whole duty is to her husband. Good-night, Marker: I do not want you to-night.'

'Of course you know best, my lady,' says Marker doubtfully. 'Good-night, my lady.'

And then all was quite silent in the old house. The mice peeped out of their little holes and sniffed at the cheese-trap; a vast company of black beetles emerged from secret places and corners; the clocks began to tick like mad. Dolly lay

awake a long time, and then dreamt of her new mamma, and
of the moonlight that evening, and of a floating sea. Mrs.
Palmer slept placidly between her linen sheets. Sarah
Francis lay awake half the night crying her eyes and her
aching heart away in bitter tears. Philippa was come. She
knew of old what her advent meant. She loved Philippa,
but with reserve and pain; and now she would claim her
Dolly, she would win her away, and steal her treasure from
her again—what chance had she, sad and sorry and silent,
with no means of uttering her love? She was a foolish,
jealous woman; she knew it, and with all her true heart she
prayed for strength and for love to overcome jealousy and
loneliness. Once in her life her difficult nature had caused
misery so great between her and her husband that the breach
had never been repaired, and it was Philippa who had brought
it all about. Now Sarah knew that to love more is the only
secret for overcoming that cruellest madness of jealousy, and
to love more was her prayer. The dawn came at last, stealing
tranquilly through the drawn curtains: with what peace and
tranquillity the faint light flowed, healing and quieting her
pain.

Dolly's new mamma's account of herself next morning
was a little incoherent. Her health was very indifferent;
she suffered agonies, and was living upon morphia when the
doctor had ordered her home without delay. She had been
obliged to come off at a few hours' notice; she didn't write.
The Admiral was fortunately absent on a cruise, or he never
would have let her go. He knew what a helpless creature she
was. She had borrowed the passage-money from a friend.
Would Lady Sarah please advance her a little now, as she
was literally penniless, and she wished to make George and

Dolly some presents, and to engage a French maid at once ?
She supposed she should hear by the next post and receive
some remittances. She was not sure, for Hawtry was so
dreadfully close about money. She did not know *what* he
would say to her running away. No doubt he would use
dreadful language, pious as he was ; *that* she was used to ;
Colonel Witherington could testify to it. . . . And then
she sighed. ' I have made my own fate ; I must bear my
punishment,' she said. ' I shall try some German baths
before his return, to brace my nerves for the—the future.'

There was something soft, harmonious, gently affecting
about Dolly's mamma. When Mrs. Palmer spoke she looked
at you with two brown eyes shining out of a faded
but charming face : she put out an earnest white hand ;
there was a charming, natural affectation about her. She
delighted in a situation. She was one of those fortunate
people whose parts in life coincide with their dispositions.
She had been twice married. As a happy wife people had
thought her scarcely aware of the prize she had drawn. As
an injured woman she was simply perfect. She did not feel
the Admiral's indifference deeply enough to lose her self-
possession, as he did. Admiral though he was, and extempore preacher, he could not always hold his own before this
susceptible woman. Her gentle impressiveness completely
charmed and won the children over.

The conversation of selfish people is often far more
amusing than that of the unselfish, who see things too *dif-
fusedly*, and who have not, as a rule, the gift of vivid
description. Mrs. Palmer was deeply, deeply interested in
her own various feelings. She used to whisper long stories
to George and Dolly about her complicated sorrows, her
peculiar difficulties. Poor thing ! they were real enough,

if she had but known them ; but the troubles that really
troubled her were imaginary for the most part. She had
secured two valiant champions before breakfast next morning, at which meal Robert appeared. He had slept upon
the crisis, and now seemed more than equal to it ; affectionate to his aunt, with whom he was charmed, readily answering her many questions, skilfully avoiding the subject of her
difficulties with the Admiral, of which he had heard before
at Henley Court. He was pleased by his aunt's manner and
affectionate dependence, and he treated her from the first
with a certain manly superiority. And yet—so she told
Dolly—even Robert scarcely understood her peculiar difficulties.

' How can he, dear fellow ? He is prejudiced by Lady
Henley—odious woman ! I can trace her influence. She
was a Palmer, you know, and she is worthy of the name.
I dread my visit to Yorkshire. This is my real home.'

Mrs. Palmer's mother, Lady Henley, had been an Alder-
ville, and the Aldervilles are all young, beautiful, helpless,
stout, and elegantly dressed. Mrs. Palmer took after them,
she said. But helpless as Philippa was, her feebleness always
leant in the direction in which she wished to go, and, in
some mysterious fashion, she seemed to get on as well as
other stronger people. Some young officer, in a compli-
mentary copy of verses, had once likened her to a lily. If
so, it was a water-lily that she resembled most, with its
beautiful pale head drifting on the water, while underneath
was a long, limp, straggling stalk firmly rooted. Only those
who had tried to influence her knew of its existence.

Dolly and George hung upon her words. George felt
inclined to go off to Ceylon on purpose to shoot the Admiral
with one of his own Colt's revolvers. Dolly thrilled with

interest and excitement and sympathy. Her mother was like a sweet angel, the girl said to her brother. It was a wonderful new life that had begun for them. The trouble which had so oppressed Dolly of late seemed almost forgotten for a time. Lady Sarah, coming and going about the house, would look with a strange half-glad, half-sad glance at the three heads so near together in the recess of the window : Philippa leaning back, flushed and pathetic ; George by her side, making the most hideous faces, as he was used to do when excited ; Dolly kneeling on the floor, with her two elbows in her mother's lap, and her long chin upturned in breathless sympathy. Admiral—jealousy—meanness—cruel—mere necessaries : little words like this used to reach Lady Sarah, creaking uneasily and desolately, unnoticed, round and round the drawing-room.

'Is it not a pity, Philippa, to put such ideas into their heads?' says Lady Sarah, from the other end of the room.

Then three pair of eyes would be turned upon her with a sort of reproachful wonder, and the trio would wait until she was out of hearing to begin again.

Mrs. Palmer was certainly an adaptable woman in some ways : one husband or another, one life or another. So long as she had her emotions, her maid, her cups of tea, her comfortable sofa, and some one to listen to her, she was perfectly happy. She carried about in herself such an unfailing source of interest and solicitude, that no other was really necessary to her ; although, to hear her speak, you would imagine her fate to be one long regret.

'My spirit is quite broken,' she would say, cheerfully. 'Give me that small hand-screen, Dolly; for *your* sake, Sarah, I will gladly chaperone Dolly to Cambridge, as Robert proposes (it must be after my return from Yorkshire) ; but

I do wish you would let me write and ask for an invitation
for you. George, poor fellow, wants me to bring Rhoda and
the Morgan girls. I do hate girls. It is really wicked of
him.'

'If that were George's worst offence——,' said his Aunt
Sarah, grimly.

'My poor boy!' said Mrs. Palmer. 'Sarah, you are not
a mother, and do not understand him. Come here, darling
George. How I wish I could spare you from going back to
those horrid examinations!'

George flushed up very red. 'I should be very sorry to
be spared,' he muttered.

Mrs. Palmer used to ask Robert endless questions about
Henley Court, and his aunt Lady Henley. 'Was she looking as weather-beaten as ever? Did she still wear plaids?
Vulgar woman!' whispered Mrs. Palmer to Dolly. Robert
pretended not to hear. 'I shall make a point of going
there, Robert,' she said, 'and facing the Henley buckram.'
Robert gravely assured her that she would be most welcome.

Welcome, my dear Robert! You cannot imagine what
an impertinent letter I have received from Joanna,' says
Mrs. Palmer. 'I shall go when it is convenient to me, if
only to show her that I do not care for anything she can
say. Joanna's style is only to be equalled by the Admiral's.
The mail will be in on Monday.'

So Philippa remained a victim, placidly sipping her
coffee and awaiting the Admiral's insulting letters. The
only wonder was that they had not burst their envelopes and
seals, so explosive were they. His fury lashed itself into
dashes and blots and frantic loops and erasures. The bills
had come in for her bracelets and mufflers and tinkling
ornaments. Had she forgotten the fate of the daughters of

O

Jerusalem, that went mincing and tinkling with their feet?
She might take a situation as a kitchen-maid for all he
cared.   She was a spendthrift, idle, extravagant, good-for-
nothing, &c. &c.   Not one farthing would he allow her,
&c. &c.; and so on.   Mrs. Palmer used to go up to her
room in high spirits to lie down to rest on the days they
arrived, and send for Colonel Witherington to consult upon
them.

She would not come down till dinner was just over, and
appeared on these occasions in a long grey sort of dressing-
gown and a *négligé* little lace cap; she used to dine off
almonds and raisins and cups of coffee, to Lady Sarah's secret
indignation.   'Oh, Sarah, *you* will not turn me away?'
Mrs. Palmer would say, leaning back in languid comfort.
Lady Sarah was very sorry, but somewhat sceptical.   She
would meet Pauline carrying French novels to the library
after scenes which had nearly unnerved them all.

CHAPTER XXIII.

THE TERRACE AT ALL SAINTS' COLLEGE.

Die Rose, die Lilje, die Taube, die Sonne,
Die liebt ich einst alle in Liebeswonne.
—Heine.

Somewhere in the fairyland of Dorothea's imagination rises a
visionary city, with towers and gables straggling against the
sky. The streets go up hill and down hill, leading by
cloisters and gateways and bywalls, behind which gardens
are lying like lakes of green among the stones and the ivy.
A thrush is singing, and the shrill echoes of some boyish
melancholy voices come from a chapel hard by. It is a
chapel with a pile of fantastic columns standing in the quiet
corner of a lane. All round the side door are niches and
winding galleries, branches wreathing, placed there by
faithful hands, crisp saints beatified in stony glory. Are
these, one is tempted to ask, as one looks at the generous old
piles, the stones that cry out now-a-days when men are
silent? They have, for the last century or two, uttered
warnings and praises to many a generation passing by;
speaking to some of a bygone faith, to others of a living
one. They still tell of past love and hope, and of past and
present charity.

But in these times charity is a destroying angel; even the

divine attributes seem to have changed, and Faith, Hope, and Charity have gone each their separate way.

To Dolly Vanborough, who had thought happiness was over for ever, it was the first great song of her youth that these old stones sang to her on her eighteenth birthday. She hears it still, though her youth is past. It is the song of the wonder of life, of the divine in the human. As we go on its echoes reach us repeated again and again, reverberating from point to point; who that has heard them once will ever forget them? To some they come with happiness and the delight of new undreamt-of sympathy, to others with sorrow and the realisation of love. . . . Its strains came with prayer and long fasting to the saints of old. This song of Pentecost, I know no better name for it, echoes on from generation to generation from one heart to another. Sometimes by chance one has looked into a stranger's face and seen its light reflected. Frank Raban saw its light in Dolly's face that day as she came out of the chapel to where her brother had left her. Just for an instant it was there while the psalm still sung in her heart. And yet the light in Dolly's face dimmed a little when she saw, not the person she had expected to see, but Mr. Raban waiting there.

' I came in Henley's place,' said he, hastily, guessing her thought. 'He was sent for by the Vice-Chancellor, and begged me to come and tell you this. He will join us directly.

Mr. Raban had been waiting in the sunshiny street while Dolly deliberately advanced down the worn steps of the chapel, crossed the flagged court, and came out of the narrow iron wicket of which the barred shadow fell upon her white fête-day dress. Miss Vanborough's face was shaded by a broad hat with curling blue feathers; she wore a pink rose in her girdle; it was no saintly costume; she was but a commonplace mortal maiden in sprigged muslin, and saints wear, as we all know, red and blue, and green stained glass and damask and goatskins; and yet Frank Raban thought there was something saint-like in her bright face, which, for an instant, seemed reflecting all her heart.

'Henley lives on my staircase,' continued Raban. 'Those pink frills are his. He makes himself comfortable, as you see.'

'I'm glad of that,' said Dolly, smiling. 'How nice it must be for you to have him so near.'

'He always takes ladies to see his rooms,' Raban continued. 'He is a great favourite with them, and gives tea-parties.'

'A great favourite!' said Dolly, warmly. 'Of course one likes people who are kind and good and clever and true and nice.'

'Who are, in short, an addition sum, made up of equal portions of all the cardinal virtues,' said Raban.

He was ashamed of himself, and yet he did not care to hear Henley's praises from Dolly. It seemed to him dishonest to acquiesce.

Dolly stopped for half a second and looked at him.

Dorothea was a tall woman and their eyes were on a line, and their looks met. My heroine was at no pains to disguise the meaning of her indignant glances. 'How can you be so ungenerous?' she said, as plainly as if she had spoken.

Frank answered her silence in words.

'No, I don't like him,' he said, 'and he don't like me; and I don't care to pretend to better feelings than I really have. We are civil enough, and pull very well together. I beg your pardon. I own he deserves to succeed,' said the young man. 'There, Miss Vanborough, this is our garden, where we refresh ourselves with cigars and beer after our arduous studies.'

Dolly was still too much vexed to express her admiration.

They all began calling to them from under the tree. John Morgan, who was of the party, was lying flat upon his broad back, beaming at the universe, and fanning away the flies. Rhoda was sitting on the grass, in a foam of white muslin and Algerian shawls. George Vanborough, privileged for the day, was astride on a wooden table ; a distant peacock went strutting across the lawn ; a little wind came blowing gently, stirring all the shadows ; a college bell began to tinkle a little, and then left off.

'Glorious afternoon, isn't it ?' says John Morgan, from the grass.

'It is like heaven,' says Dolly, looking up and round and about.

Rhoda's slim fingers clasp her pearl locket, which has come out again. They were in the shade, the sun was shining hot and intense upon the old garden. The roses, like bursting bubbles, were breaking in the heat against the old baked bricks, upon rows of prim collegiate flowers : lilies, and stocks, and marigolds. There was a multiplicity of sweet scents in the air, of shadows falling on the lawns (they flow from the old gates to the river) ; a tone is struck, an insect floats away along the garden wall. With its silence and flowers, and tremulous shades and sunshine, I know no sweeter spot than the old garden of All Saints'.

The gardener had placed seats and a bench under the old beech-tree for pilgrims to rest upon, weary with their journeys from shrine to shrine. Mrs. Palmer was leaning

back in a low garden-chair ; the sweep of her flowing silks
seemed to harmonise with her languid and somewhat melancholy grace. Rhoda was helping to open her parasol (the
parasol was dove-coloured and lined with pink). There was
a row of Morgans upon the bench ; Mrs. Morgan upright in
the midst, nicely curled and trimmed with satin bows and a
white muslin daughter on either side.

It all happened in a moment : the sky burnt overhead,
the sun shone upon the river, upon the colleges, with their
green gardens : the rays seemed to strike fire where they
met the water. The swans were sailing along the stream in
placid state, followed by their grey brood, skimming and
paddling in and out among the weeds and the green stems
and leaves that sway with the ripple of the waters ; a flight
of birds high overhead crossed the vault of the heavens and
disappeared in the distance. Dorothea Vanborough was
standing on the terrace at the end of the old college garden,
where everything was so still, so sweet, and so intense that
it seemed as if time was not, as if the clocks had stopped on
their travels, as if no change could ever be, nor hours nor
seasons sweep through the tranquil old place.

They were all laughing and talking ; but Dolly, who was
too lazy and too happy to talk, wandered away from them a
little bit, to the garden's end, where she stood stooping over
the low wall and watching the water flow by ; there was a
man fishing on the opposite bank, and casting his line again
and again. In the distance a boat was drifting along the
stream, some insects passed out towards the meadows
humming their summer drone, a wasp sailed by. Dolly was
half standing, half-sitting, against the low terrace wall ; with
one hand she was holding up her white muslin skirt, with
the other she was grasping the ledge of the old bricks upon

which the lichen had been at work spreading their gold and grey. So the girl waited, sunning herself; herself a part of the summer's day, and gently blooming and rejoicing in its sweetness like any rose upon the wall.

There are blissful moments when one's heart seems to beat in harmony with the great harmony : when one is oneself light and warmth, and the delight of light, and a voice in the comfortable chorus of contentment and praise all round about. Such a minute had come to Dolly in her white muslin dress, with the Cam flowing at her feet and the lights dazzling her grey eyes.

Mrs. Morgan gave a loud sneeze under the tree, and the beautiful minute broke and dispersed away.

' I wonder what it can be like to grow old,' Dolly wonders, looking up ; ' to remember back for years and years, and to wear stiff curls and satinette ? ' Dolly began to picture to herself a long procession of future selves, each older and more curiously bedizened than the other. Somehow they seemed to make a straight line between herself and Mrs. Morgan under the tree. It was an uncomfortable fancy. Dolly tried to forget it, and leant over the wall, and looked down into the cool depths of the stream again. Was that fish rising ? What was this ? Her own face again looking up from the depth. Then Dolly turned, hearing a step upon the gravel, to see Robert Henley coming towards her. He was dressed in his college cap and gown, and he advanced, floating balloon-like, along the terrace. He looked a little strange, she thought, as he came up to her.

' I couldn't get away before,' he said. ' I hope you have been well looked after.'

' Yes, indeed. Come and sit down here, Robert. What

In the College Garden.

a delicious old garden this is! We are all so happy! Look
at those dear little swans in the river!'

'Do you like the cygnets?' said Robert, abruptly, as he
looked her full in the face, and sat down on the low wall
beside her. 'Do you remember Charles Martindale?' he
asked; 'whom we met once at John Morgan's, who went out
to India? He is coming home next October.'

'Is he?' said Dolly. 'Look at that little grey cygnet
scuttling away!'

'Dolly,' said Henley, quickly, 'they sent for me to offer
me his place, and I—I—have accepted it.'

'Accepted it?' said his cousin, forgetting the cygnets,
and looking up a little frightened. Will you have to go to
India and leave everybody?'

Her face changed a little, and Robert's brightened,
though he tried to look as usual.

'Not everybody,' he said. 'Not if ——' He took the
soft hand in his that was lying on the wall beside him.
'Dolly! will you come too?' he said.

'Me?' cried the unabashed Dolly. 'Oh, Robert, how
could I?'

'You could come if I married you,' said Robert, in his
quiet voice and most restrained manner. 'Dearest Dorothea,
don't you think you can learn to love me? It will be nearly
five months before I start.'

It was all so utterly incomprehensible that the girl did
not quite realise her cousin's words. Robert was looking
very strange and unlike himself; Dolly could hardly believe
that it was not some effect of the dazzle of light in her own
eyes. He was paler than usual; he seemed somehow stirred
from his habitual ways and self. She thought it was not
even his voice that she heard speaking. 'Is this being in

·love ? ' she was saying to herself. A little bewildered flush came into her cheeks. She still saw the sky, and the garden, and the figures under the tree ; then for a minute everything vanished, as tangible things vanish before the invisible,— just as spoken words are hushed and lose their meaning when the silent voices cry out.

It was but for a moment. There she stood again, staring at Robert with her innocent, grey-eyed glance.

Henley was a big, black-and-white melancholy young man, with a blue shaved chin. To-day his face was pale, his mouth was quivering, his hair was all on end. Could this be Robert who was so deliberate ; who always knew his own mind ; who looked at his watch so often in church while music was going on ? Even now, from habit, he was turning it about in his pocket. This little trick made Dolly feel more than anything else that it was all true—that her cousin loved her—incredible though it may appear—and yet even still she doubted.

' *Me*, Robert ? ' repeated Dorothea, in her clear, childish tones, looking up with her frank yet timid eyes. ' Are you *sure* ? '

' I have been sure ever since I first saw you,' said Henley, smiling down at her, ' at Kensington, three years ago. Do you remember the snowball, Dolly ? '

Then Dolly's eyes fell, and she stood with a tender, puzzled face, listening to her first tale of love. She suddenly pulled away her hand, shy and blushing.

The swans had hardly passed beyond the garden-terrace ; the fisherman had only thown his line once again ; Dolly's mamma had time to shift her parasol ; that was all. Henley waited, with his handsome head a little bent. He was regaining his composure ; he knew too much of his cousin's uncompromising ways to be made afraid by her silence. He stood pulling at his watch, and looking at her—at the straight white figure amid dazzling blue and green; at the line of the sweet face still turned away from him.

' I thought you would have understood me better?' he said, reproachfully.

Still Dolly could not speak. For a moment her heart had beat with an innocent triumph, and then came a doubt. Did she love him—could she love him? Had he then cared for her all this time, when she herself had been so cold and so indifferent, and thinking so little of him? Only yester-day she had told Rhoda she would never marry. Was it yesterday? No, it was to-day, an hour ago. . . . What had she done to deserve so much from him?—what had she done to be so overprized and loved? At the thought quick upspringing into her two grey eyes came the tears, sparkling like the diamonds in Rhoda's cross.

' I never thought you thought'—Dolly began. ' Oh, Robert! you have been in earnest all this time, and I only —only playing.'

' Don't be unhappy,' said her cousin. ' It was very natural; I should not have wished it otherwise. I did not want to speak to you till I had something worth your acceptance.'

' All this long time!' repeated Dolly.

Did the explanations of true love ever yet run smooth? ' Dolly!' cried Mrs. Palmer, from under the tree.

' Hulloa, Robert!' shouted George, coming across the grass towards them.

' Oh, Robert!' said Dorothea, earnestly, unexpectedly, with a sudden resolution to be true—true to him and to herself, ' thank you a thousand times for what you have told me : only it mustn't be—I don't care enough for you, dear Robert! You deserve —— '

Henley said not a word. He stood with a half-incredulous smile ; his eyes were still fixed on Dolly's sweet face ; he did not answer George, who again called out something as he came up. As for Dolly, she turned to her brother and sprang to meet him, and took his arm as if for protection, and then she walked quickly away without another look, and Henley remained standing where she had been. Instead of the white-muslin maiden, the cygnets may have seen a black-silk young man, who looked at his watch, and then walked away too ; while the fisherman quietly baited his line and went on with his sport.

CHAPTER XXIV.

ROSES HAVE THORNS AND SILVER FOUNTAINS MUD.

Love me with thine hand stretched out,
Freely, open-minded,
Love me with thy loitering foot,
Hearing one behind it.

THE doors of the old Library at All Saints' were open wide
to admit the sunshine: it lighted up the starched frill
collars of *Fundator noster* as he hung over the entrance. It
was good stiff starch, near four hundred years old. The
volumes stood in their places, row upon row, line after line,
twinkling into the distant corners of the room; here and
there a brass lock gleamed, or some almost forgotten title in
faded gold, or the links of the old Bible chained to its oaken
stand. . . . So the books stood marshalled in their
places: brown, and swept by time, by dust, brushed by the
passing generations that had entered one by one, bringing
their spoils, and placing them safe upon the shelves, and
vanishing away. What a silent Babel and medley of time,
and space, and languages, and fancies, and follies! Here
and there stands a fat dictionary, or prophetic grammar, the
interpreter of echoes to other echoes. So, from century to
century, the tradition is handed down, and from silent print
and signs it thrills into life and sound. . . .

Those are not books, but living voices in the recess of the
old library.   There is a young man stumping up and down
the narrow passage, a young woman leaning against a worm-
eaten desk.   Are they talking of roots, of curves? or are
they youthful metaphysicians speculating upon the unknown
powers of the soul?

'Oh! George,' Dolly says, 'I am glad you think I was
right.' .

'Right!   Of course you would have been very wrong to
do otherwise,' says George, as usual, extremely indignant.
'Of course you are right to refuse him : you don't care for
him ; I can see that at a glance.   .   .   .   It is out of the
question.   Poor fellow! He is a very good fellow, but not
at all worthy of you.   It is altogether preposterous.   No,
Dolly,' said the young fellow, melting ; 'you don't know —
how should you ?—what it is—what the real thing is.   Never
let yourself be deceived by any Brummagem and paste, when
the real Koh-i-noor is still to be found—a gem of the purest
water,' said George, gently.

Dolly listened, but she was only half convinced by
George's earnestness.   'I would give anything that this had
not happened,' the young man went on.   Dolly listened, and
said but little in answer.   When George scolded her for
having unduly encouraged Robert, she meekly denied the
accusation, though her brother would not accept her denial.

'Had she then behaved so badly? Was Robert unhappy? Would he never forgive her? Should she never
see him again ?' Dolly listened sadly, wondering, and leaning against the old desk.   There was a book lying open upon
it—the History of the Universe—with many pictures of
strange beasts and serpents, roaring, writhing, and whisking
their tails, with the Garden of Eden mapped out, and the

different sorts of angels and devils duly enumerated. Dolly's mind was not on the old book, but in the world outside it; she was standing again by the river and listening to Robert's voice. The story he told her no longer seemed new and strange. It was ended for ever, and yet it would never finish as long as she lived. She had thought no one would ever care for her, and he had loved her, and she had sent him away; but he had loved her. Had she made a mistake, notwithstanding all that George was saying? Dolly, loving the truth, loving the right, trying for it heartily, in her slow circuitous way, might make mistakes in life, but they would be honest ones, and that is as much as any of us can hope for, and so, if she strained at a gnat and swallowed a camel, it will be forgiven her. George's opposition was too vague to influence her. When he warned her against Henley, it sounded unreasonable. Warning! There was no need of warning. She had said no to her cousin. Already the terrace seemed distant miles and miles off, hours and hours ago, though she could see it through the window, and the swans on the river, and the sunlight striking flame upon the water: she could hardly realise that she had been there, and that with a word and a hasty movement she had sent Robert away of her own deliberate will.

'Yes,' said George, coming up and banging his hand down upon the big book before her; 'you were right, Dolly. He isn't half good enough for you. This is not like the feeling that I and Rhoda ——'

But Dolly interrupted him almost angrily. 'Not good enough! It is because he is too good, George, that I—I am not—not worthy of him.'

It was more than she could bear to hear George speaking so.

Was Robert unhappy? had she used him ill? The thoughts seemed to smite her as they passed. She began to cry again—foolish girl!—and George, as he watched her worthless tears dribbling down upon the valuable manuscript, began to think that perhaps, after all, his sister had wished him to blame, instead of approving of her decision. He was bound to sympathise, since she had kept his secret. ' Don't, Dolly,' he said ; ' you will spoil the little devils if you cry over the book.' He spoke so kindly, that Dolly smiled, and began to wipe her eyes. It was not a little thing that George should speak so kindly to her again. When she looked up she saw that he was signalling, and bowing, and waving his cap through the open window.

' It is the girls. They ought not to miss our college library,' he said, gravely ; and then he walked towards the door, to meet a sound of voices and a trampling of feet.

As for Dorothea, with a sudden shy impulse she escaped, tears, handkerchief, and all, and disappeared into the most distant niche of the gallery : many footsteps came sounding up the wooden staircase, and Henley's voice was mingling with the Miss Morgans' shrill treble.

' How funny to see so many books ! ' said Zoe, who was a very stupid girl. (Clever people generally make the same remarks as stupid ones, only they are in different words.)

' What a delicious old place ! ' cried Rhoda, coming in. She was usually silent, and not given to ecstasies.

' Why didn't John bring us here before ? ' said Cassie. ' I do envy you, Mr. George. How nice to be able to read all these books ! '

' I am not so sure of that,' said George, laughing.

Meanwhile, Zoe had stumped up to the desk, where the history of the whole world was lying open.

'Why, look here,' she said; 'somebody has been reading, I do believe. How funny!'

As for Henley, he had already begun to examine the pictures that hung over every niche. He did not miss one of them as he walked quickly down the gallery. In the last niche of all he found the picture he was in search of. It was not that of a dignitary of the church. It was a sweet face, with brown crisp locks, and clear grey eyes shining from beneath a frown. The face changed, as pictures don't change, when he stood in the arch of the little recess. The pale cheeks glowed, the frown trembled and cleared away. She wondered if he would speak to her or go away. Henley hesitated for an instant, and—spoke.

'Dolly, that was not an answer you gave me just now. You did not think that would content me, did you?' he said; and as he looked at her fixedly, her eyes fell. 'Dolly, you do love me a little?' he cried; 'you cannot send me away?'

'I thought I ought to send you away,' she faltered, looking up at last, and her whole heart was in her face. 'Robert, I don't know if I love you; but I love you to love me,' she said. And her sweet voice trembled as she spoke.

He had no misgivings. 'Dearest Dolly,' he said, in a low voice. 'In future you must trust to me. I will take care of you. You need not have been afraid. I quite understood your feelings just now, and I would not urge you then. Now . . .' He did not finish the sentence.

When Dolly, the frigid maiden, surrendered, it was with a shy reluctant grace. Hers was not a passionate nature, but a loving one; feeling with her was not a single simple emotion, but a complicated one of many impulses: of self-

P

diffidences, of deep, deep, strange aspirations, that she herself could scarcely understand. Humility, a woman's pride, the delight of companionship and sympathy, and of the guidance of a stronger will: a longing for better things. All these things were there. Ah! she would try to be worthier of him. It was a snow and ice and fire maiden who put her trembling hand into Robert's, and whom he clasped for an instant in his arms.

Meanwhile some of the party had straggled off again to the hotel after Mrs. Palmer. George was to escort the young ladies, who seemed determined to stay on turning over the manuscripts; the unlucky Zoe was babbling innocently, knocking over stools and playfully pulling Latin sermons and dictionaries out of their places on the shelves. George, while he made himself agreeable in his peculiar fashion, was wondering what was going on at the farther end of the library. He longed to tell Rhoda and ask her advice; but that tiresome Zoe was for ever interrupting. Was this a very old book? Did he like Greek or Latin best? She thought it all looked very stupid. Was Rhoda coming to the hotel to rest before dinner? And so on. Rhoda must have guessed what was in George's mind, for presently she started away from the page over which she was leaning, and went to the window.

'Shall we go out a little way?' she said, gently. 'One would like to be everywhere to-day.'

'I'm sure we have been everywhere,' said Zoe.

'I know you are tired. I shall not allow you to come, dear Zoe,' said Rhoda, affectionately. 'You must rest; I insist upon it. You look quite worn out. Mr. George, will you help me?' And Rhoda began struggling with a heavy chair, which she pulled into the window. And here is

a stool,' said Rhoda, 'for your feet. We will come back
for you directly. My head aches ; I want a little fresh
air.'

'Oh, thank you,' said Zoe, doubtfully. '*Do* I look tired,
Rhoda? I am sure . . .' But Rhoda was gone before
she had time to say more. Zoe was not sure if she was
pleased or not. It was just like Rhoda: she never could
understand what people wanted, really ; she was always
kissing them and getting them chairs out of the way. No
doubt she meant to be kind. Rest! anybody could rest for
themselves. What was that noise ? 'Who is there?' says
Zoe, out loud, but there was no answer. Yes, she wanted to
be with the others. Why did they poke her away up here ?
by leaning out of the open window she could just see the ivy
wall, and the garden beyond. There was no one left under the
tree. They were all gone: just like them. How was she to
find her way to the hotel! It was all very well for Rhoda,
who had George Vanborough at her beck and call; they
knew well enough *she* had nobody to take care of her, and
they should have waited for her. That was what Zoe thought.
There was that noise again, and a murmur, and some one
stirring. Poor Zoe jumped up with her heart in her mouth ;
she knocked over the stool; she stood prepared to fly ; she
heard some one whispering ; they might be garotters, ghosts,
proctors—horror! Her terrors overpower her. Her high
heels clatter down the wooden stairs, out into the sunny,
silent court, where her footsteps echo as she runs—poor
nymph flying from an echo! George and Rhoda are walking
quietly up and down in the sunshine just beyond the ivy
gate: their two shadows are flitting as they go. John
Morgan is coming in at the great entrance. Zoe rushes up
to him, panting with her terror.

'Oh, John,' she says, 'I didn't know where to go. Why don't you stop with me? I was all alone, and . . .'

'Why, Zoe, tired already! Come along quick to the hotel,' says John, 'or you won't get any rest before dinner.'

They caught up the Morgans on their way, and met Raban, coming out of Trinity. Meanwhile Robert and Dorothea are leisurely following along the street. Henley had regained his composure by this time, and could meet the others with perfect equanimity. Not so his cousin. So many lights were coming and going in her face, so many looks and apparitions, that Robert thought every one must guess what had happened, as they came into the common sitting-room, where some five-o'clock tea was spread. But there is nothing more true than that people don't see the great facts that are starting before their very eyes, so busy are they with the details of life. Mrs. Palmer was trying to disentangle the silk strings of her bag as they came in (she had a fancy for carrying a bag), and she did not observe her daughter's emotion.

Then came a clatter of five-o'clock teacups at the hotel; of young men coming and going, or waiting to escort them according to the kindly college fashion. Dolly was not sorry that she could find no opportunity to speak to her mother. Mrs. Palmer's feelings were not to be trifled with; and Dolly, in her agitation, scarcely felt strong enough to bear a scene. Robert stayed for a few minutes, rang the bell for hot water, helped to move a horsehair sofa, to open the window.

What foolish little memories Dolly treasured up in after-life of tea-making and tea-talking. Poor child, her memories were not so very many, but nothing is small and nothing is great at times.

Frank Raban stood a little apart talking to Rhoda,

whose wonderful liquid eyes were steadily fixed upon him. George, on the sofa by his mother, was alternately biting his lips, frowning at Dolly over her tea and love-making, and at Rhoda and her companion.

'Darling George, cannot you keep your feet still?' said Mrs. Palmer. 'Are you going, Mr. Raban? Shall we not see you again?'

'I shall have the honour of meeting you at dinner,' said Raban, stiffly. 'I would come and show you the way, but Mr. Henley has promised to see you safe.'

Every one seemed coming into the room at once, drinking tea, going away. There seemed two or three Georges: there were certainly two Dorotheas present. Henley only was composed enough for them all, and twice prevented his cousin from pouring all the sugar into the milk-jug.

In the middle of the table there was a plateful of flowers, arranged by the waiter. Robert took out a little sprig of verbena, which he gave to Dorothea. She stuck it in her girdle, and put it away, when she got home, between the leaves of her prayer-book, where it still lies, in memory of the past, a dried-up twig that was once green and sweet. Rhoda, after Raban had left her, came up with her tea-cup, and, for want of something to do, began pulling the remaining flowers out of the dish.

'I can't bear to see flowers so badly used,' said Rhoda, piling up the sand with her quick, clever fingers. 'George, will you give me some water?'

In a few minutes the ugly flat dishful began to bloom quite freshly.

'That is very nicely done,' George said, sarcastically. 'Why didn't you get Raban to help you to arrange the flowers, Rhoda, before he left?'

'We were talking, and I didn't like to interrupt him,' said Rhoda. ' I was asking him all about political economy.'

George's ugly face flushed.

' Are you satisfied that the supply of admiration equals the demand ? ' said George.

' George, how can you talk so ? ' says Rhoda.

An hour later they were all straggling down the narrow cross-streets that led to the college again.

Dolly came, walking shyly by her lover's side; Mrs. Palmer leant heavily upon John Morgan's arm. Every moment she dropped her long dress, and had to wait to gather the folds together. Surely the twilight of that summer's day was the sweetest twilight that Dolly had ever set eyes upon. It came creeping from the fields beyond the river, from alley to alley, from one college to another. It seemed to the excited girl like a soft tranquillising veil let down upon the agitations and excitements of the day. She watched it growing in the old hall, where she presently sat at the cross-table under the very glance of the ubiquitous *Fundator*, who was again present in his frill and short cloak, between the two deep-cut windows.

The long table crossed the hall, with a stately decoration of gold and silver cups all down the centre ; there were oaken beams overhead ; old college servants in attendance. The great silver tankards went round brimming with claret and hock, and with straggling stems of burrage floating on fragrant seas.

By what unlucky chance did it happen that some one had written out the names of the guests, each in their place, and that Dolly found a strange young don on one side of her plate, and Raban on the other ? Henley did not wish to excite remark, and subsided into the place appointed for him, when he found that he was not to sit where he chose.

'Drink, Dolly,' said George, who was sitting opposite to her; 'let us drink a toast.'

'What shall I drink?' asked Dolly.

'Shall we drink a toast to fortune?' said George, leaning forward.

'I shall drink to the new President of the College of Boggleywollah,' says John Morgan, heartily.

Dolly raised her eyes shyly as she put her lips to the enormous tankard and sipped a health.

As for Raban, he did not drink the toast, although he must have guessed something of what had happened. He never spoke to Dolly, though he duly attended to her wants, and handed bread, and salt, and silver flagons, and fruit, and gold spoons: still he never spoke. She was conscious that he was watching her. In some strange way the dislike and mistrust he felt for Henley seemed reflected upon poor Dorothea again. Why had she been flirting and talking to that man? She, of all women, Robert Henley, of all men, thought Raban, as he handed her a pear. Mrs. Palmer looked at Dorothea more than once during dinner. The girl had two burning cheeks; she did not eat; she scarcely answered the young don when she was spoken to by him; but once Henley leant forward and said something, then she looked up quickly. Stoicism is after all but a relic of barbarous times, and may be greatly over-rated.

Dolly had not yet grown so used to her thick-coming experience that she could always look cold when she was moved, dull when she was troubled, indifferent when her whole heart was in a moment's decision. Later it all came easier to her, as it does to most of us. As the ladies left the dining-room Henley got up to let them out, and made a little sign to Dolly to wait behind. Being in a yielding mood, she lingered a minute in the anteroom, looking for her cloak, and allowed the others to pass on. Henley had closed the door behind him and come out, and seemed to be searching too. It was very dark in the anteroom, of which the twilight windows were small and screened by green plants. While her aunt was being draped in bournouses by Rhoda, and Mrs. Morgan's broad back was turned upon them, Dorothea waited for an instant, and said, 'What is it, Robert?' looking up with her doubtful, yet kindly glance.

'Dear Dorothea, I wanted to make sure it was all true,' said Robert, with one of the few touches of romance which he had experienced in all his well-considered existence. 'I began to think it was a dream, and I thought I should like to ask you.'

'Whether it is all a dream?' said Dolly, almost sadly. 'It is not I who can answer that question; but you see,' she added, smiling, 'that I have begun to do as you tell me. They will think I am lost.' And she sprang away, with a little wave of the hand.

CHAPTER XXV

GOOD-NIGHT.

> Love us, God! love us, man! we believe, we achieve.
> Let us live, let us love,
> For the acts correspond :
> We are Glorious, and Die.
>
> —E. B. B.

'Good-night, dearest Dolly,' whispered Henley, as they all stood waiting for their train in the crowded station. 'You can tell your mother as you go home.'

'Here, Dolly! jump in,' cried John Morgan, standing by an open railway-door; 'your aunt is calling you.'

'I can't come up till Tuesday,' Henley went on in a low voice, 'but I shall write to your mother to-night.'

He helped her into the dark carriage: everybody seemed to lean forward at once and say good-night; there was a whistle, a guard banged the door, Mrs. Palmer stretched her long neck through the window, but the train carried her off before she could speak her last words.

Dolly just saw Henley turning away, and George under a lamp-post; then they were gone out of the station into the open country; wide and dim it flowed on either side into the dusk. The day had come to an end—the most wonderful day in Dolly's life. Was it a real day; was it a day out of somebody else's existence? As Dolly sat down beside her mother she had felt as if her heart would break with wonder and happiness; it was not big enough to hold the love that was her portion. He loved her! She had floated into some new world where she had never been before; where people had been living all their lives, thought Dolly, and she had never even guessed at it.

Had her mother felt like this? Had Frank Raban's poor young wife felt this when he married her? So she wondered, looking up at the clear evening sky. Might not death itself be this, only greater still and completer—too complete for human beings? Dolly had got her mother's hand tight in hers. 'My dear child, take care, take care!' cried Mrs. Palmer, sharply; 'my poor fingers are *so* tender, Mr. Morgan; and Dolly's is *such* a grip. I remember once when the Admiral, with his great driving gloves' . . . . Her voice sank away, and Dolly's mamma began telling John Morgan all about one episode in her life.

Meanwhile, Dolly went on with her speculations. How surprised Aunt Sarah would be; how surprised she was herself. Dolly had had a dream, like most young maidens, formless, voiceless, indefinitely vague, but with a meaning to it all the same, and a *soul;* and here was Robert, and the soul was his, and he loved her! 'Thanks, half-way up,' murmured Mrs. Palmer to a strange passenger who did not belong to the party.

'Tired, Zoe?' said John to his sister: 'a little bit sleepy, eh?'

'Everybody thinks I'm always tired,' said Zoe, in an aggrieved tone: 'Rhoda made me rest ever so long when I didn't want to; she popped me down on a stool in that stupid old library, and said I looked quite worn out, and then she was off in a minute, and I had to wait, oh ! ever so long, and I was frightened by noises.'

'Poor Zoe !' said John, laughing.

' It was too bad of her ; and then they all kept leaving me behind,' continued Zoe, growing more and more miserable, ' and now you say it has been too much for me : I am sure I wouldn't have missed coming for anything.'

'Next time we go anywhere you keep with me, Zoe,' said John, good-humouredly, ' and you shan't be left behind.'

' I think we are all tired,' said Mrs. Palmer, languidly, ' and we shall be thankful to get home. Dolly, my darling, you don't speak ; are you quite worn out too ? '

Dolly looked out from her dreams with a glance of so much life and sweetness in her bright face—even the dim lamp-light could not hide her happy looks—that her mother was struck by it. ' You strange child,' she said, ' what are you made of ? You look brighter than when we started.'

' Dolly is made of a capital stuff called youth and good spirits,' said John Morgan, kindly.

The rest of the journey was passed in shifting the windows to Mrs. Palmer's various sensations. They all parted hurriedly, as people do after a long day's pleasuring, only Dolly found time to give Rhoda a kiss. She felt more kindly towards her than she had done for many a day past. Rhoda looked curiously, and a little maliciously, into Dolly's face. But she could not read anything more than she guessed already.

Mrs. Palmer was greatly disturbed to find herself driving home alone with Dolly in the hansom.

' I am afraid of cabmen. I am not accustomed to them. John Morgan should have come with me,' Mrs. Palmer said. ' I am sure the Admiral would not approve of this ! Ah ! he will be over. Dolly, darling, ask the man if he is sober. Dear me, I wish Robert was here.'

Dolly, too, was wishing that Robert was there instead of herself. Her heart began to beat as she thought of what she had to say. She looked up at Mrs. Palmer's pale face in the bright moonlight through which they were driving homewards; through streets silver and silent and transformed. They come to the river and cross the bridge; the water is flowing, hushed, and mysterious: the bridge throws a great shadow upon the water; one barge is slowly passing underneath the arch. The dim, distant crowd of spires, of chimneys, and slated roofs, are illumined and multiplied by strange silver lights. Overhead a planet is burning and sinking where the sun set while they were still in the college garden. The soft moon-wind comes sweeping fresh into their faces, and Dolly from this trance awakens to whisper, 'Mamma! I have something to tell you—something that Robert——'

'He will throw us over! I know he will!' interrupts Mrs. Palmer, as the cab gave a jolt. 'It is quite unsafe, Dolly, without a gentleman.'

Poor Dolly forced herself to go on. She took her mother's hand: 'Dear mamma, don't be afraid.'

'He was not sober. I thought so at the time,' cried Mrs. Palmer, with a nervous shriek, as they came off the bridge.

Then the cab went more quietly, and Dolly found words to tell her news. So the hansom drove on, carrying many agitations and exclamations along with it. The driver from his moonlit perch may have heard the sounds within. Mrs. Palmer spared herself and Dolly no single emotion. She was faint, she was hysterical, she rallied, she was overcome. Why had she not been told before? she had known it all along; she had mentioned it to the Admiral before her departure;

he had sneered at her foolish dreams. Dolly would never have to learn the bitter deception of some wasted lives. Cruel boy! why had he not told her? why so reserved?

'He feared that it would agitate you,' Dolly said, feeling that Robert had been right. 'He told me to tell you now, dear.'

'Dear fellow, he is so thoughtful,' said Mrs. Palmer. 'Now he will be my son, Dolly, my real son. I never could have endured any one of those Henley girls for him. How angry Lady Henley will be. I warned Robert long ago that she would want him for one of them. Dolly, you must not be married yet. You must wait till the Admiral returns. He must give you away.'

When Dolly told her that Robert wanted to be married before he left for India, Mrs. Palmer said it was preposterous. He might have to sail any day,—that Master told her so; the fat old gentleman in the white neckcloth. 'No, my Dolly, we shall have you till Robert comes back. Let the man keep the shilling for his own use.'

They had reached the turnpike by this time, with its friendly beacon-fire burning, and the red-faced man had come out with three pennies ready in his hand. Then by dark trees, rustling behind the walls of the old gardens; past the palace avenue-gates, where the sentry was pacing, with the stars shining over his head; they come to the ivy-gate at home, and with its lamp burning red in the moonlight. Marker opened the door before they had time to ring.

'Softly, my dear,' said Marker to Dolly, in a sort of whisper. 'My lady is asleep; she has not been well, and—'

'Not well!' said Mrs. Palmer. 'How fortunate she did not come. What should we have done with her? I am quite worn out, Marker; we have had a long day. Let Julie make me a cup of coffee, and bring it up to my room. Good-night, my precious Dolly. Don't speak to me, or I shall scream!'

'Marker, is Aunt Sarah ill?' said Dolly, anxious, she knew not why.

'Don't be frightened, my dear,' said Marker; 'it is nothing; that is, the Doctor says she only wants rest.'

Dolly went up to her own room, flitting carefully along the passage, and shading her light. Lady Sarah's door was closed. Mrs. Palmer was safe for the night, with Julie in attendance. Dolly could hear their voices, as she went by. In her own little room all was in order, and cool and straight for her coming. The window was open, the moonlight fell upon her little bed, where she had dreamt so many peaceful dreams, and Dolly set her light upon the window-seat, and stood looking out. She was half radiant still, half saddened. All the sights and sounds of that long, eventful day were passing before her still : ringing, dazzling, repeating themselves on the darkness. . . . . Was it possible that he loved her—that she loved him? The trees rustled, the familiar strokes of the church clock came striking twelve, swinging through darkness into silence. 'Do I love him? I think so,' said Dolly to herself. 'I hope so.' And with an honest heart, she told herself that all should be well. Then she wondered if she should sleep that night ; she seemed to be living over every single bit of her life at once. She longed to tell Aunt Sarah her wonderful story. A daddy-longlegs sailed in at the open window, and Dolly moved the light to save its straggling legs ; a little wind came blowing in, and then Dolly thought she heard a sound as of a door below opening softly. Was her aunt awake and stirring? She caught up the light and crept down to see. She could hear Julie and Mrs. Palmer still discoursing.

There is something sacred about a sick-room at times. It seems like holy ground to people coming in suddenly out of the turmoil and emotion of life. Dolly's excitement was hushed as she entered and saw Lady Sarah lying quietly stretched out asleep upon a sofa. It had been wheeled to the window, which was wide open. The curtain was flapping, all the medicine bottles stood in rows on the table and along the shelves. There lay Sarah, with her grey hair smoothed over her brown face, very still and sleeping peacefully—as peacefully as if she was young still, and loved, and happy, with life before her: though, for the matter of that, people whose life is nearly over have more right to sleep at peace than those who have got to encounter they know not what trials and troubles—struggles with others, and, most deadly of all, with that terrible shadow of self that rises with fresh might, striking with so sure an aim. What does the mystery mean? Who is the familiar enemy that our spirit is set to overcome and to struggle with all the night until the dawn? There lay poor Sarah's life-adversary, then, nearly worn, nearly overcome, sleeping and resting while the spirit was travelling I know not to what peaceful regions.

Dolly crept in and closed the door. Lady Sarah never stirred. A long time seemed to pass. The wind rose again, the curtain flapped, and the light flickered, and time seemed creeping slowly and more slowly to the tune of the sleeping woman's languid breath. It was a strange ending to the long, glittering day, but at last a flush came into Sarah Francis's cheeks, and she opened her eyes. . . . A strange new something was in that placid face—a look. What is it, that first look of change and blurr in features that have melted so tranquilly before us from youth to middle-age, or from middle-age to age, modulating imper-.

ceptibly? The light of Dolly's own heart was too dazzling
for her to be in a very observant mood just then.

'Is that my Dolly?' said the sick woman.

Dolly sprang forward. 'Oh! I am so glad you are
awake,' said the girl. 'Dear Aunt Sarah, has your sleep
done you good? Are you better? Can you listen to something? Can you guess?' And she knelt down so as to
bring her face on a level with the other; but she couldn't
see it very plainly for a dazzle between them. 'Robert says
he loves me; and, indeed, if he loves me I must love him,'
Dolly whispered; and her face fell hidden against the pillow,
and the mist turned to haze. Some bird in the garden outside began to whistle in its sleep. A belated clock struck
something a long way off, and then all was silence and darkness again.

Lady Sarah held Dolly close to her, as the girl knelt
beside her. 'Do you care for him? Is it possible?' said
Lady Sarah, bewildered.

Dolly was hurt by her doubt. 'Indeed I do,' she
answered, beginning to cry once more, from fatigue and
excitement.

One of the two women in that midnight room was young,
with the new kindling genius of love in her heart, and she
was weeping; the other was old, with the first knell of death
ringing in her ear; but when Dolly looked up at last she saw
that her aunt was smiling very tenderly. Lady Sarah
smiled, but she could not trust herself to speak. She had
awakened startled, but in a minute she had realised it all.
She had felt all along that this must be. She had not
wished for it, but it was come. It was not only of Dolly and
of Robert that Lady Sarah thought that night; other ghosts
came into the room and stood before her. And then came

every day, very real, into this dream-world—Marker with a
bed-chamber candlestick, walking straight into conflicting
emotions, and indignant with Miss Dolly for disturbing her
mistress. She had been shutting up and seeing to Mrs.
Palmer's coffee. She was scarcely mollified by the great
news. Lady Sarah was awake; Dolly had awakened her.

'Let people marry who they like,' said Marker; 'but
don't let them come chattering and disturbing at this time
o' night, when they should a' known better.'

Q

CHAPTER XXVI.

GOOD-MORNING.

Qu'un jeune amour, plein de mystère,
Pardonne à la vieille amitié.

DOLLY passed through the sleeping house, crept by the
doors, slid down the creaking stairs, into the hall. The
shutters were unopened as yet, the dawning day was bolted
out, and the place was dark and scattered over with the
shreds of the day before. The newspaper lying on the hall
table, the pieces of string upon the ground, a crumpled
letter, and the long brown-paper coffin in which the silk for
her new gown had come home the night before. Each day
scatters its dust as it hurries by, and leaves its broken ends
and scraps for the coming hours to collect and sort away,
dust of mind, and dust of matter. The great kaleidoscope
of the world turns round once in its twenty-four hours; the
patterns and combinations shift and change and disperse into
new combinations. Perhaps some of us may think that, with
each turn, the fragments are shaken up and mixed and
broken away more and more, until only an undistinguishable
uniform dazzle remains in place of the beautiful blue and red
and golden stars and wheels that delighted our youth.

Dorothea gave a cautious pull to the bolt of the outer

A MORNING REVERIE.

door and opened it, letting a sudden sweet chill rush of
light and fresh air into the closed house, where they had
all been asleep through the night. What a morning! All
her sudden fears seemed lightened, and she jumped across
the step on to the gravel walk, and looked up and round and
about. Dark green, gold, glistening bricks, slanting lights,
and sweet tremulous shadows; the many crowding house-
roofs and tree-tops aflame in the seven-o'clock sunshine, the
birds flapping and fluttering, the mellow old church clock
striking seven: the strokes come in solemn procession across
the High Street and the old brick-walled garden, and pass
on I don't know to what distant blue realms in the vault
overhead.

She stopped to look at a couple of snails creeping up
among the nails in the wall. I think she then practised a
little mazourka along the straight garden walk. She then
took off her hat and stopped to pin back some of the russet
of which I have spoken, then she looked up again and drew
a great breath; and then, passing the green beech and the
two cut yew-trees, she came to the placid pond in its stone
basin at the end of the garden. There it lay in its darkness
and light. There were the gold-fish wide-awake, darting
and gaping as they rose to the surface; and the water
reflected the sky and the laurel-bushes, and the chipped
stone edge of the basin. When Dorothea came and looked
over the brink she saw her own smiling, disjointed face
looking up at her. It was not so bright a face as her own,
somehow. It looked up grey and sad from out of this
trembling, mystical looking-glass. What was it? A cloud
passing overhead, a little, soft, fleecy, white cloud bobbing
along, and then some birds flying by, and then a rustle
among the leaves. It was only a moment, during which it

had seemed to her as if the throb of nature beat a little
more slowly, and as if its rhythm had halted for an instant ;
and in that moment the trouble of the night before, the
doubt of herself, came back to her. Sometimes Dorothea
had wondered, as others have done before her, if there is
such a thing as real happiness in nature. Do clouds love to
sail quickly on the wind ? Are pools glad to lie placid
refracting the sunshine ? When the trees rustle, is it just a
chatter and a quiver, or the thrill of life answering life?
The thought of a living nature without consciousness had
always seemed to her inexpressibly sad. She had sometimes
thought how sad a human life might be that was just a
human life, living and working and playing, and coming to
an end one day, and falling to the ground. It was, in truth,
not very unlike the life she might have led herself, and now
—now she was alone no longer. There was a meaning to life
now, for Henley loved her. She thought this, and then,
seeing a spider's web suddenly gleam with a long lightning
flash, she turned with another glad spring of youth to the
light.

On the table, lay a letter sealed and stamped and
addressed—' Miss Vanborough, Church House, Kensington.'
It was for her. There was no mistaking it. Her first love-
letter. There it lay in black and in white, signed and
dated and marked with a crest. Robert must have written
it the night before, after they had left.

A few minutes ago, in the fresh morning air, it had all
seemed like a dream of the night ; here were tangible signs
and wonders to recall her to her allegiance.

Dolly took it up shyly, this first love-letter, come safe
into her hands from the hands which had despatched it.
She was still standing reading it in the window when Lady

Sarah, who had made an effort, came in, leaning on Marker's arm. The girl was absorbed; her pretty brown curly head was bent in the ivylight, that dazzled through the leaves; she heard nothing except the new voice speaking to her; she saw no one except that invisible presence which was so vividly before her. This was the letter :—

My DEAREST DORA,—I write you one line, which will, I hope, reach you in the morning. You are gone, and already I wish you back again. Your sweetness, your trust in me, have quite overpowered me. I long to prove to you that I am all you believed me, and worthy of your choice. Do not fear to trust your happiness to me. I have carefully studied your character. I know you even better than you know yourself; and when you hesitated I could appreciate your motives. I feel convinced that we have acted for the best. I would say more, but I must write to your mother and to Lady Sarah by to-night's post. Write to me fully and without reserve.

Ever yours, dearest Dora,

R. V. H.

Inside Dolly's letter was a second letter, addressed to the Lady Sarah Francis, sealed and addressed in the same legible hand. This was not a love-letter; nobody could reasonably be expected to send two by the same post :—

My DEAR LADY SARAH,—Dora will have informed you of what has occurred, and I feel that I must not delay expressing to you how sincerely I trust that you will not disapprove of the step we have taken. Although my appointment is not a very lucrative one, the salary is increasing; and I shall make a point of insuring my life before leaving England, for our dear girl's benefit. I do not know whether Dorothea is herself entitled to any of her father's fortune, or whether it has been settled upon George; perhaps you would kindly inform me upon this point, as I am most anxious not to overstep the line of prudence, and my future arrangements must greatly depend upon my means. You will have heard of my appointment to the presidentship of the College of Boggley-wollah. India is a long way off, but time soon passes to those who are able to make good use of it; and I trust that in the happiness of one so justly dear to you, you will find consolation for her absence.

Believe me, my dear Lady Sarah, very truly yours,

R. HENLEY.

P.S.—My widow would be entitled to a pension by the provisions of the Fund.

This was what Dolly, with so much agitation, put into her aunt's hand, watching her face anxiously as she read it.

'May I read it ?' said Dolly.

'It is only business,' said Lady Sarah, crumpling it up,
and Dolly turned away disappointed, and began to pour out
the tea.

It was a very agitated breakfast, happy and shy and
rather silent, though so much had to be said. Mrs. Palmer
came drifting in, to their surprise, before breakfast was over,
in a beautiful white wrapper with satin bows. She also
had received a letter. She embraced Dolly and Lady Sarah.

'Well, what do you say to our news, Sarah ? I have
heard from our dear Robert,' said she. 'You may read his
letter—both of you. Sarah, I am sorry to hear you have
been ailing. If it would not be giving too much trouble—
I have been so upset by all this agitation—I should prefer
coffee this morning. I was quite frightened about myself
last night, Dolly, after I left you . . . . Dear me, what
memories come back to one. Do you remember our marriage, Sarah, and . . . . ? '

'Pray ring again, Dolly,' said Lady Sarah, abruptly,
and she went to the door and called Marker, shrilly and
impatient.

'There is no one but me,' says Mrs. Palmer, pulling out
her frills with a deep sigh, ' who cares for those old stories.
The Admiral cannot endure them.'

Dolly's cup of happiness, so full before, seemed overflowing
now, it spread and spread. Happiness and sorrow overflow
into other cups besides our own. John Morgan looked in
opportunely to hear the news and to ask how they all were:
his hearty congratulations came with a grateful sense of
relief. Dolly longed for sympathy in her happiness. She
was glad to be a little stunned by the cheerful view he took

of what must be so sad as well as so sweet. The news spread rapidly.

Old Sam came up with a shining face and set down the copper coal-scuttle, the better to express his good wishes. Eliza Twells tumbled down the kitchen-stairs with a great clatter from sheer excitement, and when Marker, relenting, came up in her big flowing apron for orders, her round face was rippling with smiles.

'God bless you kindly, Miss Dolly, my dear,' said the good old woman, giving her a kiss on each cheek. 'I never took up with a husband myself, but I don't blame ye. It is well to have some one to speak our mind to. And did he give you a ring, my dear?'

Dolly laughed and held up her two hands. 'No ring, Marker. I don't like rings. I wish one could be married without one.'

'Don't say that, dearie,' said Marker, gravely.

CHAPTER XXVII.

LOVE LANE FROM KENSINGTON TO FULHAM.

Where are the great, whom thou wouldst wish to praise thee?
Where are the pure, whom thou wouldst choose to love thee?
Where are the brave, to stand supreme above thee,
Whose high commands would cheer, whose chiding raise thee?
Seek, seeker, in thyself, submit to find
In the stones bread, and life in the blank mind.
                                        —A. T. CLOUGH.

ROBERT came up to town on the Tuesday, as he had promised
Dolly. As he came along, he told himself that he had
deserved some reward for his patience in waiting. He had
resisted many a sentimental impulse, not wishing to distract his mind until the summer term was over. He might
almost have trusted himself to propose at Easter, and to go
on calmly with his papers, for he was not like George, whose
wandering attention seemed distracted by every passing
emotion. Robert's stiff black face melted a little as he
indulged in a lover-like dream. He saw Dolly as she would
be one day, ruling his household, welcoming his guests,
admired by them all. Henley had too good taste to like a
stupid woman. Nothing would ever have induced him to
think of a plain one. He wished for a certain amount of
good-breeding and habit of the world. . . . All these
qualifications he had discovered in his cousin, not to

speak of other prospects depending on her aunt's good pleasure.

Old Sam opened the door, grinning his congratulations.
Robert found Dolly sitting with her mother on the terrace.
Philippa jumped up to meet him, and embraced him too
with effusion.

'We were expecting you,' she said. 'I have *much* to say
to you; come with me.' And clasping her hands upon his
arm, she would have immediately drawn him away into the
house, if Robert had not said with some slight embarrassment, 'Presently, my dear aunt, I shall be quite at your
service; but I have not yet spoken to Dolly.' Dolly did not
move, but waited for Robert to come to her—then she
looked up suddenly.

Dolly's manner was charming in those days—a little
reserved, but confident and sympathetic, a little abrupt at
times, but bright and melancholy at once. Later in life
some of its shadows seemed to drown the light in her honest
face; her mistakes made her more shy, and more reserved;
she caught something of Henley's coldness of manner, and
was altered, so her friends thought.

I don't, for my own part, believe that people change.
But it is not the less true that they have many things in
them, many emotions and passing moods, and as days and
feelings follow, each soul's experience is written down here
and there, and in other souls, and by signs, and by work
done, and by work undone, and by what is forgotten, as
well as that which is remembered, by the influence of to-
day, and of the past that is not over. Perhaps, one day, we
may know ourselves at last, and read our story plainly
written in our own and other people's lives.

Dolly, in those days, was young and confident and undismayed. It seems strange to make a merit as we do of youth, of inexperience, of hardness of heart. Her untroubled young spirit had little sympathy for others more weary and wayworn. She loved, but without sympathy; but all the same, the brightness of her youth and its unconscious sweetness spread and warmed, and comforted those upon whom its influence fell.

Dorothea Vanborough was a woman of many-changing emotions and sentiments; frank to herself, doubting herself all the while; diffident where she should have been bold, loving the right above all things, and from very excess of scruples, troubled at times, and hard to others. Then came regret and self-abasement and reproach, how bitter none can tell but those who, like her, have suffered from many and complicated emotions—trusting, mistrusting, longing for truth, and, from this very longing, failing often. She loved because she was young and her heart was tender and humble. She doubted because she was young and because the truth was in her, urging her to do that which she would not have done, and to feel the things that she would not have felt. But all this was only revealed to her later, only it was there from the beginning. Dolly was very shy and very happy all these early days.

Frank Raban thought Dolly careless, hard in her judgments, spoiled by the love that was showered upon her; he thought she was not kind to Rhoda. All this he dwelt upon, nor could he forget her judgment upon himself. Poor Raban acknowledged that for him no judgment could be too severe, and yet he would have loved Dolly to be pitiful; although she could now never be anything to him—never, so long as they both lived. When the news came of her engagement, it was a pain to him that he had long expected, and that he accepted. One failure in life was enough. He made no advance; he watched her; he let her go, foolish man! without a word. Sometimes Rhoda would talk to him about Dolly. Frank always listened.

'She does not mean to be cold. Indeed, I don't think so—I am so used to her manner that I do not think of it,' Rhoda would say. 'Dear Dolly is full of good and generous impulses. She will make Robert Henley a noble wife if he only gives in to her in everything. I would I were half as good as she is; but she is a little hasty at times, and wants every one to do as she tells them.'

'And you do as everybody tells you,' said Raban.

And to do Rhoda justice, she worked her fingers to the bone, she walked to poor people's houses through the rain and mud; she was always good-tempered, she was a valuable inmate in the household. Zoe said she couldn't think how Rhoda got through half what she did. 'Here, there, and everywhere,' says Zoe, in an aggrieved voice, 'before I have time to turn.'

Notwithstanding the engagement, the little household at Church House went its usual course. Lady Sarah had followed her own beaten ways so long, that she seemed, from habit, to travel on whether or not her interest went with her. Those old days are almost forgotten now, even by the people who lived in them. With a strange, present thrill Dolly remembers sometimes, as she passes through the old haunts of her early youth, a past instant of time, a past state of sentiment, as bygone as the hour to which it belonged. Passing by the old busy corner of the church not long ago, Dolly remembered how she and Robert had met Raban there one day, just after their news had been made public. He tried to avoid them, then changed his mind and came straight up and shook hands, uttering his good wishes in a cold, odd manner, that Dolly thought almost unkind.

'I am afraid my good wishes can add little to your happiness, but I congratulate you,' he said to Robert; 'and I wish you all happiness,' he said to Dolly; and then they were all silent for a minute.

'You will come soon, won't you?' said Dolly, shyly.

'Good-by,' said Frank Raban, walking away very quickly.

He had meant to keep away, but he came just as usual to Church House, and was there even more constantly. Lady Sarah was glad of his companionship for George, who seemed in a very strange and excited state of mind.

The summer of '54 was an eventful summer; and while Dolly was living in her own youthful world, concentrated in the overwhelming interests that had come of late, in old and the new ties, so hard to grasp, so hard to loose, armies were marching, fleets were sailing, politicians and emperors were pondering upon the great catastrophe that seemed imminent. War had been declared; with it the great fleets had come speeding across the sea from one horizon to another. The events of the day only reached Dolly like echoes from a long way off, brought by Robert and by George, printed in the paper. Robert was no keen politician. He was too full of his own new plans and new career. George was far more excited, and of a more fiery temper. Frank Raban and George and he used to have long and angry arguments. Raban maintained that the whole thing was a mistake, a surrender to popular outcry. George and Robert were for fighting at any price: for once they agreed.

'I don't see,' said George, 'what there is in life to make it so preferable to anything else, to every sense of honour and of consideration, of liberty of action. Life, to be worth anything, is only a combination of all these things ; and for one or any of them I think a man should be willing to play his stake.'

'Of course, of course, if it were necessary,' said Henley, 'one would do what was expected of one. There is my cousin, Jonah Henley, joining his regiment next week. I confess it is on different grounds from you that I approve of this war. I do not like to see England falling in the—a— estimation of Europe : we can afford to go to war. Russia's pretensions are intolerable ; and, with France to assist us, I believe the Government is thoroughly justified in the course it is pursuing.'

'I don't think we are ready,' said Raban, in his odd, constrained voice. 'I don't think we *are* justified. We sit at home and write heroic newspaper articles, and we send out poor fellows by rank and by file to be pounded at and cut to mincemeat, for what ? to defend a worn-out remnant of a past from the inevitable advance of the future. Suppose we put things back a hundred years, what good shall we have done ? '

'But think of our Overland Route,' said Henley ; 'suppose the future should interfere with the P. and O.'

There were green lanes in those days leading from the far end of that lane in which Church House was built to others that crossed a wide and spreading country : it is not even yet quite overflooded by the waves of brick—that tide that flows out in long, strange furrows, and never ebbs away. Dolly and Henley went wandering along these lanes one fine afternoon ; they were going they knew not where ; into a land of Canaan, so Dolly thought it : green cabbages, a long, gleaming canal, hawthorn hedges, and a great overarched sky that began to turn red when the sun set. Now and

then they came to some old house that had outstood storms
and years, fluttering signals of distress in the shape of old
shirts and clothes hung out to dry; in the distance rose
Kensington spires and steeples; now and then a workman
trudged by on his way home; distant bells rang in this
wide, desolate country. Women come tramping home from
their long day's work in the fields, and look hard at the
handsome young couple, Dolly with cast-down eyes, Robert
with his nose up in the air. The women trudge wearily
home; the young folks walk step by step into life. The
birds cross the sky in a sudden flight; the cabbages grow
where they are planted.

They missed the Chelsea Lane. Dolly should have
known the way, but she was absorbed and unobservant, and
those cross-ways were a labyrinth except for those who were
well used to them. They found themselves presently in the
Old Brompton Road, with its elm-trees and old gable roofs
darkening against the sunset. How sweet it was, with red
lights burning, people slowly straggling like themselves,
and enjoying the gentle ease of the twilight and of the soft
west wind. Dolly led Henley back by the old winding road,
with its bends and fancies; its cottages, within close-built
walls; and stately old houses, with iron scroll-work on their
garden gates, and gardens not yet destroyed. Then they
came to a rueful row of bricks and staring windows. A
young couple stood side by side against the low rail in front
of their home. Dolly remembered this afterwards; for the
sky was very splendid just then, and the young woman's
violet dress seemed to blaze with the beautiful light, as she
stood in her quaint little garden, looking out across the
road to the well-remembered pond and some fields beyond.
Along the distant line of the plains great soft ships of

vapour were floating; the windows of the distant houses flashed; the pond looked all splendid and sombre in its shady corner. The evening seemed vast and sweet, and Dolly's heart was full.

'Are you tired?' said Robert, seeing that she lingered.

'Tired? no,' said Dorothea. 'I was looking at the sky, and wondering how it would have been if you had gone away and never —— ?' She stopped.

'Why think about it?' said Robert. 'You would have married somebody else, I suppose.'

He said it in a matter-of-fact sort of way, and for a moment Dolly's eyebrows seemed to darken over her eyes. It was a mere nothing, the passing shadow of a thought.

'You are right,' said Dolly, wistfully. 'It is no use thinking how unhappy one might have been. Have you ever been very unhappy, Robert?' Now that she was so happy, Dolly seemed, for the first time, to realise what sorrow might be.

'A certain young lady made me very unhappy one day not long ago,' said Robert, 'when she tried to freeze me up with a snowball.'

This was not what Dolly meant: she was in earnest, and he answered her with a joke; she wanted a sign, and no sign was given to her.

They had just reached home, when Robert said, with his hand on the bell: 'This has not been unhappy, has it, Dolly? We shall have a great many more walks together when I can spare the time. But you must talk to me more, and not be so shy, dearest.'

Something flew by as he spoke, and went fluttering into the ivy.

'That was a bat,' said Dolly, shrinking, while Robert

stood shaking his umbrella-stick among the ivy leaves ; but it was too dark to see anything distinctly.

'I hope,' said Robert, sentimentally, 'to come and see you constantly when this term is over. Then we shall know more of each other, Dora.'

'Don't we know each other?' asked Dolly, with one of her quick glances ; 'I think I know you quite well, Robert —better than I know myself almost,' she added, with a sigh.

When they came into the drawing-room the lamp was alight, and George and Rhoda were there with Lady Sarah. George was talking at the very pitch of his melancholy voice, Lady Sarah was listening with a pale, fixed face, like a person who has made up her mind.

Rhoda was twirling her work round and round her fingers. She had broken the wool, and dropped the stitches. It was by a strong effort that she sat so still.

'Here is George announcing his intentions,' said Lady Sarah, as they came in. 'Perhaps you, Robert, will be able to preach good sense to him.'

'Oh, Aunt Sarah!' Dolly cried, springing forward, 'at last he has told you. . . . Has Rhoda?' Dolly's two hands were clasped in excitement. Lady Sarah looked at her in some surprise.

There was a crash, a scream from Rhoda. The flower-glass had gone over on the table beside her, and all the water was running about over the carpet.

'My dress—my Sunday best!' cried Rhoda. 'Lady Sarah, I am so sorry.'

Dolly bent over to pick up the table, and, as she did so, Rhoda whispered, 'Be silent, or you will ruin George.'

'Ruined?' said Robert. 'Your dress is not ruined,

Rhoda. I speak from experience, for I wear a silk gown myself.'

'George says he will not take my living,' said Lady Sarah. 'He wishes to be —— What do you wish to be, George?'

George, somewhat confused, said he wished to be a soldier —anything but a clergyman.

'You don't mean to say you are going to be such a — that you refuse seven hundred a year?' said Henley, stopping short.

'Confound it!' cried George, 'can't you all leave a poor fellow in peace?' And he burst out of the room.

'Come here, Dolly,' said Mrs. Palmer, from a distant corner of the room; 'make this foolish darling do as his aunt wishes. I am sure the Admiral would quite feel as I do.'

'Seven hundred a year,' said Lady Sarah. 'Wretched boy! I shall sell the presentation.'

'Oh, Robert!' said Dolly, 'he is right if he can't make up his mind. I know Aunt Sarah thinks so.'

Dolly could not help being vexed with Robert. He shrugged his shoulders, said that George would regret his decision, and went on to talk of various plans that he himself had at heart, just as if George had never existed.

'I want you to trust Dolly to me for a few days,' said he. 'I want to take her down to Smokethwaite with my aunt. She must see Jonah before he leaves. They all write, and urge her coming.'

Lady Sarah agreed, with a sigh, and her eyes filled with tears. She turned away abruptly to hide them.

Many and many were the tears she wiped away, for fear Dolly should see them. George's whole body was not so

R

dear to her as Dolly's little finger. She blamed herself in vain afterwards, when it was too late. Sometimes she could hardly bear to see her niece come into the room with her smiling face, and she scarcely answered when the sweet girl's voice came echoing and calling about the house. Could it be true that it was going, that sweet voice? Laughing, scolding, chattering, hour by hour—were the many foot-steps going, too, and the rustle of her dress, and the look of her happy eyes? was the time already come for Dolly to fly away from the old nest that had sheltered her for so short a time? She seemed scarcely to have come—scarcely to have begun her sweet home song—and already she was eager to go!

But Rhoda had come up, looking very pale, to say good-night. As she said good-by, Dolly followed her out, and tried to put in some little word for George. 'Rhoda, he has been true to himself,' she whispered; 'that is best of all—is not it?'

'Let him be true to himself, by all means,' said Rhoda.

She was thoroughly out of temper. Dolly had not im-proved matters by talking about them. George came out of the oak room prepared to walk back with her. 'No, thank you,' said Rhoda, trembling very much. 'I won't trouble you to come home with me.'

She was tying her bonnet and pinning on her shawl in an agitated way. George watched her in silence. When she was ready to go, he held out his hand. 'Good-night,' he said.

'Good-night,' said Rhoda, hurrying off without looking up, and passing out into the street.

It was unbearable. If George loved her he might do as she wished. But he would sacrifice nothing—not one fancy.

Her Uncle John was a clergyman. It was a very high calling. Rhoda thought of the pretty little parsonage-house,
and the church, and the cottages all round about, only waiting to be done good to, while the apples were baking on the
trees and cakes in the oven, all of which good things George
had refused—George, who did not know one bit what he
was doing, nor what it was to scrape, and starve, and live
with dull, stinted, scraping people. She was quite tired of
it all. It was not a real life that she led; it was a housekeeper's situation, just like Aunt Morgan. She had done
her best, and she had earned a rest, and she would not begin
all over again. George might be as true as he liked. Rhoda
ran up the steps of the old brown house in a silent passion,
and gave a sharp pull at the bell. Yes, she hated it all.
She was utterly tired of it all—of the noisy home, of Aunt
Morgan's precepts and flannels. She could hear the clink
of plates in the dining-room, where the inevitable anters of
cheese and cold meat were set out on the shabby table-cloth,
where her Aunt Morgan stood in her black cap and stiff
brown curls, carving slice after slice for the hungry curate.
'You are late, Rhoda,' said her aunt. 'I suppose you
stayed to late dinner with your friends?'

'No; but I am not hungry,' said Rhoda, shrinking away.

'Why, Rhoda, what is the matter?' said John, kindly,
and he held out his big hand to her.

CHAPTER XXVIII.

UNBORN TO-MORROW AND DEAD YESTERDAY.

> Alas, thrice-gentle Cassio,
> My advocation is not now in tune;
> My lord is not my lord; nor should I know him,
> Were he in favour, as in humour, alter'd.
>   —OTHELLO.

WHATEVER Lady Sarah may have thought, Mrs. Palmer used
to consider Dolly a most fortunate girl, and she used to say
so, not a little to Lady Sarah's annoyance.

'Extremely fortunate,' repeats Dolly's mamma, looking
thoughtfully at her fat satin shoes. 'What a lottery life is!
I was as pretty as Dolly, and yet dear Stanham had not anything like Robert's excellent prospects. Even the Ad——
Don't go, Sarah.'

Poor Lady Sarah would start up, with an impatient
movement, and walk across the room to get away from
Philippa's retrospections. They were almost more than she
had patience for just then. She could scarcely have found
patience for Philippa herself, if it had not been that she
was Dolly's mother. What did she mean by her purrings
and self-congratulations? Lady Sarah used to feel most
doubtful about Dolly's good fortune just when Philippa
was most enthusiastic on the subject, or when Robert

himself was pointing out his excellent prospects in his lucid way.

Philippa would listen, nodding languid approbation. Dolly would make believe to laugh at Robert's accounts of his coming honours; but it was easy to see that it was only make-believe incredulity.

Her aunt could read the girl's sweet conviction in her eyes, and she loved her for it. Once, remembering her own youth, this fantastic woman had made a vow never, so long as she lived, to interfere in the course of true love. True love! Is this true love, when one person is in love with a phantom, another with an image reflected in a glass? True love is something more than phantoms, than images and shadows; and yet stirred by phantoms and living among shadows, its faint dreams come to life.

Lady Sarah was standing by the bookcase, in a sort of zigzag mind of her own old times and of Dolly's to-day. She had taken a book from the shelf—a dusty volume of Burns's poems—upon the fly-leaf of which the name of another Robert Henley was written. She holds the book in her hand, looks at the crooked writing—'S. V., from Robert Henley, May, 1808.' She beats the two dusty covers together, and puts it back into its place again. That is all her story. Philippa never heard of it, Robert never heard of it, nor did he know that Lady Sarah loved his name—which had been his father's too—better than she loved him. 'Perhaps her happiness had all gone to Dolly,' the widow thought, as she stood, with a troubled sort of smile on her face, looking at the two young people through a pane of glass; and then, like a good woman as she is, tries to silence her misgivings into a little prayer for their happiness.

Let us do justice to the reluctant prayers that people offer up. They are not the less true because they are half-hearted and because those who pray would sometimes gladly be spared an answer to their petitions. Poor Lady Sarah! her prayers seemed too much answered as she watched Dolly day by day more and more radiant and absorbed.

'My dear creature, what are you doing with all those dusty books? Can you see our young people?' says Mrs. Palmer, languidly looking over her arm-chair. 'I expect Colonel Witherington this afternoon. He admires Dolly excessively, Sarah; and I really think he might have proposed, if Robert had not been so determined to carry her off. You dear old thing, forgive me; I don't believe she would ever have married at all if I had not come home. You are in the clouds, you know. I remember saying so to Hawtry at Trincomalee. I should have disowned her if she had turned out an old maid. I know it. I detest old maids. The Admiral has a perfect craze for them, and they all adore him. I should like you to see Miss M'Grudder—there never was anything so ludicrous, asthmatic, sentimental—frantic. We must introduce Miss Moineaux to him, and the Morgan girls. I often wonder how he ever came to marry a widow, and I tell him so. It was a great mistake. Can you believe it?—Hawtry now writes that second marriages are no marriages at all. Perhaps you agree with him? I'm sure Dolly is quite ready to do so. I never saw a girl so changed—*never*. We have lost her, my dear; make up your mind to it. She is Robert, not Dolly any more—no thought for any one else, not for *me*, dear child! And don't you flatter yourself she will ever . . . Dear me! Gone? What an extraordinary creature poor Sarah is! touched, certainly; and *such* a wet blanket!'

Mrs. Palmer, rising from her corner, floats across the room, sweeping over several footstools and small tables on her way. She goes to the window, and not caring to be alone, begins to tap with her diamond finger upon the pane, to summon the young couple, who pay not the slightest attention. Fortunately the door opens, and Colonel Witherington is announced. He is a swarthy man, with shiny boots, a black moustache; his handkerchief is scented with Esse-bouquet, which immediately permeates the room; he wears tight dogskin gloves and military shirt-collars. Lady Sarah thinks him vulgar and odious beyond words; Mrs. Palmer is charmed to see him, and graciously holds out her white hand. She is used to his adoration, and accepts it with a certain swan-like indifference.

People had different opinions about Mrs. Palmer. In some circles she was considered brilliant and accomplished, in others, silly and affected. Colonel Witherington never spoke of her except with military honours. 'Charming woman,' he would say; 'highly cultivated; you might give her five-and-twenty at the outside. Utterly lost upon that spluttering, old psalm-singing Palmer. Psalms are all very well in their *proper* place—in the prayer-books, or in church; but after dinner, when one has got a good cigar, and feels inclined for a little pleasant conversation, it is *not* the time to ring the bell for the servants, and have 'em down upon their knees all of a row, and up again in five minutes to listen to an extempore sermon. The Admiral runs on like a clock. I used to stay with them at the Admiralty House. Pity that poor woman most heartily! Can't think how she keeps up as she does!'

Little brown Lady Henley at Smokethwaite would not have sympathised with Colonel Witherington's admiration.

She made a point of shrugging her shoulders whenever she heard Philippa's name mentioned. 'If you ask me,' she would say, 'I must frankly own that my sister-in-law is not to be depended on. She is utterly selfish; she only lives for the admiration of gentlemen. My brother Hawtry is a warm-hearted, impulsive man, who would have made any woman happy. If he *has* looked for consolation in his domestic trials, and found it in religious interests, it is not I who would blame him. Sir Thomas feels as I do, and deeply regrets Philippa's deplorable frivolity. I do not know much of that poor girl of hers. I have no doubt Robert has been dazzled by mother and daughter. They are good-looking, and, as I am told, thoroughly well understand the art of setting themselves off to the best advantage. I am fond of Robert Henley; but I cannot pretend to have any feeling for Dorothea one way or another. We have asked them here, of course. They are to come after their marriage. I only hope my sister-in-law appreciates her daughter's good luck, and has the sense to know the value of such a man as Robert Henley.'

Mrs. Palmer was perfectly enchanted with her future son-in-law. He could scarcely get rid of her. Robert, with some discomposure, would find himself sitting on his aunt's sofa, hand-in-hand, listening to long and very unpleasant extracts from her correspondence. 'You dear boy!' Mrs. Palmer would say, with her soft, fat fingers firmly clasped round his; 'you have done me good. Your dear head is able to advise my poor perplexed heart. Dolly, he is my prop. I give you up, my child, gladly, to this dear fellow!' These little compliments mollified the young man at first, although he found that by degrees the tax of his aunt's constant dependence became heavier and heavier. Briareus himself could scarcely have supplied arms to support her unsparing weakness, to hand her parcels and footstools about, to carry her shawls and cushions, and to sort the packets of her correspondence. She had the Admiral's letters, tied up with various-coloured ribbons, and docketed, 'Cruel,' 'Moderately Abusive,' 'Apologetic,' 'Canting,' 'Business.' She was always sending for Robert. Her playful tap at the window made him feel quite nervous.

Mrs. Palmer had begun to knit him a pair of muffetees, and used slowly to twist pink silk round ivory needles. Lady Henley laughed very loud when she heard this. 'Poor Robert! He will have to pay dearly for those mittens,' she said.

For a long time past Mrs. Palmer had rarely left the house, but the trousseau now began to absorb her; she used to go driving for long hours at a time with Dolly, in a jaded fly—she would invite Robert to accompany them—to Baker Street Bazaar, to Soho Square, to St. Paul's Churchyard, back again to Oxford Street, a corner shop of which she had forgotten the number. On one occasion, after trying three or four corner shops, Robert called to the coachman to stop, and jumped out. 'I think Dolly and I will walk home,' he said, abruptly; 'I'm afraid you must give up your shop, Aunt Philippa. It is impossible to find the place.'

Poor Dolly, who was longing to escape, brightened up, but before she could speak, Mrs. Palmer had grasped her tightly by both hands. 'My dear Robert, what a proposal! I could not *think* of letting Dolly walk all the way home. She would be *quite* done up. And it is *her* business, her shopping, you know.' Then reproachfully and archly, 'And I *must* say that even the Admiral would scarcely have deserted us so ungallantly, with all this work on our hands, and all these parcels, and no servant. You dear fellow, you really must not leave us.'

Robert stood holding the door open, and looking particularly black. 'I am very sorry indeed,' he said, with a short laugh, 'but you will be quite safe, my dear aunt, and you really seem to have done enough shopping to last for many years to come.' And he put out his hand as a matter of course, to help Dorothea to alight.

'But she *cannot* leave me,' says Philippa, excitedly; 'she would not even wish it. Would you, my child? I never drive alone—never; I am afraid of the coachman. It is most unreasonable to propose such a thing.'

'I will answer for your safety,' persisted Robert. 'My dear aunt, you must get used to doing without your Dolly now. Come, Dora, the walk will freshen you up.'

'But I don't want to walk, Robert,' said poor Dolly, with a glance at her mother. 'You may come for me to-morrow instead. You will, won't you?' she added, as he suddenly turned away without answering, and she leant out of the carriage-window, and called after him, a little frightened by his black looks and silence. 'Robert! I shall expect you,' she said.

'I shall not be able to come to-morrow, Dora,' said Henley, very gravely; and then, raising his hat, he walked off without another word.

Even then Dolly could not believe that he was seriously angry. She saw him striding along the pavement, and called to him, and made a friendly little sign with her hand as the brougham passed close by a place where he was waiting to cross the road. Robert did not seem to see either the brougham nor the kind face inside that

was smiling at him.   Dorothea's eyes suddenly filled up
with tears.

'Boorish! Boorish!' cried Mrs. Palmer, putting up both
hands.   'Robert is like all other men, they leave you at any
moment, Dolly—that is my experience,—bitterly gained—
without a servant even, and I have ever so much more to do.
There is Parkins and Gotto's for India-paper.   If only I had
known that he was going to be so rude, I should have asked
for old Sam.'   Mrs. Palmer was still greatly discomposed.
'Pray put up that window, Dolly,' she said, 'and I do wish
you would attend to those parcels—they are falling off the
seat.'

Dolly managed to wink away her tears as she bent over
the parcels.   Forgive her for crying!   This was her first
quarrel with Robert, if quarrel it could be called.   She
thought it over all the way home, surely she had been
right to do as her mother wished—why was Robert
vexed?

Philippa was in a very bad humour all that evening.
She talked so pathetically of a mother's feelings, and cf the
pangs of parting from her child, that Lady Sarah for once
was quite sorry for her—she got a little shawl to put over
Philippa's feet as she lay beating a tattoo upon the sofa.
As for Dolly, she had gone to bed early, very silent and out
of spirits.

That evening's post brought a couple of letters; one
was from George to his mother, written in his cranky,
blotted handwriting :—

Cambridge: All Saints' College.

DEAREST MAMMA,—I am coming up for a couple of days.   I have, strange
as it may sound, been working too hard.   Tell Aunt Sarah.   Love to Dolly.

Yours affectionately,

GEORGE.

The other was for Dolly, and Marker took it up to her in her room. This letter flowed in even streams of black upon the finest hot-pressed paper:

DEAREST DORA,—I was much disappointed that you would not come with me, and condemned me to that solitary walk. I hope that a day may come, before very long, when your duty and your pleasures may seem less at variance to you than at present; otherwise I can see little chance of happiness in our future life.

Yours,

R. V. H.

'Was he still vexed?' Dolly, who had relented the moment she saw the handwriting, wrote him a little note that evening, by moonlight, and asked Marker to post it.

I could not leave Mamma all alone (she wrote). I wanted to walk home with you— couldn't you see that I did? I shall expect you to come to luncheon to-morrow, and we will go wherever you like.—D.

Dolly lay awake after this for a long moonlight hour. She was living in what people call the world of feeling. She was absorbed, she was happy, but it was a happiness with a reserve in it. It was peace indeed, but Dolly was too young, her life had been too easy, for peace to be all-sufficient to her. She had found out, by her new experience, that Robert loved her, but in future that he would rule her too. In her life, so free hitherto, there would be this secret rule to be obeyed, this secret sign. Dolly did not know whether on the whole she liked the thought, or whether she resented it. She had never spoken of it, even to Robert. 'You see you have to do as you are told,' Henley sometimes said; he meant it in fun, but Dorothea instinctively felt that there was truth in his words—he was a man who held his own. He was not to be changed by an impulse. Dolly, conscious of some hidden weakness in her own nature, deified obstinacy, as many a woman has done before her, and made excuses out of her own loving heart for Henley's selfish one.

It was summer still, though August had come again; the Virginian creepers along the west wall glowed; crimson-tinted leaves fell in golden rain, the gardener swept up golden dollars and fairy money into heaps and carted them away; the geraniums put out shoots; the creepers started off upon excursions along the gravel-paths: it was a comfortable old-fashioned world, deep-coloured, russet-tinted, but the sun was hot still and burning, and Dolly dressed herself in white, and listened to every bell.

The day passed, however, without any sign of Robert, or any word from him. But George walked in just as they were sitting down to luncheon. He looked very pale and yellow, and he had black lines under his eyes. He had been staying down at Cambridge, actually reading for a scholarship that Raban had advised his trying for. It was called the Bulbul scholarship for Oriental languages, and it had been founded by an enlightened Parsee, who had travelled in Europe in shiny boots and an oilskin hat, and who had been so well received at Cambridge that he wished to perpetuate his name there.

George had taken up Persian some time ago, when he should have been reading mathematics. He was fond of quoting the 'Roubaiyát' of Omar Khayyam, of which the beautiful English version had lately appeared. It was this poem, indeed, which had set him to study the original. He had a turn for languages, and a fair chance of success, Raban said, if he would only go to bed, and not sit up all night, with soda-water and wet towels round his head. This time he had nearly made himself ill, by sitting up three nights in succession, and the doctor had him sent home for a holiday.

'My dear child, what a state your complexion is in! How ill you look!' said his mother. 'It is all those horrid examinations!'

Restless George wandered out into the garden after dinner, and Dolly followed him. She began to water her roses in the cool of the evening, and George filled the cans with water from the tank and brought them to her. Splashing and overflowing, the water lapped into the dry earth and washed the baked stems of the rose-trees. George said suddenly, 'Dolly, do you ever see Raban now, and do you still snub him?'

'I don't snub him,' said Dolly, blushing. 'He does not approve of me, George. He is so bitter, and he never seems satisfied.'

George began to recite—

> 'Ah, love! could you and I with fate conspire
> To grasp this sorry Scheme of Things entire,
> Would we not shatter it to bits, and then
> Remould it nearly to the Heart's Desire?

There is Robert at last, Dolly.'

Dolly looked wonderingly at her brother. He had spoken so pointedly, that she could not help wondering what he meant; but the next moment she had sprung forward to meet Henley, with a sweet face alight.

'Oh, Robert, why have you been so long coming?' she said. 'Did you not get my note?'

CHAPTER XXIX.

UNDER THE GREAT DOME.

Fantasio—'Je n'en suis pas, je n'en suis pas.'

—A. DE MUSSET.

THE wedding was fixed for the middle of September. In October they were to sail.

Dolly was to be married at the Kensington parish church. Only yesterday the brown church was standing—to-day a white phœnix is rising from its ashes. The old people and the old prayers seem to be passing away with the brown walls. One wonders as one looks at the rising arches what new tides of feeling will sweep beneath them, what new teachings and petitions, what more instant charity, what more practical faith and hope. One would be well content to see the old gates fall if one might deem that these new ones were no longer to be confined by bolts of human adaptation, against which, day by day, the divine decrees of mutation and progress strike with blows that are vibrating through the aisles, drowning the voice of the teachers, jarring with the prayers of the faithful.

As the doors open wide, the congregations of this practical age in the eternity of ages, see on the altars of to-day new visions of the time. Unlike those of the fervent and mystical past, when kneeling anchorites beheld, in answer to

their longing prayers, pitiful saints crowned with roses and
radiant with light, and vanishing away, visions of hearts on
fire and the sacred stigmata, the rewards of their life-long
penance; to-day, the Brother whom we have seen appears to
us in the place of symbols of that which it hath not entered
into the heart of man to conceive. The teaching of the
Teacher, as we understand it now, is translated into a new
language of daily toil and human sympathy; our saints are
the sinners helped out of the mire; our visions do not
vanish; our heavenly music comes to us in the voices of
the school-children; surely it is as sweet as any that ever
reached the enraptured ears of penitents in their cells.

If people are no longer on their knees as they once were,
and if some are afraid and cry out that the divine images of
our faith are waxing dimmer in their niches; if in the
Calvaries of these modern times we still see truth blas-
phemed, thieves waiting on their crosses of ignorance and
crime, sick people crying for help, and children weeping
bitterly, why should we be afraid if people, rising from their
knees, are setting to their day's work with honest and loving
hearts, and going, instead of saying, ' I go,' and remaining
and crying, ' Lord, Lord.'

Once Dolly stopped to look at the gates as she was
walking by, thinking, not of Church reform, in those old
selfish days of hers, but of the new life that was so soon to
begin for her behind those baize doors, among the worm-
eaten pews and the marble cherubs, under the window, with
all the leaden-patched panes diverging. She looked, flushed
up, gathered her grey skirts out of the mud, and went on
with her companion.

The old days were still going on, and she was the old
Dolly that she was used to. But there was this difference

now. At any time, at any hour, coming into a room suddenly she never knew but that she might find a letter, a summons, some sign of the new existence, and interests that were crowding upon her. She scarcely believed in it all at times; but she was satisfied. She was walking with her hand on Robert's strong arm. She could trust to Robert —she could trust herself. She sometimes wondered to find herself so calm. Robert assured her that, when people *really* loved each other, it was always so; they were always calm, and, no doubt, he was right.

The two were walking along the Sunday street on their way to St. Paul's. Family groups and prayer-books were about; market-carts, packed with smiles and ribbons, were driving out in a long train towards the river. Bells far and near were ringing fitfully. There is no mistaking the day as it comes round, bringing with it a little ease into the strain of life, a thought of peace and home-meeting and rest, and the echo of a psalm outside in the City streets, as well as within its churches.

Robert called a hansom, and they drove rapidly along the road towards town. The drifting clouds and lights across the parks and streets made them look changed from their usual aspect. As they left the suburbs and drove on towards the City, Henley laughed at Dorothea's enthusiasm for the wet streets, of which the muddy stones were reflecting the lights of a torn and stormy sky. St. Clement's spire rose sharp against a cloud, the river rolled, fresh blown by soft winds, towards the east, while the lights fell upon the crowding house-tops and spires. Dolly thought of her moonlight drive with her mother. Now, everything was alight and awake again; she alone was dreaming, perhaps. As they went up a steep crowded hill the horse's feet slipped at every step.

'Don't be afraid, Dora,' said Robert, protectingly. Then they were driving up a straiter and wider street, flooded with this same strange light, and they suddenly saw a solemn sight; of domes and spires uprearing; of mist, of stormy sky. There rose the mighty curve, majestically flung against the dome of domes! The mists drifting among these mountains and pinnacles of stone only seemed to make them more stately.

'Robert, I never knew how beautiful it was,' said Dolly. 'How glad I am we came! Look at that great dome and the shining sky. It is like—" see how high the heavens are in comparison with the earth!"'

'I forget the exact height,' said Robert. 'It is between three and four hundred feet. You see the ball up at the top—they say that twenty-four people ——'

'I know all that, Robert,' said Dolly, impatiently. 'What does it matter?'

'I thought it might interest you,' said Robert, slightly huffed, 'since you appear to be so little acquainted with St. Paul's. It is very fine, of course; but I myself have the bad taste to prefer Gothic architecture; it is far more suitable to our church. There is something painfully—how shall I express it?—paganish about these capitals and pilasters.'

'But that is just what I mean,' said Dolly, looking him full in the face. 'Think of the beautiful old thoughts of the Pagans helping to pile up a Cathedral here now. Don't you think,' she said, hesitating, and blushing at her own boldness, 'that it is like a voice from a long way off coming and harmonising now with ours? Robert, imagine building a curve that will make some one happy thousands of years afterwards. . . .'

'I am glad it makes *you* happy, my dear Dorothea. I

tell you I have the bad taste not to admire St. Paul's,' Robert
repeated ; ' but here is the rain, we had better make haste.'

They had come to an opening in the iron railings by this
time, and Robert led the way—a stately figure—climbing the
long flight of weather-worn steps that go circling to the peri-
style. Dolly followed slowly : as she ascended, the lights
seemed to uprise, the columns to stand out more boldly.

'Come in,' Robert said, lifting up the heavy leather
curtain.

Dolly gave one look at the city at her feet, flashing with
the many lights and shadows of the impending storm, and
then she followed him into the great Cathedral.

They were late. The evening service was already begun,
and a voice was chanting and ringing from column to column.
' Rejoice in the Lord alway,' it sang, ' and again I say, again
I say unto you, rejoice ! rejoice ! ' A number of people were
standing round a grating, listening to the voice, but an old
verger, pleased with the looks of the two young people,
beckoned to them and showed them up a narrow stair into a
little oaken gallery, whence they could look down upon the
echoing voice and the great crowd of people listening to it ;
many lights were burning, for it was already dark within the
building. Here a light fell, there the shadow threw some
curve into sudden relief ; the rolling mist that hung beyond
the distant aisles and over the heads seemed like a veil, and
added to the mystery. The music, the fire, the arches overhead, made Dolly's heart throb. The Cathedral itself seemed
like a great holy heart beating in the midst of the city.
Once, when Dolly was a child in the green ditch, her heart
had overflowed with happiness and gratitude ; here she was a
woman, and the future had not failed her—here were love
and faith to make her life complete--all the vibration of fire

and music, and the flow of harmonious lines, to express what
was beyond words. . . .

'Oh! Robert, what have we done to be so happy?' she
whispered, when the service was over and they were coming
away in the crowd. 'It almost frightens me,' the girl said.

Robert did not hear her at first; he was looking over the
people's heads, for the clouds had come down, and the rain
was falling heavily.

'Frighten you,' said Robert presently, opening his umbrella; 'take my arm, Dolly; what is there to frighten you?
I don't suppose we are any happier than other people under
the same circumstances. Come this way; let us get out of the
crowd.'

Robert led the girl down a narrow lane closed by an iron
gate. It looked dark and indistinct, although the west still
shone with changing lights. Dolly stood up under a doorway,
while the young man walked away down the wet flags to look
for a cab to take them home. The rain fell upon the pavement, upon the stone steps where Dolly was standing, and
with fresh cheeks blooming in the mist, and eyes still alight
with the radiance and beauty of the psalm she had been
singing in her heart. 'I don't suppose we are any happier
than other people.' She wished Robert had not said that, it
seemed cold, ungrateful almost. The psalm in her ears
began to die away to the dull patter of the rain as it fell.
What was it that came to Dolly as she stood in the twilight
of the doorway—a sudden chill coming she knew not from
whence—some one light put out on the altar?

Dolly, strung to some high quivering pitch, felt a sudden
terror. It was nothing; a doubt of a doubt—a fear of a
terror—fearing what—doubting whom?

'The service was very well performed,' said Robert,

coming up. ' I have got you a cab.' He helped her in, and then, as he seated himself beside her, began again: ' We shall not have many more opportunities of attending the Cathedral service before we start.'

Dolly was very silent ; Robert talked on. He wondered at her seeming want of interest, and yet he had only talked to her about her plans and things that she must have cared to hear. ' I shall know definitely about our start to-morrow, or the day after,' he said, as the cab drew up at the door of Church House. Poor Dolly ! She let him go into the drawing-room alone, and ran up to her own little nest upstairs. The thought of the possible nearness of her departure had suddenly overwhelmed her. When it was still far off she had never thought about it. Now she sat down on the low window-sill, leant her head against the shutter, and watched the last light die out above the ivy wall. The garden shadows thickened ; the night gathered slowly ; Dolly's heart beat sadly, oh ! how sadly. What hopeless feeling was this that kept coming over her again and again ? coming she knew not from what recesses of the empty room, from behind the fleeting clouds, from the secret chambers of her traitorous heart ? The voice did not cease persecuting. ' So much of you that lives now,' it said, ' will die when you merge your life into Robert's. So much love will be more than he will want. He takes but a part of what you have to give.' The voice was so distinct that she wondered whether Marker, who came in to put away her things, would hear it. Did she love Robert ? Of course she loved him. There was his ring upon her finger. She could hear his voice sounding from the hall below. . . . Were they not going off alone together to a lonely life, across a tempestuous sea ? For a moment she stood lost, and forgetting that her feet were still upon the home-hearth and that the far-off sea was still beating upon distant shores. Then she started up impatiently, she would not listen any more. With a push to the door she shut her doubts up in the cupboard where she was used to hang her cloak, and then she came slowly down the wooden stairs to the oak-room below.

Dolly found a candle alight, a good deal of darkness, some conversation, a sofa drawn out with her mamma reposing upon it, Robert writing at a table to Mrs. Palmer's dictation.

'My child,' said Mrs. Palmer, 'come here. You have been to St. Paul's. I have been alone the whole afternoon. Your Aunt Sarah never comes near me. I am now getting this dear fellow to write and order a room for us at Kingston. I told you of my little plan. He is making all the arrangements. It is to be a little *festa* on my husband's birthday; shall we say Tuesday, if fine, Robert? The Admiral will hear of it, and understand that we do not forget him. People say I have no resentment in my nature. It is as well, perhaps, that I should leave untasted a few of the bitter dregs of my hard lot,' continued Mrs. Palmer, cheerfully. 'Have you written to Raban, Robert? My George would wish him remembered.'

'Oh, don't let us have Raban, Aunt Philippa,' said Robert. 'There will be Morgan, and George, and your little friend Rhoda will like to come,—and any one else?'

'I am thankful to say that Mrs. Morgan and those dreadful two girls are going into the country for two days; that is one reason for fixing upon Tuesday,' says Mrs. Palmer. 'I don't want them, Dolly, dearest. Really the society your poor aunt lives in is something too ludicrous. She will be furious; I have not dared tell her, poor creature. I have

accepted an invitation for you on Wednesday. Colonel
Witherington's sister, in Hyde Park Gardens, has a large
dinner-party. She has asked us all three in the kindest
manner. Colonel Witherington called himself with the note
this afternoon. I wanted him to stay to dinner. I'm afraid
your aunt was vexed. Robert, while you are about it, just
write a line for us all to Mrs. Middleton.'

Robert wrote Mrs. Palmer's notes, sealed, and stamped
them, and, betweenwhiles, gave a cheerful little description
of their expedition. 'Dolly was delighted with the service,'
said he ; ' but I am afraid she is a little tired.' Then he got
up and pulled an arm-chair for her up to the fire, and then
he went back and finished putting up Mrs. Palmer's correspondence. He was so specially kind that evening, cheerful, and nice to Mrs. Palmer, doing her behests so cleverly
and naturally, that Dolly forgot her terrors and wondered
what evil spirit had possessed her. She began to feel warm
and happy once more, and hopeful, and she was unaffectedly
sorry when Henley got up and said he must go.

He was no sooner gone and the door shut than Mrs.
Palmer said, languidly, ' I think I should like Frank Raban
to be asked, poor fellow. It will please Rhoda, at all events.
Just write, dear.'

Dolly blushed up crimson. She had not seen him since
that curious little talk she had had with George.

' But Robert doesn't wish it, mamma,' said Dolly.

' Nonsense, child. I wish it. Robert is not your husband
yet,' said Mrs. Palmer ; ' and if he were ——'

' Shall I bring you a pen and ink ? ' Dolly asked, shyly.

' Just do as I tell you, dearest,' said her mother, crossly.
' Write, " Dear Mr. Raban,—My mother desires me to write
and tell you with what pleasure she would welcome you on

Tuesday next, if you would join a small expedition we are meditating, a water-party, in honour of Admiral Palmer's 57th birthday." '

'That is not a bit like one of my letters,' said Dolly, finishing quickly. 'Where can Aunt Sarah be ? '

'I am sure I don't know, my dear. She left in the rudest manner when Witherington called. I have seen nothing of her.'

Lady Sarah was sitting upstairs alone—oh, how alone ! —in the cheerless bedroom overhead, where she used to take her griefs and her sad mistrusts. They seemed to hang from the brown faded curtains by the window; they seemed to haunt all round the bed, among its washed-out draperies ; they were ranged along the tall chimney-piece in bottles. Here is morphia and chlorodyne, or its equivalent of those days ; here is the 'linament'—linament for a strained heart! chloroform for anxious love ! Are not each one of those the relics of one or another wound, reopening again and again with the strains of the present. Sarah's hands are clasped and her head is bent forward as she sits in this half-darkness—leaden grey without, chill within—by the empty hearth. Did Robert love Dolly ? Had he love in him ? Had she been right to see him through Dolly's eyes ?

Just then the door opens, and Dolly, flushed, brightening the dull twilight, comes into the room.

'Come down directly, you wicked woman,' she says. 'You will be catching cold here all by yourself.'

SAD MUSINGS.

CHAPTER XXX.

WAVE OR FLAME.

And you have gained a ring.
What of it ? 'Tis a figure, a symbol, say
A thing's sign.

—R. Browning.

How sweet they are, those long sunset evenings on the river !
the stream, flowing by swift and rippling, reflects the sky—
sometimes, in the still glooms and depths of dying light, it
would seem as if the sky itself reflected the waters. The
distant woods stand out in bronzed shadow ; low sunset fires
burn into dusk beyond the fringe of trees ; sudden sweet
glooms fall upon the boats as they glide in and out by dim
creeks and ridges. Perhaps some barge travels past through
the twilight, drawn by horses tramping along the towing-
path, and dragging against the sky. As the boats float
shorewards, peaceful sights and sounds are all about, borne
upon the flowing water.

'I am so sorry it is over,' said Dolly, tying on her
straw hat.

The sun was setting, a little star was shining overhead,
the last bird had flown home to its nest. Robert pushed
them right through a bed of rustling reeds on their way to
the landing-place. It was crowded with dancing boats

many people were standing along the shore; the gables of
the 'Red Lion' had been all aglow for a few minutes past.
They could hear the laugh of a boating-party scrambling to
land. Here and there heads were peeping from the bridge,
from the landing-places and windows; some twinkled with
the last sunset gleams, others with lights already burning.
Dolly had been silent for the last half-hour, scarcely listening
to its desultory talk. They had exchanged broadsides with
George and John Morgan in the other boat; but by degrees
that vigorously-manned craft had outrun them, rounded a
corner, and left them floating mid-stream. Robert was in no
hurry, and Frank was absent, and sometimes almost forgot
to row. Looking up now and then, he saw Dolly's sweet face
beaming beneath her loose straw hat, with Hampton Court
and all its prim terraces for a background.

'You are not doing your share of the work, Raban,
by any means,' said Robert, labouring and not over-
pleased.

'Oh, let us float,' murmured Mrs. Palmer. She was
leaning over the side of the boat, weighing it heavily down,
and dabbling one fat white hand in the water; with the
other she was clasping Dolly's stiff young fingers. 'Truant
children!' she said, 'you don't know your own happiness.
How well I remember one evening just like this, Dolly, when
your papa and I were floating down the Hooghly; and, now
that I think of it, my Admiral Palmer was with us—he was
captain then. How little we either of us thought in those
days. The Palmers are so close one needs a lifetime to
understand their ways. I should like to show you a letter,
Mr. Raban, that I received only this morning from my sister-
in-law, Joanna—was that a fish or a little bit of stick?
Sweet calm! Robert, I am thankful you have never been

entangled by one of those ugly girls at Smokethwaite. I know Joanna and her——'

'There was never any thought, I assure you,' interrupted Robert, not displeased, and unable to refrain from disclaiming the accusation. 'My aunt has always been most kind; she would never have wished to influence my inclinations—she is very much tried just now, parting from Jonah, who joins his regiment immediately. They are coming up to London with him next Saturday.'

'Ah! I know what it is to part from one's child,' said Philippa, tapping Dolly's fingers. 'I am glad to hear Joanna shows *any* feeling. My Dolly, if it were not to Robert, who is so thoughtful, should I be able to bear the thought of parting from you? Take care—pray take care. You are running into this gentleman's boat. Push off— push off. Ah! ah! thank you, Mr. Raban. Look, there is John Morgan. I wish he were here to steer us.'

'Don't be frightened, dear,' said Dolly, still holding her mother's hand, as the little rocking-boat made towards the steps, where John Morgan was standing welcoming them all with as much heartiness as if they were returning from some distant journey, and had not met for years. Some people reserve themselves for great occasions, instead of spending their sympathies lavishly along the way. Good old John certainly never spared either sympathy or the expression of his hearty good-will. I don't know that the people, who sometimes smiled at his honest exuberances, found that he was less reliable when greater need arose, because he had been kind day after day about nothing at all. He saved Mrs. Palmer from a ducking on this occasion, as she pre- cipitately flung herself out of the boat on to his toes. Frank Raban also jumped on shore. Robert said he would take the *Sarah Anne* back to her home in the boat-house.

'Then I suppose Dolly will have to go too,' said Mrs. Palmer, archly; and Dolly, with a blush and a smile, settled herself once more comfortably on the low cushioned seat. She looked after her mother trailing up the slope, leaning on the curate's arm, and waving farewells until they passed by the garden-gate of the inn. Frank Raban was slowly following them. Then Dolly and Robert were alone, and out on the river again. The lightened boat swayed on the water. The air seemed to freshen, the ripples flowed in from a distance, the banks slid by. Robert smiled as he bent over the sculls. How often Dolly remembered the last golden hour that came to her that day before the lights had died away out of her sky, before the waters had risen, before her boat was wrecked, and Robert far away out of the reach of her voice!

There were many other people coming back to the boat-house. The men were busy, the landing was crowded, and the *Sarah Anne* had to wait her turn. Robert disliked waiting extremely. He also disliked the looks of open admiration which two canoes were casting at the *Sarah Anne*.

'There are some big stones by the shore, Dolly,' said Robert. 'Do you think you could manage to land?'

'Of course I can,' said active Dolly; 'and then you can tie the boat to that green stake just beyond them.' As she stood up to spring on shore, she looked round once more. Did some instinct tell her that this was the end of it all, and the last of the happy hours? She jumped with steady feet on to the wet stone, and stood balancing herself for a moment. The water rippled to her feet as she stood, with both hands outstretched, and her white dress fluttering, and all the light of youth and happiness in her radiant face. And then with another spring she was on land.

'Well done!' said one of the canoes. Robert turned round with a fierce look.

When he rejoined Dolly, he found her looking about in some distress.

'My ring, my pretty ring, Robert,' she said, 'I have dropped it.' It was a ring he had given her the day before. Dolly had at last consented to wear one, but this was large for her finger.

'You careless girl,' said Robert; 'here are your gloves and your handkerchief. Do you know what that ring cost?'

'Oh, don't tell me,' said Dolly; 'something dreadful, I know.' And she stood penitently watching Robert scrambling back into the boat, and overthrowing and thumping the cushions. And yet, as she stood there, it came into her mind how many treasures were hers just then, and that of them all a ring was that which she could best bear to lose.

One of the canoes had come close into shore by this time, and the young man, who was paddling with his two spades, called out, saying, 'Are you looking for anything? Is it for this?' and carefully putting his hand into the water he pulled out something shining. The ring had dropped off Dolly's finger as she jumped, and was lying on a stone that was half in and half out of the water, and near to the big one upon which she had been standing.

'How very fortunate!' exclaimed Henley from the boat.

Miss Vanborough was pleased to get back her pretty trinket, and thanked the young man with a very becoming blush.

'It is a very handsome coral,' Robert said; 'it would have been a great pity to lose it. We must have it made smaller, Dora. It must not come off again.'

Dolly was turning it round thoughtfully and looking at the Medusa head carved and set in gold.

'Robert,' she said once more, 'does happiness never frighten you?'

'Never,' said Henley, smiling, as she looked up earnestly into his face.

The old town at Kingston, with its many corners and gables, has something of the look of a foreign city heaped upon the river-side. The garden of the old inn runs down with terraces to the water. A side-door leads to the boat-houses. By daylight this garden is somewhat mouldy; but spiders' webs do not obtrude on summer evenings, and the Londoners who have come out of town for a breath of fresh air, stroll along the terraces, and watch the stream as it flows, unconscious of their serenity. They come here of summer evenings, and sit out in the little arbours, or walk along the terraces and watch the boats drift with the stream. If they look to the opposite banks they may see the cattle rearing their horned heads upon the sunset, and the distant chestnut groves and galleries of Hampton Court at the bend of the river.

Near the corner of one of these terraces, a little green weather-cocked summer-house stands boldly facing the re-gattas in their season, and beyond it again are a steep bank and some steps to a second terrace, from whence there is the side-door leading to the boats.

On this particular evening Frank Raban came quietly zigzagging along these terraces, perhaps with some vague hope of meeting Dorothea on her return.

There are some years of one's life when one is less alive than at others, as there are different degrees of strength and power to live in the course of the same existence. Frank was not in the despairing state in which we first knew him, but he was not yet as other people are, and in hours of depression such as this, he was used to feel lonely and apart. He was used to see other people happy, anxious, busy, hurrying after one another, and he would look on as now, with his hands in his pockets, not indifferent, but feeling as if Fate had put him down solitary and silent, into the world— a dumb note (so he used to think) in the great music. And yet he knew that the music was there—that mighty human vibration which exists independent of all the dumb notes, cracked instruments, rifted lutes, and broken lyres of which we hear so much, and he had but to open his ears to it.

Two voices, anything but dumb, were talking inside the little summer-house. Raban had scarcely noticed them as he came along, listening with the vaguest curiosity, as people do, to reproaches and emotions which do not concern them; but presently, as he approached the summer-house, a tone struck him familiarly, and at the same instant he saw a dark figure rush wildly from the little wooden house, and leap right over the side of the terrace on to the path below; and then Frank recognised the frantic action—it could only be George. A moment afterwards a woman— he knew her too—came out of the summer-house and stood for an instant panting against the doorway, leaning with her two hands against the lintel. She looked pale, troubled; her hair was pushed back from her white face; her eyes looked dark, beautiful. Never before had Raban seen Rhoda (for it was Rhoda) so moved. When she saw him

a faint flush came into her cheeks. She came forward a
few steps, then she stopped short again.

She was dragging her silk mantle, which had fallen off.
One end was trailing after her along the gravel.

'Mr. Raban, is that you?' she said, in an agitated way.
'Why did you come? Is it—is it nearly time to go? Is
Mrs. Palmer come back? Oh, *please* take me to her!' And
then she suddenly burst into tears, and the long black silk
mantle fell to the ground as she put out two fluttering
hands.

Raban had flung his cigar over the terrace after George.

'What is it?' he said, anxiously. 'Can I help you in
any way? What has happened?'

The young man spoke kindly, but in his usual matter-
of-fact voice; and Rhoda, even in her distress, wondered at
his coldness. No one before ever responded so calmly to
whom she had appealed.

'Oh, you don't know,' she said; 'I can't tell you.' And
the poor little hands went up again with a desperate
gesture.

Raban was very much touched; but, as I have said, he
had little power of showing his sympathy, and, foolish
fellow, doing unto others as he would be done by; he only
said, 'I have guessed something before now, Miss Parnell.
I wish I could help you, with all my heart. Does not Miss
Vanborough know of this? Cannot *she* advise? . . .'

Rhoda was in no mood to hear her friend's praises just
then.

'Dolly,' cried Rhoda, passionately, 'she would have every
one sacrificed to George. I *would* love him if I could,'
she said, piteously, 'but how *can* I? he frightens me and
raves at me; how can I love him? Oh! Mr. Raban, tell

me that it is not wrong to feel thus?' And once more the
fluttering hands went up, and the dark wistful eyes gazed
childishly, piteously into his face. Rhoda was looking to
Frank for the help that should have come to her from her
own heart; she dimly felt that she must win him over, that
if he would he could help her.

Rhoda pitied herself sincerely, she sobbed out her history
to Frank with many tears. 'How can I tell them all?'
she said; 'it will only make wretchedness, and now it is
only I who am unhappy.'

Was it only Rhoda who was unhappy? George, flying
along the garden half distracted, aching, repentant, might
have told another story. She had sent him away. He
would do nothing that she wished, she said, he would not
accept the independence that Lady Sarah had offered him,
Rhoda did not believe in his love, she only wanted him to
go, to leave her. Yes, she meant it. And poor George had
rushed away frantic and indignant. He did not care where
he went. He had some vague idea that he would get a
boat and row away for ever, but as he was hurrying headlong
towards the boat-house he saw Dorothea and Robert coming
arm-in-arm up the little path, and he turned and hurried
back towards the inn. Dolly called to him, but he did not
answer. Rhoda had sent him away, poor Dolly could not
call him back. Robert shrugged his shoulders.

'Why do you do that?' said Dolly, annoyed; 'he looked
quite ill.'

T

CHAPTER XXXI.

A BOAT UPON THE WATER.

Ich stand gelehnet an den Mast,
Und zählte jede Welle.
Ade! mein schönes Vaterland,
Mein Schiff, das segelt schnelle!

Ich kam schon Liebchen's Haus vorbei,
Die Fensterscheiben blinken;
Ich guck' mir fast die Augen aus,
Doch will mir Niemand winken.

Ihr Thränen bleibt mir aus dem Aug,
Dass ich nicht dunkel sehe.
Mein krankes Herz, brich mir nicht
Vor allzugrossem Wehe!
—HEINE.

GEORGE was shivering and sick at heart; the avenue led to a door that opened into the bar of the hotel, and George went in and called for some brandy. The spirits seemed to do him good; no one seeing a clumsy young fellow in a boating dress tossing off one glassful of brandy after another would have guessed at all the grief and passion that were tearing at his poor foolish heart. Rhoda had sent him away. Had he deserved this? Could not she read the truth? Poor timid faithless little thing. Why had he been so fierce to her, why had he told her he was jealous? George had a curious quickness of divination about others, although he

was blind about his own concerns. He had reproached
Rhoda because she had been talking to Frank, but he knew
well enough that Frank did not care for Rhoda. Poor
child, did she know how it hurt him when she shrank from
him and seemed afraid? Ah! she would not have been so
cruel if she had known all. Thinking of it all he felt as if
he had had some little bird in his rough grasp, frightened
it, and hurt its wings. Then he suddenly said to himself
that he would go back and find his poor frightened bird and
stroke it and soothe it, ask it to forgive him. And then he
left the place, and as hastily as he had entered; there was a
last glass of brandy untasted on the counter, and he hurried
back towards the terrace. He passed the window of the
room where Mrs. Palmer was ordering tea from the sofa.
Dolly, who had just come in, saw him pass by; she did not
like his looks, and ran out after him, although both Robert
and her mother called her back. George did not see her
this time; he flew past the family groups sitting out in the
warm twilight; he came to the terrace where he had been a
few minutes before, and where the two were still standing—
Raban, of whom he had said he was jealous, Rhoda, whom
he loved—the two were slowly advancing, Frank's square
shoulders dark against the light and Rhoda's slight figure
bending forward; she was talking to Raban as she had so
often talked to George himself, with that language of earnest
eyes, tremulous tones, shrinking movements—how well he
knew it all. What was she saying? Was she appealing to
Frank to protect her from his love and despair, from the
grief that she had done her best to bring about? Rhoda
laid her hand upon Raban's arm in her agitation.

It maddened George beyond bearing, and he stamped
his heavy foot upon the gravel. Some people passing up

from the boats stared at him, but went on their way; and
Frank, looking up, saw George coming up swinging his
angry arms; his eyes were fierce, his hat was pushed aside.
He put Rhoda aside very gently, and took a step forward
between her and George, who stood for a minute looking
from one to another, as if he did not understand, and then
he suddenly burst out, with a fierce oath : ' Who told you to
put yourself in my way ? ' And, as he spoke, he struck a
heavy blow straight at Raban, who had barely time to parry
it with his arm.

It was an instant's anger—one of those fatal minutes
that undo days and months and years that have gone before ;
and that blow of George's struck Rhoda's feeble little fancy
for him dead on the spot, as she gave a shrill cry of ' For
shame ! ' and sprang forward, and would have clung to
Raban's arm. That blow ached for many and many a day
in poor Dorothea's heart, for she saw it all from a turn
of the path. As for Frank, he recovered himself in an
instant.

' Go back, George,' he said; ' I will speak to you
presently.'

He did not speak angrily. His voice and the steady
look of his resolute eyes seemed to sober the poor reprobate.
Not so Rhoda's cry of, ' Go, yes go, for shame ! '

' Go ! What is it to you if I go or stay ? Am I in your
way ? ' shouts George. ' Have you promised to marry him
too ? Have you tortured him too, and driven him half mad,
and then—and then —— Oh, Rhoda, do you really wish me
gone ? ' he cried, breaking down.

There was a tone in his voice that touched Raban, for
whom the cry was not intended. Nothing would have
melted Rhoda just then. She was angry beyond all power

of expression. She wanted him gone, she wanted him silent; she felt as if she hated him.

'You are not yourself; you are not speaking the truth,' said the girl, in a hard voice, drawing herself up. Then, as she spoke, all the brandy and all the fury seemed to mount once more into George's head.

'I am myself, and that is why I leave you,' he shouts; 'you are heartless: you have neither love nor charity in you, and now I leave you. Do you hear me?' he cried, getting louder and louder.

Any one could hear. Dolly could hear as she came hurrying up from the end of the terrace to the spot where her poor boy stood shouting out his heart's secret to unwilling ears. More than one person had stopped to listen to the angry voice. The placid stillness of. the evening seemed to carry its echo along the dusky garden bowers, out upon the water flowing down below. Some boatmen had stopped to listen; one or two people were coming up through the twilight.

'He is not sober,' said Rhoda to Dolly. She spoke with a sort of cold disgust.

Dolly hardly heard her at the time. All she saw then was her poor George, with his red angry face—Frank trying to pacify him. Should she ever forget the miserable scene? For long years after it used to rise before her; she used to dream of it at night—of the garden, the river, the figures advancing in the dark.

Dolly ran up to her brother, and instinctively put out her arms as if to shield him from every one.

'Come, dear; come with me,' she said flurriedly; 'don't let them see you like this.'

'It would shock their elegant susceptibilities,' cries the

irrepressible George; 'it don't shock them to see a woman playing fast-and-loose with a poor wretch who would have given his life for her—yes, his life, and his love, and his heart's blood!'

Dolly had got her arms tight round George by this time. She had a shrinking dread of Henley seeing him so—he might be coming, she thought.

'Robert might see you. Oh, George, please come,' she whispered, still clinging to him; and suddenly, to Dolly's surprise, George collapsed, with a sigh. His furious fit was over, and he let his sister lead him where she would.

'Go down by the river-side,' said Raban, coming after them; 'there are too many people the other way.' He spoke in a grave, anxious tone, and as the brother and sister went their way, he looked after them for a moment. Dolly had got her arm fast linked in George's. The young man was walking listlessly by her side. They neither of them looked back; they went down the steps and disappeared.

The place was all deserted by this time; the disturbance being over, the boatmen had gone on their way. The two went and sat down upon a log which had been left lying near the water-side; they were silent; they could see each other's faces, but little more. He sat crouching over with his chin resting on his hands. Dolly was full of compassion, and longing to comfort; but how could she comfort? Such pain as his was not to be eased by words spoken by another person. When George began to speak at last, his voice sounded so sad and so jarred from its usual sweetness that Dorothea was frightened, as if she could hear in it the echo of a coming trouble.

'I wanted that woman to love me,' he said. 'Dolly, you don't know how I loved her.' He was staring at the stream with his starting eyes, and biting his nails. 'We have no luck, either of us,' he said; 'I don't deserve any, but you do. Tell Frank I'm sorry I struck him; she had made me half mad; she looks at me with those great eyes of hers, and says, "Go!" and she makes me mad: she does it to them all. . . . But now I have left her! left her! left her!' repeated ugly George, with a sort of sob. 'What does she care?' and he got up and shook himself, as a big dog might have done, and went out a step into the twilight, and then came back.

'Thank you, old Dolly, for your goodness,' he said, standing before her. 'I can't face them all again, and Robert with his confounded supercilious airs. I beg your pardon, Dolly; don't look angry. I see how good you are, and I see,' he said, staring her full in the face, 'that we have been both running our heads against a wall.'

He walked on a little way, and Dolly followed. She could not answer him just then. She felt with a pang that George and Robert would never be friends; that she must love them apart; even in heart she must keep them asunder.

They had come to the place where not an hour ago she had jumped ashore. The boat was still there, as they had left it—tied to the stake. The boatmen were at supper, and had not yet taken it in. 'What are you doing?' said Dolly, as George stopped, and began to untie the rope; 'George, be careful.'

'The fresh air will do me good,' he said; 'don't be afraid; I'll take care, if you wish it;' then he nodded, and got into the boat, where the sculls were lying, and he began to shove off with a rattle of the keel upon the shore. 'I will leave the boat at Teddington,' he said, 'and walk home. Good-night! good-by!' he said. A boatman hearing the voices, came out of the boat-house close by, and while Dolly was explaining, the boat started off with a dull plash of oars falling upon dark waters. George was rowing very slowly, his head was turned towards the garden of the inn. There were lights in the windows, and figures coming and going; the water swirled against the wall of the terrace; the scent of the rhododendrons seemed to fill the air and to stifle him as he passed; a bird chirped from the darkness of some over-hanging bushes. He could hear his mother's voice: 'Robert! it is getting late; why don't they come in to tea? I must say it is nasty stuff, and not to compare to that delicious Rangoon flavour.' He paused for a moment; her voice died away, and then all was silent. The evening was growing chill; some mists were rising. George felt the cool damp wind against his hot brow as he rowed doggedly on—past the lights of the windows of the inn, past the town, under the darkness of the bridge.

He left them all behind, and his life and his love, he thought, and his mad passion; and himself, and Dolly, and Rhoda, and all the hopeless love he longed for and that was never to be his. There were other things in life. So he rowed away into the darkness with mixed anger and peace in his heart. What would Rhoda say when she heard he was gone? Nothing much! He knew her well enough to know that Dolly would understand, but her new ties would part them more entirely than absence or silence.

There is a song of Schubert's I once heard a great singer sing. As she sang, the dull grey river flowed through the room, the bright lamp-lit walls opened out, the mists of a closing darkness surrounded us, the monotonous beat of the rowlocks kept time to the music, and the man rowed away, and silence fell upon the waters.

So Dolly stood watching the boat as it disappeared along the dark wall; for a time she thought she heard the plash of the oars out upon the water, and a dark shade gliding away past the wharves, and the houses that crowd down to the shore.

She was saying her prayers for her poor boy as she walked back slowly to join the others. Robert met her with a little remonstrance for having hidden away so long. She took his arm and clung to it for a minute, trembling, with her heart beating. 'Oh! Robert; you won't let things come between us?' said the girl greatly moved; 'my poor George is so unhappy. He is to blame, but Rhoda has been hard upon him. Have you guessed it all?' 'My dear Dolly,' said Robert, gravely, 'Rhoda has told us everything. She is most justly annoyed. She is quite overcome. She has just gone home with her uncle, and I must say. . . .' 'Don't, don't say anything,' said Dolly, passionately bursting into tears, and her heart went out after her poor George rowing away along the dark river.

CHAPTER XXXII.

TRUST ME.

'How tired we feel, my heart and I!
—E. B. Browning.

The much-talked-of tea was standing, black as the waters of oblivion, in the teapot when they rejoined Mrs. Palmer. Philippa was sitting tête-à-tête with Raban, and seemed chiefly perturbed at having been kept waiting, and because John Morgan had carried off Rhoda.

'I can't think why he did it,' said Mrs. Palmer, crossly; 'it is much pleasanter all keeping together, and it is too silly of that little Rhoda to make such a disturbance. As if George would have said anything to annoy her with all of us present. Tell me, what did really happen, Robert? Why was I not sent for?'

'I am afraid George was a good deal to blame,' said Robert, in a confidential voice. 'I only came up after the fracas, but, from what I hear, I am afraid he had been drinking at the bar. Dolly can tell you more than I can, for she was present from the beginning.'

Dolly was silent: she could not speak. Frank looked at her and saw her blush painfully. He was glad that Miss Vanborough should be spared any farther explication, and

that Mrs. Palmer beckoned him into a window to tell him
that the Admiral had the greatest horror of intemperance,
and that she remembered a fearful scene with a kitmutghar
who had drained off a bottle of her eau-de-Cologne. 'Dear
George, unfortunately, was of an excitable disposition. As
for the poor Admiral, he is perfectly ungovernable when he
is roused,' said Mrs. Palmer, in her heroic manner. 'I have
seen strong men like yourself, Mr. Raban, turn pale before
him. I remember a sub-lieutenant trembling like an aspen
leaf: he had neglected to call my carriage. Is it not time
to be off? Dolly, what have I done with my little blue
shawl? You say George is *not* coming?'

'Here is your little blue shawl, mamma,' said Dolly,
wearily. She was utterly dispirited: she could not understand her mother's indifference, nor Robert's even flow of
conversation: she forgot that they did not either of them
realise how serious matters had been.

'It is really too naughty of George,' was all that Mrs.
Palmer said; 'and, now that I think of it, he certainly told
me he might have to go back to Cambridge to-night, so we
may not see him again. Mr. Raban, if you see him, tell
him —— But, I forgot,' with a gracious smile, 'we meet
you to-morrow at the Middletons'. Robert tells me my
brother and his family are come to town this week. It will
be but a painful meeting I fear. Dolly, remind me to call
there in the morning. They have taken a house in Dean's
Yard, of all places. And there is Madame Frisette at nine.
How tiresome those dressmakers are.'

'Is Madame Frisette at work for Dorothea?' asked
Robert, with some interest.

Dolly did not reply, nor did she seem to care whether
Madame Frisette was at work or not. She sat leaning back

in her corner, with two hands lying listless in her lap, pale through the twilight. Frank Raban, as he looked at her, seemed to know, almost as if she had told him in words, what was passing in her mind. His jealous intuition made him understand it all; he knew too, as well as if Robert had spoken, something of what he was *not* feeling. They went rolling on through the dusk, between villas and dim hedges and. nursery-gardens, beyond which the evening shadows were passing; and all along the way it seemed to Dolly that she could hear George's despairing voice ringing beyond the mist, and, haunted by this echo, she could scarcely listen with any patience to her companion's ripple of small talk, to Mrs. Palmer's anecdotes of Captains and Colonels and anticipation of coming gaiety and emotions. What a season was before her! The Admiral's return, Dolly's marriage, Lady Henley's wearing insinuations—she dreaded to think of it all.

'You must call for us to-morrow at half-past seven, Robert, and take us to the Middletons'. I couldn't walk into the room alone with Dolly. I suppose Joanna, too, will be giving some at-homes. I shall have to go, however little inclined I may feel.'

'It is always well to do what other people do,' said Robert; 'it answers much best in the long run.'

He did not see Dolly's wondering look. Was this the life Dolly had dreamt of? a sort of wheel of commonplace to which poor unquiet souls were to be bound, confined by platitudes, and innumerable threads, and restrictions, and silences. She had sometimes dreamt of something more meaningful and truer, something responding to her own nature, a life coming straighter from the heart. She had not counted much on happiness. Perhaps she had been too happy to wish for happiness; but to-night it occurred to her again what life might be—a life with a truth in it and a genuine response and a nobler scheme than any she had hitherto realised.

Frank heard a sigh coming from her corner. They were approaching the street where he wanted to be set down, and he, too, had something in his mind, which he felt he must say before they parted. As he wished Dorothea good-night he found a moment to say, in a low voice, 'I hope you may be able to tell Lady Sarah everything that has happened, without reserve. Do trust me. It will be best for all your sakes;' and then he was gone before Dolly could answer.

'What did he say?' said Robert Henley. 'Are you warm enough, Dolly? Will you have a shawl?'

He spoke so affectionately that she began to wonder whether it was because they were not alone that he had been cold and disappointing.

They reached the house, and old Sam came to the door, and Robert helped to unpack the wrecks of the day's pleasures—the hampers, and umbrellas, and armfuls of crumpled muslins. Then the opportunity came for Robert to be impulsive if he chose, for Mrs. Palmer floated upstairs with her candle to say good-night to Lady Sarah. She was kissing her hand over the banisters, and dropping all the wax as she went along.

Robert came up to Dolly, who was standing in the hall. 'Good-night,' he said. 'It might have been a pleasant day upon the whole if it had not been for George. You must get him to apologise to Rhoda, Dora. I mean to speak very plainly to him when I see him next.'

His calmness exasperated her as he stood there with his

handsome face looking down a little reproachfully at her
flushed cheeks and sparkling eyes.

'Speaking won't do a bit of good, Robert,' she said,
hastily. 'Pray don't say much to him ——'

'I wonder when you will learn to trust me, Dora,' said
her cousin taking her hand. 'How shall we ever get on
unless you do?'

'I am sure I don't know,' Dolly answered, wearily; 'we
don't seem to want the same things, Robert, or to be
going together a bit.'

'What do you mean?' said Henley. 'You are tired
and out of spirits to-night.'

With a sudden reaction Dolly caught hold of his arm,
with both hands. 'Robert! Robert! Robert!' she said,
holding him fast and looking as if she could transform him
with her eyes to be what she wanted.

'Silly child,' he answered, 'I don't think you yourself
know what you want. Good-night. Don't forget to be ready
in time to-morrow.'

Then he was gone, having first looked for his umbrella,
and the door banged upon Robert and the misty stars, and
Dolly remained standing at the foot of the stairs. Frank
Raban's words had borne fruit as sensible words should do.
'Trust me,' he had said; and Henley had used the same
phrase, only with Robert 'Trust me' meant believe that I
cannot be mistaken; with Frank 'Trust me' meant trust
in truth in yourself and in others. Dolly, with one of those
quick impulses which come to impressionable people, suddenly
felt that he was right. All along she had been mistaken.
It would have been better, far better, from the beginning,
to have told Lady Sarah everything. She had been blinded,
over-persuaded. Marker came up to shut bolts and put out

the lights. Dolly looked up, and she went and laid her tired head on the old nurse's shoulder, and clung to her for an instant.

'Is anything the matter, my dearie?' said Marker.

'Nothing new,' Dolly said. 'Marker, George is not come home. I have so much to say to him! Don't bolt the door, and please leave a light.'

But George did not come home that night, although the door was left unbolted and the light kept burning on purpose. When the morning came his bed was folded smooth, and everything looked straight and silent in his room, which was orderly as places are when the people are away who inhabit them.

CHAPTER XXXIII.

CIRCUMSTANCE.

Tho largost minds, still oarthward bont, aro small,
Who, knowing much, aro ignorant of all.
　　　　　　　—HAMILTON AÏDÉ.

FOR some days before the picnic Mrs. Palmer and Julie had
been absorbed in the preparation of two beautiful garments
that were to be worn at Mrs. Middleton's dinner, and at a ball
at Bucklersbury House, for which Mrs. Palmer was expecting
an invitation. Lady Sarah had written at her request to ask
for one. Meanwhile the dresses had been growing under
Julie's art; throwing out fresh flounces and trimmings, and
ribbons, hour by hour, until they had finally come to perfection, and were now lying side by side on the bed in the
spare room, ready to be tried on for the last time.

'Must it be *now*, mamma?' said Dolly. 'Breakfast is
just ready, and Aunt Sarah will be waiting.'

'Julie, go downstairs and beg Lady Sarah not to wait,'
said Mrs. Palmer, with great decision.

Julie came back, saying that Miss Rhoda was with Lady
Sarah below, and asking for Miss Dolly.

'Presently,' said Mrs. Palmer. 'Very pretty, indeed,
Julie!' Then she suddenly exclaimed, 'You cannot imagine
what it is, Dolly, to be linked to one so utterly uncongenial,

you who are so fortunate in our dear Robert's perfect sympathy and knowledge of London life. He quite agrees with me in my wish that you should be introduced. Admiral Palmer hates society, except to preach at it—such a pity, is it not! I assure you, strange as it may seem, I quite dread his return.'

Dolly stood bolt upright, scarcely conscious of the dress or the pins, or her mother's monologue. She was still thinking over the great determination she had come to. George had not come back, but Dolly had made up her mind to tell Lady Sarah everything. She was not afraid; it was a relief to have the matter settled. She would say no word to injure him. It was she who had been to blame throughout. Her reflections were oddly intermingled with snips and pricks other than those of her conscience. Once, as Julie ran a pin into her arm, she thought how strange it was that Mr. Raban should have guessed everything all along. Dolly longed and feared to have her explanation over.

' Have you nearly done ? Let me go down, Julie,' said Dolly, becoming impatient at last.

But Julie still wanted to do something to the set of the sleeve.

And while Julie was pinning poor Dolly down, the clock struck nine, and the time was over, and Dolly's opportunity was lost for ever. It has happened to us all. When she opened the dining-room door at last she knew in one instant that it was too late.

The room seemed full of people. Lady Sarah was there; Mrs. Morgan bristling by the window; Rhoda was there, kneeling at Lady Sarah's knee, in some agitation : her bonnet had fallen off, her hair was all curling and rough. She started up as Dolly came in, and ran to meet her.

U

'Oh! Dolly,' she said, 'come, come,' and she seized both her hands. 'I have told Lady Sarah everything; she knows all. Oh! why did we not confide in her long ago?' and Rhoda burst into tears. 'Oh, I feel how wrong we have been,' she sobbed.

'Rhoda has told me everything, Dolly,' said Lady Sarah, in a cold voice—'everything that those whom I trusted implicitly saw fit to conceal from me.'

Was it Aunt Sarah who had spoken in that cold harsh-sounding tone?

'Rhoda has acted by my advice, and with my full approval,' said Mrs. Morgan, stepping forward. 'She is not one to look back once her hand is to the plough. When I had seen George's letter—it was lying on the table—I said at once that no time should be lost in acquainting your aunt, Dolly. It is inconceivable to me that you have not done so before. We started immediately after our eight-o'clock breakfast, and all is now clearly understood, I trust, Lady Sarah; Rhoda's frankness will be a lesson to Dolly.'

Poor Dolly! she was stiff, silent, overwhelmed. She looked appealingly at her aunt, but Lady Sarah looked away. What could she say? how was it that she was there a culprit while Rhoda stood weeping and forgiven? Rhoda who had enforced the silence, Rhoda now taking merit for her tardy frankness! while George was gone; and Dolly in disgrace.

'Indeed, Aunt Sarah, I would have told you everything,' cried the girl, very much agitated, 'only Rhoda herself made me promise ——'

'Dolly! you never promised,' cried Rhoda. 'But we were all wrong,' she burst out with fresh penitence; 'only, Lady Sarah knows all, and we shall be happier now,' she said, wiping her eyes.

'Happy in right-doing,' interrupted Mrs. Morgan.

'Have we done wrong, Aunt Sarah? Forgive us,' said Dolly, with a touching ring in her voice.

Lady Sarah did not answer. She was used to her nephew's misdeeds, but that Dolly—her own Dolly—should have been the one to plot against her cut the poor lady to the heart. She could not speak. 'And Dolly knew it all the time,' she had said to Rhoda a minute before Dolly came in. 'Yes, she knew it,' said Rhoda. 'She wished it, and feared ——' Here Rhoda blushed very red. 'George told me she feared that you might not approve and do for him as you might otherwise have done. Oh! Lady Sarah, what injustice we have done you!'

'Perhaps Dolly would wish to see the letter,' said Mrs. Morgan, offering her a paper; there was no mistaking the cramped writing. There was no date nor beginning to the note :—

I have been awake all night thinking over what has happened. It is not your fault that you do not know what love is, nor what a treasure I have wasted upon you. I have given you my best, and to you it is worthless. You can't realise such love as mine. You will not even understand the words that I am writing to you: but it is not your fault, any more than it is mine, that I cannot help loving you. Oh, Rhoda, you don't care so much for my whole life's salvation as I do for one moment's peace of mind for you. I see it now—I understand all now. Forgive me if I am hurting you, for the sake of all you have made me suffer. I feel as if I could no longer bear my life here. I must go, and yet I must see you once more. You need not be afraid that I should say anything to frighten or distress you. Your terror of me has pained me far more than you have any conception of. God bless you. I had rather your hands smote me than that another blessed.

'It is most deplorable that a young man of George's ability should write such nonsense,' said Mrs. Morgan.

Poor Dolly flushed up and began to tremble. Her heart ached for her poor George's trouble.

'It is not nonsense,' she said, passionately; 'people call

what they cannot feel themselves nonsense. Aunt Sarah, you understand, though they don't. You must see how unhappy he is. How can Rhoda turn against him now? How can she after all that has passed? What harm has he done? It was not wicked to love her more than she loved him.'

'Do you see no cruelty in all this long deception?' said Lady Sarah, with two red spots burning in her cheeks. 'You must both have had some motive for your silence. Have I ever shown myself cold or unfeeling to you?' and the flushed face was turned away from her.

'It was not for herself, Lady Sarah,' said Mrs. Morgan, wishing to see justice done. 'No doubt she did not wish to injure George's prospects.'

Dolly was silent. She had some dim feeling of what was in Lady Sarah's mind; but it was a thought she put aside—it seemed unworthy of them both. She was ashamed to put words to it.

If Dolly and her aunt had only been alone all might have been well, and the girl might have made Lady Sarah understand how true she had been to her and loyal at heart, although silent from circumstances. Dolly looked up with wistful speaking eyes, and Lady Sarah almost understood their mute entreaty.

The words of love are all but spoken when some one else speaks other words; the hands long to grasp each other, and other fingers force them asunder. Alas! Rhoda stood weeping between them, and Mrs. Palmer now appeared in an elegant morning wrapper.

'My dearest child, Madame Frisette is come and is waiting,' said Dolly's mamma, sinking into a chair. 'She is a delightful person, but utterly reckless for trimmings. How do you do, Mrs. Morgan; why do you not persuade Lady Sarah to let Madame Frisette take her pattern, and—— ? '

But, as usual, Lady Sarah, freezing under Mrs. Palmer's sunny influence, got up and left the room.

Rhoda, tearful and forgiven, remained for some time giving her version of things to Mrs. Palmer. She had come to speak to Lady Sarah by her aunt's advice. Aunt Morgan had opened George's letter as it lay upon the breakfast-table, and had been as much surprised as Rhoda herself by its contents. They had come to talk things over with Lady Sarah, to tell her of all that had been making Rhoda so unhappy of late.

' I thought she and you, Mrs. Palmer, would have advised me and told me what was right to do,' said the girl, with dark eyes brimming over. ' How can I help it if he loves me ? I know that he might have looked higher.'

' The boy is perfectly demented,' said Mrs. Palmer, ' to dream of marrying. He has not a sixpence, my dear child —barely enough to pay his cab-hire. He has been most ridiculous. How we shall ever persuade Lady Sarah to pay his debts I cannot imagine ! Dolly will not own to it, but we all know that she does not like parting with her money. I do hope and trust she has made her will, for she looks a perfect wreck.'

' Oh, mamma ! ' entreated poor Dolly.

Mrs. Palmer paid no heed, except to say crossly, ' I do wish you had shown a little common sense. Dolly, you have utterly injured your prospects. Robert will be greatly an-noyed ; he counts so much upon dear Sarah's affection for you both. As for me, I have been disappointed far too often to count upon anything. By the way, Dolly, I wish you

would go up and ask your aunt whether that invitation has
come to Bucklersbury House.   Go, child; why do you look
so vacant ? '

Poor Dolly !   One by one all those she trusted most
seemed to be failing and disappointing her.   Hitherto Dolly
had idealised them all.   She shrank to learn that love and
faith must overcome evil with good, and that this is their
reward even in this life, and that to love those who love you
is not the whole of its experience.

Rhoda's letter, miserable as it was, had relieved Dolly
from much of her present anxiety about George.   That
hateful dark river no longer haunted her.   He was unhappy,
but he was safe on shore.   All the same, everything seemed
dull, and sad, and undefined that afternoon, and Robert
coming in, found her sitting in the oak-room window with
her head resting on her hand and her work lying in her lap.
She had taken up some work, but as she set the stitches, it
seemed to her,—it was but a fancy—that with each stitch
George was going farther and farther away, and she dropped
her work at last into her lap, and reasoned herself into some
composure; only when her lover came in cheerfully and
talking with the utmost ease and fluency, her courage failed
her suddenly.

' What is the matter; why do you look so unhappy ? '
said Robert.

' Nothing is the matter,' said Dolly, ' only most things
seem going wrong, Robert; and I have been wrong, and
there is nothing to be done.'

' What is the use of making yourself miserable ? ' said
Robert, good-naturedly scolding her; ' you are a great deal
too apt, Dolly, to trouble yourself unnecessarily.   You must
forgive me for saying so.   This business between George

and Rhoda is simply childish, and there is nothing in it to distress you.'

'Do you think that nothing is unhappiness,' said Dolly, going on with her own thought, 'unless it has a name and a definite shape?'

'I really don't know,' said Henley. 'It depends upon . . . What is this invitation, Dora? You don't mean to say the Duchess has not sent one yet?' he said in a much more interested voice.

'There is only the card for Aunt Sarah. I am afraid mamma is vexed, and it is settled that I am not to go.'

'Not to go?' Robert cried; 'my dear Dolly, of course you must go; it is absolutely necessary you should be seen at one or two good houses, after all the second-rate society you have been frequenting lately. Where is your mother?'

When Mrs. Palmer came in, in her bonnet, languid and evidently out of temper, and attended by Colonel Witherington, Robert immediately asked, in a heightened tone of voice, whether it was true that Dolly was not to be allowed to go to the ball.

Philippa replied in her gentlest accents that no girl should be seen without her mother. If an invitation came for them both, everything was ready; and, even at the last moment, she should be willing to take Dorothea to Bucklersbury House.

'Too bad,' said the Colonel, sitting heavily down in Lady Sarah's chair. 'A conspiracy, depend upon it. They don't wish for too much counter-attraction in a certain quarter.'

'One never knows what to think,' said Mrs. Palmer, thoughtfully; 'I have left a card this afternoon, Robert, upon which I wrote a few words in pencil, to explain my connection with Sarah. I wished to show that I at least was not unacquainted with the usages of civilised society. Kindly hand me that *Peerage.*'

'My dear Aunt Philippa,' cried Robert, walking up and down in a state of the greatest perturbation, 'what induced you to do such a preposterous thing? What will the Duchess think of us all?'

Mrs. Palmer, greatly offended, replied that she could not allow Robert to speak to her in such disrespectful tones. The Duchess might think what she chose; Dolly should not go without her.

CHAPTER XXXIV.

WHITE ROSES.

If thou must love me, let it be for nought
Except for love's sake only.

SOME one sent Dolly a great bunch of white roses that afternoon ; they came in with a late breath of summer—shining
white with dark leaves and stems—and, as Dolly bent her
head over the soft zones, breathing their sweet breath, it
seemed to carry her away into cool depths of fragrance. The
roses seemed to come straight from some summer garden,
from some tranquil place where all was peace and silence. As
she stood, holding them in her two hands, the old garden at
All Saints' came before her, and the day when Robert first
told her that he loved her. How different things seemed
already—the roses only were as sweet as she remembered
them. Every one seemed changed since then—Robert
himself most of all ; and if she was herself disappointed, was
she not as changed as the rest ?

But these kind, dear roses had come to cheer her,
and to remind her to be herself, of all that had gone
before. How good of Robert to think of them ! She wished
they had come before he left, that she might have thanked
him. She now remembered telling him, as they were

driving down to the river, that no roses were left in their garden.

'Very pretty,' said her mother. 'Take them away, Dolly; they are quite overpowering. You know, Colonel Witherington, how much better people understand these things at Trincomalee : and what quantities of flowers I used to receive there. Even the Admiral once ordered in six dozen lemon-shrubs in tubs for my fête. As for the people in this country, they don't do things by halves, but by quarters, my dear Colonel.'

Mrs. Palmer was still agitated, nor did she regain her usual serenity until about six o'clock, when, in answer to a second note from Lady Sarah, the persecuted Duchess sent a blank card for Mrs. Palmer to fill up herself if she chose.

When Dolly came to say good-night to Lady Sarah she held her-roses in her hand : some of the leaves shook down upon her full white skirts; it was late in the summer, and the sweet heads hung languid on their stalks. They were the last roses that Dolly wore for many and many a day.

'So you are going,' said Lady Sarah.

'Yes,' said Dolly, waiting for one word, one sign to show that she was forgiven : she stood with sun-gilt hair in the light of the western window. 'Dear Aunt Sarah, you are not well. You must not be left all alone,' she went on timidly.

'I am quite well—I shall not be alone,' said Lady Sarah. 'Mr. Tapeall is coming, and I am going to sign my will, Dolly,' and she looked her niece hard in the face. 'I shall not change it again whatever may happen. You will have no need in future to conceal anything from me, for the money is yours.' And Lady Sarah sighed, deeply hurt.

Dolly blushed up. 'Dear Aunt Sarah, I do not want your money,' she said. 'You could never have thought——'

'I can only judge people by their deeds,' said Lady Sarah, coldly still. 'You and George shall judge me by mine, whether or not I have loved you;' and the poor old voice failed a little, and the lips quivered as she held up her cheek for Dolly to kiss.

'Dear, dearest,' said Dolly, 'only forgive me too. If you mean that you are going to leave me money, I shall not be grateful. I have enough. What do I want? Only that you should love us always. Do you think I would marry Robert if he did not think so too?'

'Mademoiselle! Madame is ready,' cried Julie, coming to the door, and tapping.

'George, too, would say the same, you know he would,' Dolly went on, unheeding Julie's call. 'But if you give him what you meant for me, dear Aunt Sarah; indeed that would make me happiest, and then I should know you forgive me.'

The door creaked, opened, and Mrs. Palmer stood there impatient in her evening dress.

'My dear Dolly, what have you got to say to Aunt Sarah? We shall be dreadfully late, and Robert is fuming. *Do* pray come. Good-night, Sarah—so sorry to leave you.'

Rather than keep dinner waiting people break off their talk, their loves, their prayers. The Middletons' dinner was waiting, and Dolly had to come away. Some of the rose-leaves were lying on the floor after she had left, and the caressing fragrance still seemed to linger in the room.

Dolly left home unforgiven, so she thought. Aunt Sarah had not smiled nor spoken to her in her old voice once since that wretched morning scene.

But, in truth, Lady Sarah was clearer-sighted than people

gave her credit for ; she was bitterly hurt by Dolly's want of confidence, but she began to understand the struggle which had been going on in the girl's mind, and so far, things were not so sad as she had imagined at first. They were dismal enough.

When Marker came to tell Lady Sarah that Mr. Tapeall and his clerks were below, she got up from her chair wearily, and went down to meet the lawyer. What did she care now? She had saved, and pinched, and laid by (more of late than any one suspected), and Dolly was to benefit, and Dolly did not care ; Robert only seemed to count upon the money. It is often the most cautious people who betray themselves most unexpectedly. Something in Henley's manner had annoyed Lady Sarah of late. He had spoken of George with constant disparagement. More than once Robert had let slip a word that showed how confidently he looked for Dolly's inheritance.

One day Mrs. Palmer had noticed Lady Sarah's eyes upon him, and immediately tried to cover his mistake. Not so Dolly, who said, 'Robert! what are you thinking of? How should we ever be able to afford a country-house if you go into Parliament?'

'Robert thinks he is marrying an heiress, I suppose,' said Lady Sarah.

'No, he doesn't,' Dolly answered ; 'that would spoil it all.'

This was all the gratitude poor Lady Sarah had saved and pinched herself to win.

Lady Sarah, as I have said, might have been a money-lover, if her warm heart had not saved her. But she was human, and she could not help guessing at Robert's comfortable calculations, and she resented them. Did she not know what it was to be married, not for herself, but for what she could bring? Was *that* to be her Dolly's fate? Never, never!

Who knows? Let her have her own way; it may be best after all, thought Lady Sarah, wearily. She was tired of battling. Let George inherit, if it so pleased them. To please them was all she had wished or hoped for, and now even the satisfaction of pleasing them in her own way was denied her. But her girl was true; this she felt. No sordid thoughts had ever come between them, and for this she thanked God in her heart.

'You may burn it, Mr. Tapeall,' said Lady Sarah, as the lawyer produced a beautiful neatly-written parchment, where Miss Dorothea Vanborough's name was emblazoned many times. 'I want you to make me another. Yes, make it directly, and I will sign it at once, and old Sam can bear witness.'

'I shall be happy to receive any further instructions,' said the lawyer; 'I shall have to take the memorandum home with me to prepare——'

'I will sign the memorandum,' said Lady Sarah. 'You can have it copied, if you like, Mr. Tapeall; but I wish to have this business settled at once, and to hear no more of it. There is a pen and some ink on that table.'

'Where did you get your roses?' said Robert to Dolly; 'I thought you told me they were over.'

'Did not you send them?' said Dolly, disappointed. 'Who can have sent them? *Not* Colonel Witherington?'

'Mr. Raban is more likely,' said Mrs. Palmer. 'Julie tells me he came to the door this afternoon.'

'How kind of him!' cried Miss Vanborough.

'It was quite unnecessary,' said Robert. 'Nobody, in society, carries bouquets now.'

'Then I am not in society,' said Dolly, laughing; but although she laughed, she felt sad and depressed.

When the door opened and Mrs. Palmer, followed by her beautiful daughter and Henley, came into the room at Mrs. Middleton's, Colonel Witherington declared, upon his honour, they quite brightened up the party. White and gracious with many laces and twinklings, Mrs. Palmer advances, taking to society as a duck takes to the water, and not a little pleased with the sensation she is creating. Dolly follows, looking very handsome, but, it must be confessed, somewhat absent. Her mother had excellent taste, and had devised a most becoming costume, and if Dolly had only been herself she would certainly have done credit to it; but she had not responded to Mademoiselle Julie's efforts—a sudden fit of dull shyness seemed to overpower her. If Frank Raban had been there she would have liked to thank him for her flowers; but Mrs. Middleton began explaining to Robert how sorry she was that his friend Mr. Raban had been obliged to go off to Cambridge. Dolly was a little disappointed. The silvery folds of her dress fell each in juxtaposition; but Dolly sat silent and pale and far away, and for some time she scarcely spoke.

'That girl does not look happy,' said some one.

Robert overheard the speech, and was very much annoyed by it. These constant depressions were becoming a serious annoyance to him. He took Dolly down to dinner, but he devoted himself to a sprightly lady on his left hand, who, with many shrieks of laughter and wrigglings and twinklings of diamonds, spurred him on to a brilliance foreign to his nature. Young as he was, Robert was old for his age, and a capital diner-out, and he had the art of accommodating himself to his audience. Mrs. Palmer was radiant sitting between two white neckcloths: one belonged to the Viscount Portcullis, the other to the faithful Witherington; and she managed to talk to them both at once.

Dolly's right-hand neighbour was an upright, rather stern, soldierly-looking man, with a heavy white moustache. He spoke to her, and she answered with an effort, for her thoughts were still far away, and she was preoccupied still. Dolly was haunted by the sense of coming evil; she was pained by Robert's manner. He was still displeased, and he took care to show that it was so. She was troubled about George; she was wondering what he was about. She had written to him at Cambridge that afternoon a loving, tender, sisterly little letter, begging him to write to his faithful sister Dolly. Again she told herself that it was absurd to be anxious, and wicked to be cross, and she tried to shake off her depression, and to speak to the courteous though rather alarming neighbour on her right hand.

It was a dinner-party just like any other. They are pretty festivals on the whole, although we affect to decry them. In the midst of the Middleton dinner-table was an erection of ice and ferns and cool green grass, and round about this circled the entertainment—flowers, dried fruit, processions of cut glass and china, with entrées, diversities of chicken and cutlet, and then ladies and gentlemen alternate, with a host at one end and a hostess at the other, and an outermost ring of attendants, pouring out gold and crimson juices into the crystal cups.

It is fortunate, perhaps, that other people are not silent always because we are sad. With all its objections—I have read this in some other book—there is a bracing atmosphere in society, a Spartan-like determination to leave cares at home, and to try to forget all the ills and woes and rubs to which we are subject, and to think only of the present and the neighbours fate has assigned for the time. Little by little, Dolly felt happier and more reassured. Where every-

thing was so commonplace and unquestioning it seemed as
if tragedy could not exist. Comedy seems much more real
at times than tragedy. Three or four tragedies befall us in
the course of our existence, and a hundred daily comedies
pass before our eyes.

Dolly, hearing her mother's silver laugh and Robert's
cheerful duet, was reassured, and she entered little by little
into the tune of the hour, and once, glancing up shyly,
she caught a very kind look in her neighbour's keen dark
eyes.

He knew nothing of her, except a sweet girlish voice
and a blush; but that was enough almost, for it was Dolly's
good fortune to have a voice and a face that told of her as
she was. There are some smiles and blushes that mean
nothing at all, neither happy emotion nor quick response;
and, again, are there not other well-loved faces which are
but the homely disguises in which angels have come into
our tents? Dolly's looks pleased her neighbour, nor was he
disappointed when he came to talk to her; he felt a kindness
towards the girl, and a real interest when he discovered her
name. He had known her father in India many years
before. 'Had she ever heard of David Fane?' Colonel
Fane seemed pleased when Dolly brightened up and
exclaimed. He went on to tell her that he was on his way
to the Crimea: his regiment was at Southampton, waiting
its orders to sail.

'And you are going to that dreadful war!' said Dolly,
in her girlish tones, after a few minutes' talk.

Colonel Fane looked very grave.

'Your father was a brave soldier,' he said; 'he would
have told you that war is a cruel thing; but there are worse
things than fighting for a good cause.'

'You mean *not* fighting,' said Dolly; 'but how can we who sit at home in peace and safety be brave for others?'

'I have never yet known a woman desert her post in the time of danger,' said Colonel Fane, speaking with gentle, old-fashioned courtesy. 'You have your own perils to affront: they find you out even in your homes. I saw a regiment of soldiers to-day,' he said, smiling, 'in white caps and aprons, who fight with some very deadly enemies. They are under the command of my sister, my brother's widow. She is a hospital-nurse, and has charge of a fever-ward at present.'

Then he went on to tell Dolly that his brother had died of small-pox not long before, and his wife had mourned him, not in sackcloth and ashes, but in pity and love and devotion to others. Dolly listened with an unconscious look of sympathy that touched Colonel Fane more than words.

'And is she quite alone now?' said Dolly.

'I should like you to know her some day,' he said. 'She is less alone than anybody I know. She lives near St. Barnabas' Hospital; and if you will go and see her some-time when she is at home and away from her sick, she will make, not acquaintance, but friends with you, I hope.'

Then he asked Dolly whether she was an only child, and the girl told him something—far more than she had any idea of—about George.

'I might have been able to be of some little use to your brother if he had chosen the army for a profession,' said Colonel Fane, guessing that something was amiss.

Dolly was surprised to find herself talking to Colonel Fane, as if she had known him all her life. A few minutes before he had been but a name. When he offered to help George, Dolly blushed up, and raised two grateful eyes.

There is something in life which is not love, but which plays as great a part almost—sympathy, quick response—I scarcely know what name to give it; at any moment, in the hour of need perhaps, a door opens, and some one comes into the room. It may be a common-place man in a shabby coat, a placid lady in a smart bonnet; does nothing tell us that this is one of the friends to be, whose hands are to help us over the stony places, whose kindly voices will sound to us hereafter voices out of the infinite. Life has, indeed, many phases, love has many a metempsychosis. Is it a lost love we are mourning—a lost hope? Only dim, distant stars, we say, where all was light. Lo, friendship comes dawning in generous and peaceful streams!

Before dinner was over, Colonel Fane said to Dolly, ' I hope to have another talk with you some day. I am not coming upstairs now; but, if you will let me do so, I shall ask my sister, Mrs. William Fane, to write to you when she is free.'

Robert was pleased to see Dolly getting on so well with her neighbour. He was a man of some mark, and a most desirable acquaintance for her. Robert was just going to introduce himself, when Mrs. Middleton bowed to Lady Portcullis, and the ladies began to leave the room.

' Good-by,' said Dolly's new friend, very kindly; ' I shall ask you not to forget your father's old companion. If I come back, one of my first visits shall be to you.'

Then Dolly stood up blushing, and then she said, ' Thank you, very much; I shall never forget you. I, too, am going away—to India—with ——' and she looked at Henley, who was at that moment receiving the parting fire of the lively lady. There was no time to say more; she put out her hand with a grateful pressure. Colonel Fane watched Dolly as she walked away in the procession. For her sake he said a few civil words to Henley; but he was disappointed in him. ' I don't think poor Stan Vanborough would have approved of such a cut-and-dry son-in-law,' the Colonel said to himself as he lighted his cigar and came away into the open street.

CHAPTER XXXV.

' ONLY GEORGE.'

Call as thou wilt, thou call'st in vain,
No voice sends back thy name again.

THOUGHTS seem occasionally to have a life of their own —a
life independent; sometimes they are even stronger than
the thinkers, and draw them relentlessly along. They seize
hold of outward circumstances with their strong grip. How
strangely a dominant thought sometimes runs through a
whole epoch of life !

With some holy and serene natures, this thought is peace
in life; with others, it is human love, that troubled love of
God.

The moonlight is streaming over London; and George is
not very far away, driven by his master thought along a
bright stream that flows through the gates and by the down-
trodden roads that cross Hyde Park. The skies, the streets,
are silver and purple; abbey-towers and far-away houses rise
dim against the stars; lights burn in shadowy windows.
The people passing by, and even George, hurrying along in
his many perplexities, feel the life and the echo everywhere
of some mystical chord of nature and human nature striking
in response. The very iron rails along the paths seemed

turned to silver. George leaps over a silver railing, and goes towards a great sea of moonlight lying among the grass and encircled by shadowy trees.

In this same moonlit stream, flowing into the little drawing-room of the bow-windowed house in Old Street, sits Rhoda, resting her head against the pane of the lantern-like window, and thinking over the events of the last two days.

On the whole, she feels that she has acted wisely and for the best. Lady Sarah seemed to think so—Uncle John said no word of blame. It was unfortunate that Aunt Morgan's curiosity should have made her insist upon reading George's letter; but no harm had come of it. Dolly, of course, was unreasonable. Rhoda, who was accustomed to think of things very definitely, began to wonder what Frank Raban would think of it all, and whether Uncle John would tell him. She thought that Mr. Raban would not be sorry to hear of what had occurred. What a pity George was not more like Mr. Raban or Robert Henley. How calm they were; while he—he was unbearable; and she was very glad it was all over between them. Lady Sarah was evidently deeply offended with him.

' I hope she will leave him *something*,' thought Rhoda. ' He will never be able to make his way. I can see that; and he is so rough, and I am such a poor little thing,' and Rhoda sighed. ' I shall always feel to him as if he were a brother, and I shall tell Mr. Raban so if ——'

Here Rhoda looked up, and almost screamed out, for there stood George, rippling with moonlight, watching her through the window from the opposite side of the street. He looked like a ghost as he leant against the railings. He did not care who noticed him, nor what other people might think of him. He had come all this way only to see Rhoda once more, and there she was, only separated from him by a pane of glass.

When Rhoda looked up, George came across and stood under the window. The moonlight stream showed him a silver figure plain marked upon the darkness. There she sat with a drooping head and one arm lightly resting against the bar. Poor boy! He had started in some strange faith that he should find her. He had come up all the way only to look at her once more. All his passionate anger had already died away. He had given up hope, but he had not given up love; and so he stood there wild and haggard, with pulses throbbing. He had scarcely eaten anything since the evening before. He had gone back to Cambridge he knew not why. He had lain awake all night, and all day he had been lying in his boat hiding under the trees along the bank, looking up at the sky and cursing his fate.

Rhoda looked up. George, with a quick movement, pointed to the door, and sprang up the steps of the house. He must speak to her now that she had seen him. For what else had he come? She was frightened, and did not move at first in answer to his signs. She was alone. Aunt Morgan and the girls were drinking tea at the schools, but Uncle John was in the study. She did not want him to see George. It would only make a fuss and an explanation— there had been too much already. She got up and left the window, and then went into the hall and stood by the door undecided; and as she stood there she heard a low voice outside say, ' Rhoda! let me in.'

Rhoda still hesitated. ' Let me in,' said the voice again, and she opened the door a very little way, and put her foot against it.

'Good-night, George,' she said, in a whisper. 'Good-night. Go home. Dolly is so anxious about you.'

'I have come to see you,' said George. 'Why won't you let me in, Rhoda?'

'I am afraid,' said Rhoda.

'You need not be afraid, Rhoda,' he said, going back a step. 'Dear, will you forgive me for having frightened you?' and he came nearer again.

'I can't—go, go,' cried Rhoda, hastily. 'Here is some one,' and suddenly, with all her might, she pushed the door in his face. It shut with a bang, with all its iron knobs and locks rattling.

'What is it?' said John Morgan, looking out of his study.

'I had opened the door, Uncle John,' said Rhoda. Her heart beat a little. Would George go away? She thought she heard footsteps striking down the street. Then she felt more easy. She told herself once more that it was far better to have no scenes nor explanations, and she sat down quietly to her evening's task in a corner of her uncle's study. She was making some pinafores for the little Costellos, and she tranquilly stitched and tucked and hemmed. John Morgan liked to see her busy at her womanly work, her little lamp duly trimmed, and her busy fingers working for others more thriftless.

And outside in the moonlight George walked away in a new fury. What indignity had he subjected himself to? He gave a bitter sort of laugh. He had not expected much, but this was worse than anything he had expected. Reproaches, coldness, indifference, all these he was prepared for. He knew in his heart of hearts that Rhoda did not care for him; and what further wrong could she do him than this injury that people inflict every day upon each other? She had added scorn to her indifference; and again George laughed to himself, thinking of this wooden door Rhoda had clapped upon his passion, and her summary way of thrusting him out.

At one time, instead of banging the door, she used to open it wide. She used to listen to him, with her wonderful dark eyes fixed on his face. Now, what had happened? He was the same man, she was the same woman, and nothing was the same. George mechanically walked on towards his own home—if Church House could be so called. He went across the square, and by a narrow back street, and he tried the garden gate, and found it open, and went in, with some vague idea of finding Dolly, and calling her to the bench beside the pond, and of telling her of all his trouble. That slam of the door kept sounding in his ears, a sort of knell to his love.

But George was in no vein of luck that night. The garden was deserted and mysterious, heavy with sweet scents in the darkness. He went down the dark path and came back again, and there was a rustle among the trees; and as he walked across the lawn towards the lighted window of the oak room, he heard two voices clear in the silence, floating up from some kitchen below. He knew Sam's croak; he did not recognise the other voice.

'Mademoiselle is gone to dance. I like to dance too,' it said. 'Will you come to a ball and dance with me, Mr. Sam?'

Then followed old Sam's chuckle. 'I'll dance with you, Mademoiselle,' he said.

George thought it sounded as if some evil spirit of the night were mocking his trouble. And so Dolly was dancing while he was roaming about in his misery. Even Dolly had forgotten his pain. Even Rhoda had turned him out. Who cared what happened to him now?

He went to the window of the oak room and looked in. Lady Sarah was sitting there alone, shading her eyes from the light. There were papers all round about her. The lamp was burning behind her, and the light was reflected in the narrow glass above her tall chimney-piece.

He saw her put out her hand and slowly take a paper that was lying on the table, and tear it down the middle. Poor Aunt Sarah! she looked very old and worn and sad. How ill he had repaid her kindness! She should be spared all further anxiety and trouble for him. Then he put out his two hands with a wild farewell motion. He had not meant her to see him, but the window was ajar and flew open, and then he walked in; and Lady Sarah, looking up, saw George standing before her. He was scarcely himself all this time: if he had found Dolly all might have ended differently.

'George?' said Lady Sarah, frightened by his wild looks, 'what has happened, my dear?'

'I have come to say good-by to you,' he wildly cried. 'Aunt Sarah, you will never have any more trouble with me. You have been a thousand thousand times too good to me!' And he flung his two arms round her neck and kissed her, and almost before she could speak he was gone. . . .

A few minutes later Marker heard a fall, and came running upstairs. She found Lady Sarah lying half-conscious on the ground.

CHAPTER XXXVI.

THE SLOW SAD HOURS.

And thou wert sad, yet I was not with thee ;
And thou wert sick, and yet I was not there.
—BYRON.

DOLLY and her mother had left the Middletons' when John Morgan drove up in a hansom, with a message from his mother to bring them back at once. The servant told him that they were only just gone, and he drove off in pursuit. Bucklersbury House was blazing in the darkness, with its many windows open and alight, and its crowds pouring in and its music striking up. Morgan sprang out of his cab and hurried across the court, and under the horses' noses, and pushed among the footmen to the great front door where the inscribing angels of the *Morning Post* were stationed. The servants would have sent him back, but he told his errand in a few hasty words, and was allowed to walk into the hall. He saw a great marble staircase all alight, and people going up; and, by some good fortune, one of the very first persons he distinguished was Dolly, who had only just come, and who was following her mother and Robert. She, too, caught sight of the familiar face in the hall below, and stopped short.

'Mamma,' she said, 'there is John Morgan making signs. Something has happened.'

Mrs. Palmer did not choose to hear. She was going in; she was at the gates of Paradise : she was not going to be kept back by John Morgan. There came a cheerful clang of music from above.

Dolly hesitated; the curate beckoned to her eagerly. 'Mamma, I must go back to him,' said Dolly, and before her mother could remonstrate she had stopped short and slid behind a diplomat, a lord with a blue ribbon, an aged countess ; in two minutes she was at the foot of the staircase, Robert meanwhile serenely proceeding ahead, and imagining that his ladies were following.

In two words, John Morgan had told Dolly to get her shawl, that her aunt was ill, that she had been asking for her. Dolly flew back to the cloak-room : she saw her white shawl still lying on the table, and she seized it and ran back to John Morgan again, and then they had hurried through the court and among the carriages to the place where the hansom was waiting.

'And I was away from her!' said Dolly. That was nearly all she said. It was her first trouble—overwhelming, unendurable, bewildering, as first troubles are. When they drove up to Church House, the front looked black, and closed, and terrible somehow. Dolly's heart beat as she went in.

Everything seemed a little less terrible when she had run upstairs, and found her aunt lying in the familiar room, with a faint odour of camphor and chloroform, and Marker coming and going very quietly. Mrs. Morgan was there with her bonnet cocked a little on one side; she came up and took Dolly's hand with real kindness, and said some

words of encouragement, and led her to the bedside. As
Dolly looked at Aunt Sarah's changed face, she gulped for
the first time one of life's bitter draughts. They don't last
long, those horrible moments; they pass on, but they leave
a burning taste; it comes back again and again with the
troubles of life.

Lady Sarah seemed to recognise Dolly when she first
came in, then she relapsed again, and lay scarce conscious,
placid, indifferently waiting the result of all this nursing
and anxious care. The struggles of life and its bustling
anxieties had passed away from that quiet room, never
more to return.

Dolly sat patiently by the bedside. She had not taken
off her evening dress, she never moved, she scarcely
breathed, for fear of disturbing her dear sick woman. If
Frank Raban could have seen her then, he would not have
called her cold! Those loving looks and tender ways might
almost have poured new life into the worn-out existence that
was ebbing away. The night sped on, as such nights do
pass. She heard the sound of carriage-wheels coming home
at last, and crept downstairs to meet the home-comers.

Dolly did not ask her mother what had delayed her when
the two came in. She met them with her pale face. She
was still in her white dress, with the dying roses in her hair.
Henley, who had meant to reproach her for deserting them
without a word, felt ashamed for once before her. She
seemed to belong to some other world, far away from that
from which he had just come. She told her story very
simply. The doctors said there had been one attack such as
this once before, which her aunt had kept concealed from
them all. They ordered absolute quiet. Marker was to be
nurse, and one other person. 'Of course that must be me

WATCHING.

mamma. I think Aunt Sarah would like me best,' she said, with a faint smile. 'Mrs. Morgan! No, dear mamma, not Mrs. Morgan.' Then suddenly she burst into tears. 'Oh, mamma, I have never seen any one so ill,' she said ; but the next minute she had overcome her emotion, and wiped her eyes.

'My dearest child, it is most distressing, and that you should have missed your ball, too!' said Philippa. 'I said all along, if you remember, that she was looking a perfect wreck. You would not listen to me. Robert, turn that sofa out of the draught. I shall not go to bed. Julie can come down here and keep me company after you go.'

'I must go,' said Robert; 'I have still some work to finish. Take care of yourself, Dora—remember you belong to me now. I hope there will be better news in the morning.'

From one room to the other, all the next day, Dolly went with her heavy heart—it seemed to drag at her as she moved, to dull her very anxiety. It was only a pain, it did not rise to the dignity of an emotion. Mrs. Palmer felt herself greatly neglected; she was taken ill in the afternoon and begged to see the doctor, who made light of her ailment; towards evening Mrs. Palmer was a great deal better. She came down into the drawing-room, and sent Eliza Twells over for John Morgan. Lady Sarah still lay stricken silent, but her pulse was better, the doctor said: she could move her arm a little : it had been lying helpless before. Faithful Marker sat by her side, rubbing her cold hands.

'Aunt Sarah, do you know me?' whispered Dolly, bending over her.

Lady Sarah faintly smiled in answer.

'Tell George to come back,' she said slowly. 'Dolly, I

did as you wished; are you satisfied?' She had gone back to the moment when she was taken ill.

'Dearest Aunt Sarah,' said Dolly, covering her hand with kisses. Then she ran down to tell her mother the good news. 'Aunt Sarah was rallying, was talking more like herself again. We only want George to make her well again. He must come. Where is he? Why does he not come?'

'Don't ask *me* anything about George,' said Mrs. Palmer, putting up her hands.

This was the day after the ball, but no George came, although Dolly looked for him at every instant. John Morgan, of his own accord, sent a second message to him and another to Raban. In the course of the day an answer arrived from the tutor: '*G. left Cambridge yesterday. Your telegram to him lying unopened.*'

CHAPTER XXXVII.

IN AN EMPTY ROOM.

Nor dare I chide the world-without-end hour.
—SHAKSPEARE.

THE next day Dolly, coming down into the garden, found
Raban with her mother, and she went up eagerly to meet
him, hoping for the news she was looking for. But news
there was none, although her mother, arm-in-arm with
Raban, had been for the last hour slowly pacing the gravel-
walks, recapitulating all their anxieties and all the complaints they had against that tiresome boy.

'The Admiral will be so shocked. I expect him hourly;
and I look to *you*, Mr. Raban, to tell me the plain truth.'

The plain truth was that Frank could discover nothing
of George. All that long day he had followed up every
trace, been everywhere, questioned every one, including
Rhoda, without result. He had come now in the faint hope
of finding him at home after all. When Dolly came to meet
them, he thought she looked anxious enough already, and he
made light of his long efforts, and shrugged his shoulders.

'I have no doubt George will turn up at Cambridge in
the course of a day or two. I have some business calls me
away. I will write immediately on my return,' he said.

Frank saw Dolly's look of surprise and disappointment as she turned away, and his heart ached for her; but what could he do? He watched her as she turned back towards the house again, walking slowly and with a thoughtful bent head.

'It is quite painful to see Dolly, she has no feeling whatever for me left,' cried Mrs. Palmer. 'Ever since dear George's conduct, I see the saddest change in her.　can do nothing. I would drive her out. Colonel Witherington offered me his sister's barouche any day, but Dolly won't hear of it. Dolly, you know, is simply impossible,' said Mrs. Palmer. 'I never knew a more desponding nature.'

'Indeed?' said Raban.

It was not his place to be sorry for her. He was not able to shield her from grief. It was not his place to think for her, to love her in her trouble. It was not for him: all this was for Robert Henley to do.

There was a great red sunset in the sky, islands floating, and lakes and seas of crimson light overhead, as Dolly walked sadly and slowly into the house, and went back to the dim sick-room.

There is no need to dwell upon the slow hours. Dolly found that they came to an end somehow. And all the time one miserable conviction pursued her—George was gone. Of this she was convinced, notwithstanding all they could say to reassure her. While they had been expecting him, and blaming him, and wondering, and discussing his plans, he had fled from them all. Dolly at first did not face the truth, for she had sat by her aunt's bedside half dull, half absorbed by her present anxiety; but when Lady Sarah began to rally a little, the thought of George grew more constant, the longing for news more unendurable; time seemed longer:

it became an eternity at last. One day she felt as if she could bear it no longer.

Robert found her looking very much moved; her cheeks were glowing, her eyes were shining blue; she had a cloak on her arm, and some white summer dress, and she began tying her bonnet-strings nervously.

'Robert, I want you to take me to Cambridge,' she said. 'I want to go now. I know I could find him—I dreamt it. Aunt Sarah wants him back directly. . . .'

'You are quite unreasonable, dearest,' said Robert, soothingly.

'I am not; I am reasonable,' poor Dolly said, with an effort at self-control. 'Mr. Raban cannot find him. Robert, let me go.' And Robert yielded reluctantly to her wish.

'Have you got a *Bradshaw* in the house?' said he.

Dolly had got one all ready, with the page turned down—she could spare but a few hours, and was in a hurry to get back.

After all, sympathy is more effectually administered by indirect means than by the crowbars of consolation with which our friends, even the kindest, are apt to belabour our grief. According to some, people don't die, they don't fall ill, they don't change, everything always goes right. Some reproach us with our want of faith; others drag it forth— that silent sorrow that would fain lie half-asleep and resting in our hearts. Poor Dolly could not speak of George scarcely even to Robert. She sat very silently in the rail-way-carriage, her hands lying listlessly in her lap, while he refuted all the fears she had not even allowed herself to realise. This state of things annoyed Robert. He hated to see people dull and indifferent. It was distressing and tiresome too.

Y

Few people were about when Robert and Dolly came
across the great triumphant court of St. Thomas, with its
gateways and many stony eyes and narrow doorways. They
were on their way to All Saints', close by. The place
seemed chiefly given over to laundresses. A freshman was
standing under the arched gateway that leads to the inner
court; he was reading some neatly-written announcement
in the glass shrine hanging outside the buttery. The oaken
doors were closed. Robert, seeing a friend crossing the
court, went away to speak to him. Dolly walked on a little,
and stood by the railings, and the flight of steps that lead
into the beautiful inner court of this great Palace of Art.
She watched the many lines flowing in waves of stone, of
mist. At the far end of the arched enclosure were iron-
scrolled gates, with green and gold, and misty veils of
autumn drifting in the gardens beyond. And then she
remembered the summer's day when she last stood there
with George, and as she thought of him suddenly his image
came before her so distinctly that she almost called out his
name. It was but an instant's impression; it was gone;
the steps were Robert's; the image was in her own mind.

'Are you tired of waiting?' said Henley. 'Now, if you
like we will go on to All Saints',' he said.

It seemed to Dolly as if she was looking at the old
summer day, dimmed, silenced, saddened, seen through
some darkened pane, as they went on together, passing
under archways and galleries, and coming at last into the
quaint and tranquil court that Dolly remembered so vividly.
There she had stood; and there was George's staircase, and
there was his name painted up, and there was his window
with its lattice.

Robert went off for the key of George's room, and Dolly

waited. It was so sweet, so sad, so tranquil, like the end of a long life. Dolly wandered in and out the narrow galleries; the silence of the place comforted her. She was glad to be alone a little bit, unconstrained, to feel as she felt, and not as she ought to feel; quietly despondent, not nervously confident, as they would all have her be. It was a crumbling, sweet, sunshiny sort of waking dream. Some gleams had broken through the clouds, and shone reflected from the many lattice windows round about the little court. She heard some voices, and some young men hurried by, laughing as they went. They did not see the young lady with the sweet sad face standing under the gallery. Chrysanthemums were growing up against the wall, with faint lilac and golden heads, the last bright tints left upon the once gorgeous palette of summer. A delicate cool sky hung overhead, and the light was becoming. brighter. Dolly passed an open door, and peeped in from the quaint gallery to a warm and darkened room, panelled and carpeted. It was dark and untenanted ; a fire was burning in the grate.

'That is Fieldbrook's room; he will give us some tea presently,' said Robert, coming up; 'but now we can get into George's.'

Robert, who seemed to have keys for every keyhole, opened an oak door, and led the way up some stone steps. George's room was on the first floor. Henley went in first, opened the window, dragged forward a chair. 'If you will rest here,' he said, 'I will go and find Fieldbrook. They tell me he last heard from George. I have to speak to the Vice-Chancellor too.' Then he was gone again, after looking about to see that there was nothing he could do for her.

Dolly was glad to be alone. She sat down in George's three-sided chair, resting her head upon her hand. She was in his room. Everything in the place seemed to have a voice, and to speak to her—'George, George,' it all said. She looked out of the little window across the court. She could see the old windows of the library shining, and then she heard more voices, and more young men hurried by, with many footsteps.

Ever after, Dolly remembered that last half-hour spent in George's rooms *with* George : so it seemed to her looking back from a time when she had ceased to hope. She went to the writing-table, and mechanically began to straighten the toys and pens lying on the cloth. There was the little dagger his mother had sent him from India years before; the desk she had given him out of her savings; and it occurred to her to open the lid, of which she knew the trick. She pushed the spring, and the top flew up with a sudden jerk, as it always did. Then Dolly saw that the box was full of papers hastily thrown in, verses, notes of lectures, and a letter torn through. 'Dearest Rh—' it began. She had no great shame looking over George's papers, a tear fell on the dear heap as she bent over the signs and ink-marks that told of her poor boy's trouble. What was this ? a letter stamped and addressed to herself. Had it been thrown in with the rest by mistake ? She tore it open hastily, with eager hands. He must have written the night of their water-party : it had no date :—

DEAREST DOLLY (said the crooked lines)—This is one more good-by, and one more service that I want you to do me; and you have never grudged any human being love or help. I am going, and before I go I shall make my will, and I shall leave what little I have—not to you—but to Rhoda, and will you see to this ? I sometimes think she has not even a heart to help her through life ; she will like my money better than me. It is quite late at night, but I cannot sleep ; she comes and awakens me in my dreams. I shall go away from this as soon as the gates are open. It is no use struggling against my fate ; others are giving their lives for a purpose, and I shall join them if I can.

I have been flung from my anchor here, and the waves seem to close over me. If I live you will hear from me. Dearest old Dolly, take warning by me and don't expect too much. God bless you!

G. V.

Will you pay Miller at the boat-house 2*l.* 10*s.* I owe him? I think I have cleared up all other scores. I will leave the papers with him. I shall not come back here any more.

That was all. She was standing with her letter still in her hand, blankly looking at it, when the door opened and Tom Morgan came in. ' " If I live." What did he mean ? " Ask at the boat-house ? " ' She laid the letter down and went on turning over the papers without noticing the young man.

Tom walked in with a broad grin and great volubility. ' Well ! ' said he, cheerfully, ' I thought it was you ! I was walking with Magniac and some others, and noticed the windows open, and I saw you standing just where you are now, and I said to Magniac, " I know that lady." He wouldn't believe me ; but I was right, knew I was. How are you and how is Lady Sarah ? Where is George ? When did he come back ? ' Then suddenly remembering some rumour to which he had paid but little heed at first, ' Nothing wrong, I hope ? ' said Tom.

' Tom ! where is this ? ' said Dolly, without any preamble, in her old abrupt way, and she gave him a crumpled bill which she had been examining.

MR. VANBUG *to* J. MILLER—
To hieir of the *Wave* twelve hours.
To man's time, &c. &c.
To now cotoing hir with tare, &c.

' I want to go there,' she said. ' Will you show me the way ? '

' To the boat-house ? ' said Tom, doubtfully, looking at the bill. ' Miller's, you mean ? '

She saw him hesita te.

'I must go,' she cried. 'You must take me. Is it Miller's? Show me the way, Tom.'

'Of course I can show you the way if you wish it,' said Tom.

He looked even more stupid than usual, but he did not like to refuse. He had to be in Hall by three o'clock, that was why he had hesitated. He had been thinking of his dinner; but Dolly began to tie on her bonnet. She hurried out, and ran downstairs, and he followed her across the court into the street. He was not loth to be seen walking with so pretty a young lady. He nodded to several of his friends with velvet bands upon their gowns; a professor went by, Tom raised his well-worn cap.

Dolly might have been amused at any other time by the quaint mediæval ways of the old place.

It was out of term-time, but there had been some special meeting of the college magnates. Crimson coats and black, square caps and tassels, and quaint old things were passing. The fifteenth century was standing at a street corner. To-day heartily shook hands with 1500 and hurried on. Dolly saw it all without seeing it. Tom Morgan tried to give her the latest news.

'That is Brown,' said he, 'the new Professor of Modern Literature.' Dolly never even turned her head to look after Brown.

'There's Smith,' said Tom: 'they say he will be in the first six for the Mathematical Tripos.'

Then they came out of the busy High Street by a narrow lane, with brick walls on either side. It led to the mill by the river, and beyond the river spread a great country of water-meadows. It was a world, not of to-day or of 1500,

but of all times and all hours. Pollards were growing at
intervals, the river flowed by dull and sluggish, the land,
too, seemed to flow dull and sluggish to meet a grey horizon. There were no animals to be seen, only these pollard-
trees at intervals, and the spires of Cambridge crowding in
the mist.

CHAPTER XXXVIII.

THE POLLARD-TREES.

Next Camus, reverend sire, went fooling slow—
His mantle hairy and his bonnet sedge,
Inwrought with figures dim, and on the edge
Like to that sanguine flower inscribed with woe.
'Ah! who hath rest?' quoth he. . . .
                                        —LYCIDAS.

MISS VANBOROUGH walked on; she seemed to know the way by some instinct; sometimes she looked at the water, but it gave her a sort of vertigo. Tom looked at Dolly with some admiration as she passed along the bank, with her clear-cut face and stately figure, following the narrow pathway. They came at last to a bend of the river where some boats were lying high and dry in the grass, and where a little boat-house stood upon a sort of jutting-out island among tall trees upspringing suddenly in the waste: tall sycamore, ivy-grown stumps, greens of every autumnal shade, golden leaves dropping in lazy showers on the grass or drifting into the sluggish stream, along which they floated back to Cambridge once more. It was a deserted-looking grove, melancholy and romantic. But few people came there. But there was a ferryman and a black boat-house, and a flat ferry-boat anchored to the shore. Some bird gave a cry and flew past, otherwise the place was still with that peculiar river silence of tall weeds straggling, of trees drooping their green branches, of water lapping on the brink.

'Is this the place you wanted?' said Tom, 'or was it the other boat-house after all?'

Dolly walked on, without answering him. She beckoned to the boatman; and then, as he came towards her, her heart began to beat so that she could scarcely speak or ask the question that she had in her mind to ask. 'Has my brother been here? Where is his letter? Is the *Wave* safe in your little boat-house?' This was what she would have said, only she could not speak. Some strange fever had possessed her and brought her so far : now her strength and courage suddenly forsook her, and she stopped short, and stood holding to an old rotten post that stood by the river-side.

'Take care,' said Tom; 'that ain't safe. You might fall in, and the river is deep just here.'

She turned such a pale face to him that the young man suddenly began to wonder if there was more in it all than he had imagined.

'It's perfectly safe I mean,' he said. 'Why, you don't mean to say ——'

He turned red; he wished with all his heart that he had never brought her there—that he could jump into the river—that he had stayed to dine in Hall. To his unspeakable relief unexpected help appeared.

'Why, there is Mr. Raban!' said Tom, as Raban came out of the boat-house, and walked across under the trees to meet them.

Dolly waited for the two men to come up to her, as she stood by her stump among the willow-trees. Raban did not seem surprised to see her. He took no notice of Tom, but he walked straight up to Dolly.

' You have come,' he said ; ' I had just sent you a tele-
graphic message.'

His manner was so kind and so gentle that it frightened
her more than if he had spoken with his usual coldness.

' What is it?' she said, 'and why have you come here?
Have you too heard . . .?'

She scanned his face anxiously.

Then she looked from him to the old boatman, who was
standing a few steps off in his shabby red flannel-shirt, with
a stolid brown face and white hair : a not unpicturesque
figure standing by the edge of the stream. Winds and rain
and long seasons had washed all expression out of old Miller's
bronzed face.

' George came here on Tuesday,' said Raban to Dolly ; ' I
only heard of it this morning. Miller tells me he gave him
a letter or a paper to keep.'

' I know it,' said Dolly, turning to the old boatman. ' I
am Mr. Vanborough's sister ; I have come for the letter,' she
said quickly, and she held out her hand.

' This gentleman come and asked me for the paper,' said
the old man, solemnly, ' and he stands by to contradict me if
I speak false ; but if the right party as was expected to call
should wish for to see it, my wish is to give satisfaction all
round,' said the old man. ' I knows your brother well, Miss,
and he know me, and my man too, for as steady a young
man and all one could wish to see. The gentleman come up
quite hearty one morning, and ask Bill and me as a favour
to hisself to sign the contents of the paper ; and he seal it
up, and it is safe, as you see, with the seal compact ;' and
then from his pockets came poor George's packet, a thin
blue paper folded over, and sealed with his ring. ' Mr.
Vanbug he owe me two pound twelve and sixpence,' old

Miller went on, still grasping his paper as if loth to give it up, 'and he said as how you would pay the money, Miss.'

Dolly's hands were fumbling at her purse in a moment.

'I don't want nothing for my trouble,' said the old fellow. 'I knows Mr. Vanbug well, and I thank you, Miss, and you will find it all as the gentleman wished, and good-morning,' said old Miller, trudging hastily away, for a passenger had hailed him from the opposite shore.

'I know what it is,' said Dolly. 'See, he has written my name upon it, Mr. Raban: it is his will. He told me to come here. He is gone. I found his letter.' She began to quiver. 'I don't know what he means.'

'Don't be frightened,' said Raban smiling, and very kindly. 'He was seen at Southampton quite well and in good spirits. He has enlisted. That is what he means. You have interest, we must get him a commission; and if this makes him more happy, it is surely for the best.'

'Perhaps you are right,' she said, struggling not to cry. 'How did you hear? How kind you have been. How shall we ever thank you!' Her colour was coming and going.

'It was a mere chance,' Raban said. (It was one of those chances that come to people who have been working un-remittingly to bring a certain result to pass.) 'Don't thank me,' he continued in a low voice; 'you have never under-stood how glad I am to be allowed to feel myself your friend sometimes.'

Raban might have said more, but he looked up, and saw Robert's black face frowning down upon them. Robert was the passenger who had hailed old Miller. For an instant Frank had forgotten that Robert existed. He turned away hastily, and went and stared into the water at a weed float-ing by. The old boatman waiting by the punt sat on the edge of the shore, watching the little scene, and wondering what the pretty lady's tears might be about. Tom also assisted, open-mouthed—the Morgan family were not used to tears. Mrs. Morgan never cried; not even when Tom broke his leg upon the ice.

Robert was greatly annoyed. He had come all the way, along the opposite bank, looking for Dolly, who had not waited for him; who had gone off without a word from the place where he had expected to find her. Not even her incoherent ' Oh, Robert, I am so sorry—I have heard, Mr. Raban has heard—he has found George for us ! ' not even her trustful, gentle look, as she sprang to meet him, seemed to mollify him. He looked anything but sympathising as he said, ' I have been looking for you everywhere.'

(' Brown must have told him,' thought Tom Morgan, who was wondering how he had found them out.)

' You really must not run off in this way. I told you all along that all this—a—anxiety was quite unnecessary. George is well able to take care of himself. If I had not met Professor Brown, I really don't know now ——'

' But what is to be done, Robert? Listen,' interrupted Dolly. ' He has enlisted; he was at Southampton yesterday.'

And together they told Henley what had happened. Robert took it very coolly.

' Of course he has turned up,' said Robert, ' and we must now take the matter into our own hands, and see what is best to be done. I really think ' (with a laugh) ' he has done the best thing he could do.'

Dolly was hurt again by his manner. Raban had said the same thing, but it had not jarred upon her.

' I see you do not agree with me,' continued Robert. ' Perhaps, Raban, you will give me the name of the person

who recognised George Vanborough? I will see- him
myself.'

'He is a man whom we all know,' said Raban, gravely,—
'Mr. Penfold, my late wife's father,' and he looked Robert
full in the face.

Dolly wondered why Robert flushed and looked uncomfortable.

'Come,' he said, suddenly drawing her hand through his
arm with some unnecessary violence, 'shall we walk back,
Dora? There are some other things which I must see about,
and I should be glad to consult you immediately.' And he
would have walked away at once, but she hung back for a
moment to say one more grateful word to Frank.

Then Robert impatiently dragged her off, and Raban,
with his foot, kicked at a stone that happened to be lying
in the path, and it fell with a circling plash into the
river.

Meanwhile, Robert was walking away, and poor Dolly,
who had not yet recovered from her agitation, was stumbling
alongside, weary and breathless. He had her arm in his; he
was walking very rapidly; she could hardly keep up with his
strides.

This was the moment chosen by Robert Henley to say:—
'I want you now to bring your mind to something which
concerns myself, Dora, and you. I came here to-day, not
only to please you, but also because I had business to attend
to. The Vice-Chancellor has, really in the most pleasant
and flattering manner, been speaking to me about my
appointment, and I have brought a letter for you.'

'I am so confused, Robert,' said Dolly.

'I will read it to you, then,' said Robert; and immediately, in a clear, trumpet-like voice, he began to do so,

stopping every now and then to give more emphasis to his sentences.

The letter was from the Board of Management of the College of Boggleywollah. They seemed to be in a difficulty. The illness of Mr. Martindale had already caused great delay and inconvenience; the number of applications had never been so numerous; the organisation never so defective. In the event of Mr. Henley's being able to anticipate his departure by three weeks, the Board was empowered to offer him a quarter's additional salary, dating from Midsummer instead of from Michaelmas: it would be a very great assistance to them if he could fall in with this proposal. A few lines of entreaty from Mr. Martindale were added.

'It will have to come sooner or later,' said Henley; 'it is unfortunate everything happening just now. My poor Dora,—I am so sorry for all the anxiety you have had,' he said, 'and yet I am not sure that this is the best thing that could happen under the circumstances;' and he attempted to take her hand and draw her to him.

Dolly stood flushed and troubled, and unresponding. She hardly took Robert's meaning in, so absorbed had she been in other thoughts. For a moment after he spoke she stood looking away across the river to the plain beyond.

'The college must wait,' said she, wearily; then suddenly—'You know I couldn't leave them now, Aunt Sarah and every one, and you, Robert, couldn't leave me. Don't let us talk about it!'

Robert did not answer immediately. 'It is no use,' he said deliberately, 'shirking disagreeable subjects. My dearest Dora, life has to be faced, and one's day's work has to be done. My work is to organise the College at Boggleywollah; you must consider that; and a woman's work is to follow her husband. Every woman, when she marries, must expect to give up her old ties and associations, or there could be no possible union otherwise; and my wife can be no exception to the general rule ——'

'Robert, don't talk in this way,' said Dolly, passionate and nervous. 'I don't want you to frighten me.'

'You are unreasonable again, dearest,' said Robert, in his usual formula. 'You must be patient, and let me settle for us both.'

Robert might have been more touched if Dolly had spoken less angrily and decidedly.

'If I put off going,' said Robert, soothingly, 'I lose a great deal more than a quarter's salary—I lose the prestige; the great advantage of finding Martindale. I lose three months, which in the present state of affairs may cause irreparable hindrance. Three months?—six months! Lady Sarah's illness may last any indefinite period: who can say how long it may last? and Lady Sarah herself, I am convinced, would never wish you to change your plans, and your mother will soon have her husband to protect her. You would not have the heart to send me off alone, Dolly. Is the alternative so very painful to you?' he said again. And Robert smiled with a calm and not very anxious expression, and looking down at her.

Suddenly it all rushed over Dolly. He was in earnest!—in earnest!—impossible. He meant her to go off now,—directly—without seeing George; without hearing from him again; while her aunt was lying on her sick bed. How could she go? He should not have asked such a sacrifice. She did not pause to think.

'No, a thousand times no, Robert!' she cried passionately. 'You *can't* go. If you love me, stay,' she said, with great agitation. 'I know you love me. I know you will do as I wish—as it is right to do.　Don't go.　Dearest Robert, you *mustn't* go.'　Her voice faltered ; she spoke in her old soft tone, with imploring looks, and trembling hands put out.　Robert Henley might have hesitated, but the ' *must not*' had spoilt it all.

'You know what pain it gives me to refuse your request,' said Robert ; 'but I have considered the subject as anxiously on your account as mine.　I—really I cannot give up my career at this juncture.　You have promised to come with me.　If you love me you will not hesitate.　You can do your aunt no real good by remaining.　You can do George no good ; and, besides, you belong to me,' said Robert, growing more and more annoyed.　'As I told you before, I must now be your first consideration ; otherwise ——' He stopped.

'Otherwise what ?' said Dolly.

'Otherwise you would not be happy as my wife,' he said, beating his foot upon the gravel, and looking steadily before him.

'Robert !' said Dolly, blushing up, 'you would not wish me to be ungrateful.'

'To whom ?' said Robert.　'You propose to postpone everything indefinitely, at a time when I had fully calculated upon being settled in life ; when I had accepted an appointment chiefly with a view to our speedy marriage.　There is no saying how long your conscience may detain us,' cried Henley, getting more and more provoked ; 'nor how many people may fall ill, nor how often George may think proper to make off.　You do not perceive how matters stand, dear Dora.'

Was this all he had to say ?　Her heart began to beat with a swift emotion.

'I understand you quite well,' she said, in a low voice. 'But, Robert, I, too, have made up my mind, and I cannot leave them, not even for you. You should never have asked it of me,' she cried, with pardonable indignation.

'I am not aware that I have ever asked anything that was not for your good as well as my own,' said Henley, in an offended tone. 'I begin to think you have never loved me, Dora, or you would not reproach me with my love for you. Who has influenced you?' said he, jealously. 'What does it all mean?'

She stopped short, and stood looking at him steadily, wistfully—not as she used to look once, but with eyes that seemed to read him through and through, until the tears came once more to blind their keen sight.

Raban, who had crossed by the ferry, and who was walking back along the opposite side, saw the two standing by the river-side, a man and a woman, with a plain beyond, and a city beyond the plain.

The sun was setting sadly grey and russet; the long day's mists dispersing; light clouds were slowly rising; turf and leaves stood out against the evening; it was all clear and sweet, and faintly coloured: a tranquil peace seemed to have fallen everywhere. It was not radiance, but peace and subdued calm. Who does not know these evenings? are they sad? are they happy? A break in the shadow. A passing medley of the lights of heaven and earth, of sweet winds and rising vapours. . . . The cool breeze came blowing into their faces, and Dolly turned her head away and looked across the river to the opposite bank. When she spoke again she was her old self once more.

She was quite calm now; her eyes no longer wet. 'Robert,' she said, 'I have something to tell you. I have been thinking things over, and I see that it is right that you should go; but it is also right that I should stay,' said Dolly, looking him steadily in the face; 'and perhaps in happier times you will let me come to you, or come back for me, and you must not—you will not—think I do not love you because of this.'

What was it in her voice that seemed to haunt him—to touch, to thrill that common-place man for one instant into some emotion? She was so simple and so sad; she looked so fair and wistful.

But it was only for an instant. 'Do you mean that you wish to break the engagement?' he asked in his coldest voice.

'If we love each other what does it matter that we are free?' said Dorothea, with a very sweet look in her face. 'You need fear no change in me,' she said, 'but I want you to be free.' Her voice failed, and she began to walk on quickly.

'Remember, it is your own doing,' she heard him say, as Tom Morgan, who had lingered behind, caught them up. 'But we will speak of all this again,' he added.

Dolly bent her head, she could not trust herself to answer.

CHAPTER XXXIX.

THUS FAR THE MILES ARE MEASURED FROM THY FRIEND.

> If I leave all for thee, wilt thou exchange,
> And be all to me? Shall I never miss
> Home-talk and blessing and the common kiss
> That comes to each in turn, nor count it strange,
> When I look up, to drop on a new range
> Of walls and floors, another home than this?
> —E. B. BROWNING.

THE three came back to All Saints' by many a winding way. Raban met them at the college gate in his rusty black gown; he had to attend some college meeting after chapel. Two or three young men were standing about expecting them.

'You will find the tea is all ready,' said Fieldbrook, gaily; 'are you sure, Miss Vanborough, that you would not like something more substantial? My laundress has just been here to ask whether you were an elderly lady, and whether you would wish your bread-and-butter cut thick or thin? Let me introduce Mr. Magniac, Mr. Smith, Mr. Irvine, Mr. Richmond; Mr. Morgan you know.'

Dolly smiled. The young men led her back across the court (as she crossed it the flowers were distilling their colours in the evening light); they opened the oak door of the very room she had looked into in the morning, and stood back to let her pass. The place had been prepared for her coming. Tea was laid, and a tower of bread-and-butter stood in the middle of the table. Books were cleared away, some flowers were set out in a cup. Fieldbrook heaped on the coals and made the tea, while Raban brought her the arm-chair to rest in. It was a pretty old oak-panelled room beneath the library. A little flat kettle was boiling on the fire; the young men stood round about, kind and cheery: Dolly was touched and comforted by their kindness, and they, too, were charmed with her sweet natural grace and beauty.

It was difficult not to compare this friendly courtesy and readiness with Robert's coldness. There was Raban ready to do her bidding at any hour; here was Mr. Fieldbrook emptying the whole canister into the teapot to make her a cup of tea; Smith had rushed off to order a fly for her. Robert stood silent and black by the chimney; he never moved, nor seemed to notice her presence. If she looked at him he turned his head away, and yet he saw her plainly enough. He saw Raban too. Frank was standing behind Dolly's chair in the faint green light of the old oriel window. It tinted his old black gown and Dolly's shadowy head as she leant back against the oaken panel. One of the young men thought of an ivory head he had once seen set in a wooden frame. As for Frank, he knew that for him a pale ghost would henceforth haunt that oriel—a fair, western ghost, with anxious eyes, that were now following Robert as he crossed the room with measured steps and went to look out for the fly.

As he left the room, they all seemed to breathe more freely. Tom Morgan and Mr. Magniac began a series of jokes; Mr. Richmond poked the fire; Mr. Irvine opened the window. Raban sat down by Dolly, and began telling her of a communication he had had from Yorkshire, from his old grandfather, who seemed disposed to take him into favour again, and who wanted him to go back and manage the estate.

'I am very much exercised about it,' said Frank. 'It is going into the land of bondage, you know. The old couple have used me very ill.'

' But of course you must go to them,' said Dolly, trying to be interested, and to forget her own perplexities. 'We shall miss you dreadfully, but you must go.'

' You will not miss me as I shall miss you,' said Frank.

And as he spoke, Robert's head appeared at the window.

'The fly is come ; don't keep it waiting, Dora,' said Robert, impatiently.

' And you will let me know if ever I can do anything for you ? ' persisted Frank, in defiance of Henley's black looks.

' Of course I will. I shall never forget your kindness,' said Dolly, quickly putting on her shawl.

The bells were clanging all over the place for an evening service. Doors were banging, voices calling, figures came flitting from every archway.

' There goes the reader ! he is late,' said Tom Morgan, as a shrouded form darted across their path. Then he pointed out the Rector, a stately figure in a black and rustling silk, issuing from a side door; and then Rector, friendly young men, arches, gable-ends had vanished, and Dolly and Robert were driving and jolting through the streets together, jolting along through explanation and misunderstanding, and over one another's susceptibilities, and over chance ruts and stones on their way to the station. He began immediately :

' We were interrupted in our talk just now ; but I have

really very little more to say. If you are dissatisfied, if you really wish to break off your engagement, it is much better to say so at once, without making me appear ridiculous before all those men. Perhaps,' said Henley, ' we may have both made some great mistake, and you have seen some one whom you would prefer to myself ? '

' You must not say such things, Robert,' answered Dolly, with some emotion. ' You know how unhappy I am. I only want you to let me love you. What more can I say ? '

' Your actions and your words scarcely agree, then,' said Henley, jealous and implacable. ' I confess I shall be greatly surprised, on my return from India at some indefinite period, to find you still in the same mind. I myself make no professions of extra constancy ——'

' Oh, you are too cruel,' cried poor Dolly, exasperated.

' Will you promise me never to see Raban, for instance ? ' said Robert.

' How can I make such a promise ? ' cried Dolly, indignant. ' To turn off a kind friend for an unjust fancy ! If you trust me, Robert, you must believe what I say. Anyhow, you are free. Only remember that I shall trust in your love until you yourself tell me that you no longer care for me.'

The carriage stopped as she spoke. Robert got out and helped her down, produced the tickets, and paid the flyman.

The two went back in a dreary *tête-à-tête* ; she wanted a heart's sympathy, and he placed a rug at her feet and pulled up the carriage window for fear of a draught. She could not thank him, nor look pleased. Her head ached, her heart ached ; one expression of love, one word of faithful promise would have made the world a different place, but he had not spoken it. He had taken her at her word. She was to be bound, and he was to be free. The old gentleman opposite never looked at them, but instantly composed himself to sleep; the old lady in the corner thought she had rarely seen a more amiable and attentive young man, a more ungracious young lady.

Once only Robert made any allusion to what had passed. 'There will be no need to enter into explanations at present,' he said, in a somewhat uneasy manner. 'You may change your mind, Dora.'

'I shall never change my mind,' said Dolly, wearily, 'but it is no use troubling mamma and Aunt Sarah; I will tell them that I am not going away. They shall know all when you are gone.'

Dolly might have safely told Mrs. Palmer, who was not often disquieted by other people's sacrifices. With Lady Sarah it was different. But she was ill, and she had lost her grasp of life. She asked no question, only she seemed to revive from the day when Dolly told her that she was not going to leave her. It was enough for her that the girl's hand was in hers.

What is Dolly thinking of, as she stands by the sick bed, holding the frail hand? To what future does it guide her? Is it to that which Dolly has sometimes imagined contained within the walls of a home; simple, as some people's lives are, and hedged with wholesome briers, and darling home-ties, and leading straight, with great love and much happiness and sacred tears, to the great home of love? or is it to a broad way, unhedged, unfenced, with a distant horizon, a way unsheltered in stormy weather, easily missed, but wide and free and unshackled? . . .

Mrs. Palmer, who troubled herself little about the future, was for ever going off to Dean's Yard, where the Henleys were comfortably established. The eldest daughter was married, but there were two lively girls still at home ; there were young officers coming and going about the place. There was poor Jonah preparing to depart on his glorious expedition. He was in good spirits, he had a new uniform. One day, hearing his aunt's voice, he came in to show himself, accoutred and clanking with chains. He was disappointed to find that Dolly was not there as he had expected. Bell admired loudly, but her mother almost screamed to him to go and take the hideous thing off. The dry, brisk-tongued little woman was feeling his departure very acutely. She still made an effort to keep up her old cynical talk, but she broke down, poor soul, again and again ; she had scarcely spirit left to contradict Philippa, or even to forbid her the house.

The first time she had seen Dolly, she had been prepared to criticise the girl ; Norah and Bell were more cordial, but Lady Henley offered her niece a kid glove and a kid cheek, and was slightly disappointed to find that Dolly's frivolity, upon which she had been descanting all the way to Church House, consisted in an old grey gown and a black apron, and in two black marks under her eyes, for poor Dolly had not had much sleep after that dismal talk with Robert. This was the day after the Cambridge expedition. Miss Vanborough was looking very handsome, notwithstanding the black marks, and she unconsciously revenged herself upon Lady Henley by a certain indifference and pre-occupation, which seemed to put her beyond the reach of that lady's passing shafts ; but one of them wounded her at last.

' I suppose Lady Sarah will be left to servants when you go ? ' says Lady Henley. ' Your mother is certainly not to be counted on · Hawtry is a much better nurse than she is.

Poor dear Philippa! she sees everything reflected in a looking-glass. Your school is a different one altogether from our plain, old-fashioned country ways.'

Dolly looked surprised; she had not deserved this un-provoked attack from the little gaily-dressed lady perched upon the sofa. Norah was very much distressed by her mother's rudeness; Bell was struggling with a nervous inclination to giggle, which was the effect it always produced upon her.

'I have no doubt mamma would take care of my aunt if it were necessary,' said Dolly, blushing with annoyance. 'But I am not going away,' she said. 'Robert and I have settled that it is best I should stay behind. We have made up our minds to part.'

The two girls were listening open-eared. 'Then she has never cared for him, after all,' thought Bell.

But Lady Henley knew better: notwithstanding a more than usual share of jealousy and cross-grainedness, she was not without a heart. Dolly's last words had been spoken very quietly, but they told the whole story. 'My dear,' said the little woman, jumping up suddenly and giving her a kiss, 'I did not know this' (there were tears shining among the new green bonnet-strings)—'my trial is close at hand. You must forgive me, I—I am very unhappy.' She made a struggle, and recovered herself quickly, but from that minute Dolly and her Aunt Joanna were good friends.

The next time Robert called in Dean's Yard he was put through a cross-examination by Lady Henley. 'When was he coming back for Dolly? what terms were they on?' Sir Thomas came in to hear all about it, and then Jonah sauntered in. 'Only wish I could get a chance,' said Jonah. Robert felt disinclined to give Jonah the chance he wished for. Lady Henley was now praising Dolly as much as she had abused her before, and Robert agreed to everything. But he gave no clue to the state of his mind. He was surprised to find how entirely Lady Henley ignored his feelings and sympathised with Dolly's determination to remain behind. He walked away thinking that it was far from his intention to break entirely with Dolly, but he had not forgiven her yet; he was not sorry to feel his liberty in his own hands again. He meant to come back, but he chose to do it of his own free will, and not because he was bound by any promise.

As for Dolly, she was absorbed, she was not feeling very much just then, she had been overwrought and overstrained. A dull calm had succeeded to her agitation, and besides Robert was not yet gone.

CHAPTER XL.

UNDER THE CLOCK-TOWER.

I will tell you when they parted.
When plenteous autumn sheaves were brown,
Then they parted heavy-hearted.
The full rejoicing sun looked down
As grand as in the days before:
Only to them those days of yore
Could come back nevermore.

—C. Rossetti.

An archway leads out of the great thoroughfare from Westminster Bridge into the sudden silence of Dean's Yard,
where Sir Thomas had taken the house of a country neighbour. It stood within the cloisters of the Abbey, over-
towered, over-clocked, with bells pealing high overhead
(ringing the hours away, the poor mother used to think).
Dolly found time one day to come for half-an-hour to see
Jonah before he left. She had a great regard for him. She
had also found a staunch friend in Norah with the grey eyes
like her own. Bell told Dolly in confidence that her mother
had intended Robert to marry Norah, but this had not at all
interfered with the two girls' liking for one another. Mrs.
Palmer, who was going on farther, set Dolly down at the
archway, and as the girl was crossing the Yard she met
Robert coming from the house. He was walking along by
the railing, and among the dead leaves that were heaped

there by the wind. Dolly's heart always began to beat now when she saw Robert. This time he met her, and, with something of his old manner, said, 'Are you in a hurry? Will you come with me a little way? I have something to say.' And he turned into the cloister: she followed him at once.

From Dean's Yard, one gateway leads to common life and to the day's work, struggling by with creaks and whips and haste; another gateway brings you to a cloister arched, silent. The day's work is over for those who are lying in the peaceful enclosure. A side door from this cloister leads into the Abbey, where, among high piles and burning windows, and the shrill sweet echoes of the Psalms, a silent voice sometimes speaks of something beyond rest, beyond our feeble mode of work and praise, and our music and Gothic-types—of that which is, but which we are not.

The afternoon service was pealing on and humming within the Abbey as Dolly and Robert walked slowly along the cloister. He was silent a long time. She tried to ask him what he had to say, but she found it difficult to speak to him now. She was shy, and she scarcely knew upon what terms they were: she did not care to know. She had said that he should be free, and she meant it, and she was too generous to seek to extort unwilling promises from him, or to imply that she was disappointed that he had given none.

At last Robert spoke. 'Dolly, shall you write to me?' he said.

'Yes, Robert, if you wish it,' she answered, simply. 'I should like to write to you.'

As she looked at him, fair and blushing, Robert said suddenly, 'Tell me, Dora, have you never regretted your decision?'

Dolly turned away—she could not meet his eyes. Hers fell upon a slab to the memory of some aged woman, who had, perhaps, gone through some such experience before she had been turned into a stone. Dolly was anything but stone. Tears slowly gathered in her eyes, and Robert saw them, and caught hold of her hand, and at that minute there came some pealing echo of an organ, and of voices bursting into shrill amens. All her life Dolly remembered that strange moment of parting, for parting she felt it to be. She must tell him the truth. She turned. 'No, Robert— never once,' she said; 'although it is even harder than I thought to let you go.'

They were standing by the door at the end of the first cloister. For the last time he might have spoken then, and told her that he only loved her the more, that distance was nothing to him, that time was nothing; but the service had come to an end, and while he hesitated a verger came out in his black gown, and the congregation followed—one or two strangers, then Jonah and Bell, with red eyes both of them, looking foolish somehow, and ashamed of being seen; then more strangers, and then with the last remaining verger, came Rhoda and Zoe Morgan, who sometimes went to church at the Abbey. They all joined the young couple and walked back to the house with them.

This was Dolly's last chance for an explanation with her cousin. The time was drawing to an end, fate came in between them now, for this very afternoon it was settled rather suddenly, at Sir Thomas's request, that Robert and Jonah should go as far as Marseilles together. This was Thursday, and the young men were to start on the Saturday evening.

Lady Henley bore up very well at first, and clenched

her teeth, and said they should all come to dinner on Friday.

'It is no use sitting alone and crying one's eyes out,' said the poor woman valiantly, and she made Sir Thomas ask a couple of Yorkshire friends to the feast. One was a county hero, in great favour with Bell. The other was Mr. Anley, Jonah's godfather. He had a great affection for the family, and regularly dined with them upon grave crises and great occasions.

Lady Henley, being liberal in her hospitality, ordered in her viands and her champagne-bottles, and the girls went to Covent Garden and bought fruit and pineapples and autumn flowers to dress the table, and poor Jonah brought in a great baked pie from Gunter's.

'It's pâté-de-foie-gras,' said he. 'My father likes it. I thought I might as well have it to celebrate the occasion.' And he held it up triumphantly.

Poor Lady Henley had almost overrated her powers of endurance, for she looked into his honest sallow face, and then suddenly got up and rushed out of the room.

'Go to her, Jonah,' said the girls, looking very pale.

Jonah came down after a little while with a very red nose, and then he went out again to buy something else. All day long he kept coming and going in cabs, bringing home one thing after another—a folding-chair, a stick to open out suddenly, a whole kitchen battery fitted into a tea-kettle, brooches for the girls, toys for his eldest sister's children. As for the contrivances, they served to make one evening pass a little less heavily, and amused them for the time, and gave them something to talk about. But soon after, all poor Jonah's possessions went down in the Black Sea, in an ill-fated ship, that foundered with far more precious freight on board than tin pans and folding-chairs.

Punctual to her time on the Friday, Lady Henley was there to receive her guests in her stiffest silks, laces, and jewels, looking like some battered fetish out of a shrine, as she sat at the head of the table.

Dolly came to dinner sorely against her will, but she was glad she had come when she saw how Jonah brightened up; and when the poor little wooden mother held up her face and kissed her.

Lady Henley said, ' How do you do ? ' to her guests, but never spoke to any of them. It was a dreary feast. Robert failed at the last moment, and they sat down to a table with a gap where his place should have been. No one ate the pie except Sir Thomas, who swallowed a little bit with a gulp; then he called for champagne, and his face turned very red, and he looked hard at his son, and drank a long draught.

Jonah quickly filled his glass, and muttered something as he tossed it off. He had got his mother's hand under the table in his long bony fingers. Lady Henley was sitting staring fixedly before her. As Jonah drank their healths, Norah gave a little gasp. Mr. Anley took snuff. One of the country neighbours, young Mr. Jack Redmayne, whom Miss Bell used to meet striding, riding, and walking round about Smokethwaite, had begun a story about some cele-brated mare; he paused for an instant, then suddenly rally-ing, went on and on with it, although nobody was listening, not even Miss Bell.

' I thought it best to go on talking,' he said afterwards. ' I hope they don't think it unfeeling. I'm sure I don't know what I said. I put my horse a dozen times over the

same gate; even old Firefly wouldn't stand such treatment.'
So the dinner went on; the servants creaked about, and the
candles burnt bright, but no one could rally, and Lady
Henley was finally obliged to leave the table.

Immediately after dinner came old Sam with his cab,
and Dolly and her mother got up to go.

'I cannot think what possessed Joanna to give that
funeral-feast,' said Mrs. Palmer, as they were putting on
their cloaks.

'Hush, mamma,' said Dolly, for Jonah was coming running and tumbling downstairs breathless from his mother's
room.

'Look here, Dolly,' he said: 'mother wants you to come
and see her to-morrow after I am gone, and don't let her
worry too much, and would you please take this?' he said.
'Please do.'

This was a pretty little crystal watch that he had bought
for her, and when Dolly hesitated and exclaimed, he added,
entreatingly, 'It is my wedding present. I thought in case
we never—I mean that I should like to give it to you
myself,' he said.

'Oh! Jonah,' Dolly answered in a low voice, 'perhaps I
may never want a wedding present.'

'Never mind, keep it,' said Jonah, staring at her hand,
'and I'll look up George the first thing. You know my
father has written to his colonel. Keep a good heart, Dolly;
we are all in the same boat.'

He stood watching the cab as it drove away under the stars.

Dolly was not thinking of Jonah any more. She was
looking at all the passers-by, still hoping to see Robert.

'He ought to have come, mamma, this last night?' she
said.

'My dear, do you ever expect a man to think of anything but his own convenience?' said Mrs. Palmer, with great emphasis.

'Oh! mamma, why must one ever say good-by?' said Dolly, going on with her own thoughts.

'I believe, even now he might persuade you to run off with him,' said Mrs. Palmer, laughing. . . . .

It was over. He was gone. He had come and gone. Dolly had both dreaded and longed to be alone with Robert, but her mother had persistently stayed in the room. It was about four o'clock when he came, and Dolly left her aunt's bedside and came down to the summons, and stood for an instant at the drawing-room door. She could hear his voice within. She held the door-handle, as she stood dizzy and weary. She thought of the Henleys parting from their son, and envied them. Ah! how much easier to part where love is a certainty; and now this was the last time—and he was going, and she loved him, and she had sent him away, and he had never said one word of regret, nor promised once to come back.

She had offered to set him free; she had said she could not leave them all. At this moment, in her heart, Dolly felt as if she *could* have left them; and as if Robert, in going and in ceasing to love her, was taking away all the light and the strength of her life. He seemed to be making into a certainty that which she had never believed until now, and proving to her by his deeds that his words were true, although she had refused to believe them. She had given him a heart out of her own tender heart, a soul out of her own loving imagination, and now where were her imaginations? Some dry blast seemed to her to be beating about

A A

the place, choking her parched throat and drying her tears. Her eyes were dull and heavy-lidded ; her face looked pale and frightened as she opened the door and walked in. 'Dolly is so strong,' Mrs. Palmer was saying, 'she has courage for us all. I do not fear for her.'

'Perhaps it is best as it is,' Henley answered a little hurriedly. ' I shall go out solely with a view to making money, and come home all the sooner. It is certainly better not to disturb Lady Sarah with leave-takings.'

He looked up and saw Dolly coming across the room, and was shocked by the girl's pale face.

'My dearest Dora,' said Henley, going to meet her, ' how ill you look; you would never have been fit for the journey.'

'Perhaps not,' said Dolly. She was quite passive, and let him hold her hand, but a cold shadow of bitterness seemed to have fallen upon her. It was a chilly August day. They had lit a small wood fire, and they now brought some coffee to warm Robert before he left. Robert was very much moved, for him.

He put down his coffee-cup untasted, and stood by the tall chimney looking down into the fire. Then he looked at his watch, and went up to his aunt and said good-by, and then he came and stood opposite Dolly, who was by the window, and looked her steadily in the face. She could not look up, though she felt his eyes upon her, and he kissed her. 'God bless you,' he said, deserting his post with a prayer, as people do sometimes, and without looking back once, he walked out of the room.

Robert left the room. Dolly stood quite still where he had left her ; she heard the servants' voices outside in the hall, the carriage starting off, some one calling after it, but the wheels rolled on. She stood dully looking through the window at some birds that were flying across the sky. There were cloud heaps sailing, and dead leaves blowing along the terrace, the bitter parching wind was still blowing. It was not so much the parting as the manner of it. She had thought it so simple to love and to be loved; she had never believed that a word would change him. Was it her fault? Had she been cold, unkind? She was very young still, she longed for one word of sympathy. She turned to her mother with a sudden impulse.

'Oh, mamma!' she said, piteously.

'I cannot think how you can have been so hard-hearted, Dolly,' said her mother. '*I* could not have let him go alone. How long the time will seem, poor fellow! Yes, you have been very tyrannical, Dolly.'

Was this all the comfort Mrs. Palmer had to give?

Something seemed choking in Dolly's throat; was it her hard heart that was weighing so heavily?

'Oh! mamma, what could I do?' she said. 'I told him he was free: he knows that I love him, but indeed he is free.'

Mrs. Palmer uttered an impatient exclamation. She had been wandering up and down the room. She stopped short.

'Free! what do you mean. You have never said one word to me. What *have* you been about? Do you mean that he may never come back to you?'

But Dolly scarcely heard her mother's words. The door had opened and some one came in. Never come back? This was Robert himself who was standing there. He had come to say one more farewell. He went straight up to her and he caught her in his arms. 'There was just time,' he said. 'Good-by once more, dearest Dora!' It was but a

moment; it was one of those moments that last for a lifetime. Dolly lived upon it for many a day to come. He
loved her, she thought to herself, or he would never have
come back to her, and if he loved her the parting had lost
its sting.

CHAPTER XLI.

I BRING YOU THREE LETTERS — I PRAY YOU READ ONE.

Nay, if you read this line, remember not the hand that writ it.

THE partings were over. Dolly lived upon that last farewell for many a day to come. Such moments are states, and not mere measures of life. Everything else was sad enough. Lady Sarah still lingered. Poor little Lady Henley in her home in Dean's Yard was yellow and silent, and fierce in her anxiety. What was it to her that Sebastopol was to fall before the victorious armies if the price she had to pay was the life of her son? She kept up as best she could, but the strain told upon her health and her temper. Sir Thomas kept meekly out of the way. The servants trembled and gave warning; the daughters could not give warning. Woe betide Norah if she were late for breakfast. Ill-fated Bell used to make *mal-àpropos* speeches, which were so sternly vented upon her that she used to go off in tears to her father. Sir Thomas himself was in an anxious, unsettled state, coming and going from his desk, poring over maps and papers, and the first of those awful broadsheets of fated names overcame him completely. He burnt the paper, and would not let it go upstairs; but how keep out the lurid gleam of Victory that was spreading over the country? Her flaming sword hung over all their heads by one single thread; it was the life of one man against the whole campaign for many of them. Hoarse voices would come shouting and shrieking in the streets; there was but one thought in everybody's mind. All day long it seemed in the air, and a nightmare in the darkness. Poor Sir Thomas had no heart to go out, and used to sit gloomily in a little back study, with a wire blind, and four pairs of boots, and *The Times* and a blotted cheque-book ; he determined at last to take his wife home to Yorkshire again. There at least some silence was to be found among the moors and the rocky ridges, and some seeming of peace.

But for a long time Lady Henley refused to go. She was nearer Jonah in London, she said. The post came in one day sooner. It must have brought news to many an anxious home. What letters they are, those letters written twenty years ago, with numbed fingers, in dark tents, on chill battle-fields, in hospital wards. All these correspondents are well and in good heart, according to their own accounts. They don't suffer much from their wounds ; they don't mind the cold ; they think of the dear people at home, and write to them after a weary night's watch, or a fierce encounter, in the gentlest words of loving remembrance. The dying man sends his love and a recommendation for some soldier's children or widow at home ; the strong man is ready to meet his fate, and is full of compassion for suffering. ' I am writing on poor ——'s sabretache. I am keeping it for his brother at home,' says one. Another has been to see his sick friend, and sends cheering accounts of his state. Then, too, we may read, if we choose, the hearty, ill-spelt correspondence of the common soldiers, all instinct with the same generous and simple spirit. There are also the

proclamations of the generals. The French announce : ' The
hour is come to fight, to conquer, to triumph over the de-
moralised columns of the enemy. The enterprise is great
and worthy of their heroism. Providence appears to be on
their side, as well as an immense armament of guns and
forces, and the high valour of their English allies and the
chosen forces of the Ottoman Empire. The noble confidence
of the generals is to pass into the souls of the soldiers.' At
the same time, as we read in the English correspondent's
letter, Lord Raglan issues his memorandum, requesting Mr.
Commissary-General Filder ' to take steps to insure that the
troops shall all be provided with a ration of porter for the
next few days.'

There is the record of it all in the old newspapers. Private
Vance's letters are not given, for Dolly kept them for her
own reading when they came at last. By the same mail
came news from the two last departing travellers. Marker,
who had brought in the letters one evening, waited in the
doorway.

' George !' cried Dolly, tearing her first envelope open,
and then half-laughing, half-crying, she read her letter out.

George seemed in good spirits. He wrote from Varna.
A previous packet must have been lost, for he said he had
written before. This was a cheerful and affectionate letter,
quite matter-of-fact, and with no complaints or railings at
fate.

' I daresay people think me a great fool,' he said, ' but,
on the whole, I don't regret what I have done, except for
any annoyance it may have caused you. If you and mamma
would go to the Horse Guards and ask for a commission for
me, perhaps two such pretty ladies might mollify the
authorities. They say commissions are not difficult to get

just now. I shall consult the colonel about it ; I am to see
him again in a day or two. I don't know why I did not
speak to him just now when he sent for me.' Then he went
on to say that his Bulbul scholarship had stood him in good
service, and his little Turkish had been turned to account.
He had already passed as second-class interpreter, and he
had got hold of some books and was getting on. 'This is
the reason why the Colonel sent for me yesterday morning.
I am Private Vance, remember, only just out of the awkward
squad. Our Colonel is a grand old man, with bright eagle
eyes, and the heroic manner. He is like one of your
favourite heroes. Do you remember Aunt Sarah's talking of
David Fane, our father's old friend? When I found out
who he was I felt very much inclined to tell him my real
name. He said to me at once, "I see you are not exactly
what you appear to be. If you will come to me in a day or
two I shall be glad to talk to you about your prospects ; in
the meanwhile don't forget what a good influence one man
of good education and feeling can exert in the ranks of a
regiment." Old Fane himself is no bad specimen of a true
knight ; we all feel the better for knowing him. He walks
with a long swift stride like a deer, tossing his head as he
goes. I have never seen him in battle, but I can imagine
him leading his men to victory, and I am glad of the chance
which has given me such a leader. I wish there were more
like him. Tell Raban, if you see him, that I am getting on
very well, and that, far from being a black sheep here, no
lambskin can compare with my pipe-clay.' Then came
something erased. 'Dearest Dolly, you don't know what
your goodness has been to me all this time. I hope Robert
appreciates his good luck. This will reach you about the
time of your wedding-day. I will send you a little Russian

belt when I can find an opportunity. My love to them all, and be kind to Rhoda, for the sake of your most affectionate

'G. V.'

There was a P.S.

'I forgot to ask you when I last wrote whether you got the letter I wrote you at Cambridge, and if old Miller gave you my packet. I bought the form in the town as I walked down to the boats; it all seems a horrid dream as I think of it now, and I am very much ashamed of that whole business; and yet I should like to leave matters as they are, dear, and to feel that I have done my best for that poor little girl. My love to old John; tell him to write. There has been a good deal of sickness here, but the worst is over.'

The paper trembled in Dolly's hand as she dwelt upon every crooked line and twist of the dear handwriting that wrote 'George is safe.'

'I told you all along it was absurd to make such a disturbance about him. You see he was enjoying himself with his common associates,' said Mrs. Palmer crossly. 'Strangely peculiar,' she added after a moment. 'Dolly, did it ever occur to you that the dear boy was a little —— ? ' and she tapped her fair forehead significantly.

'He was only unhappy, mamma, but you see he is getting better now,' said Dolly.

The next time Dolly saw Rhoda she ran up and kissed her, looking so kind that Rhoda was quite surprised and wondered what had happened to make Dolly so nice again.

CHAPTER XLII.

RACHEL.

Shepherd, what's love, I pray thee tell ?
It is that fountain and that well
Where pleasure and repentance dwell ;
It is perhaps that saucing bell
That tolls all into heaven or hell.
And this is love as I heard tell.

IT was not only in the hospitals at Varna that people were anxious and at work at the time when George wrote. While the English ships were embarking their stores and their companies, their horses and their battalions, transporting them through surf and through storm to the shores of the fierce Russian Empire ; while Eastern hospitals were organising their wards, nurses preparing to start on their errand ; while generals were sitting in council,—an enemy had attacked us at home in the very heart of our own great citadel and store place, and the peaceful warriors sent to combat this deadly foe are fighting their own battles. Cholera was the name of the enemy, and among those who had been expecting the onslaught, haranguing, driving companies of somewhat reluctant officials, good old John Morgan had been one of the most prominent. His own district at Kensington was well armed and prepared, but John Morgan's life at Kensington was coming to an end,

and he had accepted a certain small living in the city called
St. Mary Outh'gate, of which the rector was leaving after five
or six years' hard work. 'It is a case of bricks' without
straw,' said the poor worn-out rector. Morgan was full of
courage and ready to try his hand. Mrs. Morgan, with a
sigh given to the old brown house and its comfortable cupboards, had agreed to move goods and chattels shortly into
the dark little rectory in the City court, with its iron gates
and its one smutty tree. To the curate's widow and mother
there was an irresistible charm in the thought of a rectory.

St. Mary Outh'gate was a feeble saint, and unable to protect her votaries from the evil effects of some open sewers
and fish-heaps when the cholera broke out—at John's
request the move was delayed. The girls remained at Kensington, while Mrs. Morgan travelled backwards and forwards
between the homes. Every day the accounts grew more and
more serious, and in the month of September the mortality
had reached its height.

John's new parish of St. Mary Outh'gate lies on the river
side of a great thoroughfare, of which the stream of carts
and wheels rolls by from sunrise until the stars set. The
rectory-house stood within its iron gates, in a court at the end
of a narrow passage. The back of the house looked into a
cross lane leading to the river. The thoroughfare itself was
squalid, crowded, bare; there was nothing picturesque about
it; but in the side streets were great warehouse cranes starting from high windows, and here and there some relic of
past glories. Busy to-day had forgotten some old doorway
perhaps, or left some garden or terrace-wall, or some old
banqueting-room still standing. It had swept the guests
into the neighbouring churchyards on its rapid way. To-day
was in a fierce and reckless mood : at home and abroad were

anxious people watching the times, others were too busy to be anxious. John was hard at work and untiring. He had scarcely had time to unpack his portmanteau and to put up his beloved books and reports. His start had been a dispiriting one. People had been dying by scores in the little lane at the back of the rectory. Mrs. Morgan herself fell ill of anxiety and worry, and had to go home. It must be confessed that the cares of the move and the capabilities of the drawing-room carpet added not a little to the poor lady's distress. Betty remained to take care of her master, and to give him her mind. John bore the old woman's scolding with great sweetness of temper. 'You do your work, Betty, and let me do mine,' said he. He had taken in two professional nurses after his mother left, and his curate, whose landlady had died of the prevailing epidemic. The two men worked with good will. John came, went, preached, fumed, wrote letters to *The Times*. Frank, who was in town, came to see him one day. He found the curate in good spirits. Things were beginning to look a little less dark, and John was one of those who made the best of chance lights. He received his friend heartily, wheeled his one arm-chair up for him, and lit a pipe in his honour. The two sat talking in the old bare black room leading into the court. John gave a short account of his month's work.

'It's over now—at least, the worst is over,' he said, 'and the artisans are at work again. It's the poor little shopkeepers I pity, they have lost everything—health, savings, customers—they are quite done up. However, I have a friend in the neighbourhood to whom I go, and Lady Sarah heard of my letter to *The Times* and sent me fifty pounds for them the other day. Dolly brought it herself. I was sorry to see her looking worn, poor dear. I think it is a pity that Mrs. Palmer takes so very desponding a view of her daughter's prospects. Dolly seemed disinclined to speak on the subject, so I did not press her, and we all know,' said the curate, in a constrained sort of voice, 'that Henley is a high-minded man, his good judgment, and sense of . . . .'

'His own merit,' said Raban, testily. 'What a thing it is to have a sense of one's own virtue. He will get on in India, he will get on in every quarter of the world, he will go to heaven and be made an archangel. He has won a prize already that he does not know how to value at its worth, and never will as long as he lives.'

John Morgan looked very much disturbed. 'I am very sorry to hear you say this. Tell me as a friend, when Mrs. Palmer declares the engagement is broken off, do you really think there is any fear of . . . .'

Frank jumped up suddenly.

'Broken off!' he cried, trying to hide his face of supreme satisfaction, and he began walking up and down the room. 'Does she say so?'

The dismal little room seemed suddenly illumined; the smoky court, the smutty-tree, the brown opposite foggy houses were radiant. Frank could not speak. His one thought was to see Dolly, to find out the truth; he hardly heard the rest of the curate's sentence. 'I have been so busy,' he was saying, 'that I have scarcely had one minute to think about it all; but I love Dolly dearly, she is a noble creature, and I should heartily grieve to hear that anything had occurred to trouble her. Are you going already?'

There is a little well of fresh water in Kensington Gardens, sparkling among the trees, and dripping into a stone basin. A few stone steps lead down to the lion's head from whence the slender stream drips drop by drop into the basin; the children and the birds, too, come and drink there. Somewhere near this well a fairy Prince was once supposed to hold his court. The glade is lovely in summer, and pleasant in autumn, especially late in the day, when the shadows are growing long, and the stems of the murmurous elm-trees shine with western gold.

Frank Raban was crossing from the high-road towards the Palace gate, and he was walking with a long shadow of his own, when he chanced to see a nymph standing by the railing and waiting while the stream trickled into the cup below. As he passed she looked up, their eyes met, and Frank stopped short, for the nymph was that one of which he had been thinking as he came along—Dorothea of the pale face and waving bronze hair.

As he stopped Eliza came up the steps of the well, bringing her young mistress the glass; it was still very wet with the spray of the water, and Dolly, smiling, held it out to Raban, who took it with a bow from her hand. It was more than he had ever hoped, to meet her thus alone at the moment when he wanted to see her, to be greeted so kindly, so silently. No frowning Robert was in the background, only Eliza waiting with her rosy face, while Dolly stood placid in the sloping light in the sunset and the autumn. Her broad feathered hat was pushed back, her eyes were alight.

'I am so glad to see you,' she said. 'You have heard our good news from George? it came two nights ago. My aunt has been asking for you, Mr. Raban. What have you been doing all this time?'

'I have been at Cambridge,' said Frank. 'I am only up in town for two days; I was afraid of being in your way. Is everybody gone? Are you alone? How is Lady Sarah?'

At the Well.

'She is better, I think. I am going back to her now,' said Dolly. 'I came here with Eliza to get her some of this chalybeate water. Will you come with me part of the way home?'

Of course he would come. He was engaged to dine at the club, and his hosts never forgave him for failing; he had letters to answer and they remained on the table. He had left John Morgan in a hurry, too much excited by the news he had heard to smoke out his pipe in tranquillity, but here was peace under the chestnut-trees where the two shadows were falling side by side and lengthening as the world heaved towards the night.

As they were walking along Frank began telling Dolly about a second letter he had received from his grandfather; he could never resist the wish to tell her all about himself; even if she did not care to hear, he liked to tell her.

'I am in an uncertain state of mind,' he said. 'Since I saw you my grandfather has taken me into favour again: after these seven years he offers me Leah. He wants me to give up driving young gentlemen and to take to sheep-shearing and farming and a good allowance. He writes to me from Harrogate. I should have a house and serve in bondage, and live upon him, and rescue him from the hands of the agents who now perform that office very effectually,' said Ruban, dryly.

'What do you mean?' said Dolly, looking at him doubtfully.

'This is what I mean,' said Frank; 'I cannot forget how badly the old people used me, and how for seven years they have left me to shift for myself. I have always failed in ambition. I shall never win Rachel,' he said, 'and I want nothing else that anybody can give me; and what is the use of putting my head under the tyrannic old yoke?'

'It is so difficult to be just,' Dolly answered, leading the way under the trees. 'When I try to think of right and wrong it all seems to turn into people and what they wish and what I would like to do for them. I wonder if some people can love by rule? And yet love must be the best rule, mustn't it? and if your poor old grandfather is sorry and begs you to go to him, it seems cruel to refuse.'

She seemed to be speaking in tune to some solemn strain of music which was floating in the air.

Frank was looking at the ground, and without raising his eyes he presently said,—'Well, I suppose you are right; I shall take your advice and give up the dry crust of liberty and try to be content with cakes and ale; such strong ale, Miss Vanborough, such heavy cakes,' he added, looking at her absently.

Dolly blushed up, hesitated: she was rather frightened by the responsibility Frank seemed to put upon her.

'Could not you ask some one else?' she said, confusedly. 'Perhaps Rachel,' she added, not without a little jealous pang, lest Rachel might be Rhoda, and her poor boy's last chance undone.

The light seemed to come from Raban's dark eyes. 'I *have* asked Rachel,' he said, in a low voice that seemed to thrill clear and distinct on her ears. 'Is it possible? do you not know it? Is not your name Rachel to me? are you not the only Rachel in the whole world for me? I never thought I should tell you this,' cried Frank, 'until just now, when I heard from John Morgan that you were free; but now, whatever your answer may be, I tell you, that you may know that you are the one only woman whom I shall ever love. My dear, don't look frightened, don't turn away. Robert Henley never loved you as I do.'

His coldness was gone; his half sarcastic, half sulky, careless manner was gone. It had given way to a sort of tender domination; the real generous fire of truth and un-selfish love, that belonged to the man and had always been in him, seemed to flash out. The music still clanged on, solemnly jarring with his words. Dolly turned pale and cold.

'I am not free; it has all been a mistake,' she said, very quickly. 'You must not speak to me of Robert like that.'

His face changed. 'Are you still engaged to him?' he asked, looking at her steadily.

'I promised to wait for him, and you have no right to ask me anything at all,' she cried, turning upon him. 'Oh, why did you—how can you speak to me so?' She spoke vehemently, passionately.

He was silent; but she had answered his eyes, not his spoken words. He saw that her eyes were full of tears. He had read her too carefully to have had much hope. He saw that she was overpowered, that she was bound to Robert still, that his wild dream of happiness was but a vision. It was no new revelation to him. 'You might have guessed it all long ago,' said he, shortly. 'But you would not under-stand me before, when I tried to tell you that I loved you. Now you know all,' he said, with a sigh. 'Forget it if you like.'

He would have left her, but Eliza had disappeared, and a crowd of people were gathered outside the gate, rough-looking Irish among them from the buildings opposite. A military funeral was passing by, the music had ceased, and the soldiers went tramping down the street in a long and solemn line; the slow fall of their feet struck upon the hard road and echoed with a dull throb. People were looking on in silence and crowding to the windows and in the doorways. As the dead man's horse was led by with the empty saddle and the boots swinging from the side, Dolly turned away pale and trembling, and Raban was glad then he had not left her. She put out her hand for a moment. She seemed blinded and scared.

Then she recovered herself quickly, and when the crowd gave way, she walked on in silence by his side until they came to the turning that led to the old house. 'Thank you,' she said, a little tremulously. 'Forgive me if I spoke harshly; it was best to tell you the truth.'

Raban had meant to leave her without a word: now he suddenly changed his mind. He held out his hand.

'Good-by, Rachel,' he said, still looking at her with silent reproach. 'Do not fear that I shall trouble and annoy you again; it would be hard to take your friendship and confidence away from me because of John Morgan's mistake.'

'How can you be my friend?' cried poor Dolly suddenly, passionate and angry once more. 'Leave me now—only go, please go.'

Henley would have been satisfied if he had been present.

Frank walked away, bitterly hurt and wounded; she seemed to resent his love as if it had been an insult. He was disappointed in Dolly, in life; the light was gone out, that one flash of happiness had shown him his own disappointment all the more plainly. We don't hope, and yet our hearts sink with disappointment: we expect nothing, but that nothing overwhelms us. And meanwhile life is going on, and death, and the many interests and changes of mortals coming and going on their journey through space. When Frank got back to Cambridge he found a telegram summoning him at once to Harrogate. It was sent by some unknown person.

People part—each carries away so much of the other's life ; very often the exchange is a hard-driven bargain, willingly paid indeed, which the poor debtor is in no inclination to resent :—a whole heart's fidelity and remembrance in sleepless nights, tendered prayers and blessings, and exchange for a little good grammar, a pleasant recollection, and some sand and ink and paper, all of which Dolly duly received that evening. All day long she had been haunted by that little scene at the well; it seemed to bring her nearer to Henley, and his letter came as an answer to her thoughts. George's letter had been for them all. Robert's was for herself alone, and she took it up to her room to read.

Robert's letter was not very short: it was sufficiently stamped: it said all that had to be said; and yet, ' How unreasonable I am! how can men feel as women do ?' thought Dolly, kissing the letter to make up for her passing disappointment. Then came a thought, but she put it away with a sort of anger and indignation. She would not let herself think of Frank with pity or sympathy. It seemed disloyal to Robert to be sorry for the poor tutor.

Lady Henley also received a blotted scrawl from Jonah by that same post, and she made up her mind at last to go home, and she sent the brougham for Dolly and her mother to come and wish her good-by. On her first arrival Dolly was pounced upon by her cousins and taken in to Sir Thomas. When she came upstairs at last, she found her aunt and her mother in full committee, apparently on good terms, and with their heads close together. The little lady was upon the sofa. Mrs. Palmer was upon the floor, in a favourite attitude. There only could she find complete rest,

she said.   Lady Henley had a great heap of Jonah's clothes
upon the sofa beside her ; she had been folding them up and
marking them with her own hands.   The drawing-room
seemed full of the sound of the bells from the towers outside,
and autumn leaves were dropping before the windows.

'Come here,' said Lady Henley, holding out her hand to
Dolly. 'I have been talking to your mother about you.
Look at her—as if there were no chairs in the room!   I
wanted to show you Jonah's letter.   Foolish boy, he sends you
his love ! I don't know why I should give the message.   You
know you don't care for him, Dolly.   Have you heard from
Robert ? Is he properly heart-broken ? ' with a sort of hoarse
laugh. 'Jonah mentions that he seems in very good spirits.'
Then Lady Henley became agitated.   Dolly stood silent and
embarrassed. 'Why don't you answer,' said her aunt, quite
fiercely. 'You can't answer ; you can't show us his letter ; you
know in your heart that it has been a foolish affair.   Your
mother has told me all.'

Lady Henley was flushed and getting more and more
excited, and, at the same time, Philippa gave one of her
silvery laughs, and starting actively to her feet, came and
put her arm round Dolly's waist.

'All ! no, indeed, Joanna.   Delightful creature as he is,
Robert tells one nothing.   Forgive me, dearest, it is a fact.
He really seemed quite to forget what was due to me, a lady
in her own drawing-room, when he said good-by to you.   I
only mention it, for he is not generally so *empressé*, and if
he had only explained himself ——'

'What have you been saying, mamma ? ' said Dolly,
blushing painfully. 'There is nothing to explain.'

'There is everything to explain,' burst in Lady Henley
from her corner ; 'and if you were my own daughter, Dolly,

I should think it my duty to remonstrate with you, and to tell you frankly what I have always said from the beginning. There never was the slightest chance of happiness in this entanglement for either of you; take the advice of an older woman than yourself. Robert has no more feeling for you than—than—a fish, or do you think he would consent to be free? Ah! if you were not so blinded. . . There is one honest heart,' she said, incoherently, breaking down for an instant. She quickly recovered, however, and Dolly, greatly distressed, stood looking at her, but she could not respond; if ever she had swerved, her faithful heart had now fully returned to its first allegiance. All they said seemed only to make her feel more and more how entirely her mind was made up.

'Robert and I understand each other quite well,' said Dolly, gravely. 'I wish him to be free. It is my doing, not his; please don't speak of this to me, or to any one else again.'

She had promised to herself to be faithful, whatever came. Her whole heart had gone after Robert as he left her. She knew that she loved him. With all her humility, the thought that she had made a mistake in him had been painful beyond measure. It seemed to her now that she was answerable for his faith, for his loyalty, and she eagerly grasped at every shadow of that which she hoped to find in him.

She walked away to the window to hide her own gathering tears. The bells had come to an end suddenly. Some children were playing in the middle of the road and pursuing one another, and a stray organ-man, seeing a lady at the window, pulled out his stop and struck up a dreary tune —'Partant pour la Syrie, le jeune et beau Dunois.' It was the tune of those times, but Dolly could never hear it afterwards without a sickening dislike. Dolly, hearing the door bang, turned round at last.

'My dear Dolly, she is gone—she is in a passion—she will never forgive you,' said Philippa, coming up in great excitement.

But she was mistaken. Lady Henley sent Dolly a little note that very evening :—

MY DEAR,—I was very angry with you to-day. Perhaps I was wrong to be angry. I will not say forgive an old woman for speaking the truth ; it is only what you deserve. You must come and see us when you can in Yorkshire. We all feel you belong to us now.

Yours affectionately,
JOANNA HENLEY.

P.S.—I see in this evening's paper that our poor old neighbours at Ravens-rick died at Harrogate within a day of one another. I suppose your friend Frank Raban comes into the property.

CHAPTER XLIII.

CRAGS AND FRESH AIR.

My prayers with this I used to charge :
A piece of land not very large,
Wherein there should a garden be ;
A clear spring flowing ceaselessly ;
And where, to crown the whole, there should
A patch be found of growing wood.
All this and more the gods have sent.
— HORACE : T. MARTIN.

THE old town of Pebblesthwaite, in Yorkshire, slides down
the side of a hill into the hollow. Rocks overtop the town-
hall, and birds flying from the crags can look straight down
into the greystone streets, and upon the flat roofs of the
squat houses. Pebblesthwaite lies in the heart of Craven,—
a country little known, and not yet within the tramp of the
feet of the legions. It is a district of fresh winds and rocky
summits, of thymy hill-sides, and of a quaint and arid
sweetness. The rocks, the birds, the fresh rush of the mountain streams as they dash over the stones, strike Southerners
most curiously. We contrast this pleasant turmoil with the
sleepy lap of our weed-laden waters, the dull tranquillity of
our fertile plains. If we did not know that we are but a
day's journey from our homes, we might well wonder and ask
ourselves in what unknown country we are wandering.

Strange-shaped hills heave suddenly from the plains; others, rising and flowing tumultuously, line the horizon: overhead great clouds are advancing, heaped in massive lines against a blue and solid sky. These clouds rise with the gusts of a sudden wind that blows into Frank Raban's face as he comes jogging through the old town on his way to the house, from which he had been expelled seven years before, and to which he was now returning as master. Smokethwaite is the metropolis of Pebblesthwaite, near which is Ravensrick. The station is on a little branch line of rail, starting off from the main line towards these rocks and crags of Craven.

Frank had come down with the Henleys, and seen them all driving off in the carriages and carts that had come down to meet them from the Court. Nothing had come for him, and he had walked to the inn and ordered the trap.

'Where art goin'?' shouts a pair of leather-gaiters standing firm upon the doorstep of an old arched house opposite.

'Ravensrick Court,' says the driver.

' 'Tis a blustering day,' says old leather-gaiters.

The driver cracks his whip, and begins to do the honours of Pebblesthwaite as the horse clatters over the stones. 'Do ye ken t' shambles?' he says, pointing to an old arched building overtopped by a great crag.

'I know it as well as you do,' says Frank, smiling.

Can it be seven years since he left? Raban looks about: every stone and every pane of glass seems familiar. The town was all busy and awake. The farmers, sturdy, crop-headed, with baskets on their arms, were chattering and selling, standing in groups, or coming in and out of shops and doorways, careful as any housewives over their pur-chases. There were strange stores—shoes, old iron, fish, all

heaped together; seven years older than when the last
market-day Frank was there, but none the worse for that.
There was the old auctioneer, in his tall, battered hat, dis-
posing of his treasures. He was holding up a horse's yoke to
competition. 'Three shillin'! four shillin'!' says he. The
people crowd and gape round. One fellow, in a crimson
waistcoat, driving past in a donkey-cart, stops short and
stares hard at the trap and at Raban. Frank knew him, and
nodded with a smile. Two more stumpy leather-gaiters,
greeting each other, looked up as he drove by, and grinned.
He remembered them too. There was the old Quaker, in his
white neckcloth, standing at the door of his handsome old
shop; and Squire Anley, walking along to the bank, all
dressed from head to foot in loose grey clothes, with his bull-
terrier at his heels. And then they drove out into the
straight country roads, under the bridge between stone
hedges, beyond which the late flames of summer green were
still gleaming,—the meadows still shone with spangling
autumn flowers. Far away in the hollow hung the smoke of
the factory, with its many windows; a couple of tall chimneys spouted blackness; a train was speeding northward;
close at hand a stream was dashing; the great trees seemed
full of birds. It was a different world from that in which he
had been basking. Frank already felt years younger as he
drove along the road,—the old boyish impulses seemed
waiting at every turn. 'Why, there goes old Brand,' he
cried, leaning forward eagerly to look after an old keeper,
with a couple of dogs, walking off with a gun towards the
hills.

Frank called after the keeper, but the wind carried away
his voice. As he drove along by each stile and corner that
seemed to have awaited his coming, he suddenly thought of

his talk with Dorothea. She had been cruelly hard to him,
but he was glad to think now that he had followed her
advice about forgiveness of injuries, and made an advance
to the poor old people who were now gone. It would have
been absurd to pretend to any great sorrow for their death.
They had lived their life and shown him little kindness
while it lasted. It was a chance now that brought him
back to Ravensrick again.

He had written an answer to his grandfather's letter and
accepted his offer, but the only answer which ever came to
this was the telegram summoning him to Harrogate. It
had been delayed on the way; and as he went down in the
train, the first thing he saw was a paragraph in *The Times*,—
' At the Mitre Hotel, Harrogate, on the 28th instant, John
Raban, Esq., of Ravensrick, Pebblesthwaite, aged 86 ; and
on the following day, Antonia, widow of the above John
Raban, Esq., aged 75.' The old squire had gone to Harrogate for the benefit of his health, but he had died quite
suddenly; and the poor lady to whom he had left everything, notwithstanding his injunctions and elaborate directions as to her future disposal of it, sank the night after his
death, unable to struggle through the dark hours.

And then came confusion, undertakers, lawyers, and
agents, in the midst of which some one thought of sending
for Frank. He was the old couple's one grandson, and the
old lady had left no will. So the tutor came in for the
savings of their long lives—the comfortable old house,
the money in the bank, the money in the funds, the ox and
the ass, and the man-servant and the maid-servant, who had
had their own way for so many years past, and preyed upon
the old couple with much fidelity. They all attended the
funeral in new suits of mourning ordered by the agent.

Frank recognised many of them. There was the old house-keeper who used to box his ears as a little boy; the butler who used to complain of him. He was oppressed by all these yards of black cloth and these dozens of white pocket-handkerchiefs; and he let them return alone to Ravensrick, and followed in the course of a day or two.

There are harsh words and unkind judgments in life, but what a might of nature, of oblivion and distraction is arrayed in battle against them; daylight, lamplight, sounds of birds and animals come in between, and turn the slander, the ill-spoken sentence and its fierce retort from its path. What do harsh words matter that were spoken a week ago? Seven days' sunshine have brightened since then. While I am railing at false friends and harsh interpretations, the clematis' flowers have starred the wavering curtain of green that shades my window from the light; the old Norman steeple has clanged the blue hours, the distant flow of the sea has reached me, with a sound of the twitter of birds in accompaniment. Is it six months ago since A. judged B. unkindly? A. and B., walking by the opal light of the distant horizon, are thinking no more of coldness and unkindness, but of the fresh sweetness of the autumnal sea.

As Frank comes driving along the well-known road, and the fresh blustering winds blow into his face, past unkind-ness matters little, every gust sends it farther away. He thinks, with a vague sense of pity, of a poor little ghost that used to run hiding and shrinking away in dark corners, a little fatalist doomed to break windows, slam doors, and leave gates ajar, through which accusing geese, sheep, ponies would straggle to convict him. He used to think they were all in one league against him. Twice a week on an average he was led up into his grandfather's study to be cross-examined and to criminate himself hopelessly before that inexorable old judge:—a handsome old man with flowing white locks and a grand manner and opinion upon every subject. If old Mrs. Raban generally supplied the opinions, the language was the Squire's own. Mrs. Raban had been a spoiled old beauty, rouged and frizzed and rustling; she disliked every one who interfered with her own importance. She adored her husband, and was jealous of him to the last. Some chance speech had set her against the poor little 'heir' as some one called him, and she had decreed that he was a naughty and stupid little boy and was to be kept in his place. There rises Frank's little doppelgänger before him, hanging his head, convicted of having broken the carriage-window, or some such offence; there sits the old judge in his arm-chair by the library-table, dignified, stately, uttering magnificent platitudes, to which the ancestor in the cauliflower wig is listening with deep attention. Frank seems to hear the echo of his voice and the rustle of his grandmother's dress as she leaves the room: but the horse starts, a partridge scuffles across the road, and he comes back to the present again.

'Yan goes,' says the driver, excitedly, standing up on his box. Then they pass a little tumbledown village, and there at a turn of the road rise the chimneys of Ravensrick, and Pen-y-ghent rearing its huge back behind them, and the iron gates, and the old avenue, and the crows flying, whirling, dancing, sliding in twos and threes and twenties— how often the little doppelgänger had watched their mystic dance. Had it been going on for seven years?

'There's t' Court,' said Frank's companion—a good-humoured, talkative man. 'T' owd Squire, he were respectit, but he let things go.' As he spoke they were passing by a cottage with a broken roof and a generally dilapidated, half-patched look; a ragged woman was standing at the door, two wild-looking children were rolling in the dust; at the same time a man on horseback, coming the contrary way, rode past them on the road. The driver touched his cap, the woman disappeared into the house.

'That's Thomas Close, t' agent,' said Frank's companion.

Frank, looking back as the carriage turned, saw a curious little scene. One of the children, who was standing in the road, suddenly stamped and clenched his little fist at the agent as he passed. The man reined in his horse, leant back, and cut at the child with his whip; the little boy, howling, ran into the cottage.

Frank asked the driver what he knew of the people in the cottage.

The man shrugged his shoulders. 'Mary Styles she is queer in her ways,' said he: 'i' t' habit o' snuffin' and drinkin'. Joe Styles he follows t' Squire's cart; t' agent give him notice la-ast Monday—he wer' down at our ya-ard wantin' work, poor chap,' said the man, with a crack of the whip. 'Thomas Close he says he will have nought nor bachelors upon t' farm. He's a ——'

'Stop,' said Frank: 'I'll get down here: take my portmanteau to the front door and tell them to pay you, and say that—a—I am coming.'

The man stared, and suddenly gave a low whistle as he drove off. Meanwhile the new Squire walked up by the back way. He crossed the kitchen-garden and got on to the terrace. How well he knew the way; the lock of the gate was easier than it used to be—the walls were greener and thicker with leaves and trellis. The old couple were coming back no more, but the beds they had planted were bright with Michaelmas daisies and lilies, and crimson and golden berries with purple leaves were heaping the terrace, where a man was at work snipping at the overgrowth of the box hedges. There was the iron scrolled gate through which you could see the distant view of Pen-y-ghent. There was the old summer-house, where he once kept a ménagerie of snails, until they were discovered by Miss Meal, his grandmother's companion. Coming out of the garden he found himself face to face with the long rows of doors and of windows—those deadly enemies of his youth; a big brown dog, like a fox, with a soft skin and a friendly nose, came trotting up with a friendly expression. It followed Frank along the back passage leading straight into the hall: it was one of those huge stone halls such as people in Yorkshire like. The man in armour stood keeping watch in his corner—the lantern swung, every chair was in its place, and the old man's hat and his dogskin gloves lay ready for him on the oak table.

Then Frank opened the dining-room door. It faced westward, and the light came sliding upon the floors and walls and shining old mirrors, just as he remembered it. There was the doctor of divinity in his gown and band, who used to make faces at him as he sat at luncheon; there was the King Charles's beauty, leaning her cheek upon her hand, and pensively contemplating the door and watching her descendants pass through. This one walks firm and quick; he does not come shuffling and with care; though give him but time enough, and it may come to that. But, meanwhile, the ancestry on canvas, the old chairs with their fat seats and slim bandy legs, the old spoons curling into Queen Anne scrolls, the books in the bookcases—all have passed out of the grasping old hands, and Frank, who had been denied twenty pounds often when he was in need, might help himself now, there was no one to oppose his right.'

The next room is the library, and his heart beats a little as he opens the door. There is no one sitting there. The place is empty and in order; the chair is put against the wall; the oracle is silent; there is nothing to be afraid of any more.

Frank, as he stands in the torture chamber, makes a vow to remember his own youth, if, as time goes on, he should ever be tempted to be hard upon others. Then he walks across to the fireplace and rings the bell. It jangles long and loud; it startles all the respectable old servants, who are drinking hot beer, in their handsome mourning, in the housekeeper's room. Frank has to ring again before anybody finds courage to come.

Perrin, the butler, refusing to move, two of the house-maids appear at last, hand in hand. They peep in at the door, and give a little shriek when they see the window open and Frank standing there. They are somewhat reassured when a very civil young master, with some odd resemblance to the old eagle-faced Squire, requests them to light a fire and show him to a room.

' I came in the back way,' he said. ' I am Mr. Raban.'

Frank declines the Squire's room, the great four-post bedstead, and the mahogany splendour, and chooses a more modest apartment on the stairs, with a pretty view of the valley.

He came down to a somewhat terrible and solitary meal in the great dining-room ; more than once he looked up at his ancestor, now too well-mannered to make faces at the heir. All that evening Frank was busy with Mr. Close. He said so little, and seemed so indifferent, that the agent began to think that another golden age was come, and that, with a little tact and patience, he might be able to rule the new Squire as completely as he had ruled the old one. Close was a vulgar, ambitious man, of a lower class than is usual in his profession. He had begun life as a house-agent. Most of the Squire's property consisted in houses; he had owned a whole street in Smokethwaite, as well as a couple of mills let out to tenants.

'I daresay you won't care to be troubled with all these details,' said the agent, taking up his books as he said good-night.

'You may as well leave them,' said Frank, sleepily. 'They will be quite safe if you leave them there, Mr. Close. I will just look them over once more.'

And Mr. Close rather reluctantly put them down, and set out on his homeward walk.

It was very late. Frank threw open the window when he was alone, and stood on the step looking into the cool blackness; hazy and peaceful, he could just distinguish the cows in the fields, just hear the rush of the torrent at the bridge down below. He could see the dewy, veiled flash of the lights overhead. From all this he turned away to Mr. Close's books again. Until late into the night he sat adding and calculating and comparing figures. He had taken a prejudice against the agent, but he wanted to be sure of the facts before he questioned him about their bearing. It was Frank's habit to be slow, and to take his time. About one o'clock, as he was thinking of going to bed, something came scratching at the window, which opened down to the ground. It was the brown dog Pixie, who came in, and springing up into the Squire's empty chair, went fast asleep. When Frank got up to go to bed, Pixie jumped down, shook himself, and trotted upstairs at his heels.

Frank took a walk early next morning. What he saw did not give him much satisfaction. He first went to the little farm near the bridge. He remembered it trim and well kept. Many a time he had come to the kitchen door and poured out his troubles to kind Mrs. Tanner, the farmer's wife. But the farmer's wife was dead, and the farm had lost its trim, bright look. The flowers were in the garden, the torrent foamed, but the place looked forlorn; there was a bad smell from a drain; there was a gap in the paling, a general. come-down-in-the-world look about the stables; and yet it was a pretty place, even in its present neglect. A stableman was clanking about the yard, where some sheep were penned. A girl with gipsy eyes and a faded yellow dress stood at the kitchen-door. She made way for Frank to pass. Tanner himself, looking shrunken, oldened, and worn out, was smoking his pipe by the hearth. He had been out in the fields, and was come in to rest among his old tankards and blackened pipes.

Frank was disappointed by the old man's dull recognition. He stared at him and tapped his pipe.

'Ay, sir,' he said, 'I know you, why not? Joe Sturt from t' "Ploo" told me you hed com'. Foalks com's and go's. T' owd Squire he's gone his way. He's com' oop again a young squire. T' owd farmer maybe will foller next. T' young farmer is a wa-aiting to step into his clogs.'

Old Tanner turned a surly back upon Frank.

'Well, good-by,' said the young landlord at last. 'If Mrs. Tanner had been alive she would have been more friendly than you have been.'

This plain-speaking seemed to suit the old farmer, who turned stiffly and looked over his shoulder.

'She wer' kind to all,' said he; 'even to gra-aspin' landlords that bring ruin on the farmer, and think nought o doublin' t' rent. I wo-ant leave t' owd pla-ace,' said Tanner. 'Ye ca-ant turn me out. I know ye would like to thraw it into t' pa-ark, but I'll pay t' la-ast farthin'. Close he wer' here again a-spyin', and he tould me ye had given him the lease. D —— him.'

'Don't swear, Tanner,' said Frank, laughing. 'Who wants your farm? what is it all about?' And then it all came out. 'There is some mistake; I will speak to Close,' Frank said, walking off abruptly to hide his annoyance.

'T' cold-blooded fella,' said old Tanner, settling down to his pipe again; but somehow it had a better flavour than before.

Close had not been prepared for Frank's early walk, and the new lease he was bringing for the new landlord to sign was already on its way to the Court. The old Squire had refused to turn Tanner out, but the lease was up, and year by year the agent had added to the rent. It was a pretty little place, capable of being made into a comfortable dwelling-house, where Mr. Close felt he could end his days in peace. Old Tanner was past his work, it was absurd of him to cling on. There had been a battle between the two, and poor old Tanner had been going to the wall.

Presently Frank forgot his indignation, for he met an old friend down the steep lane that led to the moor.

James Brand was a picturesque figure, advancing between the hedges this bright September morning. He had heavy gaiters, a gun was slung across his shoulders, and a lurcher was leaping at his heels. The old fellow was straight and active, with two blue eyes like pools, and a face as seamed and furrowed as the rocks among which he lived.

'Thought ye wer' ne'er coomin', Mr. Frank,' said he, quietly; 't' wife she sent me to look,' and he held out a horny hand.

He was very quiet: he turned silently and led the way back to the little stone house built against the slope of the hill. The two trudged together: the keeper went a little ahead. Every now and then he looked over his shoulder with a glance of some satisfaction. Frank followed, stooping under the low doorway that led into the old familiar stone kitchen, with the long strings of oat-cake hanging to dry, its oak cupboard and deep window-sills, the great chimney, where Mrs. Brand was busied. Frank remembered everything: the guns slung on the walls, the framed almanack, the stuffed wild-fowl, the gleam of the mountain lake through the deep window, the face of his old nurse as she came to meet him. People who have been through trouble, and who have been absorbed in their own interests, sometimes feel ashamed when time goes on and they come back to some old home and discover what faithful remembrance has followed them all along, and love, to which, perhaps, they never gave a thought. If old things have a charm, old love and old friendship are like old wine with a special gentle savour of their own.

Frank had always remembered the Brands with kindness: once or twice at Christmas he had sent his old nurse a little remembrance, but that was all; he had never done anything to deserve such affection as that which he read written upon her worn face. Her eyes were full of tears as she welcomed him. She said very little, but she took his hand and looked at him silently, and then almost immediately began to busy herself, bringing out oat-cake and wine from an oak chest that stood in the window.

c c 2

'There is the old oak chest,' said Frank, looking about; 'why, nothing is changed, James!'

'We do-ant change,' said James, looking about, with a silent sort of chuckle. Neither he, nor the old dame, nor the stout-built stone lodge were made to change. It was piled up with heavy stones; winter storms could not shake it, nor summer heats penetrate the stout walls.

This part of Craven country flows in strange and abrupt waves to the east and to the west. Rocks heap among the heather, winds come blowing across the moors, that lie grey and purple at mid-day, and stern and sweet in the evening and morning; rivers flow along their rocky beds, hawks fly past, eagles sometimes swoop down into this quaint world of stones and flowers.

Frank, standing at the door of the keeper's lodge, could look across to the court and to the hills beyond where the woods were waving; some natural feeling of exultation he may have felt, thinking that all this had come to him when he least expected it; well, he would do his best, and use it for the best; he thought of one person who might have told him what to do, with whom, if fate had been propitious, he would gladly have shared these sweet moors and wild-flowers, these fresh winds and foaming torrents, but she had failed him, and sent him away with harsh words that haunted him still.

James, when they started again, brought him a light for his pipe, and the two trudged off together. James still went ahead. The dogs followed baying.

'So t' Squoire's in his grave,' said James. 'He were a good friend to us,' he said. 'I'm glad no strangers coom t' fore. Ye should a' cottoned oop t' old man, Mr. Frank.'

'What could I do, James?' said Frank, after a moment's

silence. 'He forbade me the house. I am only here now by a chance. If there had been a will, I should probably have been far away.'

'T'wer' no cha-ance,' said old James. 'He ne'er thought o' disinheritin' ye ; he were a proud ma-an. T'wer' a moonth sin' I last saw t' ould man. He said, "Wall! I'm a-going from Pebblesthwaite. Ye'll hav' another master, James, afore long ; tell him t' thin the Walden wood, and tak' Mr. Fra-ank down t' hollow whar t' covers lie." He took on sorely ne'er seeing ye, sir.'

Frank turned very red. 'I wish I had known it sooner, James.'

Frank came home from his talk with his keeper in a softened and grateful mind. The thought that no injustice had been meant, that his grandfather had been thinking of him with kindness, touched him, and made him ashamed of his long rancour. Now he could understand it all, for he felt that in himself were the germs of this same reticence and difficulty of expression. The letter he had thought so unkind had only meant kindness. It was too late now to regret what was past, and yet the thought of the dead man's goodwill made him happier than he could have supposed possible. The whole place looked different, more home-like, less bristling with the past ; the lonely little ghost of his childhood was exorcised, and no longer haunted him at every turn.

Frank, notwithstanding his outward calm, was apt to go to extremes when roused, and, after a few mornings spent over accounts with Mr. Close, he gave that gentleman very plainly to understand that, although he did not choose to criticise what had passed, he wished his affairs to be con-ducted, in future, in an entirely different manner. The cottages were in a shameful state of disrepair; the rents were exorbitantly high for the accommodation given.   .   .

Mr. Close stared at Frank.   The young Squire must be a little touched in the head.   When Raban, carried away by his vexation, made him a little speech about the duties of a country gentleman and his agent, Mr. Close said, ' Very true, sir.   Indeed, sir ?   Jest so.'   But he did not understand one word of it, and Frank might just as well have addressed one of the fat oxen grazing in the field outside.

' You will find I have always studied your interests, sir,' said Mr. Close, rubbing his hands, ' and I shall continue to do so.   Perhaps you will allow me to point out that the proposed improvements will amount to more than you expect. You will have heavy expenses, sir.   Some parties let their houses for a time : I have an offer from a wealthy gentleman from Manchester,' said the irrepressible Close.

Frank shortly answered that he did not wish to let the house, and that he must arrange for the improvements.   A domestic revolution was the consequence, for when the new master proposed to reduce the establishment, the butler gasped, choked, and finally burst into tears.   He could not allow such aspersions upon his character.   What would his old master and mistress have said ?   His little savings were earned by faithful service, and sooner than see two under-footmen dismissed, he should wish to leave.

Mrs. Roper, the housekeeper, also felt that the time was come for rest and a private bar.   She had been used to three in the kitchen, and she should not be doing her duty by herself if she said she could do with less.

Raban let them all go, with a couple of years' wages. For the present he only wanted to be left alone.   He stayed on with a groom and a couple of countrywomen sent in by

Mrs. Brand. They clattered about the great kitchen, and their red shock heads might be seen half a mile off. Of course the neighbours talked: some few approved; old friends who had known him before troubled themselves but little; the rest loudly blamed his proceedings. He was a screw: he had lived on a crust, and he now grudged every halfpenny. He was cracked (this was Mr. Close's version); he had been in a lunatic asylum; he had murdered his first wife.

When the county began to call in friendly basket-carriages and waggonettes, it would be shown in by Betty and Becky to the library and the adjoining room, in which Mr. Raban lived. Frank had brought the lurcher away from the keeper's lodge; it had made friends with the foxy terrier, and the two dogs would follow him about, or lie comfortably on the rug while he sat at work upon his papers. The periwigged ancestor looked on from the wall, indifferently watching all these changes. One table in the window was piled with business papers, leases, cheque-books, lawyers' letters in bundles. A quantity of books that Frank had sent for from London stood in rows upon the floor. After the amenities and regularities of the last few years, this easy life came as a rest and reinvigoration. He did not want society. Frank was so taken up with schemes for sweeping clean with his new broom, that he was glad to be free for a time, and absolved from the necessity of dressing, of going out to dinner, and making conversation. He would open his windows wide on starry nights. The thymy wind would sough into his face; clear beam the solemn lights; the woods shiver softly. Does a thought come to him at such times of a sick woman in an old house far away, of a girl with dark brows and a tender smile, watching by her bedside?

People who had been used to the pale and silent college tutor in his stuff-gown, might scarcely have recognised Frank riding about from farm to farm in the new and prosperous character of a country gentleman, be-gaitered and be-wideawaked. The neighbours who exclaimed at the shabbiness of Mr. Frank's indoor establishment might also, and with more reason, exclaim at the regiment of barrows and men at work, at the drains digging, roofs repairing, fences painting. The melancholy outside, tumble-down looking houses were smartening up. The people stood at their doors watching with some interest and excitement the works as they hammered on.

Frank superintended it all himself. He was up to his waist in a ditch one day when the Henley party drove past in the break on their way to call at Ravensrick. They left a heap of cards—Sir Thomas and Lady Henley, Mr. Jonah Anley, Captain Boswarrick—and an invitation for him to dine and sleep the following day. The red-headed girls took the cards in, and grinned at the fine company; the fine company grinned in return at Sukey.

'Why, what sort of society can he have been used to?' cried little Mrs. Boswarrick. She was the eldest daughter: a pretty, plump little woman, very much spoilt by her husband, and by her father, too, whose favourite she was.

'He has evidently not been used to associate with butlers and footmen,' said Mr. Anley.

'Hulloh!' shouted Sir Thomas, as he drove out at the park-gates. Look there, Anley! he is draining Medmere, and there is a new window to the schools. By Jove!'

'Foolish young man!' said Mr. Anley, 'wasting his substance, draining cottages and lighting school-rooms!' and he looked out with some interest.

'Then, Uncle Jonah, you are foolish yourself,' said Bell.

'Are you turned philanthropist, Uncle Jonah?' said Mrs. Boswarrick. 'I wish some one would take me and Alfred up. What have you been doing?'

'I make it a rule never to do anything at the time that can be put off till the morrow,' said Mr. Anley, apologetically. 'My cottages were tumbling down, my dear, so I was obliged to prop them up.'

'He bought them from papa,' said Bell. 'I can't think why.'

'It is all very well for bachelors like you and Raban to amuse yourselves with rebuilding,' said Sir Thomas, joining in from his box in an aggravated tone; 'if you were a married man, Anley, with a wife and daughters and milliners' bills, you would see how much was left at the end of the year for improvements.'

'To hear them talk, one oughtn't to exist at all,' says Mrs. Boswarrick, with a laugh.

CHAPTER XLIV.

WHITE WITH GAZING.

The tender heart beat no more; it was to have no more pangs, no more
doubts, no more griefs and trials: its last throb was love!

—PENDENNIS.

The Harbingers are come: see, see their mark!
White is their colour. . . .

—G. HERBERT.

FRANK accepted Lady Henley's invitation and arrived at
Henley Court just before dinner-time one day. The place lies
beyond Pebblesthwaite, on the Smokethwaite road. It was a
more cheerful house than Ravensrick—a comfortable, modern,
stone-piled house, built upon a hill, with windows north and
south, and east and west, with wide distant views of valleys
and winding roads and moors. Through one break of the
hills, when the wind blew south, the chimneys of Smokethwaite stood out clear against the sky; at other times a
dull black cloud hung over the gap. The garden was charming: on one side a natural terrace overhung the valley; a
copper beech rustled upon the lawn; and a few great
chestnut-trees gave shade in summer to the young people
of the house, to the cows browsing in the meadow, who
would come up to the boundary fence to watch Miss Bell's
flirtations with gentle curiosity, or the children at play, or

to listen to Sir Thomas reading out the newspaper. He had a loud voice and a secret longing for parliamentary distinction. When he read the speeches he would round his periods, address Lady Henley as 'sir,' and imagine himself in his place, a senator in the company of senators. He was a stupid man, but hospitable, and popular in the neighbourhood, far more so than Lady Henley, who was greatly disliked. Bell was fast, handsome. Norah was a gentle, scatter-brained creature, who looked up to everybody; she especially adored her sister, Mrs. Boswarrick, who had captivated Captain Boswarrick one evening at a York ball, where she had danced down a whole regiment of officers. The captain himself was a small and languid man, and he admired energy in others. If Sir Thomas was fond of thundering out the debates, Captain Boswarrick had a pretty turn for amateur acting and reciting to select audiences. Some one once suggested private theatricals.

'Never while I live,' said Lady Henley, 'shall there be such mummeries in this house. If Alfred chooses to make a fool of himself and repeat verses to the girls, I have no objection, so long as he don't ask me to sit by.'

'I never should have thought of asking you to sit by, Lady Henley,' drawled Alfred.

When Frank was announced, he found the young ladies in fits of laughter, Captain Boswarrick declaiming in the middle of the room, with Squire Anley and Mr. Redmayne for audience. Everybody turned round, and the performance suddenly ceased when he entered. The Squire nodded without getting up.

'How d'ye do?' said Mrs. Boswarrick, holding out half-a-dozen bracelets. 'Mr. Raban forgets me, I can see. Sit down. Alfred hates being interrupted. Go on, Alfred!'

Captain Boswarrick's manner would quite change when he began to recite. He would stamp, start, gesticulate, and throw himself into the part with more spirit than could have been reasonably expected.

And now, with a glance at his wife, he began again with a stamp, and suddenly pointing—

> That morn owd York wor all alive
> Wi' loal an' merry hearts;
> For t' country foalks com' i' full drive
> I' gigs an' market-carts,
> An' girt lang trains, wi' whistlin' din,
> Com' w-w-whirrlin' up.

The little captain, suiting the action to the word, raised his arm with some action to represent the train. It was caught from behind by a firm grasp. Frank had not seen that he had been followed into the room by a stout little man in bran-new clothes, who joined the circle.

'Take care,' said the stranger,—he spoke with a slight Yorkshire accent. 'What are you about, yo'ng man? What is all this? Very fascinating, very brilliant, very seductive, very much so, but leading to—what?' with a sudden drop of the voice, and the hand he held. Bell went off into a shriek of laughter.

Captain Boswarrick flushed up. He might have resented the interruption still more if he had not been somewhat mollified by the string of compliments.

'Leading to —— You would have heard all about it, Mr. Stock, if you had not stopped him,' said Mr. Anley.

'Shall I make my meaning plainer?' said the little man, not heeding the interruption. 'Shall I tell you what I mean? Social intercourse, music, poetry,—dazzling, I own. I, too, have experienced the charm; I, too, have studied to please; but I have also discovered the vanity of vanities; so will you one day. A fact, though you don't believe me.'

'But in the meanwhile, Mr. Stock, don't grudge us our fun,' said Bessie Boswarrick, coming to the rescue.

'I don't grudge it; far from it,' said the stranger; 'I was just like you all once; now—I am not afraid of ridicule—I can give you something better than that; better than that, better than that. You can choose between us: *his* poetry, *my* plain speaking. I'm a plain man,—a very plain man; he, brilliant, highly educated.'

Captain Boswarrick scarcely knew how to accept all these compliments and in what sense to take them. Mr. Anley listened with the profoundest gravity. Bell giggled and stuffed her handkerchief into her mouth; but everybody was glad when the door opened and Lady Henley came in, making a diversion. The scene was getting embarrassing.

'After dinner, dear Mr. Stock,' said Joanna, courteously, 'we shall be glad to hear *anything* you may have to say. Let us leave them to their folly, Mr. Raban. Do you know your neighbour?—our excellent friend and minister?'

Frank was quite prepared to make Mr. Stock's acquaintance—he was an amateur preacher, a retired cavalry officer, living not far from Ravensrick—but he found himself carried off by Sir Thomas. The baronet had been in town that week, and was in a communicative mood. He had seen the ladies at Church House, who had asked after Raban. The Admiral had been heard of from Gibraltar.

'He has been writing in the most ill-judged way to know the exact state of affairs between Dolly and my nephew Robert,' Sir Thomas said confidentially. Sir Thomas always reflected the people with whom he had been living. 'I found my sister greatly overcome—hers is a nervous suscep-

tibility, almost amounting to genius, but *not* under control.'
And then, dropping his oratorical tone of voice, he went on
to say that they all seemed much disturbed and greatly in
want of cheering; that he had promised to run up again.
'Lady Sarah still lingering, poor thing,' he added. 'She
has a most devoted nurse in my young niece.'

Frank asked as indifferently as he could how Miss Vanborough was looking.

'Not so blooming as I could wish,' said Sir Thomas.
'Far from it. My wife is anxious that our friend, Mr Stock,
should impart some of his admirable ministration to her,
but we cannot expect her to leave home at present.'

Mr. Stock's ministration seemed to have won over the
simple baronet, whose conversation was deeply interesting to
Frank, for he went on alternately praising Mr. Stock and
talking about Dolly. Sir Thomas was not the discreetest of
men. 'I had a—some painful explanation with my niece,'
he continued, lowering his voice (people seem to think that
is a sort of charm against indiscretion); 'to you, who are
such an old friend, I may safely say that I do *not* like this
vagueness and uncertainty in a matter which so closely
concerns Dolly's happiness. The engagement seems to be
neither on nor off. . . . She tells me that Robert is
free, but she seems to consider herself bound. . . . I
have thought it best to write to him plainly on the subject.
. . . My wife, as you know, wishes the engagement
entirely broken . . . at least I think so. . . .'

The baronet suddenly stopped short, and looking rather
foolish, began to talk of Mr. Stock again.

Lady Henley was not so absorbed in her conversation
that she had not overheard Sir Thomas's too candid confidences.
She was shaking her head at her husband over her shoulder.

Frank moved away, and went and stared through one of the windows. Once more hope came to dazzle him. In some moods people grasp at faintest dreams. There was everything smiling, shining, every ridge seemed illuminated; there lay the happy valley flooded with sunlight, life, brightness. Children's voices reached him, and meanwhile the recitation had begun again. 'Yan morn in May,' the Captain was saying. But a loud dinner-bell brought it all to a close.

The sun had set, they had all done dinner. Norah used to feed the cows of an evening with oat-cake prepared for Sir Thomas, and she now came out into the twilight, calling to her favourites, who stood expecting with their horns rearing against a golden streak. One bolder than the rest was making a hissing noise to attract attention, as Norah came out with her oat-cake. She called her favourites by name and softly stroked their long noses over the railings. Mr. Redmayne followed soon after, advancing with some precaution.

'Miss Norah,' he said, ' Mr. Stock is putting the drawing-room chairs in order—he evidently expects a large congregation. A Miss M'Grudder has come. Is it absolutely necessary that one should be present, or may one stop here and feed the cows?'

'I must go in,' said Norah, demurely. 'Here is the oat-cake, Mr. Redmayne,' and so saying she put the remains into his hand and tripped hastily away.

Mr. Redmayne, however, preferred to follow Miss Norah. Frank came out as the two went in together—he did not want to be present at the oration. He was distracted and thinking of many things.

Those few words of Sir Thomas had given him a strange

longing to go back, if only for a day, to see Dolly again.
He thought of his old friend also lying stricken. He had
been very forgetful all these days past, and his conscience
reproached him, and his inclination spoke too. There was
an early train from Smokethwaite—he had business in town ;
why should he not go ?   Cruel girl ! was she sad, and could
he do nothing to help her ?

As Frank walked up and down in the twilight, he would
hear the boom of Mr. Stock's voice through the open
drawing-room windows.   When they started a hymn, the
cows, who are fond of music, all crowded up to listen.   As
for Frank, he was in charity with all men, and prepared to
believe that all that people did was good.   If Mr. Stock
liked to give a peculiar expression to the faith which was in
him, Raban for one had no mind to quarrel with it.   His
own was a silent belief : it seemed growing with happier
emotions that were overflooding his heart, but it found its
best expression in silence.   He took leave of his hosts that
evening when he went upstairs to bed.

The servant had put Frank into Jonah's room.   It was
a mistake—and Lady Henley did not know of it.   There were
the poor boy's pistols, his whips, on the wall boxing-gloves
and foils.   He had somehow got hold of one of those photographs of Dolly of which mention has been made, and
hung it up over his chimney.   There were a few books on the
shelf, Captain Mayne Reid, *Ivanhoe*, a few old school-books
and poetry-books, and Frank took one down.   Frank
thought very kindly of poor Jonah as he looked about at
his possessions.   He was a long time before he could get to
sleep, and he got up and lighted his candle and read one of
the books off the shelf—it happened to be Kingsley's *Andro-
meda*—till he fell asleep.   Then it was only to dream a con-

fused dream: Jonah fighting desperately with some finny
monster, like that one on Lady Sarah's tiles, Dolly chained
to a rock, and calling for help, while Mrs. Palmer and the
Admiral stood wringing their hands on the shore. Was this
George coming to their help? The monster changed to
mist, out of which came lightning and thunder—the
lightning was the gleam of a sword. The thunder shook
the air; the mists parted; George, pale and wounded,
stretched out his hand and gave Raban the sword; he looked
weary with the fight; Frank in his dream rushed forward
and struck wildly; the monster gave a horrible scream. He
started up wide awake. He had left his window open; the
morning mist had filled the room, but the scream was a real
one; it was in his ears still. It came from the room below;
there was a stir of voices, then all was silent again.

When Frank came down to an early breakfast in the big
dining-room he asked the butler if any one had been ill in
the night. 'I heard a scream,' he said.

'It is my lady in her sleep,' the man answered. 'She
often do scream at night since Mr. Jonah left.'

'I want my man called,' said Frank; 'I am going to
town by the early train.'

As Frank was changing carriages at one of the stations,
the London train went by, and he thought he saw a glimpse
of a familiar face; a grey kid glove was waved. Surely it
was Mrs. Palmer, on her way to Henley Court!

From DOROTHEA VANBOROUGH *to* ROBERT HENLEY, ESQ., *Calcutta.*

I HAVE been hoping for a chance letter, but none has come since that last one
from Alexandria. Aunt Sarah is asleep; the house is empty, and I am writing
to you in the oak-room by the window. Dear Robert, what shall I say in
answer to your letter? That I do trust you; that I do know how to love you,
and that you in turn must trust me. I could almost scold you for what you
say about Mr. Raban if I did not think that you are only unfair because you

love me. I never see him now. He is in Yorkshire; so is mamma—she is gone for a couple of days. As for me, I cannot leave Aunt Sarah, who depends upon me more and more. I had a long talk with my uncle before he left. He asked me a great many questions about you. He tells me he has written. I do not know what he has written; but please send him a nice letter. Dear Robert, it is so painful to me to be cross-questioned about your affection for me. I must speak honestly and without disguise to you of all people in the whole world, and so I will confess that if I had known all ——

Dolly, who had written thus far, looked up, for old Sam came into the room with a card.

'It's Mr. Raban, Miss,' said he.

Dolly blushed up crimson. 'I—I can't see him, Sam,' she answered. 'Aunt Sarah is asleep. Say I am engaged.'

Sam came back with Frank's card. 'Mr. Raban is in town till Monday, Miss.'

'Put down the card, Sam,' said Dolly, and she bent her head over her letter and went on writing.

Frank walked away disappointed. 'She might have spared five minutes to a friend who had come a hundred miles to see her,' he said to John Morgan that evening, as they walked back together to Frank's hotel. The waiter met Frank with a note, which had been left during his absence.

Raban suddenly brightened up; he read a few words, very stiff, very shy. 'Lady Sarah heard he had called, and wanted to see him; would he come the following day at five o'clock?' It was signed, 'Yours truly, Dorothea Vanborough.'

'Well,' said John Morgan, 'that is Dolly's writing, isn't it?'

'Yes,' said Frank. 'Lady Sarah wants to see me. As for Miss Vanborough, she seems to be studying the art of keeping old friends at a distance.'

'Nonsense,' said Morgan, 'since she asks you to go. What is the matter with you?'

The second time old Sam let Frank in at once, and showed him into the drawing-room. 'My lady will be ready directly,' he said.

Frank waited his summons; when he was tired of waiting he stepped out upon the terrace, attracted by the beauty of the autumnal evening, and wondering what inexpressible charm the old home had for him. Ravensrick, with all the graces of possession, did not seem to him so much like home as this silent old house where he had no right, no single stake; where the mistress lay stricken, and parting from this world; where Dolly lived, but where her heart's interest was not. Already strangers were speculating upon the fate of the old house, and wondering who would come there after Lady Sarah's death. And yet Frank Raban, as he paced the terrace, felt a tranquil satisfaction and sense of completeness that existed for him in no other place.

When Dolly came into Lady Sarah's room to tell her that Frank was there, Marker, who had been sitting in a corner, got up gently and left the room. Lady Sarah was not asleep; she was sitting up on her sofa by the window, of which the sash was half raised to let in the air. Her grey hair was hanging loose; grey though it was, it fell in shining silver curls about the withered face.

'Is that you, Dolly? I have had a dream,' she said, a little wildly. 'Your father was standing by me and we were looking at a river, and George was a child again, and I held him in my arms, and when I looked into his face it was like the face of that Raphael child at Dresden. Look out,' she said, beginning to wander again, 'and tell me if the river is there.'

Dolly unconsciously obeyed, and looked out at the garden, in its shifting, changing lights and tremulous tones of radiance and golden-sombres. She could almost have imagined her aunt's dream to be true if Frank Raban had not been walking on the terrace. She looked back.

'Dear Aunt Sarah, it is the sunset that made you dream.'

' It was a dream,' said Lady Sarah, ' but I think I have sometimes seen that river before, Dolly. Christian and Christiana and all the company have crossed it.' Then, smiling: 'I am afraid I have been a tiresome old pilgrim at times.' She pushed back her grey hair and lay looking into the girl's face. ' It is nearly over now,' she said.

Dolly tried to speak, but some sudden tears seemed to choke her, and Lady Sarah stroked her hand.

' Try to be a thankful woman, Dolly,' she said. ' God has blessed you and given you love and trust in others. I see now where I failed.' Then, in her usual tone, she said, ' I should like to see Frank Raban again.'

Dolly was beginning to say that she would go for him, when Lady Sarah suddenly cried,—' Open the window wide! open! let the river come in.'

Dolly, frightened, threw open the pane, and, as she did so some evening bell began to ring from a distant chapel, and a great flight of birds passed across the sky.

The next minute Frank from the terrace below heard a cry. It was Dolly calling for help.

' I am here,' he answered, and, without waiting to think, he sprang up the old oak staircase, and hurried along the passage to the door of Lady Sarah's room.

It was all dark in the passage, but the sun was in the room. Dolly was holding up her aunt in her arms; her strength seemed to be failing. Frank sprang to help her, and together they raised her up. A little soft breeze came in at the window, and Lady Sarah opened her eyes. She was still wandering.

'Is this George?' she said. 'I have been waiting for you, dear.'

Then she seemed to recognise Frank, and she let her hand fall upon his sleeve.

'Ah! he will take care of Dolly,' she whispered, 'for this is ——'

A quick silent brightness came into her face: it may have been some change in the sunset lights. She was dead— lying in a serene and royal peace   .   .   .

CHAPTER XLV.

WHAT AUNT SARAH LEFT FOR DOLLY.

> . . . One that was a woman, sir;
> But, rest her soul—she's dead!
> —SHAKSPEARE.

FOR an hour Frank kept watch alone in the empty rooms below. The doctor had come and gone. He said, as they knew he would, that all was over, there was nothing more to be done for Sarah Francis.

Frank had been for the doctor. He had sent a telegram to Mrs. Palmer; then he came back and waited below in the twilight room, out of which the mistress was gone for ever.

When death enters a house there is a moment's silence; then comes the silent tumult that follows death, everybody scared and bustling to the door, acquaintances leave their own names on bits of pasteboard, friends write notes, relations encamp in the dining-room, the pale faces of the living come and look at the place out of which a life has passed away. Servants come and go, busy with the fussy paraphernalia. It means kindness and honour to the dead, but it seems all contrived to make sorrow grotesque and horrible instead of only sorrowful.

When the rush of strangers and of neighbours came, it pushed in between Frank and the solemn silence up above.

'How had he come there?' they asked him. 'What had the doctor said?' 'How old was Lady Sarah?' 'Was it known how things were left?' Then Frank heard Mrs. Morgan sending out for black-edged paper in a whisper, and he started up and left them, for it all jarred upon him and he could bear it no longer.

He went up and stood for a minute at the door of the room where he had left Dolly in her first burst of grief. At the moment the door opened softly, and Marker came out. Frank turned away, but in that instant he saw it all again. The light had passed away, but some stars were shining through a mist, and Dolly was kneeling in the silver shadow, with a pale upturned face.

There was no sound. As Frank walked away he thought of two peaceful faces in that upper chamber. Death might be in that room, but sorrow waited abashed for a time in the presence of the Peace of Peace.

Alas! though Dolly's friend was faithful and strong, and would gladly have saved her from all sorrow and wiped all tears from her eyes, it was in vain he wished her good wishes; poor Dolly's cup that day was filled to the very brim with a draught more bitter than she knew of as she knelt in that silent room.

The sun had set upon a day long to be remembered, when a great victory was won. Since mid-day the guns had been thundering along the heights, the waters of the Alma were crimson in the sunset. The long day was over now, the heights were won, the dreadful guns were silent; but all that night men were awake and at work upon the battle-field, sailors from the fleet and others bringing help to the wounded, carrying them to the shore, and burying the dead.

*　　　*　　　*　　　*　　　*

They laid Lady Sarah in her grave one quiet autumn day, and came away silently. The blinds were drawn up when they got back to Church House, all the windows were open, the people who had not loved her came and went freely now; it struck Dolly strangely to hear Mrs. Palmer calling Julie over the stairs. There was a little water-colour of Lady Sarah in her youth, with a dislocated arm and a harp, that George and Dolly had often laughed over together. Now, as she took it down from the niche by the window in the oak room, a sudden burst of longing tears came raining over her hands and the glass, dimming the simpering lady in water-colours. Dolly felt at that minute how much she would have given to have had a fuller explanation with her aunt. A complete clearing up between them had never come in words, and yet the look of Lady Sarah's tender eyes following her about the room, the clasp of that silent hand seemed to say, ' I understand, I trust you,' more plainly than words. ' I have done as you wished,' she had said. Was George forgiven too ?

And now at least there were no more hidden things between them, and all was peace in that troubled life. It seemed hard to Dolly at this parting time to be separated from the two she most loved—from Robert and from George —who would have shared her grief. Her long watch had told upon her strength and spirits ; every sound made her start, and seemed the harbinger of bad news. She had a longing fancy, of which John Morgan told Frank one day : she wanted to go off to the East, to be allowed to nurse her brother on the spot, and she would learn as others had done if need be. John Morgan spoke of a friend, Mrs. Fane, who had a home for training nurses ; would he not take her there one day ? John Morgan agreed to take Dolly to Mrs.

Fane's if she wished it. He was glad to do anything she told him, but as for her scheme, they were all opposed to it. She was not strong enough to bear much fatigue. And so, as the kindest people do, they condemned her to ease, to rest of body, to wearing trouble of mind.

'We should have her laid up, sir, if we let her go,' said John Morgan ; 'and she is a good girl, and has promised to wait patiently until she hears from George. Robert, I am sure, would greatly disapprove of such a plan.'

'I have been thinking of going to the East myself,' said Frank, who had made up his mind for about two seconds. 'Some men I know are taking out stores in a yacht, and want me to join them. If you see Miss Vanborough—I never see her—will you tell her I am going, and will find out her brother . . . ? '

'You had better tell her yourself,' said John Morgan. 'I am sure she would like to know it from you.' Frank only shook his head.

Frank Raban used to come to Church House every day ; he saw Sir Thomas, who had come up ; he saw Mrs. Palmer ; but, except once, he never saw Dolly. Sometimes he could hear her step turn at the door, once he saw her black dress as she walked away. One day, having gone upstairs, summoned by Mrs. Palmer, he looked through a window and caught sight of Dolly in the distance, sitting wrapped in a shawl, on the bench at the garden-end, alone, by the pond where she and George used to go together. She knew Raban was in the house. She waited there until he was gone.

What strange feeling was it that made her avoid Frank. Raban of all the people that came to the house? Was she not generous enough to forget what had passed that day by the fountain ?

'You are quite cold, my dear child,' said her mother, when Dolly came in pale and shivering. 'Why did you not come in before?'

She had asked herself that very question that day. It was one she could not answer. It was no want of trust in him, no want of gratitude for his kindness, that made her unkind. This much she told herself. She acted by an instinct, and she was right to follow it. She belonged to Robert. She had deliberately given him her word, her love, her trust. It was not a half fidelity, a half love that she had promised, and she would be true to her word and to herself. Only it seemed to be her fate, and to come round again and again in her life, short as it was, that what she loved should be at variance with what she felt; that, loving truth, and longing for one simple and uncomplicated response and sympathy, she found herself hesitating, fearing to look forward, living from day to day with a secret consciousness of something that she would not face.

This was the saddest time of Dolly's life. Brighter days were to come; hours that she had not yet dreamt of were in store for her; but the present was cold and drear: and though chill winds of spring help to ripen a heart for happiness in later life as well as the warm summer rays, Dolly could not know this yet.

One thing remained to be done. It interested no one less than those principally concerned. Lady Sarah's will was to be read; and Frank received a note from Mr. Tapeall, inviting him to come to Church House at a certain time. To-day, thanks to the lawyer's letter, he met Dolly at last. She was coming downstairs as he was crossing the hall. Her black dress made her look older, more stately. She seemed to him to change every time he met her now; and yet when she spoke she was herself again. She smiled a little, gave him her hand. She seemed inclined to say something, but she stopped short, and walked on into the drawing-room, where the others were already waiting. The Morgans were there, and Rhoda, all sitting silently round the room.

It was a dull and dismal afternoon : the rain splashed, the sky came down in gray, vaporous glooms ; the red tape was the most cheerful thing in the room. Mr. Tapeall sat untying his parcels at the table ; Sir Thomas, with a silver pencil-case and crossed legs, was prepared to listen attentively, and make notes, if necessary. Mr. Tapeall looked round. 'We are all here,' he said, drawing in his chair. ' It is unfortunate that Admiral Palmer should not have been able to arrive in time.'

As Mr. Tapeall looked round, Mrs. Palmer replied, with a languid shrug, ' We are used to do without him, Mr. Tapeall. I had proposed that he should meet me at Paris, but of course he makes his usual difficulties. What a climate ! ' she said. ' Just look at the atmosphere ! And yet the Admiral wishes to keep us in this dreadful country ! '

' Dear Philippa, this is not the moment. If you will kindly listen to our excellent—to Mr. Tapeall,' Sir Thomas began, in his oratorical voice.

Mrs. Palmer put on the resigned air, and murmured something about the climate, with an expressive glance at the window ; Dolly sat listening, looking down, and quite silent ; Frank thought of the first time he had seen her sitting by the fire. Mr. Tapeall began. 'Lady Sarah had intended to execute a more formal document, which I have had prepared from the memorandum in my possession,' said he, ' of which I will, with your permission, at once proceed to read the contents.'

And so in the silence, by Mr. Tapeall's voice, Sarah Francis spoke for the last time in a strange jargon that in her lifetime she had never used. Her house at Kensington, in the county of Middlesex; her house in Yorkshire, in the parish of Pebblesthwaite; all other her messuages, tenements; all her personal property, monies invested in Government or landed securities, her foreign bonds, &c. &c., she left to her nephew, George Francis Vanborough, of All Saints' College, Cambridge. If he should die without issue or a will, it was to revert to Dorothea Jane Vanborough, of Church House, in the parish of Kensington, to whom she left her blessing, and, at the said Dorothea's own wish, nothing but the picture in the dining-room, as a token of affection, confidence, and most loving remembrance, and her trinkets. There were also legacies:—250*l.* to the Rev. John Morgan; 275*l.* to Frank Raban, Esq.; and, to Philippa's utter amazement and surprise, the sum of 5,000*l.* to Philippa, the wife of Admiral Hawtry Palmer, which was to revert to Dolly at her mother's death. There were legacies to Marker and old Sam. Mr. Tapeall and Frank Raban were appointed trustees and executors.

'But the will is not signed,' said Sir Thomas, making a note.

'The memorandum is signed and attested,' said Mr. Tapeall. 'Lady Sarah had proposed making me sole trustee, but to that I objected; she then suggested Mr. Raban. Each person present seemed going on with a separate train of thought, as I ventured to point out to her ladyship.'

'I *quite* understand,' said Dolly, starting up and looking suddenly bright and beaming. 'I am so glad,' she said, and her eyes filled with tears.

'My dear child, we deeply feel for you,' said Mrs. Morgan, stepping forward with a heavy foot.

Raban too glanced rather anxiously; but he was re-assured : there was no mistaking the look of relief and content in the girl's face. It was as if her aunt had spoken; a sign to Dolly that she had forgiven the past; and George must come home now, he must be happy now ; all was as she wished, his long disgrace was over; she clasped her two hands together.

Mr. Tapeall continued—'The whole thing has been complicated by previous trusts and claims, making it desirable that the estate should be administered by a business man. This was Lady Sarah's reason for making me trustee,' said Mr. Tapeall. ' For the present my co-trustee's presence will not be necessary,' and he politely bowed to Frank Raban.

'Thomas, did you hear ? 5,000l.!' cried Mrs. Palmer. ' The poor dear extraordinary old thing must have lost her head. Why, we *detested* each other. However, it is quite right ; yes, it would have been a thousand pities to dwell upon trifles. As for my poor Dolly, I must say I do not at all see why George is to have all those things and Dolly nothing at all. Dolly, what *will* Robert say, poor fellow ? *How* disappointing. Come here, dearest, and let me give you a kiss.'

Dolly smiled as she bent over her mother. 'I did not want it, mamma ; you will let me live with you.' And then, as she raised her head, her eyes met Raban's anxious glance with a frank smiling answer.

Rhoda sat perfectly bewildered and amazed. Was George heir after all ? Was this a part that Dolly was acting ? Everything to George. Rhoda began to think vaguely that there was George's chair, his carpet, his four walls, and there

might have been her carpet, her chair. It might have been
hers. Her head seemed going round; she was in a rage
with herself, with her Aunt Morgan, with everybody. As for
Dolly, she did not know about poverty. How admiringly
Mr. Raban had looked at her. How strangely Dolly was
behaving. After all, thought Rhoda enviously, hearing
Mrs. Palmer chatter on to Mr. Tapeall, Dolly would be cared
for.

'Certainly, winter abroad,' Mrs. Palmer was saying. 'I
require change and rest and a warmer clime, Mr. Raban.
You must bring George back to us at Paris. So you really
go to-morrow! What a curious sum she has left you;
really the poor dear seems peculiar to the last. How much
did you say, Mr. Tapeall—5,000*l.*—is it only 200*l.* a year?'

'Mr. Vanborough should be communicated with at once,'
said Mr. Tapeall. 'I presume he has left no instructions?'

Mrs. Palmer here began shaking her head emphatically.
'He had nothing to leave,' she cried. 'Nonsense, Dolly:
that paper you have is nothing at all. Yes, Mr. Raban, we
must meet at Paris,' she continued, changing the subject,
'when you come back, as you say, to see to poor Sarah's
affairs. It is, however, quite enough that I should be
attached to any one or any thing ——'

'Philippa,' said Sir Thomas, coming up with a note he
had just made, 'Tapeall wishes to know something more
about this paper of George's. Do you know anything of it?'

'Oh! you may tell Tapeall to burn it,' said Mrs. Palmer,
indifferently. 'It is nothing.'

'I think it is a will, mamma,' said Dolly, steadily. 'I
will give it to Mr. Tapeall, and he can judge.' And she left
the room to fetch the paper.

'You know nothing of business, my dear Philippa,' said

the baronet, with a grim smile. 'Tapeall must not burn wills that are sent to him to keep.'

'Shall I ask him to give it back to me?' said Mrs. Palmer, rapidly, in a low voice. 'It is only some whim of the boy's. He could not know of poor Sarah's extraordinary arrangements, putting everything out. How childish of Dolly to have spoken of the paper to Tapeall. Pray don't make so much noise with your fingers,' for the baronet, who had many restless little tricks, was drubbing the table energetically.

Frank came up to take leave, and no more was said at the time. He was to be away for two months, and meanwhile Mr. Tapeall had promised to act for him.

Mrs. Palmer was very much annoyed with Dolly. She treated her with great coldness, and, to show her displeasure, invited Rhoda to come out with her for a drive every day. As they went along she used to ask Rhoda a great many inconsistent questions, which Rhoda could not in the least understand. Rhoda wondered what she meant.

One day they drove to Gray's Inn. Mrs. Palmer said she liked to explore odd nooks. Then she had a chance idea, and stopped the carriage at Mr. Tapeall's office, and went up to see him. She came down smiling, flushed, and yet almost affectionate in her manner to the grim, bald-headed lawyer, who followed her to the door.

'Do as you like, dear Mr. Tapeall. As a mother, I should have treasured the memorandum. Of course, your scruples do you the greatest credit. Good-morning.'

'A complete fool, my dear,' said she, with a sudden change of manner to Rhoda, as the carriage drove off; 'and as for your friend Dolly, she has not common sense.'

'Would he not do what you wanted?' said Rhoda, won-

deringly. 'What a stupid, tiresome man. But oh, Mrs.
Palmer, I'm afraid he heard what you said.'

'I do not care if he did.   He would do nothing but bob
his vulgar bald head,' cried Mrs. Palmer, more and more
irate. 'Coachman, drive to Hyde Park Gardens; coachman, go to Marshall and Snellgrove's. I suppose, Rhoda,
you would not know your way home from here on foot?'
said Mrs. Palmer, very crossly. 'Of course I must take you
back, but it is quite out of the way. What is that they are
crying in the street? It ought to be forbidden. Those
wretched creatures make one quite nervous.'

As Rhoda waited at the shop door, she heard them still
crying the news; but two people passing by said, 'It is
nothing. There is no news;' and she paid no more heed to
the voices.   But this time there was truth in the lying
voices. News had come, and the terrible details of the
battle were all in the paper next day.

Sir Thomas came to the house early, before any one was
up, and carried off the papers, desiring the servants to let
no one in until his return. He came back in a couple of
hours, looking fagged and wearied. He heard with dismay
that Dolly had gone out. Mrs. Palmer was still in her
room. Terrible news had come, and words failed him to
tell it.

CHAPTER XLVI.

THE SORROWFUL MESSAGE.

I have no wealth of grief; no sobs, no tears,
Nor any sighs, no words, no overflow,
Nor storms of passion ; no reliefs ; yet oh !
I have a loaden grief, and with it fears
Lest they who think there's nought where nought appears
May say I never loved him.
—Hon. Mrs. Knox.

DOLLY was with John Morgan. At that minute they were coming up the steps at the end of a narrow street near the Temple. The steps led up from the river, and came from under an archway. The morning was fine, and the walk had brought some colour into Dolly's pale cheeks as she came up, emerging from the gloom of the arch. John thought he had not seen her look so like herself for a long time past. Dolly liked the quaint old street, the steps, the river beyond, the alternate life and sleep of these old City places.

As they came along, John Morgan had been telling Dolly something that had touched her and made her forget for a time the sad preoccupations from which she found it so difficult to escape. He had been confiding in her—George had known the story he told her—no one else. It was a melancholy, middle-aged episode of Mrs. Carbury's faith-

E E

lossness. 'She had waited so long,' said poor John, 'and
with so much goodness, that it has, I confess, been a blow
to me to find that her patience could ever come to an end.
I can't wonder at it, but it has been a disappointment. She
is Mrs. Philcox now. Philcox is a doctor at Brighton. . . .
It is all over now,' said John, slowly, 'but I was glad to
leave Kensington at the time.'

'I am so sorry and so glad, too, for she could not have
been at all worthy of you,' cried Dolly, sympathising. 'Of
course, she ought to have waited. People who love don't
count time.'

'Hush, my dear girl,' said John. 'She was far too good
for me, and I was a selfish fool to hope to keep her. How
could I expect her to wait for me? What man has a right
to waste a woman's life in uncertainty?'

'Why, I am waiting for Robert,' said Dolly.

John muttered uncomfortably that that was different.
'Robert is a very different person to me,' said John. 'This
is the house.'

'What a nice old house,' said Dolly. 'I should like to
live here for a little.' John rang at the bell. It was a door
with a handsomely carved lintel, over which a few odd bow-
windows were built out to get gleams of the river. There
was a blank wall, too, leading to the arch; the steady stream
of traffic dinned in the distance of the misty street end.

Mrs. Fane lived in one of the streets that lead out of the
Strand. At one time she had worked for the Sisters of St.
James, who lived not far off; but when, for various reasons,
she ceased to become an active member of the community,
she set up a little house of refuge, to which the Sisters often
sent their convalescents. She had a sick kitchen for people
who were leaving the hospitals, weak still and unfit for their

work : mutton-chops and words of encouragement were
dealt out to them ; a ground-floor room had been fitted up
as a reading-room, in which she gave weekly banquets of
strong congou and dripping-cake, such as her guests
approved. She was a clever, original-minded woman ; she
had once thought of being a Sister, but life by rule had
become intolerable to her, and she had gone her own way,
and set to work to discover a clue of her own in the labyrinth
in which people go wandering in pursuit of the good intentions which are said to lead to a dreary terminus. London
itself may be paved with good intentions for all we know.
Who shall say what her stones might cry out if they had
voices. But there they lie cold and hard and silent, except
for the monotonous roll of the wheels passing on from
suburbs to markets, to docks, and to warehouses, those cities
within a city.

Charlotte Fane's clue in the labyrinth was a gift for other
people's happiness, and a sympathy that no sorrow could
ever over-darken. She had not been beautiful in her youth,
but now in her middle age all her life seemed written in her
kind face, in the clear brown eyes, in the gentle rectitude of
her understanding sympathy. Some human beings speak to
us unconsciously of trust and hope, as others, in their inner
discordance, seem to jar and live out before our very eyes
our own secret doubts and failings, and half-acknowledged
fears.

I have a friend, a philosopher, who thinks more justly
than most philosophers. The other day when he said, ' To
be good is such a tremendous piece of luck,' we all laughed,
but there was truth in his words, and I fear this luck of being
born good, does not belong to all the people in my little
history. John Morgan is good. His soul and his big body are

at peace,·and evenly balanced. Everything is intensely clear
to him. The present is present, the past is past. Present
the troubles and the hopes of the people among whom he is
living; past the injuries and disappointments, the failures
and grievances of his lot; once over they are immediately
put away and forgotten. Charlotte Fane's instincts were
higher and keener, perhaps, than the curate's, but she, too,
was born in harmony with sweet and noble things.

'Yes,' said Morgan, 'I come here whenever I want help
and good advice. There are a few sick people upstairs that
I visit. Mrs. Fane will show you her little hospital. Two
of her nurses have just gone out to the East. She has been
nursing some cholera patients with great success. I sent a
letter to *The Times* on the subject; I don't know if they have
put it in; I have not seen the paper to-day.' As he spoke,
there came a sudden, deep, melodious sound.

'That is Big Ben,' said John. 'Three-quarters. We are
late.' The strokes fell one by one and filled the air and
echoed down the street; they seemed to sound above the
noise and the hurry of the day.

Dolly remembered afterwards how a man with an organ
had come to the end of the street and had begun playing
that tune of Queen Hortense's as they went into the house.
The door was opened by a smiling-looking girl in a blue
dress with some stiff white coiffe and a big apron.

'Mrs. Fane expected them; she would be down directly;
would Mr. Morgan go up and speak to her first? Mrs. Connor
was dying they feared. Would the lady wait in the nurses' sitting-room?' The little maid opened the door into a back room
looking on to a terrace, beyond which the river flowed.
There was a bookcase in the room: some green plants were
growing in the window, a photograph hung over the chimney

of one of Mr. Royal's pictures. Dolly knew it again, that silent figure, that angel that ruled the world ; she had come face to face with the solemn face since she had looked at the picture two years ago in the painter's studio. Seeing it brought back that day very vividly—the young men's talk in the green walk : how Rhoda startled her when she came from behind the tree. The clocks were still going on tolling out the hour one by one and ringing it out with prosy reiteration, some barges were sailing up the river, some children were at play, and the drone of that organ reached her occasionally ; so did the dull sound of voices in the room overhead. She saw two more white caps pass the window. She had waited some minutes, when she saw a paper lying on a chair, and Dolly, remembering John's letter to *The Times*, took it up and looked to see if it had been inserted. The letter was almost the first thing she saw, and she read it through quietly. It was signed ' Clericus,' and advocated a certain treatment for cholera. Long afterwards she talked it over quite calmly ; then she turned the page. A quarter of an hour had passed by, for the clock in the room had begun to strike twelve. Did it strike into her brain ? Did the fatal words come with a shriek from the paper ? What was this ? For a minute she sat stunned, staring at the printed words—then she knew that she had known it all along, that she never had had hope not for one instant since he left them. For one minute only she could not believe that harm had happened to him, and that was the minute when she read a list printed in pitiless order—' Killed on the 20th of September ; wounded at the battle of the Alma ; died on the following day of wounds received in action, Captain Errington Daubigney, Lieutenant Alexander Thorpe, —th Regiment, Ensign George Francis Vanborough. . .'

There were other names following, but she could read no
more. No one heard her cry, 'My George, oh, my George!'
but when the door opened and two nurses came in quietly in
their white coiffes and blue dresses, they found a poor black
heap lying upon the floor in the sunlight.

*   *   *   *   *

I heard a sailor only the other day telling some women
of his watch on the night of the Alma, and how he had
worked on with some of the men from his ship, and as they
went he searched for the face of a comrade who came from
his own native town. 'His friends lived next door to us,'
said Captain B——, 'and I had promised his mother to look
after him. I could hear nothing of the poor fellow. They
said he was dead, and his name was in the papers; and they
were all in mourning for him at home, when he walked in
one day long after. They found it harder to tell his mother
that he was alive than that he was dead.' Alas! many a
tender heart at home had been struck that day by a deadly
aim from those fatal heights for whom no such happy shock
was in store.

'If it had not been for George,' Jonah afterwards wrote
to his mother, ' you would never have seen me again.'

On that deadly slope, as they struggled up through the
deadly storm of which ' the hail lashed the waters below into
foam,' Jonah fell, wounded in the leg, and as he fell the
bugles sounded, and he was left alone and surrounded. A
Russian came up to cut him down. He had time to see the
muzzle of a gun deliberately aimed. Jonah himself could
hardly tell what happened. Suddenly some soldier, springing
from behind, fired, and the gun went up, and Jonah was able
to struggle to his feet. He saw his new ally run one man
through with his bayonet, and then, with his clenched fist,

GRIEF-STRICKEN.

strike down a third who had come to close quarters. It was
a gallant rescue. When a moment came to breathe again
Jonah turned. 'Thank you, my man,' he gasped. The man
looked at him and smiled. Jonah's nerves were sharpened,
for even in that instant he recognised George dressed in his
private's dress : his cap had gone, and he was bareheaded.

As Jonah exclaimed, he was carried on by a sudden rush
from behind ; he looked back, and he thought he saw
George leap forward and fall. It was a sudden rally—a
desperate push—men fell right and left. The Colonel, too,
was down a few paces off, and then came a blinding crash.
Jonah himself was knocked over a second time by a spent
shell. When he came to himself, he was being carried to
the rear, and the tide of battle had swept on.

That night, while Dolly was at home watching in the
mourning house, two men were searching along a slope
beyond a vineyard, where a fierce encounter had taken
place. A village not far off had been burned to the ground;
there were shreds and wrecks of the encounter lying all
about. Some sailors came up with lanterns and asked the
men what they were doing.

'They were looking for a man of their own corps. The
Colonel had been making inquiry,' said the two soldiers. A
reward had been offered—it was to be doubled if they
brought him in alive.

'A gentleman run away from his friends,' said one of
the men. 'There is an officer in the Guards has offered
the money; he's wounded himself, and been carried to the
shore.'

'Do you take money for it?' said one of the sailors,
turning away, and then he knelt down and raised some one
in his arms, and turned his lantern upon the face.

It was that of a young fellow, who might have seemed asleep at first. He had been shot through the temple in some close encounter. There was no mark except a dull red spot where the bullet had entered. He had been lying on his back on the slope, with his feet towards the sea; his brows were knit, but his mouth was smiling.

'Why, that's him, poor fellow!' said Corporal Smith, kneeling down and speaking below his breath. 'So he's dead: so much the worse for him, and for us too—twenty pound is twenty pound.'

'Here is a letter to his sweetheart,' said one of the sailors, laying the head gently down, and holding out a letter that had fallen from the dead man's belt.

'Miss Vanbur — Vanborough; that's the name,' said Smith.

The sailors had moved on with their lanterns: they had but little time to give to the dead in their search for the living; and then the soldiers, too, trudged back to the camp.

All that night George lay still under the stars, with a strange look of Dolly's own steadfast face that was not there in life. It was nobler than hers now, tear-stained and sorrowing, in the old house at home. Afterwards, looking back, it seemed some comfort to Dolly to remember how that night of mourning had been spent, not discordantly separated from her George whom she had loved, but with him in spirit.

All that night George lay still under the stars. In the morning, just at sunrise, they laid him in his grave. A breeze blew up from the sea in the soldiers' faces, and they could hear the echo of some music that the French were playing on the heights. Some regiment was changing quarters, and the band was playing 'Partant pour la Syrie,' and the music from the heights swelled over the valley. Then the armies passed on to fresh battle, leaving the soldiers who had fallen lying along the valley and by the sea.

Jonah, on board ship, heard a rumour that George had been found desperately wounded, but alive. When he came back to the camp he found, to his bitter disappointment, that it was but a vain hope. George's name was on the list of the officers who had died of their wounds on the day after the battle. That unlucky reward had made nothing but confusion. Smith and his companion declared they had found him alive and sent him to the shore to be taken on board. He must have died on the way, they said. Jonah paid the twenty pounds without demur when the men came to claim it. The letter they brought made their story seem true. Jonah asked them a few questions. 'Did he send me this letter for his sister?' he said: 'was he able to speak?'

Jonah was choking something down as he tried to speak quietly.

'He sent his duty, sir,' said Smith, 'and gave me the letter. He said we should meet in a better world.'

'Did he use those words?' said Jonah, doubtfully. Something in the man's tone seemed odd to him.

Smith gained courage as he went on. 'He couldn't speak much, poor gentleman. Joe can tell you as well as me. He said, "Smith, you are a good fellow," says he, didn't he, Joe?'

Joe did not like being appealed to, and stopped Smith short. 'Come along,' he said, gruffly, 'the Captain don't want you now.'

Jonah let them go. He was giddy and weak from illness, and overcome. He began to cry, poor fellow, and he did not want them to see it; he walked up and down, struggling with his grief. His was a simple, grateful heart.

Colonel Fane, too, saw the men, who had gained confidence, and whose story seemed probable : they said nothing of the money that Jonah had offered. Poor George's commission had come only the day before the battle. Colonel Fane sent his name home with the list of the officers who had fallen. He thought of the sweet-looking girl, his old friend's daughter, and remembered their talk together. His heart ached for her as he wrote her a few words of remembrance and feeling for her sorrow. His praise of George was Dolly's best comfort at that miserable time, and the few words he enclosed written by her brother on the very morning of the battle.

CHAPTER XLVII.

FROM HEART OF VERY HEART.

Silent silver lights and darks undreamed of,
Where I hush and bless myself with silence.
—R. Browning.

It was as well perhaps that the cruel news should have
come to Dolly as it did, suddenly, without the torture of
apprehension, of sympathy. She knew the worst now, she
had seen it printed for all the world to read; she knew the
worst even while they carried her upstairs half conscious;
some one said 'higher up,' and then came another flight,
and she was laid on a bed and a window was opened, and a
flapping handkerchief that she seemed to remember came
dabbing on her face. It was evening when she awoke,
sinking into life. She was lying on a little bed like her
own, but it was not her own room. It was a room with a
curious cross corner and a window with white curtains,
through which the evening lights were still shining. There
was a shaded green lamp in a closet opening out of the
room, in the corner of which a figure was sitting at work
with a coiffe like that one she had seen pass the window as
she waited in the room down below.

A low sob brought the watcher to Dolly's side. She

came up carrying the little shaded lamp. Dolly saw in its light the face of a sweet-looking woman that seemed strangely familiar. She said, 'Lie still, my dear child. I will get you some food,' and in a few minutes she came back with a cup of broth, which she held to her lips, for to her surprise Dolly found that her hands were trembling so that she could not hold the cup herself.

'You must use my hands,' said the lady, smiling. 'I am Mrs. Fane. You know my brother David. I am a nurse by trade.'

And nursed by these gentle hands, watched by these kind eyes, the days went by. Dolly 'had narrowly escaped a nervous fever,' the doctor said. 'She must be kept perfectly quiet; she could not have come to a better place to be taken care of.'

Mrs. Fane reminded Dolly one day of their first meeting in Mr. Royal's studio. 'I have been expecting you,' she said, with a smile. 'We seem to belong to each other.'

Marker came, and was installed in the inner closet. One day Mrs. Palmer came bursting in with much agitation and many tears; she had one grand piece of news. 'The Admiral was come,' she said; 'he should come and see Dolly before long; but Mrs. Palmer's visit did the girl no good, and at a hint from Mrs. Fane, the Admiral also kept away. He left many parcels and friendly messages. They were all full of sympathy and kindness, and came many times a day to the door of the nurses' home. But Mrs. Fane was firm, and after that one visit from Mrs. Palmer she kept every-one out, otherwise they would all have wished to sit by Dolly's bed all day long. The kindness of leaving people alone is one which warm-hearted people find least easy to practise; and, in truth, the best quiet and completest rest comes with a sense of kindness waiting, of friends at hand when the time is come for them.

One evening, when Dolly was lying half asleep, dreaming of a dream of her waking hours, a heavy step came to the door, some one knocked, and when Marker opened with a hush! a gruff voice asked how Dolly was, and grumbled something else, and then the step went stumping down to the sitting-room below. When Dolly asked who had knocked, Marker said, ' It was only an old man with a parcel, my dear. I soon sent him off,' she added, complacently.

Dolly was disappointed when Mrs. Fane, coming in, in the morning, told her that the Admiral had called the night before. He had left a message. He would not disturb the invalid. He had come to say that he was ordered off to Ireland on a special mission. He had brought some more guava jelly and tins of turtle soup, also a parcel of tracts, called ' The Sinners' Cabinet.' He told Mrs. Fane that he was taking Mrs. Palmer into Yorkshire, for he did not like leaving her alone. He also brought a note for Dolly. It was a hurried scrawl from Philippa :—

Church House, October 30.

DARLING,—My heart is torn. I am off to-morrow morning by cock-crow, *of course*, travelling in the same train, but in a *different carriage*, with my husband. This is his arrangement, not mine, for he knows that I cannot and will not submit to those odious fumes of tobacco. Dearest, how gladly would I have watched by your pillow for hours had Mrs. Fane permitted the mother that one sad privilege ; but she is trained in a sterner school than I. And, since I must not be with you, come to me without delay. They expect you— your room is prepared. My brother will come for you at a moment's notice. You will find Thomas a far pleasanter travelling companion than Joanna (with whom you are threatened). *Do not hesitate between them.* As for the Admiral, he, as usual, wishes to arrange everything for everybody. Opposition is useless until he is gone. And heaven knows I have little strength wherewith to resist just now.

There was a P.S.

You may as well get that memorandum back from Tapeall if you can.

Dolly was not used to expect very much from her mother.
Mrs. Fane was relieved to find that she was not hurt by Mrs.
Palmer's departure; but this seemed to her, perhaps, saddest
of all, and telling the saddest story. Her mother had sent
Dolly baskets of flowers, Mrs. Morgan called constantly with
prescriptions of the greatest value. Mrs. Fane had more
faith in her own beef-tea than in other people's prescriptions. She used to come in to see her patient several times
a day. Sometimes she was on her way to the hospital in
her long cloak and veiled bonnet. She would tell Dolly
many stories of the poor people in their own homes. At
certain hours of the day there would be voices and a trampling of feet on the stairs outside.

'It is some more of them nurses,' said Marker, peeping
out cautiously. 'White caps and aprons—that's what this
institootion seems to be kep' for.'

Marker had an objection to institootions. 'Let people
keep themselves to theirselves,' she used to say. She could
not bear to have Dolly ill in this strange house, with its
silence and stiff orderly ways. She would gladly have
carried her home if she could, but it was better for Dolly
to be away from all the sad scenes of the last few months.
Here she was resting with her grief—it seemed to lie still
for a while. So the hours passed. She would listen with a
vague curiosity to the murmur of voices, to the tramp of
the feet outside; bells struck from the steeples round about,
high in the air and melodiously ringing; Big Ben would
come swelling over the house-tops: the river brought the
sound to Dolly's open window.

Clouds are in the sky, a great heavy bank is rising
westward. Yellow lights fall fitfully upon the water,

upon the barges floating past, the steamers, the boats; the great spanning bridge and the distant towers are confused and softened by a silver autumnal haze; a few yellow leaves drop from the creeper round the window; the water flows cool and dim; the far distant sound of the wheels drones on continually. Dolly looks at it all. It does not seem to concern her, as she sits there sadly and wearily. Who does not know these hours, tranquil but sad beyond words, when the pain not only of one's own grief, but of the sorrow of life itself, seems to enter into the soul. It was a pain new to Dolly, and it frightened her. Some one coming in saw Dolly's terrified look, and came and sat down beside her. It was Mrs. Fane, with her kind face, who took her hand, and seemed to know it all as she talked to her of her own life, talked to her of those whom she had loved and who were gone. Each word she spoke had a meaning, for she had lived her words and wept them out one by one.

She had seen it all go by. Love and friendship had passed her along the way; some had hurried on before, some had lagged behind, or strayed away from her grasp, and then late in life had come happiness, and to her warm heart tenderest dreams of motherhood, and then the final cry of parting love and of utter anguish and desolation, and that too had passed away. 'But the love is mine still,' she said, 'and love is life.'

To each one of us comes the thought of those who live most again, when we hear of a generous deed, of a truthful word spoken; of those who hated evil and loved the truth, for the truth was in them and common to all; of those whose eyes were wise to see the angels in the field at work among the devils. . . . . The blessing is ours of their love for great and noble things. We may not all be gifted with the divinest fires of their nobler insight and wider imagination, but we may learn to live as they did, and to seek a deeper grasp of life, a more generous sympathy. Overwhelmed we may be with self-tortures, and wants, and remorses, swayed by many winds, sometimes utterly indifferent from very weariness, but we may still return thanks for the steadfast power of the noble dead. It reigns unmoved through the raving of the storm; it speaks of a bond beyond death and beyond life. Something of all this Mrs. Fane taught Dolly by words in this miserable hour of loneliness, but still more by her simple daily actions. . . . The girl, hearing her friend speak, seemed no longer alone. She took Mrs. Fane's hand and looked at her, and asked whether she might not come and live there some day, and try to help her with her sick people.

'Did I ever tell you that, long ago, Colonel Fane told me I was to come?' said Dolly, smiling.

'You shall come whenever you like,' said Mrs. Fane, smiling, 'but you will have other things to do, my dear, and you must ask your cousin's leave.'

'Robert! I don't think he would approve,' said Dolly, looking at a letter which had come from him only that morning. 'There are many things, I fear. . .' She stopped short and blushed painfully as one of the nurses came to the door. Only that day Dolly had done something of which she feared he might disapprove. She had written to Mr. Tapeall, in reply to a letter from him, and asked him to lose no time in acting upon George's will. She had a feverish longing that what he had wished should be done without delay.

There is a big van at the door of the house in Old Street : great packing-cases have been hoisted in ; a few disconsolate chairs and tables are standing on the pavement; the one looking-glass of the establishment comes out sideways, and stuffed with straw ; the creepers hang for sole curtains to the windows; George's plants are growing already into tangle in the garden ; John's study is no longer crammed with reports,—the yery flavour of his tobacco-smoke in it is gone, and the wind comes blowing freshly through the open window. Cassie and Zoe are away in the country on a visit; the boys are away ; Rhoda and Mrs. Morgan are going back to join John in the City. The expense of the double household is more than the family purse can conveniently meet. The gifts the rector has to bestow are not those of gold or of silver.

They have been working hard all the morning, packing, directing : Rhoda showing great cleverness and aptitude, for she was always good at an emergency ; and now, tired out, with dusty hands and soiled apron, she is resting on the one chair which remained in the drawing-room, while Mrs. Morgan, downstairs, is giving some last directions. Rhoda is glad to go ; to leave the old tiresome house ; and yet, as she told Dolly, it is but the old grind over again, which is to recommence, and she hates it more and more. Vague schemes cross her mind—vague and indirect regrets. Is she sorry for George ? Yes, Rhoda is as sorry as it is in her nature to be. She put on a black dress when she heard he was dead ; but again and again the thought came to her how different things might have been. If she had only known all, thought Rhoda, naïvely, how differently she would have acted. As they sat in the empty room, where they used to make music once, she thought it all over. How dull they had all been! She felt ill and aggrieved. There was Raban, who never came near her now. It was all a mistake from the beginning. . . . Then she began to think about her future. She had heard of a situation in Yorkshire—Mrs. Boswarrick wanted a governess for her children. Should she offer herself? Was it near Ravensrick she wondered? This was not the moment for such reflections. One of the men came for the chair on which she was sitting. Rhoda then went into the garden, and looked about for the last time, walking once more round the old gravel-walk. George's strawberry-plants had spread all over the bed; the verbena was green and sprouting; the vine-wall was draped with falling sprays and tendrils. She pulled a great bunch down and came away, tearing the leaves one by one from the stem. Yes, she would write to Mrs. Boswarrick, she thought.

Old Betty was standing at the garden door. 'T' missus was putten her bonnet an,' she said; 't' cab was at door; and t' poastman wanted to knaw whar' to send t' letters: he had brought one,'—and Betty held out a thick envelope, addressed to Miss Parnell.

It was a long letter, and written in a stiff round hand, on very thick paper. Rhoda understood not one word of it at first; then she looked again more closely.

'As she stood there reading it, absorbed, with flushed cheeks, with a beating heart, Mrs. Morgan called her hastily. 'Come, child,' she said, 'we shall have to give the cabman another sixpence for waiting!' but Rhoda read on, and Mrs. Morgan came up, vexed and impatient, and tapped her on the shoulder.

'Don't,' said Rhoda, impatiently, reading still, and she moved away a step.

'Are you going to keep me all day, Rhoda?' said Mrs. Morgan, indignant and surprised.

'Aunt Morgan,' said Rhoda, looking up at last, 'something has happened.' Her eyes were glittering, her lips were set tight, her cheeks were burning bright. 'It is all mine, they say.'

'What do you mean?' said the old lady. 'Were the keys in the box, Betty?' Rhoda laid her hand upon her aunt's arm.

'George Vanborough has left me all his money!' she said in a low voice. For a moment her aunt looked at her in amazement.

'But you mustn't take it, my dear!' said Mrs. Morgan, quite breathless.

'Poor George! it was his last wish,' said Rhoda, gazing fixedly before her.

Mr. Tapeall was a very stupid old man, weaving his red tape into ungracious loops and meshes, acting with due deliberation. If an address was to be found in the Red Book, he would send a clerk to certify it before despatching a letter by post. When Dolly some time before had sent him George's will, he put it carefully away in his strong box; now when she wrote him a note begging him to do at once what was necessary, he deliberated greatly, and determined to write letters to the whole family on the subject.

Mrs. Palmer replied by return of post. She was not a little indignant when the old lawyer had announced to her that he could not answer for the turn which circumstances might take, nor for the result of an appeal to the law. He was bound to observe that George's will was perfectly valid. It consisted of a simple gift, in formal language, of all his property, real and personal, to Rhoda. By the late 'Wills

Act' of 1837, this gift would pass all the property as it stood at his death; or, as Mr. Tapeall clearly expressed it, ' would speak as from his death as to the property comprised therein.' Mr. Tapeall recommended that his clients should do nothing for the present. The onus of proof lay with the opposite side. Mr. Raban had promised to ascertain all particulars, as far as might be : on his return from the Crimea they would be in a better position to judge.

Mrs. Palmer wrote back furious. Mr. Tapeall had reasons of his own. He knew perfectly well that it was a robbery, that every one would agree in this. It was a plot, she would not say by whom concocted. She was so immoderate in her abuse that Mr. Tapeall was seriously offended. Mrs. Palmer must do him the justice to withdraw her most uncalled-for assertions. Miss Vanborough herself had requested him to prove her brother's will and carry out his intentions as trustee to her property. He considered it his duty to acquaint Miss Parnell with the present state of affairs. Mr. Tapeall happened to catch cold and to be confined to his room for some days. He had a younger partner, Mr. Parch, a man of a more energetic and fiery temperament, and when, in Mr. Tapeall's absence, a letter arrived signed Philippa Palmer, presenting her compliments, desiring them *at once* to destroy that will of her son's, to which, for their own purposes, no doubt, they were pretending to attach importance, Mr. Parch, irritated and indignant, sat down then and there and wrote off to Mrs. Palmer and to Miss Rhoda Parnell by that same post.

The letter to Mrs. Palmer was short and to the purpose. She was at liberty to consult any other member of the profession in whom she placed more confidence. To Miss Parnell, Mr. Parch related the contents of his late client's will.

CHAPTER XLVIII.

AN EXPLANATION.

So innocent arch, so cunning simple.

—TENNYSON.

LADY SARAH had left much more than anybody expected. She had invested her savings in houses. Some had sold lately at very high prices. A builder had offered a large sum for Church House itself and the garden. It was, as Mr. Tapeall said : the chief difficulty lay in the proof of George's death. Alas for human nature! after an enterprising visit from Rhoda to Gray's Inn (she had been there before with Mrs. Palmer), after a not very long interview, in which Rhoda opened her heart and her beautiful eyes, and in the usual formula expressed her helpless confidence in Mr. Tapeall's manly protection, the old lawyer was suddenly far more convinced than he had been before of the justice of Miss Parnell's claims. Her friend and benefactor had died on the 21st. He was Lady Sarah's heir, he had *wished* her to have this last token of his love, but she would give everything up, she said, rather than go to law with those whom she must ever revere, as belonging to him.

Mr. Tapeall was very much touched by her generosity.

' Really, you young ladies are outvieing each other,' said

he. 'When you know a little more of the world and money's use——'

Rhoda started to go.

'I must not stay now; but then I shall trust to you *entirely*, Mr. Tapeall,' she said. 'You will always tell me what to do? Promise me that you will.'

'Perhaps, under the circumstances,' said Mr. Tapeall, hesitating, 'it might be better if you were to take some other opinion.'

'No, no,' said the girl, 'there is no division between us. All I wish is to do what is *right*, and to carry out dear George's wishes.'

It is not the place here to enter into details which Mr. Tapeall alone could properly explain. It was after an interview with him that Dolly wrote to Rhoda:—'Mr. Tapeall tells me of your generous offer, dear Rhoda, and that you are ready to give everything up sooner than go to law. Do not think that I am not glad that you should have what would have been yours if you had married my brother. I must always wish what he wished, and I write this to tell you that you must not think of me: my best happiness now is doing what he would have liked.'

To Dolly it seemed, in her present morbid and over-wrought state, as if this was a sort of expiation for her hardness to Rhoda, whom George had loved, and indeed money seemed to her at that time but a very small thing, and the thought of Church House so sad that she could never wish to go back to it. And Robert's letters seemed to grow colder and colder, and everything was sad together.

Frank came to see her one day before she left London; he had been and come back, and was going again with fresh supplies to the East; he brought her a handful of dried grass from the slope where George had fallen. Corporal Smith had shown him the place where he had found the poor young fellow lying. Frank had also seen Colonel Fane, who had made all inquiries at the time. The date of the boy's death seemed established without doubt.

When Frank said something of business, and of disputing the will, Dolly said,—'Please, please let it be. There seems to be only one pain left for me now—that of not doing as he wished.' People blamed Raban very much afterwards for having so easily agreed to give up Miss Vanborough's rights.

The storm of indignation, consternation, is over. The shower of lawyers' letters is dribbling and dropping more slowly. Mrs. Palmer had done all in her power, sat up all night, retired for several days to bed, risen by daybreak, gone on her knees to Sir Thomas, apostrophised Julie, written letter after letter, and finally come up to town, leaving Dolly at Henley Court. Dolly was in disgrace, direst disgrace. It was all her fault, her strange and perverted obstinacy, that led her to prefer others to her own mother. The Admiral, too, how glad he would have been of a home in London. How explain her own child's conduct? Dear George had never for one instant intended to leave anything but his own fortune to Rhoda. How could Dolly deny this? How could she? Poor Dolly never attempted to deny it. Sir Thomas had tried in vain to explain to his sister that Dolly had nothing whatever to do with the present state of the law. It was true that she steadily refused to put the whole thing into Chancery, as many people suggested; but Rhoda, too, refused to plead, and steadily kept to her resolution of opposing everything first.

'Painful, indeed, very painful,' said Mr. Stock, 'but

absolutely necessary under the circumstances; otherwise I should say' (with a glance at poor pale Dolly), 'let it go, let it go, worm and moth, dross, dross, dross.'

'Mr. Stock, you are talking nonsense,' said Mrs Palmer, quite testily.

Then Mrs. Palmer came to London with Sir Thomas, and all day long the faded fly—it has already appeared in these pages—travelled from Gray's Inn to Lincoln's Inn, to the Temple, and back to Mr. Tapeall's again. Mrs. Palmer left a card at the Lord Chancellor's private residence, then picked up her brother at his Club, went off to the City to meet Rhoda face to face, and to insist upon her giving up her ill-gotten wealth. She might have spared herself the journey. Rhoda had left the Rectory. John Morgan received Mrs. Palmer and her companion with a very grave face. Cassie and Zoë left the room. Mrs. Morgan came down in an old cap looking quite crushed and subdued. The poor old lady began to cry.

John was greatly troubled: he said, 'I don't know how to speak of this wretched business. What can you think of us, Mrs. Palmer?'

'You had better not ask me, Mr. Morgan,' said Mrs. Palmer. 'I have come to speak to your niece.'

'I am sorry to say that Rhoda has left our house,' John said; 'she no longer cares for our opinion : she has sent for one of her own father's relations.'

'Perhaps you can tell me where to find her?' said Mrs. Palmer, in her most sarcastic tone. She thought Rhoda was upstairs and ashamed to come down.

'Oh! Mrs. Palmer, she is at Church House,' burst in Mrs. Morgan; 'we entreated her not to go. John forbade her. Mr. Tapeall gave her leave. If only Frank Raban were back!'

Mrs. Palmer gave a little shriek. 'At Church House already! It is disgraceful, utterly disgraceful, *that* is what I think. Dolly and all of you are behaving in the most scandalous ——'

'Poor Dolly has done no harm,' said Morgan, turning very red. 'She has not unjustly and ungratefully grasped at a quibble, taken what does not belong to her, paid back all your kindness with ingratitude . . .'

Good-natured Sir Thomas was touched by the curate's earnestness. He held out his hand.

'You, of course, Morgan, have nothing to do with the circumstances,' said he. 'Something must be done; some arrangement must be made. Anything is better than going to law.'

'If Mrs. Palmer would only see her,' said Mrs. Morgan, earnestly. 'I know Rhoda would think it most kind.'

'I refuse to see Miss Parnell,' said Mrs. Palmer, with dignity. 'As for Tapeall, Thomas, let us go to him.'

'They certainly do not seem to have profited by Rhoda's increase of fortune, living on in that horrible dingy place,' Sir Thomas said, as the fly rolled away towards Gray's Inn once more. On the road Mrs. Palmer suddenly changed her mind, and desired the coachman to drive to Kensington.

'Do you really propose to go there?' said Sir Thomas, rather doubtfully.

'You are like the Admiral, Thomas, for making difficulties,' said Mrs. Palmer, excitedly, and calling to the coachman to go quicker.

It was late in the afternoon when they reached the door of Church House. A strange servant opens to them; a strange stream of light comes from the hall, where a bright chandelier had been suspended. The whole place seemed different already. A broad crimson carpet had been put down; some flowers had been brought in and set out on great china jars. Mrs. Palmer was rather taken aback as she asked, with her head far out of the carriage-window, whether Miss Parnell was at home.

The drawing-room door opens a little bit, Rhoda listens, hesitates whether or not to go out, but Mrs. Palmer is coming in, and Rhoda retreats, only to give herself room to advance once more as the two visitors are ushered in. The girl comes flying from the other end of the room, bursts out crying, and clings kneeling to Philippa's dress.

'At last,' she says. 'Oh, Mrs. Palmer, I did not dare to hope, but oh! how good of you to come!'

'Good, indeed! No, do not thank *me*,' said Mrs. Palmer, drawing herself up. 'Have you the face, Rhoda, to meet me—to wish to see me after all the harm you have done to me and to my poor child? I wonder you dare stay in the same room with me!'

Rhoda did not remark that it was Mrs. Palmer herself who had come to her. Her eyes filled with big tears.

'What have I done?' she said, appealing to Sir Thomas. 'It is all theirs, and they know it. It will *always* be theirs. Oh, Mrs. Palmer, if you would only take it all, and let me be your—your little companion, as before!' cried the girl, with a sob, fixing those wonderful constraining eyes of hers upon Philippa. 'Will you send me away—I, who owe everything to you?' she said. And she clasped her hands and almost knelt. The baronet instinctively stepped forward to raise her.

'Do not kneel, Rhoda. This is all pretence,' cried Mrs. Palmer. 'Sir Thomas is easily deceived. If the Admiral were here he would see through your—your ungrateful duplicity.' Rhoda only persisted. How her eyes spoke! how her hands and voice entreated!

'You would believe me,' she said, 'indeed, you would, if you could see my heart. My only thought is to do as you wish, and to show you that I am not ungrateful.'

'Then you will give it all back,' said Mrs. Palmer, coming to the point instantly, and seizing Rhoda's hand tight in hers.

'Of course I will,' said Rhoda, still looking into Mrs. Palmer's eager face. 'I have done so already. It is all yours; it always will be yours, as before. Dear Mrs. Palmer, this is your house; your room is ready: I have put some flowers there. It is, oh, so sad here all alone! the walls seem to call for you! If you send me away I don't know what will happen to me!' and she began to cry. 'My own have sent me away; there is no one left but you, and the memory of his love for me.'

I don't know how or where Rhoda had studied human nature, nor how she had learnt the art of suiting herself to others. Mrs. Palmer came in meaning to speak her mind plainly, to overwhelm the girl with reproach; before she had been in the room two minutes she had begun to soften. There was the entreating Rhoda: no longer shabby little Rhoda from the curate's house, but an elegant lady in a beautiful simple dress, falling in silken folds; her cloud of dark hair was fashionably frizzed; her manner had changed—it was appealing and yet dignified, as befitted an heiress. All this was not without its effect upon Philippa's experienced eye.

Rhoda had determined from the first to win Mrs. Palmer over, to show the world that hers was no stolen wealth, no false position. She felt as if it would make everything comfortable both to her own conscience, which was not over easy, and to those from whom she was taking her wealth, if only a reconciliation could be brought about; what need was there for a quarrel—for going to law, if only all could be reconciled. She would do anything they wished—serve them in a hundred ways. Uncle John, who had spoken so unkindly, would see then who was right; Aunt Morgan, too, who had refused to come with her, would discover her mistake. There was a certain triumph in the thought of gaining over those who had most right to be estranged, so thought Rhoda, unconsciously speculating upon Dolly's generosity, upon Mrs. Palmer's suddenness of character.

'This is all *most* painful to me,' Philippa cried, more and more flurried. 'Rhoda, you cannot expect——'

'I expect nothing—nothing, only I ask *everything*,' said Rhoda, passionately, to Sir Thomas. 'Oh, Mrs. Palmer, you can send me away from you, if you will; or you can let me be your daughter. I would give up everything; I would follow you anywhere—anywhere—everywhere!'

Mrs. Palmer sank, still agitated, into the nearest armchair. It was a new one of Gillow's, with shining new cushions and castors. Rhoda came and knelt beside it, with her lustrous eyes still fixed upon Mrs. Palmer's face. Sir Thomas cleared his throat; he was quite affected by the little scene. Mrs. Palmer actually kissed Rhoda at parting.

CHAPTER XLIX.

SHEEP-SHEARING.

Ba, Ba, black sheep,
Have you any wool?
Yes, Master, that I have,—
Three bags full.

LADY HENLEY had always piqued herself upon a certain
superiority to emotion of every kind,—youth, love, sorrow had
seemed to her ridiculous things for many years. This winter,
however, had changed the little wooden woman and brought
her grief and anxiety, and revealed secrets to her that she
had never guessed before. Often the very commonest facts
of life are not facts, only sounds, until they have been lived.
One can't listen to happiness, or love, or sorrow—one must
have been some things in order to understand others. Lady
Henley married somewhat late in life—soberly, without
romance. Until then, her horse, her dog, her partner at the
last ball, had been objects of about equal interest. She had
always scouted all expressions of feeling. She had but little
experience ; and coldness of heart comes more often from
ignorance than from want of kindness or will to sympathise.

Sometimes the fire of adversity warms a cold heart, and
then the story is not all sorrowful. The saddest story is that
of some ice-bound souls, whom the very fires of adversity

cannot reach. Poor Dolly sometimes felt the chill when
Philippa, unconscious of the stab, would say something, do
some little thing, that brought a flush of pain into her
daughter's cheek.

The girl would not own it to herself, but there is a whole
life reluctant as well as a life consenting. The involuntary
words, the thoughts we would not think, the things we
would not do, and those that we do not love, are among the
strongest influences of our lives. Dolly at this time found
herself thinking many things she would gladly have left
unthought, hoping things sometimes that she hated herself
for hoping, indifferent to others that all those round about
her seemed to imagine of most consequence, and that she
tried in vain to care for too. When Philippa began to recover from her first burst of hysteric grief, her spirits
seemed to revive. They were enough to overwhelm Dolly at
times, for she had inherited her mother's impressionability,
and at the same time her father's somewhat morbid fidelity.

Lady Henley's dislike to her sister-in-law made her clear-
sighted as to what was going on, and she tried in many ways
to shield the girl from her mother's displeasure and incessant
worry of recrimination. With a view to Jonah's possible
interest, she had regretted Dolly's decision not to dispute
the will as much as Mrs. Palmer herself, but she could not
see her worried.

'Philippa is really too bad,' she said one day. 'Thomas,
can't you do something—send for some one—suggest something?'

Sir Thomas meekly suggested Robert Henley.

'The very last person I should wish to see,' cried Lady
Henley, sharply. 'Bell, did you ever know your father
understand anything one said to him?'

Lady Henley's concern was relieved without Sir Thomas's assistance. Before the end of the winter Mrs. Palmer had left Henley Court and firmly established herself at Paris. Dolly remained behind. It was Philippa's arrangement, and Dolly had been glad to agree to her cousins' eager proposal that she should stay on at Henley for a time. Nobody quite knew how it had happened, except, indeed, that Philippa had intended it all along; and she now wrote in raptures with the climate, so different from what they had been enduring in Yorkshire. But Joanna did not care for climate —her Palmer constitution was not susceptible to the influence of atmosphere.

All through that sad winter Dolly stayed on in Yorkshire. Their kindness was unwearied. Then, when the snow began to melt at last, the heavy clouds of winter to lighten, when the spring began to dawn, and the summer sun and the sweet tones of natural things to thrill and stir the world to life, Dolly, too, began to breathe again; she could not enjoy all this beauty, but it comforted her, nevertheless.

The silence of the country was very tranquillising and quieting. She had come like a tired child, sad and over-wearied. Mother Nature was hushing her off to sleep at last. She spent long mornings in the meadows down by the river; sometimes her cousins took her for walks across the moors, but to Dolly they seemed more like birds than human beings, and she had not strength for their ten-mile flights.

' You know what our life is,' she wrote to Robert, ' and I need not describe it. I try to help my uncle a little of a morning. I go out driving with my aunt, or into the village of an afternoon with Norah; the wind comes cutting through the trees by the lodge-gate—all the roads are heavy with snow. Everything seems very cold and sad—everything except their kindness, which I shall never forget. Yesterday Aunt Joanna kissed me, and looked at me so kindly that I found myself crying suddenly. Dear Robert, she showed me the letter you wrote her. I cannot help saying one word about that one word in it in which you speak of your doubting that I wish for your return. Why do you say such things or think such unjust thoughts of me? Your return is the one bright spot in my life just now. Did I not tell you so when you went away? If I have ever failed, ever loved you less than you wished, scold me, dear Robert, as I am scolding you now, and I will love you the more for it. You and I can understand, but it is hard to explain, even to my aunt, how things stand between us. I trust you utterly, and I am quite content to leave my fate to you.'

She sat writing by the fire on her knee as she warmed herself by the embers. She paused once or twice and looked into the flame with her sweet dreamy eyes. Where do people travel to as they sit quietly dreaming and warming their feet at the fire? What long, aimless journeys into other countries, into other hearts! What strange starts and returns! Dolly finds herself by the little well in Kensington Gardens, and some one is there, who says things in a strange voice that thrills as Robert's never did. Does he call her his Rachel? Is love a chord? It had seemed to her one single note until Frank Raban had spoken. Is this Robert who is saying that she is the one only woman in all the world for him? Dolly blushes a burning blush of shame all alone as she sits in the twilight when she discovers of what she had been thinking.

'What are you burning, Dolly?' said her aunt, coming in.

WRITING AND DREAMING.

It was her letter that Dolly had thrown into the fire. It had seemed to her false somehow, and yet she wrote another to the same effect next day.

Mr. Anley was going to Paris, and Dolly was to go with him. On the last day before she left her uncle took her for a drive. He had business beyond Pebblesthwaite, and while he went into a house Dolly wandered on through an open gate, and by a little path that led across a field to a stream and a great bleating and barking and rushing of waters. It was early spring. As she came round by the bridge she saw a penned crowd of sheep, a stout farmer in gaiters was flinging them one by one into the river, they splashed and struggled in vain ; a man stood up to his waist in the midst of the stream dowsing the poor gentle creatures one by one as they swam past. The stream dashed along the narrow gully. The dogs were barking in great excitement. The sheep went in black and came out white and fleecy and flurried, scrambling to land. Young Farmer Rhodes stood watching the process mounted on his beautiful mare ; James Brand, with the lurcher in a leash, had also stopped for a moment. He looked up with his kind blue eyes at Dolly as she crossed the bridge, and stood watching the rural scene. The hedges and the river banks were quivering with coming spring, purple buds and green leaves, and life suddenly rising out of silent moors. James Brand came up to where Dolly was standing. He stood silent for an instant, then he spoke in his soft Yorkshire tones :

' T' ship doan't like it,' he said. ' T' water's cold and deep, poor things. 'Tis not t' ship aloan has to be dipped oft-times and washed in t' waters of affliction,' moralised James, who attended at the chapel sometimes.

Just then Sir Thomas came up. He knew James Brand

and Farmer Tanner too ; he had come to buy some of these very sheep that were now struggling in the water; and he turned and walked on with Tanner towards the little farm. Dolly would not go in, she preferred waiting outside. All the flowers were bursting into blaze again in the pretty garden. Geraniums coming out in the window, ribës and lilies, dandies, early pansies, forget-me-nots, bachelor's buttons, petunias, all the homely garland of cottage flowers was flung there. Beyond the walls were the chimneys of a house showing among the trees. Some men were working and chopping wood. The red leaves of last winter's frost still hung to the branches. Brand was coming and going with his dog at his heels, and he stopped again, seeing Dolly standing alone ; she had some curious interest for him. She had rallied that day from a long season of silent depression. The spring birds seemed to be singing to her, the grass seemed to spread green and soft for her feet, the incense to be scenting the high air ; it was a sweet and fresh and voiceful stillness coming after noise and sorrow and con-fusion of heart. The farmer's garden was half flower, half kitchen garden ; against one wall, rainbowed with moss and weather stains, clustered the blossom of a great crop of future autumn fruits ; the cabbages stood in rows marshalled and glistening too. The moors were also shining, and the birds whistling in the air.

'Dolly,' said Sir Thomas, coming out fussily, 'I find Raban is expected immediately. I will go up to the house and leave a note for him. I thought you had been here before,' said Sir Thomas, as Dolly opened her eyes. This then was Ravensrick.

The worthy baronet was not above a condescending gossip with James Brand, as they walked up to the house.

The number of men employed, the cottages, the school-master's increase of salary. 'Nice old place,' Sir Thomas said, looking round: then he went on—

'We must have a lady at Ravensrick some of these days.'

'Wall,' said old Brand, 'he were caught in t' net once, Sir Thomas; 'tis well nigh eno' to make a yong man wary. They laid their toils for others, as ye know, but others were sharper than he —— '

'Yes, yes; what a very pretty view,' said Sir Thomas, hastily pointing to a moor upon which a great boulder of rock was lying.

'That is t' crag,' said Brand; 'there's a watter-fo' beyond. I ca' that ro-mantic; Mr. Frank were nigh killed as a boy fallin' fra t' side. . . . . I have known him boy and man,' the old fellow went on, with unusual expansion, striking his gun against a felled tree; ' none could be more fair and honourable than my ma-aster; people slandered him and lied to t' Squire, but Mr. Fra-ank scorned to take mean adva-antage o' silly women, and they made prey of him. . . . .' They had reached the garden by this time, where old Mrs. Raban used to take her daily yards of walking exercise, and where the old Squire used to sun him-self hour after hour.

The ragged green leaves of the young chestnuts were coming out, and the red blossoms of the sycamore, and the valley was full of light and blending green. But the house looked dark and closed, only one window was open. It was the library window, and Sir Thomas walked in to write his note. And Dolly followed, looking round and about; she thought to herself that she was glad to have come—glad to have heard the old keeper's kindly praise of his young master. Frank must be her friend always, even though she never saw him again. The manner of his life and the place of it could never be indifferent to her. But she must never see him again, never think of him, if she could help it.

The door opened suddenly, and Dolly started from the place where she had been standing; it was only Becky of the beacon head, who had come in to ask if anything was wanted.

'We must be off,' said Sir Thomas; 'my compliments to Mr. Raban and this note. Tell him we hope to see him as soon as he can conveniently come over. Your poor Aunt is very anxious always,' he said to Dolly in an explanatory voice, and then he stepped out through the window again, where Brand was still waiting.

Dolly looked back once as she left the room. 'Good-by,' she said in her most secret heart. 'Good-by, forgive me if I have ever wronged you.' As she went out, her dress caught in the window, and with an impatient, hurried movement she stooped and disentangled it.

As they were driving off again, Sir Thomas complacently announced that the works at Medmere were certainly a failure. 'One would not think so from his manner; but Raban is a most incautious man,' said he; 'we must come again when you come back to us, Dolly. Perhaps a certain traveller will be home by then,' he added, good-naturedly.

'I shall be gone before Mr. Raban comes back,' said Dolly.

'Robert—Robert. I was speaking of Robert, of course,' said Sir Thomas, pulling at the reins.

Dolly blushed crimson as she stooped to look for a glove that she had dropped. That night again she awoke suddenly in a strange agony of shame for her involuntary slip. It seemed to reveal her own secret heart, from which she fain would fly; she had promised to be true, and she was not false, but was this being true?

What is it that belongs to a woman of a right, inalienably, as to a man probity, or a high-minded sense of honour—is it for women, womanliness and the secret rectitude of self-respect? My poor Dolly felt suddenly as if even this last anchor had failed, and for a cruel dark hour she lay sobbing on her pillow. Then in the dawn she fell asleep.

CHAPTER L.

TEMPERED WINDS.

Oh, all comforters,
All soothing things that bring mild ecstasy,
Came with her coming.
—G. ELIOT.

FRANK RABAN arrived that evening. The fires were burning
a cheerful greeting; the table was laid in the library; his
one plate, his one knife and fork, were ready. After all, it
was home, though there was no one to greet him except the
two grinning maidens. The dogs were both up at the lodge.
As Frank was sitting down to dinner he saw something black
lying in one of the windows. He picked it up. It was a
glove. Becky roared with laughter when Frank asked her
if it was hers; she was setting down a huge dish with her
honest red hands. *Her* gloves ! ' They were made o' cotton,'
she said ; ' blue, wi' red stitchens'.' She suggested that ' this
might be t' young lady's; t' gentleman and t' young lady
had come and had walked about t' house wi' James Brand.'

' What gentleman ?—what young lady ? ' asked Raban.

' A pale-faced young lady in bla-ack cloathes,' said Becky.
' T' gentleman were called Sir Tummas. James Brand, he
knawed.'

' Sir Thomas ! A pale young lady in black ! '

Frank stuck the little glove up on the tall chimney.   It seemed a welcoming hand put out to greet him on his return.   He had guessed to whom the glove belonged even before he saw a little inky D marked in the wrist.

'So she had been there!'   While he had been away life in its fiercest phases had met him, and at such times people's own feelings and histories seem to lose in meaning, in vividness, and importance.   When whole nations are concerned, and the life of thousands is the stake by which the game is played; then each private story seems lost, for a time, in the great rush of fate.   Frank had been twice to the East during that winter.   He had seen Jonah, he had disposed of his stores.   The little yacht had done her work bravely, and was now cruising in summer seas, and Raban had come home to his sheep and his furrows—to his old furrows of thought; how curiously the sight of that little glove brought it all back once more.

As Frank rode along the lanes, it was difficult to believe that all was tranquil as it seemed.   That no ambush was lurking behind the hedges; that the rumble of carts travelling along with their load from the quarry was no echo of distant guns; that no secret danger was to be dreaded.   This was the second morning after his arrival.   The sunshine which Dolly had liked seemed to him also of good omen. The lilacs were coming into flower, the banks were sparkling with flowers: primroses and early hyacinths, summer green and summer light were brightening along the road.   Frank rode quietly along on his way to the Court, sure of a welcome from Lady Henley, for had he not seen Jonah?   Bloom, little flowers, along the path; sing, little birds, from overarching boughs; beat, honest heart, along the road that leads to the goal of thy life's journey!

Lady Henley was the first person he saw when he rode into the park. Sunshiny though it was, she was tucked up in some warm furs and sitting on the lawn in front of the house.

'How do you do?' said Lady Henley. 'My husband told me you were expected back. I hoped you might come. Well, have you brought me any news?'

When Lady Henley heard that Jonah was looking well, that Frank had seen him ten days before, had dined with him in his hut, she could not make enough of the messenger of good tidings. He must stay to luncheon; he must come to dinner: he must see the girls. The luncheon bell rang double-loud in Frank's honour, and Frank was ushered in; Norah and Bell bounced in almost immediately; an extra plate was set for Frank. The butler appeared and the page with some smoking dishes on a tray. That was all. Frank looked up in vain, hoping to see the door open once more.

'I am so sorry Sir Thomas is gone up to town with Mr. Anley,' said Lady Henley. 'It is some tiresome business of my sister-in-law's. My niece started with them this morning. We have had her all the winter, poor thing. It is really most provoking about the property, and how Philippa can have made it up with that Parnell girl I cannot imagine. They are inseparable, I hear. Just like Philippa. Dolly is going on to Paris immediately with the Squire to join her mother—quite unnecessary. Have you heard that Robert Henley is expected back? It seems to me every one is gone mad,' said Lady Henley. 'He has only been out six months. . . .'

Frank asked how Miss Vanborough was looking.

Bell immediately volunteered a most dismal account.

'I am sure Dolly will go into a decline if some one does

not cheer her up. Norah and I have done our best. We wanted to take her to the York ball, and we wanted to take her to Lynn Gill, and across the moor to Keithburn, and we tried to get her to come out huntin' one day. What she wants is stirring up, and so I told papa; and, for my part, I'm not at all sorry Robert is to come home,' says Bell.

Mamma was evidently very much annoyed.

' What is the use talking nonsense, Bell ? Robert would have done much better if he had stayed where he was, and Dolly too,' said Lady Henley. ' Everybody seems to have lost their head. Here is a letter from the Admiral. He is in town, on his way to America. He wants to meet Dolly : he will just miss her. As for Hawtry, I think he is possessed. Not that I am at all surprised, poor fellow,' said Lady Henley, expressively. ' We know what he finds at home . . .'

Frank went back very much dispirited after his luncheon. It was later in the day, and the flowers and the sunshine seemed to have lost their brightness ; but when he got home the little glove was still on the chimney-piece, with limp fingers extended.

The Hôtel Molleville stands in one of the back streets near the English Embassy at Paris. One or two silent streets run out of the Faubourg St. Honoré, and cross and recross each other in a sort of minuet, with a certain stately propriety that belongs to tall houses, to closed gates, enclosed courtyards, and high roofs. There is a certain false air of the Faubourg St. Germain about this special quarter. Some of the houses appear to have drifted over by mistake to the wrong side of the Seine. They have seen many a dynasty go by, heard many a shriek of liberty ; they stand a little on one side of the march of events, that seem to prefer the main thoroughfares.

The Hôtel Molleville is somewhat less stately than its companions. The gates are not quite so lofty ; the windows have seen less of life, and have not been so often broken by eager patriotism. It belongs to a noble family that is somewhat come down in the world. The present marquis, a stout, good-humoured man, had been in the navy in his youth, and there made friends with the excellent Admiral Pallmere, at whose suggestion he had consented to let a little apartment on the first floor to his lady, who had elected to reside in Paris during her husband's absence.

Paris comes with a cheerful flash of light, a sudden multitudinous chorus. The paved streets rattle, the voices chatter, the note is not so deep as the hollow London echo that we all know, that slow chord of a great city.

Dolly and the Squire come driving along from the station with many jingles and jolts. Little carriages rattle past. It is evening playtime for those in the street. The shops are not yet closed; there is a lady sitting in every little brilliant shrine along the way. They drive on ; they see long rivers of lamps twinkling into far vistas ; they cross a great confluence of streams of light, of cries of people.

'Here we are at the Madeleine,' says Mr. Anley, looking out.

In another ten minutes they have driven on and reached the English Embassy. Then, with a sudden turn that sends old Marker with her parcels tumbling into Dolly's lap, they drive up a side street and stop at the door of the house where Mrs. Palmer is living.

'I shall call and see how you are in the morning,' says

Mr. Anley, helping Dolly out.   He would have accompanied
her upstairs, but she begged him to go on.

The door of the house opens ; Dolly and Marker come
into a *porte-cochère* pervaded with a smell of dinner that
issues from an open door that leads into a great lighted
kitchen, where brazen covers and dials are shining upon the
wall, where a dinner is being prepared, not without some
excitement and clanking of saucepans.   The cook comes to
the door to see Dolly go by.   A *concierge* comes forward,
and Dolly runs up the polished stairs.   It all returns to her
with strange vividness.

Dolly rang at the bell, and waited on the first landing,
as she had been desired.   A man in a striped waistcoat
opened the door, and stared in some surprise at the young
lady with her parcels and wraps, and at the worthy Marker,
also laden with many bags, who stood behind her young
mistress.

'Does Mrs. Palmer live here ?' Dolly said, speaking
English.

The man in stripes, for all answer, turned, drew a curtain
that hid an inner hall, and stood back to let them pass.   The
hall was carpeted, curtained, lighted with hanging lamps.
Dolly had not expected anything so luxurious.   Her early
recollections did not reach beyond the bare wooden floors
and the china stoves in the old house in the Champs Elysées.
She looked round wondering, and she was still more surprised when the servant flung open two folding-doors and
signed to her to pass.

She entered, silently treading on the heavy carpet.   The
place was dim, warm with a fragrant perfume of flowers : a
soft lamp-light was everywhere, a fragrant warmth.   There
was a sense of utter comfort and luxury : tall doors fast

closed, draperies shining with dim gold gleams, pictures on
the walls, couches, lace cushions ; some tall glasses in beautiful old frames repeated it all—the dim light, the flowers'
golden atmosphere. In the middle of the room a lamp hung
over a flower-table, of which the tall pointed leaves were
crimsoning in the soft light, the ferns glittering, a white
camelia head opening to this alabaster moon.

The practical Dolly stopped short. There must be some
mistake she thought. A lady in a white dress was standing
by the chimney, leaning against the heavy velvet top; a
gentleman also standing there was listening with bent head
to something she was saying. The two were absorbed. They
did not notice her, they were so taken up with one another.
Dolly had expected to find her mother and the Admiral.
She had come to some wrong place. For an instant she
vaguely-thought of strangers. Then her heart gave a warning
thump before she had put words to her thoughts. She was
standing under the lamp by the great spiked leaves, and she
suddenly caught hold of the marble table, for the room
seemed to shake.

'Who is it, Casimir ?' said the lady, impatiently, as the
servant came up to her.

The tall gentleman also looked up.

Dolly's dazzled eyes were gazing at him in bewildered
amazement. He had quickly stepped back when the man
approached, and he now turned his full face and looked at
Dolly, who could not speak. She could only stand silent,
holding out her trembling hands, half happy, half incredulous.
It was Robert—Robert, whom she had thought miles away—
Robert, whose letter had come only the day before--Robert,
who had been there with Rhoda, so absorbed that even
now he scarcely seemed to recognise Dolly in her travel-

worn black clothes, looking like a blot upon all this splendour.

This, then, was the moment for which she had waited, and thought to wait so long. He had come back to her. ' Robert ! ' she cried at last.

Perhaps if they had been alone, the course of their whole lives might have been changed ; if their meeting had been unwitnessed, if Casimir had not been there, if Rhoda had not come up with many an exclamation of surprise, if all those looking-glasses and chairs and tables had not been in the way. . . . Robert stood looking down from the length of his six feet. He held a cold hand in his. He did not kiss Dolly, as he had done when he went away. He spoke to her, but with a slight constraint. He seemed to have lost his usual fluency and presence of mind. He was shocked at the change he saw. Those few months had worn her radiant beauty. She was tired by the journey, changed in manner. All her sweet faith and readiness to believe, and all her belief in Henley, had not made this meeting, to which she had looked forward as ' her one bright spot,' anything like that which she had expected. Something in Robert's voice, his slight embarrassment, something in the attitude of the two as she had seen them when she first came in and thought them strangers, something indefinite, but very present, made her shy and strange, and the hand that held her cold fingers let go as Rhoda flung her arms affectionately round her. Then with gentle violence Dolly was led to the fire and pushed down into a satin chair.

' I only came last night,' said Henley. ' I was afraid of missing you, or I should have gone to meet you.'

' We expected you to-morrow, Dolly,' interrupted Rhoda, in her sweet voice : ' we were so surprised to see *him* walk in ;' and she quietly indicated Henley with a little motion of the head.

'Everybody seems to have been running after everybody else. I am ashamed of myself for startling you all,' said Robert, jerking his watch-chain. 'It is a whole series of changes. I will tell you all about it, Dolly, when you are rested. I found I could get leave at the very last instant, and I came off by the steamer. I wrote from Marseilles, but you must have missed my letter. This is altogether a most fortunate, unexpected meeting,' he added, turning to Rhoda.

Henley's utter want of tact stood him in good service, and made it possible for him to go on talking. Dolly seemed frozen. Rhoda was very much agitated. There seemed to be a curious understanding and sympathy between Robert and Miss Parnell.

'Have you seen your mother?' said Rhoda, putting her white hand upon Dolly's shoulder. 'How cold and tired you must be? Who did you come with, after all?'

'I came with—I forget,' said Dolly. 'Where is mamma?' and she started up, looking still bewildered.

'Your mother lives next door. I myself made the same mistake last night,' said Robert, and he picked up Dolly's bags and shawls from the floor, where she had dropped them. Rhoda started up to lead the way.

'You may as well come through my room,' she said, opening a door into a great dim room scented with verbena, and all shining with lace frills and satin folds. A middle-aged lady in a very smart cap, who was reading the paper by the light of a small lamp, looked up as they passed. Rhoda carelessly introduced her as Miss Rougemont.

'My companion,' she said, in a low voice, as she opened

another door. 'She is very good-natured and is never put out by anything.'

Dolly followed straight on over the soft carpets, on through another dark room, and then another, to a door from whence came a gleam of light.

As Rhoda opened the door there came the sudden jingling of music and a sound of voices ; a man met them carrying a tray of refreshments ; a distant voice was singing to the accompaniment of a piano. Julie stood at a table pouring out coffee ; she put down the pot with an exclamation : 'Good heavens, mademoiselle! Who ever would have thought——?' Some one came up to ask for coffee, and Julie took up her pot again.

'How stupid of me to forget!' said Rhoda. 'It is your mother's day at home, Dolly. I will send her to you. Wait one minute.'

Poor Dolly, it was a lesson to her not to come unexpectedly.

'Madame *will* be distressed,' said Julie, coming forward, 'to receive Mademoiselle in such a confusion! The gentlemen all came ; they brought music ; they want coffee at every instant, or *thé à l'Anglaise*.'

As she spoke a little fat man came up to the table, and Julie darted back to her post.

Meanwhile the music went on.

> 'Petits, petits, petits oiseaux!'

sang a tenor voice—

> 'Jolis, jolis, jolis, petits!'

sang a bass—

> 'Jolis, petits, chéris!'

sang the two together.

But at that instant, with a rush, with a flutter, with her hair dressed in some strange new style, Mrs. Palmer at last appeared and clasped Dolly, with many reproaches.

'You naughty child, who *ever* expected you to-day! and the Admiral started off to meet you! How provoking. A wreck! utterly tired out! Come to your room directly, dearest. It is quite ready, only full of cloaks and hats. Here, Rhoda, cannot you take her in?'

'Never mind the cloaks and hats, mamma,' said Dolly, with a smile. 'I had rather stay here; and Julie will give me and Marker some coffee.'

'Marker! Good gracious! I had forgotten all about Marker,' exclaimed Mrs. Palmer.

CHAPTER LI.

'SING HOARSE, WITH TEARS BETWEEN.'

Sing sorrow, sing sorrow, triumph the good.
—AGAMEMNON.

ROBERT had come back from India prepared to fight Dolly's battle. Although expressing much annoyance that this disagreeable task should have been left to him, he remembered Rhoda as an inoffensive little thing, and he had no doubt but that she would hear reason, if things were clearly put before her. She was too much in her right to be expected to give up everything, but Robert had but little doubt that he should be able to effect a compromise; he had lived long enough to realise how much weight one definite, clearly-expressed opinion may have in the balance. It was most fortunate that his official duties should have brought him home at this juncture. Dolly must consent to be guided by him. He was in some sense her natural protector still, although he felt at times that there was not that singleness of purpose about his cousin which he should have wished to find in the woman whom he looked upon as his future wife. At this time he had no intention of breaking with her. He wished to keep her in suspense. She deserved it: she had not once thought of him; she had behaved most childishly—

H H

yielded where she should have been firm, sacrificed everything to a passing whim; she had been greatly tried, of
course, but even all this might have been partly avoided if
she had done as he recommended. So thought Robert as he
was tying his white neckcloth in the glass at his hotel. The
gilt frame reflected back a serious young man and a neatly-
tied cravat, and he was satisfied with both. He came back
to a late dinner with Rhoda after Mrs. Palmer's Thursday
Afternoon had departed, taking away its cloaks and hats.
Signor Pappaforte was the last to go. M. de Molleville took
leave. Mrs. Palmer, needless to say, was charmed with the
Molleville family—counts, marquises, dukes. They all lived
in the house, overhead, underfoot. Mdme. la Comtesse was
a most delightful person. M. le Comte was the only one of
the family she did not take to, M. le Comte being a sensible
man, and somewhat abruptly cutting short Mrs. Palmer's
many questions and confidences.

The table was prettily laid in the big dining-room; the
lamp-light twinkled upon the firmament of plates and silver
spoons, and. the flowers that Rhoda had herself arranged.
She was waiting for her guests. Robert having, as in duty
bound, first rung at his aunt's door, and learned from Julie
that Mademoiselle was resting, and that Madame was dressing still, came across to the other apartment, where all was
in order and ready to make him comfortable. Rhoda was
sitting in her usual place on the little low chair by the fire.
She had taken off her white dress—she had put on a velvet
gown; in her dark hair were two diamond stars: they shone
in the fire-light as she sat thoughtfully watching the little
flame. 'Have you brought them?' she said, without looking round. 'Are you alone? Come and sit down here and
be warmed while you wait.'

Rhoda's voice was like a bell, it rang so clear ; when she was excited it seemed to rise and fall and vibrate. At other times she would sit silent ; but though she sat silent, she held her own. Some people have this gift of voiceless emotion, of silent expression. Rhoda was never unnoticed : in her corner, crossing a street, or passing a stranger in a crowded room, she would mark her way as she passed along. It was this influence which had haunted poor George all his life, which made itself felt now as it had never done before. Rhoda now seemed suddenly to have bloomed into the sweetness and delicate brightness which belongs to some flowers, such as cyclamen and others I could name. She had been transplanted into clear air, into ease of mind and of body ; she suddenly seemed to have expanded into her new life, and her nature had kindled to all sorts of new and wonderful things. Many of these were to be bought with silver and gold ; it was not for affection, nor for the highest emotions, that little Rhoda had pined : hers was the enthusiasm of common-place : it was towards bright things of every kind that this little flame spirit turned so eagerly. Sometimes A gets credit for saying what B may have thought and felt, what C has lived for years with courage and self-denial ; then comes a Rhoda, who *looks* it all without an effort or a single word, and no wonder that Robert and many others were struck by her strange beauty and touched by her gentle magnetism of expression and of grace.

Henley came up, and without any hesitation established himself in the warm corner she indicated. The stiffness he had undoubtedly felt when they first met had worn off since that ' business talk '—so Rhoda called it ; and now he did not know whether it was business or pleasure as he listened to Rhoda's low song of explanation, and watched her white

fingers opening to the fire. Signor Pappaforte's tenor was
not to compare to Rhoda's soft performance. Perhaps I am
wrong to use such a word ; for, after all, she was as genuine
as Dolly herself in her way—as Dolly who had fallen asleep,
and was far away in spirit, dreaming a little dream of all
that had happened that day.

Rhoda resumed their conversation quite naturally. ' We
may be interrupted,' she said earnestly, ' and there is one more
thing I want to say to you. You know better than I do ;
you must judge for me. I always hoped that when you came,
all would be arranged. I know nothing of business,' she said,
smiling. ' I only know that I like my pretty things, and
that it makes me happy to live here, and to have my flowers
and my nice dresses and fresh air. Is it wrong ? It seems a
sort of new life to me ; ' and a wistful face was gently upraised.
' If Dolly wishes it I will give it all back—everything,' said
Rhoda, who knew that she was pretty safe in making this
generous offer, and she smoothed the soft velvet fold wistfully
with her fingers, as if she felt it was no longer her own. ' Dolly
refused, when I begged her to take it all long ago,' she added.
' Now I wish she had agreed before I became accustomed to
this new life. I confess that I do not like to look back.
Serge and smoke and omnibuses all seem more horrid than
ever.'

Robert scarcely knew how to answer the poor little thing.
' Did you offer to give it all up ? ' he said, starting up, and
walking up and down with long strides to hide his embarrassment. ' I was never told of it, or I should certainly have
ac —— Dolly should have told me,' he said quickly—all
his embarrassment turning into wrath against Dolly.

' Don't blame her,' said Rhoda, in a low voice ; ' she is
so generous, so noble. I can understand her refusing for

herself; though I think if I had loved any one as—as Dolly must love—I should have thought of his interest first of all, and not of my own impulse. I know people might say it is very foolish of me and weak-minded,' she said, faltering.

'They could only say that *you* were a true woman, and respect you for your generous devotion,' said Robert, taking her hand. He dropped it rather awkwardly as Miss Rougemont came into the room, followed almost immediately by Mrs. Palmer.

'That tired child of mine is still asleep,' said Mrs. Palmer. 'Marker wouldn't let me awaken her.'

'Then perhaps we had better not wait,' said Rhoda, whose dark eyes were never more wakeful. 'Ring the bell, Miss Rougemont.'

So Rhoda and her guests sat down with a very good appetite to dinner; she charmed them all by her grace as a hostess. Miss Rougemont, who was not a guest, discreetly retired as soon as the meal was over.

Robert passed a very disturbed night. It was near twelve o'clock next morning when he rang at the door of his aunt's apartment. Dolly had been expecting him for a long time. The baker, the water-carrier with his clanking wooden pails, Mr. Anley's familiar tones, inquiring whether Miss Vanborough was '*engagée*'—every ring, every voice had made her heart beat. Robert found Mr. Anley still sitting with Dolly. They were by an open window full of spring flowers. The cheerful rattle of the street below, the cries of itinerant vendors, the noisy song of a bird in the sunshine, and the bright morning light itself poured into the room in a great stream of dazzling motes and gold, through which the girl came blushing to meet her kinsman.

'I am afraid your long sleep has not rested you,' he said,

looking at her hard, as she stood in the slanting stream, all illuminated for an instant—her rough hair radiant, her black gown changed to a purple primrose mist ; then she came out of the light into every day, and again he thought how changed she was.

'I have brought you some violets,' and he gave her a bunch that he held in his hand. Robert thought Dolly changed. How shall I describe her at this time of her life ? The dominant radiance of early youth was gone ; a whole lifetime had come into the last few months. But if the brightest radiance was no longer there, a less self-absorbed person than Robert Henley might have been touched by the tender sweetness of that pale face. Its peaceful serenity did not affect him in the same way as Rhoda's appealing glances ; it seemed to tell of a whole experience far away, in which he was not, and which, in his present frame of mind, only seemed to reproach him.

Dorothea had no thought of reproach. She was a generous girl, unselfish, able to forgive, as it is not given to many to forgive. She might remember, but malice was not in her. Malice and uncharitableness as often consist in the vivid remembrance of the pang inflicted, as in that of the blow which caused it. Dolly never dwelt long upon the pain she had suffered, and so, when the time came to forgive, she could forgive. She had all along been curiously blind to Robert's shortcomings ; she had taken it for granted that she was in fault when he asserted the fact with quiet conviction ; and now in the morning light she had been telling herself (all the time Squire Anley had been talking of his plans and benevolent schemes for a dinner at a café, presents for half the county, etc. etc.) that perhaps she herself had been surprised and embarrassed the night before, that Rhoda was looking on, that Robert was never very expansive or quick to say all that he really felt, that this would be their real meeting.

The kind squire soon went off pleased at the idea of a happy lovers' meeting. He knew that there had been some misunderstanding. He looked back as he left the room, but the stream of light was dazzling between them, and he could not see their faces for it.

He might have stayed; his presence would have been a relief, so Dolly thought afterwards, to that sad sunshiny half-hour through which her heart ached so bitterly. She grasped the poor little bunch of violets tight in her fingers, clenching the bitter disappointment. It was nothing that she had to complain of, only everything. Had sorrow opened her eyes, had her own remorse opened her eyes?

' I did not think,' Robert was saying, ' I should see you so soon again, Dora. Poor Lady Sarah, of course, one could not expect. . . . I remember driving away,' he added, hastily, as her eyes filled, ' and wondering when I should get back; and then—yes, Marker called the cab back. I was glad of it afterwards. I had just time to come in and say good-by again. Do you remember?' And he tried to get up a little sentiment.

Dolly looked up suddenly. ' Why did Marker call you back, Robert?' she asked, in a curious voice.

' I had forgotten my great-coat,' said Robert. ' One wants all one's wraps in the sunny Mediterranean. How pleasant this is! Is it possible I have ever been away?' And then he sat down in an affectionate attitude by Dolly on the green velvet sofa. He would not scold her yet; he would try kindness he thought. He asked her about herself, tried to reproach her playfully for her recklessness in money matters, spoke of his own prospects, and the scheme which had brought him home. Martindale had resumed his old post at the college for six months. It is not necessary here to enter into all Robert's details. He spoke of a growing spirit of disaffection in the East, and suddenly he discovered that Dolly was no longer listening.

'Why do you tell me all this, Robert?' she said, hoarsely, forgetting the rôle of passive acquiescence she had promised herself to play.

It hurt Dolly somehow, and wearied her to talk to Robert upon indifferent subjects. The hour had come—the great hour that she had dreaded and longed for—and was this all that it had brought? Sometimes in a tone of his voice, in a well-known look, it would seem to her that reconciliation was at hand; but a word more, but a look more, and all separation was over for ever—all reproach; but neither look nor word came. The key-note to all these variations of feeling never sounded. Poor Dolly hated and loved alternately during this cruel hour; loved the man she had loved so long, hated this strange perversion of her heart's dream. We love and we hate—not the face, nor the voice, nor the actions of this one or that one, but an intangible essence of all. And there sat Henley, talking very pleasantly, and changed somehow. Was that Robert? Was this herself? Was Robert dead too, or was it her own heart that was so cold.

Rhoda met her leaving the room some few minutes after.

'I have come to fetch you to luncheon,' said Miss Parnell. 'Is Mr. Henley there?' I see you have got your violets, Dolly. Miss Rougemont and I showed him the way to the flower-market. We met at the door. I am afraid she kept him too long. It was very wicked of her.'

Mrs. Palmer joined them at luncheon. Miss Rougemont carved and attended to their wants. Dolly was grateful for a Benjamin-like portion that she found heaped upon her plate, but she could not eat it. Everything tasted bitter somehow. Miss Rougemont was an odd, battered woman, with an inexpressive face ; but she was not so insensible as Rhoda imagined. More than once during luncheon Dolly found her black rolling eyes fixed upon her face. Once, watching her opportunity, the companion came close up to Dolly and said, in a low voice, ' I wished to say to you that I hope you do not think that it was I who detained Mr. Henley this morning. Miss Parnell, who rarely considers other people's feelings, told me that she had told you that *I* ——' Dolly blushed up.

' He came in very fair time,' she said, gently. Miss Rougemont did not seem satisfied. ' Forgive me,' she said. ' I am old and you are young. It is well to be upon one's guard. It was not I who detained Mr. Henley.' She meant well, poor woman ; but Dolly started away impatiently, blushing up with annoyance. How dare Miss Rougemont hint, and thrust her impertinent suspicions before her ?

Squire Anley, with his loose clothes flying, with a parcel under each arm, with bonbons enough in his pockets for all the children in Pebblesthwaite, a list of names and addresses in his hand, was inquiring his way to a dressmaker, Mademoiselle Hays, whose bill he had promised Mrs. Boswarrick to pay. (Squire Anley often paid Mrs. Boswarrick's bills, and was repaid or not, as the case might be. At all events, he had the satisfaction of seeing the little lady in her pretty Paris dresses.) All day long the sunshine has been twinkling, carriages are rattling cheerfully over the stones, sightseers are sightseeing, the shops are full of pretty things.

Lord Cowley has just driven out of the great gates of the British Embassy, and the soldier has presented arms. Flash goes the bayonet in the sunshine. Squire Anley, looking about, suddenly sees Dorothea on the other side of the street, and crosses to meet her.

'Alone?' said he. 'This is very wrong. What are you doing? Where is everybody?'

'I am not alone,' said Dolly; 'they are in that shop. Rhoda went in to buy something, and she called Robert to give his advice.'

The Squire opened his eyes.

'It was very exemplary of Robert Henley to go when he was called,' he said, laughing. 'And where are you all going to?'

'I have to take some money from Mrs. Fane to a sick man in the English Hospital,' Dolly said. 'It is a long way off, I'm afraid. Mamma thought it too far, but they are coming with me.'

Here Robert came out of the shop to look for Dolly.

'I did not know you had stayed outside,' he said in his old affectionately dictatorial way, drawing her hand through his arm. 'I should have scolded you, but I see you have done us good service.' And he shook hands with the Squire.

'I was on my way to try and find you,' said the Squire. 'I have ordered dinner at the "Trois Frères" at six. Don't be late. I am the most punctual of men, as Miss Dolly knows by sad experience.'

'Punctuality always seems to me a struggle between myself and all eternity,' said Dolly, smiling.

Robert looked at his watch, and then back at the shop. 'There is nothing more necessary,' he said. 'I promised Rhoda to come for her again in twenty minutes. She

is divided between blue and sea-green. I am afraid we shall
be almost too late for the hospital to-day. Can't you come
back, Dolly, and help her in her choice?'

Dolly's face fell.

'I can't wait; I *must* go,' she said. 'The man is expecting his money to get home, and Mrs. Fane is expecting
him.'

'To-morrow will do just as well, my dear Dolly. You
are as impetuous as ever, I see,' said Robert. 'We can't
leave Rhoda alone, now that we have brought her out.'

'To-morrow *won't* do,' cried Dolly, and she suddenly let
go his arm. '*I* will go alone. I am used to it. I must
go,' she insisted, with a nervous vehemence which surprised
Mr. Anley. It was very unlike Dolly to be vexed about
small matters.

But here Rhoda, smiling, came in turn from the door of
the shop. She was dressed in violet and lilac and bright
spring colours; in her hand she held a little bunch of
flowers, not unlike that one which Robert had given Dolly
at her suggestion.

'What is all this? Now we are going to the hospital?'
she said. 'I should have had my pony-carriage to-morrow
—that was my only reason for wishing to put off the expedition.'

A large open carriage with four places was passing by;
Robert stopped it, and they all three got in. Mr. Anley
watched them as they drove away. He did not quite like the
aspect of affairs. He had thought Dolly looking very sad
when he met her standing at the shop door. What was
Rhoda being so amiable about? He saw the lilac bonnet
bending forward, and Dolly's crape veil falling as the carriage
drove round the corner.

CHAPTER LII.

AN ANDANTE OF HAYDN'S.

On admire les fleurs de serre,
Qui, loin de leur soleil natal,
Comme des joyaux mis sous verre,
Brillent sous un ciel de crystal.

—T. GAUTIER.

THE carriage drove through the Place de la Concorde. The
fountains were tossing and splashing sunlight, the shadow of
the Obelisk was travelling across the pavement. The old
palace still stood in its place, with its high crowding roofs,
and shadows, and twinkling vanes. The early green was in
every tree, lying bright upon avenues and slopes. It was
all familiar—every dazzle and echo brought back Dolly's
youthful remembrance. The merry-go-rounds were whirling under the trees. 'Tirez—tirez,' cried the ladies of
the rouge-et-noir tables. 'For a penny the lemonade,'
sang an Assyrian-looking figure, with a very hoarse voice,
and a great tin box on his back. Then came Guignol's
distant shriek, the steady roll of the carriages, and a
distant sound of music as a regiment came marching across
the bridge. The tune that they were playing sounded like
a dirge to poor Dolly's heart, and so she sank back silently
and let down her crape veil.

Meanwhile Rhoda and Robert were talking very happily together. They did not see that Dolly was crying behind her veil.

The hospital is a tranquil little place at the end of long avenues of plane-trees that run their dreary lengths for miles out of the gates of Paris. A blouse, a heap of stones, a market cart—there is nothing else to break the dreary monotone of straight pavement and shivering plane-tree repeated many hundred times. Sometimes you reach a cross-road: it is the same thing again. They came to the iron gates of the hospital at last, and crossed the front garden, and looked up at the open windows while they waited for admission. A nurse let them in without difficulty, and opened the door of a great airy, tranquil ward, where three or four invalids in cotton nightcaps were resting. The windows opened each way into silent gardens. It was all still and hushed and fresh; it must have seemed a strange contrast to some of the inmates. A rough, battered-looking man was lying on his back on his bed, listlessly tracing the lines of the ceiling with his finger. It was to him that the nurse led Dolly. 'This is Smith,' she said; 'he is very anxious to go home to England.'

The man hearing his name, sat up and turned a thin and stubbly-bearded face towards Dolly, and as he looked at her he half rose to his feet and stared at her hard: while she spoke to him, he still stared with an odd frightened look that was not rude, but which Dolly found embarrassing.

She hastily gave him the money and the message from Mrs. Fane. He was to come back to the home in —— Street. The nurse who had nursed him in the Crimea had procured his admission. He had been badly wounded; he was better, and his one longing was to get to England again.

He had a little money, he said. He wanted to see his boy
and give him the money. It was prize-money—the nurse
had it to take care of; and still he went on staring at
Dolly.

Dolly could not shake off the impression of that curious,
frightened look. She told the Squire about it when they
met at the café that evening, as they sat after dinner in the
starlight at little tables with coffee and ices before them,
and cheerful crowds wandering round and round the arcades
—some staring at the glittering shops, others, more sentimentally inclined, gazing at the stars overhead. Mrs. Palmer
was absorbed in an ice.

Voices change in the twilight as colours do, and it seemed
to Dolly that all their voices had the cadence of the night,
as they sat there talking of one thing and another. Every
now and then came little bursts of revelry, toned down and
softened by the darkness. How clear the night was ! What
a great peaceful star was pausing over the gable of the old
palace !

The Squire was giving extracts from his Yorkshire correspondence. 'Miss Bell said nothing of a certain report
which had got about, to the effect that she was going to be
married to Mr. Stock.' ('Pray, pray spare us,' from Mrs.
Palmer.) But Bell did say something of expecting to have
some news for the Squire on his return, if Norah did not
forestall her with it. 'Mr. Raban is always coming. He is
out riding now with papa and Norah; and we all think it an
awfully jolly arrangement, and everybody is making remarks
already.'

'One would really think Joanna had brought up her girls
in the stables,' said Mrs. Palmer. 'I am sure I am very
glad that Norah is likely to do so well. Though I *must* say

I always thought Mr. Raban a poor creature, and so did you, Dolly.'

'I think he is one of the best and kindest friends I ever had,' said Dolly, abruptly.

'Nonsense, dearest,' said her mother. 'And so you really leave us,' continued Mrs. Palmer, sipping the pink and green ice, with her head on one side, and addressing Mr. Anley.

'I promised Miss Bell that I would ride with her on Thursday,' said the Squire; 'and a promise, you know . . .'

'It is not every one who has your high sense of honour,' said Mrs. Palmer, bitterly. 'Some promises—those made before the altar, for instance—seem only made to be broken.'

'Those I have never pledged myself to, Madam,' said the Squire, rubbing his hands.

'If some people only had the frankness to promise to neglect, to rob and to ill-use their wives, one could better understand their present conduct,' Mrs. Palmer continued, with a raised voice.

'A promise—what is a promise?' Rhoda asked in her clear soft flute; 'surely people change their minds sometimes, and then no one would wish to keep another person bound.'

'That is a very strange doctrine, my dear young lady,' said Mr. Anley, abruptly. 'Forgive me, if I say it is a ladies' doctrine. I hope I should not find any price too dear for my honour to pay. I am sure Henley agrees with me.'

Robert felt the Squire's eyes upon him: he twirled his watch-chain. 'I don't think it is a subject for discussion,' he said, impatiently. 'A gentleman keeps his word, of course, at a—every inconvenience.'

'Surely a mosquito?' exclaimed Mrs. Palmer. As she spoke, a sudden flash of zigzag light from some passage over-

head suddenly lighted up the table and the faces of the little
party assembled round it; it lit up one face and another,
and flickered for an instant upon Rhoda's dark head: it
flashed into Robert's face, and vanished.

And in that instant Dolly, looking up, had seen Rhoda,
as she had never seen her before, leaning forward breathless,
with one hand out, with beautiful gloomy eyes dilating and
fixed upon Robert; but the light disappeared, and all was
dark again.

They were all silent. Robert was recovering his ruffled
temper. Mr. Anley was calling for the bill. Dolly was still
following that zigzag ray of light in the darkness. Had it
flashed into her dreams? had it revealed their emptiness,
and that of my poor Dolly's shrine? Even Frank Raban was
gone then. A painful incident came to disturb them all as
they were still sitting there. The noise in the room overhead had been getting louder and louder. Mr. Anley suggested moving, and went to hurry the bill. Presently this
noisy window was flung open wide, with a sudden loud burst
of shrieks and laughter, and remonstrance, and streams of
light—in the midst of which a pistol-shot went off, followed
by a loud scream and a moment's silence. Mrs. Palmer
shrieked. Robert started up exclaiming. Then came quick
confusion, rising, as confusion rises, no one knows how nor
from whence : people rushed struggling out of the café,
hurrying up from the four sides of the quadrangle: a table
was overturned. Rhoda flung herself upon Robert's arm,
clinging to him for protection. Dolly caught hold of her
mother's hand. 'Hush, mamma, don't be frightened,' she
said, and she held her fingers tight. In all the noise and
flurry and anxiety of that moment, she had again seen Robert
turn to Rhoda with undisguised concern. He seemed to

have forgotten that there was any one else in all that crowd
to think of. The Squire, who had been but a few steps
away, came hurrying back, and it was he who now drew
Dolly and her mother safe into the shelter of an archway.

The silence of the summer night was broken, the placid
beam of the stars overhead put out by flaring lights—and
anxious, eager voices, that were rung on every side. 'He
has killed himself'—'He wounded her,' said some. 'Wounded
three,' said others. 'She shot the pistol,' cried others. Then
came a man pushing through the crowd—a doctor. 'Let
him pass, let him pass!' said the people, surging back to
make way. Squire Anley looked very grave as he stood
between the two ladies and the crowd: every minute it grew
more dense and more confused. Robert and Rhoda had been
swept off in a different direction.

Afterwards they learnt that some unhappy wretch, tired
of life and ashamed of his miserable existence, had drawn
out a pistol and attempted to shoot himself that night as
they were sitting under the window. His companions had
thought he was in fun, and only laughed until he had drawn
the trigger. They were thankful to escape from the crowd,
and to walk home through the cheerful streets, rattling and
flaring among these unnumbered tragedies.

The pistol-shot was still in Dolly's ears, and the ray of
light still dazzling in her eyes, as she walked home, following
her mother and the Squire.

As she threaded her way step by step, she seemed to be
in a sort of nightmare, struggling alone against the overwhelming rush of circumstances, the remorseless partings
and histories of life—threading her way alone through the
crowds. The people seemed to her absorbed and hurrying
by. Were they too alone in the world? Had that woman

passing by been deceived in her trust ? Dolly was surprised
at the throb in her heart, at the curious rush of emotions in
her mind. They were unlike those to which she was used.
' Your part is played,' said some voice dinning in her ears.
' For him the brand of faithless coldness of heart; for him
the discredit, for him the shame of owning to his desertion.
You are not to blame. You have kept your word; you have
been faithful. He has failed. Explanations cannot change
the truth of facts. Even strangers see it all. Mr. Anley
sees it. Now at last you are convinced.'

Dolly followed her mother and Mr. Anley upstairs.
Rhoda and Robert were not come in. Mr. Anley, looking
very grave, said he would go and look for them. Philippa
flung herself wearily upon the drawing-room sofa : the fire
was burning, and the little log of wood crumbling in
embers. Dolly raked the embers together, and then came and
stood by her mother. ' Good-night, mamma,' she said. ' I am
tired ; I am going to bed,' she said, in a sort of fixed, heavy way.

' It is your own fault,' answered her mother, bursting out
in vague answer to her own thoughts. ' Mr. Anley says that
Robert is behaving very strangely. If you think he is
too attentive to Rhoda, you should tell him so, instead
of looking at me in that heavy, disagreeable way. You
know as well as I do that he means nothing ; and
you are really so depressed, dearest, that it is no wonder a
young man prefers joking and flirting with an agreeable
girl,' and Mrs. Palmer thumped the cushions. ' Give me a
kiss, Dolly,' she said. To do her justice, she was only scolding her daughter out of sympathy, and because she did not
know what other tone to take.

Dolly did not answer. She felt hard and fierce ; a sort of
scorn had come over her. There seemed no one to go to now

—no, not one. If George had been there, all would have been so different, she thought; and then his warning words came back to her once more.

Dolly put her hand to her heart and stood silent until her mother had finished. There was pain and love and fire in a heart like poor Dolly's, humble and passionate, faithful and impressionable, and sadly tried just now by one of the bitter trials that come to young lives—blows that seem to jar away the music for ever. Later comes the peaceful possession of life, which is as a revelation when the first flare of youth has passed away; but for Dorothea that peaceful time was not yet. Everything was sad. She was not blind. She could understand what was passing before her eyes. She seemed to read Robert's secret set plainly before her. She had stopped Miss Rougemont more than once when she had begun some mysterious word of warning; but she knew well enough what she would have said.

'A man must keep his word, at every inconvenience,' said Robert.

Perhaps if Frank had never spoken, never revealed his story, Dolly might still have been unconscious of the meaning of the signs and words and symbols that express the truth.

Marker asked no questions. She brushed Dolly's long tawny mane, and left her at last in her white wrapper sitting by the bed.

'Are you well, my dearie?' said the old woman, coming back and stroking her hair with her hand.

Dolly smiled, and answered by holding up her face to be kissed, and Marker went away more happy.

Whatever she felt, whatever her secret determination may have been, Dolly said not one word neither to her mother nor to her friend the Squire. She avoided Miss

Rougemont's advances with a sort of horror. To Robert and Rhoda she scarcely spoke, although she did not avoid them. Robert thought himself justified in remonstrating with her for her changed manner.

'I am waiting until I know what my manner should be, Robert,' said Dolly, bitterly.

Robert thought Dolly very much altered indeed. As Dolly shrank back more and more into herself, Rhoda seemed to bloom and brighten—she thought of everybody and everything, she tried in a hundred ways to please her friend. Dolly, coming home lonely and neglected, would find, perhaps, fresh roses on her toilet. ' Miss Rhoda put them there,' Marker would say, grimly, and Dolly would laugh a hard sort of laugh. But all this time she said no word, gave no sign.—' For *them* should be the shame of confessing their treachery,' said this angry sullen demon that seemed to have possessed the poor child. And all the while Robert, serene in his ultimate intentions and honourable sentiments, came and went, and Rhoda put all disagreeable thoughts of the future away. She had never deliberately set herself to supplant her friend, but she had deliberately set herself to win over Henley, and, if possible, to gain his support to her claims. It had seemed an impossible task. Rhoda was surprised, flattered, and bewildered to find how easily she had gained her wish, how soon her dream had come true. There it stood solid and complacent before her, laughing at one of her sallies; Rhoda began to realise that this was, of all dreams, the one she believed in most. It was something for Rhoda to have found a faith of any sort. At all events, there was now one other person besides herself in Rhoda's world. If Dolly was cross, it was her own fault. Miss Rougemont, too, had been disagreeable and prying of late

—she must go. And as for Uncle John, if he wrote any more letters like that last one which had come, she should burn them unread.

No one ever knew the struggle that went on in Dolly's mind all through these bright spring days, while Rhoda was dreaming her tranquil little visions, while Robert was agreeably occupied, flirting with Rhoda, while they were all coming and going from one pleasant scene to another, and the roses were blooming once more in the garden at All Saints', while Signor Pappaforte was warbling to Mrs. Palmer's accompaniment, and Frank Raban, riding across the moors, was hard at work upon one scheme and another. He did not know it, but the crisis had come.

It was a crowded hall, a thousand people sitting in silent and breathless circles. An andante of Haydn's was in the air. It was a sweet and delicate music, both merry and melancholy, tripping to a sunshiny measure that set everybody's heart beating in time. There was a childish grace about the strain that charmed all the listeners to a tender enthusiasm. It made them cry and laugh at once; and though many sat motionless and stolid, you might see eyes shining and dilating, as mothers' eyes dilate sometimes when they watch their children at play. The childless were no longer childless while that gentle, irresistible music shook from the delicate strings of the instruments; the lonely and silent had found a voice; the hard of heart and indifferent were moved and carried away; pent-up longings were set free. Other strings were sounding with the Haydn; and it was not music, though it was harmony, of some sort that struck and shook those mysterious fibres that bind men and women to life. The hopelessness of the lonely, the mad longings of the parted, the storm of life, all seemed appeased. To Dolly, it was George's voice that was speaking once again. ' Peace, be still,' said the music, and a divine serenity was in the great hall where the little tune was thrilling.

In former times men and women assembled in conclave to see wild beasts tearing their prey; to-day it was to listen to a song of Haydn's—a little song, that did not last five minutes.

It had not ended when Rhoda whispered something into Robert's ear.

While the music was lasting Dolly was transported; as it ended her mind seemed clear. She was at peace, she understood it all, all malice and uncharitableness seemed *dissolved*—I know no better word—pangs of wounded pride, bitterness of disappointed trust, shame of unfulfilled promise —such things were, but other things, such as truth, honest intention, were beyond them, and Dolly felt at that moment as if she could rise above her fate, above her own faults, beyond her own failures. She would confess the truth to Robert: she had meant to be faithful to him; she had failed; she would take what blame there was upon herself, and that should be her punishment. She was too keen-sighted not to understand all that had been passing before her eyes. At first wounded and offended, and not unjustly pained, she had determined to wait in silence, to let Henley explain his own intentions, acknowledge his own short-comings.

But something more generous, more truthful, impelled her now to speak. Rhoda and Robert were whispering. ' Hush,' Dolly said, and she laid her hand upon Robert's arm. He started a little uncomfortably, and then began suddenly to nod his head and to twirl his umbrella in time. Rhoda

buttoned her long gloves and leant back in a pensive attitude. Dolly sat staring at the violins, of which the bows
were flowing like the waves of a spring-tide on either side
of the circle: beyond the violins were the wind instruments
and the great violoncellos throbbing their full hearts. There
was instant silence, then a clapping of hands and a sort of
murmur and sigh coming from a hundred breasts. As it
all died away, Dolly stood up and turned to Robert: an
impulse came to her to do now what was in her heart, to
wait no longer.

'Robert ——' her voice sounded so oddly that he started
and half rose, looking down at her upturned face. 'Robert,
I want you to listen to me,' said Dolly. 'I must tell you
now when I can speak. I see it all. You were right to
doubt me. I know it now. I have not been true to you.
You must marry Rhoda,' she said; then, stopping short,
'I'm not jealous, only I am bewildered. . . I am going
home. . . Don't come with me; but you forgive me,
don't you, Robert?'

There was a sudden burst from some overture—the music
was beginning again. Before Robert could stop her, Dolly
was gone; she had started up, she had left her seat, her
gloves were lying on the ground, her veil was lying on the
bench, but it was too late to follow or to call her back; the
people, thinking she was ill, had made way for her, and
closed in round the door

'What has happened?' said Rhoda. 'Is she ill or angry?
is she gone? Oh, what has happened? Don't leave me
here alone, let me come too. . .'

Robert flushed up. 'The eyes of the whole place are
upon us,' he muttered: then came something like an oath.

'Hush, silence,' said the people behind.

Robert bit his lip and sat staring at the conductor's rod; every now and then he gave a little impatient jerk of the head.

Rhoda waited her time; he had not followed Dolly. The music went on; not one note did she hear; the time seemed interminable. But Robert, hearing a low sigh, turned at last; he did not speak, but he looked at her.

'You are angry?' whispered Rhoda.

'Why should I be angry with you?' he answered, more gently.

CHAPTER LIII.

THAT THOU ART BLAMED SHALL NOT BE THY DEFECT.

> Yesterday *this* day's madness did prepare,
> To-morrow's silence, triumph, or despair.
> Drink! for you know not whence you came, nor why;
> Drink! for you know not why you go, nor where.
> —OMAR KHAYYÁM.

ONCE, as Dolly was hurrying away through the passages to the great front entrance, she looked back, for she thought she heard Robert's step coming after her. It was only Casimir, the servant, who had been loitering by a staircase, and had seen her pass. She came to the great wide doors of the music-hall, where the people were congregated, the servants carrying their mistresses' carriage cloaks over their arms, the touters and vendors of programmes. The music was still in her ears; she felt very calm, very strange. Casimir would have darted off for the carriage if she had not stopped him.

'Is Mademoiselle indisposed? Shall I accompany her?' he asked.

But although Dolly looked very pale, she said she was not ill; she would go home alone: and when she was safely seated in the little open carriage he called for her, the colour came back into her cheeks. She leant back, for she was very tired. As she drove along she tried to remember what had happened, to think what more would happen, but she could

not do so. It was a feeling, not an event, that had moved
her so ; and the outward events that relate these great unseen
histories to others are to the actors themselves of little consequence. As for the future, Dolly could scarcely believe in
a future. Was anything left to her now ? Her life seemed
over, and she was scarcely twenty ; she was sorry for herself.
She did not regret what she had done, for he did not love
her. It was Rhoda whom he loved ; Rhoda who seemed to
have absorbed everything, little by little. There was nothing
that she had spared. Dolly wondered what they would say
at the Court. She thought of Frank Raban, too. If the
Squire's news was true, Frank Raban would be thinking no
more of her, but absorbed in other interests. Even Frank—
was any one faithful in life ? Then she thought of George :
he had not failed : he had been true to the end, and this
comforted her.

Everything seemed to have failed with her, and yet—how
shall I explain it ?—Dolly was at peace with herself. In her
heart she knew that she had tried, almost tried to do her
best. No pangs of conscience assailed her as she drove home
through this strange chaos of regrets and forgetfulness. Her
hands fell into her lap as she leant back in the little carriage :
it was bringing her away through the dull rattle of the streets
to a new home, a new life, swept and garnished, so it seemed
to Dolly, where everything was strange and bare—one in
which, perhaps, little honour was to be found, little credit.
What did she care ! She was too true a lady to trouble
herself about resentments and petty slights and difficulties.
They had both meant to do right. As for Rhoda, Dolly
would not think of Rhoda just then, it hurt her. For
George's sake she must try to think kindly of her ; was it for
her to cast a stone ? Dolly came upstairs slowly and steadily,

opened the door, which was on the latch, and came in, looking
for her mother. Miss Vanborough had never, not even in
the days of her happy love, looked more beautiful than she
did as she came into the little sitting-room at home. A light
was in her face; it was the self-forgetful look of someone who has passed for a moment beyond the common
state of life, escaping the assaults of selfish passion, into
a state where feeling is not destroyed but multiplied
beyond itself. In these moods sacrifice scarcely exists.
The vanities of the world glitter in vain, discord cannot
jar, and in the midst of tumult and sorrow souls are at
peace.

Mrs. Palmer was not alone; the Squire was there. He
had brought news. He had been detained by a peremptory
telegram from Norah—'*Jonah arrives Paris to-morrow;
mamma says, remain; bring Jonah home*'—and Jonah,
who had come almost at the same time as the telegram, had
accompanied the Squire, and was waiting impatiently enough
hoping to see Dolly. He had been somewhat bored by the
little elderly flirtation which had been going on for the last
half-hour between his aunt and his godfather (which sort of
pot-pourri, retaining a certain faint perfume of bygone roses,
is not uncommon); but he did not move, except to go and
stand out upon the balcony and stare up and down the street;
he was leaning over the slender railing when Dolly came in,
and so it happened that at first she only saw the Squire
sitting by her mother's easy-chair. She gave him her hand.
He stood holding it in his, and looking at her, for he saw
that something had happened.

'Alone!' said Mrs. Palmer. 'Is Robert with you? I
have some news for you; guess, Dolly;' and Philippa looked
archly towards the window.

Dolly looked at her mother. ' I left them at the concert,' she said, not asking what the news was.

' What made you leave them ? Why do you stare at me like that?' cried Mrs. Palmer, forgetting her news. ' Have you had another quarrel? Dolly, I have only just been saying so to Mr. Anley ; under the circumstances you really should *not*—you *really* should —— '

' It has all been a mistake, mamma,' said Dolly, looking up, though she did not see much before her. ' Everything is over. Robert and I have parted, quite parted,' she repeated sadly.

' Parted !'· exclaimed the Squire ; ' has it come to this ? '

' Parted ! ' cried poor exasperated Philippa. ' I warned you. It is your own fault, Dolly; you have been possessed all along. Mr. Anley, what is to be done ? ' cried the poor lady, turning from one to the other. ' Is it your doing or Robert's ? Dolly, what is it all about ? '

Dolly did not answer for an instant, for she could not speak.

The Squire began muttering something between his teeth, as he strode up and down the room with his hands in his pockets.

' Take care, you will knock over the jardinière,' cried Mrs. Palmer.

Dolly's eyes were all full of tears by this time. As he turned she laid her hand upon the old man's arm. ' It is my doing, not his,' she said. ' You must not be hard upon him ; indeed it is all my doing.'

' It is your doing now, and most properly,' said the Squire, very gravely, and not in the least in his usual half joking manner. ' I can only congratulate you upon having got rid of that abominable prig ; but you must not take it all upon yourself, my poor child.'

Dolly blushed up. 'You think it is not my fault,' she said, and the glow spread and deepened ; 'he was not bound when he left me, only I had promised to wait'—then with sudden courage, 'You will not blame him when I tell you this,' she said : 'I have not been true to him, not quite true—I told him so ; it was a pity, all a pity,' she said, with a sigh. She stood with hanging hands and a sweet, wistful, tender face ; her voice was like a song in its unconscious rhythms, for deep feeling gives a note to people's voices that is very affecting sometimes.

'You told him so—what will people say ? ' shrieked poor Mrs. Palmer ; 'and here is Jonah, whom we have quite forgotten.'

Jonah was standing listening with all his honest ears. It seemed to the young soldier that he also had been listening to music, to some sweet sobbing air played with tender touch. It seemed to fill the room even after Dolly had left it ; for when she turned and suddenly saw her cousin it was the climax of that day's agitation. She came up and kissed him with a little sob öf surprise and emotion, tried to speak in welcome, and then shook her head and quickly went away, shutting the door behind her. As Dolly left the room the two men looked at one another. They were almost too indignant with Henley to care to say what they thought of his conduct. 'Had not we better go?' said Jonah, awkwardly, after a pause.

But Mrs. Palmer could not possibly dispense with an audience on such an occasion as this ; she made Jonah promise to return to dinner, she detained the Squire altogether to detail to him the inmost feelings of a mother's heart; she sent for cups of tea. 'Is Miss Dolly in her room, Julie?' she asked.

'Yes, Madame; she has locked the door,' said Julie.

'Go and knock, then, immediately, Julie; and come and tell me what she says, poor dear.'

Then Mrs. Palmer stirs her own tea, and describes all that she has felt ever since first convinced of Robert's change of feeling. Her experience had long ago taught her to discover those signs of indifference which .... The poor Squire listens in some impatience.

Meanwhile Robert and Rhoda are driving home together from the concert, flattered, dazzled, each pursuing their own selfish schemes, each seeing the fulfilment of small ambitions at hand, and Dolly, sitting at the foot of her bed, is saying good-by again and again. The person she had loved, and longed to see, and thought of day after day and hour after hour, was not Henley, but some other quite different man, with his face, perhaps, but with another soul and nature. .... That Robert, who had been so dear to her at one time, so vivid, so close a friend, so wise, so sympathetic, so strong, and so tender, was nothing, no one—he had never existed. The death of this familiar friend, the dispersion of this familiar ghost seemed, for a few hours, as if it meant her own annihilation. All her future seemed to have ended here. It was true that she had accused herself openly of want of faithfulness; but the mere fact of having accused herself seemed to make that self-reproach lighter and more easy to bear. After some time she roused herself; Marker was at the door and saying that it was dinner-time, and Dolly let her in and dressed for dinner in a dreamy sort of way, taking the things, as Marker handed them to her, in silence, one by one. The Squire and Jonah were both in the sitting-room when Dolly came in in the white dress she usually wore, with some black ribbons round her waist, and tied into her bronze hair. She did not want to look as if she was a victim, and she tried to smile as usual.

'You must not mind me,' she said presently, in return for the Squire's look of sympathy. 'It is not to-day that this has happened; it began so long ago that I am used to it now.' Then she added, 'Mamma, I should like to see Robert again this evening, for I left him very abruptly, and I am afraid he may be unhappy about me.'

'Oh, as to that, Dolly, from what the Squire tells me, I don't think you need be at all alarmed,' cried Dolly's mamma: 'Jonah met him on the stairs with Rhoda, and really, from what I hear, I think he must have already proposed. I wonder if he will have the face to come in himself to announce it.'

Both Jonah and the Squire began to talk together, hoping to stop Mrs. Palmer's abrupt disclosures; but who was there who could silence Mrs. Palmer? She alluded a great deal to a certain little bird, and repeatedly asked Dolly during dinner whether she thought this dreadful news could be true, and Robert really engaged to Rhoda?

'I think it is likely to be true before long, mamma,' said Dolly, patiently: 'I hope so.'

She seemed to droop and turn paler and paler in the twilight. She was not able to pretend to good spirits that she did not feel; but her sweetness and simplicity went straight to the heart of her two champions, who would have gladly thrown Robert out of the first-floor window if Dolly had shown the slightest wish for it.

After dinner, as they all sat in the front room, with wide-evening windows, Julie brought in the lamp. She would have shut out the evening and drawn down the blinds if they had not prevented her. The little party sat silently watching the light dancing and thrilling behind the house-tops; nobody spoke. Dolly leant back wearily. From time to time Mrs. Palmer whispered any fresh surmise into the Squire's ear: 'Why did not Robert come? Was *she* keeping him back?'

Presently Mrs. Palmer started up: a new idea had occurred to her. She would go in herself, unannounced: she would learn the truth: the Squire, he too, must come. The Squire did as he was bid: as they left the room Jonah got up shyly from his seat, and went and stood out on the balcony. Dolly asked him whether there was a moon.

'There is a moon rising,' said the Captain, 'but you can't see it from where you sit; there from the sofa you can see it.' And then he came back, and wheeled the sofa round, and began turning down the wheel of the lamp, saying it put the moonlight out.

As the lamp went out suddenly with a splutter, all the dim radiance of the silver evening came in a soft vibration to light the darkened room. One stream of moonlight trickled along the balcony, another came lapping the stone coping of the window: the moon was rising in state and in silence, and Dolly leant back among her cushions, watching it all with wide open eyes. Jonah's dark cropped head rose dark against the Milky Way. As the moon rose above the gable of the opposite roof a burst of chill light flooded the balcony, and overflowed, and presently reached the foot of the couch where Dolly was lying, worn out by her long day.

Robert, who had been taking a rapid walk on the pavement outside, had not noticed the moon: he was preoccupied

by more important matters. Rhoda's speeches were ringing
in his ears. Yet it was Dolly's fault all along; he was
ready to justify himself; to meet complaint with complaint;
she might have been a happy woman. He had behaved
honourably and forbearingly; and now it was really unfair
that she should expect anything more from him, or complain
because he had found his ideal in another and more feminine character.

Dolly had heard the roll of the wheels of the carriage
that brought Robert and Rhoda home, but she had not
heard the short little dialogue which was being spoken as
the wheels rolled under the gateway. The two had not
said much on the way. Rhoda waited for Robert to speak.
Robert sat gazing at his boots.

'One knows what everybody will say,' he said at last very
crossly.

'The people who know you as I do will say that Dolly
might have been a happy woman,' Rhoda answered; 'that
she has wrecked her own happiness;' and then they were
both again silent.

Rhoda was frightened, and trembled as she looked into
Robert's offended face. She thought that the end of it all
might be that he would go—leave her and all other complications, and Rhoda had not a few of her own. If he were to
break free? Rhoda's heart beat with apprehension; her
feeling for Robert was more genuine than most of her feelings, and this was her one excuse for the part she had played.
Her nature was so narrow, her life had been so stinted, that
the first touch of sentiment overbalanced and carried her
away. Dolly possessed the genius of living and loving and
being to a degree that Rhoda could not even conceive; with
all her tact and quickness she could not reach beyond her-

K K

self. For some days past she had secretly hoped for some such catastrophe as that which had just occurred. She had taken the situation for granted.

'One sometimes knows by instinct what people feel,' she said at last. 'I have long felt that Dolly did not understand you; but then, indeed, you are not easy to understand.' And Robert, raising his eyes from his boots, met the beautiful gloom of her speaking eyes.

One has sometimes watched a cat winding its way between little perils of every sort. Rhoda softly and instinctively avoided the vanities of Robert's mind; she was presently telling him of her troubles, money troubles among the rest. She had spent more than her income; she did not dare confess to Mr. Tapeall; she felt utterly incapable of managing that fortune which ought never to have been hers—which she was ready to give up at any hour.

'Cleverer people than I am might do something with all this money,' said Rhoda. 'Something worth doing: but I seem only to get into trouble. You say you will help me, but you will soon be gone.'

'I shall be always ready to advise you,' said Robert. 'If there is anything at any time——'

'But when you are gone?' said Rhoda, with great emotion.

There was a pause; the horses clattered in under the gateway.

'You must tell me to stay,' said Robert in a low voice, as he helped Rhoda out of the carriage.

As the two slowly mounted the staircase which Dolly had climbed, Jonah, coming away from his aunt's apartment, almost ran up against them. Robert exclaimed, but Jonah passed on. What did Rhoda care that he brushed past as if

he had not seen them ?   She was sure he had seen them, and
Rhoda had her own reasons for wishing no time to be lost
before her news was made public.   She had won her great
stake, secured her prize : her triumph was not complete
until others were made aware of all that had happened.   She
urged Robert to tell his aunt at once.

' It is only fair to yourself.   Dolly will be telling her
story—dear Dolly, she is always so kind; but still, as you
have often said, there are two sides to a question.   I am
afraid your cousin passed us intentionally,' said Rhoda.   ' Not
that I care for anything now.'

' Let us have our dinner in peace,' said Robert; ' and
then I will tell them anything you like,' and he sank down
comfortably into one of the big arm-chairs, not sorry to put
after dinner out of her mind.   While he was with Rhoda he
was at ease with himself, and thought of nothing else; but
he had vague feelings of a conscience standing outside on the
landing and ready to clutch him as he passed out of the
charm of her presence.

He did not go straight off to his aunt when he left
Rhoda, and so it happened that he missed Mrs. Palmer when
she burst in upon Rhoda and Miss Rougemont.   The resolute
Robert was pacing the pavement outside and trying to make
up his mind to face those who seemed to him now more like
life-long enemies than friends.   He took courage at last and
determined to get it over, and he turned up the street again
and climbed the staircase once more.   Philippa had left the
hall-door open, and Robert walked in as he had been used to
do ; he opened the drawing-room door.   He was angry with
Dolly still, angry with her mother, and ready to resent their
reproaches.   Robert opened the drawing-room door and
stopped short at the threshold. . . .

The room was not dark, for the bright moonlight was pouring in. Dolly was still lying asleep. A log burnt low in the fire-place, crimsoning the silver light. Robert was startled. He came forward a few steps and stood in the darkened room looking at the sleeping girl: something in her unconsciousness, in the utter silence, in the absence of reproach, smote him as no words of blame or appeal could have done. His excuses, his self-assertions, of what good were they here—who cared for them here? She scarcely moved, she scarcely seemed to breathe; her face looked calm, it was almost like the face of a dead person; and so she was—dead to him.

For an instant he was touched; taken by surprise; he longed to awaken her, to ask her to forgive him for leaving her; but as he stood there a dark figure appeared in the open window; it was Jonah, who did not speak, but who pointed to the door.

At any other time Robert might have resented this, but to-night something had moved his cold and selfish heart, some ray from Dolly's generous spirit had unconsciously reached him at last. He turned away and went quietly out of the room, leaving her sleeping still.

He did not see her again; two days later she left for England.

CHAPTER LIV.

HOLY ST. FRANCIS, WHAT A CHANGE IS HERE!

If when in cheerless wanderings dull and cold,
A sense of human kindliness hath found us,
We seem to have around us
An atmosphere all gold.
—A. Clough.

TWELVE o'clock is striking in a bare room full of sunshine. A woman, who is spending her twelfth year in bed, is eating tripe out of a basin ; another sitting by the fire is dining off gruel ; beds and women alternate all down the ward ; two nurses are coming and going, one of them with a black eye. Little garlands of paper, cleverly cut out, decorate the place in honour of some Royal birthday. Two little flags are stuck up against the wall and flying triumphantly from the farther end of the room. A print of the Royal Family, brilliantly coloured, is also pinned up. Mrs. Fane is walking down the middle of the workhouse infirmary with a basket on her arm, when one of the old women puts out a wrinkled hand to call her back.

' Ain't we grand, mum ? ' says the old woman, looking up. ' It does us all good ; ' and she nods and goes on with her gruel again.

' How is Betty Hodge to-day ? ' says Mrs. Fane. The old woman points significantly.

All this time some one has been lying quite still at the further end of the room, covered by a sheet.

'At eight o'clock this morning she went off werry comfortable,' says the old woman. 'Mrs. Baker she is to scrub the steps now ; the matron sent word this morning.'

That is all. In this infirmary of the workhouse it is a matter of course that people should die. It does not mean a black carriage, nodding feathers, nor blinds drawn, and tombstones with inscriptions. It means, ease at last, release from the poor old body that used to scrub the steps so wearily day after day. There it was, quite still in the sunshine, with the garlands on the wall.

'*I* shan't be long,' said the old tripe-woman, sententiously. 'She has been expecting to go for months. A friend has sent her a shroud and some silver paper ready cut ; she says it is all ready, and she has seen the priest.'

'Ah ! Mrs. Blaney, you are a sufferer,' says the nurse with the black eye. 'She can't eat, mum, but she likes her cup of tea ;' and the nurse, who also likes her cup of tea, eyes the little packet which she sees coming out of Mrs. Fane's basket, and fetches a canister, into which she elaborately shakes the refreshing shower.

Mrs. Fane hurries on, for she has a guest at home expecting her, and a tea-party organising for that afternoon, and she has still a visit to pay in the men's ward. Some one brought her a message—a man called Smith wanted to speak to her ; and she walked along the whitewashed walls and past check blue counterpanes, looking for her petitioner. By one of the high windows of the ward lay a brown haggard face, with a rough chin, and the little old slip-shod messenger pointed to attract Mrs. Fane's attention. She remembered the man at once. He had come to see her not long before.

She had sent him some money to Paris—his own money, that he had given to a nurse to keep. Mrs. Fane looked with her kind round eyes into the worn face that tried to upraise itself to greet her.

'I am sorry to see you here,' she said. 'Did you not find your friends?'

'Gone to America,' gasped the man.

'You know I have still got some of your money,' said Mrs. Fane, sitting down by the bedside.

'It were about that I made so bold as to hask for to see you, mum,' said the man. 'I have a boy at Dartford,' he went on, breathing painfully. 'He ain't a good boy, but I've wrote to him to go to you, and if you would please keep the money for him, mum—three pound sixteen the Reverend calc'lated it—with what you sent for my journey here. I had better have stopped where I was and where the young lady found me. Lord! what a turn she giv' me. I know'd it was all up when I seed her come in.'

He was muttering on vacantly, as people do who are very weak. Mrs. Fane's kind heart ached for his lonely woebegone state. She took his hand in hers—how many sick hands had she clasped in her healing palm—but poor Smith was beyond her help.

'I see a young fellow that died beside me at the battle of the Alma,' said Smith, 'and when that young lady came up, as you might be, it brought it all back as it might be now. He was a gentleman, they said; he weren't half a bad chap.'

'Who are you speaking of?' said Mrs. Fane, not quite following.

'They called him George—George Vance,' said the man; 'but that were not his name no more than Smith is mine.'

'I have heard of a man of that name who was wounded at the Alma; I did not know that he had died there,' said Mrs. Fane. Her hand began to tremble a little, but she spoke very quietly.

Smith hesitated for a minute, then he looked up into the clear constraining eyes that seemed to him to be expecting his answer. 'It ain't no odds to me now,' he said, hoarsely, whether I speak the tru—uth or not; you're a lady, and will keep the money safe for my poor lad. Captain Henley he offered a matter o' twenty pound if we found poor Vance alive. He were a free-handed chap were poor Vance. We know'd he would not grudge the money. . . . And when the Roosians shot him, poor fellow, it wasn't no odds to him.'

Mrs. Fane looking round saw the chaplain passing, and she whispered to the old attendant to bring him to her.

'And so you said that you had found him alive, I suppose?' said Mrs. Fane, quickly guessing at the truth.

'Well, mum, you ain't far wrong,' said Smith, looking at his thin brown fingers. 'There was another chap of our corps died on the way to the ships. It were a long way to carry them down to the shore: we changed their names. We didn't think we had done no great harm; for twenty pound is twenty pound; but I have heard as how a fortune was lost thro' it all—a poor chap like me has no fortune to lose.'

'It was the young lady you saw who lost her fortune,' said Mrs. Fane, controlling herself, and trying to hide her agitation. 'You did her great injury, you see, though you did not mean it. But you can repair this wrong. I think you will like to do so,' she said, 'and—and—we shall all be very much obliged to you.' 'Mr. Morgan,' Mrs. Fane continued, turning to the chaplain, who had come up to the bedside, 'here is a poor fellow who wishes to do us a service,

and to make a statement, and I want you to take it down.'
She had writing materials in her basket. She often wrote
the sick people's letters for them.

'What is it, my man,' said the chaplain; but as he
listened his face changed. He gave one amazed and significant glance at Mrs. Fane, then biting his lips and trying
to seem unmoved, he wrote and signed the paper; Mrs.
Fane signed it; and then, at her request, poor bewildered
Smith feebly scrawled his name. He did it because he was
told: he did not seem to care much one way or another for
anything more.

'Joe can tell you all about it,' he said. 'Joe Carter—he
has took his discharge. I don't know where he is— Liverpool may be.'

John Morgan could hardly contain his excitement, and
his umbrella whirled like a mill, as he left the workhouse.
'You *are* a good woman; you *have* done a good morning's
work,' said the chaplain, as he came away with Mrs. Fane;
'say nothing more at present. We must find out this Joe
who was with him. Whatever we do let us be silent and
keep this from that wretched, scheming girl.'

Afterwards, it turned out, that it would have been better
far if John Morgan had spoken openly at the time; but his
terror of Rhoda's schemes was so great that he felt that if
she only knew all, she would lay hands on Joe, carry off
Smith himself, make him unsay all he had said. 'There is
no knowing what that woman may not do,' said Morgan. 'She
wrote to me; I have not answered the letter. Do you know
that the marriage is actually fixed? I am very glad that
you have got Dolly away from that adder's nest.'

'So am I,' said Mrs. Fane, beaming for an instant; she
had long ago taken Dolly to her heart with a confused

feeling of some maternal fibre strung, of something more tender and more enduring than the mere friendship between a girl and an older woman.

I cannot help it if most of those who knew my Dolly persisted in spoiling her. She wanted every bit of kindness and sunshine that came in her way. And yet she was free from the strain that had wrenched her poor little life, she need no longer doubt her own feelings, nor blind herself to that which she would so gladly escape.

The morbid fight was over, and the world was at peace. It was at peace, but unutterably sad, empty, meaningless. When people complain that their lives are dull and have no meaning, it is that they themselves have no meaning. Dolly felt as if she had been in the thick of the fight, and come away wounded. 'I may as well be here as anywhere else,' she had said that moonlight evening when poor Jonah had entreated her in vain to come away with him.

Dolly would not go back to Henley; she had her own reasons for keeping away. But next morning, when an opportune letter came from Mrs. Fane, Dolly, who had lain awake all night, went to her mother, who had slept very comfortably, and said, 'Mamma, if you can spare me, I think I will go over to England with the Squire and Jonah for a little time, until the marriage is over.' Mrs. Palmer was delighted. 'To Yorkshire? Yes, dearest, the very best thing you can do.'

'Not to Henley, mamma,' Dolly said; 'I should like, please, to go to Mrs. Fane's, if you do not object.'

'What a child you are,' cried Mrs. Palmer; 'you prefer poking yourself away in that horrid, dismal hospital, when poor Jonah is on his knees to you to go back to Henley with him.'

' Perhaps that is the reason why I must not go, mamma,' said Dolly, smiling. ' I must not have any explanations with Jonah.' Mrs. Palmer was seriously angry, and settled herself down for another nap.

So Dolly came to England one summer's afternoon, escorted by her faithful knights. All the streets were warm and welcoming ; the windows were open, and the shadows were painting the pretty old towers and steeples of the city ; some glint of an Italian sky had come to visit our northern world.

John Morgan met her at the train, Mrs. Fane stood on the door-step to welcome her, the roar of the streets sounded homelike and hopeful once more.

As for Lady Henley she was furiously jealous when she heard of Dolly in London, and with Mrs. Fane. She abused her to everybody for a fortnight. Jonah had come home for two days and then returned to town again. ' That is all we get of him after all we have gone through,' cried poor Lady Henley ; ' however, perhaps there is a good reason for it ; all one wants is to see one's children happy,' said the little lady to Mr. Redmayne, who was dining at the Court.

John Morgan lost no time in writing to his confessor, Frank Raban, to tell him of the strange turn that events had taken. ' I entreat you to say no word of this to any one,' said Morgan. ' I am afraid of other influence being brought to bear upon this man that we are in search of, and it is most necessary that we should neglect no precautions. Dolly's interests have been too carelessly served by us all.' Raban was rather annoyed by this sentence in Morgan's letter. What good would it have done to raise an opposition that would have only pained a person who was already sorely tried in other ways? Frank somewhat shared Dolly's

carelessness about money, as we know. Perhaps in his
secret heart it had seemed to him that it was not for him to
be striving to gain a fortune for Dolly—a fortune that she
did not want. Now he suddenly began to blame himself and
determined to leave no stone unturned to find the evidence
that was wanted. And yet he was more estranged from
Dolly at this moment than he had ever been in his life
before. He had purposely abstained from any communication with her. He knew she was in London and he kept
away.

Frank Raban was a man of a curious doggedness and
tenderness of nature. When he had once set his mind to a
thing he went through with his mind. He could not help
himself any more than some people can help being easily
moved and dissuaded from their own inclinations; only he
could not help listening to the accounts that now reached
him of the catastrophe at Paris, and feeling that any faint
persistent hope was now crushed for ever.

Lady Henley's wishes were apt to colour her impression
of events as they happened. According to her version, it was
for Jonah's sake that Dolly had broken with Robert. It was
to Jonah that Dolly had confided her real reason for parting
from her cousin. 'You know it yourself, Squire. It was
painful, but far better than the alternative.'—'Miss Vanborough's confidences did not extend so far as you imagine,
my dear lady,' said Mr. Anley: 'I must honestly confess
that I heard nothing of the sort.'

Lady Henley was peremptory. She was not at liberty to
show her son's last letter, but she had *full* authority for her
information. She was not in the habit of speaking at
random. Time would show. Lady Henley looked obstinate.
The Squire seemed annoyed. Frank Raban said nothing;

he walked away gloomily; he came less and less to the
Court; he looked very cross at times, although the work he
had taken in hand was prospering. Whitewashed cottages
were multiplying, a cricket-field had been laid out for the
use of the village, Medmere was drained and sown with
turnip-seed. Frank was now supposed to be an experienced
agriculturist. He looked in the *Farmer's Friend* regularly.
Tanner used to consult him upon a variety of subjects. What
was to be done about the sheep? Pitch plaster was no
good, should they try Spanish ointment? Those hurdles
must be seen to, and what about the flues and the grinders
down at the mill?

Notwithstanding these all-absorbing interests, Frank no
sooner received Morgan's letter, with its surprising news, than
he started off at once to concert measures with the Rector.
' Joe' was supposed to be at Liverpool, and Frank started for
Liverpool and spent a fruitless week looking up all the dis-
charged and invalided soldiers for ten miles round. He
thought he had found some trace of the man he was in
search of, but it was tiresome work, even in Dorothea's
interest. John Morgan wrote that Jonah was in London,
kind and helpful. Foolish Frank, who should have known
better by this time, said to himself that they could have
settled their business very well without Jonah's help. Frank
did him justice, and wished him back in Yorkshire. May he
be forgiven. Diffidence and jealousy are human failings,
that bring many a trouble in their train. True love should
be far beyond such pitiful preoccupations : and yet, if
ever any man loved any woman honestly and faithfully,
Frank Raban loved Dorothea: although his fidelity may
have shown want of spirit, and his jealousy want of common
sense. Dolly had vaguely hoped that Raban might have

written to her, but the jealous thought that she might show Jonah his letter had prevented him from writing. John Marplot wrote that Jonah was often in S—— Street. Why did not the good Rector add that it was Mrs. Fane who asked him to come there? Dolly was rather provoked when Jonah reappeared time after time; one day he offered himself to join them in a little expedition that Mrs. Fane had planned. Mrs. Fane was pleased to welcome the Captain and the Rector too. Six hours of country were to set John Morgan up for his Sunday services. Dolly looked pale, some fresh air would do her good, said her friend. 'Do I want to be done good to?' said Dolly, smiling.

Dolly was standing out on the balcony, carefully holding her black silk dress away from the dusty iron bars. It was a bright gentle-winded Sunday morning, and the countless bells of the district were jangling together, and in different notes calling their votaries to different shrines. The high bell striking quick and clear, the low bell with melancholy cadence, the old-fashioned parish bell swinging on in a sing-song way: a little Catholic chapel had begun its chime an hour before. From the house doors came Sunday folks—children trotting along, with their best hats and conscious little legs, mammas radiant, maid-servants running, cabs going off laden. All this cheerful jingle-jangling filled Dolly's heart with a happy sadness. It was so long since she had heard it, and it was all so dear and so familiar, as she stood listening to it all, that it was a little service in her heart of grateful love and thanks—for love and for praise; for life to utter her love for the peace which had come to her after her many troubles. She was not more happy outwardly in circumstance, but how much more happy in herself none but she herself could tell. How it

had come about she could scarcely have explained; but so
it was. She had ceased to struggle; the wild storm in her
heart had hushed away; she was now content with the fate,
which had seemed to her so terrible in the days of her girlhood. Unloved, misunderstood, was this her fate? she had
in some fashion risen above it—and she felt that the same
peace and strength were hers. Peace, she knew not why;
strength coming, she scarcely knew how or whence. It was
no small thing to be one voice in the great chorus of voices,
to be one aspiration in the great breath of life, and to know
that her own wishes and her own happiness were not the
sum of all her wants.

CHAPTER LV.

SEE YOU NOT SOMETHING BESIDE MASONRY ?

> And this I know: whether the one true light
> Kindle to love, or wrath consume me quite,
> One flash of it, within the Tavern caught,
> Better than in the Temple lost outright.

ON the Friday before they were to start on their little expedition, Mrs. Fane was busy; Dolly had been sitting alone for some time.

She suddenly called to old Marker, asked her to put on her bonnet and come out with her. Dolly made Marker stop a cab and they drove off; the old nurse wanted to turn back when she found out where Dolly was going, but she could not resist the girl's pleading looks. 'It will do me good, Marker,' said Dolly, 'indeed it will. I want to see the dear old place again.'

All that morning she felt a longing to see the old place once more: something seemed to tell her that she must go. One often thinks that to be in such a place would bring ease, that the sight of such a person would solve all difficulties, and one travels off, and one seeks out the friend, and it was but a fancy after all. Poor old Church House! All night long Dolly had been dreaming of her home, unwinding the skeins of the past one by one. It may have been a fancy that brought Dolly, but it was a curious chance.

They had come to the top of the lane, and Dolly got out and paid her cab. Her eyes were dim with the past, that was coming as a veil or a shroud between her and the present. She had no faint suspicion of what was at hand. They walked on unsuspiciously to the ivy gate : suddenly Marker cried out, and then Dolly too gave a little gasp. What cruel blow had fallen? what desecrating hand had dared to touch the dear old haunt? What was this? She had not dreamt *this*. The garden wall, so sweet with jessamine, was lying low, the prostrate ivy was struggling over a heap of bricks and rubbish, tracks of wheel-barrows ran from the house to the cruel heap, the lawn was tossed up, a mound of bricks stood raised by the drawing-room windows; the windows were gone, black hollows stood in their places, a great gap ran down from Dolly's old bed-room up above to the oak room on the terrace, part of the dining-room was gone : pathetic, black, charred, dismantled, the old house stood stricken and falling from its foundation. Dolly's heart beat furiously as she caught Marker's arm.

'What has happened?' she said ; 'it is not fire—it is— oh, Marker, this is too much.'

Poor Marker could not say one word ; the two women stood clinging to each other in the middle of the garden walk. The sky was golden, the shadows were purple among the fallen bricks.

'This is too much,' Dolly repeated a little wildly, and then she broke away from Marker, crying out, 'Don't come, don't come.'

The workmen were gone : for some reason the place was deserted and there was no one to hear Dolly's sobs as she impatiently fled across the lawn. Was it foolish that these poor old bricks should be so dear to her, foolish that their

fall should seem to her something more than a symbol of all
that had fallen and passed away? Ah no, no. While the
old house stood she had not felt quite parted, but now the
very place of her life would be no more; all the grief of
that year seemed brought back to her when she stopped
short suddenly and stood looking round and about in a
scared sort of way. She was looking for something that
was not any more, listening for silent voices. Dolly!
cried the voices, and the girl's whole heart answered
as she stood stretching out her arms towards the ulterior
shores. At that minute she would have been very glad to
lie down on the old stone terrace and never rise again. Time
was so long, it weighed and weighed, and seemed to be
crushing her. She had tried to be brave, but her cup was
full, and she felt as if she could bear no more, not one heavy
hour more. This great weight on her heart seemed to have
been gathering from a long way off, to have been lasting
for years and years; no tears came to ease this pain. Marker
had sat down on the stone ledge and was wiping her grief in
her handkerchief. Dolly was at her old haunt by the pond,
and bending over and looking into the depth with strange
circling eyes.

This heavy weight seemed to be weighing her down and
drawing her to the very brink of the old pond. She longed
to be at rest, to go one step beyond the present, to be lying
straight in the murky grey water, resting and at peace.
Who wanted her any more? No one now. Those who had
loved her best were dead; Robert had left her : every one
had left her. The people outside in the lane may have seen
her through the gap in the wall, a dark figure stooping among
the purple shadows; she heard their voices calling, but she
did not heed them; they were only living voices : then she

heard a step upon the gravel close at hand, and she started back, for, looking up, she saw it was Frank Raban, who came forward. Dolly was not surprised to see him. Everything to-day was so strange, so unnatural, that this sudden meeting seemed but a part of all the rest. She threw up her hands and sank down upon the old bench.

His steady eyes were fixed upon her. 'What are you doing here ? ' he said, frightened by the look in her face, and forgetting in his agitation to greet her formally.

'What does it all matter ? ' said Dolly, answering his reproachful glance, and speaking in a shrill voice : ' I don't care about anything any more, I am tired out, yes, very tired,' the girl repeated. She was wrought up and speaking to herself as much as to him, crying out, not to be heard, but because this heavy weight was upon her, and she was struggling to be rid of it, and reckless—she must speak to him, to anybody, to the shivering bushes, to the summer dust and silence, as she had spoken to the stagnant water of the pond. She was in a state which is not a common one, in which pain plays the part of great joy, and excitement unloosens the tongue, forces men and women into momentary sincerity and directness carries all before it ; her long self-control had broken down, she was at the end of her powers— she was only thinking of her own grief and not of him just then. As she turned her pale stone-cut face away and looked across the low laurel bushes, Frank Raban felt a pang of pity for her of which Dorothea had no conception. He came up to the bench.

'Don't lose courage,' he said—'not yet ; you have been so good all this time.'

It was not so much what he said which touched her, as the way in which he said it. He seemed to know how terribly she had been suffering, to be in tune even with this remorseless fugue of pain repeated. His kindness suddenly overcame her, and touched her; she hid her face in her hands and burst out crying, and the tears eased and softened her strained nerves.

'It was coming here that brought it all back,' she said; 'and finding ——' Her voice failed.

'I am very sorry,' he said. 'How can I forgive myself. It is all my ——' He turned quite pale, stopped abruptly, and walked away for a few steps. When he came back he spoke almost in his usual voice, and then and there began to tell Dolly all that had happened, of the curious discovery which Mrs. Fane had made, of Smith's confession, and of all that it involved, that she was now the one person interested in the property, that Rhoda Parnell had no single right to Lady Sarah's inheritance. He told her very carefully, sparing her in every way, thinking of the words which would be simplest and least likely to give pain.

'We ought to have told you before,' he repeated. 'We meant to spare you until all the facts were clearly ascertained. We have made a fatal mistake, and now I am only adding to your pain.'

But the tears with which Dolly listened to him were not bitter, his voice was so kind, his words so manly and simple. He did not shirk the truth as some people sometimes do when they speak of sorrow, but he faced the worst with the simplicity and directness of a man who had seen it all very near. 'Please don't blame yourself,' she said.

If there are certain states of mind in which facts seem exaggerated, and every feeling is over-wrought, it is at these very times that people are most ready to accept the blessings of consolation. 'Peace, be still,' said the Divine Voice, speaking to the tossing waves. And voices come, speaking in human tones to many a poor tempest-tossed soul. It may be only a friend who speaks, only a lover perhaps, or a brother or sister's voice. Love, friendship, brotherhood give a meaning to the words. Only that day Dolly had thought that all was over, and already the miracle was working, the storm was passing from her heart.

It all seemed as a dream in the night, when she thought it over afterwards. She had not seen Frank again, but to have seen him once more made all the difference to her.

CHAPTER LVI.

THE PLAY IS PLAYED, THE CURTAIN DROPS.

In tho battlo of life are we all going to try for the honours of championship ?
If we can do our duty, if we can keep our place pretty honourably through the
combat, let us say 'Laus Deo' at the end of it, as the firing ceases and the
night falls over the field.—ROUNDABOUT PAPERS.

COLONEL FANE was not a rich man, but he had a house which
had been his father's before him, and to which he returned
now and again in the intervals of service. It stood at a bend
of the river, and among hollows and ivy. He looked forward
to ending his work there some day, and resting for a year or
two. In the meanwhile the old house was often let in
summer, and Mrs. Fane looked after the repairs and necessary renovations. She sometimes spent a few hours among
the sedges and shady chestnut-trees. She loved the old
place—as who does not love it who has ever been there ?—
and discovered this sleeping bower, where one may dream of
chivalry, of fairy land, or of peace on earth, or that one is
sunshine, or a river washing between heavy banks ; or turn
one's back to the stream and see a pasture-country sliding
away towards the hills, through shade and fragrant hours,
with songs from the hedges and mellow echoes from the distant farms.

The little party came down, not unprepared to be happy.

Mrs. Fane, who never wasted an opportunity, had also brought a little girl from her orphanage, who was to remain for a time with the housekeeper at Queensmede—that was the name of the old house. The child was a bright little creature, with merry soft eyes flashing in wild excitement, and the kind lady was somewhat divided between her interest in some news that John Morgan was giving her and her anxiety lest little Charlotte, her god-daughter, should jump out of window.

' We have to thank the Captain here,' said John Morgan, ' for finding the man we were in search of; his evidence fully bears out poor Smith's dying declaration. I have sent to Tapeall,' said John, shaking his head. ' I find that, after all my precautions, Rhoda got a hint from him last week. However, it is all right—thanks to the Captain—as right as anything so unfortunately managed can ever be.'

' I don't deserve any thanks,' said Jonah. ' Poor Carter found me out. He wanted to borrow 10s.'

' When did all this happen ? ' said Mrs. Fane.

' Only yesterday,' answered the Rector. ' I telegraphed to Raban—poor fellow, he had gone off to Shoeburyness on some false scent ; I left word at home in case he should call.'

Dolly stooped down and held up little Charlotte to see the pretty golden fields fly past, and the sheep and the lambs frisking.

' Are they gold flowers ? ' said the little girl. ' Is that where ladies gets their money ? Is you going to be very rich ?'

Dolly did not answer ; she had scarcely heard what they all were saying, so many voices were speaking to her, as she watched the flying fields and frisking lambs. Was it all to be hers? The old house was gone—and this was what she most dwelt upon—money was but little in comparison to the desolate home. Could she ever forgive Rhoda this cruel blow? Ah! she might have had it all, if she had but spared the dear home. A letter had come from Robert only that morning, and all this time Dolly was carrying it unopened in her pocket, failing courage to break the seal and open up the past.

Shadows and foreboding clouds were far away from that tranquil valley, from the shady chestnut-tree beneath which Dolly is sitting, resting and shading her eyes from the light.

When the banquet is over they get up from their feast and stroll down to the river side, through the silent village into the overgrown meadow, where green waving things are throwing their shadows, where an old half-ruined nunnery stands fronting the sun and the silver river beyond the fields.

There were nuns at Queensmede once: one might fancy a Guinevere ending her sad life there in tranquil penitence; a knight on his knees by the river; a horse browsing in the meadow. The old building still stands among wild-flowers and hay, within sight of the river bend; the deserted garden is unfenced, and the roses, straggling in the field, mingle their petals with the clover and poppies that spring luxuriantly. The stable is a gabled building with slender lancet windows, with open doors swinging on the latch. The nuns have passed out one by one from the Lady House, so they call it still. Dolly peeped in at the dismantled walls and pictured their former occupants to herself—women singing and praying with pale sweet faces radiant in the sweet tranquillity of the old place, and yet their life seemed thin and sad somehow. It was here that she found courage at

last to read Robert's letter as she stood in the doorway.   She
pulled it out and broke the seal:—

My Dear Dorothea,—

Notwithstanding all that has happened, I still feel that it is no common tie of friendship and interest which must always bind us together, and
that it is due to you that I myself should inform you of a determination which
will, as I trust, eventually contribute to everybody's happiness. After what
you said to me it will, I know, be no surprise to you to have heard that I have
proposed to Rhoda, and been accepted by her; but I am anxious to spare your
learning from anybody but myself the fact, that we have determined to put on
our marriage, and that this letter will reach you on our wedding day.

Your friend Rhoda has entirely thrown herself upon my guidance, and
under the circumstances it has seemed advisable to me to urge no longer
delay. My affairs require my presence in England; hers also need the
most careful management. I am not satisfied with the manner in which
certain investments have been disposed of—notwithstanding some—perhaps
not unnatural reluctance on her part. I propose returning to Church
House immediately after our wedding, where, let me tell you, my dear
Dora, you will ever find a hearty welcome, and a home if need be, although
I am anxious to forget the past, particularly under my present circumstances. I cannot but recall once more to you how differently events might
have turned out. I have never had an opportunity of explaining that to
you, but I hope you do me the justice to believe that it was not your
change of fortune which affected my decision to abide by your determination. I have been most anxious to assure you of this. It was your want
of trust which first made me feel how dissimilar we were in many ways,
how little chance there was in my being able to influence you as a husband. Forgive me for saying that you did not understand my motives, nor
do entire justice to the feelings which made me endeavour to persuade you
for your own advantage as well as mine. If you had come to India when
I wished it much anxiety to yourself and much sorrow would have been
spared you. Now it is too late to think of what might or might not have
been, only this fact remains, and do not forget it, dear Dora, that you will
never have a more sincere friend nor one more ready to advise and assist
you in any difficulty than

Your affectionate cousin,

R. Henley.

Rhoda (did she know I was writing) would unite in most affectionate
love. I find her society more and more congenial and delightful to me.

· 'What are you reading, Dolly?' said Jonah, coming up.
'I ought to know that confounded blue paper. Has that
fellow the impudence to write to you?' Then he asked
more shyly, 'May I see the letter?'

'No, dear Jonah,' Dolly said, folding it up. 'It is a kind letter, written kindly.'.

Then she looked hard at him and blushed a little. 'This is his wedding day,' she said ; 'that is why he wrote to me.'

Dolly would not show her letter to any one, except to Mrs. Fane. She felt that it would be commented on ; she was grateful to Robert for writing it ; and yet the letter made her ashamed now that she began to see him not as he was, but to judge from another standard, and to look at him with other people's eyes. In after days she scarcely ever spoke of him even to her nearest and dearest. To-day she merely repeated the news. No one made any comment in her hearing. They were anxious at first, but Dolly's face was serene, and they could see that she was not unhappy.

One thing Mrs. Fane could understand. Robert evidently knew nothing of the destruction of Church House.

'I am glad Robert had nothing to do with it,' said Dolly, with a sigh.

'Will you come wiss me,' said little Charlotte, running up and taking Dolly's hand. Miss Vanborough was not sorry to leave the discussion of Robert's prospects to others, and she walked away, with the little girl still holding by her hand, and went and stood for a minute on the bridge, looking down at the river and the barge floating by; it slid under her feet with its cargo of felled wood, and its wild and silent human cargo, and then it went floating away between the summer banks.

The waters deepened and wavered. Tall waving grasses were also floating and dragging upon the banks, crimson poppies starting here and there, golden iris hanging their heads by the river. Little Charlotte presently ran away, and, half sunk in the grasses, stood struggling with a daisy.

TRANQUIL SECLUSION.

A sunshiny man came leading a horse from the sleepy old barn that stood beyond the Lady House. Its old bricks were hung with green veils, and with purple and golden nets of lichen and of moss.

Dolly stopped—was it a burst of music? It was a sweet overpowering rush of honeysuckle scent coming from the deserted garden. In this pastoral landscape there was no sound louder than the lap of the water, or the flowing gurgle of the pigeons straggling from one to another moss-grown ledge. Chance lights stole from the sedge to the grassy banks, from the creek by sweet tumbled grasses to the deserted old grange. Round about stood the rose-trees, flowering in the wilderness, dropping their blossoms ; the swallows were flying about the eaves ; the daisies sparkled where they caught the sunlight.

While Dolly and little Charlotte were gathering their flowers Frank Raban, who came walking along the fields by the river, had joined the others by the Lady House. Morgan's telegram had summoned him back to London, and his message had brought him on to Queensmede.

' Where is Miss Vanborough ? ' he asked presently.

' Don't you see her on the bridge ? ' said Jonah, pointing.

Frank walked on a few steps. He saw her standing on the bridge, high above the torrent. Then he saw her come slowly along, followed by her little companion. . . .

They were walking slowly away from the field and the deserted garden. As they all straggled slowly homewards with shadows at their feet, the old ivy buttresses of the walls were beginning to shine with vesper light, with deeper and crisper lines in the pure illumination all around. Dolly thought of Haydn's andante again, only here it was light that brought music out of all these instruments ;

silences, perfumes, and heavy creepers from the bewildering, sweet old place, overflown with birds, heaped up and falling into hollows.

Frank walked silently beside Dolly. He had come prepared to sympathise, full of concern for her, and she did not seem to want his help or to care for it any more. That day by the pond, when she had first turned to him in her grief, he had felt nearer to her than now, when in her reserve she said no word of all that he knew she must be feeling. Could this be pride? Did she show this indifferent face to the world, was she determined that no one should guess at the secret strain? Was she treating him as the first come acquaintance? It was very proper, no doubt, and very dignified, but he was disappointed. He could not understand it. She must be unhappy, and yet as he looked at her face he saw no effort there—only peace shining from it. She had stopped before a garland of briony that was drooping with beautiful leaves, making a garland of shadows upon the bricks. She pointed it out to him.

'It is very pretty,' said Raban, 'but I am in no appreciative mood;' and he looked back at Jonah, who came up just then, and began admiring. Why was Jonah always with her? Why did he seem to join into all their talk. Frank was jealous of Jonah, but he was still more jealous of Dorothea's confidence. There seemed to be no end to Dolly's cousins. Here was Jonah, to whom she had already given more of her confidence than to him; Jonah, who had served her effectually, while he, Frank, had done nothing; worse than nothing; Dolly, who was walking along, still looking at the bunches of briony she had gathered. It was not a very heroic mood, and I am truly ashamed of my hero's passing ill humour, coming as it did at this inopportune

moment to trouble Miss Vanborough's tardy happiness. And
yet somehow it did not trouble her; she saw that Frank was
silent and gloomy, but with her instinct for idealising those
she loved, she supposed there was some good reason for it,
and she felt that she might perhaps even try to find out what
was amiss; it was no longer wrong to take an interest in all
that affected him—even Dolly's conscience allowed this—
and, when the others walked on, in her sweet voice she asked
'if anything was wrong,' and as she spoke her grey eyes
opened kindly. Dolly loved to take care of the people she
loved. There was a motherly instinct in all her affection.

'My only concern is for you, and for the news that Jonah
Henley has told me,' said Frank; 'but you did not tell me
yourself, so I did not like to speak of it to you.'

Dolly sighed—then looked up again. 'I do not know
how to talk of it all,' she said, 'and that is why I said
nothing.'

'You are right!' Frank answered; 'when one comes to
think of it, there are no words in common language to
——'

'Please don't,' said Dolly, pained; then she added, 'I
have been so unhappy, that I must not ever pretend to feel
what I am not feeling. Perhaps you may think it strange, I
am happy, not unhappy, to-day. You are all so kind; everything is so kind. I hope they too will have a great deal of
happiness in their lives. Is not Jonah calling us?' Jonah
was waiting for them at the gate of the house, and waving a
long, shadowy arm, that seemed to reach across the road.

'Happiness,' said Frank, lingering, and bitter still, and
looking round. 'This is the sort of thing people mean, I
suppose; green pastures and still waters, and if one can be
satisfied with grass, so much the better for oneself; one may

enjoy all the things one didn't particularly want—and watch another man win the prize; another perhaps who doesn't even——' Frank stopped short—what was he saying? he might be giving pain, and he hated himself and his ill humour, jarring and jangling in the peaceful serenity.

But Dolly finished the sentence calmly enough. 'Who doesn't care for it; perhaps the prize isn't worth having,' she said very slowly. She did not think of herself until she had spoken; then suddenly her heart began to beat, and she blushed crimson; for her eyes met his, and his looks spoke plainly enough—so plainly, that Dolly's grey orbs fell beneath that fixed dreamy gaze. It seemed to look through her heart. Could he read all that she was thinking? Ah! he might read her heart, for she was only thinking as she stood there of all her friend's long fidelity and steady friendship. What had she ever done to deserve it all. And her heart seemed to answer her thought with a strange silent response. Now she might own to herself the blessing of his unfailing friendship; it was no longer a wrong to any human being. Even if she were never anything more to him, she might openly and gratefully accept his help and his interest; acknowledge the blessing, the new life it had brought her. She had struggled so long to keep the feeling hidden away, it was an unspeakable relief to have nothing more to conceal from herself nor from others—nothing more. She knew at last that she loved him, and she was not ashamed. What a journey she had travelled since they had stood by the spring that autumn day, not a year ago; what terrible countries she had visited, and had it come to this once more? Might she love now in happiness as well as in sorrow? Was she not happy standing in this golden hollow, with the person whom she loved best in all the world? No other human

being was in sight, nothing but the old shady village, floating into overflowing green, the sleepy haycocks, the empty
barn, the heaping ivy on the wall, the sunlight slanting
upon the silence. She did not mean to speak, but Frank, in
this utter silence, heard her secret thought at last. ' Don't
you know ? ' said Dorothea. ' Oh ! Frank, don't you know ? '
Did she speak the words or look them ? He could scarcely
tell, only with unutterable tenderness and thankfulness in
his heart he knew that she was his, that life is kind, that
true hearts do come together, that one moment of such
happiness and completeness lights up a whole night's wild
chaos, and reveals the sweetness of a dawning world.

Jonah, who had gone on with Mrs. Fane, came to the
door to call them again, but they did not see him, and he
went back into the house, where Mrs. Fane and John Morgan were hard at work upon an inventory.

' Here, let me help you,' said Jonah ; ' I'm not too clumsy
to count teacups.' Little Charlotte made herself very useful
by carrying a plate from one chair to another. She finally
let it drop, and would have cried when it broke, if the good-
natured young captain had not immediately given her the
ink to hold. This mark of confidence filled her with pride,
and dried her tears. ' Sall I 'old it up very high ? ' she
said. ' Can you draw a ziant ? I can, wiss your pen.'

It took them nearly an hour to get through their task,
and by this time the tea was ready in the library, the old-
fashioned urn hissing and steaming, and Jonah and John
Morgan were preparing to set out on their journey home.
Frank went with them, and then when he was gone Dolly
told her friend her story, and the two sat talking until late
into the starlight.

Two days afterwards an announcement appeared in *The*

Times, and the world learnt that Robert Henley and Miss Rhoda Parnell had been married at the British Embassy at Paris by special licence by the Bishop of Oronoco. The next news was that of Dolly's marriage to Frank Raban. Pebblesthwaite was very much excited. Lady Henley's indignation was boundless at first, but was happily diverted by the news of her favourite daughter Norah's engagement to Mr. Jack Redmayne.

James Brand's blue eyes twinkled a kindly sympathy, when the letter came announcing Frank's happiness. He came up to be present at the wedding. It was in the little city church with its smoke-stained windows. John Morgan's voice failed as he read the opening words and looked down at the bent heads of the two who had met at last hand-in-hand. ' In perfect love and peace,' he said ; and, as he said it, he felt that the words were no vain prayers.

He had no fear for them, nor had they fear for each other. Some one standing in the drizzle of the street outside saw them drive off with calm and happy faces. It was Robert Henley, who was passing through London with his wife. Philippa, who saw him, kissed her hand and would have stopped him, but he walked on without looking back. He had been to Mr. Tapeall's that morning, after a painful explanation with Rhoda—Rhoda, who was moodily sitting at the window of her room in the noisy hotel, and going over the wretched details of that morning's talk. It was true that she had sold Church House, tempted by the builder's liberal offer, and wanting money to clear the many extravagances of her Paris life ; it was true that she had concealed the lawyer's letter from Robert in which she learnt that her title to the property was about to be disputed. She had hurried on their wedding, she had won the prize for which

her foolish soul had longed; it was not love so much as the
pride of life and of gratified vanity. These things had
dazzled her, for these things this foolish little creature had
sacrificed her all. Dolly might have been happy in time,
even married to Robert, but for Rhoda what chance was
there? Would her French kid gloves put out their primrose
fingers to help her in her lonely hours? would her smart
bonnets crown her home with peace and the content of a
loving spirit? She lived long enough to find out something
of the truth, and to come to Dolly one day to help her in her
sorest need. This was long after, when Dolly had long been
living at Ravensrick, when her children were playing round
about her, and the sunshine of her later life had warmed and
brightened the sadness of her youth. What more shall I
say of my heroine? That sweet and generous soul, ripening
by degrees, slow and credulous, not embittered by the petty
pains of life, faithful and tender and vibrating to many
tones, is no uncommon type. Her name is one that I gave
her long ago, but her real names are many, and are those of
the friends whom we love.

Church House was never rebuilt. At Dolly's wish a row
of model lodgings, with iron balconies, patent boilers, ventilators, and clothes hanging out to dry on every floor, have
been erected on the site of the place where Lady Sarah lived,
and so the kind woman's dreams and helpful schemes have
come true.

'We could not put back the old house,' said Dolly, 'and
we thought this would be the next best thing to do.' The
rooms are let at a somewhat cheaper rate than the crowded
lodging-houses round about. People, as a rule, dislike the
periodical whitewashing, and are fond of stuffing up the
ventilators, but otherwise they are very well satisfied.

* M M

Dolly did not receive many wedding presents. Some time after her marriage, Rhoda sent Dolly a diamond cross; it was that one that Frank Raban had given her many years before. She was abroad at the time, and for many years neither Rhoda nor Dolly met again. Mrs. Palmer used to write home accounts of Rhoda's beauty and fashion from Ems, and other watering-places where she used to spend her summers.

The Admiral, who was still abroad, made it an especial point, so Philippa declared, that she should spend her summers on the Continent.

One day Mrs. Raban was turning out some papers in a drawer in her husband's writing-table, when she came upon a packet that she thought must belong to herself. They were written in a familiar writing that she knew at once, for it was Henley's. They were not addressed, and Dolly could not at first imagine how these letters had come there, nor when she had received them. As she looked she was still more bewildered. They were letters not unlike some that she had received, and yet they had entirely passed from her mind; presently turning over a page she read, not her own name on the address, but that of Emma Penfold, and a sentence—'It is best for your welfare that we should not meet again,' wrote Henley. 'I am not a marrying man myself: circumstances render it impossible. May you be as happy in your new life. You will have an excellent husband, and one who . . . .'

'What have you got there?' said Frank, who had come in.

'Oh, Frank, don't ask me,' said Dolly, hastily going to the fire that was burning in the grate and flinging the packet into the flames; then she ran up to him, and clung hold of his arm for a minute. She could not speak.

Frank looked at the burning packet—at the open drawers—and then he understood it all. ' I thought I had burnt those letters long ago,' he said; and stooping he took his wife's hand in his and kissed it.

* * * * *

As I write the snow lies thick upon the ground outside, upon the branches of the trees, upon the lawns. Here, within, the fire leaps brightly in its iron cage; the children cluster round the chair by the chimney corner, where the mother sits reading their beloved fairy tales. The hearth was empty once—the home was desolate; but time after time, day by day, we see the phœnix of home and of love springing from the dead ashes; hopes are fulfilled that seemed too sweet to dream of; love kindles and warms chilled hearts to life. Take courage, say the happy to those in sorrow and trouble; are there not many mansions even here? seasons in their course; harvests in their season, thanks be to the merciful ordinance that metes out sorrow and peace, and longing and fulfilment, and rest after the storm.

Take courage, say the happy—the message of the sorrowful is harder to understand. The echoes come from afar, and reach beyond our ken. As the cry passes beyond us into the awful unknown, we feel that this is, perhaps, the voice in life that reaches beyond life itself. Not of harvests to come, not of peaceful home hearths do they speak in their sorrow. Their fires are out, their hearths are in ashes, but see. it was the sunlight that extinguished the flame.

THE END.

ALSO AVAILABLE FROM THOEMMES PRESS

Her Write His Name

This series makes available the forgotten works of neglected women writers whose literary contributions have been overshadowed by those of a more famous male relative. These diverse and intriguing authors can now be valued in their own right and not for the insight they give to the work of men whose name they share.

New introductions provide the social context for these writings and explain why these authors should now be allowed to shine in their own right.

Old Kensington *and* The Story of Elizabeth
Anne Isabella Thackeray
With a new introduction by Esther Schwartz-McKinzie
ISBN 1 85506 388 3 : 496pp : 1873 & 1876 editions : £17.75

Shells from the Sands of Time
Rosina Bulwer Lytton
With a new introduction by Marie Mulvey Roberts
ISBN 1 85506 386 7 : 272pp : 1876 edition : £14.75

Platonics
Ethel Arnold
With a new introduction by Phyllis Wachter
ISBN 1 85506 389 1 : 160pp : 1894 edition : £13.75

The Continental Journals 1798-1820
Dorothy Wordsworth
Edited with a new introduction by Helen Boden
ISBN 1 85506 385 9 : 472pp : New edition : £17.75

Her Life in Letters
Alice James
Edited with a new introduction by Linda Anderson
ISBN 1 85506 387 5 : 320pp : New : £15.75

Also available as a 5 volume set : ISBN 1 8556 384 0
Special set price : £70.00

For Her Own Good – A Series of Conduct Books

Cœlebs in Search of a Wife
Hannah More
With a new introduction by Mary Waldron
ISBN 1 85506 383 2 : 288pp : 1808–9 edition : £14.75

Female Replies to Swetnam the Woman-Hater
Various
With a new introduction by Charles Butler
ISBN 1 85506 379 4 : 336pp : 1615–20 edition : £15.75

A Complete Collection of Genteel and Ingenious Conversation
Jonathan Swift
With a new introduction by the Rt Hon. Michael Foot
ISBN 1 85506 380 8 : 224pp : 1755 edition : £13.75

Thoughts on the Education of Daughters
Mary Wollstonecraft
With a new introduction by Janet Todd
ISBN 1 85506 381 6 : 192pp : 1787 edition : £13.75

The Young Lady's Pocket Library, or Parental Monitor
Various
With a new introduction by Vivien Jones
ISBN 1 85506 382 4 : 352pp : 1790 edition : £15.75

Also available as a 5 volume set : ISBN 1 85506 378 6
Special Set Price: £65.00

Subversive Women

The Art of Ingeniously Tormenting
Jane Collier
With a new introduction by Judith Hawley
ISBN 1 8556 246 1 : 292pp : 1757 edition : £14.75

Appeal of One Half the Human Race, Women, Against the Pretensions of the Other Half, Men, to Retain them in Political, and thence in Civil and Domestic, Slavery
William Thompson and Anna Wheeler
With a new introduction by the Rt Hon. Michael Foot and Marie Mulvey Roberts
ISBN 1 85506 247 X : 256pp : 1825 edition : £14.75

A Blighted Life: A True Story
Rosina Bulwer Lytton
With a new introduction by Marie Mulvey Roberts
ISBN 1 85506 248 8 : 178pp : 1880 edition : £10.75

The Beth Book
Sarah Grand
With a new introduction by Sally Mitchell
ISBN 1 85506 249 6 : 560pp : 1897 edition : £18.75

The Journal of a Feminist
Elsie Clews Parsons
With a new introduction and notes by Margaret C. Jones
ISBN 1 85506 250 X : 142pp : New edition : £12.75

Also available as a 5 volume set : ISBN 1 85506 261 5
Special set price : £65.00

ESTHER SCHWARTZ-MCKINZIE
is presently working on nineteenth-century British and American women writers. She is especially interested in how women defined themselves and their relations to one another in their fiction, essay and journal writing from this period. A graduate of Bard College, she is currently completing a Ph.D. at Temple University.

Marie Mulvey Roberts is a Senior Lecturer in literary studies at the University of the West of England and is the author of *British Poets and Secret Societies* (1986), and *Gothic Immortals* (1990). From 1994 she has been the co-editor of a Journal: 'Women's Writing; the Elizabethan to the Victorian Period', and the General Editor for three series: *Subversive Women, For Her Own Good*, and *Her Write His Name*. The volumes she has co-edited include: *Sources of British Feminism* (1993), *Perspectives on the History of British Feminism* (1994), *Controversies in the History of British Feminism* (1995) and *Literature and Medicine during the Eighteenth Century* (1993). Among her single edited books are, *Out of the Night: Writings from Death Row* (1994), and editions of Rosina Bulwer Lytton's *A Blighted Life* (1994) and *Shells from the Sands of Time* (1995).

COVER ILLUSTRATION
'Signing the Register' by *Edward Blair Leighton*
Cover designed by Dan Broughton